Wolf Born
THE COMPLETE SERIES

MICHELLE MADOW

DREAMSCAPE
PUBLISHING

WOLF BORN
The Complete Series

Published by Dreamscape Publishing

Copyright © 2025 Michelle Madow

ISBN: 9798308596899

This book is a work of fiction. Though some actual towns, cities, and locations may be mentioned, they are used in a fictitious manner and the events and occurrences were invented in the mind and imagination of the author. Any similarities of characters or names used within to any person past, present, or future is coincidental.

All rights reserved. No part of this book may be used or reproduced in any manner whatsoever without written permission from the author. Brief quotations may be embodied in critical articles or reviews.

Blood Moon

STAR TOUCHED: WOLF BORN 1

For the readers in my Facebook group, who asked to read about a specific type of magic. I hope you enjoy it!

Ruby

"RUBY GRACE!" Luna exclaims, grabbing my hand as I step out of the bathroom. "Connor and Brandon asked us to play beer pong."

My heart skips a beat at Connor's name.

Truth be told, he's half the reason I've stayed at the party this long. Actually, who am I kidding? He's the whole reason I'm still here.

Luna knows him better than I do. She's my best friend and college roommate, and for the past few years, she's been coming to this small town in the Adirondack Mountains for ski trips.

I only met him a few hours ago, but that was enough. He's tall. Muscular. And the proud owner of a pair of dark eyes that sent a cold shiver through me the instant I saw them.

As for Brandon—the other beer pong contestant—I can't remember who he is.

I do know this: I'm terrible at sports. And my lack of coordination is unlikely to impress Connor.

"Are you sure you want me to be your partner?" I ask Luna.

"They asked for the birthday girl," she says, grinning.

"Are there any other birthday girls?"

Instead of answering, she digs her nails into my upper arm and pulls me out of the house and into the backyard, where twenty or so people are chatting in circles and lounging in the steaming hot tub.

I shiver in the winter clothes Luna loaned me and glance up at the sky, where the full moon glows overhead. It seems bigger than usual, casting down an eerie light. Maybe that's normal up here in New York. I wouldn't know. This is one of the few times I've ever left Florida.

Most of the people outside are wearing all-leather clothing that shouldn't give them nearly enough warmth in early January. Some of the girls even have skirts on, their legs bare except for boots that reach their knees.

"How are they not freezing?" I ask, running my hands up and down my arms to chase away the chill.

Luna shrugs. "They grew up around here. They're probably used to it."

It's as good of an answer as any, and as we saunter over to the ping-pong table on the deck, I can't help but notice the heads turning to follow us.

I almost feel like prey.

But they're not looking at me. They're looking at Luna, with her light blonde hair and tall, willowy frame. My best friend looks like she belongs on a runway in Milan—not on her way to a game of beer pong at a house party in a small town.

In her presence, I'm just part of the background. What I have going for me are my eyes—the unique turquoise color gets some second looks and compliments—and my brains. But I don't like being the center of attention, so I'm perfectly happy letting Luna take the spotlight.

We approach the ping-pong table, where pyramids of red plastic cups are ready to go on each end.

"There she is." A guy with light brown hair heads over to me and drops a ping-pong ball in my hand. He must be Brandon. His eyes roam up and down my body, and I take an uneasy step back, not wanting to give him the wrong idea. "It's only fair for the birthday girl to shoot first."

"Sure." I hurry to the opposite side of the table, glad to put some space between us.

On the other side of the table, Connor crosses his arms over his black leather jacket and glowers at me, as if he's annoyed I'm even here.

"Are you going to take your shot or not?" he snarls.

His antagonistic tone takes me by surprise, but I manage to compose myself. "I'm just analyzing my competition," I say, trying to sound cool and collected even though my heart's beating so fast that it's about to burst out of my chest.

I center myself and line up my shot, glad to have something to focus on besides the intense way Connor continues to stare at me.

I take a deep breath, and with a flick of my wrist, throw the ball in what I hope will be a perfect arch.

Instead of landing in one of the cups, the ball hits Connor directly in the crotch.

Oh.

My.

God.

My face flushes with embarrassment.

"Keeping your eyes on the prize?" he asks, and my cheeks burn even more.

Everyone's staring at me, waiting for my response. Even Luna, who's usually quick to back me up on everything, is sitting this one out.

I have two options. Own it and try to fire back, or embrace the embarrassment and apologize.

I'm not usually one to fire back, but I'll probably never see these guys after tonight.

Maybe it's time to be daring for a change.

"You call that a prize?" I tilt my head slightly and give Connor a small smile that I hope looks flirty and mischievous.

There's a second of utter silence, like a record stopping, and I immediately question my sudden moment of boldness.

Because Connor's glaring at me like he wants to rip my head off my body. And from the way some of the guys nearby crack their knuckles and move in like hawks, I have a feeling they wouldn't stop him.

His gaze sweeps around at the onlookers surrounding us, who look ready to obey whatever command he gives them. His arm muscles tighten, he clenches his jaw, and I wonder if I should run before he and his friends attack me like a pack of wolves.

His eyes stop on Luna, and his voice is a whisper, but still clear in the night. "Continue."

She bites her lip and glances over at me, question in her eyes.

I nod at her to take her shot. I've probably lost any chance I might have had with Connor—if I even had one at all—but hopefully we can move forward and forget this awkwardness ever happened.

She squares her shoulders and tosses the ball, but it goes far too far, flying past the end of the table and landing a few feet behind the guys.

Strange.

Unlike me, Luna's a natural at sports.

"What was that?" I ask her.

"I *might* have taken a tequila shot or two while you were in the bathroom." She giggles, and I'm surprised, since Luna's not the type to get drunk at parties. She'll nurse a can or two of hard seltzer throughout the night, but that's all.

A few girls wander by, and I can't help thinking about them like gazelle, moving slowly and gracefully as they graze on their Solo cups, their stares lingering on Conner a little too long. A particularly pretty one with light red hair doesn't even try to hide her leering.

He smiles at her, igniting an angry fire in me.

What's wrong with me?

I barely even know this guy.

Somehow, I force myself to refocus on the game. Both guys miss their next shots, and I wonder if they're going easy on us.

When it's our turn, I grip the ball, trying to ignore the alcohol buzzing in my head. Above, the moon glows like a lantern, half covered in shadow.

That's strange.

"The moon was full a bit ago," I tell Luna, my voice low.

"There's a lunar eclipse tonight. It won't be long until it'll be blocked completely," she says, and as the shadow continues to creep across the moon, shivers prickle up my neck.

"Come on, Scarlet," Brandon goads me. "Your turn."

"It's Ruby," I correct him.

He rolls his eyes. "Oh, my bad. Still though, it's your turn, Ruby-Scarlet."

I miss my shot, as does Luna with hers.

The guys obliterate us in their next round. Soon, all our cups are gone, the beer they once held sloshing in our stomachs. The alcohol makes me feel far more relaxed and warmer than when the game began, and Luna's eyes are glassy and unfocused.

Brandon holds his hands up. "That's game, ladies! Time for the victors to claim our prizes." He saunters over me, his gaze fixed to my chest. "Want to join me in the hot tub?"

I take a step back.

"No, thanks," I reply, trying not to inhale his beer breath.

He grabs my wrist and jerks my body toward his.

"What's the matter? No bathing suit? That's okay." He lowers his face closer to mine. "We're not shy around here."

"I said no." I try to free myself from his grip, but he's stronger than he looks.

Feeling slightly panicked, I glance around and search for Luna, but she's disappeared.

A split-second later, Connor is somehow by Brandon's side. He wraps a hand around his friend's bicep, squeezes, and Brandon's hand goes limp.

"Don't touch her," Connor growls, staring down at Brandon like he's ready to throw him down if he so much as thinks about moving.

"It's all good," Brandon says sheepishly, even though I take the opportunity to give him what I hope is a particularly withering glare. "We're just having some fun."

"I don't think she's having fun." Connor stares at Brandon, who looks down and away, shrinking before my eyes.

"Whatever, man," Brandon says under his breath. "She isn't even one of us. You want her? Take her."

He yanks his arm out of Connor's grip, glances back at me with hate and resentment, and strides over to the hot tub.

But my attention is on Connor. His dark eyes lock onto mine, swirling with such intensity that I can barely breathe. There's only a foot of space between us, and the fog from our breath in the freezing air is so close that it's nearly touching. His body feels magnetic, like it's latching onto mine and drawing me closer with a force I can't resist.

The moment's cut short when the red-headed girl from earlier glides over and frowns at me. She places her hand on Connor's shoulder, as if to claim him for herself. "Hi," she whispers to him, pressing herself against his chest.

Every cell in my body urges me to rip her off him. But I stand strong, not wanting to make another scene.

He yanks his gaze away from mine and looks down at her, his eyes softening. "That game got me all riled up," he murmurs, and he brushes his lips against hers as if he can't get enough of her. "Want to go inside?"

"Always." She gives me a victorious smile and flips her hair over her shoulder, leading him away from me and into the house.

He doesn't look back at me, and my heart sinks with disappointment.

He has a girlfriend. Of *course* he has a girlfriend. I shouldn't have expected anything less.

Anyway, it doesn't really matter. In a few days, Luna and I will be back in our dorm at the University of Florida for another semester of classes, all thoughts of everyone in this town forgotten.

Speaking of Luna, I don't see her anywhere. But she can't have gone far. So, I dig my phone out of my jacket pocket and tap to call her, grateful for the gloves she loaned me that let the screen sense my fingers.

It rings a few times, then goes to voicemail.

I don't bother leaving a message. Instead, I switch to send her a text. But as I begin tapping out the message, my head throbs and the letters blur, making it hard to see what I'm doing.

It's not the beer. It can't be. Or maybe—

The pounding in my head intensifies, and my stomach swirls. I can't keep the sick feeling down. Everyone at the party is chattering, but their voices blend together until the sounds assault my brain like strobe lights.

Did Conner and Brandon drug the beer?

My stomach clenches and thrashes, and I flee the deck to the edge of the woods, not wanting anyone to see me be sick. Along the way, my phone slips from my hand, falling into the snow.

Desperate for something to ground me, I look to the moon.

It's full again, the shadow gone.

But it's red. Blood red, like something out of a nightmare.

How's that possible?

I don't know, but a moment later, pain hits me like a freight train. Light sears through my brain, and I keel over as my bones shatter and break through my skin, shredding me apart from the inside out.

I try to scream, but no sound comes out.

Then, as suddenly as it came on, the torture stops and I'm running through the woods, the bare trees blurring like paint strokes in the corners of my eyes. I don't know where I'm going, but I'm running on instinct, deeper and deeper into the forest, so far that I have no idea how I'll ever find a way out.

Let go of control, a voice inside me urges. *Hand it over to me.*

The voice is quiet, but familiar in a way I can't explain.

No, I think, trying to resist.

Relax, she coaxes. *I can help you, but only if you let me.*

I can't explain why, but I believe her.

And so, trusting my instincts, I surrender control and hand it over to her.

The next thing I know, I'm lying on the ground, staring up at the sky. The moon is full again, but the red is gone, leaving it a perfectly normal color. Totally normal… except I swear I see the outlines of a *wolf* carved into its surface.

I blink, and a person shimmers into view above me.

Luna?

No. They're both blonde, but this person's hair is so blonde that it's practically silver. Her eyes are violet, unlike Luna's warm brown ones, and her pale skin is supernaturally dewy. She's barely corporeal—she seems more like an angel than a person—and if I squint, she shimmers in the moonlight.

Her hair blows in the wind like silver ribbons, and she reaches down, pressing her thumbs against my temples. "Everything's going to be okay," she whispers, her voice musical and soothing. "But I need you to remember that no matter what happens, don't tell them your eyes aren't brown."

Before I can ask what she means, electricity explodes in my head, bright white light floods my vision, and everything goes dark.

Ruby

SUNLIGHT WARMS MY FACE, and as I slowly float back into consciousness, fear floods my body as the events of the past few days fill my memories.

Luna inviting me to go skiing with her in the Adirondacks. Lying to my parents and telling them I was going back to school a week early, but coming to New York with Luna instead. Luna trying to teach me how to ski, eventually giving up, and the two of us going back to the hotel for an early dinner.

A guy approaching us at the restaurant and inviting us to a party at his house.

Connor.

His dark, mysterious eyes float through my mind, and my heart does that skipping thing it always seems to do at the thought of him.

But he has a girlfriend. The redhead. And I have much more to worry about than my crush on a guy I can't have.

Like how I felt so sick that I collapsed near the woods in his backyard.

Now, my bed is cold beneath me. But there's no pillow under my head, and no comforter covering my body.

And, most startlingly, my clothes are cold and damp.

My eyes shoot open, and I'm staring up at the sky, the sun peeking out behind the bare tree branches and casting them in bright silhouettes.

No.

I push myself up, use my hand as a visor to block the light from my eyes, and look around.

I'm in the middle of the woods, with no evidence of civilization anywhere around me. It's just me, the birds chirping, and the occasional squirrel climbing up a tree. A breeze passes by, blowing my hair across my face, and the air is fresh and clean in the way it only gets up in the mountains.

Which means everything I remember from last night—drinking all that beer with the guys, stumbling to the edge of the woods, and my body exploding in unfathomable pain—was real.

I vaguely remember a woman being here with me last night, but she's nowhere to be seen.

I have no idea what's happening, but one thing's for sure—I need to get out of here.

I reach into my jacket pocket for my phone, but there's nothing there. I'm not even wearing a jacket anymore.

Shouldn't I be freezing?

As I continue looking around, unease settles over me. Because without that jacket, I shouldn't have survived the night. I should have died of hypothermia.

Yet here I am, very much alive, and feeling far more refreshed than I should after all the beer I drank last night.

I need to get back to the hotel.

Except I have no idea where the hotel is. The only thing nearby is probably Connor's house.

Connor—who drugged me.

No. Who *might* have drugged me.

Logically, I shouldn't go back there. Situations like this are how people end up on the news, declared missing until they're found dead.

If they're ever found at all.

But the way Connor looked at me last night when he warned Brandon not to touch me flashes through my mind. He was so protective. And for reasons I can't pinpoint, I know he'd never hurt me. Brandon might, but not Connor.

I'll be safe at Connor's.

Since it didn't snow last night, I look around for my footsteps, figuring I can follow my path back to Connor's house.

There's no trace of them.

There are, however, paw prints so large that I can't imagine what animal they might belong to.

Follow them, a voice echoes through my mind.

I recognize the voice.

It's the one from last night. The one that asked me to let go of control and hand it over to her.

It's not normal to hear voices. It's especially not normal to listen to them.

Brandon *must* have drugged my beer.

But something pulls at me to trust her, and since I don't have any better ideas, I stop fighting and do as asked.

I wander for at least thirty minutes. Then, eventually, the roof of Connor's house comes into view.

Please don't be a serial killer, I think, and I follow the last of the prints to the end of the tree line and step into his backyard.

It's trashed. Totally and completely *trashed.*

I make my way to where I stumbled over to during my last minutes at the party and spot the remains of my jacket on the ground.

It looks like someone stuffed a bomb inside of it and that it *exploded.*

Why would someone destroy it like that? Sure, it wasn't the best jacket in the world, but it certainly didn't deserve to be mutilated.

Dazed and feeling like I'm in a strange dream, I pick up what I can of the jacket, forge my way through the red plastic cups and beer cans littering the ground, and step onto the back deck.

A memory of the red-headed girl leading Connor inside flashes in my mind, and hot anger courses through my body.

They don't belong together, the voice from earlier whispers in my mind.

No.

I *cannot* deal with voices in my mind on top of all the other insane things going on here. So, I push the voice down and approach the glass doors. The blinds on the inside are closed, along with the blinds on all the windows, so I can't see into the living room. It's like someone turned the house into a cave.

It's something a serial killer would do.

But Connor's *not* a serial killer.

Yes, there's something undeniably dangerous about him. He was hot and cold last night, and from the way he pulled Brandon away from me, he's clearly strong enough to overpower anyone who gets in his way.

But I can't imagine him hurting me.

And so, not wanting to overthink it any further, I shake off my nerves and knock.

At first, all is silent.

I knock again.

A light in a second-floor window turns on.

There's no movement beyond that, and I wait for what feels like the longest few minutes of my life. Then the blinds on the sliding door open slightly, and a pair of dark brown eyes I'd recognize anywhere peek through the slits.

Connor.

Time stands still, and we stand there staring at each other, neither of us moving.

Eventually, he closes the blinds again, and I worry he's going to ignore me and go back up to his room.

Instead, he opens the door and slides it open.

He's wearing plaid cotton pajama pants, as if he's ready for Christmas morning, and a plain gray t-shirt. His hair is messy, but in the way that makes it look like he styled it to make it seem like he rolled out of bed instead of having *actually* just rolled out of bed, and he smells like a warm campfire on a cold night.

The redhead sits on a chair behind him, her arms crossed over her chest and her eyes narrowed at me. Her hair is also disheveled, but in the sexy sort of way that makes it clear I interrupted them in the middle of an activity she was less than thrilled to be pulled away from.

Meanwhile, my clothes are wet from the snow, I'm cold, and I don't even want to know what the rest of me must look like after my impromptu night in the woods.

"What do you want?" The redhead sneers, disdain dripping from her tone.

"Autumn," Connor warns, and I'm glad to finally have a name to put to her haughty face.

"What?" she asks. "A tourist you invited to your party last night re-appeared at your doorstep, looking like she spent the night sleeping in the woods. It's perfectly normal to ask her what she wants."

Connor ignores her as he sizes me up, concern flickering in his eyes. "*Did* you sleep in the woods?" he asks.

Embarrassment rolls over my skin at the way they're looking at me—like I'm a rodent that crawled up onto his doorstep begging for crumbs.

It's humiliating, but I need to answer instead of just standing here saying nothing.

"Yeah." I bite my lip and lower my gaze, since it sounds crazy. Especially because I have no idea how I got there. "I think."

Connor continues to study me, as if he isn't sure what to make of this.

"What do you mean that you *think* you did?" Autumn says. "You either got lost in the woods and passed out, or you didn't. There's really nothing in between."

"I did. But I didn't mean to," I say, and the rest pours out of me before I can stop myself. "I drank too much, and I went to the edge of the backyard, and then the moon turned red, and then I was waking up in the middle of the woods. Someone else was there, but I didn't—"

Alarm crosses Connor's face. "You saw the blood moon?" he asks.

"Yeah," I say. "It was hard to miss."

"You shouldn't have been able to see it." His body goes rigid, and he's somehow guarded and confrontational at the same time.

"Well, I did," I say, because I know what I saw. I might be feeling like I'm going crazy, but I can't be going *that* crazy.

He studies me again, as if he's seeing something different this time, then steps aside. "You need to come in and sit down," he says. "Because we clearly have a *lot* to talk about."

Ruby

I TAKE the seat across from Autumn. Immediately afterward, I realize it was a bad decision, since now we'll be facing each other the entire time, and she's all but shooting daggers at me with her eyes across the table.

"Did either of you see Luna last night?" I ask, praying one of them can tell me something helpful, since Luna wouldn't have left the party without me.

"The last time I saw her was after our game," Connor says. "Then I was sort of…" he trails off, as if he regrets whatever he was about to say.

"He was busy for the rest of the night," Autumn finishes. "In his room. With me." She sits forward, like she's about to bring her claws out, and the warning is clear.

She's either staking her territory on Connor, or trying to incite jealousy in me. Probably both.

But I'm too concerned about my best friend to care.

"I need to call her." I look to my destroyed jacket, then remember I dropped my phone before blacking out.

I hurry out of the house and follow the path I made last night, relieved to find my phone face-down in the snow.

I pick it up, but it doesn't turn on.

"Crap." I tap the screen to no avail, harder and harder, frustration coursing through my veins when it remains black.

Desperate, I hold down the power button as hard as I can. But still, nothing.

It's dead. Maybe permanently, since I have no idea if iPhones can survive a night buried in the snow.

"Ruby," Connor says from behind me, apparently having followed me out. He reaches for my shoulder, but stops himself before touching me. "It's freezing out here. Come back inside."

"No. I need to call Luna," I say, and I press the power button again, even though I know it's futile.

"Your phone isn't working." He sounds so stupidly calm, and he reaches forward to take it from me, but stops himself again. "We'll figure this out. Just come back inside. Please."

I shouldn't trust him.

But his eyes are so warm and concerned, and every instinct in my body urges me to believe he'll keep me safe.

Being around Connor calms me. And even though I haven't even known him for twenty-four hours, I believe him when he says he'll help.

"Fine." I release a defeated breath, stand up, and follow him back inside.

Autumn is still sitting at the table, arms crossed, as hostile as ever.

I think about asking one of them to borrow their phone, but I haven't memorized Luna's number. Why would I when it's stored in my phone? And she doesn't use social media, so I can't contact her there.

"I need to charge my phone." I hold up the dead phone and wait for one of them to offer me their charger.

Plus, once my phone's juiced up, I can call an Uber and get out of here.

"Sure," Connor says. "There's a charger in my room. I'll grab it and bring some warm clothes down for you. You look like you could use them."

"Thanks," I say, and we stare at each other, silent for a few seconds. He's giving me the same look from last night—the one that takes my breath away—and I feel so captured in his gaze that I can't move.

"I texted Jax," Autumn tells Connor, breaking whatever moment was happening between us. "He'll be over soon."

Connor steps back and snaps back into focus. "Good," he says, and they share a silent look, giving me the distinct feeling that they know something I don't. "Can you get the coffee started?"

"No problem." She gives me a final glare, flips her hair over her shoulder, and heads to the coffee maker on the counter.

Without another word, Connor hurries up the stairs, leaving me and Autumn alone.

I brace myself for the claws to come out, but she simply turns her back to me and starts making the coffee. The beans smell delicious, and I take a deep breath, somehow feeling warmer already.

"Who's Jax?" I ask, because even though Autumn doesn't seem like she wants to talk, I'm too curious to not say anything.

"Connor's grandfather," she says, keeping her back to me.

"Why's he coming over?"

"You'll see when he gets here." She returns to her task, clearly not wanting to chat any further.

Point taken.

Needing something to do with my hands, I try to turn my phone on again, but it remains as dead as ever.

Luckily, Connor returns less than a minute later. He's carrying plaid pajama bottoms that look like the ones he has on, a long-sleeve t-shirt, and a phone charger.

"Here you go." He plops the items on the table instead of handing them directly to me. "These are too small for me. If you tie the pants tightly, they might be able to stay up."

"Thanks." I reach for the charger first, stick it into the nearest socket, and plug in my phone.

I press the power button again, hold my breath, and wait for it to turn on.

Nothing happens.

So I jiggle the charger in the phone's socket, as if moving it around will fix whatever's broken in there.

"It's not working." My voice breaks, and it takes all my effort to not throw the phone across the room in frustration.

"It was buried in the snow," Connor says calmly. "The socket is probably wet. It won't be able to charge until it dries off."

"How do we dry it off?"

"Remove the plug so it can air out," he says. "Other than that, we just have to wait."

"How long?" I remove the plug and fan my hand around the socket, praying it'll dry quickly.

"Last time it happened to me, it took about half a day."

"No." My heart drops, all hope of contacting Luna sometime soon gone.

"You're safe here," he promises, firm and steady. "We're going to make breakfast. In the meantime, how about you change into those dry clothes?" He glances at them again, and I shiver at the reminder of how cold I am.

I also don't mind the idea of having some space to get my thoughts somewhat together.

"Sure." I pick up the pajamas and pull them close. "Where's the bathroom?"

"Down the hall and to the right."

I make my way there and close the door behind me. It's a standard powder room, decorated in generic browns like I'd expect from a guy living alone, and I go about changing into Connor's pajamas.

They smell like a campfire on a winter's night—exactly what *he* smells like—and I tie the pants as tightly as possible. They're loose, but as he predicted, they do stay up. And even though my underwear is damp, I keep them on, since anything else feels way too intimate for whatever's going on here.

Once satisfied that the pants aren't going to fall down, I turn around to see how I look.

Big mistake.

As Autumn said, I look like I spent the night sleeping in the woods. My hair is matted with the occasional twig in it. There are circles under my eyes. As for my eyes themselves...

I lean closer to the mirror, balancing my hands on the sides of the sink and staring at my reflection in shock.

The eyes looking back at me aren't mine.

They're brown.

Not turquoise.

I blink a few times, feeling like I'm seeing a stranger in the mirror, and glance at the ceiling to check the lighting. It's a normal yellow bulb. Nothing that would make my eyes change color.

No one's eye color changes overnight—or at all. It's impossible.

I take a deep breath and try to calm myself. I must be seeing things that aren't here. Maybe Brandon *did* drug my beer, and this is a residual side effect of whatever he put in it.

If so, I need to snap myself out of it.

I run the water, making it as cold as possible, hold my hands under it, and drink. After guzzling down as much as I can, I pat some of it onto my face, too.

But when I look back up at my reflection, nothing's changed.

No matter what happens, don't tell them your eyes aren't brown, the woman's voice from last night echoes in my mind.

Did she do this to me?

How would she do that? Why? And who was she?

I don't know. But every bone in my body urges me to trust her.

What else can I do? Tell Connor and Autumn—and Connor's grandfather—that my eyes changed color overnight? They'll think I'm crazy.

Maybe I am.

Or maybe I'll wake up soon and this will have been a long, strange dream.

Until then, I have to stay calm until my phone dries out and can charge. I'm sure I'll have loads of texts from Luna. She's probably back in town and has already told the cops I'm missing. I just need to hold tight until then.

So I gather my wet clothes and return to the kitchen.

The only person there is Autumn, who seems totally at home at the stove as she cooks breakfast.

"Where's Connor?" I ask, and my stomach rumbles at the delicious smell of bacon.

But I'm a vegetarian.

My parents are vegetarians, and I've been one my entire life. Never in my wildest dreams have I found the smell of bacon to be *delicious.*

"Jax got here, and Connor's talking with him in the other room," Autumn says.

"Oh," I say. "Okay." I plug the charger back into my phone, but still, no luck.

Crap.

I reach for my coffee, which is now lukewarm, and drink it as I wait for Connor to come back.

"Where are you from again?" Autumn asks, surprising me by attempting conversation.

"South Florida," I answer.

"Where in South Florida?"

"Naples. In the Southwest."

"Hm." She presses her lips together, studies me, and returns to scrambling the eggs.

"Have you been?" I ask, hoping to fill the awkward silence.

"No," she says. "And I've never met anyone else from there."

"It's a small town."

"I'm sure it is," she says in disdain.

I get the distinct feeling that the conversation is over, so I go back to sipping my coffee and wait.

Eventually, Connor returns with a man who's equally as tall as he is… and who looks *far* too young to be anyone's grandfather. I'm not the best at guessing ages, but I'd put him in his mid-forties, at the most. It also doesn't hurt that he's wearing tight dark jeans and a leather jacket. His skin is tan like Connor's, and his features are sharp and strong, making it obvious they're related.

Jax takes a long, deep breath, his eyes locked on mine.

I try to hold his gaze, but unease prickles my spine, and I glance down at my broken phone in defeat.

He lets out a sound of satisfaction, and I look back up at him.

"You saw the blood moon last night," he says, not bothering with introductions.

"It was hard to miss." I shrug, unsure why it's such a big deal that I saw the moon turn red, given that anyone outside would have seen it.

"The blood moon wasn't visible to human eyes," he says simply.

The meaning behind his words only half-registers. "Excuse me?"

"Only supernaturals were able to see the blood moon," he says. "Which means you're one of us. A wolf shifter, to be precise, given the story of yours that Connor just told me."

Ruby

I STARE at him like he's gone mental.

Because either he's gone mental, or I have. Probably me, given everything that's happened this past day.

"You truly had no idea," Jax observes.

"You just said that I'm a wolf shifter," I repeat, unable to believe the words coming out of my mouth.

"Correct."

"I want to go back to the hotel."

They're playing a joke on me. They *have* to be.

Then again, I read a lot of books—many of them fantasy. Everything that happened to me is in line with what happens to wolf shifters in the books I read.

This has to be a dream. The most realistic dream I've ever had, but once I wake up, it'll fade like all dreams do.

"You don't believe us," Connor says.

I glance back at Autumn, who's cooking so much food that you'd think she's preparing a feast.

"I'm not a *wolf shifter*," I say, unable to believe we're having this conversation. "I drank too much last night, wandered into the woods, and passed out. That's all."

"You saw the blood moon," Jax repeats.

"It was up in the sky." I motion to the ceiling. "*Everyone* outside saw it."

"Only supernaturals could see it," he repeats his statement from earlier.

I hear him, but I don't truly *hear* him.

"This is crazy," I finally say.

"You need to relax and listen to me," he says, and calmness floats through my veins, as if my body's obeying him without my consent. "You're a wolf shifter. It seems the blood moon made you shift for the first time."

I pause to soak it in.

This can't be possible.

"You're lucky you were here when it first happened instead of... where are you from again?" he asks, as if this is a totally normal conversation.

"Southwest Florida," Autumn supplies for me.

"There aren't any packs in Florida." Jax clears his throat and looks at me curiously. "Where are your parents from?"

"They're from Florida. The panhandle," I clarify, even though basically no one has been to the panhandle—including me. Neither of my parents have any family left, so there was never any reason to visit their hometown.

"They're human?" Jax asks.

"Of course they're human."

"Hm," he muses, and I can tell he doesn't believe me.

Just like I don't believe him.

Although, I have to admit that I'm curious...

"If you're really wolf shifters, then shift." I motion to the center of the room, ready to put this craziness to rest. "Right here, right now."

"Sure. Although I don't think the kitchen is the right place to do it," Connor says, and he strolls over to the back doors, opens them, and leaps onto the deck.

One moment he's a human, then he's leaping through the air... and then he's landing on all fours and turning to face me.

As a wolf.

An actual wolf nearly twice the size as any wolf I've ever heard of, with inky black fur that gleams in the sunlight and eyes so intense that it's like they're gazing into my soul.

My breath catches in my chest, and I freeze, unable to believe what I'm seeing.

I simply stare at the majestic wolf that was Connor a few seconds ago, my mind barely able to process the fact that he changed forms in front of my eyes.

"You have to be kidding me," I mumble, bracing myself to wake up from this stupidly realistic dream at any moment.

"I assume that's proof enough for you?" Jax says, and Connor shifts back into human form, strolls into the kitchen, and shuts the door behind him as if he didn't just shift into a supernatural creature in broad daylight.

I think back to the paw prints I followed back to the house. They were large—about the same size as a wolf around Connor's size would have. There were no regular footprints leading up to where I passed out in the woods. Which means...

"I shifted into a wolf last night."

I can't believe I'm saying it, let alone considering it.

Yet... here we are.

"Yes. It sounds like that's what happened," Jax says.

"And you came here because you're the alpha." I swallow, realizing that's why it was so hard for me to meet his eyes without lowering mine in submission.

"You catch on quick," he says.

"I like to read."

"Books rarely get everything right, but it makes sense that you'd be drawn to read about your kind," he says.

I glance at my ruined jacket, then back to where Connor is standing fully clothed.

"Only natural items can shift with us—ones that are either made from animals or come from the earth," Connor explains. "That jacket is polyester. Thus why it..." He trails off and makes a motion with his hands of a bomb exploding, with a sound to match.

"Right," I say, surprising myself with how easily I'm handling this. "How many of you are there?"

"In the Pine Valley pack?" Jax asks, and I nod. "Almost a hundred. We're the biggest pack in the area. Over half of us are here in town, and the rest are serving as Guardians in cities across the country."

I blink, unsure exactly what he's talking about. "Guardians?"

"You'll learn more later," he says. "But first, your parents. Are you sure they're not shifters?"

"I'm sure," I say. "I think they would have told me otherwise."

"I'll have the witches look into it," he says.

"The witches," I repeat, dumbfounded. "Of course there are witches. I guess it wouldn't make sense for shifters to be the only supernaturals out there."

"Precisely." Jax either doesn't catch onto my sarcasm, or he's ignoring it. "Which is good, since until we learn what pack you were born into, you're our responsibility. You'll be safe and provided for here in Pine Valley."

"How can we be sure she's not lying?" Autumn sneers, and I notice she's finished cooking breakfast and has placed the food into bowls and plates, buffet-style on the countertop.

"A lie that big is something I'd be able to smell," Jax says. "She's not lying."

"Hold up." I raise a hand for them to stop talking, and they look to me to continue. "I'm not staying here."

"You have to stay here." Connor growls and grips the back of the chair in front of him so tightly that I worry it might break. "You're one of us."

"But my parents…"

"We're your family now." His voice is hard and final, filling the room with crackling tension.

Autumn looks back and forth between the two of us, her forehead creased with worry.

She hesitates for a moment, as if fighting an internal battle, then glides to Connor's side and links her arm with his. "Connor's right," she says. "You're untrained, and it's going to take time for you to learn how to shift on command. Until you do, you're a liability to everyone out there. Like Jax and Connor said—you're our responsibility now."

She strains when she says the last part, but Connor steps closer to her and gives her an appreciative nod, and she relaxes a bit.

Jax gives them an approving look, then gets up and starts helping himself to the breakfast display on the counter.

Connor's watching me, waiting for my reaction, but I can't tear my gaze away from Autumn. She looks so smug standing next to him—as if she owns him.

The two of them together are *wrong*.

I feel it deep in my bones.

It should be me standing next to him, touching him in a way that's so casual, yet intimate at the same time.

Not her.

I don't know where the thought comes from. I shouldn't feel this way about someone else's boyfriend.

But I can visualize myself standing next to him instead of her, my arm linked with his as he stands close by my side. I can *literally* see myself there—my brown hair replacing Autumn's red, my heart-shaped face there instead of her oval one, and the silky slip nightgown she's wearing changing into Connor's pajamas loosely draped around my small frame.

She moves closer to him, he glances over at her… and his eyes widen in alarm, as if whatever he's seeing startled him into shock.

Ruby

AUTUMN FLINCHES BACK. "WHAT?" she asks, and at the sound of her voice, the fantasy of myself standing next to Connor shatters.

Connor glances at me, studying me for a few painfully long seconds, then returns his focus to Autumn. "Nothing," he says, and he pulls her closer and kisses her head, which seems to placate her.

But he looked so startled...

He couldn't have seen what I did, of me standing there instead of Autumn.

Could he have?

I shake the thought away. The idea of Connor and I sharing some sort of weird vision is insane. My imagination's getting the best of me. It has to be.

Before I can think about it further, Jax brings his breakfast plate piled high with food over to the table and plops down into the chair next to mine.

My stomach growls as the mouth-watering smell of it floats over to me.

"You should eat," he says, stabbing a sausage with his fork. "You have to be starving after your first shift."

My stomach growls again, and since he's right—I *am* starving—I get up and help myself to some of the food. Connor and Autumn help themselves as well, and I can't help but feel like Connor is staying as far away from me as possible as he does.

When we sit back down, Connor glances at my plate and frowns.

"What?" I ask, annoyed at how something as small as the food I chose for breakfast bothers him.

"You didn't take any meat." He motions to his plate, which has bacon, ham, *and* sausage on it.

All three of them took so much meat that it fills over half their plates.

"I'm a vegetarian," I say, cutting into the toast piled with eggs and beans that I made for myself.

"Seriously?" Autumn stares at me like I've grown a second head, spears a sausage with her fork, and takes a bite of it.

"Yeah. Seriously."

Connor just smirks, snaps a crispy piece of bacon in half, and starts eating it.

"Why's this such a big deal?" I ask, looking back and forth between them in irritation.

"Now that you've shifted, you're not going to last long as a vegetarian," he says. "Our wolves need meat to survive."

I want to say he's wrong, but the bacon smells even more delicious up close than it did from the other side of the kitchen. I'm practically salivating as I stare at it... and at the stupidly sexy sight of Connor eating it.

Jax stops eating and studies me. "It's not natural for our kind to refuse meat," he says.

"My parents are vegetarians," I explain. "I've been one my entire life."

"Are you sure you're not adopted?"

"If I was adopted, they would have told me," I say, although after everything I learned this morning, I don't sound as confident as I'd like to be.

"Except that you're a shifter," he says. "After our first shift, we need meat to survive. Not eating it will slowly kill us. Which means your parents are human."

My stomach drops, and I stare down at the barely touched toast concoction on my plate, suddenly not hungry anymore.

Is Jax right? Have my parents been lying to me for my entire life? Are they not really my parents?

No. They're my parents no matter what. They raised me.

But if he's right, it means they lied to me about my blood heritage.

I don't want it to be true.

However, now that he's saying it, I feel stupid for not suspecting it earlier. Neither of my parents share my eye color *or* my hair color. I always chalked it up to recessive genes, especially because other than that, there aren't any other glaring differences in our features.

"You look shocked," Jax observes.

"Can you blame me?"

He chuckles, and Connor tosses a piece of bacon onto my plate.

"Try it," he dares, his eyes light and teasing. "You might like it."

A large part of me yearns to pick it up and take a bite.

Do it, the voice from last night insists.

No, I think back.

Somehow managing to get myself together, I slide the plate away from me and force myself to think about something else.

"What are we going to tell my parents?" I ask, since they're right that I can't go back home like everything's normal. The thought of staying here for a few weeks makes my chest tighten with anxiety, but the last thing I need is to wolf out like I did last night and hurt someone, especially someone I love. "And what about Luna?"

"The witches are experienced in handling supernatural relations with the human world," Jax says. "They'll investigate it and come up with a plan. I need you to hang tight while they do. Once everything's figured out, you'll be the first to know."

"Okay," I say, since there's not much more I can ask. "Thanks."

"Like I said, you're our responsibility now," he repeats. "I'm the alpha of this pack, and it's a role I take seriously. Everyone here is taken care of under my watch, including our guests. You're safe here. I promise."

"Thanks," I say again, and I look to Connor, as if I need his assurance as well.

He's glowering at me, just like he did at the party last night.

"What?" I ask, fed up with his stupid mood swings and how he can't decide if he wants to help me or hate me.

He motions to my plate. "You're not eating."

"I'm not hungry."

"You shifted for the first time last night and slept in the woods." He stares at me in challenge, so intensely that I wonder if he's going to reach across the table and stuff that piece of bacon down my throat. "You need to eat."

I don't want to give in.

But despite having lost my appetite after the discussion about my parents, my hunger suddenly returns with double the force as before.

"Fine," I concede, and he nods, apparently pleased. "But I'm not touching that bacon."

Ruby

"Let's go outside and see how much earth magic you have," Jax says after we finish eating.

"Earth magic?" I ask.

"Shifters are connected with the element of earth," he explains. "We can harness it from the time we're young, at various ages dependent on the strength of the shifter. The amount of elemental magic we have determines our place in the pack."

"That's not in any of the books I read," I say.

"Fiction doesn't get everything right." He stands, leads the three of us outside, and points to the ground. "Sit," he tells me, making me feel like a dog being given a command.

Autumn crosses her arms and smirks, and I can tell she's hoping I'll fail.

Jax's instructions are tough to resist, so I sit crisscross on the ground, determined to do well enough at whatever he's about to ask me to do to wipe that smirk off Autumn's face.

Connor's as stoic and hard to read as ever.

Jax sits about three feet across from me, and Connor and Autumn situate themselves on both sides between us, so we're in a circle. The sun's up, making it warmer outside than last night, especially since I'm no longer wearing wet clothes.

"Close your eyes and connect with the earth," Jax instructs, and I do as asked, focusing on the grass and dirt beneath me.

I don't feel anything magical—no tingles, no buzz of energy from the ground—but I'm not sure if that's supposed to happen, or if it's also something that's only in books. So I focus on grounding myself, remaining still and calm, trying to do as directed.

"Open your eyes," Jax says after about five minutes pass.

I look to Connor, my breath catching when our eyes lock. But, remembering that Autumn is watching us like a hawk, I focus on Jax instead, who's holding a small pile of dirt in his hands as if it's something holy.

"Cup your hands together like this," he says, and I create a small bowl with my hands, mirroring his position.

Slowly, he pours about half of the dirt into my waiting hands. Then he pulls his arms closer to himself, and I do the same, bringing my elbows to my waist so the dirt is right in front of me.

"Watch," he says, and the dirt rises about two inches above his palms, forming a sphere the size of a tennis ball. It swirls around, and the sunlight bounces off the minerals in the soil, making it sparkle as it moves. There's even a green glow around it—magic come to life.

I'm in awe, amazed that something as simple as *dirt* can be so beautiful.

"You won't have as precise of control over it as I do," he says. "But I want you to try levitating it in your hands."

"Child's play." Autumn smiles smugly.

I narrow my eyes at her, then look down at the pile of dirt in my palms. It doesn't have the same magical quality as the one in Jax's hands. It simply looks like dirt.

Float, I think, trying to connect it with my palms and make it obey my command.

Nothing happens, so I hold my breath and push harder, willing it to follow my order.

"Connect with the earth below you," Jax says. "Pull its magic into your body and release it into the dirt in your hands."

"Okay." I focus on the ground, but don't feel the magic he spoke of.

Eventually I give up and try getting the dirt in my hands to float again.

It doesn't work.

"Do you feel any magic?" Jax probes.

I frown and try again. "No," I admit, unable to look at Autumn.

The disappointment in Connor's eyes makes me want the ground to open beneath me so I can disappear inside of it. Not like I'd be able to make that happen, since I have no magical connection to it to speak of.

Jax allows the sphere of dirt floating above his hands to fall back into his palms, and he pours it back onto the ground.

I pour out mine as well, since I'm clearly not getting anywhere with trying to do anything magical to it.

Jax eyes me up and down, like he's sizing me up.

I failed.

I don't need to see his expression to know it's true.

"Come inside," he says, and we do as instructed, taking our seats around the table. "I'll place you with one of the omega families," he continues. "They'll help you find a job during your stay here. You're very pretty, so I'm sure many of the royal families will be happy to have you serve in their household."

"You want me to be a *servant?*" I do a double-take, unable to believe I'm hearing this correctly.

"Serving in a royal household is the most prestigious position an omega can hope for," he says.

"I thought I was a guest here."

"You are. But given that you have no magic, you won't be training to be a Guardian, and you need to pull your weight somehow."

"I know how to wait tables," I volunteer quickly, desperate to find another solution. "I occasionally help out at the restaurant where my mom works."

"Your mom's a waitress?" Autumn scrunches her nose, like it's a bad word.

"She is." I hold her gaze, daring her to say a nasty thing about it. My parents work hard, and I refuse to let a snob like her put them down.

"We have two restaurants in pack territory," Connor says. "I'll check if there's an opening at either one of them."

"Thanks," I say in relief.

"No problem."

"I also want to take some online classes," I tell Jax. "I don't want to get behind in school."

He watches me like I'm a lost puppy, and I have a feeling I'm not going to like whatever's coming next. "I need you to realize something, Ruby," he says slowly, and I place my hands on my knees to brace myself. "Once you learn how to shift, you can go wherever you please. But you're not going to fit in with the human world anymore. You see, shifters have an instinctive need to be part of a pack. Once we figure out what pack you were born into, you'll likely choose to live with them, or you'll decide to remain with us. Both options will be open to you, but I'm confident that as you spend more time here, you'll realize you belong with your own kind and not with the humans."

"Once I'm ready, I'm returning to my life," I say, since he has no way of knowing what I'll decide, even if he thinks otherwise. "And I'm not dropping out of school."

I haven't chosen a major yet, but I'm not giving up on my education. Neither of my parents are college-educated, and it's their biggest dream for me to get my degree. I refuse to let them—or myself—down.

"Like you said, Ruby won't be training as a Guardian," Connor jumps in. "I don't see what an online class or two will hurt, as long as it doesn't interfere with her getting her job done."

Jax pauses to think, and I hold my breath, praying he'll say okay.

"Until the witches get everything settled, you can't have any contact with the outside world," he finally says. "No computer. And no phone." With that, he picks my phone off the table, tightens his grip, and crushes it.

The glass breaks, and the phone twists so much that it's nearly unrecognizable.

He drops it onto the table in a mangled heap, and the cuts on his hand quickly heal, leaving his skin good as new.

A ball of panic rises in my throat, followed by raging hot anger. "Why did you do that?" I ask, staring at the twisted metal in shock and disbelief.

That phone was my only way to connect with my parents and Luna, and now it's gone.

"The witches will cover up your disappearance," he says. "They're experts with this sort of thing. We can't have you reaching out to humans and ruining everything."

"I wasn't going to ruin anything," I say. "I just want my parents and best friend to know I'm okay."

And I want to know that *they're* okay.

His gaze is hard and unwavering. "I'm the alpha of this pack. You're my responsibility now, and I promise that everything will be figured out soon enough," he says, and I hate how assured his calm tone makes me feel. It's like he's casting a spell on me, and I try to fight it, but the anger I felt when he crushed my phone is gone. "In the meantime, I know what family I want you to stay with during your time here. I'll call them and drop you off there soon. But first, there's a mess in here from breakfast, and you need to do your job and clean it up."

Just like that, I realize that any respect Jax might have had for me went out the window the moment I couldn't connect with earth magic. In his mind, I'm an omega.

A servant.

He's destroyed my one way of connecting to the outside world, and a sickening feeling rises in my throat at the realization that he's keeping me prisoner here.

I need to learn how to shift as quickly as possible. Then I can leave and take whatever I can of my life back.

Although I can't deny the sinking feeling that Jax is right. Even if I could reach out to my family and friends, what would I say? I have no idea. Because last night, everything changed. Pretending otherwise would be impossible.

Which means as much as I hate it and want to fight it, nothing in my life will ever be normal again.

Connor

AFTER RUBY and my grandfather leave, Autumn and I go back to my room, presumably to finish what we were starting before Ruby pounded on the back door and interrupted our fun.

She sits on the end of the bed, and her eyes are hard. She's aggravated, just like she was when we were all in the kitchen.

"What's wrong?" I ask, even though I have a pretty good idea what's wrong.

"I don't like the way you look at her," she cuts to the chase.

"Ruby?" I say casually, as if the undeniably beautiful girl didn't send my head spinning the moment I saw her.

As if I didn't imagine her taking Autumn's place while we were standing in the kitchen. As if I didn't wish I was staring into her brilliant turquoise eyes instead of my girlfriend's warm hazel ones.

But Ruby's eyes aren't really turquoise. She was clearly wearing color contacts last night. The contacts wouldn't have shifted with her, which is why her eyes are back to their natural brown. The turquoise suited her better than her real eye color, although she won't be needing contacts anymore, since she surely has perfect wolf vision now that she's had her first shift.

"Who else would I be talking about?" Autumn asks, snapping me out of my thoughts of Ruby's eyes.

An excellent question.

I need to put an end to this conversation—quickly.

"How do I look at her?" I smirk and take my shirt off, hoping to distract Autumn's train of thought. Especially because my girlfriend looks as sexy as ever sitting on my bed in her silk pink nightgown, her cheeks flushed from being so emotionally heated.

"You look at her like you want to rip her clothes off."

So much for distracting her. Autumn is nothing if not outspoken and determined. It's one of the many reasons I was drawn to her all those years ago and decided to make her mine.

"There's only one person whose clothes I want to rip off," I say. "And she's sitting on my bed in front of me."

It's a lie.

I don't want it to be, but it is. However, whatever attraction I feel toward Ruby is irrelevant. I'd never act on it. I care about Autumn, and I wouldn't hurt her like that.

Besides, once Autumn turns nineteen, the mate bond will form between us, and I won't be attracted to anyone else ever again.

I prowl over to Autumn and pull her into a kiss, her lips soft and familiar as they move against mine. But there's something different about the way she's kissing me. She's more reserved, as if she's unsure about how much I want her.

Autumn's never unsure about anything.

I don't like it, and as her future mate, it's my job to put a stop to it.

So I pull slowly away from her and look into her eyes, determined to wipe any trace of doubt away from them.

"What?" she asks, soft and curious.

"You're my future mate," I tell her. "You're the strongest magic user of our kind in decades, you're a better fighter than many of the Guardians who have been serving for years, and I admire your fierceness and determination more than anything. We made a promise to each other all those years ago because we're meant to be together, and I never want you to doubt that. I never want you to doubt *me*."

Guilt floods through me after I say the words. I think back to the moment I pulled Brandon off Ruby—the trusting way the girl looked at me, and how *right* it felt to protect her.

How I purposefully avoided touching her, multiple times.

Just to be safe.

"You're right," she says. "I trust you, and I love you, just like I know you love me."

"Good," I say. "Because no one on the planet could ever compare to you. Especially not that little omega. She'll learn her place in the pack soon enough. Just you wait."

The words taste like metal in the back of my throat, but I swallow the bitterness down.

At least they do their job and appear to placate Autumn.

"Hopefully Jax figures out who her true pack is soon, so she can be out of our hair," Autumn says.

"Agreed," I say, even though I don't like the thought of Ruby leaving so quickly.

After all, she shifted for the first time in our territory.

She belongs to us.

But I need to stop thinking about her. Because Autumn is here in my bed, ready to let me do whatever I want to her. That little omega should be the last thing on my mind.

"Take this off." I pull at the strap of Autumn's nightgown, and she gives me a mischievous smile and follows my command, letting it drop into a pile around her feet.

"Better?" She tilts her head and bites her lower lip, teasing me with her naked body.

"I can't wait until your birthday so I can truly make you mine," I say, and then I push her down onto the bed, hover above her, and force myself to drive the thought of Ruby's hypnotizing eyes out of my mind as Autumn and I finally finish what we started when we woke up this morning.

Ruby

Jax barely speaks to me as he drives me to the small ranch house at the end of town where I'll be staying for the time-being.

I don't mind the lack of conversation. I'm so angry at him over my phone that I don't want to speak to him, either. He might claim to be looking out for me, but I think the only thing he cares about is getting me out of the way as soon as possible.

As for Connor, I have no idea what to make of him. It's like he can't decide if he wants to be welcoming, indifferent, or irritated at me.

Being attracted to him shouldn't be enough of a reason to make me trust him. Especially because Autumn wants to claw my eyes out if I so much as look at him. And I mean that literally, given the whole shifter thing and all.

I don't know when all of *that* will set in, but it certainly hasn't happened yet. It feels like I'm in an alternate reality. Like I'm living in one of the books I read instead of in real life.

I follow Jax inside the dreary house, and he brings the omega family up to speed about what's going on. They're a family of three—two parents and a sixteen-year-old daughter. They tell him they're more than happy to take me in, although I don't know if it's because they *want* to host me, or because it's their job as omegas to follow their alpha's command.

The mother—Felicity—looks at Jax with a timid sort of desire in her eyes, and I can't help but think that there's history between the two of them.

She looks heartbroken when he leaves.

"Thanks for letting me stay here," I tell them as he pulls out of the driveway. "This has all been very…" I pause, searching for a word to describe what it feels like to have my entire world turned upside down in less than twenty-four hours. "Shocking," I settle on, even though it doesn't come close to describing the myriad of emotions waging war inside my body.

"You can stay in my room," the daughter—Penny—offers. She's bouncing with excitement, clearly happy to have a guest stay in the house with them.

"Don't be silly," her father—Garrett—says. He's a short man with dirty blond hair and a matching scruffy beard, and he was drinking a beer when we arrived, even though it's before noon. "We're not hosting royalty. Ruby is an omega, like us. She'll sleep on the couch."

Apparently viewing the decision as settled, he sits down on the big armchair in the living room, turns on the TV, and returns to his beer.

I nearly growl at his swift dismissal, but given that I don't have anywhere else to go or stay, I rein it in.

Causing fights with these people isn't going to get me home any faster.

"I appreciate the offer, but I'm fine on the couch," I tell Penny, since they're being nice by taking me in at all. Plus, it's not her fault that her father's acting like a jerk.

"Okay." She pouts. "But you're going to need some clothes, and I think you're about the same size as me. Want to come try some stuff on?"

"That'd be great," I say, and Felicity gives me an encouraging smile before I follow Penny to her room.

The room isn't large, and the furniture is falling apart in places, but she's brightened it up with flowers and plants anywhere the light hits.

"I thought omegas couldn't use earth magic?" I ask.

"We can't," she says. "But I'm perfectly capable of growing and taking care of plants. And I'm never going to stop trying to use magic. Who knows—maybe after I have my first shift, everything will change."

"Does that ever happen?"

"Not really." She shrugs. "But it doesn't stop me from hoping. Just like how I'm going to train to be a Guardian up until our final exam, even though most omegas don't bother, since we're never chosen."

"Jax mentioned the Guardians a few times," I say. "What exactly are they?"

Her blue eyes light up, and she's clearly excited to fill me in. "We start training to be Guardians in our first year of high school," she begins. "Then, after graduation, we do an intense year of training to prepare for the big test. If we perform well on the test, we're sent to a city to serve as a Guardian for the next twenty years. Some cities—usually the bigger ones—are more dangerous than others. The shifters who perform the best on the test are sent to those. If you fail, you stay in pack territory and serve the pack."

"Wow." I take a moment to let it all sink in. "What makes a city dangerous?"

I'm guessing that since shifters are sent to guard the cities, she doesn't mean your average bank robber or mugger.

"Supernatural activity," she confirms. "Mainly vampires. Sometimes the occasional dark witch or fae, but we need approval from the covens to go after those."

"The covens?"

"Each pack serves a witch coven," she explains. "They make the rules, and we follow their rules to keep the world safe."

"So, shifters are soldiers."

"Exactly."

"Interesting," I say, still trying to wrap my mind around the fact that there are actual vampires in cities across the country.

It makes me appreciate the fact that I grew up in a small Florida beach town.

Penny pulls some clothes from her closet that she thinks will fit me. Her casual style is similar to mine, and I'm grateful for that as I try things on.

Eventually, her mom knocks on the door to check on us.

"Don't you have homework to do?" she asks Penny.

"It's Saturday," Penny says, rolling her eyes. "I can do it tomorrow."

"You'll do it now," she says. "Ruby, would you like to help me prepare lunch?"

It feels like an instruction more than a request. So I say okay, and we make our way into the small, dingy kitchen, where she gets the ingredients out for whatever she's about to prepare. I don't cook often—we live mainly on cereal, sandwiches, and microwave meals in my house—so I watch and wait for instructions.

"Penny's really nice," I say, wanting to break the silence.

"Let me guess—she told you she wants to be a Guardian?" she asks.

"She did."

Felicity lets out a sad sigh. "I'm glad she's so motivated, but I'm worried about how hard it's going to be when she doesn't get selected," she says.

"It's that impossible for omegas to be chosen?" I ask.

"No magic, no chance," she says. "No matter how good of a physical fighter you are, omegas aren't deserving of being blessed by the gods. Some even think of us as cursed."

There's a sadness in her worn eyes, and it hurts my heart to see her so broken.

"That's awful," I say. "I'm sorry."

"You'll get used to it," she says. "It's not bad here. We're given food and shelter, and we're kept safe by the pack as long as we provide for them. There are far worse fates than being an omega."

"But you're allowed to leave if you want?"

"Technically, yes," she says. "But few want to. It's too dangerous out there, especially for lone wolves with no magic. The ones who leave tend to never be heard from again."

I shiver, not liking the sound of that.

"Anyway, let's get started." She gives me a forced smile. "We're making a casserole. It should be more than enough for both lunch and dinner."

"Is there meat in it?" I ask, remembering the incident at breakfast.

"Of course there's meat in it." She looks at me like I'm crazy, and I know she's waiting for an explanation of my question.

"I'm a vegetarian," I tell her.

Her brows knit, and I can see I've absolutely befuddled her. "Well." She takes a deep breath, like she doesn't know what to say. "We can keep a section of the casserole meat-free. But now that you've shifted, you're eventually going to need to eat meat. You're not going to survive otherwise."

"So I've been told," I say, and while she still looks confused, she doesn't say anything more on the subject.

As we prepare lunch, she turns the television to a local news station. An overly greased up middle-aged man in a cheap navy suit sits at the desk, fake concern shining in his eyes.

"We just received word that a second person has gone missing," he says, keeping his expression solemn in a way that looks overly practiced.

I pause what I'm doing and stare at the television, prepared to see my face displayed on the screen.

Instead, it's an attractive man with blond hair and bright blue eyes.

"Jason Cook, age twenty-five, was snowboarding in the back bowls yesterday and never came home," he says. "If you have any news of his whereabouts, please come to the police station immediately. Jason is the second person to go missing in the past three days, preceded by Carly Katz, who went out for a jog near her home in the eastern part of town and never returned." Another photo flashes on the screen—a twenty-two-year-old woman of Native American descent with short hair and mysterious gray eyes. "Again, if you have any information about where either of them might be, please go to the police." He clears his throat, and then continues, "In other news, get ready for higher temperatures next week as a warm front passes through the area…"

He continues to talk about the weather, but I tune him out, my mind on the two missing people.

"Do you think it could be vampires?" The word feels ridiculous after it comes out of my mouth, but after everything I learned, I have to consider the possibility.

Felicity tsks at my question. "Vampires can't get into Pine Valley," she says. "The witches maintain a barrier spell around the town to keep them out, and they've never gotten through."

"Hm," I say. "Then could it be a shifter?"

She balks in offense. "Shifters don't attack humans, or eat humans," she says. "Whatever's going on with those people is a human crime. If our witches find out otherwise, they'll give us instructions for their decided course of action. Until then, we proceed as normal."

"So, you follow everything the witches tell you to do?"

"That's our job," she says proudly. "It's why they created us in the first place."

"They created you?" I ask, becoming more intrigued by the second.

"A long time ago, in the Dark Ages, when the vampires started to get out of control," she says. "We've protected the witches since, and they provide for us in return. But enough on all of that." She picks up the remote and changes the channel to Home and Garden Television. "It's far more important for you to learn what to expect on a day-to-day basis around town, and this casserole isn't going to make itself."

Connor

THE GUYS and I were supposed to go into town tonight for drinks at our favorite bar. College still hasn't started up yet for most of the east coast, which means a lot of human girls around our age are still on vacation here. They were hoping for a final night of trying to get lucky before the season slows down.

But the pent-up energy I have after the events of this morning with Ruby and Autumn is insane. So, I call off our Saturday night plans for a last-minute training session. As the grandson of the alpha—which makes me the future alpha of the pack—the guys have no choice but to listen.

Brandon's already had a beer or three, but I don't let him off the hook. In a real-world scenario, if a vampire attacks the city we're serving, we'd have to fight them no matter how much we had to drink. It's why Guardians aren't allowed to drink on the job.

We're pretty lax about it in our final year of training, which some also call our final year of freedom, but there's no time like the present for a reminder about why our rules exists in the first place.

We practice only with knives and claws, and after two hours go by, I notice the guys getting antsy.

"That's enough for tonight." One of my jobs as future alpha is to anticipate the needs of my pack, so I pull my claws back into my left hand Wolverine-style and sheathe my knife with my right. "Good session."

Brandon's breathing heavily, his hair soaked with sweat. "There's talk around town about that girl from last night," he says. "The hot one we beat at beer pong. Scarlet."

"Ruby," I correct him, and I curl my fingers into fists, waiting for him to continue.

"Yeah, her," he says. "She's staying with that omega family with the hot daughter that lives at the edge of town. The Lawrences."

I'm immediately on guard.

"Where did you hear that?" I ask, even though I'm not surprised. Shifters are naturally social, so word spreads fast around here.

"Garrett Lawrence. He was drinking at the pub earlier, and I heard him talking to some of the other omegas. He says Ruby didn't know she was a shifter until shifting last night at the party. Apparently she was adopted or something. She's also an omega, so she's staying with them until a more permanent situation is arranged for her."

His eyes go hungry at that last part, putting my nerves on edge as an intense need to protect her sets in.

"What's it to you?" I ask.

"So, you knew about it?" one of the other guys—Tyler—speaks up. His identical twin Thomas stands next to him, quiet as he waits for my response.

"Of course I knew," I say. "Jax and I dealt with her this morning. Like you heard, she's staying with the Lawrence's until we learn more about her heritage."

"And you didn't think to tell us?" Brandon blows out a frustrated breath.

"I didn't think it was relevant," I say, although the moment it's out of my mouth, I know it's a lie.

It's not that it isn't relevant.

It's because after the way Brandon treated Ruby last night, I wanted to keep her a secret from him for as long as possible.

"She's an *omega*," he says, as if he hasn't already made that clear. "A hot one. One we haven't had a chance to have any fun with yet."

Anger fires through me, and I have an intense urge to punch that arrogant look off his face.

Instead, I take a few long breaths to compose myself. "You know the rules," I say, sharp and clear. "Everyone in this pack gets the respect of giving their consent—including omegas."

The same can't be said for how some of the other packs treat their omegas, especially the more feral ones out west. But the Pine Valley pack is civilized and law-abiding. We value rules and structure above all else. That means respecting even the lowest members of our pack by not treating them like toys for us to play with.

"Ruby and I are only just starting to get to know each other." Hunger flashes in Brandon's eyes again, and he rubs his hands together, glancing back at Tyler and Thomas for their support. "She was shy last night, but I bet she just needs a bit of breaking in."

Another surge of red-hot anger passes through me, and the next thing I know, I've tackled Brandon to the ground and my knife is out, the flat end of it flush against his throat.

Fear flashes in Brandon's eyes, followed by challenge.

"Don't touch her," I growl, and I glance up at the twins to make sure they get the message as well. "She's mine."

Brandon simply raises an eyebrow. "What do you mean that she's *yours?*" he says, his voice scratchy thanks to my knife pressing on his windpipe.

Shit.

It's a good question. The words escaped my mouth on instinct, and I scramble for a believable explanation.

"I mean that once she learns her place as an omega, she'll be serving me, and by extension, my family." I raise the knife and slowly release my hold on him. "Giving her anything but the utmost respect is an offense not just to her, but to the ruling family of this pack."

Brandon raises his hands in defeat. "Chill, man," he says. "I didn't know."

"Now you do."

We both stand up, and I glance to the twins again.

They lower their eyes in respect.

Good. Message received loud and clear.

Brandon removes a twig from his hair and tosses it to the ground. "So, what does Autumn think about the little omega coming to live with you?" he asks.

A good question.

Especially because *I* didn't even know this was going to happen until saying it right now. But no matter what, Autumn and I must present a united front. It's our responsibility as the future leaders of this pack.

"I have Autumn's full support," I lie. "Ruby shifted for the first time on my property, and she came to me for help, which makes her my responsibility."

The reason sounds flimsy, but it's true.

Why else do I feel so protective over the little omega who showed up at my door this morning, scared and confused, begging for help?

Being protective is the instinct of an alpha, especially for the most vulnerable in the pack.

There's nothing more to it than that.

There *can't* be.

"As the future alpha, it's my duty to take care of my pack," I add, trying to convince them as much as myself. "Out of all of us, Ruby needs more help than anyone."

"It doesn't change the fact that a woman who's not your girlfriend will be living in your house until you move to the city to become a Guardian," Tyler points out.

I glare him into silence.

"Autumn is my future mate. She's not threatened by a little omega servant girl," I say, although I flash back to how concerned she was in my room this morning after Ruby left, and I'm not so sure about that.

But it doesn't matter. Like I just told them, all will be well after Autumn and I officially become mates.

Thomas has been quiet throughout all of this—he's always been the most introspective of the four of us—so when he speaks, we all turn to listen.

"What makes you so sure that you and Autumn will be mates?" he asks softly.

I narrow my eyes at him, angry at him for questioning such a thing.

Tyler and Brandon watch me carefully, also curious about my answer.

"Autumn is the strongest magic user of our kind in generations," I remind them. "I'm the strongest fighter, and our future alpha. We make sense together. You know it, as does everyone else in this pack who's supported us for the past few years."

"I'm aware of that," Thomas says sadly. "But sometimes loving someone isn't enough."

He's talking about his ex-girlfriend, Kara. The one he loved, then never heard from again after she mated with a member of the nearby Spring Creek pack and left to live with them.

She broke his heart, and he hasn't been the same since.

"You and Kara were only together for a few months," I point out.

"And in those few months, I loved her with every piece of my soul." His eyes are open and honest, and I feel for him, truly.

But it doesn't change the fact that his relationship with Kara was very different from my relationship with Autumn.

"I know you loved her," I say carefully. "But Autumn and I chose each other. We made a promise to each other. We're the strongest members of this pack, and we're going to stand by each other, whether we're fated mates or not."

I've never shared this with anyone.

But telling them makes the pact Autumn and I made feel more real. It gives me more of a reason to stand by my promise than ever.

I'm a man of my word, and I will never betray her.

"You'd really go against fate?" Thomas asks.

It's quiet in the clearing, the only sound the chirping of the crickets in the nearby forest. Thomas's question hangs in the air, and I feel Tyler and Brandon's continued curiosity as they wait for my answer.

"I'll do whatever's necessary to strengthen our pack, and Autumn is powerful, respected, and deserves to stand by my side." I stand strong, daring them to question me again.

For the first time in the years we've been friends, Brandon's expression is unreadable to me.

"You're the future alpha," he finally says. "Whatever you say goes."

I simply nod at him, and he lowers his gaze in deferral, as my beta should.

Tyler clears his throat and shuffles in discomfort. "So, how about those beers?" he asks with a chuckle, although no one laughs with him.

"You guys go," I say. "I'm done for the night."

I shift into my wolf form before they can ask anything more, intending to go straight home. But after that confrontation, I need to blow off some steam.

So I run through the woods with no destination in mind, eventually coming to a stop when I realize where I've ended up.

The house at the end of town where Ruby is staying with the Lawrence's.

Connor

My senses are enhanced while in wolf form, so I can hear the Lawrence's and Ruby chatting from where I'm standing in the backyard. The small window that I assume is in the kitchen is cracked open, so I smell what they're eating—some sort of hot dish with ground beef.

The teen girl who Brandon referred to as their "hot daughter"—Penny—is asking Ruby what it's like to go to school in the human world.

Brandon might not have known Penny's name, but I make it my personal mission to know the names of everyone in the pack, along with general details about them. Someday they'll be *my* pack, and a good alpha knows enough about all their pack members to ensure we live in happiness and harmony.

The window is high up—it's the type that's usually above the kitchen sink—so I can't see inside. But there's a tree in the backyard with a trunk and branches thick enough for climbing. It's far enough from the house that I should be able to climb it without them seeing me, especially since it's night.

I shift into human form behind the trunk, climb it so swiftly that I make zero noise, and settle in the branches about six feet above the ground. From up here, I see Ruby, Penny, and Felicity eating what looks to be some sort of casserole.

Has Ruby given in and started eating meat yet?

I hope so.

I can't tell with my human eyes, so I shift my eyes into the eyes of my wolf. Partly shifting is an advanced skill, and one we can't hold for extended periods of time, but it's useful in moments like this.

With my wolf vision, I see them as clearly as I would if I was with them in the room.

Ruby is so beautiful that she takes my breath away. There's something so sweet and innocent about her, but thoughtful and grounded at the same time. Her warmth pulls me into her orbit whenever I'm around her, and even now, I ache to knock on the door and check on her to see how she's been settling in.

She smiles at something Penny says, and seeing her like that makes me smile as well.

I shouldn't feel this way about someone I just met.

The only time I've ever heard about anyone feeling this sort of attraction to someone is when they're initially around their mate. That urge to touch them... to ignite the mate bond...

My wolf's excitement grows as he urges me to dig deeper into the feeling.

No, I shake the thought away.

Ruby is *not* my mate.

Autumn and I share the sort of deep trust that only forms when two people have spent years getting to know each other. She's my number one ally in life—someone who will stand by my side no matter what.

Autumn would never betray me, and I'll never betray her by giving in to whatever pull I feel toward Ruby.

Mate bonds don't form until first touch. If Ruby is my mate, all I have to do is make sure to never touch her.

Except I scrambled back at training and told the guys that I intended on having Ruby serve at my house as an omega.

I'll have to think up a reason to tell them about why I changed my mind. Because I can't let myself get within arm's length of that girl, let alone have her live in my house.

On top of that, despite what I told them, Autumn wouldn't be happy with Ruby staying with me.

I'll think of something.

Suddenly, Ruby turns her attention away from Penny and glances out the window.

I duck behind the trunk quickly enough that there's no chance she had time to see me, especially because it's dark and she's only using human vision. But I stay perfectly still just in case, holding my breath and making no sound.

Eventually, I peek around the tree, relieved that she's returned to answering Penny's questions about the human world.

I need to get out of here.

But there was a reason I came up here. I need check to see if Ruby's eating meat yet.

So I zero in on the plates on the table, easily making out the chunks of ground beef on Penny and Felicity's plates.

There's no meat on Ruby's plate. Just noodles, vegetables, and cheesy sauce.

She's eating a glorified mac and cheese.

Stupid girl. She's going to slowly starve her wolf if she keeps this up. Eventually she'll crack, but until then, weakening herself isn't going to do her any favors.

As it is, the smell of their food makes my stomach growl. It's been hours since I've eaten, on top of the calories burned by training. Not only do I need to get out of here to make sure they don't notice me, but I need food.

More than that—I'm fired up and need to hunt.

So I take a leaping jump out of the tree, shift into wolf form, and run into the woods, following the scent of a nearby deer that's about to become my dinner.

* * *

After releasing my stress with a good old-fashioned hunt, my belly is full and my excess energy is sated. I run back home in wolf form, only shifting back to human form when I reach the door.

My phone buzzes in my pocket as it receives the texts I missed while out. It's impossible to truly apply science to the laws of magic, but the consensus is that since phones are made mainly of metals derived from the earth, they're able to shift with us as easily as simple pieces of jewelry.

I get inside, grab a sports drink from the fridge, and check my phone.

There's a missed call from Autumn, followed by a text.

The guys told me you went on a run instead of coming out. Everything okay?

I curse, realizing I didn't tell Autumn I wasn't going to be at the bar, because I was so consumed with my conflicted feelings about Ruby. She tried being relaxed about it in her text, but I know Autumn. She's organized and a good communicator, like I normally am.

She isn't happy about this.

Sorry, I reply. *Had a lot on my mind and needed to clear my head.*

It's not a lie. But it's also not a good enough explanation, and I know it.

Her reply comes quickly.

Anything you want to talk about? I can come over if you want.

There's a lot I want to talk about. But I can't talk about it with her. I can't talk about it with *anyone*.

Autumn's always been the person I go to with anything. Whenever I need to get something off my chest, she listens patiently. She can somehow tell the difference between when I need to vent and when I need to brainstorm solutions. She's always been my rock, no matter what.

Ruby's arrival might as well have kicked that rock off a cliff and buried it deep in the ocean.

A part of me hates her for it. Because I can't talk to Autumn about Ruby, which means I have no one to go to about this, and it's lonely as all hell.

I look back at her text.

Is there anything I want to talk about?

Yes.

But I can't say that.

All good, I write instead. *I'm just going to relax and go to bed.*

The type bubbles start on her end. They continue for a while, and I can barely breathe as I watch them, bracing myself for anything.

Then they stop.

I hover my thumbs over the keyboard. I want to assure her that everything's okay, but how can I say that when I'm not sure it's true?

Luckily, the text bubbles start again, and she sends the message.

Okay :(

That can't be all she was typing before. Whatever she was about to say, she changed her mind and sent that instead.

My chest hollows with guilt.

I could tell her that I changed my mind and invite her over, but honestly, I'm not in the mood. And I don't want her to press for more information about what's bothering me, since I'm not ready to share it.

I can't imagine *ever* being ready to share it.

Somehow, I have to push my conflicted feelings aside and act like everything's normal tomorrow. Hopefully it won't be long until Autumn chalks this up to my having a bad day and forgets about it.

Sorry, I apologize again. *I'll see you tomorrow. Sleep well.*

You too, she says, but as I lay down in bed and start drifting off, those bright turquoise eyes are the last things I see before falling asleep.

Ruby

Penny watches a lot of television—mainly teen dramas—and all through dinner, she wouldn't stop asking me about the human world. Answering her questions kept my mind off all the craziness from the past twenty-four hours, so I engaged myself in the conversation as best as possible.

We finish eating, and Penny's dad still isn't back from the bar. She and her mom don't talk about his absence—I have a feeling this is normal around here—so I don't bring it up, either.

"Do you want to shower and change?" Penny asks after we finish cleaning up.

The last time I showered was before Luna and I headed to the hotel bar, and given that I spent last night in the woods, I'm sure I've smelled better in my life.

Hopefully I'll get word about Luna soon. Penny and Felicity wouldn't let me use their phones—they said they couldn't go against Jax's orders—and I don't know their passcodes to try to steal their phones and use them myself.

I wish there was something I could do other than waiting for Jax to pass on whatever the witches tell him, but until that happens, I need to hang tight.

"Ruby?" Penny tries to catch my attention.

"Sorry," I say. "I was thinking."

"What about?"

"About my friend," I say. "Luna. I'm worried about her."

"Jax will let us know when he has news," Felicity says what I already know. "In the meantime, I agree with Penny that you should take a shower."

Wow—I *really* must smell.

"Sure," I say, and Penny gets me set up with pajamas and towels, and I head to the bathroom to clean up.

They were right. The warm shower feels amazing. I shampoo my hair twice to get out all the grime, digging into my scalp extra hard, then move onto lathering the puff with lavender soap to clean my body.

I glance down to wash my stomach and spot a large smudge of mud on my hip.

Gross. I apparently got dirtier in my night in the woods than I realized.

But when I examine it closer, it's obvious that it's not mud.

It looks like a brown henna tattoo of the North Star. It's about an inch long, with eight points coming out of the center.

I stare at it in shock, as if it'll go away the more I focus.

Unsurprisingly, nothing changes.

I scrub it with the puff, but it doesn't come off. So I use my nail and scratch at it instead, but all I do is leave the skin around it pink and irritated.

This isn't possible.

I'd remember if I got a henna tattoo, and I'd *certainly* remember if I got a real tattoo.

Then again, my eyes are now brown instead of turquoise, and I shifted into a wolf last night. What's one more weird thing to add on top of everything else?

I finish the shower quickly, then change into the pajamas Penny supplied. I don't consider yoga pants and tight workout tops to be "pajamas," but that's what she wears, and I'm not in any position to be picky.

I knock on her door once I'm finished, and she invites me in, looking me up and down. "You okay?" she asks.

"Yeah," I say quickly. "Thanks for the clothes."

"No problem." She doesn't add anything more, and I can tell she knows I want to talk with her about something.

I almost show her the star mark on my hip. But I'm not supposed to tell anyone about my natural eye color, and my instinct tells me to keep the star a secret, too.

"Are wolves connected to the North Star?" I ask instead.

"No." Her brow creases in confusion. "Why?"

"No reason," I say, since asking anything more than that might cause suspicion. "Do you want to watch TV? I know you said you're a fan of Elementals, and I think there was a new episode last night."

"Yes!" she all but squeals. "Do you want popcorn?"

"We just ate…"

"I know." She rolls her eyes. "But buttery popcorn is a great dessert."

"I'm more of a chocolate girl," I say. "But sure. Popcorn sounds great."

She gets to making it, and I flip on the TV in the living room, which is set to the local news channel. Again, the faces of the two missing people flash across the screen, with the newscaster reminding people to go to the police if they have any information about their whereabouts.

Hopefully it's not my and Luna's faces up there next.

"Creepy, isn't it?" Penny asks as she joins me on the couch with a giant bowl of popcorn.

"Yeah," I say. "Do you guys not have any way of helping the police find them? Can you shift into wolves and try to track them down by scent?"

"Maybe," she says. "But we try not to get involved in human affairs. Our job is to keep the supernatural world under control, and we let the humans handle their problems themselves."

"But you could be helping them…"

"The witches make the rules—not us." She picks up the remote, switches to the streaming channels, and selects *Elementals*. "Ready?"

"Yeah," I say, but even though it's a great episode, I can't focus on it. My brain's too busy thinking about all the craziness that's happened in the past day.

And when we wrap up and go to bed, it's Connor's dark brown eyes that I see in my mind before falling asleep.

Ruby

I SPEND the entire next day watching television with Penny. Her dad went into town to watch a football game with his friends, so we have the television to ourselves.

It's unproductive.

I should be trying to learn more about the pack and the town. Or trying to learn how to shift, or trying again with earth magic. But I'm tired, and my brain feels numb and sluggish. It's like I'm glued to the couch, and it's easier to zone out than to get stuck in a loop of repetitive anxious thoughts about the fact that my life as I knew it doesn't exist anymore.

Someone rings the doorbell, and Penny looks at the front door, confused.

"Are you expecting someone?" I ask.

"No. At least, I don't think so," she says. "Maybe my mom is?"

But Felicity looks equally as confused as she hurries from the kitchen—where she was making dinner—to answer the door.

Connor stands in the entrance, and his eyes immediately go to me.

My breath catches in my chest, and I feel more trapped in his gaze than I've been to the couch all day. But I force myself to stand, not wanting him to see me as weak, although so much blood rushes from my head that it takes effort to not fall over.

"Connor." Felicity all but lowers herself into a curtsy. "I assume you've come to check on Ruby?"

"I have." He's still looking at me instead of at Felicity, his eyes burning into my soul.

I have no idea what to say.

Luckily, Felicity continues. "Your timing is perfect—I'm just finishing up making dinner," she says. "Do you want to join us?"

"Did you make enough?" he asks.

"It's sloppy joes on the menu tonight, and there's more than enough. Plus macaroni and cheese for Ruby," she adds, glancing over at me in concern.

I give her a small smile, grateful to her for going out of the way for me.

"Sloppy joes are my favorite," Connor says, and a few minutes later, we're all gathered around the kitchen table as Felicity doles out our food.

The macaroni and cheese looks good—extra cheesy, just how I like it.

But the smell of the sloppy joes makes my mouth water.

Connor's sitting across from me, his eyes boring into me as we go over the initial pleasantries.

"I have good news," he says to me after Felicity sits down to join us.

"Yes?" I stop eating my food, waiting for him to continue.

"There's an opening for a waitress position at Park Tavern," he says. "You'll start tomorrow afternoon."

Park Tavern—the sports bar where Penny's dad is watching the game with his friends right now.

"Thanks," I say, although I'm so tired that I can't imagine being on my feet all day.

Concern splashes over his face. "What's wrong?"

"Nothing." I force a smile, hoping I look bright-eyed and awake. "I'm good."

"She hasn't gotten up from the couch all day," Penny outs me, and I give her a look to tell her to stop, but she either doesn't understand or doesn't care. "I think it's because she isn't eating meat."

Connor puts down his sandwich and studies me. "Is this true?"

"I've been tired," I admit. "But I'll be fine tomorrow after a good night's rest."

A lie. Because from the way my stomach growls at the mention of meat, and how a part of me wants to reach forward and snatch that sandwich from Connor's plate, I have a feeling that Penny's onto something.

I glance at Felicity, but she simply shrugs.

"You look exhausted. Sick," she says. "I think they're right. It's why I made extra beef tonight."

"I'm fine." I shovel a forkful of mac and cheese into my mouth in protest, but it's frustratingly unsatisfying.

"Do you feel sluggish? Hazy?" Connor asks. "Like you have severe brain fog?"

"I'm fine," I repeat, although it doesn't sound convincing, not even to me.

"You're literally starving the wolf side of your body," he says, apparently unwilling to drop this. "It won't get better unless you eat meat."

"When you put it that way, it sounds like I'm a vampire deprived of blood," I say.

"It's a good comparison," he says, and he gets up, prepares another sloppy joe, and drops it onto my plate. "Eat."

It's a command—not a request.

My mouth waters again at the smell of meat, my stomach growls, and every cell in my body is screaming at me to pick up that sandwich and devour it.

Connor sits back down, his eyes locked on mine.

Felicity and Penny look back and forth between us, silently waiting.

I try to keep my breaths shallow to stop myself from smelling the meat, but it's no use. They're right. I know they are. I've never felt this sluggish in my life, and Connor's description of what I'm going through was right on the nose.

Eat it, my wolf says, and I realize I haven't heard from her all day. *We need it. We're no good to anyone when we're this weak.*

She's right, too. How am I supposed to get out of here if I barely have enough energy to stand?

I won't. I'll lay around on the couch and starve.

I refuse to dig my own grave.

So I pick up the sandwich, take a giant bite of it… and it's *the* most delicious thing I've ever eaten in my life. Energy floods my veins as it fills me up like no food ever has before, and soon, the entire thing is gone.

Felicity is already coming over with another, and I devour it as well.

Once finished, I feel more satiated than I have after any other meal in my life.

"Good?" Connor asks with a satisfied smirk.

"Yeah," I admit, and I pick at the mac and cheese, but it has zero appeal after that sloppy joe.

He continues eating his sandwich, and I can tell by the way he occasionally glances at me that he thinks he won.

Which, admittedly, he sort of did.

"Have you heard anything about Luna?" I ask, praying the answer is yes.

"I have," he says, and with that, all thought of my food is forgotten.

"Where is she? Is she okay? Can I talk to her?" The questions come out in a rush, and I watch him closely, as if it'll encourage him to answer them faster.

"She's okay." He brings out his phone, taps the screen a few times, and places it on the center of the table. "See for yourself."

I pick it up and see a photo of Luna walking through campus. She's wearing all black, and she's heading toward the library steps. Even though her face is angled away from the camera, I know it's her.

I slide to the next photo, and there's Luna sitting on a bench in one of the courtyards in a similar black outfit, reading a book.

I tap on the photo and see it's dated from this morning. There are a few others, all of Luna around campus, with various time stamps. They end in the afternoon.

"What happened to her?" I ask, since it's absurd that she simply flew back to campus and is acting like everything's normal.

"Jax spoke to the witches after dropping you off here, and they headed to the hotel where the two of you were staying," he says. "They used their magic to get into Luna's room, and she was still sleeping when they found her. They said she looked like she'd had a rough night."

"You expect me to believe that she headed back to the hotel without me, like it was no big deal?"

"She said she was drunk," he says. "She didn't remember getting back."

I almost tell him that's impossible. Luna doesn't get blackout drunk. Then again, I've never seen her drink as much as she had during the party.

"What happened from there?" I ask, since I'm not going to stop asking questions now that I'm finally getting some answers.

"They used a spell to alter her memory. She now believes she came here to ski alone, and that you left the country a week ago to study abroad. The witches were able to get her to give them enough information about where to find your parents, and they now believe the story as well."

Alarm rushes through me. "They spoke to my parents?"

"Relax," he says. "Your parents are fine. The situation is handled."

He shows me more photos, these ones of my parents, with time stamps about four hours after the photos of Luna. The photos are taken from outside a window of our house, and I'm relieved to see that they look okay.

I drop the phone back down on the center of the table. "How am I supposed to know these are real?" I ask.

"You're just going to have to trust me," he says. "Like my grandfather told you, you're being treated as a member of this pack until we learn more about your heritage. We look out for our own, no matter what."

I glance at Penny, and she nods in encouragement.

I don't like this. Something about it feels off in a way I can't explain.

But getting on the bad side of this pack won't do me any favors. It might be best to just nod and agree until I figure out how to get out of here.

"Where do they think I'm studying?" I ask, since the more information I can get, the better.

"Perth, Australia. One of the farthest places away from Florida you can get."

"And why do they think they haven't heard from me since I left?"

"Time zone changes? Jet lag? The length of the trip?" He shrugs. "I don't know. That's the sort of thing the witches figure out. But like I said, they're experts at dealing with supernatural relations with the human world, and they have this handled."

It sounds sketchy to me.

"So, you just follow the witches' rules without questions?" I ask.

"The witches and the wolves have a symbiotic relationship. Rules are what have kept the supernatural world in order for over a thousand years," he says, his expression stone cold. "It's our job as shifters to enforce them."

He's clearly not changing his mind, so I go back to picking at my mac and cheese.

The silence is insanely tense, but Penny breaks in, stopping it from getting even more awkward.

"What's it like to train as a Guardian?" she asks Connor, her tone light in comparison to the previous conversation. "Have you killed any vampires yet?"

"Not yet," he says with a small smile. "We don't kill any vampires until we've passed our final test and are serving in the city streets."

"Then how do you know if you can kill them or not?"

"Consider our first year in the city to be the *actual* final test," he says. "Although I suppose that every vampire we face is a test."

"It sounds exciting." She frowns, her gaze lowering to her food. "I wish I could be a Guardian."

"Penny," Felicity warns.

"Sorry." Penny shrugs, although she doesn't sound sorry. "It's the truth."

Another awkward silence descends upon the table, but this time, no one tries to break it. Instead, we focus on finishing our food as quickly as possible.

Eventually, everyone's done, and Felicity starts collecting our plates.

"I need to speak with you," Connor suddenly says to me. "Alone."

My stomach flips at the thought of being alone with him. "Why?"

"Because there's something I want to tell you privately."

I feel like an idiot after he says it. Of course he wouldn't ask to speak to me alone otherwise.

"You can go to my room," Penny pipes in, and when she looks back and forth between me and Connor, it's obvious from her expression that she thinks something's going on between us.

Logically, I know there isn't. There can't be. He has Autumn, and Penny's filled me in on enough that I know royals—especially alphas—don't date omegas. The only exception is if they mate, which happens rarely, and when it does happen, it's not viewed upon highly at all.

"Ruby, do you remember where Penny's room is?" Felicity asks, snapping me back into focus.

My cheeks blush, since the house is small enough that I'd have to be an idiot to not remember where it is. "I do," I say, and I push out my chair and walk down the hall, trying not to think too hard about the sound of Connor's footsteps behind me, and about how this will be the first time the two of us will ever be alone together.

Nothing's going to happen, I tell myself, and I open the door to Penny's room and step aside, letting Connor go first.

He hurries through, staying as far as possible from me and barely looking at me. It's like he thinks I have the plague, but that doesn't stop tingles from rushing down my spine as he passes.

And even though every logical thought says he'll never see me as anything other than an omega, from the way he sucks in a sharp breath when there are only inches between us, I can almost swear he feels the electricity there, too.

Connor

THAT WAS CLOSE, I think after making my way through the door.

I should have insisted she enter first. Then there would have been no chance of accidentally coming into contact.

I can't risk slipping up like that again.

Technically, I shouldn't still be here. I already did what I came here to do—passing along my grandfather's message about her parents and Luna. There's no need to stay around for any longer.

But I saw the way her pale face filled with color after eating that meat, how the hollows under her eyes disappeared, and how much more focused she seemed than earlier.

What if she isn't an omega? What if she couldn't harness earth magic because she was nutritionally deficient? What if her body was using up all its energy to keep her alive, so she hadn't been able to expend an ounce more to connect with the earth?

If I left without answers, I wouldn't stop wondering. And I hate the thought of leaving her with omegas if she has more potential than that. Especially because if she isn't truly an omega, Brandon and the other guys will leave her alone.

I need to know the truth for my own sanity and peace of mind.

So, here I am, alone with her in Penny's dingy room.

It's dangerous territory. But I feel a thrill of excitement about it at the same time.

She shuts the door and crosses her arms, remaining near it as if she might need to make a quick exit. The tight yoga pants and tank top combination she's wearing accentuates all her curves, and as I drink her in, my mind wanders to my dream last night.

The dream where she wasn't wearing any clothing at all, where I felt her warm skin against mine, and she melted into my arms as I claimed her as my own.

The memory makes my body pulse with animalistic need.

Touch her, my wolf's voice echoes in my mind. *Take her as ours.*

My blood pumps faster, and it takes every effort to stay where I am.

She's not ours, I tell my wolf. *Autumn's ours.*

How can we know if we don't try?

My eyes are locked on Ruby's, and from the way her breathing slows and her cheeks flush, I have a feeling she's fighting her desire as much as I am mine.

Just a touch, my wolf continues to goad me. *So we can know for sure.*

No.

I need to stop this.

Now.

I don't want to know, I think, and I push my wolf down, step back, and rein in my desire. Even though I've never been as attracted to anyone as I am to Ruby, I don't know her. These feelings aren't real. They're lust—not love.

I'm stronger than such basic, primal instincts. I will *not* let wolf control me.

My loyalty to Autumn is too strong for me to hurt her like that.

At the thought of my girlfriend, I snap myself back into focus.

"Why are we here?" Ruby asks me, and she's breathing normally again, apparently yanked out of the spell as well.

"I wanted to talk to you," I say.

"I gathered that."

She says nothing more, waiting for me to explain. I have no idea how she's remaining so calm. I've never known of a shifter who grew up without knowing what they are. Everything she's been through these past two days is basically unheard of.

Her bravery and strength in such a difficult, likely scary situation is highly admirable.

"I want to test your magic again," I tell her.

She raises an eyebrow in an unfairly tempting way. "I thought I didn't have any magic."

There's a hint of challenge in her tone, and even though I haven't proven anything yet, I have a strong feeling that I was right to do this.

I glance around the room, since I was so focused on Ruby that I hadn't paid attention to my surroundings. It's a tiny room, with a twin bed, one nightstand, and a small bookshelf. The window is small, only allowing a bit of natural light inside, but a bunch of plants are lined up on the windowsill anyway.

Even omegas have a natural draw toward greenery, and I'm happy to see that Penny isn't an exception.

I pluck a barely budding rose from one of the pots, examine it, and turn to face Ruby again. "The meat made you stronger," I say. "Visibly so. Now that you've fed your wolf, I want to see if your inability to connect with earth magic yesterday was a mistake."

I walk over to hand her the rose, but stop myself when I'm halfway there.

If I hand it to her, I'll risk touching her.

So I lay the rose on the gray, carpeted floor between us instead.

"Thank you?" She says it as a question, glancing at the budding rose and back at me.

"Pick it up," I tell her. "Make it bloom."

She gives the flower a wary look. "Okay," she finally says, and then she kneels to pick it up.

The little tank top she's wearing doesn't leave much to the imagination, especially while I'm staring down at her from above. My breath hitches, desire coursing through me, and I force myself to look at the wall until Ruby is safely standing again.

"Are you okay?" she asks, and she has the audacity to sound *amused.*

"I'm fine." I don't feel a need to add any more than that. Instead, I stare at the rose, waiting for her to start.

The sooner she proves she isn't an omega, the sooner I can get out of here and go on a run to shed all this excess energy that builds inside me whenever I'm in Ruby's presence.

She brushes the stem of the rose with her fingers, studying it. "How am I supposed to do this?" she asks.

"It's hard to explain how to use magic. It's more of an instinct than anything else," I tell her. "But you should connect with the flower's energy. Imagine it opening up so the petals inside it can be free to grow and bloom."

"All right." She studies the rose bud again, although she keeps glancing up at me, checking to see if she's doing it right.

Am I distracting her?

Is it wrong of me to like it if I am?

"Close your eyes and picture it blooming in your mind," I say.

"Here goes nothing," she says, and she takes a deep breath and closes her eyes.

The skin between her brows furrows as she concentrates, and I find myself studying her face. It's heart-shaped, and her features are delicate, making her look almost more fae than shifter. Her entire frame is delicate, but there's also a strength to her that makes her seem unbreakable. And when a ray of light shines through the window, warming her skin, there's a glow to her that's downright radiant.

Energy buzzes between us, and the pull I feel to her is unreal. I want to take her hands in mine and let my magic flow into her, so she can get a taste of what it feels like and recreate it herself.

But I can't do that. I can't touch her.

I *won't* touch her.

Suddenly, the rosebud flickers.

It slowly starts to open, and I lean forward in excitement. "There you go," I say. "Keep going. Just like that."

She opens her eyes, her gaze meeting mine, and the rose returns to its original state.

She looks down at the bud in confusion. "What happened?" she asks.

"It was starting to bloom," I say, but then I think back to *exactly* what happened.

The energy I felt between us. My urge to reach out and help her.

Did she actually do anything? Or did I unconsciously project my magic onto the rose because of how badly I wanted this to work?

"Did you feel anything before you opened your eyes?" I ask.

"I was picturing the rose blooming, like you told me to," she says. "I felt a tingle in my head."

"Anything in your palms?"

"No." She flips her hand over and studies her palm. "Was I supposed to?"

Her hand is so small.

I want to reach for it and find out if her skin is as soft as it looks.

But I need to control myself. I'm a person who follows logic—not emotions. And even if Ruby isn't an omega, what should it matter to me? She technically stopped being my problem the moment my grandfather dropped her off with the Lawrence's. Once he figures out what pack she belongs to, she'll be out of here, and this pull I feel toward her will fade into oblivion.

Hopefully he gets answers sooner rather than later.

Until then, I need to stay as far away from her as possible, to escape this driving force inside me that's begging me to take her in my arms and claim her as mine.

Ruby

I'M WAITING for Connor to answer my question, but he's staring at my hand, his mind gone to another place.

"Conner?" I say, and he snaps back into focus. "Was I supposed to feel something in my hand?"

"You were." His words are clipped and harsh, as if he's angry at me for failing to make the rose bloom. "My grandfather's assessment of you yesterday was correct. You're an omega."

His disappointment in me is clear, and I hate the way he's looking at me. As if I'm worthless. Lower than dirt.

I place the rose at my side and leave it there, not wanting to see the evidence of my failure for a second longer.

But this isn't right. He's wrong about me. I'm not an omega. I feel it with every inch of my soul.

"I have to go," he says, making his way slowly to the door.

He can't leave.

If he leaves now, who knows when I'll be able to talk to him again? Especially because the entire time we've been alone in this room together, there's been a burning question I've been dying to ask him.

I need answers, and as the grandson of the alpha, he might know enough to give them to me.

"Wait," I say, relieved when he stops and looks at me to go on.

It's now or never.

"I'm not an omega," I say quickly, continuing before I can second-guess myself. "In the shower last night, I found this." I pull the waistband of my yoga pants down to reveal the North Star on my hip.

He studies it in silence for a few seconds.

His expression is unreadable. I have no idea what he's thinking, but instead of asking, I wait for him to speak first.

"You have a tattoo," he finally says.

"I don't," I say. "I have no idea what this is, but it wasn't here before I shifted."

"Are you sure?"

"Yes." I all but roll my eyes. "I'm sure."

He reaches out his hand, fingers outstretched, but quickly pulls back. "I've never seen anything like that in my life," he says.

Disappointment floods me, but I'm not going to give up that quickly. "Have you ever heard of a shifter being marked?" I ask.

"No." He studies me a bit longer, his eyes raking over every inch of my body, and his gaze hardens.

Any hint of friendliness is gone.

All that's left is suspicion.

He backs away, as if I'm an enemy, and for the first time in his presence, I feel cold, raw fear.

I release my waistband, covering the mark again. "You know what it means," I say steadily, since he wouldn't act this way if he didn't.

"I don't."

"Then why are you looking at me like that?"

He relaxes slightly, but it's too late to hide his true reaction. "How am I looking at you?" he asks, distant and cold.

"Like I've done something wrong."

He inhales, and his eyes soften again. "You haven't done anything wrong," he says smoothly—too smoothly. "You were right to show me this. I'll help you figure out what it means. Just hold tight, okay?"

The mark buzzes so much that it stings.

It's warning me. I'm not sure what it's warning me about, but his suspicion is setting me on edge, and my gut instinct says I need to get out of here.

The shifters stick to the laws and rules the witches put on them. From my conversations with Penny and Felicity, I know that if there's one thing the shifters hate more than anything else, it's the unknown.

Showing this to him was a mistake.

I feel like an idiot for trusting him.

"Sure," I somehow manage to say. "Thanks."

"Anytime." He smiles grimly, and my heart pounds with anxiety. "Goodnight, Ruby."

"Night," I say, and he hurries out of the room, leaving me alone and confused.

I don't believe that he doesn't know what the mark means. He wouldn't have looked at me like that if he didn't.

And whatever it means, it isn't anything good.

He's undoubtedly going to tell someone about it. Probably Jax. And if Jax was unfriendly to me when he decided I was an omega, what's going to happen when he finds out about this?

More importantly, how stupid was I to trust Connor? I've known him for less than two days. It's like he's cast a spell on me, making me open up when I should be on guard, and I don't like it one bit.

I'm standing there in a daze when Penny bursts into the room.

"What happened?" she asks.

"I'm not sure." I stare at the door where Connor just left, wishing I could go back in time and stop myself from showing him the mark.

She walks over and kneels to pick up the budding rose. "What were you doing with this?"

"Oh. That," I say, relieved to be reminded about why Connor brought me in here before things went south. "Connor wanted me to try using earth magic again."

"And…"

"I couldn't." I shrug. "Looks like I'm an omega. Like you." I try to smile, but I'm sure it looks forced.

"I'd say that being an omega isn't bad, but…" she trails off, since the rest of the sentence goes without saying.

"Have you ever wanted to get out of here?" I ask. "To leave and never come back?"

"I don't know." She shifts uncomfortably. "Sure, I've thought about it. But where would I go? I'd never fit into the human world, and no pack would take in a runaway omega. I belong to the Pine Valley pack, and I will for the rest of my life."

"You talk about it like you're their property," I say.

"As an omega, I basically am."

After she says it, the reality of my situation sets in. If I stay in Pine Valley, I'll be trapped here, like Penny and the other omegas. Or worse, if Connor's reaction to my star mark is anything to go by.

I need to get out.

I glance at the window, set in my decision, then look back at Penny. "It's been a long day," I tell her, yawning for emphasis. "I'm exhausted. Will you let me sleep in here tonight? Alone?"

The corners of her lips turn up into a small smile. "Are you saying you want me to sleep on the couch?"

"Would you mind?" I hold my breath, praying she'll say yes.

She glances at the rosebud in her hand, and I worry I've overstepped my welcome.

"Sure," she finally says. "Just promise me one thing."

"What's that?"

"Try not to kill any more of my plants."

Ruby

PENNY'S DAD comes back around nine, and everyone goes to bed at ten, since Penny has school in the morning and her parents have work.

I should be going to bed as well, to make sure I'm well-rested for my first day working at Park Tavern. But there won't be a first day at Park Tavern for me, since I'll hopefully be well on my way back to Florida tomorrow.

I wait until after midnight, when I'm sure everyone is asleep. Then I grab a fleece from Penny's closet and a pair of sneakers. The shoes are a size too big, but I tie them tightly enough that it should hopefully be okay.

I'm as careful as possible as I remove the plants and flowers from the windowsill, placing them gently on the floor next to me.

My body is a bundle of nerves as I stare at the window. I can't mess this part up. If they hear me, it's game over. So I steady my hands, unlock the window, and slowly push it up to open it.

It creaks, and I pause and hold my breath, praying they didn't hear. Penny's parents sleep with the television on, but who knows what she can hear from the living room?

It'll be okay, I think, trying to talk myself down.

If she comes in, I'll tell her I needed to let in some fresh air. She'll probably ask why her plants are on the floor, but I could say I was being extra careful to not knock them over.

A minute passes, then another, and another.

No one comes in, and I give a silent thanks to whatever force in the universe is looking out for me.

Pretty sure I'm in the clear, I open the window the rest of the way, slowly enough to not make any more noise. The crisp winter air feels fresh, like it's welcoming my escape. And while it's not the biggest window in the world, I'm small enough that I'm able to scoot through it without making any noise.

I land on the ground, crouching next to the house so no one can see me through the windows, and my heart pounds with exhilaration.

I did it.

I'm out.

But I still have a long way to go.

Even though it's likely a long shot, I close my eyes and call on my wolf.

If we're going to figure out to shift on command, now would be a great time to make it happen, I think.

As strange as it is, I feel her *bristle* inside me, as if her fur's standing on end.

No.

I don't hear her voice, but her disagreement reins me in, stopping me from shifting.

Come on. I grind my teeth together and try to push out of my skin to recreate the feeling I had when I shifted two nights ago.

She pulls me back again. And while she doesn't say anything, a picture floats through my mind.

Connor. Specifically, how concerned he was when he realized how tired I was feeling, and how he looked out for me by insisting I eat meat.

He fed my wolf, and she loves him for it.

She doesn't want to leave him. To be honest, a part of me doesn't want to leave him, either.

But the way he looked at me when he saw the star mark burns in my mind—like I'm his enemy—and I know I need to get out of here.

Luckily, my wolf doesn't seem to have any physical control over me when I'm in human form. And while it would be nice to have her help, I can do this on my own.

Not wanting to waste any more time, I sprint across the backyard and into the trees. The moon is full enough that it casts light into the forest, and since the tree branches are bare of leaves, I have enough light to see as I hurry deeper into the woods.

I was hoping to shift and use my wolf's natural sense of direction to find my way back to town, but since that's not happening, it's time for the backup plan.

The main town is at the bottom of the mountain, which means I need to follow the mountain down. Once there, I can go to the hotel or to the police station, get in touch with my parents, and have them buy me a plane ticket home.

It's far from a perfect plan. If anyone realizes I'm gone, wolves have a strong sense of smell and will likely be able to track me down. But it's the best I've got.

Staying in the same place isn't helping anything, and overanalyzing my plan isn't doing my nerves any favors. So I look both ways and run down the mountain as fast as I can go, which ends up being decently fast, given that I've never been much of an athlete. I don't even find myself running out of breath.

It *has* to be thanks to my newfound wolf powers.

Eventually, I hit a stream. The water's flowing down the mountain, so I can likely follow it into town.

Then an idea strikes me.

I've seen enough movies and television shows to know that when someone's being tracked by animals, the animals lose their scent if they get into water and run with the water.

There are, however, a few issues with the idea. Firstly, I won't be able to trek through the water for long, since it's likely freezing. Secondly, if I'm followed into the water, they'll probably be able to smell where I left the water and pick up my trail from there.

What if I do something unexpected and run upstream instead of downstream? Then, once I'm a decent way up the stream, I can resume my journey on land and throw off anyone who might be tracking my path.

As far as plans go, especially ones created on a whim, it doesn't feel terrible.

So I step into the water and suck in a sharp breath at how *freezing* it is. It's like pins poking my skin, but after about a minute of trudging upstream, the pain numbs and I can't feel my feet and shins anymore.

If I keep this up for too long, I might get hypothermic.

I'll give it ten minutes. Maybe fifteen, depending on how I feel.

Then I'll continue down to town, get in touch with my parents, and finally go home.

Connor

I RUN in my wolf form until after midnight, happy to release all thoughts of Ruby and the mysterious mark she showed me at the Lawrence's house.

My wolf doesn't want to turn Ruby in. He doesn't want to resist our pull toward her.

But my wolf is wrong. He's affected by whatever dark magic Ruby is casting on us, just like I am.

Autumn is going to be our mate.

The sooner we figure out what Ruby truly is, the better.

Eventually, I end up at my grandfather's house and shift back into human form. His lights are off, but it doesn't matter. As alpha, he's responsible for this pack and what happens in our territory, no matter what time it is.

Turning Ruby in tears at my heart, but I push the feeling down. I only feel this way because of whatever she's doing to me. Turning her in is the right thing. Not just for me, but for Autumn, and for the pack.

They're my priority. Not Ruby.

And so, set in my decision, I march up to my grandfather's doorstep and ring the bell.

He answers less than a minute later. Even though he's in his pajamas, he's alert and ready to go, as an alpha always should be.

I aspire to be just like him someday.

"Connor." He opens the door wider and looked me up and down. "Come in."

I step into his large living room—even though my grandfather lives alone, he has the biggest house in town—and start pacing. My wolf continues to protest what I'm about to do, and moving around helps me control him.

"Something's bothering you," my grandfather observes, as calmly as ever.

He doesn't say anything more. He simply leaves space for me to speak.

I force myself to stay still, take a deep breath to calm myself, and face my grandfather. "I visited Ruby and told her what you asked me to," I say. "We spoke privately, and she showed me a mark on her hip that she got after her shift, in the shape of a star."

I wait for a hint of recognition on his face.

There's nothing.

"Do you know what it means?" I ask.

"I've never heard of such a thing happening to any of our kind," he finally says.

"I wonder if she isn't our kind," I propose what I've been thinking since leaving on my run. "There's something different about her. Something..."

I want to say *magnetic*, but I don't want to share the draw I feel toward Ruby with anyone. Not even my grandfather.

"I can't explain it," I say instead. "But I don't think she's what she appears to be."

My heart twists at how I'm betraying her.

But I'm doing this for my pack. My loyalty is to my pack.

Ruby isn't one of us.

"I need to see it," my grandfather decides, swiftly and surely. "We'll go there now."

"It's past midnight..." I trail, not liking the thought of barging in on them like that.

"I'm the alpha of this pack." His eyes narrow, warning me not to speak against him. "If I want to go there now, then the Lawrence's will wake up and let me see her now."

"Fine," I say, and I hold his gaze to make it clear that what I'm going to say next is a statement and not a question. "But I'm going with you."

* * *

We take his car to the Lawrence's, since it can get there faster than we can while running as wolves. Minus the flickering of a television in one of the bedrooms, all the lights inside their house are out.

"What are you going to do to her?" I ask, keeping my voice low.

"It'll depend on what she says when we speak with her."

"That's fair," I say, and we get out of the car, and he slams the door so loudly that an owl hoots nearby in response.

He rings the doorbell, and Penny answers a few seconds later. Her hair is tangled, and her eyes are half awake. But she snaps to it when she sees my grandfather, her mouth forming into an O of surprise.

"Jax," she says. "What are you doing here?"

Her parents hurry over, and they look equally surprised by my grandfather's late-night call.

"Let me guess—it's about Ruby," Garrett says, continuing before my grandfather can reply. "I knew that girl was only going to bring us trouble."

"I need to see her." My grandfather marches inside before they can invite him in. "Where is she?"

"She's in my room," Penny says quickly, and she leads the way to the room where I spoke with Ruby privately a few hours earlier.

She opens the door, and cold air rushes out of it. It smells like trees, and the window is open, the plants on the sill set down on the floor.

Ruby's nowhere to be found.

Stupid girl.

People run when they're guilty. She's only making things worse for herself when we inevitably drag her back from wherever she's run off to.

"She left." My grandfather turns his angry gaze to me. "What did you say to her?"

"Nothing," I snap, although that's not actually true. "I said I'd help her figure out what the mark means, and that she should hang tight until I do."

"Then she's clearly incapable of listening to her superiors," he growls. "But we'll find her. She couldn't have gotten far."

"On it," I say, and the window's too small for me to fit through, so I run out the front door, shift into wolf form, and follow Ruby's deliciously sweet scent into the forest.

I need to get to her first.

Because I don't know what my grandfather will do to her if he catches her before I do, and I have zero intention of finding out.

Ruby

I CAN ONLY RUN in the stream for about ten minutes before the cold seeps into my bones and slows me down.

Hopefully it'll be enough that if anyone's tracking me, they'll lose my trail. So I step out of the water and run down the mountain again, relieved when I spot lights from the town poking through the trees in the distance.

I'm almost there.

I'll have a lot more to worry about once I'm back home, but for now, I need to get out of the Pine Valley pack's territory. If I let my mind wander beyond that, I'll crack from the pressure of it all.

I just have to take it one step at a time.

I hurry down the mountain, getting so close to the town that I can all but taste freedom.

Then I slam into a wall, my shoulder luckily stopping me from getting whammed in the face. The impact pushes me back, and I trip over my feet and land on my butt on the snow-packed ground.

When I look back up, there's nothing there. No wall—nothing.

Once the throbbing in my shoulder calms down, I reach forward. My fingers hit some sort of invisible wall, and when I push on it, it doesn't budge.

The Lawrence's mentioned a magical barrier around the main town to keep out the vampires. I'd think this is it, but I haven't reached the main town yet.

If this is a barrier, then it must be a second one inside the main barrier, possibly to protect wolf territory.

To keep people out… and to apparently keep them in.

Panic clings to my lungs, tightening until I can barely breathe. I'm trapped in here. There's no way out.

Maybe.

Because I'm assuming that this thing wraps around the entire pack territory.

There's only one way to find out if I'm right. I have to follow it and search for a break.

So I get up and brush the snow off my legs, realizing that along with my sneakers and the bottoms of my thin yoga pants being soaked from the stream, the rest of my pants are now damp as well.

If I hadn't survived the night sleeping in the snow, I'd think I was risking freezing to death. But being a wolf shifter has its advantages, like tolerating cold weather better than humans, so I keep my hand on the invisible barrier and walk alongside it.

I don't get far before something snaps in the trees off to the side.

Crap.

Someone's there.

The trees are thick, so I have no idea how I know that. But I *feel* their presence behind me, and I know it's a person and not an animal.

But there are a lot of trees here. Maybe I can hide until they pass, which will be better than making noise and alerting them to my presence.

So I lean against one of the trees—the trunk is wider than I am—and go as quiet as possible.

Don't see me, don't see me, don't see me, I repeat in my mind, praying to whatever gods are out there that they'll help keep me safe.

I don't move. I barely even breathe. I just focus on blending with the woods and becoming invisible.

A beautiful black wolf emerges from the trees.

Connor.

After seeing him shift at his house, I'd recognize him anywhere.

He sniffs in my general direction, but doesn't seem to see me.

It's too late to move from my hiding spot. It would only draw attention. I need to stay hidden and hope he moves on quickly.

Then there's the more important question—what's he hunting for? I want to think it's something as simple as a late-night snack, but I've been out here for a while. Did he somehow realize I sneaked out, and is searching for me?

He turns his head and looks straight at me, although his brown eyes that gleam in the moonlight seem unfocused. He sniffs a few times and looks around the area, but somehow doesn't seem to see me.

My heart's pounding a million miles a minute, so loudly that he must hear it.

Why's he pretending not to see me? Because he *must* be pretending. There's no way he could miss me from this distance.

Maybe there's an entire search party out here, and someone else is watching him.

Does he want me to escape? Is he going to return to the search party and lie to them, telling them he didn't see me?

I'd think so, but he gives no hint that I should play along.

I don't know how, but he truly doesn't see me.

It's impossible. But a lot of impossible things have happened to me recently. So, not wanting to test my luck, I remain still, focusing on going unnoticed and unseen.

Suddenly, Connor's wolf sprints toward me in a flash, shifts into his human form, and he body slams me down to the ground so hard that he knocks the wind out of me.

I gasp, trying to get air back into my lungs, and try to roll out from under him. But he grabs my wrists, pinning me to the ground with so much strength that I can't move.

That's not the only reason I can't move.

Because the skin on my wrists that his fingers are wrapped around buzzes with so much energy that it feels like our bodies are being fused together. It's like the matter that makes him up is melding with mine, and when his eyes glow yellow, I suddenly know without a doubt that this beautiful man above me will forever be the center of my world.

Connor

Electricity crackles through my body, and Ruby glows like an angel below me, her silky brown hair splayed around her head like a halo as she gazes up at me with amazement and desire.

Her eyes glow yellow, and smokey magic travels between our eyes, linking our souls. Our hearts beat in tandem, and in that moment, there's no one else in the world that matters but *her*.

My wolf howls in excitement inside me at the feeling of being complete.

There's no greater joy for a shifter than finding our other half. It doesn't happen to all of us. This is the moment my wolf and I have wanted for our entire lives, and it feels better than I ever could have imagined.

The pull to Ruby is magnetic, and I lower myself down to her, ready to finally feel her soft lips on mine. My body pulses with desire, and I need to claim this beautiful woman, right here and right now, and lose myself in her for days.

From the awestruck way she's looking up at me, I know she'd let me if I tried.

Good. She should let me do anything I want to her. Because she belongs to me.

My mate.

The thought feels warm and right, and as her soft breath mingles with mine, she's so tantalizing... so *tempting*.

No.

An image of Autumn flashes through my mind, and I snap myself into focus and force myself to pull back.

This can't be happening.

It's everything I wanted to avoid.

It's why I was extra careful to keep Ruby at arm's length and never touch her. I was doing so well. But one slip-up a moment ago, and all that effort was for nothing.

I moan in frustration. Because my mate is underneath me, our faces inches away from each other's... and I can't let myself kiss her.

Why is the universe doing this to me?

It's the devil's work. It must be. Why else does Ruby have that mark on her hip, and how else could she have done whatever she just did?

Anger overruns my desire, and I happily let it.

"How did you do that?" I growl, satisfied when her eyes widen in surprise at the sudden shift of my energy.

"How did I do what?"

I push her wrists into the snow-covered ground—hard. "You know what I'm talking about."

"I truly don't," she says, begging me to believe her. "All I know is that your eyes glowed, and then there was that mist between us, and my skin's on fire where you're touching me." She swallows, then gets herself together enough to continue. "I don't know what's happening, but I think you do, and I want you to tell me."

My heart softens at how frail and innocent she sounds, yet fiery at the same time. Every bone in my body urges me to believe her. To help her.

But I don't. Because what she just did… no shifter has that type of magic. Not ever in the history of our kind.

"I'm not talking about that," I say. "I'm talking about how you were invisible."

The words sound crazy, but I can't deny what I saw.

Well, what I *didn't* see.

Realization shines in her eyes.

She knew.

Obviously she knew. She was the one who did it.

But she's still staring up at me like a deer in the headlights, like she's worried I'll break her if she so much as tries to move.

"Is that why you didn't see me?" she asks, her voice barely louder than a whisper.

Is she scared?

I want to loosen my grip around her wrists, take her in my arms, and figure this out together. She needs me. I hear it in her voice and see it in her eyes. There's a reason why she shifted for the first time on my land, and why she came to my door for help.

It's because she's mine, and she knows it.

Ours, my wolf's voice echoes in my mind.

But still… she's not one of us. And I can't let myself forget it.

"You expect me to believe you don't know what you did?" I ask.

"I didn't know," she insists. "I swear it. I don't even believe it myself…"

"You're lying," I say, although I know in my heart that she isn't. Because a lie that big is something I'd smell, like rusted metal in the back of my throat.

Still, I don't loosen my hands around her wrists. I can't risk her running. I could easily catch up to her, but she belongs to me, and she's not going anywhere until I have answers.

"I didn't do anything," she repeats, firmer than before. "Besides, if I was invisible, how did you see me well enough to pounce on me?"

"I didn't see you. I smelled you." I inhale slowly, since her scent—like roses on a spring day—is so unmistakably *hers*. "And you forgot to hide your shadow."

"What do you mean?" she asks, even though I think it's pretty damn obvious what I mean.

I also know she isn't asking because she's confused. She's asking because she wants me to further explain.

How I know these things, I don't know.

Except that's a lie.

I'm in tune with her feelings because of the bond.

The bond that must be some sort of cruel mistake.

"You hid yourself," I say slowly. "You blended into the trees like a perfect camouflage. But the moon's almost full, the tree branches are bare, and my sight in wolf form is impeccable. Your shadow was there on the snow in front of you, plain as day."

"Okay." She takes a deep breath, gathering her thoughts. "You're saying I was invisible. I guess I can maybe believe it, because you really didn't seem like you saw me. But how was I able to do it?"

"I don't know," I say. "But if you're going to go all superhero on me, you really should have done it *right*."

She laughs at that, and I can't help but smile, too.

Then the pieces click together, and I can't believe I didn't realize it sooner.

This isn't the first time she's done something like this.

"When I tackled you, you flickered back into existence," I say, unable to believe what's about to come out of my mouth. "Just like when you created the illusion of the rose opening up... and the illusion of yourself standing by my side in the kitchen instead of Autumn."

Ruby

CONNOR IS HOLDING ME DOWN, pinning my wrists to the ground, with no hint of letting go.

And, while I never thought I'd be into this sort of thing, it's hot as hell. Especially the way his dark eyes feel like they're cutting into my soul.

"You think I'm making you see things?" I ask, caught majorly off-guard by his accusation.

"Or *not* see things," he mutters.

"With the whole invisibility thing."

"Yes. That." He studies me closer, like I'm a mystery for him to figure out. "The question is—are you only making *me* see things, or can you do it to other people as well?"

He still seems to think I know more about this than he does.

Well, he's wrong. And somehow, I need to make him see it.

"I wouldn't know, since I didn't realize I was doing anything at all until you pointed it out right now," I say.

I prepare myself for him to accuse me of lying again, but he doesn't.

"I'm telling you the truth," I add, praying he'll believe me.

"I know." He doesn't sound happy about it, but at least it's a step forward.

Feeling him relax a bit, I try to wiggle free. But he's strong, and he stops me before I can.

"Ruby." The intense way he says my name sends shivers down my spine. "Your mark and your magic are unheard of. I'm going to bring you back to my grandfather's, because I have no other choice right now, and I need you to go along with everything he wants. Fighting him will only make this more difficult. Do you understand?"

"You told him about the mark." My chest pangs with betrayal, even though I expected him to do as much. It's why I ran in the first place.

It's just that now, after whatever happened to us when we touched, the betrayal stings worse than I imagined.

"It was my duty as a member of the pack." He lowers himself closer to me, as if it will help me better understand, but all it does is send waves of desire through my body. "I wouldn't turn on my pack just because a pretty little omega wants me to keep her secret."

Ouch.

"I'm not an omega," I say swiftly, the words feeling *right* after I speak them. "I have magic. Maybe not earth magic, but it's still magic. Which, according to everything I've learned so far, means I'm not an omega."

"Hm." He pauses, considering it. "You might be right."

"I *am* right."

There are only a few inches between our faces, and his breaths are slow and calculated, as if he's fighting every instinct to stop himself from getting closer.

I know the feeling, because I'm experiencing the same thing.

I've never had a boyfriend. At least not anything serious. No guy has ever caught my interest, and I always thought I might end up being an old cat lady—minus the fact that I don't like cats.

No one has ever set my insides on fire like Connor's doing right now.

"What did you do to me?" I barely speak louder than a whisper, afraid that anything sudden might push him away.

His eyes harden, but he doesn't move. "I don't know what you're talking about," he says stiffly.

"When you touched me, it was like an electric shock. Your eyes turned yellow," I say. "There was some sort of smoke or magical haze that *connected* us together."

He glares down at me, silent. But I don't say anything more, leaving space for him to answer my question.

"I needed to stop you from getting away," he finally says.

"So you used magic to hold me down?"

"I did."

I don't know why, but there's something off about his answer. It doesn't feel right. However, I'm not sure accusing him of lying is going to get me far right now.

"Whatever you did wasn't earth magic," I say steadily.

"It wasn't," he agrees, his eyes glinting with warning. "Which is why you can't tell anyone about it."

"So you're asking me to tell no one about your magic, even though you're going to tell your grandfather about mine?"

It hardly sounds fair to me.

"My grandfather is going to figure out your secret one way or the other," he says. "But as long as you keep what I did to you to yourself, I'll keep you safe in return."

"Why should I believe you?"

"Because in case you didn't notice, I'm all you've got right now."

Tension crackles between us, and I know he has me cornered.

"Great." I huff. "You're all I've got, and you're threatening me and pinning me to the ground."

He says nothing. Instead, his grip around my wrists tightens, his pupils dilate with desire, and he gets so close that I swear he's about to kiss me.

I'm lightheaded, and his heart is pounding so hard that I can feel it.

Mine's beating at the same rate. And despite the voice in the back of my mind reminding me that he has a girlfriend, I need his kiss more than anything in the world.

For a moment, I think he's going to give me what I need.

But instead of kissing me, he growls and pushes himself off me.

The sting of rejection floods my veins, and coldness travels through my body now that he's no longer touching me.

I sit up in a daze and try to catch my breath.

"Don't tell anyone else in the pack what you did with your magic, either," he says. "It's not their business unless my grandfather makes it their business."

"Your grandfather doesn't *have* to know," I say, even though I know getting him to keep anything from his alpha is a lost cause. "You don't have to tell him."

"You're right. I don't have to do anything," he says. "But I assume you want answers?"

"I do."

"Then you need to lay low—if you're even capable of doing that—and let me help you get them."

Connor

Ruby starts to stand up, and even though I want to help her, I don't. Because each time I touch her, I'll feel more drawn to her. And I refuse to let that happen.

Best scenario is that my grandfather figures out what her mark and magic means, and she goes far, far away from here. The farther she is, the weaker the bond between us will be.

But for the time being, she's my responsibility. And, like all my responsibilities, I won't take it lightly.

"Your shoes and pants are wet," I observe now that she's standing.

"I walked in the stream to hide my path," she says. "So, yeah. They got wet."

I look her up and down to see if she's injured, relieved that she appears to be okay. She looks more than okay—she looks *strong*. Determined. Proud.

Three very admirable qualities, along with the fact that she seems to be intelligent as well.

At least the universe didn't have the audacity to give me a weak, stupid mate.

"You went upstream instead of downstream, even though it's not the direction of the town," I say.

"I thought it might throw you off my path." She shrugs. "Apparently, I thought wrong."

"It was the less obvious choice," I say. "My grandfather went downstream, but I had a feeling you might go upstream. We split up to cover more territory."

I also had a gut feeling she'd go upstream—like I could sense her tracks, even through the water. Which makes sense now that I know we're mates.

"Not like I could get out of here anyway." She frowns. "I hit that invisible wall."

"The barrier," I tell her.

"That's what I thought it was."

"After the witches heard about your arrival, they thought it best to keep you in pack territory until you learn how to control your shifts," I say. "They were apparently right, given that you were close to leaving town and putting endless people in danger—including your friends and family, if you got that far. What were you *thinking?*"

I don't realize how angry I am until the words come out.

"I was thinking that when you saw my mark, you looked at me like I was evil, and I had no idea what you were going to do to me," she says. "I felt like I was in danger. I needed to get out of here."

She's not wrong, which is why I don't correct her. Especially since I'm still not convinced she's not a sorceress or demon. The mate bond made me soft to her—it made me want to protect her no matter what—but I need to continue to be on guard.

"I'll keep you safe until we figure out what the mark means," I say simply. "You have my word."

She raises an eyebrow. "And if you don't like what we find out?"

"We'll deal with that if it comes to it."

She nods, looking surprisingly satisfied. Which makes sense, since the mate bond will make her feel like she should trust me, just like it's making me feel like I should trust her.

"In the meantime, you need to come back with me to my grandfather's," I continue. "As long as you cooperate, you won't get hurt."

I hope it's true.

I'll do everything in my power to make *sure* it's true.

"You're making it sound like he might kill me," she says, dark fear crossing her eyes.

My heart twists at the thought of it. Even though we've only known each other a few days, I can't imagine my life without Ruby in it. I want to learn what makes her smile, what makes her laugh, and I want to be someone she's comfortable coming to for anything she needs. I want to be here for her in every possible way. I want her to feel safer with me than she does with anyone else.

I want to get to know her like I've gotten to know Autumn all these years.

But I feel like I'm betraying Autumn for simply *thinking* about it.

Maybe it'll be easier if I let my grandfather kill her. If he does it before Ruby and I consummate the bond, the bond will be destroyed. I'll be free from this curse the universe forced on me, and free to be with Autumn without Ruby getting in the way. It will hurt at first, but Autumn and I will be happy together, and I'll get over it eventually.

I hate myself for thinking it.

Especially because Ruby's watching me with those wide, innocent eyes of hers, waiting for me to say something.

I won't resort to having her killed. Autumn and I chose each other. We promised to be together even if either of us formed a mate bond with someone else. I care about her, and I refuse to break that promise.

I'm strong enough to resist the mate bond with Ruby. I won't accept anything else.

"Connor?" Ruby says, my name sounding musical when it escapes her lips.

"My grandfather's not going to kill you," I promise, since even if he *wants* to kill her, I'll make sure he fails.

We'll kill him before he kills her, my wolf's voice growls in my mind.

Disgust rolls through me at the fact that my wolf would consider killing a man who's not just our grandfather, but our alpha.

Neither of them is going to die—at least not by my hand, I think, and then I successfully bury my wolf deep down inside myself, where he can't assault me with such treasonous thoughts anymore.

I bring myself back to the present, where I just promised Ruby I'll keep her safe at all costs.

"I need you to come back with me," I tell her. "Please."

She says nothing for a few seconds, and I have no idea what to do if she refuses.

"You promise I'll be safe with you?" she asks, and from the willingness in her tone, I know I've won.

"I promise." I don't have to think twice about it.

"Okay." She nods and takes a deep breath, and for the first time since pinning her down, I feel somewhat relieved. "Then by all means, lead the way."

Ruby

JAX'S HOUSE is a log cabin mansion that reminds me of the ski lodge I stayed at with Luna. The inside is decently modern, with tall ceilings, wooden floors, paneled walls, and large windows.

Instead of feeling rustic, it feels majestic.

I know Jax is the alpha, but I didn't realize that also means he's rich, especially since Connor's house is decently modest.

"A gift from the witches," Connor explains.

"Where do the witches live?" I ask.

"They're near town. They don't need land like we do, since they don't shift and go on runs."

"But don't the Guardians live in cities for twenty years?" I ask, since Penny talked about the Guardians constantly.

"A sacrifice to keep the supernatural world in order," he explains. "Guardians who return home after the required twenty years are gifted ample land and living space as a thank you for their service." He motions at Jax's giant house for emphasis.

"Got it." I shiver and wrap my arms around myself, suddenly aware that I've been dripping water onto Jax's luxurious Turkish rug.

"You need to shower and warm up," Connor says. "I'll grab you some of my grandmother's old clothes."

When he says it, I realize he's told me nothing about his grandmother. Or his parents, for that matter.

"Is your grandmother..."

"She's dead," he finishes. "It happened when I was a baby, at the same time as my parents. I grew up in this house with my grandfather, and he gave me my own place when I started high school."

My heart breaks for him, especially given the sadness in his eyes when he says it. "I'm sorry," I say carefully. "That sounds awful."

"It was a long time ago." He tries sounding nonchalant about it, but I can tell it hurts him. "You can shower in my old room. Come on."

He's already halfway up the steps, and I follow his lead. His bedroom here is similar to the one in his current house—a king-sized bed with a green comforter, lots of wooden furniture, and floors to match. His shelves are lined with books, and I smile at the fact that he likes to read. Maybe we have more in common than I initially thought.

"There should be towels and stuff in there." He motions to the ensuite bathroom. "I'll leave some of my grandmother's clothes in here for you for when you're done. I'll wait to let my grandfather know we're back here until you're finished, but I still recommend you be quick about it."

"Sure," I say, still in a daze after everything that happened tonight. "Thanks."

"Anytime."

Connor's bathroom is all marble and traditional, with a walk-in shower more luxurious than any other shower I've seen in my life. It's the sort of shower you'd expect to find in a five-star hotel.

I finish up in ten minutes, wrap myself in a fluffy towel, and catch my reflection in the mirror.

My brown eyes startle me every time I see myself. Because who was that woman in the woods? Why did she change my eye color? And how did she do it?

I know she told me to tell no one, but eventually I'm going to need answers. Especially since the answers are probably related to my star mark and illusion superpower.

Thankfully, the clothes Connor set out for me are regular loungewear—not old lady pajamas. I brush my finger over my star mark, as if it can give me good luck, then get dressed and head back downstairs.

Connor's made coffee, and I follow the scent into the kitchen. It's a huge kitchen with marble countertops and an island in the center, and he pours me a cup when I enter. He looks amazing in his low-slung jeans and tight t-shirt, and it takes all my effort to not obviously check him out as he hands me my steaming mug.

He ensures his fingers don't brush mine.

Disappointment flutters in my chest, and I sit at the table, trying to put a lid on my crazily intense attraction to him.

He joins me at the table, taking the seat across from me. "I texted my grandfather's beta when I heard you coming downstairs," he says. "He'll track down my grandfather, let him know you're here, and my grandfather will come over."

"You mean wolves can't speak in each other's minds?" I ask.

"No." He chuckles. "That would be a bit intrusive. Don't you think?"

"I suppose so."

I'm also relieved that no one can see into my mind—especially Connor. I'd want to sink into the floor and disappear forever if he knew how much I've been pining over him since the night we met.

We're both silent, and I have no idea what to say to fill the space.

"Looks like the clothes fit," he says. "From what I've heard about my grandmother, she'd be glad for her stuff to finally get some use around here."

"What happened to her?" I ask, realizing only a second later that it might be an insensitive question. "Sorry. You don't have to answer that."

"It's okay," he says. "Everyone in the pack knows. You should know as well."

I sip my coffee and wait for him to continue.

"My parents were some of the best Guardians of their time, along with their best friends, Xavier and Abigail," he begins. "They served their twenty years in New York City, came back here to settle down, and my mom soon gave birth to me."

"Because shifters aren't fertile until they hit forty," I repeat what Penny told me in one of her many lessons about their kind.

No—not *their* kind.

Our kind.

"Exactly," he says. "Everything was going well for them until Xavier's sister Jessica disappeared while serving as a Guardian in the city. We didn't know it at the time, but Jessica had secretly been in a relationship with one of the vampires in New York—Dominic."

"I thought the Guardians were supposed to kill the vampires?" I ask.

"Our relationship with vampires is complicated," he says. "There are two types of vampires that live in the city. The uptown vampires, and the downtown vampires. The uptown vampires have an organized clan, and an uneasy alliance with us. They keep willing humans as blood slaves and don't cause chaos in the city. In return, we let them be. The downtown vampires, however, are a different story. They're more spread out, and some of them hunt to kill. The majority of Guardians are stationed downtown so we can keep them under control."

"So there are good vampires, and bad vampires," I say.

His eyes darken. "There are no good vampires," he says. "Vampires have no soul. There are only rabid vampires, who are consumed with bloodlust, and vampires who can keep their urges under control. Neither are good, but we maintain an uneasy truce with the latter as long as they remain civilized."

"Got it," I say. "Which clan was Dominic in?"

"The downtown vampires," he says, and for some reason, I'm not surprised.

"And what happened with him and Jessica?"

"They were together secretly," he continues what he started to tell me earlier. "But then a new shifter was assigned to be a Guardian in the city, and he and Jessica formed a mate bond. Soon afterward, Jessica disappeared."

"Dominic's doing?" I guess.

"Correct. He wanted her for himself, so he turned her into a vampire, since that's one of the two main ways to destroy a mate bond."

"What's the other?" I ask.

"Death."

His body stiffens, chills travel up my spine, and the tension in the room is so strong that I can barely breathe.

"Anyway, it wasn't long until the New York Guardians learned what happened to Jessica," he continues. "They tracked down Dominic and killed him, but Jessica escaped before they found her."

"Did they want to kill her, too?" I ask, appalled at the thought of the Guardians killing one of their own.

"Either Jessica chose to become a vampire, or she was turned against her will," he says. "If it was by choice, she betrayed her people, and the punishment is death. If it was against her will, she lost her soul. All Guardians make a vow that it's better to die than live without a soul, so it was their duty to reunite her body with her soul so she could receive safe passage to the Underworld."

"Oh. Wow." It sounds barbaric to me, but then again, I've never come face-to-face with a vampire.

He nods grimly, then continues, "Jessica returned to Pine Valley, hid out in a cave outside town, and got word to her brother Xavier about her location. It's unclear what she said to him, but Xavier decided to help Jessica escape. Abigail was in a nearby pack before mating with Xavier—the Spring Creek pack—and that pack is suspected of being vampire sympathizers. So, she agreed with Xavier to help Jessica. However, my grandfather and grandmother knew something wasn't right, and they followed Xavier and Abigail to the cave. It was their duty to release Jessica from the curse of being a vampire, but Xavier was desperate to save his sister, so he and Abigail turned on my grandparents. A fight broke out between the five of them in the cave, and my grandfather was the only one who made it out alive."

He speaks neutrally while he relays the story, like he's keeping the facts separate from his feelings.

"That's awful." I blink a few times as I take it in. "I'm so sorry."

There's a *lot* that's awful in there, including how Xavier was expected to help murder his sister, but I don't feel like my opinion about that would be appreciated right now.

"Like I said, it happened a long time ago," Connor says. "My grandmother died while upholding her vow to the Guardians. She died a hero."

"She sounds like a strong woman," I say.

"She was."

I want to ask about the Spring Creek pack—the ones he called vampire sympathizers—but the front door opens before I can.

My lungs tighten, and my heart races.

There's only one person it can be.

Jax.

And even though Connor promised to keep me safe, I have no idea what the alpha of this pack might want with me once he learns about my strange, mysterious, and possibly dangerous magic.

Ruby

JAX BURSTS into the kitchen and stares me down, looking insanely intimidating in his leather pants and biker jacket.

"Stand up and show me the mark," he commands.

There's something supernaturally forceful about his voice, and I find myself standing up without realizing it, my hand going to the waistband of my pants to pull it down.

Before I finish, he snarls, his angry gaze going straight to Connor.

"She's in her clothes," he growls, and I worry he's about to rip out his grandson's throat.

"Ruby's clothes were wet from walking in the stream," Connor explains, slowly and steadily. "She needed to change."

Jax holds Connor's gaze for what feels like an entire minute, and neither Connor nor I say a word. "Don't touch her stuff ever again," he finally warns, and his stormy eyes return to me. "The mark. Now."

There's no point in resisting, so I pull the waistband down just far enough so he can see the star inked on my hip.

Jax steps forward and studies it, his fingers hovering above the eight-pointed symbol.

"This wasn't here before your shift?" he asks.

"No."

"And you don't know what it means?"

"No."

He inhales, sniffing the air, and I remember what Connor said about being able to smell lies.

I wonder if that's a skill I'll be able to learn, too.

He breathes out and stares me down, and I brace myself for more questioning. "Very well," he says instead, and he takes out his phone, snapping a picture of the mark. "I'll show it to the witches so they can investigate. In the meantime, you'll stay in one of the guest rooms here."

"I'll stay here as well," Connor volunteers.

Jax's gaze bores into Connor, like he's trying to figure out why he cares.

"I want to learn how to shift, and Connor wants to help me," I say before Jax can question Connor—or worse, tell him to leave. "The sooner I can shift, the sooner I can go home."

Jax sits down and stretches, cracking his knuckles one-by-one. "You're not going home," he says. "Not ever."

"What do you mean?" I ask, even though it's pretty clear what he means.

I just don't want it to be true.

"I think you should sit down." Connor motions to an empty armchair, and I get a feeling that I'm not going to like whatever they have to say.

"Sure," I say, trying to sound calm as I take a seat, even though my insides feel like they're trying to jump out of my skin, needing to escape.

I watch Jax, waiting.

"Yesterday, I sent Connor to the Lawrence's to tell you that your family and friends think you're spending the semester abroad," he begins. "However, that isn't the truth."

I swallow down a giant ball of worry in my throat. "Okay..." I say, wrapping my fingers around the armchair and gripping it tight, as if it can hold me steady.

"The truth is that to the outside world, you're considered dead," he says simply.

No.

The world around me freezes, my blood turns to ice, and my heart stops. I can't breathe. I can barely think, let alone process the meaning behind his words.

It can't be true.

I look to Connor, and while he looks pained, I doubt it compares to the horror and anger burning through my veins.

"You lied to me," I say to him, betrayal stabbing at my heart.

"You weren't ready for the truth." His voice is strained, and from the sad way he's looking at me, I can tell he's ashamed about what he did.

Good.

He deserves to be.

"We were going to wait until you were more settled in," Jax says. "But after that stunt you pulled tonight, you're clearly stronger than we gave you credit for."

I think he's trying to give me a compliment, but it's so backhanded that it falls on deaf ears.

"It's being said that you died in a drunk driving accident in Florida late Saturday night," he continues, either not noticing that he's sent me into shock, or not caring.

His words buzz in my mind, barely making sense.

"I wasn't in Florida on Saturday night," I say. "I was here."

"Your friend Luna doesn't remember coming here with you," he says. "She believes you both went back to school early for intersession week, which is the lie you told your parents."

"How?" I ask, unable to find any other words.

"The witches spoke with Luna, and she answered their questions, since she wanted to help them find you," he says. "Then they used their magic to make her believe the lie they spun was the truth."

"And then they convinced her that I'm *dead*?"

It's crazy.

It can't be real.

How much power do the witches have to be able to pull off something like that?

"Correct." He gives me a small smile, like he's proud of me for figuring it out. "The story is that you went to a bar next to campus, and when you were walking home, you were hit by a truck while walking across the street."

My eyes widen, since I wasn't expecting *that*.

"I thought you said it was a drunk driving accident." It's a silly thing to focus on, but I need something solid to hold onto. Otherwise, the reality of what this means will hit me like an *actual* truck, and I'm not sure I can handle it without breaking down completely.

"The truck driver was drunk," he says. "There was so much damage to the body he hit that it was impossible to identify on sight. Two of our witches, however, came forward as witnesses and confirmed it was you."

"No."

"Yes." He taps on his phone screen and holds it out to me. "Here's the article. See for yourself."

I reach for the phone, but he pulls it back.

"No touching," he says.

I glare at him, then read the article.

Everything in it is as he said.

As I read, it's so quiet that I can practically hear the silence. My eyes tear up, and a sob threatens to escape my throat, but I push it down. I refuse to let them see me cry.

After reading the article another time, I somehow gather myself enough to speak.

"They made this truck driver hit a person," I say, my words hollow to my ears.

"Another witch was behind the wheel," he steadily explains. "After the job was completed, they ensured the actual truck driver—who was, in fact, drunk—believed he was there the entire time."

"So, they ran over an innocent girl and made a man believe he killed her."

It's so disgusting that I think I might be sick, but again, I swallow it down.

I refuse to lose my composure in front of Jax.

I won't let him see me as weak.

Jax holds my gaze, his expression hard. "These are the lengths we must go to ensure our world remains a secret. You might not understand it now, but you will in time."

"It's not right."

"It's *necessary*," he growls. "We have our rules, and we abide by them, no matter what."

I remain steady and narrow my eyes. "You blindly follow whatever the witches tell you to do," I say, my voice sounding venomous to my ears.

"Enough!" He slams his hand down on the table, and I jump in my seat. "Someone needs to keep you under control, and while you're here without knowledge of your true pack, I'm your alpha. You may not understand it yet, but I look out for my own. Right now, that includes you. Which is why I'm bringing this photo of your star mark to the witches so we can learn what it means—for the sakes of you, the pack, and the supernatural world as a whole."

There's so much rage racing through my body that I fear I might snap and try to strangle that superior look off his face on the spot.

But even though I'm new here, I know better than to attack the alpha.

"You're one of us now," he continues, as if he's trying to ram it into my brain. "It's time for you to leave the human world behind and take your place in this pack."

"You mean my place as an omega," I say darkly.

"Precisely."

Again, he gives me that smug smile. But it doesn't irritate me as much as before, since even though my magic isn't earth magic, it *is* magic.

Which means I'm not an omega.

It's a card I have hidden up my sleeve. And even though I don't know what to do with that card quite yet, I do intend on using it. I just need to wait for the right moment.

This isn't it.

And if I want to continue to keep my magic secret, I need to pretend I'm truly an omega.

So I lean back in my chair and lower my gaze like a good, submissive wolf. "I understand," I say softly.

It doesn't sound believable to me, but when I glance up, Jax looks appropriately satisfied.

"I hoped you would," he purrs. "Now, I'll show you to your room. It's almost three in the morning, and after your adventure tonight, I'm sure you're tired."

My eyes suddenly feel heavy, and as much as I don't want him to be right, I know he is. Plus, after everything he just told me, I wouldn't mind some space to process what this means for my family and best friend.

They think I'm dead.

It doesn't feel real.

Someday, it won't be real. Because someday, I'll set this right. I'll see them again. I'll make sure of it.

But that day isn't today.

I glance over at Connor, annoyed that seeing his face brings me a bit of comfort. "You're definitely staying here, too?" I ask.

"I wouldn't dream of doing anything else."

My gratitude for him fills me with warmth, and I want to run over to him and hug him. I want to sink into his arms and have him tell me everything's going to be okay. Just the thought of it brings me relief, especially because he's looking at me like he wants to comfort me as well.

But as much as I want to go to him, I need to remember that while he promised to help me, his allegiance is to the pack. He's not on my side. His loyalty will always be to his grandfather first.

To his alpha.

And it's best that no matter what happens, I don't let myself forget that.

"Thank you. Truly. It means a lot," I tell him, and then I let him show me to the guest room, where I fall asleep faster than should be possible after the life-changing revelations of tonight.

Ruby

I'M WOKEN the next morning by someone knocking on my door. The knock is jolting—I was sound asleep—and I pull the comforter over my head to block out the noise.

I want to slip back into the oblivion of my dreams so I can avoid reality for as long as possible.

But whoever's there knocks again—louder this time.

"Ruby?" Connor calls through the door. "Are you awake?"

I throw the comforter off my head, open my eyes, and sigh in irritation. "I am now," I say.

Sunlight peaks through the blinds, and a glance at the clock on the nightstand shows it's just past nine.

Six hours of sleep. I can technically survive on that, but from the exhaustion I feel right now, I could easily sleep for six more.

"Can I come in?" Connor asks.

"No." I have bedhead and my eyes are crusty, and as silly as it is, I don't want Connor seeing me like this.

"No problem," he says, and I'm relieved he didn't burst in anyway. "My grandfather just left to talk to the witches. I'm going to start making breakfast. Can you come down when you're ready? With my grandfather gone, it's the perfect time for us to see what you can do with that new magic of yours."

"What do you mean?" I ask, my brain still half-awake.

"I mean that as far as I'm aware, every time you've used your magic, you haven't been aware you're doing it," he says. "We need to see if you can control it, and try to figure out its limitations. All *before* my grandfather comes back. So, the sooner you're able to drag yourself out of bed, the better."

I sit up and rub the sleep out of my eyes. Because as much as I want to go back to bed, I need to learn about my magic, and I can't deny that Connor's idea is a good one.

"Fine." I huff. "Give me five minutes."

"That's what I was hoping you'd say," he says, and while I can't see him, I can practically hear the smile in his voice. "I'm making bacon. From the way you were staring at it the other day like it was about to drive you feral, I have a pretty good feeling you're going to like it."

* * *

It takes me ten minutes to freshen up and get downstairs.

The kitchen smells *amazing,* and the bacon tastes incredible. So does the sausage patty and the ham.

My parents are going to be appalled when they find out I've been eating meat.

No. They won't be.

Because they'll be too shocked about the fact that *I'm not dead.*

I drop the bacon onto my plate, suddenly not hungry anymore, and glare at Connor.

"What?" he asks.

"You lied to me."

He places his fork down, regret splattered across his beautiful face. "I know," he says. "I'm sorry."

"You told me my parents thought I was studying abroad," I continue, barely hearing his half-hearted apology. "Meanwhile, they thought I was dead—and you knew it."

My stomach swirls from just saying it, and I focus on swallowing a few times to make sure the breakfast meats stay put.

"I know," he repeats, and he breathes out slowly, gathering his thoughts. "Look—everything changed last night in the forest. I'm on your side now."

"Why?" I ask. "Because we know I'm not an omega?"

Hurt crosses his eyes, and he looks like he wants to say no. But he stops himself, pauses, and recollects himself.

"I don't know," he says instead. "But when I realized what you were doing with your magic, I realized how special you are. If we figure out exactly what you can do and how to control it, you can use your magic to help this pack. You might even be able to become a Guardian."

"Last night, you were worried that your grandfather might want me dead. Now you think he'd let me become a Guardian," I deadpan, since after everything Penny told me about how intense Guardian training is, it sounds crazy.

"I don't know," he says again, and I'm getting *really* tired of hearing him say that.

"What *do* you know?" I ask, watching him in challenge.

He sits straighter, daring me to back down. "I know that I kept my word to you that I'd protect you, and I didn't tell my grandfather about your magic," he says. "As it is now, I don't know what my grandfather is going to find out from the witches. But if they connect your star mark to your illusion magic, we're going to have to show him that your magic can be beneficial to our kind. We have to prove you're useful to the pack."

"Or what? He'll kill me?"

"I won't let him kill you," he growls, and from his tone, I have a feeling he'll go to *any* length to keep that promise.

I don't need to be able to smell lies to know he's telling me the truth.

On top of that, he's right. I need to learn more about my magic. He's willing to help me do that right now, and it would be crazy for me to refuse.

After all, if I end up in a position where I need to defend myself, this illusion magic is my best method of protection.

"Okay," I finally say. "I'm in."

"Great." He gives me a knowing smile with those incredibly sexy lips of his, as if he knew I was going to agree this entire time. "What were you thinking when you went invisible?" he asks.

"I was thinking that I didn't want you to see me," I say simply. "I was *begging* the universe to not let you see me, and praying I could somehow blend into the forest."

"Interesting," he contemplates. "What about with the rose?"

I flash back to the moment in Penny's room and think about what was going through my mind during it. "I was picturing the rose blooming, like you told me to do, and begging the universe to make it happen so I didn't have to be an omega."

"Hm." He frowns. "And what about when you made me see you next to me in the kitchen instead of Autumn?"

My cheeks heat at the memory, and I glance down at my plate, embarrassed at the idea of telling him the truth.

"Ruby." My name sounds lyrical when he says it, his voice sending shivers up my spine. "I can only help you if you're honest with me."

When I meet his gaze again, his pupils are dilated, and he's looking at me like he's hungry for my next words.

I was wishing that you were looking at me the same way you were looking at her.

It's embarrassing. I don't want to tell him.

But keeping it from him isn't going to do either of us any good. Plus, it's pretty obvious what I was thinking, given what was going through my mind the other two times I used my magic.

"Fine," I say, willing my voice to remain as steady as possible, so he won't see my embarrassment.

Here goes nothing.

"I was wishing that I was the one standing next to you instead of Autumn."

Ruby

Connor nods in acceptance, and if he's surprised, he doesn't show it. "Were you *picturing* yourself standing there?" he asks.

There's no point in denying it.

"I was."

"Okay." He doesn't appear fazed, but one thing I've learned about Connor in the short time I've known him is that he's good at controlling his emotions. "There's a pattern here. Each time you created an illusion, you wished for something to happen, and pictured it happening at the same time."

"That sounds right."

"So, we're getting somewhere." He picks up his coffee, takes a thoughtful sip, and places it back down. "What does it feel like when you use this magic?"

I think back to all three times in question.

What connects them?

"My brain tingled a bit," I realize.

"What do you mean?"

"I mean that it tingled a bit." I'm not sure how else to explain it, and I search for another word to help get it across. "It buzzed. Like electricity, but it didn't hurt."

He pauses to think, studying me like I'm a puzzle he's trying to figure out. "It sounds similar to how it feels when we use earth magic," he says. "But it happens in your brain instead of your body and palms."

"I've never used earth magic, so I wouldn't know," I say.

"I do know," he says, stronger now. "And even though I'm no expert, my guess is that your magic is coming from your mind instead of your body. So, it's mental magic instead of physical magic."

He watches me, waiting for me to confirm it.

"You *are* the expert on this," I correct him. "You've known about magic your entire life. I only learned about it two days ago."

Two days.

It feels like far longer than that.

"I've never heard of this kind of magic, which is why I'm far from an expert, but let's continue to roll with my theory," he says.

"Sure," I say. "I have nothing else to roll with."

Oh my God.

Did I really just say that?

Maybe this "mental magic" of mine is driving me mental.

"What next?" I ask, changing the subject. "Any other questions for me?"

"No more questions—at least not at this moment," he says. "Because I want you to recreate what you did those other three times, right here, right now."

"You make it sound so easy," I say.

"You have natural talent." He smiles, like he's proud of me and believes in me. "You can do this."

His encouragement is warm and contagious, and with him smiling at me like that, I believe I can do this, too. "All right." I straighten my shoulders, ready for anything. "What should I try first?"

He studies my face so intensely that I feel like a piece of artwork on display, and it takes all my effort not to look away. "When I realized you transformed Autumn to look like you, the first thing that popped into my mind was that you could be a useful spy for the Guardians," he says carefully.

A spy.

I'm not sure how comfortable I am with that. But like he pointed out earlier, if the shifters see me as having a purpose, they're less likely to try harming me.

Anything that helps keep me safe is good in my book.

"So, you want me to make myself look like someone else?" I ask.

"The previous times you used your magic, you were experiencing intense emotions." He clears his throat and looks away, as if something about that makes him uncomfortable. But when he refocuses on me, he's back to business. "Let's start smaller and work our way up from there."

"Sounds like as good of a plan as any," I say. "Do you have something specific in mind?"

He tilts his head and studies me so intensely that I squirm a bit in my seat. "Have you ever thought about going blonde?" he asks.

"My dad's blond," I say. "My mom's a redhead."

Like Autumn, I think, although I don't say it out loud.

"Brown hair's perfect on you," he says with so much passion that my heart leaps into my throat. "But let's see if you can make it blonde."

"Sure." I take a deep breath and close my eyes.

I need my hair to turn blonde, I think at the same time as I imagine what I might look like if I dyed my hair.

I don't need him to say anything to know nothing's happening.

But failure isn't an option.

So I take a deep breath, center myself, and try again.

I need to learn how to use this magic, and I want my hair to turn blonde, I try again, and I focus harder on what I'd look like as a blonde. *Please. Work this time. Make me blonde.*

The tingly sensation spreads through my brain, and I smile, knowing it's working.

Once finished, I open my eyes and pull a piece of my hair over my shoulder to take a look.

It's the same blonde color I was imagining—the white blonde that the Targaryen's have in Game of Thrones. And it's startlingly realistic, as if it's truly dyed instead of just being an illusion.

"Hey there, Stormborn," Connor teases with a glint of amusement in his eyes.

"You're a Game of Thrones fan?" Out of everything going on, that's the last thing that should surprise me, but it does.

"Why so surprised?" he asks.

"I don't know." I can't help but smile. "You just seem like such a… jock."

He runs his fingers through his silky brown hair, and I have a sudden urge to feel it for myself, although I somehow manage to control myself and stay in place. "You're not wrong," he says. "But you also might find that you and I have more in common than you think."

The way he's looking at me makes heat rush to my cheeks, and I take a sip of my now-cold coffee to cool down.

"Can you change it back?" he asks.

"What?"

"Your hair." He chuckles, and I have a feeling he knows exactly what effect he's having on me. "Make it brown again."

"Right." I try to shake off whatever spell he put me under, although I doubt it'll ever go away. He's stolen a piece of my heart, and as crazy as it is, I don't think I'll ever get it back. "Sure. Of course."

I barely think about wanting to remove the illusion—let alone close my eyes—before the tingles travel through my mind once more.

I examine a strand of my hair again, relieved to find that it's back to its normal color.

"Reversing it was easier than creating it," I tell him, proud of myself for completing his first challenge.

"It looked so realistic." He leans forward, as if he wants to touch it, but he stops himself and leans back in his seat.

Disappointment fills me when he does.

"Now try it with your eyes," he says, jolting me back to focus.

"Why my eyes?" I'm immediately on-guard, since my eyes aren't exactly the color they should be to start with.

"Easy." He gives me a small smile, as if we share a secret, and it makes my heart flutter like crazy. "Because they looked really beautiful when they were turquoise."

Ruby

My heart stops in my chest.

He knows.

Of course he knows.

But I assumed it might come to this, which is why I have a lie ready and waiting.

"You mean like the contacts I wore to your party?" I ask, trying to sound as nonchalant as possible.

"Exactly," he says, not seeming to think it's strange in the slightest. "I guess you haven't needed the contacts since the shift?"

"They weren't prescription." I shrug. "I just liked the way they looked."

It seems like a safer bet than assuming the shift would change my vision, since if that doesn't happen to other shifters, it would be yet another thing suspicious and different about me.

"I liked the way they looked, too." He sounds mesmerized, and my breathing slows at the way he's looking at me, but he quickly snaps back to attention. "Not like the brown isn't pretty," he scrambles. "It is. Your natural eye color is great."

I tilt my head slightly, amused by how he's tongue-tied over his words.

"Don't worry about it," I say, and he relaxes slightly. "I prefer the turquoise as well."

"I guess you wouldn't wear those contacts if you didn't." He gives me a sheepish smile.

"Exactly."

We're both quiet for a few seconds, and the tension buzzing between us amplifies. My heart pounds, and I freeze, not wanting to break this moment.

From the intense way he's looking at me, he seems to feel the same way.

But he shakes himself out of it and glances out the window, and just like that, the moment's gone.

"Anyway, now that you have this magic, you might not need contacts to change your eye color," he says, and the energy between us dims, although it's not fully gone. "Give it a go."

"All right," I say, and I close my eyes, imagining myself with my natural eye color. This is easier to do than when I changed my hair, especially because I love my natural eye color and wish I could have it back.

But no matter how hard I picture it and wish for it, my magic doesn't buzz through my mind.

When I open my eyes again, I know they're unchanged.

Connor's frown supports my assumption.

"Try again?" he says.

"Sure." I close my eyes and do as asked, but again, nothing happens.

"Hm." He presses his lips together in contemplation. "Maybe you used up your magic for the day."

"What do you mean?"

"Magic is a muscle," he explains. "We can only use so much before we run out of energy. We like to compare it to running. Some people have more of a natural ability for long distance running than others. Training increases endurance, but eventually, everyone will run out of steam and need a break to recharge."

"That makes sense," I say. "But I feel like I can do more. Let me try something that might be easier."

"Go for it."

I close my eyes, then open them again. Because while I closed my eyes with the rose and my hair color, I was looking directly at Autumn when I saw myself standing in her place.

I hold my hands in front of myself and look at my nails. The white polish is chipped and in desperate need of getting redone, so I picture a fresh manicure in my mind and try to project the image into reality.

My brain tingles, and in seconds, the white polish looks brand new—just like it did in my mind.

"So, you didn't hit your limit," Connor says. "You made that look easy."

"It *was* easy," I say. "Maybe eyes are harder to change?"

Or maybe I can't change them because brown isn't their color to start with.

"Possibly," he says, and he's staring into my eyes so deeply that I can't move. "I have another idea."

"What's that?" I ask.

"So far, your illusions have built off things that already exist—or made them disappear, in the case of making yourself invisible," he says. "I wonder if you can create something out of nothing."

"Like what?" I ask, interested in exploring this idea further. "Make it look like there's an apple in the center of the table?" It's the first thing that pops into my mind, and while it's random, I'm curious now that he's brought it up.

"It's worth a try," he says, motioning to the space on the table between us.

"Okay." I take a deep breath, stare at the center of the table, and imagine a shiny red apple sitting in the center of it. I can easily picture the apple in my mind—I've always had excellent recollection of what things look like, along with a great imagination—and I focus on *projecting* the image of it onto the table.

My brain tingles, and the apple shimmers into existence just like I pictured it, down to the specific downward turn of the stem.

"The shadow," Connor reminds me, and his voice is low, as if he doesn't want to break the spell.

"Right." I note the direction the light is shining and try to imagine the shadow the apple would cast in it.

A shadow appears, but it's unnaturally long.

I try to adjust it, and it's too short.

Ugh.

I do a bit of experimentation, and eventually, the shadow looks natural enough that I don't think someone would question it.

"You can work on that," Connor says.

"I will."

I continue to focus on the apple, and my mind tingles as I hold the illusion in place. It's easier to hold it there than to create it. But if I stop focusing, I'm sure it will disappear, just like what happened with the illusion of the rose blooming and my invisibility.

The apple looks so solid that it's impossible to tell it isn't real, and I reach forward, wanting to know what my creation feels like.

Connor apparently has the same idea, because he reaches for it at the same time as I do.

The apple isn't tangible, and our fingers go straight through it, connecting in the middle.

Electricity buzzes from my finger where it touches his, up my arm, and all the way to my mind.

The apple blinks out of existence.

All that's left is my index finger wrapped around Connor's.

Neither of us of is letting go.

I don't *want* to let go. Because his touch gives me warmth and safety, as if he's filling my soul with a light that I never knew I needed.

Our eyes are locked, and our breathing slows, so our chests are rising and falling at the same time. With our fingers intertwined, it feels like our bodies are one, and I can't bring myself to pull away.

He, however, doesn't have the same feeling, because he yanks his finger out of mine and pulls his arm back to his side.

The longing in his eyes turns to disgust. "I'm with Autumn," he says, and the reminder breaks my heart. "This needs to stop."

"What even *is* this?" I ask.

"It's nothing," he growls. "Absolutely nothing."

From the way he says it, I wonder if he's trying to convince himself as much as he's trying to convince me.

"Autumn is my girlfriend," he repeats, as if he's trying to drill it into my brain. "I'm not going to let you get between us."

"I'm not trying to."

It's true—I'm *not* trying to.

It's more like an invisible force is bringing us together, and I know it's affecting him as much as it is me.

He wouldn't be so combative if it wasn't.

His body stiffens, and his eyes go hard. "It doesn't matter if you're trying to get between us or not," he says. "Because once my grandfather figures out what pack you were born into, you're going to leave Pine Valley for good and live with them instead."

His words are a blow to my heart, and ice floods my veins, numbing me to the core.

"You want to get rid of me," I say.

"I think it would be for the best." He remains as cold as ever, as if he's a different person than the one who was helping me learn how to use my magic for the past hour. "Don't you?"

No.

The thought of living somewhere far away from Connor tears at my soul. Which is ridiculous, since we barely know each other.

It's probably one of those trauma-bond connections that are in books and movies. I just went through a massive change in my life, and Connor's been helping me understand it.

A part of me might even be feeling like I can rely on him. Like I can trust him.

But I'm not about to tell him all—or *any*—of that. Especially given how coldly he's watching me right now.

"Sure." I try to shrug it off, hoping to look as unaffected as he does. "Whatever."

He's silent for a few seconds, and I wonder if the careless manner of my words hurt him.

A part of me hopes it did—just a little bit.

Because I couldn't have hurt him even half as much as he did me.

"I think that's enough for today," he finally says, standing up and running his fingers through his hair. "I'm going to go check on Autumn. You can continue testing things out with your magic here, or there's the TV in the living room, if you'd rather do that."

Don't leave, I want to say.

I want to continue practicing my magic with *him.*

But I'm not about to beg for his company, especially given the circumstances.

"Sounds good," I say instead, feeling like I'm listening to someone else speaking instead of myself. "Thanks."

"Anytime." He nods, gives me one last glance, then is out of there before either of us can say another word—all but shattering my heart in the process.

Connor

I RUN through the woods to Autumn's house, hoping that being in my wolf form will help me escape the torrent of thoughts swirling in my mind. But my wolf is eerily quiet, which is making my thoughts impossible to shut out.

I want to help Ruby. Truly, I do.

But every moment I spend with her increases the pull of the mate bond. If I didn't get out of there when I did, I don't know what would have happened next.

No—I do know.

It would have been something I'd deeply regret for the rest of my life.

At least I helped Ruby learn more about her magic. That has to count for something.

As for what her mark and her magic might mean... that's an entirely different can of worms, and I have no idea what to make of it. Now that I know we're mates and have spent more time with her, I don't think she cast some sort of spell on me. I think she's telling the truth about not knowing what the mark means, and I don't think the mark means anything bad.

Why would she be my mate if it did?

My mate.

Ruby is my fated mate.

I can't keep this from Autumn. She and I promised to always be honest with each other, and that we'd stay together even if we found out we had a mate that wasn't each other.

I'm a man of my word, and I'm keeping my promise to remain loyal to Autumn no matter what.

Before I know it, I'm exiting the woods, shifting back into human form, and heading toward Autumn's house where she lives with her parents. Her house is on a hill, so the basement is actually a semi-basement, with one half aboveground with a sliding door entrance to the inside. The basement is basically a mini-apartment, and she's lived down there since starting high school, to assert her independence to her parents.

My girl is strong like that. A born leader. I've always admired her strength and determination—those qualities are two of the many that will make her the perfect partner to stand by my side when I'm the alpha of this pack.

They're qualities that Ruby has, too. But Ruby's softer and warmer, and there's something about her that makes me feel welcome and safe in a way Autumn never has. Being around Ruby makes me feel like I've come home.

The thought feels like a betrayal to my girlfriend, so I push it from my mind and continue forward.

I see Autumn through the sliding glass door, at the kitchen table with the codex of rules for Guardians in front of her. We have a test next week, and Autumn is the most diligent student I know. She looks beautiful with her red hair draped over her shoulder, ensconced in memorizing the responsibilities of the Guardians, and she's oblivious to the fact that I'm standing out here watching her.

No one in the pack locks our doors, since it would show distrust, so I slide the door open and step inside.

She looks up and smiles, and my heart breaks knowing that what I'm about to tell her will wipe that happiness from her face in an instant.

"Hi," she says. "I missed you last night."

It's impossible not to notice the tinge of worry in her tone.

Autumn is never insecure, and it makes me uneasy to see her like this.

"Sorry I didn't call," I say, since I know that's what she means. She and I call each other every night, but so much was going on last night that I couldn't pick up my phone. "Something happened. Something big."

I formed a mate bond with the new girl.

Autumn's going to be devastated. After I tell her, our relationship will never be the same.

"Want to sit?" she motions to the chair next to her, and I'm unable to look her in the eyes as I sit down.

Instead, I look at the codex laid open on the table. She's reading about shifters who get their wolves—and therefore their magic—stripped by witches, and how they're never supposed to set foot into pack territory or the Guardian safe houses in the cities again.

Her eyes flit to the page as well. "I don't understand what could make a shifter want to do such a thing," she says.

"It's an insult to our birthright," I agree, and we stare at the book in silence, as if mourning all the shifters who threw away their heritage like it meant nothing.

"Anyway," she says, moving uncomfortably in her chair. "What's going on?"

I dread what I'm about to do, but I need to get on with it. The sooner, the better.

"It's about Ruby," I say, and Autumn stiffens after hearing her name.

The warmth disappears from her face, and I suddenly realize that if she knows the truth, she might never show me that warmth again. She might never kiss me the same way again or trust me the same way again.

Ruby could be a wall standing between us forever.

Despite all our promises to be honest with each other no matter what, I might lose Autumn because of this.

Again, I curse the universe for putting me in this god-awful position. My heart is being split in two, and I have no idea what to do about it.

"What about her?" she finally says, slowly and cautiously.

She's my mate.

The words are on the tip of my tongue, but I can't bring myself to say them. Not when it might erase the openness in Autumn's eyes when she looks at me for forever.

But I can't bring myself to lie to her, either.

For now, telling her half of the truth will have to do. Because now that I've come this far, I have to tell her something important. She'll be suspicious otherwise.

The only thing I can think to tell her to make sense of why I barged in like this without warning is Ruby's secret.

Autumn is loyal to me. She'll keep Ruby's secret if I ask her to. I have zero doubts about it.

"Promise me you won't tell anyone," I say, dreading what I'm about to do. But I choose Autumn over Ruby, and this is how I'm going to show it to her.

I owe Ruby nothing.

I owe Autumn *everything*.

"I promise." She leans forward, her beautiful eyes wide as she waits for me to continue.

I take a deep breath, then force out the words.

"Ruby has magic." A knot forms in my chest after I say it, but I push myself to continue, needing to prove I'm more loyal to the girlfriend I *chose* than to the mate who was unwelcomely thrust upon me. "It's not earth magic. She has a different type of magic."

"Oh?" Autumn raises a perfectly arched eyebrow, and I can tell she's intrigued.

"She can make people see things that aren't there," I say, and the awful feeling of betrayal grows the more I speak, tasting like metal in the back of my throat.

This is wrong.

I shouldn't have come here.

I shouldn't be telling her this.

But it's too late to take it back now.

"What can she make people see?" Autumn is calm—scarily calm. She glances at the codex, as if we might find answers there, but I've read the book front to back and know there's nothing in it that will help make sense of Ruby's ability.

"It's all illusions, so they're not tangible. It's nothing dangerous," I backtrack, since I don't want Autumn to think Ruby's a demon, like I did when I saw her mark. "She made a rose look like it bloomed. She changed her hair color to blonde. And she made it look like there was an apple in the center of a table, even though there was nothing there."

I hold back the part about Ruby making it look like she was standing in Autumn's place, since I don't want to stir up jealousy between them. And I don't tell Autumn about how Ruby can make herself invisible, because I don't want Autumn to worry that Ruby could be spying on her—or on anyone.

"How do you know all of this?" she finally asks.

"My grandfather sent me to the Lawrence's yesterday to see if I could try again to see if Ruby has earth magic." It's not a lie, but it's close enough to the truth that she shouldn't question it. "She couldn't make a rose bloom, but she could create the *illusion* that the rose bloomed. We tested it some more, but she got scared, and she tried to run last night, so my grandfather's having her stay at his house for the time-being."

"He knows what she can do?"

"Not yet," I say. "But as my future partner who will stand by my side when I'm the alpha of this pack, I owe it to you to tell you what's going on. And I trust you to keep it secret until we decide how to move forward."

Autumn says nothing for a few seconds, and I worry she's going to question one of the many holes in the story—especially why I feel the need to keep Ruby's secret from the pack's alpha.

Then she looks down and picks at her cuticles, which is something she only does when she's nervous.

"What's wrong?" I ask, and I take her hands in mine, to show her she's safe with me.

When she looks back up, her hazel eyes are wide and vulnerable. "You just called me your future partner," she says, and she glances down before continuing. "Not your future mate."

Shit.

She's right. Before this moment, I've only ever referred to her as my future mate.

Now that I know she'll never be my mate, it feels wrong to say it out loud.

But she's watching me, waiting for an answer, and I need to figure out a way around this—quickly.

"Don't you think 'partner' is more meaningful?" I ask. "It means we chose each other, instead of the universe forcing us together."

I pray she believes it.

Which she should, since it's true.

"I guess." She continues to study me, and I have a sudden wave of doubt if she truly believes me or not. "Thanks for telling me the truth about Ruby," she says, and while I'm surprised by the change of subject, I'm glad she seems to be putting the partner/mate switch-up behind us. "Would you mind if I try helping out with her?"

"Help out how?" I ask, on edge about the two of them being near each other, never mind alone together.

"You said she still hasn't demonstrated any earth magic," she says, sounding more and more confident as she speaks. "I'm the strongest magic user in the pack for decades. If she has even a trace of earth magic inside her, maybe I can help bring it out."

"You'd do that for her?"

"It's our duty as pack members—and as future leaders—to ensure that all members of the pack are trained to their maximum potential," she says, and she glances at the codex, as if looking for approval for following our laws so diligently. "If she has earth magic along with illusion magic, she'll be a major asset to us. I'm happy to help in any way I can."

A wave of love and appreciation for Autumn rolls through me at how she's putting the pack above her own biases toward Ruby. It's one of the many reasons why I chose her, and why I'll continue to choose her as the one to stand by my side for the rest of our lives.

"That's really generous of you," I say. "Thank you."

"Anytime." She slowly gets out of her chair, lowers herself onto my lap, and buries her fingers through my hair as she looks deeply into my eyes.

Desire courses through me, and I'm no longer focused on anything other than her hips pressing against mine.

"Now, I think I need a break from studying," she says, and she lowers her lips to mine, and all thoughts of anything other than the current moment disappear around me.

But when I close my eyes, it isn't Autumn's face I see in my mind.

It's Ruby's.

And I can't get rid of the worry eating at my soul that unless I go to extremes, I might never be able to shut out the mate bond, no matter how hard I try.

Ruby

I'M PRACTICING CREATING illusions of objects and trying to make their shadows look natural when the front door opens and someone walks inside.

I immediately drop the illusion of the small potted cactus I was working on.

Is Connor back already? Does he want to apologize for telling me he wants me out of here as soon as possible?

God, I hope so. I keep seeing the cold look in his eyes when he told me he wants me to leave Pine Valley, and I feel rejected all the way down to my soul.

But even though I want Connor to be the one who walks into this room, I know it's likely Jax returning after talking to the witches.

Dread pools in my stomach at what Jax might have discovered, and my bones rattle with fear at the thought of being alone with him.

But I have to believe that Connor wouldn't have left me alone here if he truly thinks Jax wishes me harm. And if Jax *does* intend me harm, I'll have to be quick on my feet and figure out a way to use my magic to get out of here.

Or I can do what Connor recommended and tell Jax whatever he wants to know. That's probably my safest bet right now.

I stand and ready myself to face Jax… but it's not Jax who enters the room.

It's Autumn. She's wearing an all-black leather outfit, and when she sizes me up, it's clear she doesn't like what she sees.

I shiver even though there are no drafts in the room.

"What are you doing here?" I ask, bracing myself for her to pounce on me and try to claw my eyes out because of the way I look at Connor.

As much as I hate it, she wouldn't be totally wrong for doing so.

"I want to help you connect with earth magic," she says, catching me majorly by surprise. "I'm the strongest magic user in generations, and Connor thought it would be a good idea for me to see if I can bring anything out of you."

"Connor sent you?" I have a hard time believing it's true, but it makes more sense than Autumn volunteering out of the kindness of her heart.

"Is that so crazy?" she asks.

"No," I say quickly. "I just thought he'd come with you."

Or did I just *want* him to have come with her?

"He has Guardian training right now. I do, too, but he wanted me to come by before Jax gets back." She looks me up and down with her sharp eyes, sizing me up. "So, are you just going to stand there, or should we head outside and get started?"

Despite my surprise, I'm in no position to turn down anyone who wants to help, no matter how intimidating they might be.

"I'm ready if you are," I say, and even though I doubt I have any earth magic, I'm glad to try again—even though Autumn looks like she'd rather throttle my throat than help me improve.

It's way warmer today than yesterday, so the snow on the ground is mostly melted, leaving wet grass and mud in its wake.

Autumn motions to the table on the deck, and I take a seat on one of the chairs. It's slightly damp, but I don't complain.

She remains standing.

"We can use our magic to manipulate more than just dirt and plants," she begins, as if she's a teacher in front of a classroom. "My go-to is something that can create far more damage."

"What's that?" I ask, half-intrigued, and half-scared.

"Rocks." She grins. "Stay still. Connor won't be happy if you end up getting hurt."

There's an edge in her voice at the last part, but she turns to face the woods and holds both palms out toward the trees before I can ask any more questions.

At first, nothing happens.

Then rocks float toward her, twelve of them in all, each one about the size of a fist. Soon they're moving in a circle around her body, as if she's the center of a giant clock, and green energy crackles around them, her red hair blowing around her as the rocks create a vortex with her in the middle of it.

Even though she's in her human form, it's clear in this moment that she's far more powerful than a mere mortal.

"Remember—stay still," she warns, and suddenly one of the rocks is hurtling in my direction faster than I can blink.

Wind whooshes by me as it passes by my face and hits the outside wall of Jax's house with a loud thump.

I flinch, and the only thing keeping me from bolting out of that chair when she throws the next rock is the knowledge that if I move, the rock might smash into my head instead of the house.

She throws another above my head, the next to the deck floor a few inches away from my right foot, and the next a few inches from my left. My heart's pounding, blood rushes to my head, and I wrap my fingers around the arms of the chair, praying for her terrifying demonstration to end soon.

I'd make myself invisible if I wasn't trying to hide my illusion magic from her.

Finally, she pauses.

Seven rocks remain. But instead of throwing them near me, she lets them fall to the ground in a circle around her feet.

I remain still, not wanting to make any sudden moves in case she tries something else.

She tosses her hair over her shoulder and smiles again, as if nothing out of the ordinary just happened. "That's one of my favorite tricks," she says brightly. "And if you keep trying to seduce my boyfriend, you might find yourself at the wrong end of one of those rocks."

My stomach drops, and my tongue feels like a brick in the center of my mouth. "You didn't come here to help me," I realize. "You came here to threaten me."

"I came here to warn you to keep your paws off my boyfriend." Her gaze is locked on mine, and she narrows her eyes, as if she's trying to get me to lower mine in submission.

My body tenses, and I instinctively know it's some sort of wolf dominance thing.

I can't let her win.

If I do, she'll consider me subservient to her. And I refuse to give her the upper hand, no matter how terrifying her magic might be.

So I stand up, wanting to be on equal footing with her.

Satisfaction courses through me when she steps back in surprise.

"You have nothing to worry about," I say, feeling stronger with each word I speak. "Because Connor wants me out of Pine Valley as soon as possible."

"As he should, given your demon illusion magic," she snarls.

Betrayal rips at my heart. "He told you?"

"Of course he told me," she says. "He trusts me with everything. I'm his future mate."

An intense feeling of *wrongness* crashes through me, and I can't stop my next words before they escape my lips.

"How do you know?"

She tenses, my question apparently catching her off-guard, and I brace myself for another rock to come flying my way.

"Connor and I are connected," she says so steadily that I fear she's about to snap. "He's going to be my mate. I turn nineteen in a few weeks, and when the mate bond ignites, he won't so much as look at you anymore."

Her words sting, but I force myself to not show it. "How does the mate bond 'ignite?'" I ask, unable to resist the need to learn more.

"You're full of questions today." She glares at me again. "Why do you want to know?"

"Why don't you want to tell me?" I challenge in return.

I don't know where this sudden boldness is coming from. But I refuse to let Autumn see me as weak, no matter how much more powerful than me she might be. So I wait for her to elaborate, knowing that if I remain silent for long enough, she'll be pressed to say *something.*

I have a sneaking suspicion—or hope—about what she might say. It's been on the back of my mind since Connor tackled me in the woods, but I thought it was too crazy to voice out loud.

Now's my opportunity to find out if I'm right, and despite the fact that Autumn is capable of killing me with a flick of her wrist, I'm not going to throw it away.

Ruby

"Fine. I'll tell you." Autumn tosses her hair over her shoulder and smiles, as if she's envisioning the moment when the mate bond between her and Connor will happen. "As soon as both shifters in the pair have turned nineteen, the bond happens at first touch," she says. "Skin-to-skin contact—it doesn't matter where. I've heard it feels like fireworks, and I've seen it happen a few times. Their eyes glow, and the magic visibly connects them. The eyes are the windows to the soul, and they're the gateways for the bond to join the souls of the mated pair together."

I'm frozen, my mind back at that moment in the woods instead of in the present where I'm standing here with Autumn.

When Connor tackled me, it was the first time he touched me.

Autumn will never mate with Connor.

Because *I'm* mates with Connor.

The reality of it hits me like a bomb, and I'm shellshocked as I soak it in.

But why did Connor lie and tell me that the magic I saw was a spell to hold me down?

The answer is painfully and unbearably obvious.

He doesn't want me to tell anyone about what happened between us because *he doesn't want anyone to know we're mates.*

And he wants me to leave Pine Valley.

He doesn't want me.

We're supposed to be destined for each other, and he doesn't even want to give me a chance.

The realization hurts deep in my soul. It's like someone's ripping out my heart, throwing it to the ground, and stomping it to smithereens. I can't focus. I can't breathe. All I can think about is the coldness in Connor's eyes when he told me he wanted me to leave town for good.

The pain is a million times worse after learning that he knows we're mates.

And I have a sneaking suspicion that if Autumn finds out, she might carry through on that threat and put me on the wrong side of one of those rocks.

Is that why Connor wants me gone? Is he trying to protect me from Autumn?

It's far better than the alternative.

But if he truly thinks she might hurt me, maybe it's best that I do whatever I can to protect myself—even if it means walking away from the person who's supposed to complete my soul.

Unless there's another option… one that might be far less painful.

"Is it possible to break a mate bond?" I ask, hoping I sound neutral and not like someone who just learned that her fated mate rejected her.

Rejected.

The word crushes my soul.

I hate the thought of severing the tie with Connor. I feel so safe around him, and I know that with him nearby, I'll always have someone in my corner.

But he rejected me, and his girlfriend will likely have it out for me if she discovers the truth. And at the end of the day, Connor and I don't really know each other yet.

Maybe it'll be for the best if we break the bond before it goes any further. Then he can have his perfect life with Autumn, and I can leave Pine Valley with nothing tying me down to this godforsaken place.

It would be a win-win.

If it's possible.

"You have a lot of questions about this," Autumn observes, tilting her head as she studies me with those unnervingly conniving eyes of hers.

"It's interesting." I shrug, hoping to look and sound casual about it. "But you don't have to tell me if you don't want to. I can always ask someone else."

Someone like Connor.

The unspoken threat hangs in the air, and I brace myself, praying that if she launches an attack, my wolf will come out and somehow know how to fend her off. If not, I can always try to go invisible again. She can't hit what she can't see.

I'm playing with fire. I know I am. But I'm desperate for answers, and I'm so shaken by what I just learned that I'm willing to push to get them.

"Not everyone meets their mate in their lifetime," Autumn finally says, and I relax at the fact that she's talking instead of trying to smash my head into a pulp. "Having a mate is a blessing from the gods. But there are occasional instances where someone wants to break their mate bond. If that person wants to keep their own magic, then the only way to break the bond is for their mate to die."

Ice-cold horror floods through me as her words set in.

Because that's *not* an option.

I can't imagine living in this world without Connor in it. The pain of the thought hurts a million times more than his rejection ever could.

"Usually they get someone to do it for them, because it's nearly impossible to kill your own mate," Autumn continues, either not noticing how much her words distress me, or not caring. "Those who try and succeed end up shattering their souls in the process."

She doesn't elaborate, and I wonder if she knows someone who's experienced such a thing.

The thought of hurting Connor at all—let alone killing him—is enough to put cracks in my soul. I can't imagine how painful it would be for someone who goes through with it.

How desperate and cruel would they have to be to resort to something so terrible?

"You said death is the only way to break the bond if they want to keep their magic," I say, wanting to keep her talking. "Is there another way? One that involves getting rid of their magic?"

"Correct. The mate bond is magic, and it feeds off magic to stay alive," she says. "If one or both of the mates get their magic stripped, the bond will sever with it."

"How does a wolf strip their magic?" I ask.

"Why?" She raises an eyebrow. "Are you interested?"

"I want to go home and get my life back," I say, although I can't bring myself to say that I'm interested in stripping my magic.

My star mark aches at the thought. Because I just got my magic. I'm just learning how to use it. My magic is a part of me, and getting rid of it would be like carving out a piece of my soul.

And now that I know about the supernatural world, I'll never be able to return to my old life, no matter how much I wish I could.

"All you have to do is ask the witches," she says simply. "The spell can only be done by extremely powerful witches, but we have some here in Pine Valley. I can take you to them if you want."

"You'd like that, wouldn't you?" I say.

"I'd be happy to help." The smile she flashes me this time is downright feral.

"Well, I'm not doing it," I say. "But thanks for the offer."

"Anytime," she says, the word dripping with venom.

She's like a poisonous snake, and I have no idea how Connor doesn't see it.

"Why are you so interested in mate bonds, anyway?" she asks, and I tense at the possibility that she's figured it out.

"You brought it up." I try to stay calm, focusing on slowing my racing heart. "It's interesting."

"It is," she agrees. "And it's highly looked down upon to try getting between someone and their mate. You understand, right?"

I push down a smile at the irony of her statement. Because if anyone's trying to get in the way of a mate bond right now, it's her.

"I do," I say, hoping I sound equally as dangerous as she does. "And I hope it goes well with you and Connor on your birthday."

I can't help but feel a slight thrill at the fact that it's going to go anything *but* well. And while I normally don't like wishing harm on people, she did threaten to smash my head in with a rock, so I don't feel overly bad about it.

"Connor and I are meant for each other. It *will* go well," she says, the confidence in her tone astounding me. "Anyway, I'm done here. I expect you know that this conversation needs to stay between us?"

She wipes the dirt off her hands, as if reminding me of her threat.

"Don't worry. I have zero interest in getting between you and your mate," I say.

It's not a lie, given that Connor isn't her mate.

She nods in approval, looking strangely satisfied. "I'm glad we worked that out," she says, and then she shifts into her wolf form and runs into the forest without looking back, somehow leaving me with more problems than I already had when I woke up this morning.

Ruby

I NEED TO FIND CONNOR.

I have to tell him that I know.

But Autumn likely went straight back to him, and I have no way of contacting him. Plus, a part of me dreads facing him. He already rejected me once, and I doubt that will change now that I know the truth. It might even make him want to get rid of me faster.

Plus, if Jax comes back and I'm not here, he'll be furious. I've already induced enough of his anger so far. I'm lucky he's letting me have free roam of the house. For all I know, he has a basement cell or something, and I don't want to risk having my freedom stripped from me even more.

Instead, I wander around, exploring a bunch of the rooms until finding the library.

The small, traditionally styled room smells like old books, and there are no windows in it, which makes it feel like a secret cave. An intricately carved wooden desk faces outward, and shelves of books both old and new climb up to the ceiling. I doubt any of them hold information about my star mark, since if they did, Jax wouldn't have needed to go to the witches. But I have nothing else to do right now, so I figure it won't hurt to poke around a bit.

The library is divided into sections—world religions, mythology from different cultures, and history, among many others. There's even a small section for fiction, and the books there appear to be surprisingly well-read.

I eventually find the section with books about shifters, and I settle in to start reading. The information in them is interesting, but there's nothing about star marks or any sort of magic that shifters have other than earth magic—not even in the books about the original shifters who were created by witches to protect the world from the ever-growing population of vampires.

I read about vampires next, tracing all the way back to the original vampire, Ambrogio. His story fascinates me, specifically because he was rejected by the woman he loved—the goddess of the moon, Selene.

I'm absorbed in the book when I hear the front door open, and I slam it closed, shoving it back into the slot where I found it. Once making sure everything in the room is exactly how I found it, I hurry out of the library, down the hall, and into the living room.

Jax is there with three people—a man, a woman, and a petite girl with brown hair and a splattering of freckles on her face. She looks slightly younger than me, and judging by her resemblance to the man and woman, she's their daughter.

All three of them radiate confidence and power.

"Ruby." Jax sizes me up suspiciously. "Where were you?"

"The library." The truth seems like the best way to go, given that I wasn't doing anything wrong, since I had free reign of the house and the doors weren't locked.

"And what were you doing in the library?" he presses.

I glance at the girl and her parents, unsure who they are and how much I should say in front of them.

"Just looking for information about the thing we were talking about earlier," I say, figuring it's vague enough to not get me into any trouble.

The girl smiles, as if she knows something I don't. "Do you mean your star mark?" she asks, her voice light and airy.

I look to Jax, and he nods to let me know it's okay to continue. "Yeah," I say, refocusing on the girl and her presumed parents. They're dressed differently than anyone I've seen in pack territory, with the girl and her mom are in conservative skirts and blouses, and her dad in slacks and a blazer. "Are you witches?"

"Correct," she says. "I'm Hazel. These are my parents, Seraphina and Perry."

"You call your parents by their first names?"

Out of everything going on here, that shouldn't be the most shocking. Yet, it somehow is.

"Hazel is the most powerful witch born in centuries," her mom—Seraphina—says. "She calls everyone by their first names, as is proper for someone of her station."

"Interesting," I say, although it's not nearly as interesting to me as the reason why they're here. "Do you know what my star mark means?"

I direct the question at Hazel, since she seems to be the one in charge here.

"I believe so," she says. "But first, can we see it?"

"Of course." I pull the elastic band of my lounge pants down slightly, revealing the mark on my hip.

They walk toward me to get a closer look. Seraphina's lips part in surprise and amazement, and she brushes her finger against the mark without bothering to ask if I mind.

I almost step back, but I stay put, since these people seem to have the answers I need, and I don't want to do anything that might offend them.

I can barely breathe as I wait for them to finish inspecting it.

"What is it?" I ask, unable to wait any longer.

"It's the mark of Selene." Seraphina steps back, and I pull my waistband up to cover the mark. "Which means you've been blessed by the cosmic goddess of the moon."

Selene.

The goddess I read about in the book.

It can't be a coincidence. If this mark is truly Selene's, I must have been drawn to that book for a reason.

"But Selene's in an eternal sleep with Endymion," I say, recalling the story of the man Selene chose to be with after rejecting Ambrogio. It's crazy to think that these ancient gods exist, but my life is full of crazy now, so I'm just rolling with it by this point. "Zeus cursed Endymion into an eternal sleep, and Selene joined him so she could be with him forever.

How could she mark me if she's sleeping? And if she's the goddess of the moon, why's her mark a star?"

"You know your history," Hazel says in approval.

"I've been doing some reading."

Respect flashes in the young witch's eyes. "Very interesting," she says. "As for your first question, you're right that Selene couldn't have marked you. But she and Endymion have many daughters. Four of them have taken on Selene's cosmic duties and rule in her place, splitting the jobs between themselves. It could have been one of them."

"As for the mark being a star instead of the moon?" I ask again.

"We wondered that as well," Seraphina says. "We believe it's because Selene and her daughters represent not just the moon, but the cosmos as a whole. The North Star—which is the specific star you're marked with—also represents fulfillment, purpose, and destiny. Being marked with it likely shows that you have an important role to play in the supernatural world. And while we don't know what that role is yet, we intend to figure it out."

"Wow," I say, stunned nearly speechless. "That's… a lot."

"It is," she agrees, but before she can say anything else, someone opens the front door and hurries into the living room.

Connor.

My heart clenches at the sight of him.

His dark hair is messy, as if he's been running. His eyes go to me first, and he studies me up and down, as if he's making sure I'm okay.

As if he cares.

You're being silly, says an inner voice that I know is my wolf. *Of course Connor cares. He's our mate.*

He doesn't want us, I think, and I push her voice down as far as possible, not wanting her to distract me from the facts.

It feels strange to talk to my wolf, since hearing voices isn't exactly something that's looked upon highly in the regular world. But Penny told me that this is completely normal, and that as I continue connecting with my wolf, I'll be able to control my shifts.

Right now, I don't care about my shifts.

I only care about getting her to shut up.

"I heard you were back with the witches," Connor says to Jax. His tone is all-business, and his concerned eyes flick to me again before returning to his grandfather. "What's going on?"

Seraphina looks to Jax in question.

"It's okay," Jax says. "My grandson already knows quite a lot. We can trust him."

"Very well." She straightens her shoulders and quickly gets Connor up to speed.

As she repeats the part about suspecting that one of Selene's daughters marked me, my thoughts flash back to the blonde woman in the woods.

"The goddess who marked me," I say, and all their eyes go to me. "I met her. Sort of. In the woods, on the night I shifted for the first time."

"The night of the blood moon," Hazel says, and I nod in confirmation. "What did she say to you?"

"She told me that everything was going to be okay," I say, purposefully omitting the part about my eye color. "Then she touched my head, and it was like an electric shock, and I passed out. I think that was the moment she marked me."

"Did she tell you her name?"

"No." I shrug. "That was all."

"Interesting," she says slowly. "Can we speak with you? Privately?"

I glance to Connor, as if I need his permission, then quickly realize that I don't. Because firstly, I don't need his approval for my decisions. Secondly, the witches are higher ranked than the wolves. What they say goes around here.

From Connor's stiff stance, he's thinking the same thing.

"You can go to the library," Jax says, and he looks to me, his eyes hard. "Since you already know where it is."

I shift uneasily on my feet, although I quickly stop and stand still again, not wanting Jax to think he intimidates me.

"Great." I give Connor a final glance, immediately regretting it after seeing his ambivalent expression.

He's a mystery to me, and I hate it.

I tear my gaze away from him, not wanting to look at him for a moment longer than necessary. Then I lead the witches to the library, my heart pounding in anticipation about what they want to ask me that can't be said in front of the others, and unsure how much to tell them when they do.

Ruby

HAZEL'S FATHER—PERRY—IS the last to enter the library, and he shuts the doors to lock us in.

Before I realize what's happening, Hazel holds her hands out, and a blaze of fire ignites in a circle around us. The flames are so high that they lick the ceiling, hot against my skin as they crackle and pop so loudly that I can barely hear my thoughts.

Panic grips my chest and throat, tightening so much that it's smothering me.

The witches are trying to kill me. They're like hungry hawks surrounding me, zeroing in on me like I'm their prey and they're ready for a feast.

I need to get out of here.

I scan the area, searching for a break between the flames, but there's nothing. The room has no windows, so there's no escape there, which means I need to run for the doors and pray to escape with the least amount of burns possible.

Better burned than dead.

I make headway for the doors, but Seraphina grabs my wrist, stopping me. Her grip is stronger than expected, and even though I try to free myself, my attempts are unsuccessful.

"Connor!" I scream his name. "Help!"

"They can't hear you," Hazel says calmly, the flickering flames reflecting in her eyes like she's the devil in disguise.

I narrow my eyes at her and try again to pull myself out of Seraphina's grip.

Again, I'm unsuccessful.

These witches are stronger than they look.

Maybe if I can manage to shift, I'll surprise them enough to get away. But when I try to connect with my wolf, I get nothing.

Seraphina pulls me closer. "We're not trying to hurt you," she says. "We're here to help you."

"By burning me alive?" I glare at her, hoping she sees my rage instead of my fear.

"Are the flames touching you?" she asks. "Are they burning you? Is there smoke in your lungs choking you?"

I take a deep breath, surprised by how clear the air feels. And while the fire is warm enough to make beads of sweat form on my forehead, it isn't so hot that it hurts. And none of the furniture in the room is catching on fire. Even the books are immune—much to my relief.

"No," I admit, relaxing slightly.

"As you know, witches control the element of fire," Hazel says, her voice clear and bright. "I created this fire, and I can easily contain it, as you see now. Nothing will burn that I don't want to burn."

"But *why* are you doing this?" I ask. "To show off how strong you are?"

"That's a plus. But it's not the reason." She gives me a small smile, seeming to enjoy this. "Do you hear how the fire crackles?"

"I do."

"It blocks out sound," she explains. "It'll prevent our conversation from being heard by anyone who's not standing in this circle."

"Oh." I gaze around at the fire surrounding us, seeing it in an entirely new light as the pieces click into place. "It's a sound barrier so Jax and Connor can't listen in on our conversation."

"Correct."

"That's... convenient," I settle on the proper word, then turn to Seraphina, whose death grip is still locked around my wrist. "You can let me go. I'm not going to run."

"A smart move." She releases my wrist, and I pull it toward my chest and step away from her.

She remains on guard for a few seconds, then relaxes when she sees I'm not going anywhere.

"What did you want to ask me?" I look to Seraphina, then Perry, then finally settle on Hazel.

"Jax told us you haven't presented with any elemental magic," Hazel says. "He thinks you're an omega. Or, as we call our witches with no elemental magic, a cinder."

"Because cinders don't give off flames," I guess.

"Exactly." She smiles again, and now that I know she's not trying to burn me alive, I have a sudden feeling that if we met in the normal world, we could become friends. "But given your star mark, we think it's highly unlikely that you have zero magic to speak of."

I glance at the floor, realizing a second later that my reaction likely gave me away.

"You can trust us," Hazel continues. "Being touched by a goddess is a gift. As witches, we value all gifts—especially rare ones. But we can't help you if you don't tell us what's going on."

I think back to my conversation with Connor. He asked me to not tell the *pack* about my magic, but he didn't say anything about the witches. Plus, he betrayed me when he told Autumn my secret. He's loyal to her. Not to me.

The witches know more than the shifters. They have more clout in the supernatural world. If anyone can help me, it's them.

I meet Hazel's gaze—her eyes are the same color as her name—and she says nothing more as she waits for me to speak.

"I only got my magic a few days ago, so I don't know much about it, but I can make people see things that aren't there," I say, feeling a wave of relief from telling her the truth. "I can create illusions."

She presses her lips together as she takes it in, and I worry she's going to think it's demon magic, like Connor seemed to when he first found out.

"Interesting," she finally says, and I release a long breath. "Show us."

No point in holding back now.

"Okay," I say, and keeping my eyes locked on hers, I use my magic to make my hair blonde, like I did while practicing with Connor.

Hazel's eyes light up like a child watching a spectacular act at a circus. "Fascinating," she says, and she looks to her parents. "Can you see it, too?"

"We can," Seraphina confirms.

"So, you're not planting the illusion in my mind," Hazel says, returning her focus to me. "You're creating it for everyone to see."

"I haven't thought about it one way or the other, but yes, I suppose that's what it feels like when I do it." I release my magic, allowing my hair to return to its normal brown, and the tingling in my brain subsides.

"I've never seen or heard of anything like this before," Hazel says, and I'm not sure if that's a good thing or a bad thing. "What more can you do?"

I tell them everything, minus making myself appear in Autumn's place. They do *not* need to know about my feelings for Connor, especially because the humiliation of admitting that my fated mate rejected me would be too much for me to bear right now.

Or ever.

"Thank you for sharing this with us," Hazel says when I'm done, and she releases her hold on her magic, the flames disappearing into thin air. "I think we're done here."

"That's it?" I ask.

Seraphina opens the door to the hall. "Follow us," she says. "We'll chat with the shifters and handle this from here."

I glance at Hazel, who nods in encouragement, and follow them back out to the living room where Connor and Jax are anxiously waiting.

Connor stops pacing, looking relieved at the sight of me.

"Is everything okay?" he asks.

"Yes," I say, even though I have more questions now than ever.

Hazel moves to stand by my side, and I feel stronger with her next to me. "Ruby's coming with us," she says confidently, as if it's already been discussed and decided.

"What?" Connor and I say at the same time.

"You can learn more from us than you can with them," she tells me. "You'll be *respected* more with us than you are with them." She directs that part to Jax, her distaste for his treatment of me clear, and I like her more by the second. "Out of all the supernatural species, the witches are the most in touch with and devoted to the gods. You've been star touched by a goddess. As far as we're concerned, that means you belong with us."

"Wow." I take a few seconds to digest what she's saying, caught completely off-guard. "I don't know what to say."

"Say yes," Connor says, watching me with total detachment.

The rejection burning through me is so intense that I can barely stand it. "You don't want me here," I say, even though I already know he feels that way, since he told me as much this morning.

"Like Hazel said, you're better off with them than with us," he says. "You've caused us nothing but trouble, and it'll be a relief to get you out of our hair."

The words are his worst gut-punch yet, hurting so badly that it feels like he's knocked the wind out of me.

He hates me.

Just the fact that I exist screws up his long-term plans with Autumn, and he *hates* me for it.

And he's completely unaware that I know the truth.

I can't leave without telling him. If he's going to reject me, then he deserves to know that I'm aware of exactly what he's doing to me.

"Understood," I say, trying to sound as aloof as he does. "But I need to talk to you first. Alone."

"I don't think that's a good idea." He keeps his gaze fixed on mine, his tone sharp with warning.

"Talk to me, or I don't go with them."

He wants me gone so badly that it seems like the best threat I can make.

"Fine," he gives in, and he glares at me, spins around, and walks toward the library, motioning for me to follow him without bothering to say another word.

Ruby

As I follow Connor to the library, I feel separated from my body, and each step fills me with dread.

What am I doing? How will it help anything to tell him that I know we're mates?

Maybe I should forget about it. Telling him won't change anything.

It won't make him want me more than he wants *her*.

My jealousy disgusts me. He met her first—he *chose* her. I have no right to him.

Wrong, my wolf says in my mind. *We're his mate. We have more claim on him than she ever will.*

The fact that my wolf thinks about us as a "we" seriously freaks me out. Does she think we're the same person? Or does she think she's a separate entity living in my body?

I don't know, but for now, I push her down as far as possible.

This is *my* body. I'm in control of it. Not her.

Suddenly I'm in the library with Connor, the door closed. He stands across the room, as far away from me as possible, as if he's afraid I might bite.

"What do you want?" he asks.

"I know about the mate bond," I say quickly, wanting to get it out before I can second-guess myself any further.

I don't know what kind of reaction I expected, but he stays perfectly still, unfazed by my statement.

His apathy hurts more than anything else possibly could have.

"How did you find out?" he asks.

"I read about it in the library."

It's a lie, but telling him I got the information from Autumn will likely do more harm than good. Especially since he might ask me about the time Autumn and I spent together, and I have zero interest in telling him that his girlfriend threatened to kill me.

I don't want it to sound like I'm trying to turn him against her.

If he ever decides to be with me, it will be because it's what he wants, and not because I tried to manipulate a decision out of him.

His breaths are slow and steady, his eyes twist with pain, and I feel a sliver of hope that he'll stop trying to fight the bond.

"This doesn't change anything. I'm not breaking up with Autumn," he finally says, shattering any hope I might have had. "Autumn and I made a promise to each other. I care about her, and I respect her. The pack views us as their future leaders. Turning away from her would be the same as turning my back on the pack."

"The pack respects mate bonds," I say, unable to stop myself from standing my ground.

I'm not trying to make him do anything, but mate bonds are sacred to wolves. I know it, my wolf knows it, and I'm sure Connor knows it, too.

It's why he's so conflicted that he looks like he's about to burst out of his skin.

"They can't respect what they don't know exists," he says steadily. "Because no one is going to know about this. Especially not Autumn."

"Don't worry. I have no intention of telling her," I assure him. "If she ever finds out, it should come from you and not me."

"I'm not breaking up with her," he repeats, as if he's trying to drill it into my brain.

Or maybe he's trying to drill it into *his* brain. As if the more times he says it, the more he won't want to do it.

"I understood you the first time you said it," I say, frustration building in my blood at the fact that I'm in this position at all. "But you never said you loved her."

"What?" He jerks back, looking truly surprised by my statement.

"You said you respect her. You said you care about her. You said you made a promise to her. But you never said you love her."

The more I say, the more I'm convinced it's true.

Or maybe I just *hope* it's true.

This whole situation is breaking my heart, and I hate it.

"Autumn and I have been together for years. Of course I love her," he says, although for reasons I can't place, I'm not convinced. "I'm a logic-oriented person, and Autumn's the logical choice for my future wife. I made a promise to her. I'm not backing out of it."

His future *wife*.

The word stings far more than I imagined it could.

"I understand," I say, because what else am I supposed to say?

I want someone who wants me. Who appreciates me.

Connor clearly doesn't. He doesn't even want to give me a chance.

Regardless of the universe trying to push us together, I deserve better than that.

"Oh," he says, sounding almost… surprised. "Thanks."

"Sure." I shrug, trying as hard as I can to not look like my heart is breaking. "I just thought it was important that before I leave, you knew that I know."

"So, you're going with them?"

"Trust me—I'm happy to get out of here."

I don't expect him to care, but he looks like I slapped him in the face. And while I don't consider myself a vengeful person, I'm glad of it.

"It's best for us to be apart," he says, quickly composing himself. "The bond will weaken the longer we're away from each other. The farther the better, but staying with the witches will do for now. And it might be enough, since we haven't consummated the bond, or even done as much as kissed."

His eyes drift to my lips, as if he wants to change that, and my heart pounds faster. A sudden thought crosses through my mind of him closing the space between us and kissing me like the world depends on it.

I'd melt into him if he did.

But despite the temptation of the mate bond, he hasn't succumbed to it and cheated on Autumn. I respect him for it. He's loyal to the people he cares about, and he keeps his promises, even if it causes him pain.

Right now, being here with him is causing *me* pain.

I need to get out of here.

"You're going to make an excellent alpha one day," I tell him, and then I hurry out of the library and go with the witches, not looking behind as I leave him standing in my wake.

Ruby

THE WITCHES LIVE across the river on the opposite side of the town, on a street with a court at the end of it, about a ten-minute drive away from the main drag. Their houses are closer together than the ones in pack territory, because unlike the wolves, they don't need open space to shift and go on runs.

Hazel and her parents live in the largest house at the end of the court. It's a white, Victorian mansion with a wraparound porch, a large turret tower, and a steep roof to cap off all three stories. It *looks* like a place where witches would live, and I can't help but wonder if it's haunted.

They set me up in a guest room that overlooks the gardens in the backyard and have me tell them about everything that happened to me these past few days over cups of tea. They listen intently as I go over every detail, not saying much. As we're finishing up, my eyelids feel like they're being weighed down by sledgehammers, and I barely make it back to the room before falling into a dead sleep.

I'm awoken the next morning by someone knocking on my door, and I glance at the clock, surprised when it says 4:30.

Why are they waking me up so early?

Except it's not pitch dark outside, like it should be at this time in the morning. Rays of dim sunlight are coming through the window.

It's sun*set*, which happens stupidly early this far north in the winter.

I slept for over twelve hours.

The knock on the door sounds again.

"Come in," I say, sitting up and running my fingers through my messy hair.

It's Hazel, and she enters with a box of delicious-smelling pizza.

"Sorry for waking you up," she says sheepishly. "It's just that you've been asleep forever, and the pizza's hot."

The room is more of a suite, and she places the pizza box on a small table near the window.

"It's from the best pizza place in town," she continues. "Extra cheese. And pepperoni. The cupped kind that holds in the grease."

My stomach growls at the mention of pepperoni, which is a meat I've yet to try.

I'm a traitor to all the vegetarians in the world. But judging by how delicious the pizza smells, I'm not sorry about it.

"Thanks," I say. "Give me a minute."

I walk across the room and enter the ensuite bathroom, which is supplied with every amenity I could ask for, down to scented candles to freshen up the space. I brush my teeth and hair, still surprised every time I see my brown eyes in the mirror. I kept my changed eye color from Hazel and her parents, since whoever marked me—apparently a daughter of the goddess Selene—instructed me not to tell anyone. Until I hear otherwise, I assume that includes the witches.

When I re-enter the room, Hazel's sitting down, and there are two bottles of Coke on the table. She looks so *normal* in her jeans and long-sleeve black top that it's hard to believe she's an all-powerful witch capable of lighting an entire room on fire.

She opens the pizza box and pulls out a massive slice. "Sit down and dig in," she says, and her eyes light up as she takes the first bite.

I join her, and she's right—the pizza is delicious. Even more so because of the grease sitting in the center of each pepperoni.

"Good, right?" she asks, and I can only nod in response as I finish chewing.

"What have you been up to all day?" I ask.

"Just a few errands. Nothing interesting." She shrugs. "I grabbed the pizza on my way home."

"Thank you. It's great," I say, which earns me a smile. "And I know I said it last night, but thank you for letting me stay here."

"You've been touched by a daughter of Selene," she says. "You deserve a place with us."

"Even though I'm a shifter and not a witch?"

"Being touched by a goddess is more meaningful than being a shifter *or* a witch." She polishes off her first slice of pizza and starts on a second, and I do the same. "You're special, and you deserve to be treated like it."

I know she's trying to give me a compliment, but it doesn't feel as great as I think she intends.

I continue eating my pizza, not saying anything.

"What's wrong?" she asks.

"I'll never fit in with the humans again," I start, figuring that's as good of a place as any. "I'm clearly not a witch, and I thought I'd eventually fit in with the shifters, but I'm pretty sure they think my magic makes me some sort of demon."

Let alone the fact that my mate rejected me, but I have zero interest in getting into *that* right now. Or ever. It would be best if I could erase all the feelings I have for Connor out of my heart for good.

Maybe the witches have a potion that can help me, but I'm not anywhere close to ready to talk about it yet. Even though Hazel feels like someone who could quickly become a close friend, I've only known her for less than a day, and I'm not one to pour my heart out to people I just met.

"You're not a demon," Hazel says, as confidently as ever.

"I know. But I'm the only person alive who's been star touched, which means I have no one." I take a large bite of my pizza, since if I'm wallowing, I should do it right and wallow into my food.

"You have me," she says, a sad look crossing her eyes. "I know a thing or two about not fitting in."

"But you're a super powerful witch," I say.

"Which makes me different. And people tend to avoid those who are different."

"What do you mean?"

"First of all, there's my parents," she starts, and she sits straighter, like she's getting ready to share a prepared speech. "They view me as a prized possession instead of an actual person, and they use me as a tool for power more than anything else. And let's not get started on the others our age in the coven. The girls shy away from me—I'm not sure if they're jealous of my magic or scared of it, but I think it's a bit of both. And the guys… well, I'm far from the most attractive of the girls for them to pick from."

"What are you talking about?" I ask, although I'm just trying to be nice. Hazel's not hard to look at, but she's someone who'd be described as "mousy" in the books I read, with no distinguishing features other than the freckles smattered across her cheeks and bridge of her nose.

"It's okay. We both know it's true." She gives me a small smile to show she's not offended, then creates ribbons of fire in her palms and plays with them, letting them slither around her fingers like pet snakes. "But beyond that, I think the guys are intimidated by my magic and don't want to be with someone stronger than they are. Why would they, when there are other, more beautiful girls to choose from who won't *emasculate* them by being so powerful?"

She brings the ribbons of fire together to form a ball of it in her hands, then closes her fingers around it so it vanishes into her palms. The remaining smoke trails up to the ceiling and disappears.

"I'm sure there's someone out there for you," I tell her, hoping to sound encouraging instead of like someone who was just rejected by her fated mate. "You just haven't met him yet."

"I'm not so sure about that," she says with a mischievous smirk.

"*Have* you met someone?" I ask.

She glances around the room, as if checking to make sure no one's listening. "If I tell you something, you have to promise to tell *no one*. Understand?"

"I promise," I say, and I lean forward, ready for her to continue, since it'll be nice to focus on someone else's drama for a change instead of dwelling on my own.

Ruby

THE TURN of the conversation feels so *normal*, like one I'd have with Luna in our dorm room, and it's surprisingly easy to forget how much my life changed in the past few days.

"I have a boyfriend," she says quickly, her eyes lighting up with excitement. "He lives in town. He's *human*." She whispers the final word, like she's risking getting in trouble simply by saying it out loud.

"Witches aren't allowed to date humans?" I ask.

I know that shifters only date shifters. But witches seem more human than shifters, so dating one doesn't seem like it would be totally outside the realm of possibility.

"Some do, although it's highly frowned upon," she says. "But I'm not a normal witch. Regular rules don't apply to me."

"I'm sorry," I say, since it clearly bothers her greatly.

"Don't be," she says, perking up again. "Benjamin's great. He doesn't know what I am, and I intend to keep it that way."

"Forever?"

"I don't know." She chews on her lower lip, as if she hasn't thought it through. "But definitely for as long as I can. If he *does* ever find out, hopefully we'll have known each other long enough that he sees me for who I am instead of as the prodigal witch who's too powerful for her own good."

"People really think that about you?" I ask.

If they think that about Hazel, who at least has elemental fire magic that witches are supposed to have, then what will they think about me and my weird magic?

Hazel and her parents said they were on my side, but what about everyone else?

"They do," she says, a trace of bitterness in her tone. "It's why they want to keep me here, even though I eventually want to go to NYC and help oversee the Guardians there. I've been cooped up for my entire life—I've never left Pine Valley. But the city seems so exciting, and I want to be part of it. I belong there. I *know* I do."

"You'll get there," I say. "I have faith in you."

"Thanks." She picks up another slice of pizza, and we both enjoy our food for a few more minutes.

As we eat, my mind drifts to Luna and my parents.

"My parents think I'm dead," I say after polishing off my third slice. "As does my best friend."

"I know," she says solemnly.

"Do you think I'll ever be able to tell them the truth?"

"I don't know." She shrugs, and my heart drops, since it's hardly a promising response. "I wish I had a better answer. But even though I'm the most powerful witch around here, I don't call the shots about anything that has to do with politics between the supernatural and human worlds."

"Got it," I say, since it was at least worth an ask.

"But there's a reason why we did what we did," she continues. "Your parents and best friend have no magic. They have no place in our world. The more distance you put between yourself and them, the safer for them it will be. Especially since you'll have more eyes on you than ever if word about your magic gets out."

"I understand," I say, since I don't want the people I love getting mixed up in the supernatural world, either. If they get hurt—or killed—because of me, I'll never forgive myself.

"I wish I had better news for you," she says.

"It's not your fault." I give her a small smile to show I truly do get it.

She looks down at her plate, and I have a feeling she wants to say something else.

"What's wrong?" I ask.

She takes a deep breath, then looks back up at me with her wide, child-like eyes. "I know I can never replace your best friend," she says hesitantly. "But if anyone knows what's it's like to be different around here, it's me. You and I are two of the most powerful people around, and I think we could be a pretty awesome duo, if we want to be."

"*You're* one of the most powerful people around," I correct her. "I'm a shifter with no earth magic who doesn't know how to shift, and I barely know what I can do with my illusion magic."

"You can use it to trick people," she says with a devious flash in her eyes. "The possibilities are endless. It's going to be fun to find out what you're capable of."

"You're going to help me?" I'm grateful, but also surprised about how easily Hazel seems to trust me.

Although considering everything she's told me, I imagine she's desperate for a friend.

"Of course I'm going to help you," she says. "You bring a lot to the table. It would be foolish to let that go to waste. Plus, the goddess who star touched you brought us together for a reason. I can help you harness your magic so you can have more power than you've ever dreamed possible. Together, we'll be unstoppable."

"I haven't had time to dream about much of anything, since I just found out about this magic a few days ago," I remind her.

She gives me a sympathetic smile. "I can't imagine how overwhelming it must be," she says. "You need a break from it all. What do you say we get out of here and have a bit of *human* fun?"

"What do you mean?"

"I'm meeting Benjamin in town in about an hour," she says. "Want to come with? I can tell him to bring his friend Tristan. Tristan's *hot*. I think you'll like him."

I can't imagine myself being attracted to anyone other than Connor, since the mate bond created a connection between us that I'll never experience again in my life.

But my other option is to stay here and brood about how the man who's supposed to be my perfect match rejected me, and how my family and best friend think I'm dead.

Wallowing in my misery will only make me feel worse.

And maybe this Tristan guy *will* help me get my mind off Connor.

I won't know if I don't try.

"Will your parents mind?" I ask.

"They'll be happy you're getting out and seeing the town," she says. "We won't be in danger there, especially with my magic to protect us."

"All right," I say, feeling more excited by the second to do something normal for a change. "When do we leave?"

Her eyes light up instantly. "Forty-five minutes," she says. "There are clothes in the dresser and makeup in the vanity. And trust me—once you see Tristan, you're going to be glad I dragged you out."

"I really hope so," I say.

"I *know* so," she says, and then she grabs the pizza box and leaves my room, giving me privacy to get ready for whatever adventure this night on the town might have in store for us.

Ruby

FORTY-FIVE MINUTES LATER, Hazel comes back into my room and looks over my all-black outfit in approval.

I've never been one to love fashion, but it's hard to go wrong with black. And she's wearing jeans and a conservative long-sleeve top, which actually makes me feel a bit *over*dressed.

"One final thing," she says, and she reaches into her back pocket and hands me an ID card. "You'll need this."

I take it from her and look at it. It's her New York ID, except it's horizontal—not vertical like the ones given to everyone under twenty-one.

A glance at the birth date makes the reason why clear.

It's a fake ID that says Hazel is twenty-three, even though there's no way that the small girl in front of me could ever pass as being older than eighteen, let alone older than twenty-one.

"Why are you giving this to me?" I ask.

"This is mine. I used it the first few times I went to this bar, but now all the bartenders know me and don't ask to see it," she says. "We could try to give them a large tip to see if they'll look the other way when you order a drink, but it'll be easier for you to just use this."

"Except I'm obviously not the one on the ID…" I say, unsure where she's going with this.

"You're not the one on the ID right *now*," she says, her lips curling up into a mischievous smirk. "But you have illusion magic. How about you put your new power to use and make it look like it's your ID instead of mine?"

It's not a terrible idea. I've never been one to drink a lot—the game of beer pong at Connor's was one of the few exceptions—but being able to forge identification cards could be a good use of my magic.

So I take the ID card, focus on the photo of Hazel, and picture myself there instead.

My brain tingles, and within seconds, I'm staring at a picture of myself.

Hazel takes the card from me and studies it. "Very cool," she says. "But why did you make your eyes turquoise?"

Crap.

I look at the photo again and use my magic to make my eyes brown.

"I usually wear color contacts." I use the same excuse I told Connor. "Not prescription—just for fun. I lost them when I shifted."

"Interesting," she says, and for a moment I worry she doesn't believe me. "You should probably change the name to yours, too."

Relieved at how quickly she dropped the subject of my eye color, I quickly make the adjustment on the ID so it says my name instead of hers.

She examines it in approval. "How long will it last?"

"I don't know," I say. "The longest I've held an illusion has been a few minutes."

She holds up the ID, as if trying to find any imperfections, then brings it back down. "I want to try something. Keep focusing on holding the illusion in place," she instructs, and then she flips the card over so the photo is face-down on her palm.

I do as asked, and continue focusing on the illusion.

When she flips it back over, it still has the photo of me instead of her.

"The illusion doesn't have to be in your field of vision for you to hold it," she says. "It makes sense, since you were able to make yourself invisible and change your hair color, and you couldn't see all those parts of yourself when you did it. But there's something else I want to try. Keep holding onto your magic."

"Okay," I say, and she turns around and leaves the room.

She closes the door, and the tingling in my brain stops. I try to reach for it again, but it's gone.

She re-enters a few seconds later.

"The illusion disappeared," I say, since I'm sure that's what happened. "I lost my hold on it when you closed the door."

"It could be a distance thing," she supposes, closing the space between us. "Or it could be because I was in a different room. We'll have to keep testing it out. But let's not tax you too much in a day. We want you to be able to create the illusion when you hand this thing over to the bartender."

"I could just order a Coke instead," I say, since I'd truly be fine with that.

"Where's the fun in that?" she says. "You have this magic—you might as well put it to use."

Her energy is infectious, and I can't help but feel excited at the prospect of applying my magic to something in the real world. I won't be hurting anyone by ordering a drink at a bar. And after everything I've been through these past few days, it might be good for me to have a little fun.

What *else* am I going to do—sit around in this witchy tower room and brood myself to death?

"I might as well start somewhere," I say, and Hazel grins at my decision.

"I knew I liked you," she says, and we finish getting ready, hop into her car, and head out to town.

* * *

The bar is cozy and rustic, with wood floors and exposed beams lining the ceilings. Vintage ski equipment decorates the walls, about half the people inside are still wearing their ski gear, and the distinct smell of yeasty beer permeates the room. It's a totally different vibe than the fancy cocktail bar at the hotel where I stayed with Luna, but I kind of like it.

Hazel nabs us two seats at the bar, in front of an impressively large display of beer offered on tap. A few televisions are mounted on the wall below the ceiling, most of them showing various sports games, and one with the local news.

The bartender walks over to us—a tall, broad man in a plaid shirt, with a bushy beard and a blue baseball cap with "Bills" written across the front in large red font.

"Hazel," he says to her, slowly filling up a pint with dark brown beer. "Who's your friend?"

He glances at me, clearly expecting me to answer even though he directed the question to her.

"I'm Ruby," I say, figuring the fewer details I give him, the better.

"Pretty name. I'm Frank," he says, and then he looks back to Hazel. "What'll it be?"

"Baby Guinness shots," she says. "Make them doubles."

He refocuses on me. "ID?"

Panic shoots through me—I've never used a fake ID before. And sure, I knew coming in that I was going to do this, but it's a totally different ballgame when put on the spot.

But the longer I wait, the more awkward it will be, so I open the purse Hazel loaned me and dig through to find the ID.

Since it was out of sight for so long, the photo reverted to being of Hazel. So I take my time, as if making sure I'm pulling out the right card, and use my magic to change the photo and name to mine.

"Here you go." I give him a smile and hand it over, focusing on keeping the illusion in place.

He brings it close to his face and squints, and I hold my breath, feeling like time's slowing down.

He's looking at it for too long. I must have messed something up.

Still, I hold the image in place in my mind, praying to the goddess that this works.

I don't even care about drinking alcohol. I just don't want to fail at my first try of using my magic in the real world.

"I think it's almost time for me to invest in some glasses." He smiles and hands the ID back to me, and I pocket it as quickly as possible. "Two baby Guinness shots, coming right up."

Ruby

"Is that a shot of beer?" I ask, since all I know about Guinness is that it's a popular beer from Ireland.

"There's no Guinness in a baby Guinness shot," he says proudly. "It's Irish cream and coffee liqueur."

"Sounds fancy."

"A baby Guinness shot is anything but fancy." He brings out two extra tall shot glasses, reminding me that Hazel asked for doubles.

"Make mine a single," I say quickly, and he gives me a nod, pulls out two bottles, and gets to work.

As he does, Hazel gives me a knowing look. "Good job," she says, and from the sparkle in her eyes, I can tell she's having a great time with this.

There's far more spunk to her than you'd guess from first look, and I like her more and more because of it. She reminds me of Luna in that way.

My chest pangs at the reminder of my best friend. But I push the thought away, focusing instead on the present, where Frank is pouring dark liqueur into a regular size shot glass like an old pro.

"Enjoy," he says, placing the double in front of Hazel and the single in front of me.

Hazel raises hers in a toast. "To new discoveries and wild adventures," she says, and I clink my glass with hers and down it in a few gulps.

It's sweet—it tastes more like a dessert than alcohol.

"That's good." I wipe a drop off my lips and place the glass back down on the table.

"Right?" Hazel looks back over at Frank. "Let's top it off with some tequila. Another double."

He looks at me for my reaction.

"I'll pass," I say, since I already completed my goal of using the ID I manipulated with my magic. There's no need to get toasted. "How about a Coke?"

"You're no fun." Hazel rolls her eyes.

"I'm not a big drinker," I say. "But you go ahead."

"Hazel's not usually this big of a drinker, either," Frank says, looking back to her. "What's going on with you? Did that boyfriend of yours break up with you?"

"Everything's good with Benjamin," she says. "It's just been a long week."

"We've all been there." Frank pours a double shot glass with tequila and slides it over to her. "Be careful. With those people going missing... well, I don't want you getting hurt."

"I can hold my own," she says, and then she holds the shot glass to her lips and downs it. "Wow." She blinks tears out of her eyes. "That's strong."

Frank puts glass of Coke in front of me and gives Hazel a look that says *I told you so.* Then he hands Hazel a cup full of water. "Might not be a bad idea to have some of this," he says.

"Thanks." She pulls the water closer, but makes no move to drink. "I'll slow down. How about a Truly?"

"You sure about that?" he asks.

"Yes. I'm sure."

"Don't blame me for your hangover tomorrow." He digs around beneath the bar and puts a white can of Truly next to Hazel's water.

She pops open the tab and takes a large sip.

It's a good thing I stopped drinking after that first shot, since I'll clearly be driving us home tonight.

"You okay?" I ask Hazel under my breath as Frank goes to help another customer.

"Sure," she says. "Why?"

"All the drinking..." I motion to the Truly as she takes another sip.

She sighs and stares down at her drink. "Benjamin's been distant these past few days," she admits, not meeting my eyes. "Something's wrong, and he won't tell me what. I thought everything was solid between us, but now I'm not so sure." She shrugs, and I fight the urge to give her a giant hug.

"I'm sorry," I say.

"Not your fault." She manages a small smile. "I just hope he'll be more normal tonight."

"I hope so, too," I say, relieved when she seems comforted by my words, even though they couldn't have been that much help.

"Hey man, turn it up," a middle-aged man sitting at a table behind us says to Frank, pointing to the television showing the local news.

The same greased up anchorman is on the screen as the other day, with the caption, "Another local woman goes missing," at the bottom of the screen.

A photo appears above his head of a pretty girl with blonde hair and striking blue eyes.

"Lindsay Davis, a twenty-three-year-old woman, was last seen during her morning shift at the Stardust Diner taking the trash out to the back of the building," he says. "She's the third local of Pine Valley to go missing, along with Jason Cook and Carly Katz."

Photos of Jason and Carly appear on the screen next to Lindsay's. The three of them are all in excellent shape and very attractive—the types that would stand out in a small town like this.

"We have every reason to think that all three of them are still alive," the anchorman continues. "The police are continuing to search for answers, and they ask that if anyone has any information that might be helpful, they go to the station to share it. In the meantime, we advise everyone in town to take precautions. Until we apprehend the person behind these abductions, try to be aware of your surroundings and not to go anywhere alone, even during the day. There's strength in numbers. The local store has generously decided to donate pepper spray to anyone who wants it, and we recommend stopping by to pick some up at your earliest convenience."

The screen flashes to the owner of the local store holding a small can of pepper spray while being interviewed, and Frank turns the volume back down.

The happy chatting from the other customers turns into low talks of worry.

"How about a round of ale on the house?" Frank offers, instantly distracting everyone from the troubling television broadcast.

Since Hazel and I are seated at the tap, he puts the first two glasses in front of us and gets busy handing more to the waitresses so they can drop them off at the tables.

Not wanting to be ungrateful, I take a sip of the light-colored beer, surprised when I don't hate it.

"What's going on with these disappearances?" I ask Hazel, hoping the witches have more information than the shifters.

"We don't know yet," she says, lowering her voice. "The boundary around Pine Valley is in place, so it isn't vampires. My parents have been interrogating the shifters and other witches in the coven, but we haven't found anything remotely suspicious. The most likely explanation is that it's an ordinary human crime. But don't worry—humans don't mess with witches or shifters. They instinctively know to keep their distance. You have nothing to worry about."

"I'm not worried about myself," I say. "I'm worried about the next person who might go missing around here." I'm unsure when I got so protective over this place, but it seems crazy for the witches and shifters to sit around doing nothing. "Can't you use your abilities to find whoever's doing this?"

"Our job is to protect the human world from supernatural occurrences, to keep our world hidden from theirs," she says. "The humans take care of their problems, and we take care of ours."

"Even if those human problems are drawing attention to the town?"

"We've been doing this for centuries," she says firmly. "We can handle it."

"Okay," I say, although it still doesn't sit right with me.

Her phone lights up with a text message, and she picks it up to read it, clearly finished with our conversation. "The guys just parked," she says, and then she waggles her eyebrows in excitement. "Are you ready to meet Tristan?"

I almost ask who Tristan is, but I quickly remember—Hazel's boyfriend's friend who she wants to introduce me to.

"Sure," I say, reminding myself to be openminded, even though Connor's face flashes through my mind, and a wave of guilt crashes over me.

As if by meeting another guy, I'm *cheating* on the man who rejected me.

It's ridiculous. I need to get a handle on my emotions. I've always wanted to fall in love, and it's not going to happen if I'm brooding over Connor for the rest of my life.

I owe it to myself to give Tristan a chance.

And when Hazel waves over the next two guys who walk in, my breath is instantly taken away by the one with light brown hair that gleams in the low lighting and golden eyes that pierce through my soul, and I wonder if moving on from Connor might not be so impossible, after all.

Autumn

I'M SITTING at the table with the Guardian codex open in front of me, researching what I've been focusing on since Connor's party—mate bonds.

Mainly, information on how to break them without killing the other person or having them volunteer to have their magic stripped, since magic can't be stripped involuntarily—at least from what I've ever learned.

Because while I don't know anything for sure... I just have a feeling. A feeling I don't want to think about too much, because it's likely just stress and nerves.

With my birthday coming up so soon, it's normal to get jittery about my mate bond with Connor. Right?

But the way he looks at that girl every time they're together... I don't like it. Not one bit. And if the worst happens, and if that feeling is right, then I want to be prepared.

It never hurts to be prepared. Especially because if I'm right, I don't want to resort to the worst.

If we have to, then we will, my wolf's voice echoes through my mind.

She's grown as attached to Connor as I have these past few years. And while we know the mate bond is holy, not *every* wolf gets a mate.

As things are now, we want *him*.

Only him.

She's okay resorting to things I don't want to think about. Things I don't want to believe I'm capable of considering, let alone doing.

Which is why there *has* to be another way.

I won't accept anything else.

So far, the codex has given me nothing I didn't already know. I sort of knew that would happen, since I've been studying this book left and right since Connor and I started dating. We're from the two strongest royal shifter families in the country, and my job as Connor's mate—as the future alpha female of this pack—involves upholding the rules and traditions of our kind.

I intend on being the best alpha our pack has ever seen.

It's what the goddess chose me to do. She wouldn't have gifted me with such powerful magic otherwise.

Leading this pack is my birthright. I refuse to let anyone take it from me, let alone that little omega… or whatever type of demon she is.

She can't take anything if she's not alive, my wolf says again.

"Stop it," I say out loud, slamming my fist onto the table next to the open book.

I might be tough, and I'm clearly powerful, but I'm *not* a murderer.

It's not going to come to that. Ruby's with the witches now. She's not one of us.

She was sent here to test the love between me and Connor. Once I turn nineteen and our mate bond solidifies, he'll forget all about her.

Still, I have to be prepared.

Just in case.

I'm ensconced in reading the codex when my phone buzzes with a text.

My heart leaps when I see it's from Connor. He's been so distant these past few days, and I hate it. Each time I see or hear from him, I pray things are about to change for the better.

I need to see you, his text says. *Come to the gazebo.*

I smile at the screen.

The gazebo is where he kissed me for the first time, when we were fourteen years old and he asked me to be his girlfriend. It's our place. It always has been, and it always will be.

We don't go there often—mainly only when one of us needs the other when there's something serious on our mind.

He's going to end things, my wolf's voice says in my head.

Ice-cold dread courses through me.

You saw the way he looked at her, she continues, goading me. *We both did.*

Shut. Up, I think back, and then I slam the book shut.

I usually trust what my wolf thinks. Her instincts are almost always correct.

I refuse to believe she's right about this one.

But there's only one way to find out.

On my way, I reply to Connor's text, and then I hurry out of the house, shift into my wolf form, and run to the gazebo perched on the side of the mountain that overlooks the town, which has a perfect view of the nearly full moon shining overhead.

Connor's already there, gazing out at the town. His dark hair glows in the moonlight, but he's barely moving, and I can tell from here that something's bothering him.

My wolf can't be right about his bringing me here to break up with me. I've given my entire heart to him—to the future of our pack.

He's *mine.*

Unwilling to put it off for any longer, I run the final few yards to the gazebo, shift back into human form, and step onto the platform.

He spins around when he hears me, his dark, serious eyes meeting mine.

He looks nervous. It's not something I've seen from him often, and I'm immediately on guard.

"Autumn," he says my name, sounding tense. "Thanks for coming."

He sounds like he's welcoming me to a business meeting—not like he's meeting the woman he loves at the spot we've always viewed as ours.

"Hi." I do my best to sound casual, and I walk toward him, but stop myself from taking his hands. "What's going on?"

Before I can comprehend what's happening, he closes the space between us and pulls me into a kiss. Not a violent one, like on the night he had me come over after midnight, but not a passionate one, either. It's soft, but distant, like he's going through the motions but doesn't really feel anything.

But that's not true. Because I do sense an emotion coming from him.

Sadness, my wolf provides for me.

I shake the thought away, step back, and look up into his soft, caring eyes that are more familiar to me than my own.

He loves me.

I know he does.

He hasn't kissed us the same way since she came to town, my wolf continues. *He doesn't want us like he used to. And there's only one way to get the Connor we know and love back. We need to get rid of her. Permanently.*

She won't stop getting in my head. She hasn't stopped since we saw Connor pull Ruby away from Brandon at the party.

She's driving me *insane*.

"I needed to see you," Connor says, and I push my wolf's nagging voice down—where it belongs.

I force a light smile. "I figured that," I say, and he smiles back, which I take as a good sign.

But he's the one who brought me here, so I wait, giving him space to say what he needs.

Instead, he drops down onto one knee, reaches into his jacket pocket, pulls out a small velvet box, and pops it open.

I suck in a sharp breath at what's inside.

It's a gold engagement ring, with a diamond in the center and two small, carved wolves flanking the gem's sides. Simple, but intricate.

It's beautiful. It's perfect. It's what I've always wanted.

Connor's staring up at me with steely determination in his eyes, and I'm trapped in his gaze, barely able to breathe.

"Autumn Blackwell," he says, and even though I'm pretty sure what's happening, I can hardly believe it. "Ever since we first kissed in this gazebo, I knew you'd be the perfect woman to have by my side to ensure that the Pine Valley pack remains the strongest in the country and continues to produce the best Guardians alive. You're a force to be reckoned with. You're confident, beautiful, smart, and strong. I've admired you since the moment we met, and it would be the greatest honor if you'd accept my proposal and agree to become my wife."

I hang onto every word, but at the same time, it passes in a blur.

Connor's proposing.

He's asking me to marry him.

This... isn't the order we planned for things to happen.

"Autumn?" he questions, and I realize I've been standing here speechless while he waits for my response.

"What about our mate bond?" I blurt out before I can think twice.

His body goes rigid—defensive. "What about it?"

Crap.

I shouldn't have said that. I might have just messed this up, all because I couldn't smile blindly, put that ring on my finger, and say yes.

Stupid, my wolf's voice echoes inside my mind.

But I don't care what she thinks. I need to speak my truth.

"Haven't we always wanted our mate bond to happen before we got engaged?" I ask, even though I know the answer is yes. We've talked about it many times before and have always agreed on the order that this would go.

His eyes harden, and I'm afraid he's going to take back the proposal.

"I changed my mind," he says firmly. "My commitment is to you, mate bond or no, and I want to marry you *before* you turn nineteen to prove it."

I think he intends for the statement to be romantic, but instead, it makes me consumed with worry.

Does he not think we're going to have a mate bond?

Correct, my wolf answers. *And you know why.*

Anger rises inside me as my wolf thinks about Ruby. I don't want to think about that girl ever again, but my wolf refuses to let it rest. I'd strangle her if she wasn't a part of me.

I need her to stop.

If she doesn't, she's going to drive me crazy. But she doesn't seem to care, and that scares me more than I'd like to admit.

I've always had control over myself and my wolf, and I won't let that change. I refuse to become prey to the animal inside me.

"Autumn?" Connor asks, and I refocus on the beautiful ring on display, which is mine for the taking.

"Yes." I stand straighter, forcing confidence into my tone. "Of course I'll marry you."

He nods, as serious as ever, and removes the ring from the box. "Hold out your hand," he instructs, and I hold my left hand out to him.

Gently, he slides the ring onto my finger. The stone sparkles in the moonlight, but the ring is slightly loose, and I make a note to myself to bring it into a shop where they can size it properly, so it won't fall off.

"It was my grandma's," he tells me. "Designed by my grandfather for the alpha female of this pack."

"It's beautiful," I say, with a true smile this time.

"Not as beautiful as you." He pockets the empty velvet box, stands, and pulls me in for a kiss.

I try to melt into his touch, but my wolf is clawing at the inside of my skin, like she's trying to break free.

I won't let her.

So I bury her deep inside myself, pull Connor onto the floor of the gazebo, and show him just how much I love him.

But my wolf's final thought won't leave my mind, and it stops me from being able to lose myself in what should be one of the happiest nights of my life.

When he proposed, he never said he loves us.

Shadow Moon

STAR TOUCHED: WOLF BORN 2

Ruby

IN THE SMALL town of Pine Valley, nestled in the Adirondack mountains of New York, I'm sitting at a bar with Hazel, the most powerful witch in the local coven. She's sixteen—three years younger than I am—and yet, her experience with magic spans a lifetime.

I, on the other hand, only found out about the supernatural world a few days ago.

It feels like an eternity since then.

Unlike Hazel, I'm a wolf shifter. However, I've only been able to shift once, and I can't use the element wielded by wolf shifters—earth.

But I'm not powerless. A different, never-before-seen magic courses through my veins.

I can create illusions with my mind.

The witches say I've been blessed by a cosmic goddess. Or, as they prefer to call it, star touched. It's a plausible theory, considering the mysterious star tattoo that materialized on my right hip the same night I received my magic, bestowed by an ethereal woman who appeared out of nowhere and disappeared just as quickly.

But other than seeing if I could create an illusion to make Hazel's fake ID have a picture of me instead of her so I could get served alcohol at the bar, she didn't bring me here to teach me more about magic.

She brought me here to introduce me to her boyfriend, Benjamin, and his best friend Tristan. Both of them *human*.

She wants to set me up with Tristan to get my mind off the craziness of the past few days.

Little does she know that there's a slim-to-none chance I'll be interested in Tristan. Because I have a mate. Connor.

A mate who *rejected* me.

The cold way Connor looked at me when he rejected me seared my heart and left a scar there for all eternity. Sure, Connor and I barely know each other, but it doesn't matter. He's my mate. The other half of my soul.

And he doesn't want me.

He hates the fact that I'm his mate, since he's promised himself to his long-term girlfriend, Autumn.

Autumn, who I'm pretty sure would rather see me dead than anywhere within Connor's vicinity. She's a powerful shifter, and she's made it abundantly clear that she could end my life with a flick of her wrist if I dare to cross her.

Luckily, the witches took me in as one of their own. They told me I can trust them, but I'm well-aware that it would be foolish to let my guard down around any supernaturals in Pine Valley—or the rest of the world.

"Ready to meet Tristan?" Hazel slurs.

She's had a lot to drink in the short time we've been here. And, from the way she's using her elbow to prop herself up on the bar, she's clearly a lightweight.

"Sure," I say, despite the wave of guilt that crashes over me at the thought of considering anyone other than Connor.

It's ridiculous. I need to get a handle on my emotions. If I ever want to experience love, I can't spend the rest of my life brooding over Connor.

I owe it to myself to give Tristan a chance.

Hazel's eyes, shimmering like liquid glass, shift toward the entrance. They light up as two guys walk in, and she waves them over.

The first has sandy blond hair and a confident stride, like he owns the place. With a broad smile, he seems like the kind of guy who could be the star quarterback of a football team, surrounded by adoring cheerleaders vying for his attention.

The other one has light brown hair, chiseled features, and golden eyes that pierce through my soul the moment his gaze locks with mine.

My breath catches in my chest.

He's mesmerizing. And from the way that a few of the other women in the bar glance over to check him out, I'm not alone in my opinion.

But his focus remains solely on me, seemingly oblivious to everyone else.

I almost reach for Hazel's arm to say something to her, but I stop myself just in time.

Because she hasn't told me what Tristan and Benjamin look like.

For all I know, the guy with the golden eyes is her boyfriend and not his best friend.

I need to snap out of it and keep my cool. Autumn already hates me for being mates with her boyfriend, even though it was totally out of my control. The last thing I need is for Hazel to think I'm pursuing hers.

The guys reach us, and the blond one takes the spot next to Hazel. The chairs at the bar are high, and he wraps an arm around the back of it, right below her shoulders.

"Hi." He smiles down at her, and she's looking up at him with total adoration. He gives her a short kiss, and she all but melts into him.

I feel a visceral sense of relief when I realize the guy with the golden eyes is Tristan, not Benjamin.

Unsure what to do with my hands—or with any part of my body—I pick up the beer in front of me and take a sip, even though it's far too bitter for my taste.

"Hi," Hazel says to Benjamin, her cheeks pink either from kissing him or all the alcohol she's consumed. Probably both. "This is my cousin, Ruby. She's visiting from out of town." She directs her attention to me. "This is my boyfriend, Benjamin, and his friend, Tristan."

At the sound of Tristan's name, I look to him again. He's standing right next to my chair, his arm only inches away from mine. I swear I can feel a surge of electricity pulsing between us.

"Ruby," he says, my name sounding like music when it escapes his lips. "It's nice to meet you."

The three of them are watching me, and it takes me a moment to realize they're waiting for me to respond.

"You, too," I say. "I'm glad Hazel dragged me out tonight."

"That makes two of us." He flashes a perfect smile, and a feeling of victory soars through my chest.

Because I'm attracted to him.

I thought it was going to be impossible to be attracted to anyone after the intensity of my connection to Connor. Nothing's supposed to be able to compare to a mate bond. But here I am, not even a day later, already proving myself wrong.

Maybe there's hope for me, after all.

The pull to Tristan isn't quite as strong as it was with Connor, but it's enough that I can work with it.

"When did you get in?" Tristan asks.

"To the bar?" I almost reach for my phone to check the time. Then I remember that I have no phone, courtesy of Jax—the alpha of the Pine Valley pack—crushing it after telling me that contacting anyone from my old life is forbidden.

Because they think I'm *dead*.

It feels like a sledgehammer to my heart every time I think about it.

So I don't think about it, instead returning my focus to Tristan.

"When did you get *into town*," Tristan clarifies, smiling again, as if he knows how he's affecting me and finds it endearing.

That makes one of us.

"Oh. A few days ago," I say, trying to sound casual about it. Hazel and I didn't work out an official story before coming here, but it's probably best to stay as close to the truth as possible.

I take another sip of my beer, grimacing at the taste.

"That bad?" Tristan asks.

"It was on the house," I explain. "They showed that news clip on TV about the third human going missing, and it got everyone pretty down, so Frank decided to lift our spirits with a round of free drinks."

Tristan raises an eyebrow, and my pulse quickens as I realize my mistake.

I referred to the missing people as *humans* instead of *people*.

No one talks like that. At least not anyone who isn't in the supernatural world.

He probably thinks I'm a total weirdo. But I can't think of anything to say that won't bring more attention to my mistake, so I stay silent.

Benjamin looks at Hazel in concern, seemingly oblivious to my slip-up. "There was another one?" he asks.

"Yeah." She frowns. "But don't worry. I'm being safe."

She reaches for her mostly finished beer and downs the remainder of it, placing the empty glass back on the bar with a resounding thud.

She sways a bit in her chair, leans against Benjamin for support, and he lowers his arm to wrap it around her waist to steady her.

"Promise me you won't go anywhere alone?" he asks her.

"I promise." She giggles, hiccups, then covers her mouth with a hand, giggling once more.

"Please be careful," he says. "For me."

"I will."

If Benjamin knew how powerful of a witch Hazel is, I doubt he'd be as concerned. Although, Hazel's so drunk that I don't know how helpful her magic would be against anyone right now—even if the person doing the kidnapping is a human like her coven believes.

One of us needs to keep a clear head, so I focus on drinking my water, accepting the role of designated driver for the night. I don't mind, since I'm not a big drinker. But when Hazel invited me out, I didn't think she was going to get this toasted.

She slides out of her chair and nearly crashes into me, managing to stop herself by grabbing onto my arm for support.

"You okay?" I ask her, even though it's a bit of a rhetorical question.

"Be right back," she mumbles, the words slurred with alcohol. "I have to go to the bathroom."

"I'll go with you," I offer, already rising from my chair to accompany her.

"No," she snaps, but then her features soften, and she smiles. "Stay here and chat with the guys. I'll be back in a minute."

Despite her unsteady state just moments ago, she navigates her way to the back of the bar with surprising grace, leaving me alone with Benjamin and Tristan.

What am I supposed to say to them?

Given the fact that I have to lie to them about practically everything going on in my life, I have no idea where to start.

Maybe I should go after Hazel anyway? But she snapped at me pretty intensely, and despite how much she's had to drink, she's still a powerful witch who can stand her ground.

She'll be back in a minute.

For now, I just have to act cool, calm, and… human.

Ruby

"How are you liking Pine Valley?" Tristan asks before I can further worry about the situation.

A tricky question.

I found out I'm a wolf shifter, was relegated to be an omega in the pack, found out I have magic that's never been seen before, my fated mate rejected me, and his girlfriend wants to kill me.

This is clearly one of those instances where honesty isn't going to be the best policy.

"It's been good," I say one of the biggest lies in my entire life. "It's different from where I grew up."

"Where's that?" He leans forward. His golden eyes are locked on mine, as if my answer will be the most fascinating thing he's ever heard.

My heart races, and I need to take a moment to remember his question.

"Naples. In South Florida," I finally say.

At least I don't have to lie about that one.

"Never been," he says, which doesn't surprise me, since Naples isn't nearly as touristy as other parts of Florida.

"Did you grow up in Pine Valley?" I ask, glancing at Benjamin. I don't want to leave him out of the conversation.

"No," Tristan says with a chuckle. "New York. Manhattan," he clarifies, as if Manhattan is a different country than the rest of New York.

"And I've never been *there*," I say, adding a bit of a laugh. "Actually, I've never left Florida before coming here."

"To stay with your cousin?"

I almost ask what he's talking about, but then I remember Hazel's lie.

"Yep," I say. "Hazel's great."

"She is," Benjamin agrees, a dreamy smile playing on his lips. He glances at the bathroom, clearly anxious for her to return.

He's smitten with her, and I'm happy for her. From the little Hazel's told me about her life, she deserves someone like him, who appreciates her for who she is instead of how much power she has.

"So, *you're* from Pine Valley?" I ask Benjamin.

"Nope," he says. "Also from Manhattan. But I have a place in Spring Creek. It's about fifty minutes away."

"I've heard of it," I say, keeping it to myself that I know about it because another pack of wolves and a coven of witches live there. A pack and coven that, from the little I've heard, don't have the best relationship with the pack and coven in Pine Valley.

"It was my grandfather's, but he passed away a few months ago and left it to me," he says.

"I'm sorry." I lower my eyes in respect, and at the mention of death, I'm suddenly reminded about how everyone I know thinks *I* died less than a week ago.

I swallow down the ball of tears in my throat, praying that neither of them asks me what's wrong.

I have no idea how to answer if they do.

"Tristan's staying with me for a few weeks to help fix the place up," Benjamin continues, seeming like he wants to avoid the topic of death as much as I do. "Might as well sell it and make some money. And share some of the profits, of course."

He glances at Tristan when he says that last part.

"Happy to help." Tristan raises his glass of what looks to be whiskey—Benjamin apparently ordered for them when Tristan and I were first chatting—and they clink their glasses together and drink.

"So, how do you two know each other?" I ask, attempting to steer the conversation away from any more awkward revelations.

As I speak, I lean closer to Tristan, unable to resist the pull I feel toward him.

From the way he gravitates toward me, I think he feels the same.

Why can't Tristan be my mate instead of Connor?

I shake the thought away. I shouldn't be obsessing over Connor when there's a charming, gorgeous guy in front of me.

Connor doesn't want me.

Tristan might.

I need to get myself together.

"We're old friends," he says simply, and as he speaks, my eyes land on the cross pendant hanging around his neck.

There's a dark red gemstone embedded into the center of it, and it's so intricate that it looks like something someone would pick up at an antique store. It's unlike anything I've ever seen, but at the same time, he pulls it off flawlessly.

"I like your necklace," I say, since I'm sure it's obvious that I'm staring at it.

"It was my brother's."

From the way he says it, I have a sinking feeling that his brother isn't alive anymore.

Why does death keep coming up over and over again? First Benjamin's grandfather, and now Tristan's brother.

I have no idea how to reply. Because while all loss is hard, the loss of a grandparent is far more typical for someone our age than the loss of a sibling. I have no way to relate to what he went through, and I know better than to attempt to try.

Tristan doesn't elaborate about his brother. Instead, his gaze drops to my lips, and I wonder if he's going to move closer and kiss me in the middle of the bar.

My heart speeds up at the thought. Especially because if he does try, I don't think I'd stop him.

"All right, guys," Benjamin breaks the silence, bringing his hands together. "I need to check on Hazel. I trust you'll be okay without me?"

He looks at Tristan, then me, then back to Tristan, his eyes swirling with mischief. He's clearly as determined as Hazel is to set the two of us up.

I'm not sorry about it in the slightest, especially because it's helping me get my mind off of Connor.

Sort of.

"Maybe it should be me..." I say slowly, even though I like the idea of having some time alone with Tristan. "I don't think people will be too happy if you barge into the ladies room."

"They're single-holers," he says with a wave of his hand. "It'll be fine."

He's gone before I can say anything more, leaving me and Tristan standing at the bar together, our eyes locked on each other's in a way that makes the butterflies in my stomach flit around like crazy.

"So, Ruby." Amusement dances in his eyes when he says my name, making it clear that he knows *exactly* what kind of effect he's having on me. "What are you normally doing when you're not visiting small towns in the mountains?"

Panic leaps in my throat at how unsure I am about what I can say without giving the truth of the past few days away.

How has Hazel kept her identity secret these past few weeks with Benjamin? I want to get to know Tristan, but how can I do it without lying about everything going on in my life? How can I have a normal, honest relationship with someone who's not in the supernatural world?

I can't.

But maybe it won't hurt to pretend. Just for tonight.

"I'm a student at University of Florida. A few hours north of Naples." I smile, forcing myself to relax and act like normal.

"What's your major?" he asks, and I'm amazed by how normal the question feels.

"I haven't picked one yet, since it's only my first year. But I think I want to study English."

Thought, I correct myself in my mind. *Past tense.*

Because I'm not sure I'll ever be able to return to school.

I'll never be able to declare a major, never be able to graduate, and will likely never be able to have a normal job.

My life before finding out that I'm a shifter is as dead as the human world thinks *I* am.

"An English major. I assume that means you enjoy reading?" he asks, and the question immediately jolts me back into present.

"I *love* reading."

We spend the next few minutes chatting about our favorite books. We have a surprising amount of them in common, and it's easy to get lost in the conversation—and in him.

Men are immediately ten times more attractive when they enjoy books.

"So, when do you head back?" he asks.

"Back where?"

"To school." He smiles with that twinkle in his eyes that I've grown to love in the short time we've been chatting. "Surely winter break is almost over?"

I take another sip of my soda, contemplating how to answer somewhat truthfully, while also not giving anything away.

"I'm taking the semester off and staying here with Hazel and her parents for a bit," I say the first thing that pops into my head. "There have been a lot of changes in my life recently, and it'll be good to get some space from it all."

"I know how that goes." He reaches for the cross hanging from his necklace, and I want to ask him more about it.

But I feel like he's about as willing to share more about his brother as I am about my family.

Meaning, he doesn't want to share anything at all.

Benjamin comes back to join us before the conversation can continue, with Hazel clutching onto his arm and nearly stumbling over her feet. There are a few drops of sweat on her forehead, and her pale face has a sickly cast of green over it.

Despite how powerful she is, she looks so fragile and small.

"Are you okay?" I ask her, even though she clearly isn't.

"I think I drank too much," she mumbles, not meeting my eyes.

No kidding, I think, although I don't say it out loud.

"Do you want to leave...?" I say instead, pointing my thumb toward the door.

We haven't been here very long, and I don't want to leave, since I'm enjoying talking with Tristan. But no matter how enticing Tristan might be, my loyalty is to Hazel. She's the closest thing to a friend I have around here, and I intend on sticking by her.

"Benjamin and I are going to sit outside for a bit so I can get some air," she says. "But it's cold out there, so I totally understand if you two want to stay in here."

She gives me a look that I know is girl code for *I want some alone time with my boyfriend, and you and Tristan seem to be hitting it off, so you should stay inside with him.*

Luna used to look at me the same way whenever we were out and she met a guy she was into.

My chest pangs with grief over the loss of my best friend, even though she's technically the one who thinks she lost me.

"We'll be right outside," Benjamin adds, pulling Hazel close. "Nothing's going to happen to us."

I glance up at the TV, knowing he's referring to the people who've gone missing. And I know he's right. They were all in secluded areas—jogging at the edge of town, snowboarding in the back of a mountain, and bringing trash out to a back alley. I saw the restaurant's outside porch when we walked in, and there was nothing unsafe about it. Cold, but not unsafe. They'll be fine.

Which is good, because I definitely want more time alone with Tristan.

Meanwhile, Benjamin's watching me, waiting.

I decide to follow my gut instinct with this one.

"Okay," I finally say. "I'll stay."

"Just what I was hoping to hear," he says.

Hazel gives me a grateful smile, and she and Benjamin head outside, leaving me alone once more with Tristan.

Ruby

I'M relieved when Tristan and I easily return to the topic we have most in common—books. And it's not just books we have in common. It's also movies, television shows, and music. Our shared interests are like invisible threads binding us together, and the energy between us builds with every sentence exchanged.

Either we share strikingly similar tastes, or he's the most well-rounded person I've ever met.

Both options are insanely attractive.

His golden eyes light up when he talks, and he leans in closer as he listens to my thoughts, the conversation flowing so easily that it isn't long before I've finished my soda. When I check my watch—an old analogue type that Hazel loaned me, since I no longer have a phone—I'm surprised to find that an hour has already passed.

"Do you want another?" Tristan asks, glancing at my now-empty glass.

The deeper meaning behind his question is clear.

Do you want to spend more time with me? Are you as captivated by this connection as I am?

"Yes," I say, not needing to think twice about my answer.

"Sticking with Coke?"

I could get something stronger to help cool my nerves. A hard seltzer, like Luna likes to drink.

It's tempting.

But I'm going to have to drive home. Plus, I'm at a bar with a guy who's basically a stranger, in a town full of wolf shifters and witches, both with reasons to fear and question me.

Maybe I shouldn't have left Hazel's side to begin with, even if she is just outside. And she is indeed still outside—a glance out the front window confirms it.

Tristan's apparently so captivating that I'm losing all logical thought around him. And despite how nice it would be to unwind with a stronger drink, I'm not going to add more alcohol into the mix. It would be basically begging for trouble.

I have enough of that as it is—in so many areas of my life that it feels impossible to keep track.

"Are you okay?" Concern flashes in Tristan's eyes, and I realize I've been thinking way longer than normal about what type of drink I want to have next.

"All good." I give him what I hope is a carefree smile. "Another Coke sounds great."

"Coming right up."

He motions to Frank, who comes over and pours me a fresh drink. He places it in front of me, and I can almost swear the bartender *winks* before moving on to help another customer.

"I never thought this would happen," Tristan murmurs, his voice velvety smooth as I take a sip of my soda.

"What do you mean?" I barely manage to whisper.

"I mean that when Hazel told Benjamin to bring me out tonight to meet you, I didn't expect us to connect like this." His eyes are locked with mine, expressive and vulnerable. It's like he's baring his soul to me, offering his heart for me to do what I want with it, and the electrifying pull between us intensifies so much that I think I'm going to explode.

"I didn't expect this, either," I admit, my cheeks growing warm with each passing moment. "It's kind of crazy how much we have in common."

"It's definitely crazy," he agrees, the corner of his mouth lifting in a small, knowing smile.

We've been slowly moving closer to each other, and as his gaze drops to my lips, my breathing slows.

What's coming over me?

It's like Tristan's casting a spell over me... and I'm more than happy to let him.

Anything to give myself a break from these past few days.

A second after making the decision, everyone but Tristan blurs into the background. It's just me and him sitting at this bar, and every inch of my skin hums with electricity as he closes the space between us and brushes his lips against mine.

Fire ignites inside me, and I kiss him back, slowly and gently. It's a sweet sort of kiss, soft and tender, as if he's expressing feelings for me that words can't say. He tastes like sugar, and I swear I'm getting a buzz from him, like he's some sort of magical elixir far more potent than any drink offered at this bar.

His fingers trace delicate patterns across my lower back, and I shiver with pleasure at his touch, my stomach flipping with excitement. I'm running my thumb over his necklace without realizing I've reached for it, and touching it is somehow so intimate, enhancing the connection between us even more.

How's this happening?

How can someone I just met have such a strong effect on me?

It shouldn't be happening, a voice growls inside me. *It's wrong.*

My wolf.

She's pushed herself out of where I locked her down, and she's angrier than ever. Her fury courses through me like bristles poking under my skin, extinguishing every ounce of pleasure I was experiencing from Tristan's touch.

Go away, I think, but it's no use. She's waging war against my feelings, and she's not going anywhere anytime soon.

No, she insists. *We belong to Connor. Not Tristan.*

Red hot anger rushes through me.

Because I don't *belong* to anyone. I decide who I want, what I want, and when I want it.

And I want to be here.

With Tristan.

We belong to our mate, she argues, refusing to give up that easily.

No.

I fight against her and try to lose myself in the moment again, but it's no use. Because as much as I hate it, my wolf's right. Connor is my mate.

I don't know what's going on here with Tristan. I think it's real—I *hope* it's real. It's so easy to talk to him that there must be something truly here.

But ultimately, does it matter?

Tristan's human, and I'm not.

Sure, our tastes in books, movies, and television are the same. But it'll never be enough. Because at the end of the day, if this spark between us turns into anything, the lies I'll have to tell him to keep my real life a secret will eventually destroy us.

It's not fair to him, or to me.

Which is why I need to end this, before it has a chance to get too far.

Ruby

I've stopped kissing Tristan without realizing it, and he pulls away, looking down at me in concern.

"What's wrong?" he asks, his brow creased as he tries to figure me out.

Tough luck with that.

"I have a bit of a headache," I say, which isn't a lie.

The way my wolf is fighting me is literally giving me a headache.

"Oh." He frowns.

"It's not you. I'm having a great time with you," I say quickly, scrambling for an excuse that might make sense. "It's just that I don't actually live here, and neither do you. I have no idea how long I'll be here, and I like you, and..." I lower my eyes and twist my fingers around themselves, hating myself more and more with every word I say.

"Okay," Tristan says simply. "I understand."

"You do?" I raise my gaze to his, not having expected him to be so accepting. Pretty much every guy I've ever interacted with would have tried to convince me to give him more of a chance.

Not Tristan.

Which is somehow making me feel even guiltier—and more attracted to him.

"Yes," he confirms, and he reaches for his credit card and slides it over to Frank before I can offer to pay for myself.

Well, technically it would be Hazel's money from the bag she loaned me. Close enough.

Tension crackles between me and Tristan, and a huge part of me wants to lean back into him and tell him that never mind, I want to keep spending time with him.

But I like him too much. The kiss proved that. And the more involved I get with him, the more it's going to hurt when I have to push him away to protect him from the truth.

Maybe Hazel can stand it with Benjamin, but after how Connor broke my heart, I refuse to torture myself any further. Add on top of that the way my wolf is fighting against me, and the difficulty of adjusting to my new life, and it's too exhausting to handle.

Coming out tonight was a mistake.

Frank brings the check, and as Tristan signs it, I can't help noticing his generous tip. A hundred percent of the total bill.

I've never seen someone tip that much. *Ever.* And that says a lot, since I've occasionally helped at the restaurant where my mom's worked since I was thirteen.

What does Tristan do for a living that he has so much money?

We chatted so much about the things we like, but I know next-to-nothing about *him*.

"Come on," he says. "Let's find Benjamin and Hazel." He reaches forward, like he wants to help me out of the chair, but then he pulls abruptly back.

My heart sinks with disappointment. But when I hop out of the seat and make sure I have all my stuff, I remind myself that it's for the best.

Nothing good can come out of starting something with Tristan.

He follows me out of the bar, making sure to open the door for me, and I'm pleasantly surprised that it's not as cold as I expected. Wolf shifters can tolerate the cold better than humans. Tristan doesn't seem overly affected either, even though he's only wearing a bomber jacket that isn't practical for this weather.

After stepping outside, I wrap my arms around myself and glance up at the nearly full moon. The sliver of shadow grounds me, bringing a sense of calm I haven't felt since meeting Tristan. It's as if the moon itself is whispering reassurances to me, telling me everything's going to be okay.

Hazel narrows her eyes when she sees us, watching us with suspicion as we approach the table.

"Hey, guys," Benjamin says. "Want to pull up some chairs?"

The patio is only about a quarter full, so there are plenty of chairs available to bring over.

"No, thanks," I say, looking back over at Hazel. "I'm actually ready to head back."

"So soon?" she asks, her brow furrowed.

"I have a headache," I say, causing her frown to deepen.

"It's probably the altitude," Tristan chimes in, shocking me even more by *supporting* my decision to leave. "Going from sea level to the mountains is a tough adjustment. Especially when you're not used to it."

I brace myself for Hazel to get angry at me for cutting her time with Benjamin short.

"That makes sense," she says instead, filling me with relief. "I'm still not feeling great, either. Do you want to drive us back?"

"I was planning on it," I say, and she happily hands over the keys to her SUV. I've never driven a car this large before, but given how much Hazel's had to drink, it's better off in my hands than in hers.

The guys walk us to the parking lot, and, unable to look Tristan in the eyes, I'm happy to let Hazel and Benjamin do most of the chatting. The walk to the car feels endless, charged with unspoken tension, and I keep glancing up at the moon for comfort.

My wolf—thankfully—is silent.

"It was nice meeting you, Ruby," Tristan says when we finally get there. "Have a safe drive home."

"Thanks." I fumble with the keys, my hands shaking as I find the button to unlock the car. "You, too."

As Tristan reaches forward to open the door for me, his arm brushes against mine.

His touch sends a jolt of electricity through me. I take a sharp breath inward, the cold air burning inside my lungs, and my eyes meet his golden ones. They're somehow even more captivating under the light of the moon, and regret fills me at the possibilities of what might have been if he wasn't human—or if I wasn't supernatural.

"I'm sorry I couldn't stay longer," I say, since it's the truth.

"Don't worry about it," he says smoothly, although his smile is tinged with sadness and longing. "Have Hazel text Benjamin when you get back, to let us know you're home."

"Will do." I slide into the car, wait for Hazel to get situated, and drive out of there without speaking another word to Tristan.

I should never speak another word to him. It would be better that way for both of us.

But I can't shake the feeling that it's not going to be as easy as that.

Connor

My girlfriend—no, my fiancée—is stunning as she stands up in front of me, bathed in the soft glow of the moonlight, her clothes pooled at her feet. She's a living goddess, and for the past few years we've been together, I've felt so lucky to call her mine.

But Autumn isn't mine.

Ruby's mine.

The mysterious, beautiful girl who burst into my life a few weeks ago, tearing apart the carefully laid plans of my future. Like a wildfire, Ruby's consumed my thoughts, and I can't seem to push her away, no matter how hard I try.

Autumn and I get dressed in the gazebo where I kissed her for the first time all those years ago—the gazebo where I proposed to her about an hour ago—and I stare out at the horizon where the mountains meet the sky. The winter air is crisp and fresh, and an owl hoots in the forest ahead.

This night should be one of the happiest in my life. Yet, there's a weight sitting on my chest that I can't shake away.

Autumn sits on the bench and twirls the engagement ring I gave her tonight around her finger. It was the ring my grandfather gave my grandmother when he proposed to her, and it's slightly too big on her. We'll have to take it into town to get it resized.

Given that I've known her for my entire life, I can tell there's something on her mind.

"Are you having second thoughts?" I ask her, guilt immediately washing over me when I realize I want her to say yes.

Probably because if she's having second thoughts, I won't feel as bad about the doubt digging into my skin like sharp fingernails refusing to let go.

She turns her gaze up at the moon, looking to it for comfort, then finally looks at me. There's something harsher about her pale features—colder. A sharp glint in her hazel eyes that I've never seen before.

"You've changed," she says softly, her voice a whisper in the night.

"What do you mean?"

I sound defensive, and she tenses up, as if preparing for a major blow. So, I sit down next to her and reach for her hand with the ring on it, relieved when she doesn't pull away.

She gazes out into the distance, as if at war with herself, unsure how to start. Eventually, she turns back to me and chews her lower lip. It's a habit she kicked a few years ago, and she looks younger and more vulnerable than ever, as if something inside of her is close to breaking.

"You can talk to me," I tell her. "I'm here for you. Always."

"I know," she says, and then she forces a small smile, and continues. "But things feel different between us recently."

"What things?" I ask, even though I know she isn't wrong.

"You don't seem as confident that we'll be mates," she starts, barely meeting my eyes. "And when I went to Jax's to help Ruby with her magic, she had all these questions about mate bonds."

I tense when she says Ruby's name… and because I fear where she might be heading with this.

"Ruby's new to the supernatural world," I say carefully. "She has questions about *everything*."

"Did you mate with her?" she asks so quickly that the words almost blend together.

The question is a punch to my gut, and for a moment, it hurts to breathe.

I can't lie to Autumn. Especially not about this.

The silence is heavy between us, the world as I know it shifting on its axis. The time it's taking me to reply is likely an answer unto itself, but I won't do Autumn the disservice of not speaking directly.

"I did."

Her expression crumples, and I want to take her in my arms to shield her from the pain I've caused. But I have no idea how that would be received. Instead, I sit there like a statue as I break the heart of the woman I thought would be by my side forever.

"This changes nothing," I tell her, even though it's more of a wish than anything else. "We promised each other that we'd stay by each other's sides, even if one of us mated with someone else. We've been together for years. You know me. You know that I stick to my word. I chose you all those years ago, and some girl I just met isn't going to change my mind about that, mate bond or no."

"But you touched her," she says, the hurt in her eyes piercing my soul.

There's no point in denying it. Skin-to-skin contact is how mate bonds first form.

"She was trying to run away," I say slowly. "But she doesn't have control over her shifts yet. She's not allowed to leave pack territory. So, I caught her and stopped her."

I think back to how Ruby used her magic to make herself invisible in the woods. How I pounced on her to force her to show herself and pinned her to the ground, and the bond that formed between us when I was hovering over her, our faces a few inches from each other's as the mate bond took hold.

The self-control it took to stop myself from fully making her mine was a test from the gods unlike any I've experienced before.

"Did you kiss her?" Autumn's voice is strained, and she looks like she's bracing herself for another blow to the heart.

This night is going downhill quickly.

I need to fix it.

I'm the future alpha of this pack. Fixing things is my job. I refuse to let Autumn or anyone else in this pack down, no matter what.

"I would never betray you like that," I tell her. "The mate bond wasn't my choice, but you are. I just proposed to *you*. You're the one I want. Not her."

"But do you still love me?"

The question takes me by surprise. Autumn has never doubted my love. She's always been the strongest, most confident woman I know.

This side of her—on edge and insecure—is one I've never seen before. It's almost like I'm looking at a stranger.

"Of course I do," I say, and she nods, blinking the shadow of doubt from her eyes.

"Good." She leans forward and kisses me, her lips soft and familiar. But there's something sad about the kiss, too. Like there's something lost between us that we'll never get back, no matter how hard we try.

When she pulls away and looks into my eyes, I can see that she feels it, too.

"We'll get through this," I tell her. "I promise."

"How can you be so sure?" The vulnerability in her question lingers in the cold night air, making the space between us feel larger than before.

I immediately regret my previous words. Because the truth is, I can't be sure. I pride myself on my logic, plans, discipline, and control, but none of those qualities allowed me to extinguish my feelings for Ruby. Sure, they helped me not *act* on those feelings, but they can't make the mate bond disappear.

I know it, and Autumn does, too.

It's why she's so doubtful—so *scared*.

As much as I hate thinking it, I'm scared, too. Scared that this mate bond with Ruby will eat away at my relationship with Autumn. It's already tearing Autumn apart, revealing a side of her I never thought existed.

I'm also scared of the feeling gnawing away at my heart that tells me that by rejecting Ruby, I'm missing out on the best person to have ever walked into my life.

The mate bond is changing me, and I hate it.

At the same time, there's an undeniable curiosity about Ruby pulling at my heart, begging me to pay it more attention. Pleading with me to give her an actual chance.

"Ruby's not coming back here," I say, trying to assure Autumn as much as myself. "Her magic has no place with us."

"Does it have a place with *anyone?*" Autumn's voice is cold and cruel, full of angry resentment.

Maybe even hatred.

My skin prickles with warning.

I've always known that Autumn's a force to be reckoned with. I just never expected that I'd ever have to protect someone from her.

"Ruby's not our concern anymore. Her place is with the witches," I say, trying to sound as calm and collected about it as possible. "They took her to live with them."

I'd been so intent on proposing to Autumn—and then on defending my mate bond with Ruby—that I still haven't told her about what happened with the witches at my grandfather's house earlier tonight.

But Autumn and I are a team.

She deserves to know everything. Even the hard stuff.

Especially the hard stuff.

"What I'm about to tell you stays between you, me, and my grandfather," I say sternly, looking her straight in the eyes so she knows I'm serious. "Understand?"

"Yes," she says, waiting patiently for me to continue.

"The witches say that Ruby has her magic because she's been blessed by a goddess," I begin. "They're calling her star touched."

"I've never heard of that before."

"Neither have I," I say. "But the witches have sources we don't, and what they said adds up with everything Ruby's experiencing. They said she belongs with them—not with us. They're going to take care of her. She isn't our responsibility anymore."

I sound cold and heartless, and Autumn studies me, her eyes searching my face for any hint of deception.

She's never doubted me. Not ever.

The possibility of that changing because of something out of my control hurts my soul on a level I've never felt before.

"How do you feel about her leaving?" she asks cautiously.

I take a few seconds to think about my response, since my next words have the power to change everything—for better or for worse.

"I'm glad she's gone." It pains me to say it out loud—or maybe that pain is because it's not as true as I want it to be. "The longer Ruby and I are away from each other, the more the bond will weaken. Eventually, it'll barely exist at all."

Autumn knows this. But I'm saying it for assurance—for both of us.

However, the unspoken words hang in the air. Because while the mate bond will weaken, it won't disappear.

She presses her lips together, and I prepare for her to argue with me. Instead, she looks away, the icy moonlight tracing the curve of her cheekbone as she gathers her thoughts.

"Okay," she finally says, surprising me.

"We're good?" My grip around her hand tightens, cautiously hopeful.

"Yes. You chose me, and I love you even more for it. We're going to be together forever." The warmth returns to her eyes, and for the first time since this conversation began, I'm seeing *my* Autumn.

The girl I've known for my entire life.

The woman who will eventually be my wife.

We can't marry her, my wolf's voice echoes in my mind, taking me by surprise and shattering my moment of peace.

I've always been in control of my wolf, just like I'm in control of everything in my life. He only comes out when I ask him to.

Who I choose to be with is my decision. Not his.

I tell him as much.

Wrong, he pushes back. *Ruby was chosen for us. She's meant for us. You know it, I know it, and Autumn knows it. Fighting fate will only make all of us miserable.*

I don't want to believe it.

But another part of me—a part I wish would disappear—can't help wondering if he's right. Because the future feels more uncertain than ever.

Still, I refuse to let the bond with Ruby destroy my loyalty to Autumn.

Autumn would never turn her back on me. I know her, I love her, and I'm not throwing what we have away as if these past few years didn't matter at all.

I'm in control here. I make my own choices. I decide my future.

And I'm not going to let fate or my wolf stand in my way.

Autumn

I GIVE Connor's hand a light squeeze to affirm that we're good.

But inside, I'm crumbling.

No—I'm already shattered.

My worst fear is true: Ruby's his mate. Connor and I will *never* be destined for each other. As long as he has that bond with Ruby, his loyalty will never be one hundred percent with me. He might tell me otherwise, but if his mate bond with her remains, she'll own a piece of his soul forever.

His eyes, once a comforting warmth, now betray him as they gaze down at me. They're filled with uncertainty. He might not say it directly, but I've known him for my entire life. He's making all these promises to me, but he isn't fully *here* with me.

My inner wolf snarls.

We have to get rid of her, she says. *It's the only way.*

Ever since that fateful night of the blood moon when Ruby stepped into our lives, my wolf has been different. Her rage is all-consuming, and it's hard to pinpoint where her fury ends and mine begins.

She wants me to kill Ruby.

I won't do it.

I don't trust Ruby. More specifically, I don't trust Ruby's magic. She isn't one of us. She never will be.

But that doesn't mean I want her dead.

I just don't want to lose the man I love because of a force of nature that neither of us can control. I believe that Connor wants to choose me, but how can I ever trust that he's truly mine when fate insists on tethering him to her?

I can't.

My wolf is right that his mate bond with Ruby needs to be broken. I just don't agree with her opinion about how to make it happen. Sure, it was fun to scare Ruby when I flaunted my powers the other day in Jax's yard, but that doesn't mean I want to murder her.

I'm not a monster.

I refuse to let my wolf turn me into one. Which means the faster I can fix this, the better.

"Will you stay with me tonight?" Connor asks, his voice soft, sweet, and hopeful.

I want to. Especially given the longing in his eyes, the promise to continue the passion we just shared in the gazebo.

But I have more pressing matters to attend to tonight.

"I have some more studying to do." I hate myself for not being honest with him, but I also know it's necessary. "We have that paper due at the end of the month, and I still haven't decided what topic I'm going to write about."

"The one about the most important value for Guardians to uphold?" he asks.

"Yes, that one," I say, since it's the only paper we have assigned right now.

Connor stiffens, his voice filling with resolve. "The answer is integrity. Understanding, respecting, and following through on our responsibility to maintain the laws of our kind. Keeping order is how we stop the world from descending into chaos. We owe it to everyone to do that, even when it means putting the law above our own wishes and desires."

The seriousness of his answer hums in the air between us. I shouldn't have expected anything less, since Connor's always been the most intense person I know.

But I'm not in the mood to discuss homework or have a deep conversation about the morals we're supposed to fall back on as Guardians. Because the faster I get out of here, the faster I can get started on what needs to be done.

"All excellent points." I smile, playfully nudging him to lighten the mood. "But I can't write the exact same thing as you."

"I know," he says, tucking a strand of my hair behind my ear. His fingers brush against my skin, sending shivers down my spine, and I'm suddenly back to when I was fourteen years old, when he asked me to be his girlfriend in this gazebo. "Your dedication to your studies is one of the many things I love about you."

My heart flutters at his words. He may not have said he loves me when he proposed to me, but he *does* love me.

We wouldn't be here right now if he didn't.

"There's only one thing I'm more dedicated to than my studies," I say, turning serious again.

"And what's that?" A playful glint dances in his eyes, as though he already knows what I'm going to say.

"You." I raise my left hand between us, the ring on my finger catching the light. "No, more than just you. The thing I'm the most dedicated to in the world is *us*."

The conviction in my tone silences him.

"I know you are," he finally murmurs. "I've never doubted you. Not for a moment."

I almost say the same back to him, but I can't. Because Ruby has planted seeds of doubts inside of me that I never thought I could experience.

I owe it to Connor and our relationship to make sure those doubts never surface again. That means giving him back his freedom to choose his future instead of leaving him to constantly be fighting the universe's pull toward something he doesn't want.

It's unnatural for mates to follow through on fully breaking their bonds. I've studied enough about mate bonds to know this.

Which leaves this responsibility to me.

I can save him from the chains of this bond. He deserves to have free will, and I'm going to do everything in my power to give it back to him.

Everything that will still allow me to live with myself when all is said and done.

"I love you," I say instead, and I lean forward to kiss him, hoping to get across all the feelings that I'm not yet ready to put into words.

Once I finish what I'm setting out to do, I'll tell him everything. He'll understand. More than that—he'll thank me for giving him back his freedom.

Until then, his feelings will be clouded by the mate bond. No matter what he might say or do, I can't let myself forget that.

"Well," he says, pulling away from the kiss to look at me again. "Don't let me keep my fiancée from her studies."

Fiancée.

Not mate.

I know he doesn't mean for the word to sting, but it does. It's a painful reminder of what will never exist between us.

Because even if I succeed in breaking his bond with Ruby, I'll never be Connor's mate.

"I have to go," I say, trying to ignore the regret gnawing at my heart for leaving Connor to sleep alone on the night he proposed. "I'll see you tomorrow."

"See you tomorrow," he repeats, and then I shift into my wolf form and run into the woods before he can see the tears glimmering in my eyes.

But I don't run home.

I can't fix things at home. I can't fix things in *Pine Valley*. Our witches have taken Ruby in, and they view her as one of their own. They don't see her as the threat that she is. They won't prioritize my feelings and desires over hers.

Which means it's time to seek help somewhere else, from someone who might share my goals.

And I know exactly who that person will be.

Autumn

THE MOONLIT SHADOWS dance around me as I race through the forest, my heart pounding with anticipation.

It takes me just over an hour to reach Spring Creek. Not only am I a stronger magic user than most shifters, but I'm also a faster runner. Only Connor and Jax can match my pace within the pack.

I've studied the map of Spring Creek, and I've always had an excellent sense of direction, so I navigate the woods with ease.

My destination soon comes into view—an ancient Victorian mansion that's been passed down for generations within the Spring Creek coven. Once a symbol of their power and influence, the grand estate now stands as a sad reminder of the coven's waning strength.

Now, only one of their witches is known to possess significant magic. Their leader, Calliope.

Hopefully her power will be enough to help me achieve what needs to be done.

And it does *need* to be done.

This is about more than securing Connor's commitment to me. It's also about protecting the Pine Valley pack from the potential fallout if the worst happens and he ends up with Ruby. Because despite Ruby's illusion magic—her *unnatural* magic—she has no earth magic. She's an omega.

On the off chance that Connor loses himself to the mate bond, the Pine Valley pack deserves better than their female leader being an omega.

She's unsuitable to lead.

What I'm trying to do will benefit us all.

Shifting back into my human form, I approach the house with determination. As I draw nearer, its state of disrepair becomes increasingly apparent. Paint peeling from the walls, uneven floorboards lining the covered porch, and crooked doors and windows that hint at years of neglect. The house exudes an eerie, almost haunted aura, making me shiver involuntarily as I prepare to confront the coven's mysterious and infamous leader.

I have no idea what to expect from Calliope.

She's notorious for thinking outside of the beaten path. Most packs look down on her because of it, since we're taught to value rules and order above all else. But the help of someone who thinks for herself is exactly what I need right now.

I refuse to let her creepy house intimidate me.

It's late, and she's likely sleeping, but this is the only time I'm able to leave Pine Valley without someone noticing I'm gone, so I hope she'll understand. And so, I straighten and make my way up the creaking stairs to the door, take a deep breath, and use the large brass knocker to signal my arrival.

The sound echoes through the cold night air, startling a few creatures in the nearby woods.

I keep my hand on the knocker, preparing to sound it again, but a light on the first floor turns on.

A silhouette moves toward the window adjacent to the door, and with a swift tug, the drapes are pulled open. Calliope's piercing gaze meets mine through the glass panes. Her silver hair flows down to her waist, and the moonlight glows against her aging skin in a way that makes her look like a ghost in a horror movie.

But I refuse to let her scare me. So, I hold her gaze steadily, as if I'm asserting my dominance to another member of the pack, unwilling to reveal even a hint of the anxiety coursing through my veins.

Finally, she releases the drapes and opens the door, its hinges groaning in protest as she reveals herself in full. She's a few inches taller than me, and her white nightgown hangs to the floor. She doesn't speak, and I shift slightly on my feet, unable to hide my unease.

However, I can't just stand here saying nothing.

If I want her to take me seriously, I have to get myself together and speak my purpose.

"Sorry for waking you up," I begin, my voice steadier than I feel. "I needed to talk to you, and this was the only time I could get here without my pack noticing I'm gone."

"You're from Pine Valley." Her voice is surprisingly youthful for a woman her age, as if time has yet to claim her spirit.

"I am."

"A wolf shifter," she says.

"Yes." I glance at the porch swing swaying eerily off to the side. "Can I come in?"

"Is anyone else with you?" Calliope's eyes sweep across the yard, her gaze sharp as she searches for any other members of my pack.

"It's just me."

She studies me again, as if trying to determine if she trusts me or not.

"They don't know I'm here," I add, even though I have no way to prove I'm telling the truth.

"And why *are* you here?" she asks.

"I'm engaged to the future alpha of the Pine Valley pack—Connor Ward—and I need your help." I lift my left hand and show her the ring, keeping my gaze locked on hers the entire time, daring her to defy me. "After you hear me out, you'll be glad I came."

She takes a few seconds to think.

"Very well," she finally decides, opening the door wide to allow me entry. "Make yourself comfortable. I'll go prepare us some tea."

* * *

I sink into the aged velvet sofa, my discomfort growing as I wait for Calliope to return from the kitchen. The cavernous living room is musty, with a Turkish rug in the center fading from age, and startling amounts of half-used candles and dusty antique clocks displayed throughout the room.

It's half past one in the morning, and it seems like the entire world is asleep, except for Calliope and me.

Finally, she returns carrying a tray with a kettle and two cups perched upon it. Setting the tray on the coffee table between us, she pours the tea and hands me my cup.

I'm not a big tea drinker—I've always been more of a coffee girl—but I know better than to refuse her offering. Still, I wait for her to drink her tea first, since she poured it from the same kettle as mine and I want to make sure she didn't add any questionable herbs into the brew.

"So, young shifter," she begins, her keen eyes studying me. "Explain why you're here, what you believe I can do for you, and why you think I'd be willing to help."

I lower my cup, my hand shaking slightly as I ready myself for what I'm about to do.

Tendrils of guilt threaten to seep beneath my skin, but I can't back down now. What I'm doing will benefit the pack in the long run.

It's the only way for Connor to be free to love the person he wants to love—*me*.

It's not the only way, my wolf reminds me.

She's right.

It's not the *only* way.

But it is a more peaceful way.

My wolf's anger is a force unlike I've ever felt before. The Pine Valley witches are on Ruby's side, and I fear if I don't get help from someone else with power—someone like Calliope—then I might succumb to my wolf's dark desires and take care of Ruby on my own.

If I do that, I'm not sure I'll ever be able to live with myself.

"A few days ago, a new girl arrived in town," I start, praying to every force in the universe that Calliope will be open to helping me. "She's a wolf shifter, but she's not one of us. Her magic is dangerous and unnatural. She's a threat to us all, and if we don't stop her, she might end up leading the Pine Valley pack by Connor's side instead of me."

The rest of the story spills out of me like a dam that's finally burst, and Calliope listens attentively, sipping her tea and studying me over the rim of her cup.

The relief that floods me after I'm done is so intense that I feel like I've reached the end of a therapy session.

"What, exactly, do you think I can do for you?" she asks when I'm finished.

"I want you to help me break the mate bond—*without* killing Ruby," I say, my voice thick with conviction.

She frowns, and my heart sinks with dread that what she has to say next isn't what I'm hoping for.

"A witch can only break a mate bond if one of the members in the pair willingly asks to be stripped of their magic," she says, confirming my fears. "From what you've told me, Ruby's not willing. I'm not quite sure I can help you."

"You're the oldest witch alive," I plead, desperation seeping into my tone. "There has to be another way. Please."

She purses her lips and sets her cup down, giving my request some thought. "I appreciate you coming to me with this information, and there might be something I can do for you," she finally says. "But it will involve a significant amount of open-mindedness on your part."

"I'm listening."

"You'll have to go against one of the core beliefs of your kind."

"Like I said—I'm listening."

Calliope raises a hand, palm-up, and with a flick of her fingers, every candle in the room ignites. The flames burn so brightly that their reflection dances in her eyes, like she's some sort of demon, and a lump of fear forms in my throat as I pray that whatever she says next doesn't make me regret coming here.

"It just so happens that you came to the right place," she says, her lips curling into a dangerous smile. "As you see, I'm growing old. It's no secret that the few remaining members in my coven are weak. But I refuse to let our line die out. Which is why, to immortalize our magic, I've made some... unorthodox alliances."

"Unorthodox, how?" I ask.

"I've joined forces with the very creatures we've been trained to hate," she says, and I swallow hard, sensing where she's heading with this.

It's why I came here, isn't it?

Because deep down, I know that while I don't have the connections to make what she's about to suggest happen, she might.

It's unspeakable. I can barely think it, let alone say it. Everything I've learned tells me that what she's likely about to propose we do to Ruby would be a fate worse than death.

If it works, and if Connor ever finds out that I was involved, I don't think he'd forgive me.

But if Calliope's proposal is what I think it is, then no one will be dead at *my* hands. And, if you don't consider someone to be dead if they still walk this earth, then they won't technically be dead.

Isn't that ultimately what I want?

"Go on," I say, wanting her to speak plainly instead of beating around the bush.

"Where do you think I'm heading with this?" she asks sweetly, and I realize she isn't going to make this easy for me.

I can do this. It goes against everything I've ever believed, but it's either this or losing the love of my life.

Connor's highest value might be integrity, but mine is determination.

And I'm determined to save our relationship, no matter what.

So I brace myself, hold her steely gaze, and say, "You're talking about working with vampires."

Her eyes twinkle with amusement and a hint of respect. "Indeed, I am. But you must understand that my involvement will come at a cost."

I hesitate, realizing the gravity of my decision. But I'm here, and I'm committed to saving my relationship with Connor, no matter the price.

"I understand," I say with a determined nod. "I'll do whatever it takes."

"As I hoped," she says, and then I sit back and listen as she lays out a plan so twisted that I wonder if I'm making a deal with the devil herself.

Ruby

"There you go," Hazel says, and as I look into her full-length mirror, the last part of my body—my feet—goes invisible.

All that remains is the reflection of her ornate four-poster bed and the window looking out to the moonlit, cloud-strewn night sky. My head buzzes with magic, but other than that, I feel perfectly normal.

I walk forward until the mirror is a few inches in front of me and raise my hand to press my palm against its cool surface. The cloudy shape of the outline of my palm appears, like the mirror is being touched by a ghost.

A knock on the door interrupts my concentration, and I shimmer back into existence. The eyes staring back at me, brown instead of their natural turquoise, have been unfamiliar since the night I received my magic.

It startles me every time I see my reflection.

For unknown reasons, the goddess who star touched me changed my eyes from their natural turquoise to brown. The last thing I remember before passing out was her instruction to tell no one that my eyes aren't naturally brown. So, even though I trust Hazel and her parents, I've kept the secret to myself.

I turn around to see who's here.

Hazel's mom, Seraphina, opens the door and peeks in. "Hope I wasn't interrupting anything," she says, soft and hesitant.

"Just Ruby making herself invisible," Hazel says, light and teasing. "No big deal."

"Glad to hear you're making progress," Seraphina says as she opens the door fully and steps inside. Her wild, curly brown hair tumbles past her shoulders, and the splattering of freckles across her cheeks and nose mirrors Hazel's. "I just received word from Jax and Connor. They want to see you."

She directs that final part to me.

My stomach flip-flops at the sound of Connor's name, and all the air leaves my lungs at once.

"Why?" I ask, my voice barely a whisper.

"He didn't say." She shrugs. "But Perry and I are finishing something up here. Hazel—would you mind driving Ruby to Jax's place?"

"Not at all," she says.

"As I thought." She nods, then returns her focus to me. "Best of luck."

She's out of there before I can ask her anything more.

I turn to Hazel, praying she has answers. "Why do they want to see me?" I ask.

"I don't know," Hazel says, but then a knowing smile crosses her face. "Maybe because he's your mate?"

I freeze in place.

Because I never told her that.

"How did you know?" I ask, since I feel like she'd see through any attempt of mine to lie.

"It would take a blind person to miss the way you look at him," she says with a gentle laugh.

"Oh." I frown, suddenly feeling exposed and vulnerable, as if my every emotion is laid bare for the world to see.

"What happened with him?" she asks.

"It doesn't matter, because he's with Autumn," I say simply. "They've been together for years. He chose her—not me. He made it more than clear that he'll *always* choose her." The ache in my heart intensifies as I say the words aloud, making them feel all too real.

She watches me with deep, knowing eyes, as if she has wisdom far beyond her sixteen years.

"You're underestimating the power of mate bonds," she finally says. "Mates are destined for each other. He's correct that the bond will weaken with distance, but unless he breaks it, he'll never truly feel complete."

Her words strike a chord within me, resonating with the emptiness I've been trying to convince myself is only temporary.

"And it'll be the same for me. I'll never feel complete," I say, tendrils of fear taking hold at the prospect of always chasing happiness but never finding it.

It's a depressing, hopeless future, and I don't want it.

"I need to break the bond," I say, determination lacing my tone.

The thought of severing the connection with Connor is a dagger in my heart. But at this point, what other option do I have? Live in despair for the rest of my life?

I refuse to accept such a grim future.

There has to be a way to make sure it doesn't happen.

"I'm afraid that breaking a mate bond is far easier said than done," she says.

"But it's possible?"

"Anything is possible. It just depends on how many sacrifices you're willing to make."

There's something sinister to her tone, and I feel like I'm seeing the dangerous witch she showed me the first time we met instead of the lovesick girl who drank too much at the bar.

I almost say I'll do anything to break the bond, but I stop myself. There are things too horrible to think about, let alone carry out.

Things like hurting Connor.

I would rather live the rest of my life with a piece of my heart belonging to him than do anything that might cause him pain.

"You look like you're at war inside yourself," Hazel observes, her keen eyes studying me. "Are you really that convinced he won't end up choosing you?"

My throat tightens, but I speak through it. "He doesn't *want* to choose me," I say. "Even if he gives into the bond, it doesn't change the fact that if it were fully up to him, he'd want her and not me."

Again, the truth of it all is a blow to my heart. A reality that will never allow me to find total happiness.

"Perhaps," she says, and my hope crumbles, since it wasn't what I wanted to hear. "But maybe instead of standing here wondering, we should go over there and listen to what he has to say ourselves?"

Her gaze lingers on me, patient and expectant.

I take a moment to gather my thoughts, but who are we kidding? Of course I'm going to say yes.

"You're right," I finally say, and she gives me a small, reassuring smile.

"I'll be there with you the entire time," she promises. "You've got this."

"Thanks," I say. "It's just… hard."

That's the understatement of the year.

I have no idea how I'm going to face Connor without feeling the pain of his rejection all over again.

Still, we might as well get this over with. Like Hazel said, the longer we stay here wondering, the worse it's going to get.

Catching sight of myself in the mirror, the dark circles under my eyes serve as a stark reminder of the toll that spending the entire day honing my magic has taken on me.

Maybe leaving this very instant isn't the best idea.

"Can I have some time to freshen up?" I ask, since if I'm going to see Connor again, I want to look my best. Hazel left some makeup in my bathroom when we got ready to go out to the bar, and it's time to put it to use again.

"I was going to suggest the same thing," she says, which makes me wonder just how tired I look. "I'll be downstairs when you're ready."

"I won't take long," I tell her, and keeping to my promise, I'm downstairs in less than fifteen minutes. Her parents are nowhere to be seen, and I can't help but wonder if they have some sort of secret chamber where they concoct potions, cast spells, and practice the ancient witchcraft that fills this house with an aura of mystery.

Hazel looks me up and down, her smile approving. "You look beautiful," she says, and even though I doubt the bit of makeup I applied can erase the stress of the past few days, I appreciate the compliment.

"Thanks," I reply, swallowing hard. "So, are you ready to get this over with?"

"As ever," she says, leading the way out of the house.

The moon casts its soft, ethereal light upon the world, making the shadows dance and shimmer as we walk to her car. With each step we take, my heart races, pounding in my ears, knowing that each step we take is another one closer to Connor.

Once inside the car, Hazel starts the engine, and we begin our drive toward pack territory.

The silence isn't doing anything to calm my nerves, so I reach for the radio and turn it on.

Hazel apparently listens to her music *loudly*, because a woman's steady voice blares through the car, making me jump.

"…still looking for information regarding Lindsay Davis, Jason Cooke, and Carly Katz," she says, and I reach for the knob again, quickly changing the station.

The familiar voice of my favorite singer fills the car, and I take a deep breath, trying to relax.

It's going to be okay, I tell myself. *There's nothing Connor can say to me that can be more shocking than everything that's happened these past few days.*

At least, I hope there isn't.

Now that there's music on, being in the car is somewhat soothing, and I lean back to watch the passing scenery through the window. The streetlights create a blur of colors that meld together like a kaleidoscope, and the trees cast eerie shadows on the pavement, their bare branches swaying in the night breeze.

After a few minutes, Hazel turns into a smaller street that I don't remember from before. It veers sharply off the path, and she pulls to the side, bringing the car to a sudden, jarring stop.

My heart pounds with anxiety.

Something isn't right.

"What's wrong?" I instinctively look over my shoulder and out the back window of the SUV, worried that someone might have been following us. I don't think there was anyone behind us, but my thoughts have been so far off that I haven't been paying the best attention.

"Sorry, Ruby," Hazel says, although she doesn't sound a bit apologetic. "But I promise this will all make sense soon."

Before I can ask what she means, there's a prick against my neck, my vision blurs at the edges, and everything goes dark.

Ruby

I wake up in bed, groggy and disoriented. For a moment, I think I'm back in my shared dorm room with Luna. My head is so heavy that it feels like it's melting into the pillow, and I don't feel like waking up to get to my first class of the day.

But I don't remember what class I have first today.

I don't even remember what day it is.

And the bed is harder than the one I have at school. The thin, itchy cover isn't nearly as thick and warm as my comforter.

As I'm lying there, the past few days slam into me at once. The last thing I remember is Hazel apologizing to me before pricking something onto my neck that knocked me out cold.

Hazel *drugged* me.

Panic kicks in, and I sit up, looking around. I'm in a small, dimly lit room with a green tasseled rug, a small table and chair, and a full bookshelf. The air is stale and oppressive, and I realize with a jolt that there are no windows.

Most startlingly, only three brick walls surround me. The fourth "wall" consists of vertical metal bars, revealing another nearly identical room beyond. There, a girl with curly brown hair pulled up in a bun sleeps, her face turned toward the wall.

I'm trapped in a prison cell.

Sure, it's a fancy prison cell, but it's still a cell.

Terror pulls at my chest, anxiety threatening to choke me. I try to swallow it down, but my mouth is as dry as a desert, so the attempt is futile.

This can't be happening.

I didn't think anything could be worse than waking up cold and alone in the woods, but I was wrong.

So, terribly wrong.

I push myself out of bed, make a mad dash to the glass of water on the table, and swallow half of it down in what feels like one large gulp. The cool liquid soothes my parched throat. There's a bagel and cream cheese on a plate next to it, but the panic clawing at my insides makes it completely unappetizing.

Especially because I think I recognize that girl's hair from the news.

I walk up to the bars of the cell, wrap my hands around them, and pull, hoping some of my supernatural strength helps me out. No luck.

"Lindsay?" I try, my voice rough with sleep.

She stirs, but doesn't wake.

"Hey, Lindsay!" a male voice calls from the cell next to hers. "There's a new girl here."

Lindsay groans, pushing herself up and rubbing sleep out of her eyes. Her t-shirt is wrinkled, as if she's been wearing it for days, and her warm brown eyes focus when they lock with mine, sad and defeated.

"You're Lindsay Davis," I say. "The one from the news."

She offers a slow nod and a weary smile. "Yeah, that's me. Didn't know about the news part, though."

"And I'm Jason," the guy in the cell next to her chimes in. "The other one from the news."

I press my face against the cold metal bars, craning my neck to get a look at him. The cell extends far enough that I can see him on the other side, also standing close to the bars. His blond hair is a disheveled mess, and his eyes are sunken and hollow. He looks like he's aged years since the photo of him they showed on TV.

"What about Carly?" I ask, expecting her to speak up from another cell.

"She's not here," Jason says. "She was gone when I woke up."

My heart sinks, and I chew on my lower lip, worried about what that could mean.

They killed her, I think, although I try to push away the thought, not wanting to jump to conclusions.

"What happened to her?" I ask.

"We don't know," Lindsay says. "They won't tell us."

"Who's 'they?'"

I already know Hazel's involved, but I have no idea who she's working with.

Jax? Connor?

My heart clenches at the thought of my mate who rejected me.

Please don't be Connor.

"Gwen," Jason says, and I feel a tinge of relief at the unfamiliar name. "Benjamin. And the witch they're working with. Hazel."

"Benjamin's not human," I say, which brings me to another realization. "Neither is Tristan."

"We haven't met a Tristan. But how do you know Benjamin?" Lindsay asks, a sudden protective edge in her tone.

"He's Hazel's boyfriend," I say. "She introduced him to me two nights ago. She said he was human."

"She lied," Lindsay says flatly.

"Yeah. I figured that out," I say, immediately cringing at how snarky I sound. "Sorry. It's just…" I pause for a second to look around the cell. "I wasn't expecting her to do *this.*"

"Knock us out and lock us down here to become living blood bags for vampires?" Jason says, stunning me into silence.

It's not possible.

Witches hate vampires. It's why they created shifters all those centuries ago—to protect themselves from vampires.

"Don't worry. It's not as bad as it sounds," he continues, his words far from comforting. "They're keeping us here to make sure we're safe. After we prove we're loyal to them, they'll let us out. Like they did for Carly."

"I thought you never met Carly?" I ask, immediately suspicious.

"I didn't," he admits. "But Gwen said Carly was able to help them with something, so they let her go. And Gwen wouldn't lie. Not to me."

I have no idea who Gwen is, but I do know he's being stupid to trust her. So, I glance at Lindsay for some insight, but she just gives a noncommittal shrug, revealing no opinion on the matter.

I'm not getting far with this.

Time to pivot to try finding out more information.

"How long have you both been here?" I ask, even though I have a bit of an idea about the timeline of events from the news.

"Three days? Maybe four?" Lindsay answers, rubbing her temples as if she's trying to squeeze out the memories. "It's hard to keep track of time in here."

Jason nods in agreement. "I've been here a few days longer than she has. I have to admit—it was a relief to get some company."

"Shut up," Lindsay says, although her voice is light and teasing. It's the sort of tone someone would use when talking to a close friend or a sibling.

"You guys knew each other before this?" I ask.

"He came into the diner sometimes," Lindsay says, reminding me that she was a waitress there who disappeared while taking trash out to the back alley. "I always thought he was a bit of a jerk, to be honest. A typical city boy with enough spare cash to move out to the mountains to become a ski bum."

"A *snowboard* bum," Jason corrects her, a smirk playing on his lips.

"Same thing." She shakes her head in mock annoyance, rolling her eyes again.

We lapse into silence for a moment, the air around us heavy with unspoken thoughts.

"They send vampires down here to feed on you?" I ask, involuntarily bringing my fingers to my neck at the thought of that being in my near future.

Horror rushes through me, and I quickly lower my hand back to my side.

"They do," Lindsay says. "Benjamin drinks from me. Gwen drinks from Jason."

"I know how I made it sound before, but don't worry—it's not so bad," Jason says, his voice taking on a more animated tone. "I mean, before Gwen fed on me, I was terrified. But it didn't hurt. And she's different. I don't know. It's hard to explain."

"You like her," I realize.

"I do," he says, running his fingers through his unkempt hair. "You'll understand when you meet her."

I shiver at the idea of meeting her. Because I don't believe him. Vampires who lock people in their basement to feed from them can't be "not so bad."

Gwen's manipulating him somehow, and I don't like it one bit.

There's also another big thing that doesn't make sense.

"You're both human?" I ask, looking from Lindsay to Jason and back again.

"As far as I know." Lindsay chuckles and glances around her cell. "That's why they're keeping us down here."

"Interesting," I say.

"You're not?" Jason guesses.

"I thought I was up until a few days ago," I say, trying to keep it simple. "Then I found out I'm a wolf shifter."

I don't have the energy to tell them about being star touched and having illusion magic, so I figure that's enough information for now.

"An actual wolf shifter?" Jason's eyes widen in amazement. "You can transform into a wolf?"

His surprise about the existence of shifters is amusing, given the casual way he was talking about vampires a few minutes ago.

"I did once, about a week ago," I tell him. "Haven't been able to since."

"Wow," he says. "That's cool."

"I guess," I say, since "cool" is far from how I'd describe these past few days.

"Can you shift into a wolf right now?" he asks.

"Didn't you hear her? She said she hasn't been able to," Lindsay says, although the intrigued look she's giving me suggests she's as curious as he is.

I reach for my wolf, figuring it can't hurt to try again, but she's silent. It's like she's hiding, trying to get as far away from this nightmare as possible.

I don't blame her.

I'm still trying when the sound of a door slamming shut interrupts my concentration. Footsteps echo from down the hall, and the three of us fall silent as we wait for whoever it is to show themselves.

Benjamin comes down the hall and stops near my cell. He has an eerie grace as he moves, and his eyes look me up and down, far deadlier and sharper than they were the night we met.

"Good morning," he says, his voice smooth and relaxed. "I see you're all getting to know each other."

I swallow hard, the hairs on the back of my neck standing on end. "Where are we?" I manage to ask, my voice steadier than I feel.

This is *not* the same Benjamin I met at the bar.

The Hazel who pulled me to the side of the road and drugged me isn't the same girl who shared a pizza with me at her house and confessed that she had a human boyfriend, either.

"Spring Creek," he says, surprising me by directly answering my question. Although, I suppose the answer isn't overly surprising, given that he and Tristan *did* tell me the other night that they're from Spring Creek.

Tristan, who I assume is one of them, too.

I was so stupid to have trusted him like I did, and to have let him kiss me. But what's even stupider are the butterflies that flutter in my stomach when I think about how much it truly felt like we connected that night, and how the entire world disappeared around us when his lips brushed against mine.

Benjamin's silent as he studies me, the smug look in his eyes downright infuriating.

It's like he's reading my mind, and I hate it.

"You're a vampire," I say what Jason and Lindsay already told me.

I want to hear it from him, not from them.

His smile is cold and predatory. "Did you really think a witch as powerful as Hazel would fall for a human?"

The amusement in his tone makes my blood boil, and I want to reach through the bars and strangle him. But I take a few deep breaths instead, controlling myself.

"And Tristan?" I ask, bracing myself for the answer I know is coming.

"You like him, don't you?" Benjamin answers my question with another question, toying with me.

I press my lips together, refusing to answer.

"I saw it when you looked at him," he continues. "The entire bar did. You need to work on hiding your emotions better, Ruby."

I nearly growl at the condescending way he says my name.

"But enough about Tristan," he says. "I didn't come down here to stand around and have a gossip session. I came down because it's breakfast time, and I'm hungry."

I step back and curl my hands into fists.

No way am I going to let this monster feed from me. I might not have any practice with combat, but if he comes near me, I *will* fight him off, if it's the last thing I do.

And he's going to regret the moment that he, Hazel, Tristan, and whoever else they're working with drugged me, kidnapped me, and threw me in this cell to begin with.

Ruby

"Don't worry, wolf girl," Benjamin taunts, his mouth twisting into another cruel smile. "I don't want you. I want her."

He strides purposefully toward Lindsay's cell. She's sitting on the bed, her eyes wide and alert. She licks her lips slightly as she gazes up at him, and even though it's crazy, it looks like she *wants* him to feed from her.

Benjamin removes a key from his pocket, and when he goes to open the door, his hand passes through something that shimmers. Only slightly, but enough for me to tell that there's a magical barrier keeping us inside.

It reminds me of the barrier that trapped me inside Pine Valley.

The cold metal bars, it seems, are just for dramatic effect. An extra level of intimidation. Which makes sense, since otherwise, we could try to barrel through anyone who tries to enter. The humans probably wouldn't have a chance of succeeding with that, but me?

Who knows.

Benjamin closes the door behind himself and walks slowly toward Lindsay, pulling me out of my thoughts.

"Stand up," he commands, and she slowly does as he asks.

I glance at Jason's cell, but he's no longer leaning against the bars, so I can't see his reaction.

Turning my attention back to Benjamin and Lindsay, I watch in horror as he moves toward her and gently wraps a hand around her neck.

I need to stop him.

Maybe I can use my illusion magic?

But what, exactly, can I do with it?

Sure, I can try making Lindsay invisible. But that won't make her non-corporal. It won't stop Benjamin from feeding off her.

"Stop," I call out to him, my voice desperate. "Feed from me instead."

It's likely the stupidest thing I've ever said in my life. It's the exact opposite of what I was thinking a minute ago when I decided to fight him off no matter what. But I'm supernatural and Lindsay's not. I heal faster than humans. And I can't help myself from thinking about Carly, and her mysterious disappearance.

I can't stand by and watch Benjamin drain Lindsay's life away.

Benjamin looks over his shoulder and sneers at me. "You're not worth the risk," he says simply, and he pushes Lindsay up against the wall, sinking what I imagine are his fangs into her neck.

She relaxes into him, and I watch in horror as he drinks his fill. Even worse—I can smell a tinge of blood in the air, like rusted metal. I take shallower breaths to block it out, but it doesn't matter. The metallic taste still lingers in the back of my throat.

Eventually, Benjamin pulls away. The twin puncture marks on Lindsay's neck heal, and she stares up at him, like she's in a trance.

"You liked that?" he asks, his voice low and seductive.

"Yes," she breathes, trembling, and she tilts her face up, like she's longing for a kiss.

He moves closer, stopping mere inches from her lips. "No, Lindsay. I have a girlfriend," he says gently. "Remember?"

Desire continues to swirl in Lindsay's eyes as she stares up at him.

"Hazel's not down here. She won't know." She tries to move closer to him, but he presses his index finger to her lips, stopping her.

"Thanks for the meal. It was quite satisfying," he says, smirking. "But I have to run."

With a final, lingering glance at Lindsay, Benjamin turns and exits her cell, locking the door behind him. He looks over at me, a smug expression plastered on his face.

"See that? She liked it," he says, nodding toward Lindsay as she sits down on the bed again, her eyes glazed and distant. "When it's your turn, you will, too."

His words send a shiver down my spine, but I refuse to let him see it.

I *hate* him.

"I thought you said I wasn't worth the risk?" I shoot back, my voice steady despite the fear gnawing inside me.

I'm unsure of the risk I pose to him, but it probably has something to do with me being a wolf shifter, star touched, or both.

"Did I say that *I'll* be the one feeding from you?" he asks, his tone dripping with condescension.

I straighten my shoulders and hold his icy gaze. "No," I say. "But who will?"

He chuckles darkly, the sound echoing through the dimly lit cells. "Do you really think I'm going to answer that?"

No. I didn't.

But I won't give him the satisfaction of admitting it.

I don't have time to push Benjamin for more information, because from the shadows of his cell, Jason speaks up.

"Where's Gwen?" he asks, gripping the bars of his cell again, craning his neck to get a better look at Benjamin.

Benjamin turns to face Jason, smirking. "Relax, Jason. Gwen fed from you last night. She'll be back tonight," he says in a way that I think is supposed to be calming, but makes my skin crawl.

Desperation shines in Jason's eyes, and he clings to the bars tighter, his knuckles turning white. "Tell her that I'm thinking about her, okay? And that I'm looking forward to seeing her."

He sounds nothing like the confident guy who was bantering with Lindsay earlier.

A cruel smile plays on Benjamin's lips, clearly amused by Jason's plea. "Sure, I'll pass along the message," he says, although from the way he seems to be mocking Jason, I don't believe him. "In the meantime, the three of you should relax. Read some of those books we gave you." He looks to me specifically when he says that last part. "I know how much you enjoy reading."

I glare at him again, since he's directly referencing my conversation with Tristan.

He's teasing me. Playing with my mind. And while I didn't think it was possible to hate him even more, he just managed to prove me wrong.

"I'll take a look at them," I say coolly, since asking him questions clearly isn't getting me anywhere. "Thanks."

He narrows his eyes at me. "You do that," he says, and then he's down the hall, up the stairs, and out of the basement before any of us can say another word to him.

I stand there in shock for a few seconds, trying to process what just happened, then turn my attention to Lindsay. She's still sitting on the bed, and she allows her hand to rest on the place where Benjamin fed from her neck.

"Lindsay," I say softly, not wanting to startle her. "Are you okay?"

A stupid question.

Of *course* she isn't okay.

"All good," she says, letting her arm fall back to her side and giving me a weak smile. "It's not as bad as it looks. You'll see."

Hell no I won't.

"We'll get out of here," I promise, even though my words feel empty.

But how will we escape? I'm just as trapped as they are. I might be supernatural, but I can't shift, I have no earth magic, and my illusion magic is all but useless to do anything to get us out.

"How?" she asks exactly what I'm wondering myself.

"I don't know yet," I admit. "But I'll figure something out."

She shrugs, and I glance at Jason, hoping he might have something to add.

He says nothing.

"Benjamin might eventually let me out," Lindsay continues. "He cares about me. I know he has a girlfriend, but that doesn't mean I'm not important to him, too."

I study her, looking for any signs of doubt, but I find nothing.

She's delusional.

That, or he did something to her when he fed from her. I'm betting on the latter. Judging by the way Jason talks about Gwen, she did the same to him, too.

The question is: how long after feeding from them will it take for the effects of whatever they did to them fade?

Will it fade?

And even though I'm not human, will it happen to me if a vampire feeds from me, too?

So many questions, and no answers.

Maybe Connor will come for me. Despite how much he hates it, we do have our mate bond. We're connected by fate, or the universe, or however it works.

What if he can sense that something's wrong, and tries to get me out of here?

Or maybe he's working with Hazel.

The intrusive thought crawls into my mind, sinking its hooks into me and refusing to let go. After all, Connor *does* want to get rid of me. He hasn't made a secret of it.

Which means the only person who can help me is myself.

Unsure what else to do, I reach for my wolf again, but trying to find her is like trying to push through molasses. My head feels fuzzy, my body weak.

How long has it been since I've eaten?

I glance at the bagel sitting on the table. It looks far from appealing, but I need to keep my strength up. Connecting with my wolf and figuring out how to better use my magic might be my only way out of this place.

And I need to do it before one of the vampires does whatever they did to Jason and Lindsay to me.

Because I've lost a lot recently, and I don't intend on losing my sanity, too.

Tristan

I WILL ALWAYS STAND by the fact that Calliope Thornhart's library in her ancestral home in Spring Creek, New York, is the best in the state. The rambling house itself, with its peeling paint and creaky floorboards, sprawls over twelve thousand square feet, not including the basement. Its library, a vast sanctuary of knowledge, harbors thousands of books, from freshly minted to ancient. Some are so old that they date back to before Gwen was turned into a vampire.

As for me, I gravitate toward science fiction. Fantasy usually hits too close to home, and I generally enjoy reading about possible futures rather than dwelling on the past.

The worn velvet armchair has come to know the shape of my body in the past few weeks, and the silence in the room is only interrupted by the occasional rustle of pages and the soft creaking of the floorboards beneath me as I shift in my seat.

That is, until an unexpected knock on the door shatters the stillness, and the person on the other side comes in before I can give her permission to enter.

Calliope. Her silver hair glints in the sunlight as she strides toward me, her boots clicking on the floor.

I'd be annoyed that she's storming in here as if she owns the place, except that she does, in fact, own the place.

I close the book, not bothering to mark it. I always remember exactly where I left off.

It always feels surreal to look at Calliope. Because even though she appears decades older than me, I'm the one who has years on her.

Many, many years. Granted, I'm nowhere near as ancient as Gwen, but if I weren't immortal, I'd have long since turned to dust.

"Good morning," I say pleasantly, despite being annoyed at the interruption.

Ever since I met *her*, I've been in no mood for anything but reading.

Ruby.

I was supposed to be the one seducing her, not the other way around. But there's something about her—something otherworldly, captivating—that has ensnared me. The memory of the sparkle in her eyes and the fire in her voice during our conversation has haunted me since that night at the bar.

I've kept this to myself, of course.

I trust Benjamin and Gwen with my life, but Calliope and the other witches?

We're supposed to be loyal to them above all else. I doubt they'd be thrilled about this new… infatuation of mine.

That's what I'm feeling for Ruby, isn't it? Infatuation. I've never been in love, but I refuse to subscribe to the naïve belief that love can be sparked at first sight. Even with shifter mate bonds, I feel like it must only be intense attraction—not love.

Love takes time, patience, work, and communication. Though I've never experienced it myself, I've witnessed enough in my long lifetime to know that much.

So why am I constantly having to remind myself of this logic now?

"Have you had your morning meal yet?" Calliope asks, never one for small talk.

"Not yet," I say. "I was trying to enjoy the quiet before the others wake up."

In truth, the thought of feeding on the animal blood I've been subsisting on lately holds little appeal. I've been reduced to feeding from animals because it's too risky to continuously feed off humans in the nearby town, but we can only stomach animal blood for so long before growing restless.

Thus why we were all relieved when Hazel suggested keeping some humans from Pine Valley here with us for consistent feedings.

"Good," Calliope says, a knowing smile playing at her lips. "Because we've brought someone for you."

At the mere mention of a human waiting for me, I set the book on the side table and rise to my feet, all irritation from the interruption vanishing in an instant.

"Take me to her," I command, my gums aching at the thought of human blood.

"Not so fast." The gleam in Calliope's eyes makes it clear she's up to something. "There's a catch you're going to want to brace yourself for."

"What catch?" I remain still and calm as I wait.

"The person we brought for you isn't a human. It's Ruby."

My breath catches in my throat, and my heart stutters.

She can't be serious.

Ruby's a shifter. She's star touched. We have plans for her. Plans that don't involve kidnapping her and locking her in the basement.

On top of that, the thought of Ruby being locked in one of those cells… well, I don't like it. Not one bit.

"Why did you bring her here?" I ask, since the idea of Ruby being captured for me to feed on is preposterous.

They wouldn't put one of us in danger like that.

Especially not *me*.

"To drink from her, of course." Calliope has the audacity to look proud of herself, as if she's just unveiled a brilliant plan.

"That's insane," I say, my voice a low growl.

It's more than insane.

It's illegal.

"There's been a change of plans," she says casually, as though she's discussing a minor inconvenience instead of breaking one of the biggest laws of the supernatural world. "We need you to make progress with Ruby sooner rather than later."

"No," I say, but she just stands there, her loose white blouse fluttering in one of the many drafts that constantly haunt this ancient house. "If I do what you're asking, I'll be marked for death. You know it. The others know it." I glance at the door, half expecting Gwen and Benjamin to burst through at any second to right this terrible wrong.

My magic stirs, tempting me to blast Calliope aside and confront the others, but she's no pushover. Despite her age, she's far from weak.

As if to emphasize this fact, she holds up her hand and conjures a ball of fire in her palm.

It's warm against my skin. Something about it calls to me to look closer, but I avert my gaze, well aware of the hypnotic effect a witch's flames can have. Especially ones created by a witch as powerful as Calliope.

"No one will ever find out," she says, snuffing out the fire as if she's already made her point. "And, if they ever do, our coven will already be the most powerful in the world. *We'll* make the laws then. You're safe with us. You're one of us. We're family now. And we're all in this together."

Tristan

Calliope's words that we're family now ring true, but still...

"I won't follow in my brother's footsteps," I say. "Especially when our plan with Ruby was going so well. I told you how... receptive she was." My heart aches at the memory of Ruby's responsiveness to my kiss, and I touch the cross pendant around my neck—the one that belonged to my brother. "This is a terrible way to gain her trust."

If reminding her of the risk to my life isn't enough, perhaps an appeal to our long-term strategy will be.

"You will never capture the girl's heart," she says plainly. "It already belongs to someone else."

"Who?" Every muscle in my body tenses, but I maintain control, never one to act impulsively out of emotion.

"I had a visit from a wolf in the Pine Valley pack," she begins. "Autumn Blackwell. The one the same age as Ruby? She says she's going to be their alpha female someday."

She watches me, waiting to see if I recognize the name.

"I don't know much about the wolves in other packs," I admit. "They all blend together to me."

All except for *her*.

But, given the fact that she's star touched, Ruby is hardly an ordinary shifter. She's far more special, and anyone with eyes can see it.

"A quick lesson about the Pine Valley pack: Autumn is in a relationship with their future alpha male, Connor Ward," Calliope says. "They've been together for years. They're engaged to be married, but a recent obstacle has appeared in their path."

"What 'obstacle?'" The words escape my mouth in an angry hiss. Once more, I have to rein in my urge to blast her against the wall. As it is, the crystals in the chandeliers chime overhead as the drafts in the room blow stronger, a testament to the magic rising inside me.

However, I've lived long enough to know that asserting force on the old witch isn't going to get me anywhere. So I release my hold on my magic, and when the chandeliers go silent again, Calliope nods in satisfaction.

"Connor has a true mate," she says, her voice cutting through the air like glass. "Ruby."

Her words strike me like a dagger to my heart, and I have to breathe deeper to ground myself.

"We need to break the mate bond before they solidify it," she continues, as if she didn't just shatter my world.

"Autumn's lying," I say, refusing to believe it. "Why else would their future alpha remain engaged to her?"

I can't bring myself to say his name.

Connor.

The name of the man whose existence threatens to derail everything we've set out to achieve.

"She's not lying. She wouldn't have agreed to my condition if she were," Calliope says, and then she proceeds to outline the terms Autumn made with her.

Terms no shifter would accept unless they were desperate to be with the one they claimed to love.

"You believe me," she says when she's done, since I'm sure my hard expression gives away that I do.

"Yes." I keep my voice steady and calm, unwilling to give into the emotions threatening to boil to the surface.

I shouldn't care this much. Ruby must have hypnotized me, the same way I'm doing to her. It's the only explanation for this... protectiveness I'm feeling for her.

The mate bond makes it so Ruby will never feel the same way for me that she does for Connor.

And yet, that knowledge makes me want her even more.

"As I'm sure you now understand, we need to break their bond as soon as possible if we want the girl to join us," Calliope continues, looking extremely satisfied with herself for catching me off-guard. "The necklace won't be enough. A blood bond will be a good start, bringing us closer to our goal, but it still won't be enough. The only thing that will be enough is—"

"If she volunteers to turn," I finish her sentence, knowing exactly where this is going.

A person can only be turned if they're willing. For me, over a century ago, it was a choice between turning or dying.

Not a difficult decision at all.

"But why would she volunteer to turn or join us?" I ask. "You've kidnapped her, locked her in a cell, and given her every reason to hate us."

"To hate *us*, perhaps." Calliope absentmindedly twirls a strand of her silver hair around her boney finger. "But we don't need her to like us. We only need her to like *you*. To *love* you. To do anything to be with you forever."

"Even though she has a fated mate." The words come out in a deadpan, since I hate that they're true.

The pendant around my neck feels like it's pulsing with emotion, as if insisting that Ruby belongs with me.

I know she isn't mine.

But I *want* her to be.

The question is—how far am I willing to go to make it happen?

"She has a fated mate who rejected her," Calliope reminds me. "The pain of a shifter being rejected by a mate is supposedly one of the worst things they can experience. It's an emptiness they'll never be able to fill. If you offer to turn her, you'll be offering her freedom from that pain. You'll be offering her love and safety. How could she possibly say no?"

I press my lips together, because even though what she's suggesting is treason, I can't deny that a large part of me yearns to have Ruby by my side—forever.

This might be my one and only chance to make that happen.

"Fine," I give in. "I'll do it. But I have one condition."

"And what's that?" Calliope asks, her eyes narrowing with curiosity.

It's hard to believe this is happening—that she's made an offer like this, and that I'm saying okay.

But it *is* happening. So, with precision, I explain exactly what I want to do after Autumn fulfills her part of the deal and delivers on her promise.

And, much to my satisfaction, Calliope says yes.

Ruby

I SPEND the next hour or so getting to know Jason, as Lindsay is sleeping again due to the blood loss she suffered at Benjamin's hands. His warm and outgoing nature is infectious—he's the type of guy who makes friends easily—and he easily chats with me about his love for snowboarding and other adrenaline-seeking activities.

He speaks fondly of his younger sister, who's studying to be a nurse, and they're clearly very close. His parents, both accomplished lawyers, have always been supportive of his passion for snowboarding, even though they don't completely understand it. Their love mirrors the support my parents have always given me, encouraging me to go for my dreams, no matter what.

My heart hurts when I think of them, like it has every time since learning that they think I'm dead.

It makes me even more determined to get Jason and Lindsay out of here, so their parents never have to suffer the pain I know mine are experiencing right now.

Suddenly, the door at the top of the stairs swings open, interrupting my conversation with Jason.

My breath catches in my chest at the sight of Tristan walking down the stairs, with Benjamin, Hazel, and a woman I haven't met yet.

Their footsteps echo in the hall, the woman's high heels clicking with authority as she takes the lead. There's something ageless about her, in her tailored blouse and black trousers, and her dark, wavy hair makes her already pale skin appear nearly translucent. Her eyes are a striking shade of violet, and from the way Jason grips the bars of his cell like a lovesick puppy, I have no doubts who this woman is.

Gwen.

But my attention is stolen by Tristan, his golden eyes piercing my soul like they did the night we met. He's wearing the same bomber jacket he had on then, and as he pins me down with his sharp gaze, his strong features tense into pure anger.

He quickly tears his focus away from me. "What's *she* doing here?" he asks Gwen, disgust dripping from his tone.

I step back, startled by how much it sounds like he hates me.

But I suppose I shouldn't be surprised. The Tristan I met before doesn't exist. That Tristan was a human, not a vampire. That night was an act to him—a game. None of what happened in that bar between us was real.

I clearly mean nothing to him.

Just like he should mean nothing to me.

"I told you we brought someone for you," Gwen replies, her accent a curious blend of British and something else.

"You were supposed to bring me a human," he says. "Ruby isn't human."

"I thought you liked her?" Hazel chimes in, her sweet demeanor from our time together at her house now hidden beneath black jeans and a tight leather jacket.

She looks like some sort of evil twin of the girl I thought I knew.

"I'm hungry," he says. "Whether or not I liked her is irrelevant. I can't feed on her. And you can't keep her here. It's… degrading, to say the least."

His eyes flick back to me, determination blazing within them.

My heart leaps with hope.

Maybe my attraction toward him wasn't so unrequited, after all.

And, if it wasn't, there might be a chance he can help get me get out of here.

"Gwen," Jason says, interrupting their conversation. "I missed you."

Gwen barely spares him a glance. "I'll join you soon," she promises, which seems to placate him for the moment. "Like Tristan, I'm hungry."

I've been a silent observer so far, and I know I should have said something by now. But begging them to let me go isn't going to convince them have a sudden change of heart. So, what else is there?

"You drugged me," I say to Hazel, going for the obvious.

"I truly am sorry about that." Her apology echoes the one from the car. "I needed to get you here, and it was the easiest way."

"You don't think I would have happily strolled into this cell?" I ask, sarcasm dripping from my words.

"Sorry," she repeats. "But this entire thing is complicated. I promise you'll understand soon."

"Understand what? That you want him to feed off my blood?" I glance back at Tristan, his icy gaze sending shivers down my spine.

So much for him not hating me.

"Don't worry," he says. "I'm not going to do it."

"This is orders from above," Gwen says. "You have to do it."

"This is *illegal*," he snarls, and a breeze passes through the stuffy hall, even though there are no windows to let it in.

Vampires have power over the element of air, I remember from everything Penny told me during the short time I stayed at her house.

Tristan clearly isn't an omega, or whatever term the vampires use to describe the members of their species who can't connect with their assigned element.

Gwen's violet eyes narrow, her lips pressed into a thin line as she regards Tristan's defiance. "No one will find out," she says. "You know the others will protect us, no matter what. They made an oath to us."

"That doesn't change the fact that if we *are* found out, I'll be hunted and killed." Tristan's voice is tight with barely contained anger, back to talking with them as if I'm not here.

My heart hammers in my chest as a desperate idea takes root in my thoughts. Maybe I should make it so I'm *not* here. At least, make it look like I'm not.

Turning invisible won't help me escape. But it might remind them that I'm *not* human—I'm star touched.

It beats standing here doing nothing.

So, I reach deep inside myself, searching for my magic. But just like when I looked for my wolf, it's like navigating through a thick fog.

Hazel's drug is still in my system.

It *must* be.

"We won't be found out," Gwen repeats. "You're my son. I care about you—I created you. Would I ever put you in danger like that?"

"You might do it for *him*." Tristan's snarl is vicious, and Gwen shoots Hazel a meaningful glance.

In a blur of motion, Hazel reaches inside her jacket, pulls out a dagger, and plunges it into Tristan's stomach.

"No!" I scream, and I'm suddenly at the very front of the cell, my hands wrapped around the bars in a desperate, unsuccessful attempt to wrench the door open.

Tristan sucks in a sharp, painful breath, his eyes wide in shock as he stares at Hazel.

Benjamin springs into action, striding towards my cell. With one hand, he hurls a blast of wind at me, propelling me back onto the bed. With his other, he retrieves the key and unlocks the door.

Determination surges through me, and I rise to my feet, ready to make a break for it.

He forces me back with another gust of wind.

At the same time, Gwen and Hazel drag Tristan over and toss him into the cell. Hazel's removed the blade, and Tristan rolls onto his back, his hands clutching the wound as crimson blood spills through his fingers.

I curse and hurry toward him, carefully moving his hands so I can get a look at the injury. As I watch, the hole in his stomach begins to knit back together, the flow of blood slowing until the wound is sealed.

Stunned, I stare at the smooth skin now visible through the tear in his black t-shirt.

Tristan uses his elbows to sit back up, and he pushes me away, eyes blazing with anger as he stares down Hazel.

She's studying the blade in her hand, which is now smeared with Tristan's blood. It's an ancient-looking thing, and her fingers wrap around the handle, hiding all but an intricately carved skull at the base.

"What did you *do?*" Tristan growls, rising and pulling at the cell bars like a caged animal.

I cautiously back away from him, my own focus also on Hazel and the others, my heart pounding with fear.

They locked me in here with a vampire.

One who hasn't yet had his breakfast.

Terror rushes through my veins. Because sure, Tristan claims to like me and not want to feed from me. But if they keep him in here with me for long enough…

"You'll eventually get hungry enough that you'll need to feed," Gwen completes my thought as Hazel returns the bloodied dagger to the inside of her jacket pocket. "Especially after losing all that blood."

"I won't do it," Tristan says, his voice strained and desperate.

"You will," Gwen says with chilling certainty. "If it comes down to feeding from her or killing her... well, I know you well enough to know what you'll choose."

"You might as well get started, brother," Benjamin says, shifting his attention back to me. "I saw the way you looked at him at the bar. You can't deny that you want it."

It sounds so vile and demeaning when he says it that way, and I want to reach through the cell bars and wring his arrogant neck.

"I want to get out of here," I say, trembling with frustration and fear, and then I turn my plea to Hazel. "You said there was something you want me to understand. I can't do that if you don't explain what it is."

"I will, eventually," she says, her eyes distant. "But you're not ready yet."

"I *am* ready," I insist, trying to remain calm despite the fact that they've locked me in here with a hungry vampire. "I've been through enough these past few days that I'm open to anything. You know that."

My heart races as I lock eyes with Hazel, searching for any hint of sympathy or understanding.

There's nothing.

So, I turn my focus to Tristan.

His jaw is set, his eyes ablaze. But despite his anger, there's an undeniable concern in his gaze as he studies me. It's as if he's torn between his instincts and whatever pull he feels toward me, weighing the consequences of defying Gwen and her ruthless plan.

I think I can get through to him.

I just need to play my cards right.

"You're not ready," Hazel repeats, snapping me back to the present. "But you will be. Soon."

With that, she turns and heads for the door, Benjamin and Gwen following close behind.

"Gwen," Jason pleads from his cell, halting her in her tracks. "Stay."

She pauses, considering his request with a cold, calculating gaze. "Don't worry. I'll be back for you," she finally says, her words a chilling promise. "For now, these lovebirds need some time to get reacquainted."

Her smile sends a shiver down my spine, and then she, Benjamin, and Hazel are up the stairs and out the door. It echoes through the dimly lit space as it slams shut, emphasizing our isolation.

I take a shaky breath, attempting to steady my racing heart. The air in the cell is stale and cold, heavy with the scent of fear and blood. It's only a matter of time before Tristan's hunger takes over.

I can't let that happen.

He wants to resist.

I just have to figure out a way to help him... or, if it comes down to it, defend myself against the monster lurking beneath his dangerously alluring surface.

I can do it.

My life—and probably Jason and Lindsay's—likely depends on it.

Ruby

Tristan leans against the cold, stone wall on the opposite side of the cell, the dim light casting shadows across his conflicted expression. He's gazing at me like I'm the most tempting thing in the world, his golden eyes smoldering with a mixture of desire and fear.

I stay put on the bed, careful not to startle him.

"You don't have to do this," I say, trying to stay calm and steady.

"I won't hurt you, Ruby." His voice is smooth as silk, laced with a dangerous edge. "I can keep it under control."

"For how long?"

My eyes dart to the dark red stain on the worn rug beneath us, the memory of Gwen's words about Tristan's intensified hunger after losing so much blood sending a shiver down my spine.

"I can last about a month without blood," he admits, running his fingers through his soft, brown hair. "I'll lose myself to the hunger in about three days. Maybe less, due to the blood loss."

Every fiber of my being goes on high alert. "What happens when you lose control?"

I swallow hard, having a feeling where this is going.

"I won't be able to resist feeding from you," he says exactly what I thought he might. "And, once I start, I won't be able to stop."

His gaze locks on mine, and I swear I can see the monster lurking beneath his perfect exterior, like a beast biding its time in the shadows.

Tristan's dangerous, and I can't let myself forget it.

"You'd kill me," I say, and his eyes harden, confirming my fear.

"We won't let it come to that." He glances at the stain on the rug, a flash of anger crossing his face. "I can't believe Hazel stabbed me."

"And I can't believe she drugged me," I snap back, my anger mirroring his.

"She wasn't supposed to do that." He reaches for the cross pendant hanging from his neck, as if looking to it for protection.

"Then what was she 'supposed' to do?" I ask.

He hesitates, his jaw clenched. "It's complicated," he says. "But trust me, Ruby, I care about you. And I swear on my brother's life that I'll never hurt you."

Silence hangs in the air between us, thick and suffocating. From the desire swirling in his eyes, I'm unsure if he wants to kiss me or kill me.

My heart races as I remember the taste of his lips, and I feel my face flush, warmth spreading through me like an all-consuming fire.

"Benjamin referred to you as his brother," I say, hoping to break the tension.

"He's not my brother by birth," Tristan says. "Gwen turned us both, so we have the same sire, but this necklace belonged to my true brother. The one who shared my blood."

"He's gone," I say carefully, not wanting to push him, but also getting the impression that he's open to talking about it.

"Murdered by shifters," he says, bitterness lacing his tone. "Their punishment for his feeding on a supernatural. They hunted him down and killed him for it."

A chill fills the air, as if his brother's spirit is in the cell with us.

"So that's why you don't want to feed from me," I say, piecing it all together. "You'll be hunted down if they find out."

"Exactly."

I can tell by how vulnerable he looks that he's telling the truth. But also...

"If they don't let us out of here, it sounds like we won't have much of a choice." I hold his gaze, daring him to lie and say otherwise.

He presses his lips together and drops his hand back down to his side. "I'll figure out a way to fix this," he promises, although I have no idea how, exactly, he'll be able to do that.

"The Pine Valley pack will eventually realize I'm gone and come looking for me," I tell him, hoping it's true.

Connor will realize I'm gone and come looking for me.

Although that would mean he cares, and he's made it more than clear that he doesn't.

"They won't," Tristan says, a hint of sympathy in his eyes. "Hazel sides with Spring Creek. So do her parents. They'll be able to hide your disappearance. Anyway, it's best that the Pine Valley pack doesn't come here, for all their sakes."

A knot forms in my stomach. "What do you mean by that?"

"If they come here, they'll be facing a force they can't imagine." He pauses, as if unsure to share more, then continues, "The Blood Coven."

My body turns cold after he says it.

"What's the Blood Coven?" I ask.

"I can't tell you more," he says, his voice tight. "I'm sorry."

I want to push him for more information. At the same time, I'm in no position to anger him, so I nod instead. "No problem," I say. "I understand."

Our conversation fades, and he sits down on the only chair in the cell, refusing to look at me. The unspoken tension crackles like a live wire between us, charged and dangerous.

My gaze drifts to the cell across from ours, where Lindsay is still sleeping. Her chest rises and falls in a peaceful rhythm, although I know that will be shattered when she eventually wakes up.

"I watched Benjamin feed on her." I lower my voice, as if not wanting her to hear, even though she's clearly not waking up anytime soon. "After he finished, she was entranced by him. Just like Jason is by Gwen."

"The blood bond," Tristan says darkly, confirming what I already suspected was true.

"How does it work?" As much as I hate it, I need to prepare myself for what might happen if Tristan and I are unable to get out of this cell and it comes down to the inevitable.

I need to stay alive, no matter what I have to do—or offer—to make it happen.

"The more a vampire feeds from someone, whether they're human or supernatural, the more that person will trust them," he tells me. "The more they'll... desire them."

He leans forward, his gaze burning with the same desire he's speaking of right now.

Even though he said he'll do everything he can to stop himself from feeding on me, I have no doubt that if I walk over there right now and offer myself to him, he wouldn't say no.

And, most disturbingly, why is a part of me... excited by the thought?

No, I think. *I don't want that. I don't want him doing to me what I watched Benjamin do to Lindsay.*

Yet, my gaze drops to his lips, and memories of our electrifying kiss dance through my mind, tempting me with the possibilities of what could happen if I let down my guard.

We both stay exactly where we are, but the space between us feels like it's growing smaller, as if something between us is trying to pull us together. A force that tugs at my soul almost as much as it did when I was around Connor.

From the way Tristan's eyes dilate and his breathing slows, I know he's feeling it, too.

How long can we possibly last in here together before giving in?

"How many times does it take?" I ask cautiously.

"The first time isn't bad," he says. "They'll shake it off in a day or two. It's why it's best for our kind to only feed from someone once, lest we have hoards of obsessed humans intent on tracking us down. It's easiest to accomplish that in large cities, which is why most of us congregate in them."

"Makes sense," I say, remembering what Penny told me about shifter Guardians being sent to cities to protect humans from the vampires that live there.

Key word: humans.

"What happens when a vampire feeds off a supernatural?" I ask, since that's the situation we're dealing with right now.

"The same bond forms with supernaturals as humans," he says. "It's why the witches and shifters are determined to keep us in line—why our feeding on any of them results in an immediate death penalty. They don't want to be bound to us. They don't want us to have that sort of control over them."

"Understandably so," I say, thinking about Connor and the bond I resent between the two of us, the one that only seems to exist for the purpose of causing us constant pain.

I'm already bound to one person. I don't need the same with another.

"I'll do everything I can to resist drinking from you," he says, his expression pained. "But I'll only last for so long, and I refuse to reach the point of killing you."

"Trust me—I don't want you to kill me, either," I say. "If it comes down to killing me or feeding from me, I want you to do the latter. I just want you to know that, before... well, when you still know it's *me* saying it and not because of anything else."

"I appreciate it," he says, and he sits back a bit in relief. "Truly."

"Why are they so determined to have you drink from me, anyway?" I ask. "They know the law. Why would they put you in danger like this?"

A shadow crosses his eyes, and he rips his gaze away from mine, conflicted and torn. Whatever truth lies behind my question haunts him.

I let the silence linger between us, giving him space to organize his thoughts.

Finally, he meets my eyes again.

"They want us to grow close," he admits. "They know about your magic, and they want you to choose to stay with us. To stay with *me*."

I stare at him in shock, unable to believe he admitted to that.

"So, let me get this straight. They imprisoned me, forced you to share this cell with me, and plan to starve you until we have no other choice than for you to either form a blood bond with me or kill me," I say, the ridiculousness of it astounding me. "All in an effort to get me to fall for you so I don't want to leave you, and therefore, not leave them?"

"I don't want this anymore than you do," he snaps, stunning me into silence. "I genuinely like you, Ruby. I didn't expect to feel anything for you, but I do. If you ever end up feeling the same way about me, do you think I want it to be because you were forced to love me? What kind of relationship would that be? How would I ever know if I could trust it or not? How would I ever know I could trust *you?*"

My mind races, trying to process everything he just said. It's a lot to take in, but one word of his hangs in the air, echoing in my thoughts.

Love.

Tristan, with his haunting, golden eyes, claiming that he likes me? That he could maybe even love me?

Sure, we had one good conversation—and one amazing kiss—but we barely know each other. This is crazy. The entire position we're in right now is positively *insane*.

The silence that stretches between us is tense and heavy, the weight of his words threatening to crush us both.

"I'm sorry," he eventually says, and he sits back, releasing a long, defeated breath. "I shouldn't have said that."

Understatement of the century.

I struggle to figure out a response, but eventually, it comes to me.

"You literally just accused a future version of me of lying about feelings that *I don't even have for you*. Ones I've never *claimed* to have for you, and ones I'm never *going* to have for you." My anger about it boils to the surface, and he flinches at my words. "So don't worry—you'll never have to wonder if I'm lying to you or not. Because if we're forced into this blood bond, and if I ever claim to love you afterward, you can trust that it's most certainly *not* true."

Hurt flashes across his features, but he masks it before I can tell if it was ever there at all.

"I understand," he murmurs, his voice cold and strained. "You'll never feel anything for me but hatred and disgust. You won't have to worry again about me thinking that anything else is possible."

My heart twists in my chest, torn between wanting to comfort him and wanting to protect myself.

But he stands and walks to the bookshelf in the far corner of the cell before I can make a choice, his back turned as he browses its contents, and I know he's closed himself off from whatever open conversation we were starting to have.

We're two strangers trapped together, the illusion of whatever connection might have existed between us shattered and scattered like broken glass.

And, in this moment, I make a promise to myself.

Tristan and I might be prisoners in this cell, and I may eventually have to let him feed from me so I can stay alive. But I will never allow myself to be a prisoner to my own heart.

Not for Tristan, not for Connor, and not for *anyone*.

I don't care if it's a blood bond, and I don't care if it's a mate bond. My thoughts belong to me, and my feelings are mine alone.

I refuse to ever accept anything else.

Ruby

As the hours tick by, Tristan and I settle into an uneasy silence. The quiet is stifling, interrupted only by the occasional rustling of pages as we immerse ourselves in books at the opposite sides of the cell, avoiding all eye contact and conversation.

There's a small bathroom attached to the cell, and I try to escape into it for a bit. But it's beyond claustrophobic, since it has no windows and is smaller than a closet, so that doesn't last very long.

I want to ask Tristan about the book he's reading—a recent work of science fiction—but I refuse to be the one to break the oppressive tension crackling in the air between us. He's the one who was a jerk to me. Sure, I reacted intensely to his words, but given the entire situation, I don't think it's crazy for me to be upset.

Lindsay eventually wakes, and I give her a summary of what happened. She seems to know better than to pry for more information than I'm willing to provide, and I'm grateful for that.

I assume Jason is brooding over Gwen's continued absence.

The day slowly fades into evening, and Hazel comes back downstairs, delivering sandwiches and bottles of water. Tristan gets nothing, since as we've all been made well-aware, his food is already in this cell with him.

Me.

Hazel's wearing the same all-black outfit as earlier, and I'm positive that the creepy dagger is still inside the pocket of her leather jacket.

I remain standing, since I'm taller than her and don't want her to feel like she's on higher ground.

"Hungry yet?" she asks Tristan.

He lowers the book he's reading just enough to meet her gaze with a glare that could cut through steel. "I'm doing fine. Thank you for asking," he says, and he quickly returns to reading, seemingly unaffected by her attempt to pick a fight with him.

"Anytime," she says, turning her attention to me. "How have you been holding up?"

She can't be serious.

And yet, she is.

I muster a fake smile. "Fantastic. Absolutely loving the five-star accommodations here. In fact, I'm considering making this my permanent residence."

She smirks at my comment. "Well, I'm glad you're enjoying your stay at the Spring Creek Inn," she says, her gaze lingering on me as though she's weighing her next words carefully.

I cut in before she can speak. "Do you let Benjamin feed from you?" I ask, curiosity getting the better of me.

Her expression falters for a moment, and then a wistful smile crosses her lips. "No." She shakes her head gently, reminding me of the fragile girl who confessed her insecurities to me over a shared box of pizza. "I love Benjamin freely, without the influence of a blood bond. There's only one vampire I'd ever let near my neck."

Her gaze locks onto mine, and I sense that she's baiting me.

"Who?" I ask, since I can't resist trying to learn more.

The mysterious smile on Hazel's face grows, and her eyes hold a hint of amusement. She glances briefly at Tristan, still absorbed in his book, before turning her attention back to me.

"You're not ready to know that yet, but you'll find out soon enough," she says cryptically, and then she reaches inside her jacket, pulling out the dagger from earlier. The intricately carved metal handle depicts a creepy, smiling skeleton with a snake coiling around its feet. The blade, now clean of Tristan's blood, gleams in the dim light as she cradles it with a tenderness that sends an icy shiver snaking down my spine.

She raises it, the tip aimed toward the ceiling, and a delicate helix of fire spirals up the blade. The dancing flames reflect in her eyes and cast flickering shadows on her face.

"What is it?" I ask, since it's clearly no ordinary dagger.

"The Blade of Erebus," she says simply, as if that should hold any meaning for me.

Although, I can *sort* of put my finger on the name, from a fantasy book I read a few years ago…

"Erebus is a god," I remember. However, my knowledge of him stops there.

"Correct." She smiles, and the fire sputters out, leaving behind a wisp of smoke that spirals toward the ceiling and a burnt scent that lingers in the air. "He's the ancient Greek god of darkness and shadow. His blade is imbued with the power of darkness, and it's been in my family for generations."

As she speaks, I feel the darkness radiating off the dagger, like it's poisoning the air around it.

"In case you're about to ask, I'm not going to let you touch it," Hazel adds.

I most definitely *wasn't* about to ask. But her words remind me that it's been a while since she drugged me. I haven't tested my magic since then, but her statement gives me an idea.

I hold my hand in front of me, palm up, and visualize the dagger floating above it. I imagine the eerie skeleton handle, the gleaming blade, and even the spiral of fire magic Hazel summoned around it.

Then I delve inside myself for my magic, relief flooding me when I sense it flowing beneath the surface. It's not as solid as usual, but it's *there*.

I call it forward. My mind tingles with the familiar sensation of my magic bending to my will, and I project the illusion of the dagger above my palm. It flickers and wavers, and it's slightly transparent, but it's a start.

I smile in satisfaction, then glance back at Tristan to see if he's watching. He hasn't seen my magic yet, and I can't deny that there's a part of myself that wants to impress him with it.

He's as engrossed in his book as ever, as if Hazel and I don't exist.

It must be a *really* good book.

Irritation surges through me, hot and fierce.

I need to stop looking at Tristan, and instead focus on what I'm doing. But when I return my attention to my palm, the illusion is gone.

"Nice try." Hazel shrugs. "But it looks like that little cocktail I gave you last night is still in your system."

I glare at her and lower my hand, not in the mood for her games. "Why are you still here?" I ask.

"I have news for you," she says, sliding the dagger back inside her jacket. "Connor and Autumn are engaged."

My stomach drops, the floor swaying beneath me.

"What?" I ask, even though her words rang painfully clear.

"Connor proposed to Autumn," she repeats. "They're going to be getting married. They haven't told the pack yet, but Jax thought it was important for my family and the other witches in the Pine Valley coven to know that a pair as strong as the two of them will be the future leaders of the pack that protects us. Given the history between you and Connor, I thought you'd want to know, too."

Ruby

I TRY to picture Connor getting down on one knee and proposing to Autumn. The image makes me feel physically ill. My heart pounds in my chest, the throbbing echoing in my ears, and my breaths become shallow and quick.

His decision is clearly a reaction to learning that I'm his mate.

It *has* to be. Why else would he be hurrying things along with Autumn? He's only nineteen, and she's only eighteen. Aren't they too young to be engaged, let alone married?

"You're upset." Hazel frowns, her voice barely cutting through the ringing in my ears.

If I didn't know any better, I'd think she genuinely feels bad about it.

Luckily, I do know better. So I swallow hard, somehow managing to hold back the tears burning behind my eyes. I refuse to let her see me as weak.

If she realizes how much she upset me, she'll rub it in even more. And I can't bring myself to look back at Tristan again. If Hazel's already told him that Connor and I are mates—which she might have, since she knew about it before bringing me here—then I don't want to see how smug he probably looks at the fact that Connor rejected me more harshly than I just rejected him.

I need to seem confident and unfazed.

"Connor and I aren't together," I say, forcing strength into my voice. "He can propose to whoever he wants."

From the way she studies me, like she's waiting for me to crumble, I can tell she doesn't buy it.

"I just thought it was important for you to know," she continues. "So you realize they're not on your side."

"Are you implying that *you're* on my side?" I ask, shocked that she might be serious.

"Is that so hard to believe?"

"I'm currently locked in your basement with a hungry vampire." I gesture around the cell in irritation. "So, yes. It's *impossible* to believe."

"Tristan won't kill you," she says simply.

"Maybe not," I say. "But he might feed off me. You know what will happen if he does."

"The blood bond."

"Yes." I stare her down, the air crackling with tension between us.

She doesn't falter.

"Your mate rejected you and is engaged to be married," she says slowly, as if I need a reminder of the news that just crushed my soul. "Would it be so bad to bond with someone else? Someone who might actually like you, and from what I saw at the bar, you like in return? Especially if it numbs the pain of being unwanted by your mate?"

Unwanted.

The word is a sledgehammer to my heart. It steals the air from my lungs, and it hurts to breathe.

But no good will come from letting her see me like this. I need to pull myself together. Now.

"I'm already bound to one person," I say slowly, steadily. "I don't want to be bound to another."

Hazel hesitates, her eyes filled with a strange mix of concern and something else I can't quite place. "Bonding with Tristan will make this easier. Give it time. You'll see," she says, and then she turns and walks away, the sound of her footsteps echoing as she leaves.

The door creaks shut behind her, and the basement is once again plunged into silence.

Throughout this entire exchange, Lindsay's been nibbling on her food as if she's watching a twisted horror movie.

"Want to talk?" she asks carefully, like she's afraid one wrong word will break me.

Honestly, she's not wrong.

"No," I say, and she lowers her gaze, not pushing further.

Stunned by the weight of Hazel's news, I sink down into the chair at the table and stare numbly at the sandwich and bottle of water on its surface. I didn't think there could be any worse feeling in the world than my fated mate rejecting me to my face.

Apparently, I was wrong. Because his getting engaged less than a week afterward is *definitely* worse.

I reach for my water, stopping at the feeling of someone watching me.

Tristan.

I'm unsure whether to be grateful or annoyed that he's gazing at me like he wants to scoop me into his arms and hold me until his touch erases every last bit of my pain.

Like Hazel said, he's capable of doing exactly that. But with his bite, not his touch.

As much as I hate to admit it, even to myself, it's tempting. So, very tempting.

"I bet you enjoyed that," I say bitterly to Tristan.

The openness in his eyes vanishes in an instant.

"Then it's a good thing I'm not a gambler, because you would have lost," he says, and his gaze shifts to the water bottle in my hand before I have a chance to respond. "I wouldn't drink that if I were you. I wouldn't eat the sandwich, either. Both are drugged. The poison will numb your magic, like it did before." A small, unexpected smile plays on his lips. "That was an impressive show of magic, by the way. I've never seen anything like it."

"It sucked," I say, although I can't deny that the compliment gives me a small sense of satisfaction.

"You'll improve," he says. "Just avoid the food and water."

"If I don't eat or drink, I'll die," I say, stating the obvious.

"You can survive for about a month without eating, and three days without drinking," he informs me. "I'm going to try getting us out of here before then."

"By reading?" I raise an eyebrow and glance at the book in his hands.

"By being patient."

He sounds frustratingly done with the conversation, and I refocus on the food and water, weighing the advice he wasn't obligated to give. "Why are you telling me this?" I finally ask.

He sets his book down on his lap, his face once again a mask of guarded emotions. "I know it's hard for you to believe, but I do care about you, Ruby. I don't want to see you hurt," he says. "But you can do with my advice as you please."

I frown, saying nothing.

Instead, I open the bottle of water, figuring it won't hurt to smell it. Hazel likely wouldn't use a detectable poison, but as a shifter with heightened senses, it's worth a shot.

The cap offers no resistance.

It's already been opened.

Tampered with.

I stare at it in annoyance. Because as much as I hate it, Tristan's right. There's a definite possibility that it's been drugged. And, if he manages to get us out of here, I won't be of good use to either of us if I can't access my magic.

"Fine," I give in, dropping the water bottle back down onto the table. "I'll starve myself. You're doing it, so I can, too."

"I believe in you," he says, and then he returns to his book, ending the conversation.

This is ridiculous. All of it.

But, in a twisted way, at least we're in it together.

Ruby

A FEW HOURS CREEP BY. Gwen comes and goes, leaving Jason fully satisfied. Lindsay knows about the food being tampered with, but she's eating it anyway. Either she doesn't think the drugs apply to her, since she doesn't have magic, or she doesn't care.

I'm struggling. Luckily, the running water in the bathroom is safe to drink. And while I do trust Tristan about the food and water bottles, the last thing I ate was the bagel this morning, and the gnawing hunger in my stomach is already becoming nearly unbearable.

Given that Tristan didn't have breakfast *and* that he lost all that blood earlier, I imagine he's suffering far worse than I am.

We're both quietly reading, the sound of rustling pages occasionally breaking the silence. However, I continuously glance over at him to check how he's holding up. I feel him doing the same to me, which makes me smile, even though I've resolved to hate him.

Minus the times when he turns the pages, he's as still as a statue as he makes his way through his book.

Suddenly, he drops it onto his lap and leans his head back on the hard wall, releasing a low groan of pain.

He's hungry. He must be.

This isn't good.

"Are you okay?" I ask hesitantly.

His jaw clenches, his voice strained when he finally meets my gaze and speaks. "The blood loss from earlier left me hungrier than usual. I haven't felt this famished in a long time."

He says it so calmly, as if he isn't admitting that he's on the verge of killing me.

I swallow hard, and my stomach growls, so hollow that it feels like it's eating away at me from the inside out.

If it's like this for me, then how much harder is it for him?

"Is there anything I can do?" I ask softly, even though there's only one answer I can think of.

Let him feed on me before he loses control and kills me.

Disgust ripples through me, since I hate the thought of giving him any bit of control over my heart.

But is my stubbornness worth my life?

From the pained look in his eyes, I suspect he's thinking the same thing.

He inhales deeply, his voice barely a whisper. "Your blood smells... delicious," he says, not really answering my question. "It's harder to resist than I thought it would be."

The admission sends a shiver down my spine, and I press myself against the wall. My heart pounds harder, the sound echoing in my ears, and I can only imagine how it taunts him further.

How much longer can we realistically carry on like this?

"I meant what I said earlier," I finally bring myself to reply. "If your hunger gets to be too much, then I want you to feed on me."

My reminder of the offer brings us both to silence.

His eyes, like golden storm clouds, seem to look right through me. "If we do that, at least I wouldn't have to worry if any feelings you develop for me are your own or due to the bond, since you've made your disgust for me quite clear," he finally says, and I stiffen at the resentment in his tone. "But no need to worry about it yet. I can hold out for a day—maybe longer."

"Are you sure?" I ask.

His features harden, his skin pales, and the hollows under his eyes darken.

"I'm sure," he says, and I sit back in defeat.

That didn't go well.

I want to reach for him, to say something to break this wall between us. But what can I do?

Nothing more than I already have. Or that I will, if it comes down to it. The best thing I can do is stay as far away from him in this small cell as possible, to try not to tempt him further.

So, we return to our books, the tension in the room thick and suffocating. But I can't focus. I force my eyes to skim the words, but my mind is elsewhere.

Two places, if I'm being honest.

One here with Tristan, trying to ignore the tension pulsing between us, the pull of this attraction that feels like it's going to end any sense of self-preservation I've ever had.

The other is back in Pine Valley, with Connor.

Hazel could be lying about his engagement to Autumn. But hoping it's not true feels more like a wish than anything else. Connor made his devotion to Autumn quite clear to me. He plans on spending the rest of his life with her. Engaged or not, what difference does it make? He chose her, and I'm going to have to deal with the pain of being rejected by my fated mate for the rest of my life.

Maybe...

I glance at Tristan, who's perfectly still as he reads, his sharp features illuminated by the faint light of a nearby lamp.

If he feels the weight of my gaze, he makes no sign of it.

Feeling as torn as ever, I look back at the book in my hands. I'm so lost in my thoughts that I'm not even bothering with trying to read the words on the page anymore.

Could Hazel be right that it's better to be bound to someone who chooses me than to someone who rejected me? I'd obviously prefer neither, but the worse of the two options is clear. Especially because being in this cell with Tristan has been making me think of

Connor less and less. I feel a pull to him, even without a blood bond, and Tristan gives me a sense of security that I never felt around Connor.

Maybe I should apologize for the way I snapped at him this morning. He does seem like he has true feelings for me. And while he could have had more tact earlier, I enjoyed my time with him at the bar, and I *definitely* felt something when we kissed.

I certainly feel an undeniable tension between us now. A smoldering fire that threatens to consume us both if neither of us addresses it.

"Tristan?" I finally say, my voice piercing the silence.

"Yes?" His response comes quickly, as if he's been waiting for me to speak.

"I'm sorry about earlier. I don't hate you."

My apology hangs there, heavy in the air, and time seems to stretch into an eternity.

His hand goes for his cross necklace, his fingers brushing over it as if seeking solace or guidance from his brother.

"Okay," he says simply. "Thanks."

I'm not sure what kind of response I was expecting, but it certainly wasn't that.

"Okay," I echo his sentiment, a strange sense of relief washing over me.

We share a look of understanding, and then return to our books as though nothing ever happened.

But something *did* happen. A shift in the air between us, like a change in the direction of a gentle breeze.

I can't pinpoint exactly what it is, but the first word that pops into my mind is *respect*. A newfound trust that Tristan will respect my wishes for as long as he can, even if it means torturing himself in the process.

As we continue reading in a strangely comfortable silence, I can't shake the feeling that this small moment of understanding might have the potential to be a solid foundation for something more between us. And, in this dark and uncertain world I've found myself in, maybe that can be enough.

Connor

Moonlight filters through the curtains, casting an eerie glow on Autumn as she sleeps beside me in my bed, wrapped in my arms. The shape of her body is familiar, the scent of her lavender shampoo one that I'll always associate with her.

My fiancée. The woman I'm going to spend the rest of my life with.

I should be at peace, but something feels off. In the darkest corner of my subconscious, I can feel it—a nagging sensation that refuses to be silenced.

I haven't been able to get rid of this feeling of *wrongness* since I watched Ruby leave Jax's house with the witches and not look back.

Of course something's wrong, my wolf's unwelcome voice taunts in my mind. *You rejected your fated mate and proposed to a woman who isn't meant to be yours.*

Autumn is mine, I think back, releasing a low, protective growl in the back of my throat.

She stirs in my arms and I pull her close, wishing we could return to the period two weeks ago when questioning the love between us seemed impossible.

I need a break from my warring thoughts. And so, using every bit of force I can, I wrangle my wolf into the deepest part of my soul and close my eyes, praying for sleep to come quickly.

As I drift off, a dream takes hold, and I find myself standing in a dimly lit basement cell. The furniture is hazy, the walls fuzzy, the ground barely there.

The only thing I see clearly is *her*.

Ruby.

My heart clenches at the sight of her—my mate, the one I rejected. She's huddled in a corner, but her beautiful turquoise eyes are sharp and brave.

"Connor," she pleads, her voice heavy with desperation. "Help me. Please."

Her eyes flick to look at something over my shoulder, and I try to turn to see what it is, but I can't budge. My feet are cemented to the floor.

A shadow moves from behind me, and an icy chill rolls over my spine. It's a creature of the night, gliding toward my mate. I can't make out his face, but I know what he is.

A vampire.

He descends upon her, and I use every ounce of force in my body to move to stop him, but it's futile. I'm trapped, an outsider looking in, watching helplessly as he lowers himself next to her and brushes her soft brown hair away from her delicate neck, exposing her smooth skin.

She doesn't resist him.

Instead, she sits there calmly, her eyes locked on mine as he sinks his fangs into her neck. Slowly, he begins to drink, draining her life force as I stand there, helpless to intervene.

This can't be happening.

I need to stop him. But when I try screaming Ruby's name, nothing comes out.

He continues to drink as I watch helplessly, a moan of pleasure escaping his throat. Eventually, she falls limply into his arms, her skin so pale that it's like looking at a corpse.

It feels like my soul is being emptied along with hers.

If he doesn't stop soon, he'll drink her dry, leaving her lifeless and cold.

No.

"Ruby!" I finally manage to scream her name.

In a burst of sheer determination, I break free of the force holding me down and rush toward the vampire, ready to shift into wolf form and use my jaws to rip the monster's head from his body.

Before I can, the dream shifts, and the basement cell fades away.

I jolt awake, my heart jumping in my chest as I sit up in bed, pushing Autumn to the side. Cold sweat dampens my brow. I can barely catch my breath, and I feel a raw ache in my vocal cords, along with the faint echo of my scream.

I didn't just call out Ruby's name in my dream.

I did in real life, too.

Autumn tentatively sits up beside me and rests a hand on my shoulder. Her touch should be warm and comforting, but I can't bring myself to look at her.

I can't bear the thought of seeing the devastation in her eyes when I do.

"What happened?" she finally asks, her voice tight and cold.

Her anger is thick in the air, and when I look over at her, she's as heartbroken as I feared.

But nothing can compete with the fear from that dream. Ruby's face, her terror, and the vampire stealing her life in front of my eyes.

Still, Autumn's watching me, waiting.

I have to tell her.

More than that, I have to act.

"It's Ruby," I say, swallowing down the guilt that logically, I shouldn't feel. "She's in danger. We have to help her."

From the hard way Autumn's looking at me, I brace myself for her to snap.

Instead, she glances out the window and composes herself. When she turns back to me, she's cool and calm. The same level-headed girl I fell in love with all those years ago.

"It was a dream," she finally says. "It wasn't real."

"It felt real."

"All right." She straightens and pulls herself together even more. "Tell me what happened."

I nod in appreciation of her offer to listen, then recount the nightmare as quickly as possible. "Ruby was in a cell. There was a vampire with her. He was drinking from her. He was *killing* her."

"You stopped him?" she asks, like she's speaking to a child.

"I couldn't move." I hate how weak and helpless the words make me feel. "All I could do was watch as he drained her dry."

It was all so vivid that I don't think I'll forget it for as long as I live.

Autumn takes a deep breath and reaches for my hand, holding it gently. I want to feel something—the connection to her that used to always be there—but her touch is cold and empty.

"Connor," she says, her voice softening. "Ruby is with the witches. The Pine Valley coven is the most powerful in the country. If she was in trouble, they would let us know."

She's right.

But I shake my head, unconvinced. The dream felt too real, too raw. I can still feel the chill that ran down my spine when I saw the vampire's shadow, and I can still see the terror in Ruby's eyes as she pleaded for my help.

On the other hand, I saw Ruby leave with the witches. They know how important she is. They wouldn't let anything happen to her.

There's only one thing I can think to do.

"I need to visit the witches and check on Ruby. I need to see her with my own eyes, to make sure she's safe."

"Connor," Autumn repeats my name, growing frustrated. "Take a deep breath and *think* for a second. Don't you think that if something was wrong, the witches would have immediately called Jax? And then he would have told you?"

Her words sink in, grounding me for a moment.

So, I pick up my phone from the nightstand and check it.

Nothing. No missed calls or messages.

"Vampires can't get through our barriers," she continues, her voice soft yet firm as she takes the phone from my hand and places it facedown onto the nightstand. "Pine Valley is the most protected town in the country. There are no vampires here."

The conviction in her voice is reassuring, but I can't shake the unsettling feeling.

"What about those humans that have gone missing?" I ask.

Autumn's eyes narrow, her expression guarded. "The witches have investigated it. It's a human crime," she says, suspicion rising in her tone. "Unless you're accusing the witches of lying to us?"

Her words hang in the air like a challenge.

Shifters are loyal to our witches. They take care of us, and we take care of them. Doubting them is the same as doubting the laws that have kept us safe for centuries. The laws I've vowed to follow to the grave.

"No," I say, and she relaxes slightly, releasing a relieved breath.

"Good. I was worried about you for a second," she says gently, and the tension between us starts to ebb. "But if you're *that* worried about Ruby, why don't you call Hazel in the morning to check in with her?"

Contacting Hazel isn't a bad plan. And while Autumn's right that it's too late to call, I also don't have to sit around doing nothing.

"I'll text her now." I pick up my phone again and open my text thread with Hazel, which isn't very long.

How's Ruby doing? I write, and then I press send.

Simple and to the point.

I watch as the message delivers.

I want to call her. I'm not sure how I'll sleep until I know for sure that Ruby's safe.

Luckily, even though it's just past midnight, the bubbles start bouncing on the screen, signaling that she's typing.

She's doing great!

I keep looking at the screen, waiting for more.

There's nothing.

"See?" Autumn says, snapping me out of my trance. "Everything's fine." She pauses, then continues. "Do you think the dream could have been a metaphor about your mate bond with Ruby?"

That idea throws me for a bit of a loop.

"What type of 'metaphor' would it be?" I ask, confused about where she might be going with this.

"I'm not experienced with dream analysis, so I don't know exactly," she says, and she glances out the window, as if looking to the moon for answers. "Maybe a part of you worries that by walking away from Ruby, you're leaving the mate bond to get drained away? The dream could be a reflection of your fear—not a sign from the universe that she's in danger."

"Interesting," I say, since she has a point. It's considered unnatural for shifters to reject our fated mates. The internal struggle is said to be one of the hardest and most haunting things a shifter experiences.

Dreams like the one I just had are proof of that.

"It'll get easier as the mate bond continues to fade," Autumn assures me. "The more you fight the bond, the weaker it will become. But if you react to this dream and go to see her again, you'll be letting the mate bond win."

She's so gentle, warm, and caring when she speaks. As if she understands exactly what I'm going through.

I glance at her left ring finger, a small reminder of the promise we made in the gazebo. We brought the ring into town to get it sized, so she's not wearing it now, but she will be soon.

Autumn is the one I chose, and I *will* stand by my commitment to her. I refuse to let the mate bond mess with my head and make me question my decision.

I won't let it control me.

"You're right," I finally say. "I need to fight it."

She smiles and pulls me closer.

"I'm here for you while you do," she says, trust and adoration shining in her eyes. "I'm here for you, always."

"I know you are," I say. "Just as I'm here for you."

Eager to leave the haunting dream behind, I lean forward and brush my lips against hers. She's immediately responsive—as she always is to my touch—and soon we're laying down on the bed again, my body hovering inches above hers.

It's not long until I lose myself in my fiancée's embrace, and much to my relief, the lingering images of the dream fade as I finally drift back to sleep.

Ruby

I WAKE up in the cell bed, this time having zero trouble remembering where I am and what's been going on. The gnawing hunger in my stomach makes it impossible to forget.

Last night, Tristan told me to take the bed. He was still reading when I went to sleep. He's still reading now, at the opposite side of the cell, although he's moved onto another book—the second of the series he started yesterday. While he reads, he's idly holding the cross pendant hanging from his neck, his thumb brushing against its textured surface as if it's his lifeline.

Watching him sitting there, absorbed in his book, it's impossible to deny how beautiful he is. Every angle of his face is shaped to perfection, and there's something timeless about him that makes him look like he could easily be the star in an old Hollywood movie.

I push myself up so I'm sitting in bed, and he raises his gaze to look at me. The hollows under his eyes have grown worse, and there's something eerily predatory in his gaze that reminds me that I'm in an increasing amount of danger every minute I'm trapped in here with him.

Still, he gives me a small, warm smile. "You're awake," he says simply.

"Did you sleep?" I ask, calmly and cautiously, as if any word I speak might cause him to break.

"A bit."

He doesn't elaborate, and I don't ask for more details. Instead, I stand and make my way to the tiny bathroom to freshen up. All the important basic hygiene items have been supplied for us, and while it's only a small thing, it's certainly one I'm grateful for.

Tristan's breath catches when I re-enter the cell, and he immediately returns to playing with his necklace.

It's a coping mechanism, I realize. *One to help him control his urge to feed on me.*

Aware of his struggle, I sit back down on the bed. It's the farthest I can possibly get from him, aside from the bathroom, which won't keep me safe for long if he decides to go on a starving rampage.

"When did you last feed?" I ask, since while he didn't feed yesterday morning, I don't know when he last ate *before* that.

He pauses for a second, releasing the necklace. "Wednesday morning," he admits.

It's Friday morning.

Two days have passed. He said he could last for three days, but with all that blood loss...

We're pushing it with timing. He's trying to hold out, but I know the facts as well as he does.

Something's going to have to give. And that "something" will have to be me.

But it's not just my life that's at risk.

"If the witches knew the details about our situation, do you really think they'd kill you for feeding on me?" I ask.

His eyes darken, as if he's lost in thought, and he places his book down on the floor. "The witches follow the law no matter what," he says. "Dominic—my brother—never fed on Jessica. They had no blood bond. They were together in secret for years, and in those years, I grew to love her like a sister. But she was a shifter, like you. She was already in love with Dominic when she met her mate. She wanted to escape the mate bond, and she wanted to be with Dominic forever... so she asked him to turn her. He did. They were so consumed by their love for each other that they thought they could leave the country and start fresh somewhere else, but they weren't even able to leave the state before being hunted down and killed by Guardians."

My mind's only halfway present for most of the time he's speaking. Because those names... Dominic and Jessica...

"Jessica was in the Pine Valley pack," I say, remembering the story Connor told me at Jax's house.

Jessica was the sister of Connor's father's best friend, Xavier. Xavier had a mate, Abigail, although Abigail was part of the Spring Creek pack before mating with Xavier.

"I didn't realize any of the Pine Valley wolves would dare to speak Jessica's name," Tristan says bitterly, reaching for his necklace again. "To them, she's more than dead. She's a traitor, wiped from existence."

Something about his words make me shiver.

"Connor told me about her," I say. "His parents and grandmother died in that cave with her."

The cave where Xavier and Abigail were helping her hide out.

"Only one person walked away from that cave alive," Tristan says, his voice dripping with pure hate. "Jax."

"I'm not the biggest Jax fan, either," I admit.

"Oh?" Tristan raises an eyebrow, waiting for me to elaborate.

"He cut me off from the outside world and asked the witches to fake my death," I say, my chest hollowing with pain as I think about what that must have done to my parents. "I understand that he doesn't want me returning to the human world until I learn how to control my shifting, but the way he went about making that happen..." Anger rages through me as I remember the way he crushed my phone, just like he crushed my parents' hearts. "He was cruel about it. And he became even crueler after realizing I'm an omega."

"You have no earth magic," Tristan says, and I nod. "But you *do* have magic. And on top of your magic, you're unique, smart, and fierce. Anyone with eyes can see it."

His compliment catches me unaware, and gratitude washes over me. I feel that magnetic pull toward him again—the one I felt at the bar—and I want to go over there and comfort him.

But it's not my comfort he needs.

It's my blood.

"Are you doing okay?" I ask.

His weak smile tells me everything I need to know. "I'm doing my best."

"So far, 'your best' means you haven't killed me or drank from me without my consent, so I'll take it," I say.

"I don't want to drink from you, no matter what," he says.

"Well, it doesn't seem like we're going anywhere anytime soon, so you're going to have to." I scoot to the edge of the bed, my heart hammering like crazy. Then I take a deep breath, forcing out the words I never thought I'd say. "And I think you should do it now, before it gets any worse."

Ruby

I hold Tristan's gaze, daring him to contradict me, the air between us crackling with electricity as the weight of my words sinks in.

He doesn't challenge me. Instead, he simply studies me, his gaze contemplative, weighing the implications of my offer.

"Are you sure?" he finally asks.

I meet his gaze steadily. "If I wasn't, I wouldn't have suggested it."

He takes a deep breath and nods. "All right. Thank you."

My face flushes as he keeps his eyes locked on mine, well-aware of the consequences this decision will have on me.

I won't lose myself to the blood bond, I promise myself. *I don't know how, but I won't.*

After all, there's no knowing *how* I'll react. I'm star touched. Blessed by a goddess. This might not affect me the same way it does for everyone else.

I have to hold onto hope that it might be true. Right now, it's the only thing I've got.

"So…" I say, laughing awkwardly. "What do I do?"

Do we do it standing? On the floor? On the bed?

Warmth radiates through me at the thoughts, since they bring forth images of us doing *far* more than his just feeding from me.

At least I know the attraction I feel for him is real, and not because of the blood bond.

"Don't move," he instructs, and then he stands up and cautiously makes his way toward me. He keeps his haunted eyes locked on mine, and I'm entranced, like I'm under some sort of spell.

My heart races as he sits down on the bed next to me, each of his moves slow and calculated. The few inches between us crackle with tension, and as he looks over at me with a mix of gratitude and apprehension, I know down to my bones that this decision was right.

I can resist the blood bond.

I won't accept anything else.

Tristan's gaze drifts to my neck, and I swallow, hard.

"It's going to be okay," he murmurs, and I can't tell if he's talking to me or himself.

I manage a small, brave smile. "Just don't drain me dry, okay?"

He chuckles softly, the sound tinged with sadness. "I promise."

"I trust you." The words slip out before I can stop them, and I'm surprised by how much I mean it.

His golden eyes flicker with surprise, the corners of his mouth curving up in a small, appreciative smile. "I was captivated by you the moment I saw you," he says, and then he adds, "Every word I've spoken, every moment we've shared… it was all real. I won't let you down. I swear it."

It was real for me, too.

The words are on the tip of my tongue, but I hold them back. "I know you won't," I say instead.

His face softens with understanding, and the silence that follows is full of shared secrets and unspoken words.

"I'm ready," I tell him, and then, with careful, measured movements, he reaches out to gently brush my hair away from my neck. His touch is cool against my skin, and I find myself leaning into it, my heart pounding in my chest. I close my eyes, inhaling deeply to steady my racing pulse, bracing myself for the sting of his fangs.

But his lips brush against my skin, and he kisses my neck softly, gently. The unexpected tenderness sends a current of warmth radiating out from the pit of my stomach. My arm winds around his back instinctively, anchoring me in this moment and steadying myself in his embrace.

Then, the sharp prick of his fangs pierces my neck.

It doesn't hurt.

Instead, a strange, almost euphoric sensation washes over me like a wave. His fingers trace their way up my spine, and he cradles the back of my head with his hand, as if I'm made of glass and he's making sure I don't break. It's a touch laced with care, brimming with an intimacy that takes my breath away.

It's the touch of someone who *loves* me.

I've never felt this vulnerable in my life, and what I said to him continues to prove true—I do trust him.

I'm not scared.

Maybe I should be, but I'm not.

As he takes what he needs from me, time slows down. The room around us fades away until all that exists is the connection between us, as if we're bound together by an invisible thread, and I never want this feeling of intimacy with him to end.

My hand drifts to his chest to run my fingers against the cross pendant hanging from his necklace. The metal feels cool against my touch, amplifying the warmth coursing through my veins, and deepening our connection. I'm consumed by him, and I lean closer into him, trusting him with my life.

Eventually, he pulls away, pressing a soft kiss to the puncture wounds before looking down at me. His beautiful golden eyes are no longer haunted, but filled with a deep, intense warmth that sends a jolt of electricity through my body. I feel like I've stripped down every layer of myself, bearing my soul to him, and that he protected it as if it was his own.

My heart's racing at a million miles a minute, and as I stare up into his loving gaze, I find myself completely and utterly speechless.

His hand reaches up to gently cup my face, his thumb tracing my cheekbone as if I'm the most precious person to him in the universe. "Thank you, Ruby," he murmurs, his eyes searching mine. "Are you okay?"

Okay?

The earth just shifted beneath my feet, and my world is spinning faster than ever.

With no idea how to accurately get across what I'm feeling right now, I take a few seconds to center myself.

"Yes," I finally manage, and I move closer to him, drawn to him in a way I've never felt with anyone before. My gaze drifts down to his lips, and I remember how soft they were when they kissed me—how warm and gentle.

I want him to kiss me again.

I close the space between us, my heart pounding in my chest, and his eyes are wide and apprehensive, but hopeful at the same time. We're so close that I can feel his breath on my lips. My hand rises to trace the outline of his jaw, and his eyes flutter shut as he leans into my touch.

Just as our lips are about to meet, I pull back.

This is the blood bond, I remind myself. *It's not real. It's not me.*

Or is it? I loved kissing him at the bar. I've been drawn to him the entire time we've been in this cell together. His drinking from me just now might have intensified those emotions, but they were already there before that.

Still, I can't let this happen.

So I pull back, and disappointment flickers in his eyes, now so dilated that they're nearly swallowed by darkness.

"Thank you," I whisper, my throat still tingling on the spot where his fangs pierced my skin. "For not killing me."

Instead of being upset, he smiles. A soft, genuine smile that sends a jolt of warmth through my chest. "You don't have to thank me for that," he murmurs, his fingers lingering in my hair, tracing soothing circles on the nape of my neck. "I could never hurt you, Ruby."

"I know," I somehow manage to say.

Suddenly, a voice cuts through our moment.

Lindsay.

"It feels good, doesn't it?" she asks, her voice dreamy. "Really, really good."

She must have woken up sometime while Tristan was feeding from me. Her eyes, distant and glazed, make me think she's lost in memories of Benjamin.

How many times has he fed from her?

Tristan recovers quickly, dropping his hand from my hair and moving back slightly.

The gap between us feels empty and cold.

"It did," I admit, unable to look at Tristan as I speak.

"Letting him feed before he lost control was a smart move," Lindsay continues. "I was wondering how long it would be before you gave in."

Of course she was. She'd kept her opinions to herself during all of this, but she was watching and listening to Tristan and me the entire time.

"Aren't you tired?" she asks, and I remember how hard she crashed after Benjamin fed from her.

"Not really." I shrug, then look to Tristan for an explanation.

"All supernaturals have fast healing," he says. "Your body has probably already replenished the blood you lost."

"But yours didn't do that after Hazel stabbed you," I point out.

"As a vampire, I lack the ability to produce my own blood," he says. "The blood coursing through my veins is all borrowed."

And now it's my blood that fills him.

The realization sends a thrill through me, binding me to him in a way I never thought possible. And, as I continue studying him, his eyes meet mine again.

No longer haunted, but full of desire.

Another wave of heat rushes through me.

Oh my God. If I don't get a handle on my emotions, I'm going to lose what little control I apparently have left.

I get up and sit at the table chair, trying to ignore the coldness I feel with each step I take away from Tristan.

"So," I turn to Lindsay, forcing myself to sound casual. "Tell me more about Ned."

She'd started talking about her boyfriend the other day, but we didn't speak much after Tristan was thrown into my cell.

"Ned…" She blinks rapidly, as if trying to grasp a fleeting memory.

"Your boyfriend?"

"Right. Of course." She gives me a strained smile, and I can tell that my question troubled her. "He's a mechanic," she starts. "We've been together for five years, and plan on getting engaged soon…"

I continue listening, but my mind is only halfway there.

Because blood bonding with Benjamin is clouding her memories of Ned, to the point where it seems like she's no longer thinking about him at all. It's unsettling.

And I can't help but wish for the same to happen with my feelings for Connor.

Ruby

I spend the rest of the day reading, trying to keep my distance from Tristan. Not because I want to lessen the temptation of my blood, but because I'm trying to reduce my own temptation to go back over to him and finish what we started with that almost-kiss.

Jason continues to brood about Gwen every moment she isn't there with him. When she does go to feed on him, it's clear from their moans, gasps of pleasure, and variety of other sounds that there's far more happening in that cell than just feeding.

Benjamin continues resisting Lindsay's kiss, and her frustration is more than evident. She spends quite a bit of time in bed, curled under the covers as she cries herself dry. But she doesn't want to talk about it, and I don't push her.

As the hours wear on, I find myself growing more and more tired. My eyelids feel heavy, the words on the pages blur, and I reluctantly close the book, marking my spot.

"I'm going to bed," I say, getting up to grab the fresh pajamas that the witch who regularly makes our deliveries—Thalia—left with my dinner.

Tristan's gaze meets mine, his eyes glowing softly in the dim light. "Sleep well, Ruby," he says, his attention quickly returning to his own book. He's seated on the cold floor, his back resting against the wall, and I can't imagine it's comfortable.

I head to the bathroom to get ready, and when I emerge, he's in the same place, still engrossed in his book.

My gaze drifts to the bed, then back to him.

"Are you tired?" I ask hesitantly.

He stops reading to turn his gaze up to look at me, and my breath hitches at the intensity burning in his eyes.

"Not yet," he says simply.

I glance back over at the bed.

I should offer. He shouldn't have to sleep on the floor for another night in a row. Sure, there's a rug, but it's thin and worn, offering no padding at all.

"Do you want the bed…" I ask, pointing awkwardly toward it.

His lips twitch into a half-smile. "Are you offering to share?"

"No," I say, stumbling over the word. "I can sleep on the floor."

"You absolutely will not." He leaves no room for argument, and I press my lips together, knowing better than to try.

Because there it is, that determination, that fierce protectiveness that makes me feel safe and cherished. My heart lurches in my chest, and I swallow hard, taking a shaky breath.

I want to make him feel as cared for as he does for me.

"You can share it," I say, barely realizing what I'm saying until the words are out of my mouth. "The bed. With me."

His eyebrows rise in surprise. "Are you sure?"

That question again. It seems to be his favorite recently.

But he's already fed on me. Sharing a bed can't possibly be any more intimate than when he pressed his lips to my neck and let my blood flow out of my body and into his.

"We've already come this far." I shrug, trying to sound casual. "Might as well add this to the list of things we've done to break the rules today."

His rich laughter fills the room, a warm, soothing sound that chases away the echoes of hesitation. "You do make rule-breaking so incredibly tempting," he says, making my cheeks heat even more.

"It's apparently a new habit of mine that I developed after coming to Pine Valley," I say, trying to keep the mood light. Then I cautiously make my way toward the bed, my breaths feeling heavier as I pull on the covers and slip beneath them, nestling myself as close to the wall as possible.

I've never shared a bed before. Not with a man… not with *anyone.*

And this bed isn't exactly large.

He rises from the floor, the fluidity of his movement a stark reminder of his vampiric nature. "Just to clarify," he says, his voice a velvet caress that sends shivers down my spine. "We're sharing a bed, not breaking it, right?"

My breath catches, my heart pounding in my chest.

He did *not* just say that.

"Relax," he says, although the images of Tristan and I entangled on the bed are far too ingrained in my mind for me to relax. "I was joking. I'll be sure to stay as far on my side as possible."

"Cool," I manage, my words stilted. "Thanks."

With a small smile playing on his lips, he gets up to grab his pajamas and get ready for bed.

I stare up at the ceiling, waiting, my body a bundle of nerves. Hopefully this doesn't turn out to be a huge mistake, but I don't think it will be.

It isn't long until he returns. I can barely bring myself to look at him as he joins me on the bed and flicks off the light. The room is plunged into darkness, and I feel him slide under the covers, making sure to keep a respectful distance between us.

I face the wall, my heart thundering in my chest.

And he has supernatural hearing. He can hear it.

He knows *exactly* the effect he has on me.

I do my best to breathe steadier and calm my heartbeat. And, as I do, I hear something I didn't expect.

His heart is racing as well.

I need to relax. Be still. Pretend I have no idea that he's being driven just as crazy as I am.

I can do this.

As I lie there, memories of our almost-kiss loop in my mind. The thought of his lips against mine only makes my heart race faster, and I clench my hands into fists, trying to push away the urge to turn towards him. It would be so easy to curl into his body, to have him wrap his arms around me, to hold me and make me feel safe in this dark, stifling cell.

But I resist.

"Goodnight, Ruby," he murmurs, his voice barely above a whisper.

"Goodnight," I reply, my voice shaky, and then I close my eyes, the warmth of Tristan's body somehow making me feel safe enough to drift off to a deep sleep.

Ruby

I GRADUALLY COME to the next morning, and the events from the night before hit me like a freight train.

The almost-kiss with Tristan. The way my heart had pounded in my chest, my nerves singing with anticipation. The disappointment in his eyes when I pulled back.

His getting into bed with me after I *offered* to share it.

I hear his breathing next to me, soft and steady.

He kept a respectable amount of distance between us all night. I had a feeling he would, and the fact that he didn't make any moves on me makes me trust him even more.

I roll over, unable to resist the pull at my chest to see what he looks like sleeping beside me.

He's so devastatingly gorgeous. Something about him urges me closer, tempting me to close the space between us and nestle myself in his arms until the world disappears around us like it did while he fed from me.

Before I can, he stirs, his eyelashes fluttering against his cheeks before his eyes slowly open. He blinks a few times before his gaze lands on me, a soft smile tugging at his lips.

"Morning, Ruby," he murmurs, his voice thick with sleep.

As he speaks, my mind replays the moment from last night. Our faces inching closer, the warmth of his breath against my skin... and then the sharp way I pulled back.

Regret tugs at my chest.

"Morning," I reply. "Thanks for not killing me yesterday."

Tristan's smile fades, replaced by a look of intense sincerity. "I never want to hurt you. I promise," he says softly, his golden eyes searching mine. "I'd never forgive myself if I did."

I believe him.

And I can't help but compare this moment to the one with Connor a few days ago when he told me he'd never choose me. The pain Connor's words caused me were the opposite of what I've been hearing from Tristan, and I can't deny that being around Tristan makes me feel... loved.

Which is crazy. He can't love me after only a few days of knowing. But still... he and I are getting off on a much better start than I did with Connor, minus how he lied about not being human, and the whole "almost killing me" part.

My gaze drifts to Tristan's necklace, its garnet centerpiece twinkling in the dim light. I can't imagine him without it. It's mesmerizing, the intricate carving begging to be touched.

But I resist.

"What's on your mind?" he asks, and his eyes search my face, pulling my attention away from his necklace and back to him.

I roll over and stare up at the ceiling, unable to figure out where to start.

"You heard what Hazel said," I begin. "About Connor—my mate—being engaged."

"I did." His voice gives away no emotion one way or another.

"He never wanted me," I say. "Not like..."

Not like you do.

The words hang in the air, unspoken but understood.

"I'm sorry," he says simply. "He has no idea what he's missing out on."

"Thanks," I say, trying to shake it off. "Anyway, I'm going to freshen up. I trust you'll still be here when I get back?" I smile at him, somehow playful despite the serious turn our conversation had taken.

"I *guess* I'll stick around," he teases. "Since you asked so nicely and all."

I roll my eyes, and instead of crawling over him, I make my way to the end of the bed and slip off.

As I freshen up, I examine my neck for any traces of yesterday's bite. There's nothing there. It's as if it never happened at all.

Eventually, I focus on my now-brown eyes, and a crazy thought pops into my mind.

Should I tell him that my eyes changed color on the night I received my magic?

Maybe he has an idea what happened.

But I quickly shake myself out of it. The goddess who star touched me specifically instructed me to tell no one. And, despite how close I'm starting to feel to Tristan, I know intrinsically that I need to listen to her.

So, I open the door and head back into the cell, finding Tristan on the bed with a book in his hands.

He looks up and smiles when he sees me, his eyes lighting up as if we weren't together only a few minutes ago.

"Miss me?" I ask, trying to keep my tone light.

"You have no idea," he says. "The minutes you were gone were pure agony."

I can't help but smile more.

"Your company isn't turning out to be as awful as I thought it would," I say, and then I head to the table, tracing my fingers across its smooth surface. There's nothing on it right now—Thalia takes the uneaten sandwiches away each day so they don't rot—but I know she'll be back soon.

Eventually, I'm sure Hazel will come down to check on us instead, to see how things are progressing between me and Tristan.

And now that I'm thinking about Hazel again...

"The Blade of Erebus," I start, and Tristan sits straighter, dropping the book onto his lap. "What does it do?"

"I'm bound to an oath to the Blood Coven to not say too much," he says with a hint of regret. "But I can tell you this: the blade is ancient. Powerful. In the hands of a witch as strong as Hazel, it can do the unthinkable."

Chills run up my spine at the word.

Unthinkable.

It's such an evasive term, vague and menacing all at once.

Can the blade warp time? Steal magic? Control the minds and bodies of others?

The final idea is somehow the most terrifying of them all.

"So, this 'unthinkable' thing the blade can do is why you, Benjamin, and Gwen joined forces with Hazel?" I guess.

"Correct," he says. "The vampires have been hunted and controlled by the witches for centuries, and the laws of the witches are designed so they can stay in power. It's time for a regime change. Hazel and the rest of the Blood Coven want to help us make that happen."

"What's in it for them?"

Given what he said, it doesn't sound like the witches would want to work with vampires, let alone help them.

"More power than they ever dreamed possible," he says, as cryptic as ever.

Suddenly, he sets the book aside and rises from the bed. He crosses the small space separating us and slides gracefully on the table to sit on top of it, taking my hands in his and gazing down at me as if he's begging me to trust him.

His touch grounds me amidst the whirlwind of my thoughts.

"They want you to be part of it," he says, firm and steady. "*I* want you to be part of it."

His eyes blaze with sincerity, and my heart leaps at the thought of having someone on my side in this crazy supernatural world who wants me there. Of being part of a group that wants me, instead of one that deems me as less than them and shames me, like how I was treated by Jax and the Pine Valley pack.

I don't want Tristan's offer to be tempting.

Yet… it is.

A ghost of a smile crosses his lips, and I can't help but wonder if he knows exactly what I'm thinking. Because something undeniable connects us together, and no matter how hard I try to fight it, there's no making it disappear.

I suddenly realize that I'm doing exactly what I promised myself I *wouldn't* do.

I'm softening to him.

The basement door opening breaks us out of the moment, and we turn to see Hazel walking downstairs with a pack full of water and food.

I pull my hands out of Tristan's, but we're still sitting incriminatingly close to each other when she's near enough to see us. I scoot my chair away from the table, but I know it's too late.

"I see you two are getting comfortable with each other." A knowing smile plays on her lips, and she focuses on Tristan. "You look healthier this morning. Much more… satisfied."

"He fed on her," Lindsay chimes in, and I glare at her. She's just getting out of bed, and she shrugs in apology, but she doesn't look like she feels all that bad about it.

"Good," Hazel says, refocusing on the two of us. "Who convinced whom?"

"It was me." I raise my chin, determined to stay strong and not let her get to me. "He didn't want to do it. He values your laws too much. Which you apparently don't, since we wouldn't be locked in here otherwise."

"Those laws won't apply to us soon." She shrugs it off, unconcerned. "But do *you* want to eat? Tristan's looking better, but you look like you could use some nourishment. I brought something hot this morning. Meatball subs."

"Who eats meatball subs for breakfast?" I ask, even though my stomach *does* rumble at the sound of it.

"Who decided that breakfast has to have a totally different menu than all other meals?" she counters, and then she drops the pack on the floor and pulls out a bottle of water and a hot, footlong sub from a familiar fast-food chain. She opens the cell door again, the magical barrier glimmering when she slides the water and food through, taking extra caution to not put any part of *herself* at risk. "Enjoy."

She glances over at Lindsay and Jason's cell, and continues, "Benjamin and Gwen will be down soon with your meals. I'm sure you're missing them deeply."

Then, without another word, she heads down the hall and up the stairs, the door closing behind her as she leaves before I can ask any questions.

Connor

Magic thrums off the forest floor as I face off against Autumn. Her eyes glint with excitement, and the wind blows her red hair around her, making her look like the supernatural force she is. We move in a calculated dance, two predators circling and ready to pounce.

The others our age in the pack who are training to be Guardians—Brandon, Tyler, Thomas, and Nicole—watch eagerly from the sidelines. They've all had their turns tonight—against me, and against each other.

I took each of them down without any trouble.

Now, it's time for the showdown I've been waiting for since the start of training today.

"Ready?" I call out, my voice echoing through the stillness.

In response, the ground beneath my feet trembles. A distinct signature of Autumn's earth magic.

"I'm always ready."

Her voice is a challenge, a dare. She holds her hands up, palms out, and a barrage of hardened soil erupts from the earth and flies straight at me.

I'm already braced for the attack, my earth magic swirling inside my veins. I latch onto the dirt she's aimed toward me, stop it mid-air, and let it fall to the ground between us.

A grin tugs at my lips. "You're going to have to try harder than that."

"Challenge accepted."

The forest floor rumbles again, but my feet are rooted to the earth. She's not going to knock me over anytime soon.

With a wicked grin, I retaliate, yanking the dirt from under her feet as if tugging a rug out from under her.

She stumbles, but catches herself before falling.

Sparring like this is tricky. We're not actually trying to harm each other—thus why we're aiming dirt at each other instead of sharp stones.

The goal is to get the other person on their back.

Which is exactly where I like Autumn to be.

We continue like this for a few more minutes, each trying to use the earth in various ways to knock the other over. Autumn's a force to be reckoned with, and I love watching her use her magic. However, we can anticipate each other's moves—a byproduct of having sparred many times before—and it's more of a choreographed dance than anything else.

Eventually, she calls upon the rocks at her feet and brings them up in an elegant spiral around her body. It's one of her signature moves, making her look like a goddess in the center of a storm, and she knows how much it riles me up to see her power on display like this.

"Show off," I say, and I prowl around her, ready to pounce the moment she lets her guard down.

"You know you love it." She gives me a devilish grin, then lets the rocks fall back down to her feet.

Game on.

I pounce, fur sprouting from my skin as I shift into my wolf form—a large, muscular creature with a sleek black coat.

Autumn, always quick to react, leaps aside with the grace of a ballerina.

In a fluid transformation that takes my breath away every time, she too shifts into her wolf form—majestic and lithe, with fiery fur that matches her hair. She's beautiful, as both a human and a wolf.

The two of us together are unstoppable.

But right now, we're fighting against each other—not together.

So, we dart and weave around each other, our movements a blur in the moonless night. Her every move is a challenge, a dare to catch her. She even gives me a playful nip two times, while still managing to evade my capture.

She's a tease, and I love her for it.

Getting more riled up by the second, I narrow my eyes at her and go in for the final pounce.

Just as I launch myself at her, she tries to do the same.

We crash together in mid-air.

Where she's lithe and graceful, I'm brute force. My jump overpowers hers, and I pin her to the ground, leaving her underbelly exposed and vulnerable.

Victory.

With the fight over, we shift back into human forms. She's sprawled beneath me, her chest heaving, her skin glowing with the thrill of the fight. We stare deep into each other's eyes, the thick tension between us exciting me even more, and a wave of desire passes through me.

If the others weren't standing around as onlookers… well, let's just say that Autumn and I wouldn't be wearing our training gear for much longer.

As it is, I lower myself further down and crush my lips to hers. But only for a second.

We are, after all, being watched.

I pause while pulling away, allowing my nose to nuzzle hers. "We're continuing this later tonight," I promise, and then I stand, holding my hand out to help her up.

Another wave of love rushes through me as I drink in the beautiful, brilliant woman who's going to be my wife. I glance at her hand—her finger is still bare as the ring gets sized—but it's been over a week since the proposal.

The magic of this moment leaves me not wanting to wait another second to share the news.

And so, I wrap my arm around her waist, pull her close, and turn to face the others.

Nicole's watching us knowingly, her light blonde hair glinting under the stars. Tyler and Thomas are careful and reserved. Brandon, however, has a smirk pasted on his face, and I suspect he knows what's coming.

"Autumn and I are engaged," I tell them, my voice strong and sure in the crisp night air. "I thought the four of you should know first."

At first, silence.

Then Tyler, Thomas, and Nicole tell us various versions of congratulations.

"When's the wedding?" Brandon asks, always the one to get straight to the point.

His question catches me off-guard. Mainly because it's a good one, and one I haven't given much thought to yet.

I glance at Autumn, her eyes shimmering with love and anticipation, and I know she'll do whatever I command.

As she should, since I'm her alpha.

I swallow, then look back to the others.

"Two weeks from now," I decide. "When the moon is full."

"Before you have a chance to mate?" Nicole asks, her confusion overpowering her hesitance to question her leader.

My focus, however, is only on one word she said.

Mate.

My chest hollows in guilt at the sound of it.

I haven't thought much about Ruby this past week. It's been a huge relief, and I assume it's because with her not around, the mate bond is weakening.

I don't want or need her shiny brown hair, warm eyes, and perfectly pouty lips in my life, distracting me from my planned future. She's been a menace to me since her arrival, and it's been good for me to have her away from pack territory.

Autumn's tense beside me, and I know she's thinking about Ruby as well.

There's still time to take this back. My wolf's thought is unwelcome in my mind. *Your previous plans are irrelevant. Autumn will never be our true mate. She's our past. Ruby is our future.*

Luckily, it's a new moon, so quieting my wolf's voice is no problem. Especially because the bond with Ruby is weakening. My wolf knows it, and I suspect he's slightly grateful for it, too.

It'll be easier this way. Better. It already *has* been easier this past week, and I believe that the longer Ruby and I remain separated, the more the pain will subside until it dwindles down to practically nothing.

Meanwhile, the others remain silent while I wrangle with my thoughts.

I stand strong and firm. "Autumn is my future wife," I say, my eyes scanning over each of them, daring them to talk back to me again. "We'll marry when I decide we'll marry. And that's going to be on the next full moon."

In the following silence, the tension wraps around us like a shroud, whispering doubts and questions.

Thankfully, they know better than to press me further.

"Well then, congratulations, Connor," Brandon says, the first to break the silence. "You too, Autumn."

From the careful, calculated way he watches me, I can't help but get the feeling that he knows the truth about what's going on here. After all, he saw my interaction with Ruby at the party. He knows how protective I became over her. How I all but claimed her as mine.

I hold his gaze until he lowers his eyes, reminding him of his place in the pack. He—and the others—submit to *me*.

Nicole and Tyler echo Brandon's sentiment, their words sincere but their eyes guarded. Thomas just nods, his expression unreadable.

"Thank you," I say simply, having no need to explain myself further.

Autumn gives me a grateful look, her fingers squeezing mine. She's my rock, my anchor, the one constant in my ever-changing world. She's loyal to me, and I won't let anything come between us.

Not even the call of a mate bond.

I pull her closer, and she leans into me, her body fitting perfectly against mine.

"I love you," she tells me, although as she says it, I swear there's a hint of guilt in her eyes.

My chest hollows at the obvious reason why. She knows she isn't my mate, and that she never will be.

I refuse to ever let her doubt herself.

"And I love you," I reply, my words a solemn vow. "Always."

I kiss her again, and when I look down at her smiling face afterward, I know I've made the right decision. Autumn is my future. She always has been, and she always will be.

"So…" Brandon says, breaking the silence. "How about a run to celebrate?"

"That's a great idea," I say, mainly because I don't want to continue this conversation, and a run is the perfect way to do that.

I give Autumn a mischievous smile, and she knows me well enough to know *exactly* what I'm thinking.

And so, keeping our hands clasped together, we turn around and leap into the air, shifting into our wolf forms at the exact same second.

The others shift behind us, Autumn and I at the head of the pack as we lead them into the forest, our howls ringing through the mountain air as we become one with the night.

In two weeks, this beautiful woman will be my wife.

And I refuse to let anything—not even my fated mate—come between us.

Ruby

Nine days.

That's how long Tristan and I have been in this cell together.

He's able to safely go two days without feeding, which means he drank from me this morning. Somehow, through sheer willpower, I've kept myself from kissing him. Sharing the bed makes it tougher, especially since a few days ago, I gave up on trying to keep myself from snuggling with him.

It feels so good to be held and cared for. With his arms around me each night, I feel so *safe*. The fact that he's been so respectful of my boundaries makes me trust him even more.

Some nights, the temptation feels like it's going to rip me apart. But I have no idea if this feeling of safety is because it's what I truly feel, or if it's the blood bond taking over.

Plus, Lindsay is still there in the cell across from us. If Tristan and I ever kiss again— and, as much as I hate it, the thought sends butterflies flapping like crazy in my stomach —I want the moment to be private.

Thalia continues to regularly give me, Lindsay, and Jason our meals. She always wears her brown hair in a loose wave down her back, and while she's pretty, it's in more of a soft way. She also doesn't talk much. But from what I've learned from Tristan, she has a decent amount of magic. Not as much as Hazel, but no one would ever describe her as weak.

I want to like her.

But I liked Hazel, and look how *that* turned out.

As for the drugged food, I eventually had to make a choice. The first option was to hold out and be so physically weak that I could barely get out of bed each day. The second was to eat it to give myself energy, accepting the fact that it's repressing my magic.

I chose the second option. Because if we ever manage to get out of here, I'm not going to do anyone any good if I can't walk up the stairs without passing out.

And I long past got over the fact that they're consistently giving me meat, even though before coming here, I was a vegetarian. The fact of the matter is that my wolf needs meat to survive.

I will *always* choose to survive.

I finish eating lunch—a hot, gooey, delicious cheeseburger—and I place the plate next to the bars of the cell, where Thalia will eventually come to take it away.

"You're really not hungry at all?" I ask Tristan, who's currently lounging on his favorite place—the bed. "For actual food?"

Even though we've had this conversation before, I can't wrap my mind around the mechanics of it.

"Not one bit," he says, his eyes dilating a bit when he looks at me. "Food tastes good, and I enjoy it greatly, but I have all I need to survive right here."

Because he has *me*.

My cheeks flush, and I take a sip of water to cool down.

"I still feel bad whenever I eat and you just sit there watching me," I say.

Instead of responding, he lifts his hand and does a little wave with his fingers, pointing them in the general direction of the book placed on the nightstand. The wind he creates blows the cover open, and the pages follow, flipping quickly until the book is halfway open.

Then, to prove his point further, he aims some of his magic at the dim light hanging from the ceiling. It swings back and forth like a pendulum, as if there's a ghost in the room with us. I feel the cool breeze on my cheeks, like a gentle caress, and the moment feels strangely intimate.

"You'd rather my magic be suppressed as well?" He raises an eyebrow, already well-aware of my answer.

"You know I don't," I say.

"Good," he says, and he adjusts himself on the bed, making himself more comfortable. "We've read a lot today. Tell me a story."

"What type of story?"

"The craziest thing that happened to you in college."

This is how our days have gone recently. Reading, and talking. Sometimes with Lindsay or Jason, but most of the time with just the two of us. Tristan's a good conversationalist, when I'm not actively trying to ignore him.

Which I haven't done since the first night he drank from me.

"Let's see," I say, wracking my mind for something I haven't told him yet. "There was that one time when Luna and I ran through the halls of our dorm naked."

"Oh?" His eyes scan my body, as if he's mentally undressing me, and my breath catches in my chest at the sudden intensity of his gaze.

I glance away and take another sip of my water.

"It wasn't on purpose," I say quickly, rushing to continue before he gets any ideas about me that aren't true. "The girls' bathroom was broken for a bit, so Luna and I decided to risk it and shower in the guys' bathroom. We thought that with the two of us there together, we'd be safe from any pranks they might try to pull."

"Then you severely underestimated the determination of college-aged boys," Tristan finishes for me, a smirk playing on his lips.

"Or overestimated their maturity," I reply rolling my eyes. There's a pause, and then I admit, "But yes, you're right. Two of them stole our towels *and* our clothes. I had no idea what to do, but Luna's always quick on her feet. She pulled both of our shower curtains down, and we ran back to our room with them wrapped around us like togas, screaming and laughing the entire time."

"That's one way to meet your neighbors," he says, smiling softly. It's a smile that reaches his eyes and warms his entire face, and I can't help but return it.

"It happened the first week of school. It was mortifying, but I guess it's more of a fond memory now. It was the moment Luna and I became best friends."

I shrug and glance away, the sadness hitting me all at once.

The air between us shifts, becoming charged and heavy.

"You okay?" Tristan asks.

"I just can't believe that Luna and my parents think I'm dead."

"I'm sorry," he says. "I know it's hard. Especially right now."

"It is," I say, since we've had enough conversations in this cell that I know he's all too familiar with the pain I'm feeling.

On the night they were turned, at the beginning of the twentieth century, Tristan, Dominic, and Benjamin were at an underground bar. They got trapped in a terrible fire. Gwen was there, and she dragged them into a back room and told them that the fire had spread too severely. There was no getting out of there alive—at least not for humans. They'd die of smoke inhalation before they could get far.

Then she quickly told them about the existence of vampires, and that she could either turn them, or they'd die.

They chose to survive.

Then they made the hard choice to let everyone they loved think they hadn't made it out, to protect them from the supernatural world.

It was the noble thing to do.

I don't think I'd have had the strength to do the same.

"What are you thinking about?" Tristan asks, yanking me out of my thoughts.

"You," I reply, the truth coming out before I can stop it. "How much I respect the decision you made after you were turned."

"If I could go back and do it again, I don't think I'd do the same thing," he says, his confession taking me by surprise. "Not after experiencing the pain I did after Dominic was killed. Nothing's worse than losing someone you love. Absolutely *nothing*. I wouldn't put my family through that again."

He's so adamant when he talks, and I can feel in the air how much love this man has inside himself to give. Tristan's the type of person who keeps his distance from most people, but when he loves, he loves fiercely.

And he loves me.

He hasn't said it, but I know it's true. I sense it with everything he does—the sound of his voice when he talks to me, warm and inviting, and the adoration in his eyes when he looks at me, as if something about me lights up the darkness he harbors deep inside his soul.

These are things I've experienced from him, first-hand, here in this cell. I'm not seeing him this way because of the blood bond. I'm seeing him this way because it's the person he's consistently shown me he is this past week we've been locked in here together.

I have a sudden urge to go over to the bed, sit down next to him, and snuggle up against him.

It's so incredibly tempting.

Why am I resisting? It's the same thing we do when we're sleeping. Is it really all that different to be so close to him during the day than at night?

Decision made, I get up from the chair and walk over him, not saying a word.

His breathing slows, and he simply watches me with those mesmerizing golden eyes of his, waiting to see what I do next.

As I settle into the bed next to him, he wraps an arm around me, pulling me close. His body is familiar and warm, and it's so incredibly easy to sink into his embrace. His heart beats steadily against my ear, a comforting rhythm that lulls my worries away, if only for a moment.

Coming over here was the right decision. I have zero doubts about it.

"Thank you," I whisper, not entirely sure why I'm thanking him. For his company, for his understanding, for his warmth?

Probably for all of it.

He doesn't say anything—he just tightens his grip around me. We stay like that for a while, the silence between us heavy with unsaid words and shared fears, but it's a comforting silence. One that speaks of understanding and solidarity.

And I've never felt this close to anyone in my entire life.

Ruby

Slowly, I tilt my head up to look at him. His gaze is intense, sending a shiver down my spine and making my heart pound faster.

Because he's looking at me with *love*. Pure, unfiltered love.

I want to kiss him. No—I want *him* to kiss *me*.

My eyes dart across the hallway, catching sight of Lindsay engrossed in her book. From her position, she can definitely peek over the pages to watch me and Tristan. I'm sure she's been doing just that.

There's not much else to do in this place.

But is it really so horrible if she sees me with Tristan? I've seen her throw herself at Benjamin every day we've been here. She's not going to judge me for kissing a vampire.

As for Jason, his cell is at an angle where he can't see to the back of mine, where Tristan and I are sitting on the bed.

And it's not like kissing Tristan is something I haven't done before.

I turn my gaze back to Tristan's. There's so much uncertainty in his eyes, along with vulnerability, as if he's torn about what to do next.

That makes two of us.

Suddenly, the sound of footsteps approaching our cell disrupts the silence.

I break away from Tristan, the moment shattered.

It doesn't make sense. It's too early for Thalia to come down to clear our lunch plates and give us dinner.

Tristan's expression mirrors my confusion, his eyes clouded with uncertainty.

The footsteps grow louder, echoing through the hall. But it's not just one person I hear. It's two.

They get closer and stop in front of my cell.

It's Hazel. She's accompanied by a man I've never seen before—tall and broad-shouldered, with a commanding presence. His eyes are a piercing ice blue, and his dark hair is cropped short.

There's an air of authority and danger about him, sending every nerve in my body on edge.

This feeling… it's familiar. It's the same instinctual alertness I felt around Jax.

I know deep in my gut that this man is an alpha wolf shifter.

I attempt to hold his gaze, but it feels like an army of ants is burrowing beneath my skin, a relentless itch that's impossible to ignore. Finally, the discomfort becomes too intense, and I'm compelled to glance down at the cold stone floor.

That uncomfortable feeling vanishes, the relief washing over me stronger than my irritation at myself for the involuntary submission.

"I didn't mean to interrupt," Hazel says, and when I look back up at her and the man, I want to rip his smirk right off his face. "I wanted to introduce you to Riven, the alpha of the Spring Creek pack."

"Ruby," he drawls, his condescending tone making me tense up further. "I've heard so much about you."

"I hope the stories were good," I say, trying to sound as nonchalant as possible. "I'd hate to think I've been boring you."

Riven's smirk widens. "I assure you—you're far too unique to be boring."

"So I've heard," I say, and then I turn my attention back to Hazel, not wanting to be a source of amusement for Riven for a moment longer. "What do you want?"

"Firstly, I wanted to check on you to see how you've been holding up," she says, and then she waits for me to respond, sounding annoyingly like she cares.

"You locked me in a cell with a vampire to force me to be his only food source, and you've been drugging everything I eat to repress my magic," I say. "How do you *think* I'm doing?"

"Are you still heartbroken?" She tilts her head slightly, curious.

"What?" I say to her, and then I glance at Tristan, since he's hardly been breaking my heart these past few days. If anything, he's been making his way into it, becoming the only light I have in this dark, dreary place.

"I'm not talking about Tristan," she says. "I'm talking about Connor. Your mate."

"Oh." I open my mouth, then close it, realization flooding my veins.

I haven't thought about Connor in a while. I did for the first few days I was locked up here, but the more time I've been spending with Tristan, the more he's been the one consuming my thoughts—and my heart.

He hasn't just been here for me physically, but emotionally as well. I've been enjoying my time with him.

It's the blood bond, I think, but deep down, I know it's more than that. Because after this past week together, I know Tristan far better than I've ever known Connor. The time we've had together is real.

It counts. A lot, actually.

From the way Hazel's eyes light up with approval, it's clear that she knows exactly what I'm thinking. "You trust each other," she says, as if she's stating a fact instead of asking a question.

"Yes." The word escapes my lips involuntarily, and I don't take it back. Because it's a truth that's been growing inside me, like a flame flickering to life from a single spark, and taking it back would be a blatant lie.

Tristan reaches for my hand and gives it an assuring squeeze.

The single motion speaks volumes.

My admission means everything to him. And, in that moment, a silent understanding passes between us, a connection deeper than words.

He loves me. I have zero doubts about it. But I release his hand, not wanting to look dependent on him in front of Hazel and Riven.

Because I'm *not* dependent on him. Just like I'm not dependent on Connor, or on anyone except for myself.

Hazel doesn't reply. Instead, she looks to Riven, giving him a silent command with a single glance.

Riven sniffs the air, a deep, deliberate inhale, his eyebrows furrowing in concentration. Then he exhales slowly, a small smirk playing at the corners of his lips.

"She's telling the truth," he declares, crossing his arms over his broad chest.

Approval washes over Hazel's face, and she gives me a genuine smile.

"Good," she says. "I knew the two of you would get along. I told you so before bringing you to that bar."

"I'd say you have a good sense of character… except for the fact that you're with Benjamin." I glance at Lindsay after saying it, thinking about how Hazels boyfriend has been toying with her this past week.

Hazel doesn't so much as flinch. "Doesn't it feel good to not be brooding over Connor anymore?" she continues, as if I didn't say a word against her boyfriend. "To care about someone who wants you in return?"

I hold her gaze, torn. Because she's right. She knows it, I know it, and there's no point in denying it.

My wolf remains dormant, repressed due to the drugged food.

"Yes," I finally admit. "And, if I had it my way, I'd get rid of the mate bond forever."

Another truth.

She glances to Riven again, who nods in confirmation that I'm not lying, and then looks back to me with the most approval she has since the day we met.

"I'm happy to tell you that we can help you with that," she says. "But first, you'll have to join us."

Ruby

"I assume that by 'us,' you mean the Blood Coven?" I ask, my voice echoing in the dimly lit chamber.

"I do," Hazel confirms.

"And why, exactly, do you think I'd ever be able to trust you?"

She sizes me up, then continues, "You can trust us. But many times, it's more important to consider who you can't trust rather than who you can."

"You mean not being able to trust someone who drugged me and threw me in a basement cell with a hungry vampire? And who's been doing the same to humans?"

"I apologized for that many times," Hazel says with a frown. "I don't know how else I can say I'm sorry."

"If you're truly sorry, then you'll let me out of here," I say.

"So you can run back to Pine Valley and tell them everything?"

I take a moment to think about it. Because the only person I *can* trust—from the limited selection of those who don't think I'm dead—is Tristan. And he's right here, with me.

On instinct, I step closer to him, my arm brushing his.

A jolt of electricity surges through me at the contact, and my breath catches in my throat.

I don't want to leave him. He's the only person in the supernatural world who's on my side and has my back no matter what. Walking away from him would be foolish, even self-destructive.

And just the thought of it makes my heart ache.

"I don't know where I'd go," I admit, unable to look Hazel in the eyes. I avoid Riven's gaze as well, who's continuing to stand by her side like a loyal guard dog.

Which, I suppose, is exactly what shifters are to witches.

"Well, you can't go back to Pine Valley," she says. "Your mate rejected you. His girlfriend—wait, his *fiancée*—hates you. Jax doesn't consider you a pack member, because your illusion magic makes you different. You have no place with them."

"And you think I have a place here?" I ask. "With you?"

"I know you do," she says, determination burning in her eyes. "If you join us, we'll protect you. You'll be able to better protect yourself, too."

There's a smugness to her smile, like she's goading me. And I'm too curious about what she's talking about to resist learning more.

"What do you mean by that?" I ask, knowingly falling right into her trap.

"I mean that the Blood Coven is the most powerful coven in the world," she says. "Soon, we'll be even more powerful. If you join us, not only will we keep you safe, but you'll share in that power, too."

"Is that why you joined them?" I ask. "Power?"

"Power, and love," she says. "Two of the most important things in the world. But you already know that. You know what it feels like to be deemed lesser—to be deemed an *omega*. And you know what love feels like—both the pain of it, and the joy of it."

Her implication is clear.

Connor is the pain.

Tristan is the joy.

And the most frustrating thing about everything she's saying is that she isn't wrong.

As I stand there, trying to process it all, Tristan links his pinkie finger with mine. It's a small gesture, but it grounds me in a way I desperately need.

"She's telling the truth," he murmurs, his cool breath against my ear making me grow warm with desire.

I swallow, feeling like I'm being pulled in countless directions, each of them threatening to rip me apart.

"Look at me, Ruby," he says, and I obey without hesitation. His golden eyes are blazing down at me, offering me a sanctuary, a guarantee that whatever he's about to say is the sincerest truth in existence. "I'm here for you. I'll protect you. Choose me, and I swear that you'll be my number one priority, always."

His number one priority.

It's exactly what Connor will never give me.

And I know, with every fiber of my being, that Tristan can—and that he *will*.

"I believe you," I say, and then turning back to Hazel, I ask, "If I say yes, will you let me out of this cell?"

"I'll have to speak with Tristan in private first," she says, noncommittal. "The others will likely want to talk to him as well. But yes, it should be possible."

Possible.

It's not a guarantee. But it's a start—a glimmer of hope in the darkness that surrounds me. And for now, it's the only lifeline I have.

"Thank you," I tell her, although I also find myself pulling Tristan closer, unwilling to let him go.

"It's going to be okay," he says, and then he releases my hand and brings both of his up to his necklace. Carefully, he lifts it off over his head and holds it out to me. "Here. Hang onto this for me, until we see each other next. Which will be soon—I swear it."

"Your brother's necklace," I say, barely louder than a whisper. "But it means everything to you."

"No," he insists. "*You* mean everything to me."

I'm rooted to the spot, my heart pounding in my chest. Because this—what he's offering me and telling me right now—holds more significance than if he were to tell me he loves me.

Taking a deep breath, I reach out and accept the necklace. As it rests in my palm, a subtle warmth radiates from it, somehow binding me to Tristan on an even deeper level.

"I'll see you soon," I tell him.

"Soon," he promises, and then he walks to the front of the cell, preparing to leave.

Hazel unlocks the door and extends her hand to him. "You know how this works," she tells him, and then he takes her hand, the usually invisible barrier shimmering slightly as he steps through.

He immediately releases her hand after crossing the barrier, and he looks back at me, his eyes filled with warmth and affection. "Once you're out of here, I'm going to take you on a proper date," he says. "One without a captive audience. And one where I can actually enjoy a meal with you instead of just watching you eat."

"You mean I won't be the food?" I tease, although I'm surprised by the disappointment I feel at the realization that I won't have to provide for him anymore.

I suppose, in a way, I kind of liked it. Providing for him. Being here for him, like he's been for me.

Knowing that he needed me.

"Not if you don't want to." He gives me a sheepish smile, and my cheeks heat at the memories of the intimate moments we've shared this past week.

I want to.

The words are on the tip of my tongue, but I hold them back.

"Don't get ahead of yourself," I say instead. "I haven't even said yes to that date yet."

A playful glint appears in his eyes, and he flashes a confident grin. "Remember, Ruby—absence makes the heart grow fonder," he says. "Unfortunately for me, I won't be gone for long enough for you to experience it yourself."

"I think my heart's fond enough for you as it is," I say automatically, which earns me another smile from him.

"Good," he says, his eyes burning with intensity again. "Although there's no way it can be as fond for me as mine is for you."

His declaration leaves me breathless.

How many different ways can this man tell me he loves me? And how does each of them manage to be even more endearing than the last?

With a final, lingering glance, he turns to leave the cell. Hazel follows him, and Riven, ever the dutiful enforcer, trails behind.

The door shuts with a heavy, resounding thud, and I'm alone with Lindsay and Jason once more.

I slip the necklace around my neck, feeling the cool metal settle against my skin. It's as if Tristan's presence envelops me, offering solace and strength in the darkness. I wrap my fingers around the pendant, and it's almost like his love for me is pulsing out of the garnet in the center, filling my soul with a sense of security and steadiness I've never felt before.

"Well," Lindsay says, breaking the silence. "That was intense."

There's a strong yearning in her eyes, and I know why. She's desperate for the type of romance with Benjamin that I share with Tristan.

I look over at her, nodding. "Yeah, it was."

Jason clears his throat, walking to the front of his cell so I can see him. The hollows in his cheeks are deepening, his eyes not quite as bright as they were when we first met. "So, what now?" he asks.

"We wait," I say, running my fingers over the cross pendant again. "Hazel and the others will talk to Tristan, and then they'll let me out of here. Once they do, I'll do everything in my power to get you guys out, too."

"You don't have to worry about us," Jason says. "Gwen hasn't spent as much time with me as you have with Tristan, but once she does, she'll realize how much I love her. Then she'll let me out of here, too."

"Right," I say, since it's impossible to argue with him about anything involving Gwen. "Of course she will."

Lindsay sits down on the floor, her back against the cold stone wall. "I hope it all works out for you, Ruby," she says. "You deserve a chance to be happy."

"So do you," I tell her. "And you will be. Soon."

"Thanks." She gives me a small smile, and I can tell she doesn't believe me.

But it doesn't matter if she believes me or not. Because I'm going to get them out of here. I'm not sure how, but I will.

We fall into a comfortable silence, and I close my eyes, finding solace in the pendant hanging around my neck. The warm pulse of it gives me hope that no matter what comes next, I'll be ready to face it head-on.

I'll learn more about the Blood Coven.

I'll make them think I want to join them.

And then I'll figure out how to have a future with Tristan—one where the two of us can finally be safe and free.

Together, forever.

Tristan

HAZEL and I step into the library, the soft creak of the door echoing through the air as she closes it behind us.

It should be a relief to be back in my favorite room in the house, the hushed whispers of knowledge and secrets enveloping me. Yet, I find myself yearning for that basement cell. Well, not particularly for the cell—but for the person who was sharing it with me.

Ruby.

From now on, my favorite room will likely be whichever one she's occupying at the time.

"You did a good job," Hazel says, yanking me out of my thoughts about Ruby. "With both the blood bond and giving Ruby the necklace."

"What would you have done if she refused to offer me her blood?" I ask the question that's been gnawing at my mind for a while now.

"Would you have allowed things to get to the point where you'd have actually killed her?" Hazel asks.

"I would have resisted for as long as possible."

"What about when it was no longer possible?"

I stare her down, daring her to push further. "I wouldn't have allowed it to get to that point."

"How would you ensure it didn't?" She raises an eyebrow and conjures a ball of fire in her palm, the flickering flames casting eerie shadows on her face.

I make sure to look into her eyes instead of directly at the flames.

She's so calm, so detached. I've always been one to keep my guard up, but it never ceases to amaze me how cold Hazel can be for someone so young. I suppose that's what happens when you're held at arm's length from everyone in your community—including your own parents—from the time you're a child.

"I would have fed from her by force," I say with a dangerous edge to my tone, since I have no shame about it.

It's true that my preference would have been for Ruby's feelings for me to have progressed naturally, without a blood bond. But it's far better for her to be bonded to me than not in this world at all.

"Without killing her," Hazel continues.

"Yes."

"Therefore, forcing the blood bond upon her."

"Yes."

I summon my air magic, feeling the cool, invisible currents swirl and dance around me, responding to my unspoken command. Then I blow it toward Hazel's flame.

The fire sputters and dies, leaving only tendrils of smoke in its wake.

It's a dangerous game—goading a witch. Especially one with as high of status as Hazel.

But I've done all that she's asked of me.

I will *not* allow her to toy with me.

"Interesting." She stands down, seeming to have gotten the answer she wanted, making no retaliation to my assertion of dominance.

"You know, it was a very interesting touch you added there," I tell her, taking back control of the conversation.

She studies me, seemingly unable to read where I'm going with this.

"What was?" she finally asks.

"Stabbing me."

"Right. That." She shrugs. "We needed it to look convincing. The entire plan would have been ruined if there had been even a hint that you knew it was coming."

"I've been alive for over a century," I remind her. "You underestimate my acting skills."

The corners of her mouth curl into a sly grin, and she tilts her head ever so slightly. "Is that what you've been doing with Ruby?" she asks. "Acting?"

My jaw clenches as I hold her gaze. "Never."

"You're in love with her," she says, as a fact and not a question.

"I am."

"I'm happy to hear that," she says. "As you know, I had a feeling the two of you would be good together. Just like me and Benjamin. And, after Ruby joins us, I want us to all be friends."

She truly does.

Benjamin entered his relationship with Hazel to bring her to our side, just like she had me do with Ruby. Hazel doesn't know it, of course. However, he loves her now—or at least I think he does. He's impressed by power, and Hazel wields it in abundance.

She's determined to be with him forever, which is why she eventually joined us. Love conquers all—even if that means conquering beliefs that were ingrained into you since childhood.

"We will all be friends," I assure her. "You and Ruby got along well before you brought her here. You just need to give her some time to adjust to all the changes."

I'm unsure if I believe it, given the way Hazel's treated her, but saying anything else won't get me anywhere right now.

"I can always get trapped with her somewhere for a week," she says with a chuckle. "It seemed to work for you."

Every muscle in my body stiffens. "You won't harm her," I warn, ready to call on my magic at a moment's notice if necessary. "Not ever."

"Relax," she says, though it does nothing to calm my nerves. "I never said I'd harm her."

"And you never will." I let the threat hang heavily in the air.

She appears unshaken. "You truly do love her," she says.

"Yes. I do."

"Do you think your feelings are returned?" she asks, continuing before I can reply. "We know she trusts you. We know she's bonded to you. But does she love you?"

It's a good question. One that I hope I have the answer to, but I have no way of knowing for sure.

"You could have asked her while Riven was there," I tell her.

"Which means she hasn't told you she loves you. Yet," she adds that final word with a twinkle in her eyes, and I have a feeling she *does* believe that Ruby loves me.

Sometimes you can simply see the love between two people when they look at each other and interact with each other. And, while I'm biased, I'd like to think that's how Ruby looks at me.

But I refuse to allow Hazel to shake me.

Still, I can't deny that she's getting under my skin. I've never been in love before, and I'm finding that I dislike the uncertainty of it all.

"She trusts me," I say, since Riven confirmed it. "And she's bonded to me."

"All true." Hazel nods, considering it.

"You completed your goal of creating a blood bond between us," I continue. "It's time to let her out of that cell. It's not like she'll be able to leave this house. You can create a boundary to keep her inside, just like you kept her inside the Pine Valley pack territory."

"I can, and I have," she says. "But I'm curious if you think that trust she has in you is because of the blood bond, or if she came upon it naturally after spending all that time with you."

Another good question. One that I'll never truly have an answer to, thanks to them forcing me to bond with her.

"There's no way to know for sure," I admit, even though it pains me. "But blood bond or no, the time Ruby and I spent together was real. And I firmly believe that if you let her out of that cell, I'll be able to make more progress with getting her to feel more comfortable with opening up about her true feelings for me."

"Why do you think that?" Hazel asks.

"Because we need her to be intimate with me," I say. "She won't be in that cell. She's too uncomfortable—both with being seen and heard by the humans, and by being locked in a cell in general. But if you allow us to be alone together—truly alone—then I believe the connection between us will deepen, and she'll open herself up to me."

"Open up what, exactly?" Hazel's eyes glitter with mischief. "Her heart, or her body?"

My glare is icy enough to wipe that smile from her face.

"For Ruby, the two will go hand and hand," I say, strongly and firmly.

Hazel watches me, waiting for a crack in my armor, one that will cause me to waver. There is none.

"Okay," she says. "I'll speak with the others. I can't force them to do anything, but I do think your point is valid, and there's a good chance they'll see things our way."

"*Our* way?" I ask, since Hazel's given no signs of us being a team.

"I don't want Ruby locked in there, either," she says, like it should have been obvious this entire time. "It makes it hard for me to continue building a friendship with her."

No kidding.

However, I sense that Hazel is sincere, so I suppress any sarcastic remarks that threaten to surface.

She wants friends. She *needs* friends. She might be powerful, but so am I—and I have a century of experience over her. Sometimes, I think she forgets that we convinced her to join us instead of the other way around. "We," as in me, Gwen, and Benjamin.

"Great," I say instead. "I'm glad we're working toward the same thing."

"As am I," she says. "Now, why don't you go grab some food in the kitchen? I'm sure it's been a pain to not be able to enjoy solid food recently. We have cheeseburgers. And tater tots. They really are the best form of potato, don't you think?"

The mention of food stirs a familiar craving inside me. Even though vampires don't need solid food to survive, it's hard to feel fully satisfied without it.

It's a habit most of us find hard to shake from our human days.

"Thank you," I say. "After watching Ruby and the humans eat this past week, I could use a bite."

"Enjoy your meal," she says. "I'll let you know when the others reach a decision. If you're not still in the kitchen when we do, I trust I'll find you here in the library?"

The message is clear—don't return to the basement until she's given me a verdict.

And, as much as I want to check on Ruby, I know better than to do anything that might jeopardize our chances. Short term, impulsive thinking rarely gets people anywhere.

"Absolutely," I say instead. "You know me well."

"You better get used to it," she says with a friendly smile, motioning for me to exit the library first. "Because we're going to know each other for a long, long time."

Ruby

I wait in my cell for what feels like the longest few hours of my life.

Are they hurting Tristan? Hazel *did* stab him, so I can't put it out of the realm of possibility.

But that wouldn't make any sense. They threw him in here with me because they wanted him to feed on me. We did exactly what they wanted. Plus, they want me to join their coven.

Which means they have no reason to punish Tristan—or me.

"Do you think he's turning on you?" Lindsay asks. She's sitting on the worn rug, her fingers nervously braiding and unbraiding the frayed fringe, her eyes focused on the repetitive task.

I stare at her in shock.

What kind of crazy question is that?

Tristan's pendant around my neck throbs with irritation, as if Lindsay's words personally offended it.

"Of course he's not turning on me." I wrap my fingers around the pendant, my lifeline that ties me to Tristan. "He loves me."

"He never said it directly."

"Come on." I roll my eyes. "You've seen us together for over a week. He's on our side."

"He's on *your* side," she says. "Not ours. You're a supernatural. We're not."

I frown, since while she has a point, I don't want to admit it.

"There's no way he'd ever turn on me," I say instead.

"Okay. Sorry I asked." She continues to focus on the fringe that she's braided and unbraided hundreds of times since we've been down here, still not looking me in the eyes.

"Don't listen to her," Jason speaks up from his cell. "He loves you. He'll be back for you."

I can't see him, but I can tell from his tone that he means it.

"Thanks," I say, and then my stomach growls, and I glance at my empty lunch plate.

Thalia should have come with our dinner by now.

Something isn't right.

Unfortunately, given my current position, there's nothing I can do about it.

So, to distract myself, I curl up in bed with a book—the first sci-fi one Tristan read while we were down here. It's a bit heavy on the spaceships and dense science stuff for my taste, and I'm too anxious to focus on reading anyway, so I just end up scanning the words without much comprehension.

Finally, the door to the basement creaks open, and Hazel comes back downstairs. She stops in front of my cell, ignoring the others, and I place the book down next to me without bothering to mark the page.

"Hey." She smiles at me, like she's talking to a friend.

"Hi…" I trail off, waiting for her to say whatever she's come down here to tell me, and bracing myself for anything.

Anything, minus Lindsay's idea about Tristan turning on us. Because while there are a lot of things that could be going on up there, I'm sure that isn't one of them.

"After talking with Tristan, I chatted with the others," she says, bouncing on her toes like a kid ready to share good news. "I fought for you, and they agreed to let you out of here."

Her voice rises with excitement at the end. She sounds genuinely happy about it, as if we've been on the same side this entire time.

"Right now?" I ask.

After so many days and nights in this cell, all of them blurred together, this barely feels real.

"Yes, right now," she says. "Dinner's almost ready, and the sisters hate it when anyone's late."

I watch, stunned, as she removes a key from her jacket pocket and unlocks my cell door. It clicks open, and she places her palm on the barrier, which shimmers and fades away.

With nothing standing between us, every hair on my body stands on end, warning me to always stay alert. Hazel's a wild card. I can't let myself forget that.

So, I rise to my feet, bracing myself for an attack.

None comes.

"I can just walk out of here?" I ask.

It seems too easy.

"Out of the cell—yes," she says. "You'll have free roam of the house from now on."

"Which means I won't be able to *leave* the house."

"We placed a boundary around it. Sorry," she says. "The others don't know you yet, so they want to spend some time with you to make sure you're on our side."

"You mean the three sisters?"

The more information I can get, the better. You never know when someone might accidentally give you something valuable that you can use against them later.

"Yep," she says. "Morgan, Zara, and Willow. They're excited to meet you."

"If you like them, then I'm sure I'll like them, too," I say, and then I go a step further and add, "You knew how much I'd like Tristan."

Hazel chuckles softly, a sparkle in her eyes. "I knew you liked him from the second you saw him," she says. "You should have seen the way your eyes lit up when he walked through the door."

"So did every other woman's at that bar," I remind her.

"They did," Hazel says. "But he was only focused on you."

My heart flutters as I remember that first moment—the way Tristan trapped me in his gaze, mesmerizing me with his beauty and charm—and I know Hazel's right. Tristan had my heart from the moment I saw him.

No vampire blood bond or dulled shifter mate bond will ever change that.

Hesitantly, I make my way to the front of the cell and step through the open door. Nothing zaps me.

I'm free.

And, even though I'm still the basement, the air feels fresher than it has in over a week. It's like a weight has been lifted from my chest, and I know I never want to be confined in such a small space ever again.

"Thank you," I say to Hazel, not needing to fake my gratitude.

"I'm glad I was the one who got to do it," she says, and again, I have the impression that she means it.

I say bye to Lindsay and Jason, and then Hazel leads me out of the basement and up the narrow, creaky staircase. The scent of fresh herbs and cooked meat wafts through the air, making my mouth water.

Even though I can't see it yet, the food smells fancy.

"Will Tristan be at dinner?" I ask Hazel, shutting the door behind us.

"No," she says, and I swallow down disappointment. "The sisters want to spend this time getting to know you without anyone else there. Other than me, of course. But don't worry—you'll see Tristan after dinner."

The assurance immediately calms me. Tristan's somewhere in this house, waiting for me.

But before seeing him again, I have to get through this dinner with three—likely evil—witches.

They want to like me, I remind myself. *Go along with whatever they say, and all will be okay.*

It's the best—and only—way I can think of to gain their trust.

"Are they okay with me wearing this?" I ask, motioning to the warm flannel pants and tank top that Thalia dropped off this morning.

"They know we haven't been giving you clothes straight from the runway," she says, and she smiles warmly, amused. "But like I said, they don't like to be kept waiting. Come on—follow me."

The house is a labyrinth of dimly lit hallways lined with antique paintings and dark wooden furniture. It's both eerie and intriguing, and it *feels* like witches live here, as if past generations of them haunt these halls. Quite literally, in the case of many of the old portraits on the walls.

Finally, we reach a set of ornate double doors that lead into the dining room. Hazel pushes them open, revealing an extravagant feast laid out on a long, polished oak table. Silver candelabras cast flickering shadows on the walls, illuminating the intricate wallpaper and high, arched ceilings, making me feel like I walked into a royal banquet.

As we enter, the three women in the room stand to greet us. Their bewitching beauty combined with the matching silver pendants around their necks that pulse with power and magic leave no question that they're powerful supernaturals. They're also dressed far more formally than I am, but there's nothing I can do about that.

I have far more important things to worry about than what I'm wearing, anyway.

So, I take a few deep breaths to steady myself, reminding myself to remain cool and calm, no matter what they might throw my way.

After all, my life may depend on it.

Ruby

"Ruby, I'd like to introduce you to the original three members of the Blood Coven," Hazel begins, and then she gestures to the petite, youthful-looking woman with sun-kissed hair that cascades in loose curls to the middle of her back. "This is Morgan."

"Hi, Ruby," Morgan says, her voice light and inviting. "We've heard so much about you."

As everyone apparently has around here, I think, although I know better than to say it out loud.

"Nothing too bad, I hope," I say instead, which earns a smile from her.

"No." Morgan smiles warmly. "Nothing bad at all."

Strangely, I believe her.

Next, Hazel introduces me to the tallest of the three. "This is Zara," she says, motioning to the woman with long, jet-black hair and piercing, fiery orange eyes. Her sharp, angular features give her an air of determination and intensity, and she stands strongly and proudly, like someone who feels like she should be well known enough to not need an introduction.

She has a small, silver flame tattoo on her left cheekbone, which she likely chose because of the elemental magic that witches possess.

Fire.

"Welcome," Zara says, her voice cool yet guarded.

"Thank you for having me." I lower my eyes, hoping the gesture will make her feel like I'm not a threat.

When I look back up, I'm relieved to find that she looks incredibly pleased with herself.

A woman who finds joy out of intimidating others.

Noted.

Hazel quickly moves on to the final sister, who has warm, amber eyes and wavy, auburn hair that frames her heart-shaped face.

By process of elimination, I know before Hazel introduces us that this is Willow.

"It's nice to meet you, Ruby," Willow says with a genuine smile. "Please, join us."

Zara's at the head of the table, her sisters flanking her sides. There are place settings next to Morgan and Willow. Clearly, one is for me, and one is for Hazel.

I want to sit next to Morgan, but I also don't want to offend Willow.

"Which seat is mine?" I ask, since it feels like the safest move to make.

"Sit next to me," Morgan says, and I'm more than happy to oblige.

They take their seats at the same time as Hazel and me, and I try to ignore the weight of their gazes. Well, mainly of Zara's gaze. Out of the three sisters, she's the only one who fits the description of "evil Blood Coven witch" that I was expecting to find when I walked through these doors.

The other two seem… nice?

Then again, Hazel seemed nice at first.

I need to keep my guard up.

Across from me, Willow reaches for her water glass to take a sip, and I notice an intricate phoenix tattoo that wraps around her left wrist.

A phoenix—a bird that rises from the ashes.

I have no doubt that the bird's relation to fire isn't an accident.

My stomach growls, and I focus on the food in the center of the table. Roasted vegetables glisten with herbs and olive oil, while tender cuts of meat sit beside steaming, fragrant rice.

When I was a vegetarian, I barely would have been able to look at the meat, which is cooked so rare that there's still blood in its center.

Now, it looks and smells like one of the most delicious foods on Earth.

But, most notably, the platters are family style. Which means that unless these witches are willing to dull their magic—which I bet they aren't—there's no way that the food is drugged.

"As you see, we have a few more members who aren't here with us this evening," Willow says, gesturing to the empty seats at the long banquet table with her left hand in a way that shows off her tattoo again. "We wanted to keep it small tonight, as to not overwhelm you, and to give us a chance to get to know each other more intimately."

"Thank you," I say, and then, because I get the impression that she wants to hear it, I add, "I like your tattoo."

She beams at the compliment. "I designed it myself."

"It's beautiful."

Before the conversation can continue, someone walks through the door. Thalia. She's wearing all black, as always, and she's carrying a bottle of red wine.

"Brunello di Montalcino," Zara says as Thalia uncorks the bottle. "It's one of the greatest Italian reds, and one of my favorites. I sent two of our shifters to bring it in from the city for this exact occasion."

The deliberate way she says it makes it clear that refusing a glass would be a great offense.

"That was very kind of you," I say instead, and she gives me a sharp smile, the silver flame tattoo on her cheek seeming to glow when she does.

I know nothing about wine, since the restaurant where my mom works in Naples is more of a "red or white" sort of place. But I know that no matter what I think of this particular vintage, I need to pretend like it's the most delicious wine I've tasted in my life.

It shouldn't be too hard, since it most likely will be. And luckily, we'll all be drinking from the same bottle, so I know it hasn't been drugged.

Thalia allows Zara to take the first taste, which she says is excellent. She moves on to pour for the rest of us—starting with me—refusing to look me in the eyes as she does.

The wine is a rich, dark red, like blood, and I can't help but think that's a reason Zara favors it.

"Thank you, Thalia," Zara says when our glasses are full and the bottle is empty. "I'll message you when we're ready for dessert."

Thalia simply bows her head slightly, then turns around and leaves without saying a word.

Zara reaches for her glass and holds it up, her silver rings glinting in the candlelight. "Now, for a toast," she says, and the rest of us raise our glasses as well. "To the one sent to us from the stars."

She holds her gaze with mine, and I know she's referring to me.

I lift my glass a few inches higher, mimicking the others, then bring it to my lips and take a sip.

The wine is an explosion of dark, velvety fruit in my mouth. The flavor somehow fills my entire head, and while I've never been a wine girl, this might be the one to change my mind.

"Well?" Zara raises a perfectly plucked eyebrow, waiting for my verdict.

"It's delicious." I savor the lingering taste as I contemplate the appropriate thing to say next. I feel like I'm in one of my fantasy novels, and I know that every word I say to this woman could be the difference between freedom and being locked back up in that basement cell. "Thank you for going to such lengths to bring it here tonight."

"My pleasure." She gives me an approving look, apparently pleased, and I relax slightly.

I can do this.

It's going to be a dance of words, and perhaps a battle of wits, but I can make these women believe they're convincing me to join their cause.

The conversation easily flows as they ask about my story—my first shift, how I discovered my magic, and the work Hazel and I did together so I could learn how to better control my powers. Even though they previously said they'd heard all about me, I suppose they wanted to hear things directly from the source.

Zara's just beginning to ask me about something I have zero desire to discuss—my mate bond with Connor—when Hazel gasps and hisses in pain, a curse ringing through the air.

All eyes are immediately on her, where she's cradling her left index finger, whimpering slightly.

"What happened?" I ask, although from the way Hazel's knife is laying in the center of her half-finished meat, it's obvious that she cut herself with it.

"It's nothing," she says, although from the way she winces when she talks, it doesn't sound like nothing. "My knife slipped. No big deal."

"Let me see," Willow says, gently taking Hazel's hand before she can protest.

Hazel's finger is slashed from her nail bed to her middle knuckle. Blood wells up, trickling down the rest of her finger, and I stare at it in shock.

How could a girl who so deftly handled the Blade of Erebus have accidentally cut herself with a dinner knife?

I have no idea, but I definitely don't think it was an accident.

Ruby

"That's not nothing," Willow says. "Let me help."

She downs the rest of her water until only a few ounces remain. Then she takes her knife to her palm, slices it open, and squeezes, allowing her bright red blood to drip into her glass.

I watch in shocked silence, unable to tear my eyes away from whatever she's doing.

"Your cut's pretty shallow, so this won't take much," she says to Hazel. Then, once her blood has colored the water like dye, she stops squeezing. Her own cut heals in seconds, and she brings the glass closer, cradling it in her hands and staring intently into the blood-filled water.

As she does, magic pulses through the room, thickening the air and creating a quiet hum in my mind.

She lifts her gaze from the glass and hands it to Hazel. "Here. Drink this."

Hazel takes the glass, wrinkling her nose as she stares down at it. Then, gathering her courage, she raises it to her lips and downs it like a shot.

I watch, transfixed, as Hazel's cut seals itself and the blood vanishes, leaving her skin smooth and unblemished.

"The Blood Coven..." I say, piecing it together. "You have blood magic. Healing magic."

"I'm the only one with healing magic," Willow says, reaching for the pitcher and refilling her glass. "Morgan can scry for things, and Zara creates powerful blood oaths."

"You always make mine sound so boring." Morgan huffs and turns to me, her green eyes bright with excitement. "I can use my blood for divination, to receive visions and messages to gain insight into the past, present, or future. The more blood spilled, the stronger and more useful the message."

"You're a prophet," I say, and when she sweeps her hair over her shoulder, I glimpse her tattoo—a small, shimmering comet behind her right ear.

"Exactly," she says. "It's not always easy to control what I see, and the universe enjoys being as cryptic as possible, but the Blood Coven wouldn't be anywhere near where we are today without my help."

"How so?" I ask.

"We're still just getting to know each other, but we'll tell you eventually," she says, grinning playfully.

I nod, figuring she'd say something like that. But it didn't hurt to ask.

"And you?" I ask, turning my attention to Zara.

It feels great to move the focus away from me and onto them. Finally, I'm learning something. A *lot* of things.

Zara swirls her wine in her glass, takes a sip, and says, "The blood oaths I create bind two individuals together, ensuring that the promises made are kept. If they're broken, the consequences are severe."

She sits back in her seat, her gaze hard.

I barely have time to process what she said before Morgan leans forward, her eyes glittering with curiosity.

"So, Ruby, why don't you show us your magic?" she asks. "We've been talking about it so much—I think it's time we see it for ourselves."

I hesitate and glance at Zara, since she seems to be the one in charge around here. "I can't use my magic right now. It's been... dulled by the drugs you've been giving me."

Zara raises an eyebrow, a small smile playing on her bright red lips. "Oh, Ruby, we stopped giving you the drugged food last night. You should be able to use your magic just fine by now."

I blink in surprise. "You did?"

"Yes," she confirms. "Go ahead. Show us what you can do."

Before agreeing to anything, I take a deep breath, steady myself, and dig deep inside myself to search for my magic.

The familiar stirrings of it respond within me. It's not as strong as it was before I was drugged, but it *is* there.

"All right," I say, relief rising in my chest at the fact that my magic is returning. "What do you want to see?"

Morgan's the first to jump in. "Make it look like Willow's tattoo is gone," she says, bright and excited, as if she amused herself with her own suggestion.

I glance at Willow to see if she's okay with it.

She pulls down her sleeve and rests her arm on the table, the detailed phoenix on display for us all to see.

"Do your best," she challenges, making me even more determined not to mess up.

"Don't worry. I will."

Steeling myself, I take a deep breath and concentrate on Willow's tattoo. It takes longer than I'm used to, but soon the energy of my magic courses through me, tingling in my mind as I direct it with my eyes toward Willow's wrist.

Using every ounce of focus to push through the traces of the drugs lingering in my system, I weave the magic around her wrist like an invisible silken thread. As the illusion takes hold, the once-vibrant phoenix fades until it vanishes completely, leaving Willow's pale skin smooth and unmarked.

She stares blankly at her now-bare wrist, a mixture of fascination and annoyance playing on her soft features. "Wow," she says, not sounding pleased with the result. "It's like it was never there."

She pokes her skin a few times, as if it will make the ink reappear. But, as Hazel and I learned from our time experimenting with what I can do, the illusion will stay in place for as long as I want it to, unless Willow leaves the room.

Zara reaches over the table, her fingers tightening around Willow's wrist, examining the skin where the tattoo used to be. "Your magic is fascinating, Ruby," she eventually says, dropping Willow's wrist and returning her sharp gaze to mine. "There's so much potential for how it can be used."

A wave of unease washes over me as I observe the calculating glint in Zara's eyes. I get the feeling that she's scheming up countless ways that my magic can be used to benefit the Blood Coven's agenda, and my heart races with the realization that I'm not just their guest—I'm their potential weapon.

Instinctively, I reach for Tristan's necklace to ground myself.

"Change it back," Willow says, breaking the silence with her harsh tone. She catches herself, softens her expression, and adds, "Please."

I nod and reverse the illusion.

The phoenix on Willow's wrist gradually reappears, as if emerging from her skin, the vibrant colors blazing back to life.

"Thank you." She examines the tattoo, her eyes narrowing as she makes sure every detail's intact. Once satisfied, she pulls her sleeve farther up her wrist than before, as if desperate to erase the memory of her tattoo's temporary disappearance.

Zara clears her throat, drawing our attention back to her. "Ruby, as I'm sure you've figured out, there's something we need your help with," she says.

No kidding.

"I'm listening," I say instead, taking another sip of my wine. The liquid does little to calm my nerves. I haven't had too much of it, since I want to keep my wits about me, but it helps to have something to do with my hands.

"I hoped you would," she says. "Because we're looking for a powerful artifact—one that we've already located, but need your magic to help retrieve."

"What artifact?" I place my glass back down on the table and lean forward, my heart pounding as I wait for the answer that might help me continue piecing together the puzzle of the Blood Coven's ultimate goal.

"One that hasn't been seen for centuries, and has been hidden in a place that will be close to impossible for us to safely reach without your help," she says, her gaze cutting through me like a sharpened blade. "The Key of Hades."

Ruby

She says it as if I'm supposed to have a general idea about what the Key of Hades is.

I don't.

"What's the Key of Hades?" I finally give in.

Zara sighs, as if she expected the question. "A powerful artifact," she repeats. "It can raise the dead."

An icy chill runs up my spine, causing the hairs on the back of my neck to stand on end. I don't know what I expected, but it certainly wasn't this.

"Who are you trying to raise from the dead?" I ask, looking around at each of them in a new light.

A darker light.

Willow takes another sip of her water, her eyes averted. Morgan uses her fork to poke at the vegetables on her plate, the clinking sound sharp in the tense atmosphere. Hazel plays around with a small helix of fire around her index finger, as if she's checking to see if her magic still works after her injury, and the fire reflects in her eyes, making her look pleased with the result.

Zara's lips curl into a secretive smile. "I'm afraid I can't tell you… yet."

My curiosity grows, and a nagging unease settles in my stomach. "When will you tell me?"

"After you gain more of our trust," she says simply. "You don't have to know how we intend to use the key to help us retrieve it."

It's a fair point, so I don't pry further.

"I understand," I say, trying to keep my voice steady. "But I'd like to know where we're going to find it."

"You, Hazel, Tristan, and Benjamin will be going to Central Park in New York City—the entrance to the Summer Court of the fae," she says, and I exhale in relief at the fact that Tristan will be coming with us.

If he's coming with us, it means they haven't hurt him or sent him away.

"You're staying here?" I ask.

"Correct."

Very interesting. It shows that the sisters don't want to risk themselves. However, they are okay with risking me, Tristan, Benjamin, and Hazel.

Of course they're okay with risking me. I'm their weapon. It's why they want me on their side, why they went to all this trouble to bring me here in the first place.

As for Hazel…

"You're going to put yourself in danger like that?" I ask, since from the little I know about the fae, they aren't friendly to other supernaturals. Luckily, the Summer Court isn't as bad as the Winter Court, which is known for being downright cruel, but the mission will still be dangerous.

"Benjamin's going, so I'm going, too." She extinguishes the fire in her hand, a wisp of smoke curling from her fingers. "Plus, you never know when a little bit of fire magic might come in handy."

Her mention of magic reminds me that they need mine.

I look to Zara again, who's taking a slow, deliberate bite of her meat. "Why *exactly* do you need me to help you so badly?" I ask her.

"We can't risk the fae knowing that the four of you are there," she answers. "You'll have to go in disguise. Your magic will make those disguises as convincing as possible."

I have a bit more wine as I take it in.

"I was only gifted with my magic a few weeks ago," I remind her. "And, for a portion of that time, I had no access to it. What makes you think I can pull this off?"

"I've worked with you enough to know that you're talented with altering appearances," Hazel chimes in. "You're more than capable of doing what we need. Especially under the pressure of our lives being on the line."

She's right—I do work best under pressure. Like when I turned invisible to stop Connor from seeing me in the woods.

Tristan's necklace pulses, as if reminding me to not dwell on Connor… and it works.

I feel no pain when I think of my mate's name.

Incredible.

"Okay. Let's say I do this," I say, and Morgan stops playing with her food, her bright eyes lighting up in excitement. "What do I get from it?"

"For starters, you won't have to stay in the lovely accommodations downstairs," Zara begins, sarcasm dripping from her tone. "But, most importantly, you'll be inducted into the Blood Coven as an equal member. Once we achieve our goal, you'll enjoy the benefits with the rest of us. And trust me when I say that the benefits will be worth it."

"I suppose that means you're not telling me what they are right now?" I ask.

"Help us retrieve the key first," she says. "Then, depending on how the mission goes, we'll let you know more."

"You'll have a family with us," Hazel adds, although it only serves to remind me that the family I've always had—my parents—thinks they'll never see me again. "We'll protect you. Which, as we've discussed, is far more than you'll ever get with the Pine Valley pack."

"I know," I say, and then for their benefit—and because it's the truth—I continue, "Jax views me as an omega and an outcast. Connor rejected me. Autumn turned me in. I will never, ever trust the Pine Valley pack, for as long as I live."

"You can trust us," Morgan says as she reaches for my hand, her fingers soft and comforting as they wrap around mine. The gesture should feel overly intimate from someone I just met, but from her, it's kind and welcoming. "The Blood Coven is a family. And we protect our family. Forever."

There's an added emphasis on the final word, as if there's far more meaning behind it than I know.

I offer her a tentative smile before pulling my hand away from hers and reaching for my water glass. The cool liquid soothes my parched throat, but it does little to quench the thirst for answers burning inside me.

"You'll also get more power," Willow repeats, something I've already heard multiple times. "A *lot* of it." She leans forward, and I can tell she wants to tell me more, but that she's holding back.

I place my water glass back on the table, my gaze sweeping over the four of them.

Zara maintains a carefully neutral expression, giving away nothing of her thoughts or desires. Morgan fidgets with one of the many gold rings on her fingers as she waits for my response. Willow devours the vegetables on her plate so quickly that I wonder if using her magic earlier drained her energy, leaving her desperate to refuel. Hazel's fingertips dance with tiny flames, her eyes challenging me from over the flickering fire. They create mesmerizing patterns, their warm glow casting an almost calming atmosphere over the dinner table.

The power in the room crackles with energy that hums and shimmers against my skin. It's a testament to the Blood Coven's strength, a force that beckons me with promises of belonging and purpose.

Maybe they're right. Maybe there's a place for me here, with them.

As I ponder their offer, my gaze drifts to the window, where the night sky stretches out like an inky canvas dotted with countless stars. And, as I stare out into the darkness, the facts of the situation resurface in my mind, a sobering reminder that these witches are not on my side.

Hazel drugged me to bring me here.

The Blood Coven locked me in a basement cell for a week.

They're kidnapping humans and keeping them captive as living blood bags for the vampires.

They forced a blood bond between me and Tristan.

At the thought of Tristan, I wrap my fingers around his pendant. It's like his love for me fills me, reminding me that he's the only one I can trust.

And he's part of the Blood Coven.

The people at this table may never feel like family to me. But Tristan?

A part of me—one that's larger than I care to admit—already feels like he is.

And the four of them are all watching me with hawk-like eyes, waiting for my decision, clearly wanting me to make one—now.

Ruby

"I'll help you find the Key of Hades," I tell them, and Hazel pulls the flames back into her fingers, looking as proud of me as she did when we were working together in my room to improve my control over my magic. "As for joining the Blood Coven... I need time to think about it."

"Understandable," Zara says. "The universe agrees. Because it's currently the new moon, when the moon is in shadow. To induct you into the coven, it needs to be a full moon. Which means you have two weeks to make your decision."

Two weeks.

She says it as if it's a generous amount of time.

But it feels suffocatingly short.

"You'll make the right decision," Hazel assures me. "Then, once you do, I'll use my magic to make your parents and best friend remember your existence."

I stare at her, shock and dread coiling in the pit of my stomach.

"What did you just say?"

"I said that I'll make your parents and best friend remember your existence."

"I heard you the first time." I raise a hand and shake my head, an unspoken plea for her to stop talking. "But they think I'm dead. Not that I don't exist."

"That's a lie," Hazel says plainly. "Another lie told to you by Jax. He didn't think you were ready to know when he first talked to you, but he wanted you erased."

"But... why?"

The full implications of what she said hasn't set in. Because if I thought it was painful for my parents and Luna to believe I was dead, the realization that they don't even remember my existence is a hundred times more agonizing.

The scent of the food on the table turns sickly sweet, and the sounds of cutlery scraping plates feel like needles against my eardrums as I wait for Hazel's response.

"He thought that if they believed you were dead, you still might eventually go back to them and tell them you're alive," Hazel explains, her eyes filled with a mix of pity and understanding. "So, he asked us to erase their memories of you instead."

The room shrinks around me as the weight of her words settles in.

"But it doesn't make sense," I say, struggling to put it all together. "Even if you're telling the truth, and my parents and Luna don't remember I existed, other people will. My mom's friends at the restaurant will have asked her how I'm doing at school. The other people in my dorm will have asked Luna where I am. They'll think that my parents and Luna have gone insane for not remembering me."

"All true," Hazel says. "Which is why, with the help of the entire Blood Coven, and with using Carly as a sacrifice, I erased your existence from the human world altogether."

I blink a few times, unable to believe what I'm hearing.

"You killed Carly," I finally say. The words taste bitter on my tongue, and I swallow hard.

Out of everything she said, it shouldn't be the one on the forefront of my mind.

Yet, it is.

"Carly didn't know it, but she had powerful blood, thanks to the deep connection to the spiritual world passed down to her through her ancestral line," Hazel continues, as if she's not admitting to *murder*. "I was able to tap into that power—albeit, in ways her ancestors would never approve of—to pull off the most impressive spell I've done to date."

"I'm erased... from existence," I say in shock, unable to look at any of them as I speak. "And you murdered someone to make it happen."

"We did," she confirms.

"How could you do that? How could you just... erase me from their lives?"

Hazel's expression softens. "I know it seems cruel, but it was Jax's decision, not ours," she says, and then she continues, her voice firm. "But I promise you, Ruby, if you decide to join the Blood Coven, I'll use my magic to reverse it all. I'll give you back the people you love. And if you need more proof that I'll follow through on this promise, Zara can forge a blood oath between us. That way, you'll know for sure that I'm telling you the truth."

"Proof," I repeat. "Yes, I need proof."

"Wonderful," Zara says, bringing her hands together. "I can create the blood oath now, if you'd like."

"No," I say, and she frowns, taken aback by my rejection. "I don't need proof that Hazel will reverse the spell. I need proof that you're telling the truth about the world forgetting my existence."

"Not the entire world," Morgan says, in what I think is an attempt to be reassuring. "It's only the human world. Not the supernatural one."

"Up until three weeks ago, the human world was the only world I knew," I snap, and she sits back, looking physically hurt by the harsh way I spoke to her.

I feel bad. I do sort of like her, and I don't want her taking the brunt of my anger and grief.

But Hazel said the entire Blood Coven participated in the spell. Morgan is part of the Blood Coven.

She's as guilty as the others.

"If it's proof you want, then it's proof you'll get," Zara says breezily, looking to Hazel. "Take her to Florida. Tomorrow. Let her see the truth with her own eyes."

"A good plan," Hazel says. "Benjamin will come with us."

"And Tristan," I add quickly.

If they're telling the truth, and I think they are, then this is going to be devastating. I want Tristan there with me. He'll be the only person left in the world who loves me.

He'll be the only person in the world—at least, in this version of it—who's *ever* loved me.

The realization makes it feel like the world's closing in on me, eating my soul alive from the inside out.

"Of course," Hazel says with another understanding smile. "And Tristan."

Zara regards me with a glint in her eyes that reflects the silver flame tattooed on her cheek. "For tonight, we've prepared better accommodations for you," she says. "A penthouse suite, if you will."

She's goading me.

"Is that a fancy way of saying the attic?" I ask.

She raises an eyebrow. "Would you prefer your cell in the basement?"

"Fine," I say, since the last thing I want to do is return to that cell—especially without Tristan in it. "I'm sure it'll be a real 'rags-to-riches' experience."

Zara smiles. "You know, I kind of like you, Ruby," she says.

That makes one of us.

"Well, Zara, the verdict's still out on whether or not I like you," I say, since she seems like a girl who can handle a little rough talk. "We'll see with time."

"Don't worry." She flashes me a dangerous smile. "After we finish what we've set out to do, the one thing we're not going to be lacking is time."

Again with the annoying cryptic stuff.

"I suppose you're not going to explain what you mean by that?" I ask.

"You're already getting to know me so well," she says. "Hazel will bring you to your room once we're done here. Now, since we're having such a lovely time here, how about we have Thalia bring us some dessert?"

Ruby

I GET NO MORE information from the four of them during dessert. Instead, Willow and Morgan are all over me, prying into my mate bond with Connor and my blood bond with Tristan. They're like a pair of high school girls, all giggles and whispers, trying to unearth the latest juicy secret.

It's nearly impossible to focus, since *everyone I've ever known has likely forgotten my existence*, but by some miracle, I manage.

After dinner, Hazel leads me up a grand staircase, and I can't help but glance around, taking in the opulent decorations and ancient artifacts that fill the creaky old mansion.

What secrets does this place hold? What dark magic courses through its foundation?

Finally, we reach the attic, and Hazel pushes open the heavy wooden door with a flourish.

It's nothing like I imagined. It's more of a royal suite than an attic, adorned with plush armchairs and a grand canopy bed. Velvet drapes add a regal touch, and tall windows with cozy reading nooks offer a view of the sprawling gardens below, which are artificially lit in the moonless night.

Zara's 'penthouse suite' comment suddenly doesn't seem that sarcastic. The place even has an ensuite bathroom. Sure, the tub, sink, and toilet scream Victorian, but Hazel assures me they're as good as new.

I'll have to see about that later.

"When will I get to see Tristan?" I ask her, since she promised I'd see him after dinner, and I intend on holding her to it.

"I was thinking we could hang out for a bit first?" she asks with a hopeful smile. "Like we used to?"

From the way she's making it sound, you'd think I stayed at her house for three years instead of three nights.

But I don't think it's going to get me anywhere to tell her no.

"Sure," I say, forcing a smile. "Sounds great."

"Cool." She saunters over to the bed and perches herself on the end, seeming genuinely pleased. "I'm so glad we're working with each other and not against each other now. We're both freaks of the supernatural world, so it makes sense for us to be friends. Don't you think?"

She watches me carefully, a silent plea in her eyes for me to agree.

I know from what she told me when we first met that she's never had any close friends.

If I can convince her that I want to be her friend—not just her friend, but her *best* friend—then it will likely increase my chances of gaining the Blood Coven's trust. The more they trust me, the more freedom they'll give me. Plus, the only thing it'll do if she thinks I hate her is make things more difficult for me.

Still, I don't want to sit next to her. So, I choose one of the plush chairs, facing her and preparing to give the performance of my life.

Hopefully the alpha wolves aren't sent to sniff out my lies.

"Ruby?" Hazel asks. "Are you okay?"

She's tenser than before. More on edge.

Time to get this show on the road.

"Yeah," I say, holding her gaze with what I hope is conviction in my eyes. "And I want you to know that I understand."

Her face brightens with hope. "Understand what?"

Looking at her now, with her small frame and the smattering of freckles on her nose and cheeks, she seems almost childlike.

But I know better. She might look like an innocent lamb, but she's a wolf through and through.

She *murdered* Carly. And she didn't sound even slightly sorry about it.

"I understand why you brought me here. I'm actually grateful for it. The Pine Valley pack..." I pause for a second, my eyes far off, because this is one part where I won't have to lie. "After everything they did to me, I'll never be able to trust them. You and the Blood Coven are more on my side than they'll *ever* be. And even though you did that spell to... erase me from existence," I say, and I swallow, hard, since it hurts to say out loud. "I know you'll reverse it. I trust you."

"Interesting." Hazel's eyes, as sharp as a hawk's, study me intently. After a brief pause, she scoots forward, the antique bed creaking under her weight. "So, tell me—how much of this is because of our chat over dinner, and how much of it is because of your connection to Tristan?"

Her question is a spider's web glistening in the moonlight, a trap waiting for unsuspecting prey.

At least, I think it's a trap.

If I was lying, I'd say it was because of our dinner conversation. That's what Hazel wants to hear—that it's about her. That she's special in some way.

But she's no fool. She's aware of the bond Tristan and I share. She orchestrated it, after all.

Probably because she thought it would make me more likely to trust the Blood Coven.

Little does she know that I didn't need the blood bond with Tristan to grow to trust him. After all that time together, I care about him.

Deeply so.

"It was Tristan," I admit, and then to make it more convincing I add, "I love him."

The words echo in the room, and strangely enough, they don't feel like a lie.

There's a beat of silence before Hazel finally speaks her eyes searching mine. "You love him?"

"I do." I reach for his necklace, the warm pendant acting as my anchor in the storm of emotions swirling within me. It's my proof, my constant reminder that this isn't an illusion. That it's not just the influence of the blood bond.

No blood bond could fabricate those stolen moments in our cell. The electric charge that pulsed between us, the trust that gradually grew… the way he cradled me in his arms every night we slept in that bed together.

And now, saying it out loud makes me feel more vulnerable than ever.

Hazel swings her feet that are dangling over the edge of the bed, like a child ready for a bedtime story. "How do you know you love him?" she asks.

"How do you know you love Benjamin?" I turn the question back to her, having a feeling she won't mind answering.

"I knew it from the moment I saw him," she says, her eyes dreamy, her tone ringing with honesty.

Her answer is a naïve confession, the kind given by someone who's never been in love before.

Not like I have any more experience than she does in the realm of love. After all the intimate, stolen moments with Tristan, I'm more convinced than ever that my feelings for Connor were lust—not love. The mate bond was nothing more than an illusion, as fake as the ones I create with my mind.

Nothing more.

"That's very romantic," I tell her, which earns me a smile. "But it was different with me and Tristan. Yes, I was attracted to him. I'd have to be blind otherwise. But we had a lot of time to get to know each other. And around him, I felt safe, cared for, cherished, and understood. I trust him. What else could that be, if not love?"

She contemplates my words, her gaze intense. "Do you think he loves you back?" she finally asks.

"Yes." The word fills me with relief after I speak it, because I know in my heart that it's true.

Her face softens as she studies me, and she tucks her hair behind her ears. "I think so, too," she says shyly.

"Now you understand why I want to see him so badly," I say. "I know it hasn't even been a day, but… I miss him."

This, too, isn't a lie.

I hold my breath, praying she'll take the bait.

She hops off the bed, a glint of mischief in her eyes. "Well then, who am I to stand in the way of love?" she says, surprising me by how easily she concedes. "I'll bring Tristan up here."

"Yes," I say. "Please."

"Anything for a friend."

With a final impish grin, she stumbles slightly as she hurries out the door, leaving me alone in the dimly lit attic.

Once she's gone, I drop my head into my hands, hardly able to believe what just happened.

I pulled it off.

But the craziest thing about all of it?

I didn't have to do much acting.

Because despite the uncertainty of this entire situation, one thing is clear to me above all else: I'm in love with Tristan. And I'm ready to face whatever comes next, as long as he's there with me, by my side, forever.

Cursed Moon

STAR TOUCHED: WOLF BORN 3

Ruby

LYING IN BED, I trace my fingers along the cross pendant Tristan gave me this morning. The piece of jewelry is a promise of sorts.

And maybe a sign.

It belonged to Tristan's brother, Dominic. He was also a vampire. But the shifter Guardians hunted him down and killed him when they learned he'd fallen in love with one of their own and turned her into a vampire so they could be together forever.

Will my fate be something like that? A tragic end just when I'm on the cusp of finding love?

Light streams past the velvet drapes, casting shadows on the hardwood floor in the attic bedroom. *My* attic bedroom. At least for now. It's a gift from the three sisters of the Blood Coven, and a huge upgrade from the basement cell they kept me in for the past ten days.

Suddenly, the door creaks open, and there he is—Tristan.

My heart races, and I drop the pendant, running into his arms before the door's fully closed behind him.

"Ruby," he murmurs, his breath cool in my ear. "I missed you."

"I missed you, too," I say, and then I reach for the necklace and pull it over my head. "Here. This belongs to you."

He makes no move to take it from me. "I gave it to you," he says. "It's yours now."

"I can't accept it." I hold his gaze, refusing to budge. "Dominic would want *you* to have it. Not me."

His golden eyes harden, and I worry he's going to refuse again.

"Take it. Please," I insist, and his fingers brush against mine as he accepts the necklace, the simple contact sending sparks shooting up my arm.

"Thank you." His voice softens, and as he secures the chain around his neck, his gaze wanders around the room. "Nice upgrade you got here. I take it the dinner went well?"

"You knew about that?"

"I did," he says. "I had a feeling you'd click with Morgan. Willow, too, to a lesser extent. Zara, however…" He trails off, leaving the rest unsaid.

"She likes me," I say. "Kind of."

"She said that?"

"In those exact words."

He waits for a punch line, but there is none.

There is, however, something else that needs to be discussed. Something far more important than if Zara's going to try becoming my new bestie or not.

"She told me more about the Key of Hades." I swallow to steady myself before continuing. "And about my parents."

"What about them?" he asks cautiously.

"Hazel wiped their memories of my existence. And it's not just them. No one in the human world remembers me. She erased me entirely."

The world around us seems to pause, and I brace myself for his questions, his shock.

"Ruby," he says instead, his voice strained. "I'm so sorry."

"You knew?"

The betrayal is a knife to my heart.

"Hazel told me today," he says. "But she'll reverse it. Zara will create a blood oath between the two of you to make sure she keeps her promise."

His gaze is locked on mine—full of hope and vulnerability—and every bone in my body urges me to believe him. Because if I can't trust Tristan, who *can* I trust? My mate rejected me, my pack doesn't want me, and the witches I thought were my allies turned on me.

Without Tristan, I have no one.

"Hazel will reverse it *if* I help them get the key," I remind him. "But I'm not making any blood oaths until I have proof that she's telling the truth."

"What kind of proof?"

"She's taking me to see my parents. Zara said you and Benjamin can come with us."

I wait anxiously for his response, praying he'll say yes.

"Of course I'll go with you," he says, and I relax instantly. "I'm here for you, no matter what."

"I know," I say. "I trust you."

"Good."

His lips are on mine in less than a heartbeat, and I'm kissing him back as if he's fresh air and I'm finally able to breathe.

We've kissed before—at the bar when we first met—but this is different. This is the kiss of two people who have shared their hopes and dreams with each other, who have seen the good and bad parts of each other's souls and still want each other anyway.

Before I know it, he guides me to the bed and eases me onto the mattress.

"Stay here with me tonight," I say, and even though we spent over a week together locked in that cell, this is different.

More intimate.

Because now, spending the night together will be a *choice*.

His fingers trace gentle patterns on my skin, each touch lighting up my nerves like fireworks. Eventually, he pulls away again to study me, his golden eyes darkened with raw emotion.

"Are you sure?" he asks.

"Yes," I say, and he crushes his lips against mine again, electricity crackling across my skin like a lightning storm.

This is perfect.

This is wrong, a voice I haven't heard in days intrudes upon the moment.

My wolf.

She's clawing her way to the surface, and her anger ripples through me, demanding to be heard.

In retaliation, I kiss Tristan deeper and try to suppress her, to shut her up and push her back down.

He shouldn't be touching us. He's not our mate, she growls, refusing to go away.

At the sound of that word—*mate*—the sting of Connor's rejection hits me again, like a needle injecting ice into my heart.

Connor's our mate. Pine Valley is our home. My wolf's aggression gathers so much strength that it's burning through me, consuming me. *The pack is our family. Tristan needs to GET OFF US.*

At her thunderous roar, I scream those final words and push Tristan off me, sending him sprawling onto the floor.

The silence that follows is deafening.

I meet his eyes and suck in a sharp, pained breath. Because he's looking at me like he doesn't know me.

Like I'm a *monster.*

"Are you okay?" he asks, and he gets up slowly, his gaze locked on mine as if he thinks I might snap at him again.

I blink a few times, trying to make sense of this.

Because he should hate me.

And yet, here he is… *concerned* about me.

"I just yelled at you and threw you off the bed," I say. "And you're asking me if *I'm* okay?"

"Yes." His voice is full of resolve as he stands at his full height before me. "Because you didn't tell me to get off *you*. You told me to get off *us*. And while I have a pretty good idea what you meant by that, I'd appreciate it if you told me yourself."

He puts his shirt back on and sits down on the bed, and I can't help noticing the space he puts between us. It's like he's protecting himself… from me.

"It's my wolf," I admit, and he nods, since I'm sure it's the answer he expected. "She doesn't like that we're together."

"Because she wants Connor."

He says it as a statement—not a question.

"She does," I say.

He says nothing for a few seconds, as if choosing his next words carefully.

"I imagine it must be difficult," he finally says. "To have someone in there with you, fighting you."

"When you say it like that, it makes me concerned for my mental health." I chuckle to lighten the tension, even though it's far from funny.

His solemn look makes me realize that he *is* concerned for my mental health.

Given what just happened, I suppose I can't really blame him.

"I'm sorry," I say. "I didn't mean to hurt you."

"If you want to hurt me, you're going to have to do far worse than a tumble off the bed," he says, and despite the lightness in his tone, I feel the weight of what just happened creating a wall between us.

I need to figure out how to control my wolf.

And I have the perfect idea for trying to do just that.

"Do you think my mate bond with Connor will keep weakening if you feed from me more often?" I ask.

If he's surprised by the proposal, he doesn't show it.

"We can try," he says cautiously. "But I want you to promise me that if you ever change your mind, for any reason, you'll tell me the second you do."

"I promise."

Somehow, while we've been talking, we've been moving closer to each other, so we're now inches apart. I don't know if he's going to kiss me or bite me, but I'd welcome either one.

Suddenly, my wolf bristles inside me, like tiny spikes trying to poke through my skin.

I won't let you do this, she says, and she sends a blast of rage through me so intense that her consciousness drowns out mine.

I lunge at Tristan.

We tumble to the floor, and he reacts quickly, flipping me over and pinning me down.

Pain shoots through my back, and I use the moment to push past my wolf and break through to the surface.

"Do it." I barely manage to speak through my wolf, who's trying to wrangle herself into control again. *"Please."*

Wind sweeps around us—Tristan's magic.

And then, with a swift, almost gentle movement, he sinks his teeth into my neck.

I gasp at the shock of his fangs piercing my skin. But then it's gone, and a soothing sensation flows through me, washing away the anger and the fight.

It's like he's sucking my wolf—and the power she has over me—out of my system. Calmness settles deep in my bones, replacing her fury with a soft, insistent pleasure.

Eventually, his grip around my wrists loosens, and he pulls away.

"I'm sorry," he says. "It was like one second you were here, and the next—"

"Don't apologize," I cut him off, and I reach up to touch my neck, where the twin puncture marks are already starting to heal. "You did what I asked you to do. And it worked."

"I didn't want it to happen like that."

"And I didn't want my wolf to try killing you." I release a small laugh and sit up. "But sometimes we have to roll with the punches. Literally."

I finally get a smile from him.

His hand moves to cradle my face, his thumb gently stroking my cheek. "You're beautiful," he says. "Even when you're trying to kill me."

My heart leaps, his touch taking my breath away.

"Will you still stay here with me tonight?" I ask, continuing before he can reply. "It's okay if you don't want to. I know it'll be hard to sleep if you're worried about being attacked at any moment."

"I'm not worried," he says, so confidently that I don't question him. "But if you feel your wolf again, I want you to tell me. Even if it means waking me up. Okay?"

"Okay," I say, and apparently satisfied with my response, he gives me a quick kiss before I head to the bathroom to get ready for bed.

I can barely look at myself in the mirror as I do. All I can think about is that I might see my wolf staring back at me.

She's not going to give up easily.

But until we come up with a better solution, Tristan drinking from me more often to keep her subdued will have to be enough.

When I come back out, Tristan's already propped up against the pillows with a book in his hand, presumably from the small bookshelf wedged in the corner of the room.

"Anything good?" I ask as I crawl into bed with him.

"It's okay-ish." He places it down on the nightstand without bothering to mark the page. "How are you feeling?"

"Tired," I say, and then I yawn, my body agreeing with my words. "Can we go to sleep?"

"I suppose I can put the book down for the night," he says. "For you."

"Your sacrifice is noted."

We share a smile, and I feel so safe with him that despite everything that's happened today, I quickly start drifting off to sleep.

Then, just when sleep is claiming me, he murmurs, "I love you, Ruby."

And that's the last thing I hear—or *think* I hear—before the world fades away.

Autumn

NOW THAT CONNOR'S told the pack about our engagement, there's only one thing for us to do.

Celebrate.

The new moon, unseen yet powerful, is ideal for an engagement party. Because new moons mean new beginnings. It's when we plant seeds for our future.

My future is Connor.

Now, and forever.

The party is perfect. Lanterns are suspended from the surrounding trees, twinkling like a thousand miniature suns. A bonfire dominates the center of the clearing, its flames dancing toward the night sky, melting the snow to reveal the muddied ground beneath it.

Others might dislike the mud, but as wolves with earth magic, we relish in it.

Connor sits next to me, his fingers entwined with mine. His gaze is fixed on the dancing flames, their light reflecting in his dark eyes, which are as serious as always.

Ever since Ruby left to stay with the witches, he's been slowly coming back to me. Now, I finally have *my* Connor back. The man I've known since we were kids, who loves me more than anyone else in the world.

I don't want to lose him again.

As I gaze into the fire, I pray that the Blood Coven follows through on their promise to break his mate bond with Ruby sooner rather than later. After they do, my future with Connor will finally be secure.

He squeezes my hand and pulls me toward him.

"Beautiful, isn't it?" he murmurs in my ear.

"It is," I reply, my gaze not on the bonfire anymore, but on him. The firelight casts flickering shadows across his face, highlighting the sharp lines of his cheekbones and the curve of his lips that I've kissed more times than I can possibly count. "But not as beautiful as you."

"Aren't I the one who's supposed to be saying that to you?" he asks with a twinkle of amusement in his eyes.

"Men can be beautiful, too." I pout, although it quickly shifts into a smile.

"Then we're both beautiful," he concludes, and he gives me a quick kiss, which ignites hooting and clapping from the crowd.

I smile against his lips. "You'd think they've never seen you kiss me before."

"They've seen me kiss my girlfriend," he says. "But now's the first time they're seeing me kiss my *fiancée*."

It's a sweet comment. But that word—fiancée—still stings. It's a reminder that I'll never be Connor's mate, and that there's nothing I can do about it.

It's not too late to take care of Ruby, my wolf says inside me, feeding off my anger at the reminder that Connor has a mate, and it isn't me.

I'm not killing her, I remind my wolf. *I can't kill her, now that she's in Spring Creek. But the Blood Coven has it handled. We have nothing to worry about.*

Whatever you say. Her irritation is intense, but controllable. Like it's been ever since I made my deal with Calliope, the leader of the Spring Creek coven.

"You okay?" Connor asks, pulling me out of my darkening thoughts.

"I'm great," I say, forcing myself to snap out of it. "Why?"

"You looked far off there for a second."

"I'm here." I give him a reassuring smile. "Just got lost in thought for a moment."

"About what?"

"About how I can't wait until two weeks from now, when I finally become your wife."

The lie comes swiftly, easily.

I've been getting much better at lying recently.

Some truths are better left unsaid, especially tonight.

As the night progresses, the laughter grows louder, the stories more animated. Our packmates revel in our joy, their happiness for us evident in their smiles and cheers.

Eventually, the conversation dies down, and a figure rises to stand.

Jax.

Connor's grandfather... and our current alpha.

Standing tall and muscular, Jax looks like he's in his upper thirties—forty, at most. His dark hair—the same brown as Connor's—is full and silky. It's the type of hair that's practically begging to be touched.

A hush descends upon the pack as he walks toward us, holding two simple crowns of laurel leaves at his side.

Connor pulls me up to stand.

Jax looks at Connor, then to me, as if he's drinking in this moment to remember forever.

"Tonight," he begins, his voice deep and resonating in the quiet night. "We celebrate not just the union of two individuals, but the promise of the continued future for our pack."

A few pack members hold their glasses up in agreement. It's not an official toast yet, but it's a party, and they're looking for any reason to drink.

Jax's gaze turns away from the crowd and back to us.

"Connor, my grandson, who I've raised as a son since soon after his birth," he starts, his voice echoing through the silent crowd as we take a moment to remember the tragic deaths of Connor's grandmother and parents.

His parents, killed by their best friend Xavier and his wife, when Xavier defended his sister—a shifter-turned-vampire—instead of following the law of the Guardians.

The law demands that any shifter turned into a vampire has their soul freed by the Guardians in the only way possible.

Death.

After a moment of silence, Jax continues.

"Connor—your dedication to learning our traditions has turned you into a man of courage, wisdom, and strength. A man who dutifully follows the laws of our kind over anything else. You're going to make a remarkable alpha for the pack someday, and a loyal husband to your bride."

Our packmates cheer, using the pause as an opportunity to enjoy more of their drinks.

Jax turns his gaze to me, and his words soften. "And Autumn," he says. "You've grown into an incredible woman. Your beauty is evident not only in your outward appearance, but also in your spirit. It shines brightly in your strength, determination, and resilience."

The depths of his blue eyes radiate intensity, and his words echo in my mind.

Strength. Determination. Resilience. Beauty.

I never realized Jax saw me that way.

"You're a force to be reckoned with—gifted by the gods with a rare combination of powerful magic and sharp intelligence," he continues. "You know your worth, and you're not afraid to fight for what you believe in. Any man would be lucky to call you his wife."

The fire flickers behind him, making him look more like a god than a mortal, and I find myself utterly speechless. Because the man standing before me is no longer the man that raised Connor. Instead, he's the alpha of our pack. Strong, dominant, and powerful, with a jawline that could cut glass and blue eyes that pierce deep into my soul.

I vaguely feel the eyes of my packmates on me, and I blink a few times, trying to snap myself out of it.

Jax must be asserting alpha willpower on me. I can't think of anything else that could have inspired this shift in the way I'm seeing him. He's toying with me. Playing with my mind.

He *has* to be.

But why?

Does he know what I promised the Blood Coven? I don't know how he could. But as our alpha, he knows far more about what's going on behind the scenes than he lets on.

Guilt creeps up the back of my throat, and I reach for Connor's hand to steady myself.

Before I know it, Jax walks closer to me and Connor, so there's less than a foot of space between us. My heart races, and I try to focus on anything other than Jax as he crowns Connor first, his powerful hands steady as they place the laurel leaves atop my fiancé's head.

"Tonight, we honor you and your future bride." He glances down at the ground, using his magic to call up the mud in a sparkling, swirling helix toward his fingers. "The earth bears witness to your promise."

Slowly, he smears lines of mud across Connor's cheeks with careful, deliberate strokes. One side, and then the other. Two lines to symbolize the joining of our two souls.

He turns to me, and I suck in a sharp breath at the intensity of his gaze.

From the way he pauses, I swear he's as entranced as I am.

"Tonight, we celebrate your unity." He places the crown on my head, and I hold my breath, as if one small movement has the power to shift the ground between us forever.

Maybe this is what it feels like for every shifter who goes through this ceremony? After all, Jax is blessing us with alpha magic. What should it feel like, if not this?

I relax a bit, feeling slightly better with that conclusion.

Again, the mud winds around Jax's fingers as he calls it forth from the earth.

This is it.

As if in slow motion, his thumb grazes my cheek, sending a tingling wave of warmth through my body. His movements are careful and deliberate, his touch firm yet gentle. And he goes slowly with me—much slower than he did with Connor.

"You look beautiful tonight," he murmurs, his voice so low that only the two of us can hear. He's staring deeply into my eyes, like he's in a trance, as captivated by this moment as I am.

It's wrong. *So* wrong.

At the same time, I don't want it to end.

"Thank you." My words are so soft that they're nearly lost in the sound of the crackling fire.

We're both silent for a few torturously long seconds.

"The earth bears witness to your promise," he finally says, and when he pulls his hand away from my face, his eyes linger on mine, full of unspoken questions.

Connor clears his throat and takes a step closer to me. "The toast?" he asks, calm, yet firm.

"I was getting to that." Jax sweeps his eyes across the crowd, and his beta stands up and kneels before him to offer him a cup of bourbon.

He then hands one to me, and another to Connor.

"To Autumn and Connor." Jax raises his cup, glances at me, and turns his focus back to the pack members gathered around the fire.

My mom and dad are in the front row. My dad's brow is furrowed in confusion, and my mom gives me a tight smile.

They noticed.

They *had* to have noticed.

But there's nothing I can say to them right now. In fact, I never want to speak about this with them at all. So, I turn my attention back to Jax.

"May your bond be as strong as the mountains surrounding us, as enduring as the rivers that flow through these lands, and as passionate as the fires that light our paths," he says. "To new beginnings."

"To new beginnings," the pack repeats in unison.

I raise the cup to my lips and force down a swallow of the bourbon. It tastes just like it smells—like gasoline.

While I'm drinking, a major realization hits me.

Jax—our alpha—looked me in the eyes for an extended period of time. I should have felt compelled to submit.

But I never once thought about lowering my gaze.

Tristan

I wake at dawn, and Ruby's still sleeping in my arms. Unlike me, she's a deep sleeper.

I, on the other hand, have been plagued with nightmares since the night I was turned into a vampire over a century ago.

As she sleeps, Ruby seems so sweet and innocent. But the way her wolf took over last night… the feral look in her eyes as she attacked to kill… I don't want it to happen again.

I need to save her from her wolf. But feeding off her twice a day—or however many times she'll need to keep her wolf subdued—isn't the answer.

Eventually, she's going to have to make a choice. Turn into a vampire to break the mate bond, or live with her wolf inside her forever.

I pray she chooses the first.

Needing a bit of time to decompress, I slip out of bed and leave the attic as quietly as possible.

Calliope is already in the kitchen when I get there, with a bowl of hot porridge in front of her on the table.

So much for having a peaceful breakfast before the rest of the house wakes up.

She looks me up and down, pulls some of her silver hair over her shoulder, and frowns. There's something eerily conniving about Calliope. She's my least favorite member of the Blood Coven, but she's a necessary piece for us to complete our goal, so I have to deal with her for now.

"You're wearing your necklace again," she says in lieu of a greeting.

"I am."

Her eyes shine with disapproval. "Zara told me that Ruby wore it to dinner last night, since you did as discussed and gifted it to her before leaving the cell."

"Ruby knows how much the necklace means to me," I say without missing a beat. "She returned the gift."

"How unbecoming." Calliope scoffs.

"It was an act of love."

"Do you truly think the girl loves you? Or are her feelings the enchantment of the necklace speaking, along with the blood bond?"

It's clear from her tone that she believes the latter.

"Ruby and I got to know each other when we were locked in that cell for over a week," I say. "We grew to care about each other. No necklace or blood bond can take that away from us."

She leans back and twirls a strand of her hair around her finger, her food forgotten. "The necklace only works when she's around it, does it not?" she presses, and I can tell by the smirk on her lips that she knows she's hitting a nerve with me.

"It does," I confirm what she already knows.

"Then you need to get her to wear it."

I wrap my hand around the cross pendant protectively. Because Ruby knows me well. She was right when she insisted that the necklace was too important to me to give away—even to someone I care about.

"I have it under control," I say to Calliope, and I walk over to the counter to grab a mug and get a pot of coffee started. Caffeine has no effect on vampires, but drinking coffee is a comfort from my time as a human. While it doesn't do anything for me physically, it does relax me mentally.

She rotates in her chair to face me. "The two of you were intimate with each other last night, were you not?" she asks.

It's a good thing the coffee isn't ready yet, because I might have spit it out at her comment. As it is, my magic rushes through me, creating a breeze through the room that fills the kitchen with the delicious scent of the fresh beans.

"She asked me to stay with her last night," I say steadily, since the level of my *intimacy* with Ruby is no one's business but ours.

"Interesting." Calliope smirks again. "Because we heard some... noises up there last night. Loud ones. It sounded like quite the wild reunion happening between the two of you."

I plop the mug onto the counter—hard. "Like I said, I have my relationship with Ruby handled. What happens between the two of us in private will remain private."

I hold my gaze firmly with hers, daring her to push me further.

"Such a gentleman," she finally says. "I do like that about you, Tristan."

The predatory way she's looking at me sets me on edge, and I suddenly want to get out of this kitchen as soon as possible.

"You can have the coffee," I say. "I'm done here."

With that, I leave and go back up to the attic, where I climb into bed with Ruby and wrap my arms around her again, wishing I could freeze time and stay with her like this forever, never having to let go.

Ruby

I WAKE to the sensation of strong arms wrapped around me.

Tristan.

As I stir, his hold on me tightens. He's awake, and probably has been for a while.

As I come to, his whispered confession from last night plays in my mind.

I love you, Ruby.

Did it really happen? Or was it just a dream?

I don't know. But I do know one thing—if he wants to tell me he loves me, he'll tell me so when I'm awake.

He doesn't love us, my wolf whispers in my mind. *And you don't love him. You think it's love, but it's just the blood bond talking.*

Instead of responding to her, I turn to face Tristan. He smiles when his eyes meet mine, and my heart flutters like it always does when he looks at me with such tenderness and care.

"Can you drink from me again?" I ask, still groggy from just waking up.

Concern flickers in his eyes. "Your wolf is back?"

"Yes."

He studies me, thinking about it, and I worry he might say no.

"You know, based on how often you're asking me to feed from you, it almost sounds like you're trying to make me fat," he finally says.

I can't help it—I laugh.

"Vampires can gain weight?" I ask, realizing that the thought had never crossed my mind.

"Just kidding," he says with a smile. "Well, we can gain weight from food, just like humans. But not from blood."

"Can you get full from blood?" I ask. "So full that you can't drink anymore?"

"We can," he says. "But I'll drink as much as I can. For you."

"Thank you," I say, and then I move my hair aside, and he does as promised. He doesn't drink as much blood as he did back in the cell, when he was going two days without meals, but it's enough to quiet my wolf.

Afterward, we lounge in bed, talking in detail about my dinner last night with the three sisters.

We're interrupted by a knock on the door, and I glance at Tristan, half-tempted to tell him to hide. But what's the point? I'm sure everyone in the house knows he stayed here last night.

Still, I move away from him, not wanting whoever's knocking to think they barged in on a more intimate moment.

"Who is it?" I ask, and I run my hands through my hair, trying to work through any tangles.

"It's me," Hazel says, and she opens the door before I can tell her she can come in.

She glances between me and Tristan and smiles.

"We were just talking," I say before she can ask what I know is on her mind.

"You don't have to validate anything to me." She steps back and holds her hands up in defense. "We're all adults here."

"You're sixteen," I remind her, and I hear Tristan suppress a chuckle.

"Technically, yes," she says, ignoring Tristan. "But I had to grow up fast. I feel like an adult."

I almost roll my eyes.

"Got it," I say instead, relieved I didn't accidentally offend her by even implying otherwise. Hazel can be unpredictable, and I'm trying to make her think I'm her friend here. "What's up?"

"Just wanted to remind you that we're leaving soon," she says. "And, I wanted to give you this."

She removes a dagger from inside her jacket and presents it to me with an encouraging smile. The sharp blade gleams silver, but my eyes are immediately drawn to the handle. There, embedded within the hilt, is a strikingly deep blue gem.

"It's beautiful." My instinct pulls me to take it from her, but I resist. "But you know I don't know how to use a dagger—or any other sort of weapon. Right?"

"I know," she says, playing with the dagger with a dangerous glint in her eyes. "But it's better to have it than to not. Especially because the gem is lapis lazuli, so it will give you protection."

I'm not one to turn down extra protection. But there's a big thing about this gift that doesn't make sense...

"The Blood Coven trusts me with a weapon?" I ask.

"We trust that if you need a weapon, your shifter instincts will help you figure out how to use it," she says. "One of the reasons shifters make such great Guardians is because you're all naturals in battles. Plus, the dagger's enspelled so it can't be used against any member of the Blood Coven. We trust you, but not *so* much that we'd hand over a weapon that can be used against us. Yet."

"I understand," I say, since I need to convince them that they can trust me with my actions, not my words. "Trust needs to be earned. It doesn't happen overnight."

"Correct," she says. "And, to that point, I want you to know that this dagger used to be mine. It was my favorite, until my parents gifted me the Blade of Erebus. Now, I'm entrusting it to you."

"Where did they get Erebus' Blade?" I ask, eager to jump on any opportunity to get information about the Blood Coven.

"It's been in the family for centuries." She waves off my question, as if I should have already known the answer. "So… do you want it or not?"

"I'd love to have it. Thank you," I say, and as I take it from her, I'm struck again by how deceptively innocent she looks. Minus the leather jacket, she hardly looks capable of cursing someone to make the world forget their existence.

"Anyway," she says, a hint of mischief in her eyes. "We have a few hours until we leave. Want to practice using your magic?"

"Always," I say, and then Tristan excuses himself, and we get to work.

Ruby

THE DRIVE from Spring Creek to my hometown of Naples, Florida, takes almost a full twenty-four hours.

Hazel, Benjamin, and Tristan take turns driving, as we don't want the trip to take any longer than necessary. Luckily, we're not stuck driving only at night, because while vampires prefer night to the day, sunlight doesn't kill them. Their eyes are sensitive to the sun, and their skin burns easily, but that's where the traditional stories end.

Every time we cross a state line and get closer to Florida, the more my anxiety grows. I'm not in the mood to talk—I'm too wrapped up in what it will be like to see my parents—and I'm grateful when Hazel puts on an audiobook for us to listen to during the drive.

I try to stay awake for as long as possible, but my eyelids eventually grow heavy, and I drift off to sleep.

When I wake, I'm snuggling with Tristan in the backseat.

"Hungry?" Hazel asks from the passenger seat, bright and awake.

"Yes," I say, but when I rub the sleep out of my eyes and look around, I immediately lose my appetite. Because we're parked in a lot that I know very, very well. One surrounded by palm trees, in front of a restaurant that looks like a large tiki-hut overlooking the water.

The restaurant where my mom works.

A quick glance at the clock in the car shows me it's just after noon.

My dad always comes into the restaurant to have lunch at this time. *Always*.

"You knew exactly when they'd both be here," I say.

"Naturally, your parents are of great interest to us," Hazel says. "We've been having someone keep an eye on them."

My entire body tenses. "What sort of 'someone?'"

"Relax," she says. "It's just two of the Spring Creek witches. They've been really enjoying their vacation in South Florida. It's a nice break from the cold in the mountains."

"They're spying on my parents," I say darkly.

"More like looking out for them," she corrects me. "It's a dangerous world out there. We have to make sure your parents are who they say they are."

"What have you found out?"

As much as I hate to admit it, I'm curious as well. Because if there's any chance of my parents also being supernatural, I want to know about it.

"Not much." She shrugs. "All we know so far is that they're definitely human. And that they're pretty boring people."

Anger surges through me, and I clench my hands into fists, wishing I could punch that smug look off Hazel's face. "Just because they're not supernatural, it doesn't mean they're boring," I say. "They're normal people living normal lives. They love each other. They love *me*."

Loved me, I correct myself in my mind.

Past tense.

They can't love a daughter they don't know exists.

"Can we just go in there and get this over with?" I ask, since I'm close to positive that the Blood Coven is telling the truth about Hazel's spell, and I know it's going to hurt even more when I see for myself.

"Absolutely," she replies, unbuckling her seat belt in preparation to get out of the car.

Benjamin, who was quietly listening to our conversation, offers me a sympathetic glance before opening the door to step outside.

He's the last person I ever thought would be sympathetic to me. But I know from the story about how he was turned into a vampire that he—and Tristan—walked away from their families to keep them safe. It's not the same thing as your family *forgetting about your existence*, but he and Tristan understand what I'm going through far more than Hazel ever could.

As we walk away from the car and through the parking lot, Tristan reaches for my hand. I know he's trying to be supportive, but I instantly pull away. What I'm about to face is for me to deal with, and me alone.

I can do this. I can be strong.

I *have* to be.

As I look around, everything is just like I remember. The salty tang of the ocean air, the warmth of the Florida sun, the faint strumming of live acoustic music, and the easy laughter of people outside enjoying their meals.

Yet, I feel more distant from it than ever. Because now that I know the truth about what I am, it's truly hitting me that the life I used to have will never be mine again.

Not even after Hazel reverses the spell.

We walk in, and I see the hostess—a girl named Carrie from my high school class who used to be somewhat of an acquaintance of mine.

She barely glances at us as she picks up the menus. "Four?" she asks, paying me no more attention than the others. No friendly smile, no asking how I've been… nothing.

It's like she's never seen me before in her life.

"Yes," I somehow manage to say. "In the bar section, please."

My mom always waitresses the bar area during the lunch shift. She specifically requests it so she can be near my dad.

"Are you sure you don't want to sit outside?" Carrie points her thumb toward the deck. "It's a beautiful day out there, and—"

"The bar," I say, cutting her off mid-sentence. "The booth all the way at the end. The one that looks out to the ocean."

She flinches at the harshness in my tone, but quickly recovers. "Sure thing," she says, and she motions for me to go ahead, since it's pretty clear from my request that I've been here before.

I turn the corner and stop in my tracks.

Because there's my dad, sitting at the far end of the bar with a beer in front of him. He's tanner than the last time I saw him, which I assume means he's been doing a lot of outdoor work recently for his handyman job. The bartender is laughing about something with him—a friend of his who comes over for dinner sometimes.

This area of the restaurant is pretty empty, so my dad glances at the four of us for a moment, then returns to his conversation.

He has no idea who I am.

My heart clenches, the twist of rejection sharper than anything I've ever felt in my life.

I want to run to him. I want to bolt out of the restaurant. I want to curl up in a corner and cry.

Instead, I look away and hurry to the booth, feeling like I'm moving on autopilot as I get situated.

"You okay?" Tristan asks, sliding in next to me.

What a loaded question.

"No," I snap. "I'm most definitely *not* okay."

His eyes flash with hurt, and he says nothing more.

Good. Because there's nothing that could possibly make me feel better right now.

Hazel reaches for the menu and starts looking through it. "So… what's good here?" she asks in what I think is an effort to diffuse the tension.

"Seafood," I say robotically. "It's what they're known for. The fish tacos are the most popular."

"I suppose I'll have to try that then," she says, although she continues browsing through her options, as if she isn't totally sold on my recommendation.

She, Benjamin, and Tristan make small talk about the menu, and I steal a few more glances at my dad. He orders another beer, chats animatedly with the bartender, and laughs at a joke I can't hear.

It's like I've walked into a nightmare.

I take a sip of my water and try to swallow down the lump of tears in my throat, but it doesn't do much to help.

And, as I wait for my mom to come to our table, I know it's just going to get harder from here.

Ruby

We could leave. I already have my proof.

But I need to see her. If I don't, I'll always wonder…

I don't have any more time to think about it, because my mom breezes through the restaurant and stops in front of our table. Her red hair flows down her back in big, wavy curls, and she gives us a bright smile that reaches her familiar hazel eyes.

Neither of my parents share my natural turquoise eye color, which always confused me. But it makes sense now, after learning that they're most likely not my birth parents.

However, my mom isn't giving me that warm smile because she recognizes me. Being happy is simply part of her personality. Even though our life here was simple—or "boring," as Hazel so eloquently put it—it's the life my parents chose, and it's always been one they loved and appreciated.

I'd be lying if I said it isn't tough to see her so happy without me in her life. I wondered if she'd show any hints that there was something missing, but she's always been the most optimistic person I know, so it's not surprising.

Also, I'm sure it would be tougher to see her hollow and miserable—a shell of the mom I've always known. Because if the worst happens, and we fail to get the key, at least I'll know that my parents are happy, and that they have each other.

"Welcome to the Salty Pelican," she says. "Have you had a chance to look at the menu?"

Hazel flashes her a friendly smile. "Actually, we were just deciding," she says. "What do you recommend?"

"Definitely the fish tacos, or the fresh snapper," she says, and I'm surprised by how *normal* she sounds. "We also have a few specials for the day…"

She rambles off the specials, but I barely hear what she's saying. All I know is that if I look at her for too long, I'll burst into tears, and then she'll ask me what's wrong, which will just make me cry some more.

"And you?" she asks, the question directed to me.

"The veggie tacos," I say automatically, forcing myself to look back up at her.

There's no spark of recognition. No hint that she's looking at her daughter.

Even though it's been a while since I last ate, I have absolutely no appetite.

"Great choice!" She writes down my order and beams at me. "I'll have these out to you shortly. In the meantime, can I get you anything else to drink?"

Hazel, always the rule-breaker, asks for a gin and tonic. She hands over her fake ID, and while I don't think my mom truly buys it, she lets it slide.

The guys order drinks as well, and I mumble that I want a Coke.

My mom gives us another smile, gathers the menus, then heads to the kitchen.

I stare off at where she disappeared, barely able to process what just happened. Because she's so similar to the mom I've always known. So much that I can almost fool myself into believing nothing's changed.

"See? It's just like I told you," Hazel says. "The spell worked."

The proud smile she's giving me makes me want to reach across the table and rip her hair out.

"I figured that out when my parents had no idea who I am," I deadpan.

"You said you wanted proof." She shrugs, as if she didn't just shatter my entire world. "So, there was your proof."

From the way she's looking at me, I can tell she wants recognition for successfully casting such a strong spell. And, while I hate being nice to her, I need to keep my end goal in mind—gaining her trust.

If that means sucking up to her, then so be it.

"That was very powerful magic," I say steadily, since it's not a lie.

"Thank you." She smiles, apparently placated by my comment. Which is a good thing, since I'm not sure how much more I could bring myself to sugar coat it right now.

Tristan reaches for my hand under the table, in a clear attempt to comfort me.

This time, I let him.

"I'll do the blood oath," I say, since there's no point in beating around the bush. "I'll help you bring back the Key of Hades, and you'll reverse the spell, like you promised."

Hazel leans back and studies me, like she's deciding if she believes me or not. "You'll do more than help us bring back the key," she says. "I'll only reverse the spell after we complete the resurrection."

"You didn't tell me that before," I say.

"Well, I'm telling you now."

"It shouldn't be an issue," Benjamin chimes in. "Once the key's with us in Spring Creek, there won't be anything stopping us from using it as soon as possible."

I frown, not loving the fact that they've added another requirement to our deal.

"What's the catch?" I ask.

"No catch," Hazel says. "Like Benjamin said—we're going to use the key as soon as possible after bringing it back to Spring Creek."

I look to Tristan for confirmation.

"It's true," he says. "You have nothing to worry about, other than helping us get the key and bringing it back to the human realm. We can handle it from there."

"So why add this extra level to the oath?" I ask.

"For another layer of protection," Hazel says, like it should be obvious. "To make sure you don't try doing anything to stop us from completing the spell."

I hate to admit it, but from their perspective, it makes sense.

"All right," I say, and I look at where my dad is eating his burger, my heart breaking all over again. "But I've seen enough here. Can we get our food to go?"

"We most certainly can," Hazel says.

After my mom wraps up our food, I tell her goodbye, give my dad a final lingering glance, and hurry out the door.

I've always appreciated my parents and everything they gave me. But as I get back into the car, I swear to myself that when they remember me, I'm never going to take their love for granted ever again.

Ruby

We get back to Spring Creek the next day.

The witches let me visit Lindsay and Jason in the cells. My visit is supervised, and I'm not allowed to say much about what's going on with me. Knowing that they're still alive is going to have to be enough for now.

That night, I go into the gardens with Hazel, Zara, Willow, and Morgan to perform the blood oath ceremony. The moon is a bright crescent overhead, and it's almost like it's smiling down at us, wishing us luck for what's about to happen next.

Zara has already cleared the space of negative energy—whatever that means—and we gather in a circle, with her in the center. She's wearing a black dress that falls to the floor, making her look extra-witchy, and the silver flame tattoo on her cheekbone glows in the moonlight.

I take a deep breath of the crisp, winter air, trying to ground myself. Thanks to my supernatural shifter side, I don't truly *feel* the cold. Neither do the witches, because of their fire magic.

Hazel gives me a reassuring smile. "Don't worry. You've got this," she says.

"I'm not worried," I tell her.

I'm just ready to get this over with.

Zara raises her arms toward the crescent moon, her dress billowing in the gentle wind, and I instinctively know it's time to start the ceremony.

"Hear us, Hecate, goddess of witchcraft." Her voice sounds beyond the garden and through the night. "Safeguard our oath tonight, for it is born of truth and blood."

My skin tingles, as if it can feel the magic answering her call.

"Willow, Morgan," Zara continues. "Step forth and protect this circle."

Willow and Morgan reach into the sleeves of their jackets, pulling out small, ceremonial daggers that gleam in the moonlight. Swiftly, they use them to prick the pads of their index fingers, so the slightest bit of blood bubbles to the surface of their skin.

Spirals of fire travel up their blades in identical helixes, and they walk to the edge of the circle, tracing its perimeter with the tips of their daggers. Flames grow out of the lines they're tracing, searing the circle into the ground.

They meet at the end point and cross their blades.

"Guarded by flame and guided by starlight, we protect this sacred space, an unbroken circle, bound by fire and by blood," they say in unison, their voices echoing through the quiet night.

They lower their daggers, and the fiery circle pulses three times before stabilizing into a warm, glowing ring of protection around us.

The earth ripples beneath me, as if it's taking on a life of its own, and warm tingles of magic travel through my feet and up my body. It's like the ground is responding to their magic, and it caresses my skin, telling me everything is going to be okay.

Its power is calming, and I take a deep breath, using it to steady myself—to ground myself.

Willow and Morgan lower their blades, and then Willow presents hers to Hazel, and Morgan presents hers to me. I take it from her, and she gives me a soft, reassuring smile before returning to her original place in the circle.

The hilt is warm from the fire, the tip of the blade red from Morgan's blood.

"Hazel, Ruby," Zara says, looking at each of us as she says our name. "Join me in the heart of our circle, cross your blades, and declare your intentions."

I hold my gaze steadily with Hazel's, and we raise our blades, bringing them together so they create an X between us.

"Ruby, you may begin," Zara says, and all eyes turn to me.

I swallow, then say, "I promise to do everything I can to help retrieve the Key of Hades from the fae realm and bring it safely back to the Blood Coven."

I look to Zara, and she nods, satisfied.

Now, it's Hazel's turn.

"I promise that after we use the Key of Hades for a successful, completed resurrection, I'll reverse the erasure spell so the world will remember Ruby's existence," she says.

"And that they'll think I'm alive—not dead," I add, not wanting to get mixed up in any nuances.

"And that they'll think she's alive, not dead," Hazel agrees, and I give her a single nod of appreciation.

After a moment of silence, Zara finally says, "As it is spoken, so let it be done."

Hazel and I repeat the phrase together, and the ground ripples under my feet.

"Next, I need each of you to use your dagger to make a horizontal cut on your left palm," Zara instructs.

Luckily, they prepared me for this part. And, since the dagger is spelled, my supernatural healing won't kick in until after the ceremony is complete.

Taking a deep breath, I lower the dagger to my palm and drag its sharp tip across my skin, giving just enough pressure for a tiny amount of blood to escape. It stings, but I breathe steadily, embracing the pain instead of fighting it.

Hazel does the same, although her cut is deeper than mine.

"Ruby's blood is now mixed with Morgan's, and Hazel's is now mixed with Willow's," Zara says, removing an identical dagger from where it's sheathed on her side. "Now, the final touch."

She uses her dagger to slice her left palm. Then she holds her hand over my palm, lets a few drops of her blood drip into the blood pooling there, and does the same for Hazel.

She pulls her hand back to her side, satisfied.

"Join your hands together," she tells us.

Hazel and I reach forward like we're about to shake each other's hands and clasp them together. The blood mixes inside our grips, its magic entering my palm and flowing through my body.

Zara rests her bleeding hand around our joined ones, the flame tattoo on her cheek almost seeming to dance in the moonlight.

"By the crimson tie that binds, by the sacred moon that shines, seal our pact in blood and light," she says, and her voice is melodic, as if woven with magic.

The center of my palm warms. From the way Hazel tightens her grip around mine, it seems like hers is doing the same.

"Let go and face your palms toward the sky," Zara instructs next, and Hazel and I do as asked.

Maybe it's magic, or maybe it's the moonlight, but the blood in my palm shimmers in a way it didn't before.

"Now, for the fun part." A hint of fiery orange swirls in Zara's eyes, and she presses one thumb in my palm and the other in Hazel's, as if the blood is ink and she's getting ready to stamp her fingerprint.

It's not too far off, because she continues by pressing the pad of her thumbs to the insides of our wrists. But when she raises them, it's not her thumbprint on our skin.

It's the symbol of the Blood Coven. An interwoven pentacle and flame.

A chill runs up my spine at the sight of it. There's something eerie about it—something dark. Like a warning.

As I look down at it, magic buzzes through the air, and the earth thrums with life. It's like the ground is reminding me that it's here with me, supporting me.

I've never felt this connected to the earth before. As an omega, I don't have earth magic. Yet, throughout this ceremony, the ground has been pulsing beneath my feet, as if it's alive.

What if Jax was wrong in thinking that I don't have elemental magic?

As the realization hits, Zara continues the ceremony, yanking me out of my wandering thoughts.

"The essence of life unites us now. Behold the bond, and accept our vow," she says, her voice echoing in the darkness.

Suddenly, the blood on my wrist *burns*. It's setting fire to my skin, branding it, so hot that I have no doubt it's going to leave a permanent scar.

Orange light radiates out of it. But it eventually dies out, and the symbol of the Blood Coven sinks beneath my skin.

Thunder rumbles from above, vibrating through my chest, and a flash of lightning brightens the sky.

As the blood oath takes hold, the air thickens with magic and promise. It's like we've struck a deal with the universe itself, and the world has agreed to hold us to our vows.

"After you've fulfilled your promises to each other, you'll be released from the oath," Zara reminds us, turning to me. "If you go against it, you'll remain erased forever."

Thunder rumbles again, as if accentuating her point.

"I understand," I say, and she gives me an approving smile.

"Good," she says. "I'm liking you more and more each day. When the time comes, you'll make an excellent addition to our coven."

"Yes, she will," Hazel agrees, her words hanging in the air like a veiled threat.

Zara smiles, sharp and dangerous, and continues with the ceremony. "By the power of flame and the essence of life vested in me, this circle is now closed," she says. "Blessed be."

"Blessed be," the others repeat in unison.

I say it a second after them, since I didn't realize this was going to be a group participation moment.

My palm tingles, the cut sealing itself, and the blood disappears.

The earth's energy gives one final pulse beneath my feet, then fades away.

Once it's gone, I know deep in my bones that if my connection to the earth during this ceremony was elemental magic, I'm keeping it to myself. No member of the Blood Coven needs to know. Not even Tristan.

It's my secret, and mine alone. Because someday, if I ever need to defend myself against them, it could benefit me to catch them unprepared.

Zara glances up at the moon one final time, as if silently thanking it for overseeing the ceremony. "The oath is complete," she says with a wicked smile. "Now, the two of you need to get some rest. Because tomorrow, you have a fae realm to enter and an ancient artifact to steal."

Ruby

THE ADRENALIN from the ceremony swirls within me as I hurry up the multiple flights of stairs and into my room in the attic. All is quiet and just as I left it, down to the unmade bed.

My parents always told me that making my bed is the best way to start the day. But honestly, I never bother, since I'm just going to sleep in it at night and mess it up all over again.

If we succeed in getting the key and Hazel reverses the spell, then I'm never going to not make my bed at home ever again.

But right now, I'm not tired. I *should* be, but as I look around at the hardwood floors and carved wooden furniture, I feel a tiny bit of magic radiating off them. It makes sense, since wood comes from trees, and trees come from the earth. In fact, the entire room buzzes with an energy that I never felt before.

Which means that connection—the raw power I felt with the earth—is still inside me.

It didn't disappear when Zara closed the circle.

The question is—can I use it? On purpose?

There's no time to try but the present.

I glance over at the bookcase on the far wall. It's littered with the usual books, pens, and trinkets... but also a collection of crystals. They're all different shapes, sizes, and colors, but now, one of them in particular is calling to me.

A particularly large, jagged piece of clear quartz.

I grab it and jump onto my bed, ready to get this experiment on the road. The crystal is cool and smooth, and it reacts to my touch, humming with energy like the ground did during the ceremony.

Now... what to do with it?

Back at Jax's house, Autumn used her earth magic to raise a group of stones from the ground and swirl them around herself like she was the center of a storm.

I doubt I can do anything as advanced as that. But there has to be something small I can try.

Maybe I can get it to hover in my hand? Just a bit? Even a few millimeters will be enough to prove to myself that I can do this—that the magic of the earth lives inside me.

I sit cross-legged, like I'm about to start a yoga class, then pick up the quartz and hold it with both of my hands. It sits in my cupped palms, ready for whatever I'm about to throw at it.

I take a deep breath, stare at it, and focus.

Float up, I tell it, trying to connect it to my mind like a live wire going from the quartz to my brain and get it to do my bidding.

Nothing happens.

Because you're not trying to use illusion magic. You're trying to use elemental magic, my wolf speaks up from inside me.

For the first time in a long time, she's supporting me instead of fighting me. And, I have to admit that it feels nice to have her on my side.

Okay, I answer her, steeling myself to try again.

This time, I picture the energy like roots growing from the wood floor beneath me, through my body, out my palms, and into the crystal. It responds to my call, humming through me just like it did during the ceremony, and I smile in victory.

Holding onto the magic, I envision it like vines growing around the crystal, willing it to obey my commands.

Float up, I try again, pushing the bottom of the crystal with the energy buzzing in my hands.

And then—just as frustration begins to nibble at my patience—it starts to work. The rock moves upward, one slow millimeter at a time, until it's floating inches above my palms.

I smile, and the crystal seems to glow brighter, glimmering in the dim light of the room as if it's celebrating my victory.

I was right.

I'm not an omega.

I have illusion magic *and* earth magic… which makes me far more of a threat than any of the others realize.

Suddenly, there's a knock on the door, breaking my concentration and sending the quartz tumbling back into my hands.

"Ruby?" Tristan says. "Morgan told me you came back up here…" He peeks inside, smiling when he sees me.

I move the crystal behind me and shove it under the blanket, hoping he didn't see it. I could always lie and say I was playing with it while thinking about the ceremony—or something like that—but it'll be easiest if he doesn't ask.

"Hey," I say quickly, hoping to sound casual and not like I was just practicing using magic I'm not supposed to have. "What's up?"

"I wanted to ask how the ceremony went." He eyes me, concerned. "And I thought it might be time for… you know."

For drinking my blood.

I curse internally.

Because if he feeds from me, it might not only mute my wolf. It might mute my earth magic, too.

Now that I've realized I have elemental magic, I don't want to give it up. The magic won't do me any good if I'm unable to access it.

You're finally thinking like a Guardian, my wolf chimes in. Her change in attitude from the other night is jolting, but I suppose she'll jump on any opportunity to stop me from letting Tristan feed from me.

"About that," I say, shifting uncomfortably. "Maybe we should take a break. Just for a bit."

Hurt splatters across his face, and I instantly realize how that might have come off.

"I don't mean that the two of us should take a break from each *other,*" I rush to explain. "It's just that my wolf hasn't come back yet, and it might be good to wait for as long as possible between feedings. Don't you think?"

Lies.

I don't like lying to him. But I've already committed to hiding my earth magic from the Blood Coven, and I stand by that decision.

Even though it means keeping the truth from Tristan, too.

"Sure." He walks over to the bed and sits next to me, studying me with concern etched across his features. "Is everything okay?"

"It's been a tough few days," I say, since at least *that's* not a lie. "And the ceremony was… intense."

"I know," he says. "Zara had us make oaths to her when we joined the coven, to make us swear to keep all the details about what we're trying to do to ourselves."

"Zara's tough, but she's smart," I say.

"She is."

He glances down at my hands, then reaches for my left one—the one I cut during the ceremony. His touch is feathery and caring as he traces his thumb in circles around my palm, and my breath catches, like it does every time he touches me.

My wolf bristles, but she doesn't fight.

Good. At least she has enough sense to know that if she tries to take over my body again, Tristan *will* stop her, and I won't be mad about it.

I look down at our entwined fingers, my mind whirling with so many questions. And even though Tristan isn't a witch, he's been alive for over a century, which means it's more than possible that he'll have answers to some of them.

I give his hand a small squeeze, then pull away.

He frowns, but only for a moment.

My wolf, on the other hand, is thrilled to not be touching him anymore.

"What happens when the witches cast the protective circle during the ceremony?" I ask.

After all, that was the first time I felt my earth magic.

And I'm determined to learn as much as I possibly can before stepping foot into the fae realm.

Ruby

TRISTAN'S FINGERS TWITCH SLIGHTLY, but instead of reaching for me again, he brings his hand back to his side. Part of me wants to close the space between us to feel connected to him, but I have more important things to worry about right now than my relationship with Tristan.

So I watch him quietly, waiting for his answer.

"Witches are at their most vulnerable when they're performing a ceremony," he eventually says. "The circle isn't only there to draw forth magic, but also to protect them."

"Protect them from what?"

"From anyone who wishes to cause them harm," he explains. "When a witch is casting a spell or performing a ritual, they're essentially opening themselves up to the universe. It strengthens them on the inside, but makes them more vulnerable on the outside."

"Do you mean that when they're casting strong magic in a circle, they're less aware of potential attacks?" I ask.

"That's the basics of it," he says. "And the circle itself is also a conduit for the magic they're channeling."

A conduit for magic...

The phrase echoes in my mind, and the pieces start coming together. Because the circle isn't just about protection. It also enhances a witch's powers, maybe even allowing them to tap into something more.

Like how I connected with my earth magic.

The witches just helped make me more powerful, and they don't even know it.

The realization sends a giddy sort of satisfaction through me.

But of course, I don't voice any of this. I simply smile and squeeze Tristan's hand, feeling him relax from my touch.

"Thanks for explaining," I say. "This is all so new to me, and it really helps to have someone I trust in my corner."

If you trust him, then why did you lie to him?

My wolf sounds insanely pleased with herself, and I do my best to shake her out of my thoughts.

"No problem." He returns my squeeze and gives me a true smile. "You know I'm always here for your magical inquiries."

His eyes flick to my neck, and I have a feeling he's thinking about another, far more intimate way he can be here for me, too. Then, before I realize what's happening, he closes the space between us and presses his soft lips to mine.

My body reacts instantly.

I want to pull him closer, lean back in bed, and finish up what we started the other night.

But—beyond the fact that if I lean back from where I'm sitting right now, I'll be lying down right on the jagged crystal—tonight isn't the right time for me to lose myself in Tristan.

Because I need to lose myself to learning as much as I can about my earth magic. I need to spend time *practicing* that magic.

In private.

"Wait." I press my hand to his chest, stopping him mid-kiss. As I do, my fingers brush against the pendant of his necklace, and desire courses through me so intensely that I want to kiss him again and not stop until we've given ourselves to each other completely.

No, my wolf snaps me out of it, and this time, I agree with her.

I need to resist the hold Tristan has over me.

"What's wrong?" He's breathing heavier now, on the verge of losing all self-control.

I pull my hand off his chest and scoot backward, the edge of the crystal poking my skin.

"It's just been a long day," I manage to say. "Between seeing my parents, and doing the blood oath… I think I just need a night to myself."

He stiffens, and his expression is no longer full of desire, but as stoic as ever. "I understand," he says simply, and even though he's trying to hide it, I can tell that being pushed away hurt him. "I hope you sleep well, Ruby. We have a big day tomorrow."

He stands up and leaves before we can talk about it further, closing the door and leaving me alone in the drafty attic.

The room feels empty without him here with me.

But then the crystal thrums with energy where I'm sitting on it, reminding me why I asked him to leave in the first place.

I have work to do.

I get up to change, since it sounds so much more appealing to practice magic in my cozy pajamas than my jeans. When I take off my red leather jacket—a gift from Morgan—the dagger Hazel gave me falls out of the inside pocket and onto the floor next to my feet.

The handle of the dagger glistens in the moonlight shining through the window. Specifically, the deep blue lapis lazuli gem embedded into it.

Seeing it there ignites an idea inside me.

I was able to control that quartz because it came from the earth. The blue gem in the dagger came from the earth as well.

If I can strengthen my earth magic enough to tune into the lapis lazuli and control it, then I might have more power over that dagger than Hazel ever could have predicted when she gave it to me.

I pick up the weapon and smile at it, as if I'm holding the key to my freedom.

Because when they locked me in that cell, I was weak. Scared. Powerless. Dependent. Trapped.

But everything I've learned since then—about myself and those around me—has lit a fire in me. And from this moment on, I refuse to be any of those things ever again.

Connor

THE VERY FIRST rays of sunlight are starting to make their way through the window when I wake up. Autumn is sleeping next to me, her hand resting on my chest, the diamond on her engagement ring sparkling.

She's so peaceful as she sleeps, her red hair strewn about like a halo on the pillow around her.

But every time I look at her these past few days, I can't help but think back to the night of our engagement party, when Jax painted the mud on her cheeks. The way he took his time, as if he didn't want to stop touching her, and how they gazed at each other like they were seeing deep into each other's souls.

I've only seen her look at one other man that way.

Me.

It's crazy. I have to be reading too much into it, and seeing something that isn't there. Because Autumn and I are *engaged*. Jax's kind words were nothing more than a courteous gesture. He was showing respect and acceptance for her, because soon she'll officially be part of our family.

Still, she shouldn't be looking at someone like that other than me. Especially not *Jax*.

How do you think Autumn felt when she saw you look at Ruby? my wolf speaks up in my mind.

The image of Ruby's face—fierce, yet laced with a subtle vulnerability—flashes in my thoughts, and it's like a physical blow.

Neither my wolf nor I have thought about Ruby much recently. I figured the mate bond was fading, thanks to the physical distance between us. But apparently my intrusive thoughts are bringing my desire for her back to the surface again.

That's different, I reply to my wolf. *Ruby's my fated mate.*

Jax, on the other hand, is a womanizer. He's probably slept with every woman who's single in the pack. Even the married ones—the ones who aren't mated—sneak glances at him when they don't think their husbands are looking.

I can't imagine him making moves on my girl.

On the other hand, he knows Autumn and I will never be mates. Maybe he views her as fair game now? Even as some sort of fun challenge?

The universe chose Ruby for us for a reason, my wolf speaks up again. *Maybe this is a reminder that we'll never truly be happy with anyone other than her.*

I rub my temples, frustrated and conflicted. This is *not* how I wanted to start my day.

But I'm too awake by now to fall back to sleep. So, I sit up and reach for my phone.

There's one text—from an unknown number.

I tap on it and read it.

I have important information about your mate, Ruby. She isn't safe. Meet me and my boyfriend at the Stardust Diner as soon as possible, and I'll tell you more. We'll be in the booth all the way in the back until noon. Come alone.

I blink a few times, trying to make sense of it.

It could be some sort of prank.

Except as far as I'm aware, no one knows Ruby's my mate other than me, Autumn, Jax, Hazel, and Hazel's parents. I have all their numbers stored in my phone, so the text can't be from any of them. Especially because they specifically said they're with their boyfriend. Maybe Hazel has a boyfriend, but I doubt it.

It could, of course, all be a lie.

But assuming so isn't a risk I want to take. Because if I don't meet them, and if something happens to Ruby because of it, I'll never forgive myself for sitting back when I could have taken action to help.

Besides, the Stardust Diner is here in Pine Valley. Nothing's going to happen to me there.

I'll be right there, I reply, and then I open my text chain with Autumn. She sleeps with her phone on do not disturb, so if I message her right now, it won't wake her up.

Woke up early and couldn't go back to sleep, so I decided to go for a morning run and grab us some breakfast. Sleep in, and I'll wake you up with your favorite bacon.

I almost press send, but then I add one more thing to the end.

I love you.

Message sent.

I head out of my house and shift into my wolf form, running to town as quickly as possible to find out who's waiting for me at the diner, and to hear what they have to tell me about Ruby.

Because I know one thing above all else: I will not rest until I know my fated mate is safe.

Connor

THE STARDUST DINER is just starting to wake up when I get there. The smell of coffee and pancakes fills the air, mixing with the hum of early morning chatter and the faint sound of an old rock song playing on the jukebox.

The hostess beams at me and reaches for the menus. "How many in your party?" she asks.

"I'm meeting some friends," I reply. "They're in the back."

"Sure thing. Enjoy your breakfast!"

She's *far* too perky for this early in the morning.

I head back and spot the booth, which is far enough away from the more popular area in the front of the restaurant that no one's going to overhear our conversation. Sitting in it is a girl with wavy brown hair, her back facing me, across from a burly guy who looks like he could be a football player.

I've seen them a handful of times before, during my few visits to Spring Creek. I remember that she's a witch and he's a shifter, but I don't recall either of their names. And while it's unprecedented for a witch to date a shifter, the supernaturals of Spring Creek have always been unconventional, so it's not entirely surprising.

I approach them, my wolf senses on high alert, and stand at the edge of the table so I'm looking down at them.

"You asked to meet?"

I don't give any more information, in case they weren't the ones who sent the text.

"I'm Thalia," she says, just as soft spoken as she looks. "This is my boyfriend, Gunnar."

Gunnar gives me a single nod.

"Connor," I say, even though they both clearly already know who I am.

"Want to sit?" She motions at the space next to Gunnar.

Gunnar moves all the way to the side, and I slide myself into the booth, folding my hands on the table.

"What was it you wanted to talk about?" I ask.

Again, I'm purposefully cryptic.

Thalia raises an eyebrow, and I have a feeling she knows exactly what I'm doing.

"Not *it*," she says. *"Who.* Ruby. Your fated mate."

My heart twists at the sound of her name.

"What does Spring Creek have to do with Ruby?"

We pause as the waitress pours me some coffee. When she asks what we want to eat, Gunnar orders an assortment of dishes for the table. Far too many than we could possibly eat, even with our shifter appetites.

When she's gone, I turn my attention back to Thalia. She's playing with a ring on her middle finger—it has a silver flame pendant on it—and I can tell she's nervous.

"I'll get to that soon," she says. "First, I have to give you important information—as much as I'm able. About my coven... and a person you think you love."

I tense and lean forward slightly.

What the hell could she possibly be getting at?

Instead of asking, I watch her carefully, waiting for her to continue.

She takes a deep breath, looks at Gunnar, and he gives her an encouraging nod. "Okay," she starts, slowly exhaling. "Like I said, I'll share as much as I can. We're under an oath to not give outsiders much information, but I'm going to try."

"Go on."

"The Spring Creek coven has expanded," she says. "Other powerful witches have joined. They call themselves the Blood Coven, and they threatened all the witches and shifters in Spring Creek to either join them or suffer the consequences."

"What sort of consequences?" I ask, and even though what she's saying sounds crazy, it's almost *too* crazy to not believe it.

"They wouldn't say," she tells me. "But I can't imagine it would be anything good."

It certainly doesn't. The name alone—the Blood Coven—already raises red flags in my mind.

She reaches for her coffee and takes a sip, her fingers tightening so much around the handle that her knuckles turn white. I'm half-worried that she's going to drop it, but she places it back on the table, steadying herself.

"They're doing the devil's work," Gunnar chimes in, his previously warm green eyes swirling with rage. "They have to be stopped."

"What exactly are they doing?" I ask, and his muscles tighten, as if he's straining against something I can't see.

"We can't say." Thalia's face pales, her breaths quickening. "I'm sorry. But you need to gather the pack and witches of Pine Valley to stop them, before it's too late."

Questions swirl through my mind—many of them about Ruby—but I have to be strategic about this conversation and learn as much from Thalia and Gunnar as possible. I've been training all my life for situations like this.

It's time to put those skills to the test.

I take a deep breath to feel them out. If they're lying, I'd be able to smell it, like rusted metal.

Nothing of the sort fills the air.

"This is all very interesting," I eventually say, as steadily as ever. "I can speak with the Pine Valley witches to see what they know."

Fear flashes in Thalia's eyes.

"You can't talk to them about this," she says.

"Why not?"

"Because their leaders—Hazel and her parents? They're members of the Blood Coven."

I stare at her like she's gone mental. "That's not possible," I say, and I take a deep breath to sniff out her lie.

Nothing.

Of course there's nothing. She and Gunnar know I'm the grandson of the Pine Valley alpha. They know I'll be able to sense if they lie.

And, since what she's saying is true…

Horror strikes me so intensely that it sucks all the air from my lungs at once.

"Ruby isn't safe with them," I say, and she nods, her brown eyes sad for me.

Eyes that are nearly the same warm shade as Ruby's.

Ruby can't stay with them for a second longer.

I bolt upright and push myself out of the booth, needing to get to Hazel's house as quickly as possible.

Thalia's hand shoots out and grabs my wrist, her grip surprisingly strong.

"Wait," she pleads.

"Let go." I try to yank my wrist out of her grip, but she refuses to release me. It's a strain for her—almost as much as it was to speak through whatever promise she made to the Blood Coven—but she's putting up a good fight.

"No. You need to listen." Her voice is sharp and commanding, a stark difference from earlier. "There's more you need to know."

"But Ruby—"

"Isn't the only one you love who's mixed up in all of this, although I do have more information about her as well."

I stop fighting her, needing to learn more. "What are you talking about?"

She watches me with sympathy, as if she knows she's about to tell me something that's going to catch me off-guard all over again and possibly tilt my entire world off-axis.

"There's something important you need to know about someone you love," she repeats. "But I'm not talking about Ruby. I'm talking about Autumn."

Connor

My anger grows at the sound of my fiancée's name, and this time when I try to pull my wrist out of Thalia's grip, she doesn't resist.

"What about Autumn?" I ask.

Thalia takes a deep breath and plays with her ring. "You need to sit down, Connor."

I glance at Gunnar, who's been pretty silent throughout all of this.

He nods in support of his girlfriend.

I re-join them at the table, keeping my eyes locked on Thalia's the entire time.

"Thank you," she says, and apparently having caught onto the break in our argument, the waitress hurries over to deliver our food. She doesn't say much, and she's quick to leave us alone so we can return to our conversation.

I ignore the food, even though it smells delicious. The only thing I care about right now is hearing what else Thalia has to say.

Gunnar's quick to dig in, but Thalia doesn't seem interested in eating, either.

"You have my attention," I tell her. "Tell me what you came here to say."

"Autumn betrayed you," she starts, and just like the rest of this little meeting, there's no scent of a lie.

My heart rises in my throat.

Because I want to learn what she means. But I also have a terrible feeling that when I do, my world will never be the same.

"What did she do?" I ask slowly, cautiously.

"She came to Spring Creek," Thalia says. "She gave us information. Well, not *us*. She gave information to the leader of our coven."

"Calliope?"

"Yes."

I take a moment to process this, because it doesn't make sense.

"When did Autumn go to Spring Creek?" I ask, since I see her every day, and there were never any signs that she did something that huge behind my back.

Although up until this past week or so, my thoughts were consumed with Ruby and the mate bond. Could I have been so wrapped up in Ruby that I missed any hints of something larger going on with Autumn?

"About fifteen days ago," Gunnar chimes in, finally deciding to take part in the conversation. "She came at night."

Fifteen days.

I know exactly what happened fifteen days ago, since it was a huge turning point in our lives.

It was the night I proposed to her.

That's why she didn't want to come back with me to my house afterward. It wasn't because she had a lot of work to do, like she claimed.

The realization makes me feel sick.

But I need to know the truth.

"What information did Autumn give you?" I ask, and while this entire conversation feels surreal, I stay grounded and focused.

"She told Calliope about Ruby being star touched," Thalia begins. "And she begged her to break the mate bond between you and Ruby, no matter what needed to be done to make that happen."

I sit there, shellshocked.

"The only way to break someone's mate bond involuntarily is for one of the mates to die," I say slowly, unable to believe this is possible.

Luckily, I know Ruby's alive. If she wasn't, I would have felt it through the bond.

I've always felt like I'm a person who's ready for anything at any time. But this is too much to wrap my head around. Because I know Autumn. She's driven, and she stops at nothing to complete her goals.

But actively taking part in murder? And not just any murder, but the murder of my fated mate?

It's too low. Because sure, Autumn's determined—just like Jax pointed out to the entire pack during our engagement ceremony. But she wouldn't…

"She wouldn't do something like that," I say, even though I know Thalia's telling the truth. Or at least the truth as she knows it.

"She would," Gunnar says. "And she has."

"I don't know the details of the deal." Thalia plays around with the scrambled eggs on her plate, even though I haven't seen her take a single bite. "Even if I did, I doubt my oath to the Blood Coven would allow me to say."

"An oath that they forced us to take," Gunnar reminds me, drilling in the fact that he and Thalia aren't truly on the Blood Coven's side.

"Understood," I say, and then I listen with growing fury as Thalia tells me about Hazel kidnapping Ruby, the Blood Coven locking her in their basement, and the worst part… forcing a blood bond between Ruby and a vampire.

The world crumbles beneath my feet with every word she speaks, until there's nothing left to stand on.

Autumn betrayed me.

Because of what she did, Ruby's in danger. My fated mate is bound to someone else. A *vampire.*

Rage swells inside me, dark and raw. Time feels like it's standing still, and I clench my hands into fists, my nails biting into my palms.

This is too much.

I've spent my entire life preparing myself for anything. That's what Guardians do. But nothing—absolutely *nothing*—could have prepared me for this.

Suddenly, there's a rumbling beneath us. Glasses and plates clink on the tables. The overhead lights flicker, and the room starts to shake.

Someone screams.

Multiple someones.

Thalia reaches for me, and she squeezes my wrist—hard.

"Connor," she says, her voice low. "Calm down."

Her voice pulls me back to reality—one where my anger channeled my earth magic without me meaning to.

I rein it in, and the ground stops shaking, although now I'm angry at myself for losing control like that.

A Guardian *never* loses control.

I take a few deep breaths, slowly getting myself together.

"I'm calm," I finally say.

The lie is so thick that I'm sure Gunnar can smell it, even though he's not of alpha blood.

Still, the tremors have stopped, so Thalia releases my wrists, satisfied.

"That was a damn big truck!" a man says from the center of the diner, where he's standing up and looking out the window for any sign of the offending vehicle.

"Wasn't a truck," an old man mutters at the bar, downing his cup of coffee. "I've lived in California. I know an earthquake when I feel one."

Luckily, he's far enough away from everyone that no one pays him any attention.

People chuckle around us and resume their meals, tension bleeding away as they dismiss the tremor as something harmless.

I can't let that *ever* happen again.

Doing something so careless—something with the potential to reveal our existence to humans—is against one of the many laws of the Guardians.

"No one will ever find out what just happened here." I look to Gunnar, then to Thalia. "Understood?"

"I'll make sure of it," she promises, and I know the subtext behind what she means.

She wants to use her fire magic to compel everyone in here to forget about what just happened.

"You're powerful enough to do that?" I ask.

"I am." She stands up and gives me a knowing smirk that looks out of place on her soft features. "Watch me."

With that, she walks around the diner, going from table to table, creating a small ball of fire in her hands when she talks to every person in there and compels them to forget about what they just felt and saw.

She finishes up with the man at the bar and the waiter serving him, then slides back into our booth.

"Happy?" she asks, pulling the last of her flames back into her palms.

"Not as happy as I'll be after you tell me the name of the vampire that fed from my mate."

"I can't do that," she says simply.

"Because of the oath with the Blood Coven?"

"Correct," she says. "Also, this vampire is now blood bonded to Ruby. Killing him won't do you any favors, unless you want your fated mate to hate you more than she already does."

"She hates me?"

Out of everything I've learned tonight, this shouldn't be so shocking.

Yet somehow, it is.

I failed my mate. And now, both of us are paying for it.

But it's not too late. As long as Ruby's still alive, I can fix this. After all, we're destined for each other. I can—and I *will*—make this right, even if it's the last thing I ever do.

"I'm coming back with you to Spring Creek," I tell them, my decision made.

"You can't do that," Thalia says. "They'll kill you."

I lean forward and hold her gaze, making myself extra clear. "You can't just tell me that your coven is keeping Ruby there against her will, and then not expect me to go after her."

"You know, we hear stories about you in Spring Creek," Gunnar says. "Aren't you supposed to be strategic and level-headed?"

My magic swirls inside me, threatening to come out again.

This time, I control it.

"I'm going after her," I repeat. "The two of you can either help me or not, but I'm not changing my mind."

"We're not asking you to change your mind," Thalia says quickly, before I have a chance to stand up. "We agree that you need to get Ruby away from the Blood Coven. If they get their way and force her into joining them, it will make them more powerful than they already are. We need to stop that from happening."

"Then you'll tell me everything I need to know to help me infiltrate Spring Creek."

"No, we won't," she says calmly. "Because we have a much better plan than that."

From the fierce way she's looking at me, I can tell she means business.

"Okay." I take a sip of my coffee and lean back in the booth. "I'm listening."

"Thank you," she says, and from there, she and Gunnar give me all the details about the plan they've concocted over the past few days.

As crazy as it is, it might actually work.

And once I get my mate safely back to Pine Valley where she belongs, I swear to every god in existence that I'm never going to let her down ever again.

Connor

I RUN BACK HOME AS QUICKLY as I can. Running in my wolf form usually does wonders to calm my nerves, but right now, nothing's going to help until I rescue Ruby and bring her back to Pine Valley.

And then we'll solidify the bond and make her ours, my wolf's voice rumbles in my head. *Forever.*

Yes, I agree. *We absolutely will.*

Shifting back into human form, I reach my backyard and catch sight of Autumn making coffee through the kitchen window. She taps her fingertips on the countertop as she waits for it to be ready, looking anxious and troubled.

Good.

Given what she's done, she should be in constant war with herself.

I've seen it a bit—the darkness that occasionally crosses her eyes recently when we talk about our future together. I assumed it was because she was insecure about the fact that I have a mate that isn't her.

Now I know it's far, far more than that.

She and I shared years of love and trust. When she shifted for the first time, I was the one who went on a run through the mountains with her. We studied for tests together, practiced using our magic together, trained together, and planned a future together.

That trust was broken in a single morning, shattered into so many pieces that it will never exist again.

I'm so disgusted by her betrayal that I don't even feel bad about the thought of ripping our future out from under her feet.

Steeling myself, I enter the kitchen, and she turns around with a huge smile on her face.

"Morning," she chirps. "How was your run?"

How can she stand there and act so innocent? I search for any sign of concern, and find nothing. It's like she put on a mask the second I came inside.

"It was… enlightening," I say, and she cocks her head, intrigued.

"How so?"

It's like I'm looking at a stranger in my girlfriend's body, and I have no idea where to even begin.

"You're brooding," she says, and she walks over to me, wraps her arms around my neck, and kisses me.

I don't kiss her back.

I just stand there, still as a statue, giving her absolutely zero acknowledgment whatsoever. Because I should be kissing my mate. Not the woman who tried to take her from me forever.

She pulls away and frowns. "Talk to me."

All I see when I look at her and all I hear when she talks are lies.

How did I miss it before? Did I trust her so much that I didn't ever bother trying to sniff out when she was lying to me or telling me the truth?

I did.

And I will never make that mistake again. Not with her, and not with anyone.

The disgust that rolls through me at her touch is all-consuming, and I shake her off me and step back.

She looks me up and down, and from the innocence in her eyes, you'd think I was the one who did something wrong instead of her.

"Where's the bacon?" She sounds so small and vulnerable that I want to grab her shoulders and shake the truth straight out of her.

I can envision it now. The fear in her eyes as my grip on her tightens, the way she'll break when she finds out that I know every terrible thing she's done, and how her world will crumble when she learns there's no future between the two of us.

Not anymore, and not ever.

My wolf snarls inside me, egging me on.

She played us. She purposefully endangered our mate. She deserves everything that's coming to her.

I clench my hands by my sides, using every bit of strength I have to stop my claws from coming out and slashing them through her skin so she can experience an inkling of the pain I'm in after she crushed my heart and stomped all over the pieces.

But I ground myself, reining in my emotions, and thus, my wolf.

No matter how much I hate Autumn, I would never lay a hand on her. I wouldn't be able to forgive myself if I did.

However, I can't deny that I'm tempted. Which means I can't stay here. I won't risk doing something I'll regret.

"I need to get out of here," I say, and I hurry to the door, grab my keys, and make my way to the car.

Where I'm heading next is too far of a journey to make in my wolf form.

"Connor!" Autumn screams my name, running after me. "Wait."

I turn around and shoot her a glare that could cut glass.

She sucks in a sharp breath and takes a few slow steps back, her big eyes finally showing the fear she should have been feeling around me this entire time.

"I'm leaving," I tell her, as if it wasn't obvious by my grabbing my keys and heading to my car.

"Wherever you're going, I'll go with you." She squares her shoulders and takes a small step forward, apparently determined to not give up. "We're a team. Always."

"Not anymore," I growl, satisfied when the last traces of hope vanish from her face.

Good. She deserves to suffer for what she did.

Not physically, but emotionally.

I give her one final glare—a warning not to follow me—jump into my Wrangler, turn the key, and peel out of there.

I don't look back at Autumn.

I can't.

And I don't bother with music. There's no song in existence that can match the anger and betrayal I'm feeling right now. Instead, I drive in silence, relief washing over me when I'm out of Pine Valley and heading south.

Eventually, my phone buzzes, shattering the quiet.

I don't need to look at the caller ID to know it's Autumn.

She's *relentless*. It used to be a quality I loved about her.

Now it's one I hate.

I tighten my grip on the steering wheel, ignoring the call. I'd crush the phone and toss it out the window if I wasn't holding onto it as a potential lifeline to Ruby.

At the thought of my mate, hope blooms in my chest that the pieces of my heart can eventually come back together. Because Ruby's my future. And I won't let anything—or anyone—stand in my way of making things right between us.

As the minutes rush on and the scenery blurs past, I make a vow. I will save Ruby. I will bring her back home.

And Autumn?

She'll have to live with the consequences of her actions for the rest of her life.

Ruby

I SLEPT SURPRISINGLY WELL without Tristan in the bed with me.

Maybe it helped that I kept the dagger on the pillow next to me, had my wolf's approval as I slid into sleep, and felt my earth magic filling a hollow spot inside me that I didn't even know existed until the witches cast that circle.

Now, I'm in a large SUV with Gwen, Hazel, Benjamin, and Tristan as Gwen drives us south.

Not to Florida this time, but to New York City.

I'd be anxious/excited about seeing such a big city for the first time, if I didn't have something else to focus on. Because earlier this morning, Gwen gave me full-body portraits of the four fae we're going to disguise ourselves as while we're in their realm.

Well, that *I'm* going to disguise us as, using my illusion magic. Gwen's a talented artist, so the drawings are incredibly detailed. Which is good, because I need to memorize as many details about these fae as possible before we get there.

Luckily, one of the benefits of my star touched magic is an exceptional visual memory.

Gwen specifically chose these fae because they're *arid* fae. They have no water magic, just like how omega wolves have no earth magic. Similarly, witches with no fire magic are called cinders, and vampires with no air magic are called voids.

Different species, but the same general idea.

And while arid fae are already outcasts, these four are even more so, for reasons Gwen didn't feel like sharing with us. The important thing is that since they're decently ostracized by others of their kind, they'll be easy targets.

I'm glad that studying the portraits gives me a good reason to not talk to the others during the car ride. I need to save as much energy as possible for what's coming tonight.

There's only one problem—neither of the female fae have brown eyes. The others know that the one feature of mine that I can't alter with my magic is my eyes, but we plan to stay as far away from other fae as possible, so it most likely won't be an issue.

Ideally, we'll be out of the fae realm tomorrow morning, with the Key of Hades in hand.

It takes nearly five hours to get to the city. As we get closer, the buildings get taller and denser, and I tear my eyes away from the portraits in my hands to gaze at the sight of the Empire State Building and the World Trade Center looming ahead of us.

The bright lights of the city are beautiful, especially at night.

Eventually, we cross a bridge into Manhattan, and I feel like a child all over again as I watch the city and the people walking down the sidewalks.

I'm mesmerized.

However, I don't think I'd ever want to live here. Thanks to what I assume is my shifter side and my affinity for earth magic, I've always liked open spaces. But that doesn't stop the thrill racing through me as I watch it all pass by before my eyes.

Gwen has zero difficulty driving the SUV through the traffic. She parks the car in a garage with ridiculously tiny spaces, and then we head out and walk across the street to a pizza place called Angelo's that Gwen said we *had* to eat at before our adventure.

She was right—the pizza is delicious. Possibly some of the best I've ever had.

The craziest thing is that while there, I'm *almost* able to pretend that my life is somewhat normal. Well, other than the fact that Gwen, Tristan, and Benjamin can't stop telling me and Hazel about what the city was like at the turn of the twentieth century, when they first lived here.

Gwen pays with cash, and then we get back into the car, driving another twenty minutes north.

"Did we really just go twenty minutes out of the way for pizza?" Hazel asks.

Gwen shrugs and gives Hazel a small smile in the rearview mirror. "I couldn't come all the way to the city and not have my favorite pizza."

She parks in another garage with stupidly tiny spaces, and we walk across the street to the Vanderbilt Gate, where we'll be entering Central Park. The black gate stands tall in the night, the swirls and crests of the ironwork standing out even under the city lights.

It *looks* like something you'd step through to enter a magical realm, like it was dropped here straight out of a fantasy novel.

"Remember—don't eat or drink anything while you're in the fae realm. And you *must* have the Key of Hades in hand before 6:00 am," Gwen reminds us.

From her tone, you'd think she didn't already tell us multiple times that the hours between 1:00 am and 6:00 am—when the park is closed—are the only times we can access the fae realm. At 6:00 am we'll be transported back to the human world, and then we won't be able to try for the key again until the park closes that night.

The more tries we make, the more likely it is that we'll get caught.

We *can't* get caught.

Being trapped in the fae realm is a possibility I'm simply not willing to accept.

"I'll see you at the meeting spot tomorrow morning," Gwen says. "For now, good luck."

At some point while we've been standing here, Tristan's moved closer to me. So close that his arm nearly brushes against mine.

"You okay?" he asks me.

"Okay as I'm going to be, given what we're about to do."

He reaches for my hand and squeezes it, and I give him a smile in return. His gesture says a lot. He's here for me. He'll keep me safe.

But I can also feel the energy of the dagger in my jacket pocket, and I know that with it, I can keep myself safe as well. I *do* trust Tristan to protect me, but I also believe in myself.

You also have me, my wolf speaks up in my mind, and I'm grateful for how agreeable she's being, even though Tristan just touched us.

She wants us to get out of this alive, too. And she's smart enough to know that attacking one of the people who's going to try keeping us alive is far from the best way to do that.

Thanks, I reply, and a comforting warmth settles through me.

I haven't tried shifting again since refusing Tristan's offer to feed from me last night—I haven't had the chance. But when we're out of the fae realm, you can bet I'll be trying again. The only reason I won't in the fae realm is because we need to blend in to stay as safe as we can, and that's hardly going to be possible if I'm prowling around in my wolf form.

But still, I know my wolf is here with me.

Just in case.

"What are we waiting around for?" Benjamin asks. "We have a hideout to get to."

He leads the way through the gate with Hazel by his side. Tristan and I follow behind.

Since it's dark out, there aren't many other people in Central Park. Even though it doesn't close until 1:00 am, it's not as safe at night as during the day, so people tend to clear out after dark.

Together, we walk along the gravel path, traversing the park until reaching a lake called Harlem Meer. It's at the northern end of the park, where the arid fae tend to live. The ones with magic are farther south.

But the four fae we're tracking are loners *and* arids, so we won't find them in the main part of the lake. So, I follow them up a rocky hill, to an area surrounded by trees that's empty of anyone but the four of us.

"This is where they live. We can camp out over there until we're transported to the fae realm," Benjamin says, pointing to an area where the trees and bushes are denser, but still have a view of the small clearing.

Since Tristan and Benjamin are the only two of the four of us who have been here before, Hazel and I let them lead the way.

We follow them over and get situated amongst the rocks and bushes. It's cold out, and without thinking about it, I find myself moving closer to Tristan for warmth.

He wraps an arm around my shoulders and pulls me close, my heart speeding up from his touch. "We've got this," he says.

"Yes," I agree. "We absolutely do."

He glances at his watch—an old analogue one that his father gave him for his birthday when he was a teen.

"How much longer?" I ask.

"An hour," he says, and we all fidget around to get ourselves as situated as possible, waiting out the final hour before the fae realm will overlap with ours, and our mission will truly begin.

Ruby

Thirty minutes to go, and the four of us have lapsed into comfortable silence. My fingers curl tighter around the dagger in my jacket pocket, its presence offering as much reassurance as Tristan's arm that's still wrapped around my shoulders.

Inside, my wolf remains watchful, ready to leap into action if necessary.

Suddenly, Benjamin lets out a startled gasp.

Before any of us can ask what's wrong, he's yanked away and dragged across the ground into the trees behind us.

We jump into action, hurrying to where he disappeared. There's a smokey, spicy scent nearby... one that's achingly familiar...

Connor.

He's kneeling next to Benjamin, holding a small syringe. With swift precision, he jabs it into Benjamin's arm.

Benjamin's eyes widen, his body goes slack, and his head flops to the ground. It's then I realize that there's something coiled around Benjamin's ankles.

Tree roots.

The roots release him and sink back into the ground. Earth magic.

Time freezes, and I stare at Connor, my heart racing, as if he's some sort of dream. It has to be a dream. Because how could he possibly know we were here?

Hazel rushes toward him, but Connor gets his claws out, ready to attack. Which turns out to be unnecessary, because it wasn't Connor she was heading toward.

Instead, she kneels beside Benjamin and gently shakes his shoulder, trying to wake him up.

My gaze returns to Connor's.

Being this close to him fills a hole in my heart that I can't believe I was almost forgetting was there.

Mate, my wolf's voice hums inside me. Every bone in her—*our*—body aches to run to him.

But the pain of Connor's rejection rises inside of me, and I stay firmly where I am.

Tristan's by my side in an instant, and the growl that rumbles from his chest mirrors my anger. Yet, he stays next to me, as if he knows better than to try laying a hand on my mate.

Hazel picks up the syringe and stands, her eyes hard as she glares at Connor. "This is mine," she says, gripping it so tightly that I'm surprised she isn't crushing it. "Where did you get it?"

Connor smiles smugly. "Let's just say that the Pine Valley pack—and coven—isn't as clueless as you think we are," he says, and then he hurries toward me and wraps his arms tightly around me, as if he's making sure I'm real.

I relax into his embrace.

My wolf hums with pleasure.

Everything else in the world other than the safety of being in Connor's arms disappears.

Eventually I pull away and stare up into his warm brown eyes. "What are you doing here?" I ask, shocked and confused and thrilled all at once.

"I heard about this crazy mission you're going on, and I wasn't about to let you risk your life without me here with you," he says, staring down at me as if he's just as amazed that I'm here as I am that he's here.

"What about Autumn?" My heart hurts when I say her name.

"I found out what she did. That she handed you over to Spring Creek." His eyes darken, and as crazy as it is, I can physically feel the pain emanating from his body. "Her betrayal is unforgivable. It's over between us."

Two weeks ago, those words would have made me the happiest person alive.

Now, it's all so much more complicated than that.

"And then you came here. To me." I know it's true, but it still doesn't feel real.

"I had to be here," he says, strong and determined. "To make sure you're safe. I'm not asking you to forgive me, because I know that's going to take time. But I let you go once, and I swear to every god in existence that I'm not going to repeat that mistake ever again."

"You do realize how much pain you caused her, right?" Tristan speaks up from next to us, yanking me out of my Connor-induced trance.

Guilt washes over me. Because the moment I saw Connor, I forgot Tristan was even there.

Because Connor's our mate, my wolf says, as if it's something I'd ever forget.

Still, none of that takes away the time Tristan and I spent together, and the bond we share.

Connor's jaw tenses as his eyes lock with Tristan's. "Is this your vampire keeper?" he asks, although his gaze doesn't move away from Tristan's as he speaks.

Tristan, however, is as calm and relaxed as ever. "I'm Tristan," he introduces himself, as if we're at a party instead of in a dark park about to go on a potentially dangerous mission. "And I'm not her 'keeper.' In case you didn't notice while you were busy *rejecting* her, Ruby's her own woman, and she doesn't belong to anyone."

His words send a bolt of appreciation through my chest.

Something flickers in Connor's eyes. Regret? Pain? Anger?

I'm half-prepared for him to let his claws out and try to rip them through Tristan's throat.

"You do know that a mate bond trumps a blood bond," Connor finally says, and he takes a step closer to Tristan, his eyes brimming with hatred. "And even though you want it—and despite what you're saying, I know you do—she'll never truly be yours. *Never.*"

He practically growls when he says the final word.

A warning.

"Stop." I step between them, arms out, ready to push away either of them if they get too close.

The word lingers in the cold winter air, and they both watch me, waiting for what I'm going to say next.

I look to Tristan, then to Connor. They both seem to be standing down—for now.

"The three of us have a lot we need to talk about," I start, which is the understatement of the century. "But I take it that both of you want to help me get the Key of Hades?"

"Yes," Connor says, at the same time Tristan says, "You know I do."

"Great." I take a deep breath, then continue. "Because if we want to succeed, then we need to get our heads in the game and focus. We can't do that if both of you are fighting about who owns me and who doesn't. Because Tristan's right—I don't belong to anyone. I'm not a possession, and I'm perfectly capable of making my own decisions."

A relaxed smile creeps onto Tristan's lips, and I turn to Connor, my heart already hurting from what I'm about to do.

"I appreciate that you're here, and I welcome your help," I say, meeting his gaze straight on. "But you rejected me. You chose Autumn. Yes, what she did was shitty and conniving and downright deceitful. You don't owe her forgiveness, and I wouldn't blame you if you never spoke to her again. But Tristan and I are together now. If you come on this mission, I need you to accept that."

Connor's features twitch, the muscles in his jaw flexing as he absorbs my words.

"I understand," he finally says, cold and distant.

A whimper of pain tries to make its way up my throat—either from me, or my wolf—but I push it down.

"I'm coming on this mission." He lifts his chin, his gaze hardening with resolve. "Whether you're with Tristan or not, it doesn't change the fact that you're my mate. I won't let you face this without me here fighting with you."

I want to run to him and feel his arms around me again.

Do it, my wolf whispers in my ear, and I feel her crawling to the surface, waiting for me to let my guard down enough to give into my primal urge to fall straight back into my mate's arms.

Try anything, and I'll tell Tristan to drink from me again, I threaten her, and she must believe me, because she backs down.

"You guys?" Hazel's voice breaks through the silence, and the three of us look to where she's still kneeling beside Benjamin's unconscious body. "As touching as this reunion is, my boyfriend's out of commission—and will be for the next few hours—and this entire park is going to turn into fae territory in less than half an hour. We need to get him out of here. Now."

"Where should we bring him?" I snap to attention, ready to do exactly what I told the guys I was going to do by focusing on our mission and putting the drama between us aside.

"We need to get him out of the park," she says. "Tristan, you'll carry him. Ruby, you need to make both of them invisible, since an unconscious man being carried out of

Central Park at this time of night is going to draw the exact sort of attention we want to avoid."

Tristan's on it in seconds, hoisting Benjamin up onto his back shoulders as if he weighs nothing.

"You're okay with Connor joining us?" I ask Hazel, even though it's pretty clear that Connor's coming along whether she says yes or not.

"I'm not exactly thrilled with it," she says. "I'm also smart enough to know when to pick my battles, and Connor's a strong warrior who will do whatever he can to ensure you make it out of here alive and complete our deal. We're more likely to succeed if we're working together. But he also just *drugged my boyfriend* to take his place in our mission, and if we don't get Benjamin to safety, you can mark my words that no one in the Blood Coven will rest until your mate here is dead."

I shiver when she's done speaking, since it's clear from her tone that it's more than just a threat—it's a promise.

"Understood," I say, and then I look over at where Tristan is carrying Benjamin, tap into my illusion magic, and make the two of them invisible.

"I don't think I'll ever get used to that," Connor mutters.

"Did it work?" Tristan asks.

"It worked," I tell him. "But try to be quiet. Because even though no one can see you, we can still hear you."

"And smell you," Connor adds, and when I glare at him, he gives me an amused smirk. "What?" he asks, my reaction apparently amusing him. "It's how I knew you were there in the woods that day."

That day.

The day I'll never forget.

When he pinned me down, touched me for the first time, and the mate bond ignited between us.

"I'll text Gwen and tell her where to find Benjamin," Hazel says.

"Make sure she doesn't follow us in here," Connor tells her.

"She won't," Tristan says, and it's weird hearing his voice, since we can't see him. "Firstly, we're in the territory of the uptown vampire clan, and she won't leave Benjamin alone and vulnerable out there like that. Secondly, we have less than twenty minutes until the fae realm takes over. She won't risk getting stuck here until dawn."

"But she'll risk *you* getting stuck here?"

"It's complicated," he says. "Now, are you guys coming? Because as far as I'm aware, Ruby can't hold the illusion magic if we're too far away from each other."

He's right, so we all hurry back to the gate. I keep an eye on Connor and Hazel the entire time, making sure one of them doesn't suddenly decide to strangle the other, but they remain on their best behavior.

"All right," Tristan says, and while I can't see him, I hear him next to me. "It's done."

I release the magic, revealing Tristan next to me and Benjamin propped up against the stone wall next to the fence, looking like a passed out drunk man in the city.

"That potion was some strong stuff," Connor says.

"Tell me about it." I glance at Hazel, remembering when she injected a dose straight into my neck.

Luckily, she's too focused on watching out for Benjamin to catch my hate-glare.

A second later, Gwen's SUV tears around the corner and stops in front of the gate. In a blink, she's out of the car, tossing Benjamin inside of it, and driving away.

"She's pissed," Hazel says, putting her phone back inside her pocket. "Just as a heads up."

"We'll sort it out later," Tristan says, glancing at his watch. "Because right now, we have fifteen minutes to get back to the lake, fill Connor in on the plan, and get ready to strike."

Ruby

"So," Hazel says to Connor when the four of us are back in position, the empty syringe in hand. "Care to tell me where and how you got *this*?"

"No, actually," Connor says simply. "I don't."

Hazel's glaring at him so intensely that I worry she's about to take the syringe and stab the pointy end into Connor's eye.

Although from the way Connor's holding her gaze—as if he's warning her that he'll break her neck if she tries—I keep my fingers around the handle of my dagger, just in case.

You can't use the dagger on any member of the Blood Coven, my wolf reminds me. *My claws, on the other hand…*

I'll keep that in mind, I tell her, even though just the thought of giving up control to let her loose is enough to make me uneasy.

If she's that eager to harm Hazel, who's to say she won't go for Tristan while she's at it?

A ball of fire ignites in Hazel's hand, the flames lighting up the anger swirling in her eyes, and she lets the charred remains of the syringe pour down to the ground.

"Fine," she says. "But don't expect me to forget about this."

"And don't expect me to forget that you turned your back on Pine Valley to join some evil blood cult in Spring Creek," Connor says, not looking the least bit worried.

"Guys," I say, snapping them back into attention. "We need to go over the plan."

"Ruby's right," Tristan says, and then as quickly as possible, he and Hazel give Connor as many details as they can fit into the next ten minutes.

Luckily for all of us, Connor's nearly finished his Guardian training, so he's prepared for being attentive for quick briefs like this.

"You're sure the four fae will be here?" Connor asks when we're done.

"Yes. This is their home," Tristan says, his voice clipped and irritated as he glances down at his watch. "Less than a minute to go."

We crouch behind the bushes in front of one of the many rocky outcrops, watching and waiting.

Connor's on one side of me, Tristan on the other. We're all invisible, but I can hear both of their breaths, their heartbeats. Connor's all fire and passion, and Tristan is warmth and comfort. And, as awkward as it might get between the three of us, one thing that I trust above all else is that both of them are on my side.

An eerie silence falls over the park, followed by a low hum in the air that sends a shiver down my spine.

It's happening.

The energy around us shifts, like the change in pressure just before a storm, and the park *transforms*.

The bare branches of the trees explode into green leaves. Flowers bloom in a burst of colors around us. The once frosty ground is now covered with lush, green grass, and the cold winter air shifts to the warm, humid breeze of a summer's night.

Incredible.

Magic is *amazing*.

It's still night time, since time in the fae realm is generally synced with ours, and our four target fae are sleeping peacefully on the grass.

The guy built like a warrior—Lorcan—is snuggling with the smallest of the females, Aeliana. Her golden hair shines even under the moonlight. Only a foot away from them are Eamon and Elysia, also sleeping. Elysia's arm and leg are wrapped around Eamon's slender frame, her silky brown hair covering his chest.

All of them are naked. A few animal-skin bladders of what smells like sweet wine are laid out around them, some empty, others not quite so.

Clearly, they had a fun night. Which is as expected, since as Gwen told us, the four of them have three favorite activities: drinking, sleeping, and… the one they were obviously doing between the drinking and the sleeping.

I stay back, keeping us invisible as Tristan and Hazel inject the fae with the same drug Hazel used on me and Connor used on Benjamin.

It's over so quickly that you wouldn't even know when the transition happened for them between regular sleeping to drugged unconsciousness.

"All right," Hazel calls out. "You can make us visible now."

I do as asked, and we stand together in the center of the clearing, around the unconscious fae.

"That stuff comes in handy a lot, doesn't it?" Connor smirks at Hazel, who's still holding her empty syringe.

She glares at him so hard that you'd think fire's about to shoot out of her eyes. Then she uses her magic to turn it into ash, and pours its remains to the ground.

"Bring them over there." She points to a space under the shadows of one of the larger outcroppings of rocks.

The guys do the heavy lifting, and I happily let them. Not that I don't have the strength to at least drag the fae over to the rocks—I'm sure I do. I just don't love the idea of manhandling anyone like that, especially given their unconscious, naked states.

I'm close to positive that Hazel, on the other hand, simply enjoys watching people do her bidding.

The four fae are now splayed out next to each other in a way that clearly makes it obvious that they're passed out and not sleeping.

"Stand back," Hazel commands. There's a look in her eyes that I recognize from one other time, when she brought me into Jax's library with her parents to tell me about being star touched, and how she created the circle of fire around us to stop anyone from eavesdropping…

She raises her hands, palms out toward the four fae, and blasts them with streams of fire so hot that it's blue in the center.

"No!" I scream, and I run to shove her down, but Tristan's arms wrap around my waist, stopping me.

I watch helplessly as the fire dies out, leaving nothing but charred bones in its wake.

I try to squirm out of Tristan's arms, but my attempts are futile.

"You can't save them," he murmurs in my ear. "They're gone."

I muster enough force to free myself, spin around, and stare up into his soft golden eyes. "You knew she was going to do that," I realize.

Connor's by my side in a second, and he reaches for my elbow to pull me away from Tristan. "Vampires don't have souls," he says. "Including your *boyfriend* right here."

I know that's what the shifters think. But after all of my time with Tristan—even if he *did* know Hazel was going to do this—I don't believe it. I *won't* believe it.

Because that would mean our time together was a lie.

"Let go." I pull myself out of Connor's grip and face Hazel, who looks rather pleased with herself. "You killed them."

"I did."

"That wasn't in the plan."

"It was in the plan." She shrugs. "Just not in the part we told you."

"Because you knew I wouldn't agree to *murder?*"

"Because I didn't want it to turn into an argument, since we weren't going to change our minds," she says. "The drugs I brew up work well on shifters, vampires, witches, and humans, but we've never been able to test it on fae. For all we know, it could have only knocked them out for an hour, or even not at all. This was our safest bet to make sure no one realizes there are two of each of us in the park tonight."

"But there had to be *some* other way…" I shake my head as I stare at their charred remains, knowing I'll forever be haunted by what I saw here tonight.

"This was Gwen's plan," Tristan says firmly.

"So what?" I glare at him again. "You just follow everything Gwen tells you?"

He flinches, but his expression quickly hardens again. "Gwen's one of the oldest vampires in the world," he says, skirting around the question. "She saved my life when she turned me. Dominic and Benjamin's too."

I look to Connor to see what he thinks of all of this, but his eyes are hard and stern. "It's already done, and we're on a time-sensitive mission. We can discuss this once we're back home." He pauses for a second, then turns to Hazel. "Promise there won't be any more surprise deviations."

"That was the only one," she says.

He takes a long breath—I can tell he's sniffing out if she's telling the truth—and nods.

"Very well," he says. "It's done now. And the longer we stay here like this, the more likely we are to get caught. So, Ruby? You're up."

Ruby

CONNOR'S RIGHT. It's done now. Getting into an argument with Hazel and Tristan will only delay us further, which would put us in more danger.

I can deal with what I just saw when we're back in Spring Creek. Compartmentalizing my feelings—both for the deaths I just witnessed and Connor's sudden reappearance in my life—is the only way I'll be able to make it through tonight without breaking down completely.

You're finally thinking like a true shifter Guardian, my wolf says in approval, and I can't help being proud about the fact that I'm doing something that pleases her.

But now, it's time to focus. What I have to do next is one of the most important parts of the plan. If I mess up, it could be the difference between us getting out of here alive or being caught before we can truly get started.

Closing my eyes, I easily recall what the four fae look like from the drawings I studied of them.

Time to do some magic.

"All right," I say, opening my eyes and stepping forward, "I need everyone to stand still. This might feel strange at first, but don't worry. It's just the illusion taking hold."

First is Connor. I ground myself and summon the image of Lorcan from my memory. His black hair, emerald eyes, and chiseled features. I reach for my magic in my mind and let it seep out, swirling around Connor like a gentle mist.

Within seconds, Connor's figure has been replaced with the illusion of Lorcan. However, even though he looks different, his eyes remain as stoic and serious as ever.

He inspects his new fae hands, which are slightly more slender than what he's used to. "Strange," he says, although his voice remains unmistakably his own.

My illusion magic can change how things look, but that's it. I can't make us truly *become* these four fae. Which means we'll still sound like ourselves, and retain our normal supernatural abilities.

"Do me next," Hazel says, stepping forward and looking me straight in the eyes.

When I look at her now, all I see is how cold she looked right before turning those four fae to ash.

Focus, Ruby, my wolf reminds me, and I feel the ground warm beneath my feet. It's as if the world is letting me know that my magic and my wolf will be here with me through everything we'll face next.

"Sure," I say, and Aeliana, the ethereal fae, comes to mind with her golden hair and violet eyes. The illusion engulfs Hazel, and standing there now is the captivating image of Aeliana, pointed fae ears and all.

Hazel's own eyes glance down at her transformed appearance, a trace of her usual confidence and power flashing through them.

"Feels like Halloween," she quips, her voice unchanged. "Which is my second favorite holiday, by the way."

I feel like she wants me to ask what her favorite is, but I don't give in.

Instead, I turn my attention to Tristan.

He holds his gaze with mine, and I can't help but notice the pain in them, as if all he wants to do is make things right between us.

I want that, too. But this isn't the time.

We have far more important things to deal with right now.

Focusing again, I envision Eamon, his auburn hair and amber eyes that aren't too far off from Tristan's golden ones, and let the magic get to work. Tristan's familiar frame is soon replaced by the illusion of Eamon, although the pain in his eyes remains.

He says nothing, giving me a small, hopeful smile instead.

I return it on instinct, then turn the magic on myself, picturing Elysia.

Brown hair, porcelain skin, and rosy cheeks. Not too far off from what I look like, but her features are sharper—more dangerous. Plus, she has pointed ears, like all fae.

I release the magic, feeling it wash over me. As it settles, I look down at my new form, relaxing as the illusion takes hold.

However, Aeliana had brilliant violet eyes, nearly as bright as the turquoise ones I had before the goddess came down from the sky and star touched me. I don't need a mirror to know that my eyes remain brown.

But there's nothing I can do about it other than pray that if we run into other fae, they won't notice.

With my transformation complete, I scan over the others, double-checking my work.

They look almost perfect—the spitting images of the fae they're supposed to be. It's uncanny. I have to remind myself that these are just illusions, and that beneath the fae-like exteriors, they're still Hazel, Tristan, and Connor.

After we leave the fae realm tomorrow morning, it'll be the last these four fae will ever be seen in this world. All that's left of them will be…

Bile rises in my throat as I think about the bones off to the corner, and I force myself to not look over there again.

Hazel reaches for a strand of her golden hair and admires it. "Maybe I should go blonde once we're back home," she says, although none of us give an opinion one way or the other.

I couldn't care less about what she chooses to do with her hair.

She deserves to have it burned to a crisp after everything she's done. Unfortunately, given her affinity for fire, I don't think it would hold.

"Looks like we're ready," Tristan says, pulling me out of my thoughts. His voice is still his own, the same one that soothed me every day and night in that cell, and I'm so incredibly grateful for that.

"I trust you know where you're going?" Connor asks him.

"I do."

"Well then, bloodsucker." He motions the path out of the clearing. "Lead the way, and try your best to not get us lost."

As we leave the clearing, I catch one last glimpse of the ashes and bones, and I make myself a promise.

I will make sure their deaths weren't in vain. I'll leave this place in the morning with the Key of Hades in hand, and then somehow, I'll stop the Blood Coven before they do something horrible that can't be reversed.

Maybe I'll have Connor's help, and maybe Tristan's, or maybe neither of theirs.

But nothing and no one is going to stand in my way.

Ruby

THE FOUR OF us are silent as we follow Tristan around the lake, toward the nearest path that will lead us to the North Woods.

The North Woods, as the name suggests, is the forest-filled part in Northern Central Park. Going through them is the only way to get to where we're heading next. According to Gwen, we're supposed to continue walking around the lake until reaching a particular path that leads into the woods, to lessen our chance of getting lost once we're in the forest.

We turn a corner, and then we see them.

A small group of fae is gathered by the lakeside, quietly lounging in the grass. They seem to be in a daze, clearly having finished off the honey wine in the empty bladders by their sides.

Crap.

Running into others wasn't in the plan.

Tristan stops walking. But Hazel, apparently not paying attention, crashes into him and releases a sound of surprise.

A silver-haired fae looks in our direction and beams. "Lorcan!" she calls out, apparently having eyes only for the fae Connor's disguised as. "Come, join us."

Another fae—a male with striking blue eyes and hair as white as snow—stumbles up to us. His gaze is locked on mine, as if he's transfixed by the sight of me.

"Elysia," he slurs, a wide grin plastered on his face. "It's been too long since we last saw each other."

Both Connor and Tristan move closer to me, as if they're trying to stake claim on me.

As if they're threatened by this drunken fae.

I keep my face impassive, but my heart is racing. Because if I speak, it won't be with Elysia's voice. It will be with mine. And I don't even know what Elysia sounded like, so I can't make any attempt to imitate her.

"I was beginning to think you'd abandoned us forever in that pleasure cave of yours," the drunk fae-boy continues, his eyes glazed, and his words garbled. "But I'm glad you came. It's much more fun out here."

He nearly trips over his feet, catching himself at the last second and looking back up at me with an impish smile.

I glance at Tristan, and he gives me nod as if he's saying, *you've got this.*

"Maybe later." I pray that the white-haired fae is drunk enough that he won't notice a difference in my voice. "We have to be on our way right now."

He pouts, his lower lip sticking out. "Promise?"

"Promise," I say, and guilt pangs through my chest.

Because after tonight, he'll never see Elysia again.

Luckily, he returns to his group by the lake and doesn't follow us as we continue toward the woods. However, he does glance over his shoulder once, as if he's hurt that we didn't want to join them.

"Good job," Connor says, and we walk in silence again until Tristan stops in front of a path leading into the woods.

The trees arch over the pathway like eerie skeletal hands, and shadows linger within the undergrowth, giving the impression of hidden creatures observing our every move.

It's just trees, I remind myself. *I have earth magic. It's going to be fine.*

I reach for my magic for reassurance, but instead of the warm comfort I was hoping for, it sends prickles along my skin.

A warning to stay away.

I glance at Connor to see if he feels it, too.

From the way he's steeled himself, his expression a mask of bravery and determination, I have an innate feeling that he does.

"Ready?" Tristan asks. If he's worried, he doesn't show it.

There's a collective nod from all of us, since we've already come this far and aren't about to turn back now, and we follow him into the woods.

The deeper we move into the trees, the quieter it becomes, until all we can hear is the soft rustle of leaves and the occasional night bird calling out in the distance. It's so dark that seeing more than ten feet ahead of us is a challenge. Without supernatural vision, I imagine it would be nearly impossible.

"Are you sure you know where you're going?" Connor asks Tristan from where he's walking close behind me.

"Yes," Tristan says, curt and final. "Benjamin and I studied these woods for years. We'll be there in about five more minutes."

Bitterness laces his voice, the undertone of what he's saying clear: we'd be better off right now if Benjamin was with us instead of Connor, per the original plan.

"You studied these woods in the human realm," Connor points out. "This is the fae realm."

"They mirror each other," Tristan snaps, making it clear that this conversation is over.

We don't get much farther until eerie laughter echoes through the woods, bouncing off the trees and wrapping around us.

I freeze, the sound sending chills down my spine.

"What was that?" I ask.

Goblins, the wind whispers through the trees.

Hobgoblins, a breeze from the other direction whispers in return.

Tristan's eyes dart around the darkness. "Hobgoblins are more mischievous than harmful," he says, staying calm. "Ignore them."

"You knew about these?" I ask.

"Like I said—they're not harmful."

Another cackle reverberates through the forest, followed by rustling in the trees, and the chattering of what sounds like a dozen small creatures.

"They might not be harmful, but they certainly don't sound innocent," I mutter, relieved when Tristan hurries up the pace.

"It's not much longer to the Blockhouse," he says as we hop across a few rocks to cross a stream.

Suddenly, a small stone whizzes through the air, narrowly missing Hazel's head.

"Hey!" she screams, ducking and pulling me down with her.

My grip on her hand tightens.

I never thought I'd find Hazel's touch comforting, but yet… here we are.

Another stone flies through the air, but Connor taps into his earth magic and sends it soaring back to where it came from.

Something yelps in the forest—hopefully whatever creature hurtled the rocks at us.

"Let's keep moving," Connor says. "I can redirect any more rocks they throw at us."

"We're not supposed to be using our elemental magic," Hazel says. "If anyone sees us, they'll know what we are."

"Would you rather have a rock to your head?" he asks.

"Fair point."

Hazel and I stand up, and I brush dirt from the bottom of my pants. Technically, I can help guard us from the stones as well, but that would mean revealing my earth magic to the three of them. Which I definitely don't want to do.

Luckily, with Connor being here, I can keep my secret for a little bit longer.

We start moving again, but something scurries across the path in front of us, making us all jump.

"It was just a squirrel," Connor says calmly. "We're fine."

"Right." I take a deep breath to calm my nerves. "Just a squirrel."

Even so, I reach inside my jacket for my dagger, making sure it's still there. Which, obviously, it is. The handle warms under my fingers, the magic from the gemstone pulsing with energy in its place next to my heart.

Between me, Hazel, Tristan, and Connor, if these fae-goblins try to truly attack, they have another thing coming.

With every step we take, the forest grows more haunted and alive. It's like the hobgoblins are controlling every noise and every creature, creating an eerie symphony of the night. But we stay the course, since we don't have time to let anything—especially our own nerves—slow us down.

I gaze around as we walk, amazed that this is all technically in the middle of a city. If someone told me we were back in the Adirondacks, in a mountain far away from civilization, I would have believed them.

"Does anyone else feel like we're going in circles?" Hazel asks as we walk by a particularly gnarled tree that I'm pretty sure we've seen before.

"We're fine. I've got this covered," Tristan says, although from the uneasy way he looks around, he doesn't look totally sure of it.

"You know, this would be a lot easier if I could shift into my wolf form," Connor says. "I could sniff out where we've been and figure out the path forward."

"We don't know what—or who—is watching us in this forest," Tristan reminds him, keeping his voice low. "We're already suspicious enough wandering around here at this time of night. We'll be walking targets if we're being led by a shifted wolf."

Connor's hands curl into fists, and while he doesn't say it, I can tell he knows that Tristan's right.

Hazel glances around uneasily. "The hobgoblins are messing with our senses," she says. "We need to focus. Believe in what we know instead of what we're being made to perceive. And I *know* we've passed that tree before."

"So do I," I chime in. "It's pretty recognizable."

A cold wind sweeps through the forest, rustling the leaves and sending a shiver down my spine.

A glance at the frustration in Tristan's eyes makes me think that the wind came from his air magic and not from the forest.

"We walked left around the tree last time," I say, trying to mitigate his irritation, but also stay practical. "How about this time we go right?"

"If we go right, we'll be walking away from the Blockhouse," Tristan says.

"But we're not making progress as it is," Hazel says. "We need to try something different."

Another high-pitched cackle erupts from somewhere above us, and a flurry of leaves descend in a whirlwind, obscuring our vision.

Tristan aims his palms around at the leaves, and they spiral around us, separating and flying back into the trees.

"If they want to scare us, they have to do better than that," he says, his hands still up and ready for another attack.

"Don't goad them," I say. "They might take it as a challenge."

From the dangerous glint in Tristan's eyes, it seems like he *wants* a challenge.

"They're trying to confuse us and steer us off course," Connor says, a thoughtful look on his face as he brings us back into focus. "Ruby's right. We need to change our approach."

I give him a grateful smile—it feels nice that he believes in me—and he nods in return.

I've got you, his eyes seem to say, and the gratitude I feel for him fills me so much that I feel like I might burst from it.

"Right it is then," Tristan says, leading the way.

There's no more laughing, and no more stones thrown. It's quiet.

Eerily so.

Suddenly, a rapid movement blurs past us. Then another, and another.

The hobgoblins.

It has to be.

I can't make out anything about them, other than the fact that they seem to be the same brown color as the trees.

"No magic," Hazel says through gritted teeth, although from the way she's clenching her fists, she's clearly aching to blast these goblins with enough fire to turn them to ash.

Just like she did to the four fae.

"This isn't getting us anywhere," Connor says as another goblin rushes ahead of us and up a nearby tree. "Hey there!" he calls out. "Come down from there. We need to talk to you."

Snickers fill the woods, coming from every direction possible.

One zips too close to me. I catch a fleeting glimpse of pointed ears, a wicked grin, and gleaming eyes before it disappears into the darkness.

They're laughing, and laughing, so much that I think my head's going to explode from the sound of it.

The magic from my dagger hums in its place near my heart, calling for me, as if it's begging for me to act...

"Screw this." I reach for my dagger at the same time as one of them runs across my path and up a tree, connect to its gemstone with my magic, and hurl the weapon toward the creature like a javelin.

Ruby

THE DAGGER GOES straight through the hobgoblin's hand, pinning it to the tree trunk with a loud *thunk* that reverberates through the forest.

It squeals, a high-pitched sound that grates on my nerves, and reaches for the handle with its other hand—presumably to pull it out.

Connor is on it in an instant, grabbing a particularly pointy tree branch and ramming it through the goblin's other hand.

The goblin squeals again and struggles in vain to free itself. But it must be pretty painful to wiggle around with both hands pinned to a tree, because it gives up quickly.

Now that the creature is relatively still, we can finally see what we've been dealing with.

It's about half my size, with wild brown hair and pointy ears. Its skin is the same texture and color as the tree bark, but like an illusion, it fades away until it's a smooth, unnatural white that glows like the moon. I can't see its face, because it was climbing up the tree when I pinned him, so we're looking at its back.

I stare at the dagger through its hand in shock, unable to believe that it *worked*.

My attack must have also scared all the other hobgoblins, because they scurry away, and all is still once again.

"Wow, Ruby," Hazel says. "Looks like those hunter instincts of yours are coming out to play."

"I don't know what happened." I shrug, unable to tear my eyes away from the struggling creature. "I got mad, and then..." I motion to the hobgoblin, since it's more than obvious what I did next.

"You did the right thing," Tristan says, and then he marches around the tree to get a look at the creature straight-on.

Hazel and I do the same.

Connor, of course, is already there.

The hobgoblin is stuck hugging the tree, thanks to both hands being impaled to it. His beady eyes are wide and alert, as if he's intelligent and not animalistic. From his features, he seems to be male. And despite his child-like size, he appears to be an adult.

Hopefully he'll be able to effectively communicate with us.

However, I'm focused on one main thing—I want my dagger back.

The gem on the handle is calling to me, and from the way my body hums with energy as it connects to the weapon, I'm close to positive that I could call it to me and have it fly straight into my palm. But I resist, not wanting to reveal my secret.

"Good job. You caught me," the little guy sneers. "Now, what do you want?"

"We need you to lead us to the Blockhouse." Connor wastes no time getting to the point.

The creature tilts his head, considering it. "And what will I get in return?"

"What do you want?" Hazel asks.

"Well, despite the fact that this dagger is causing me considerable pain," he starts, glancing pointedly at the blade embedded in his hand. "I can't help but appreciate its craftsmanship. I want it."

"Absolutely not," I say. "That dagger is *mine*."

I don't even care that Hazel is the one who gave it to me. Or that it's spelled to not harm any members of the Blood Coven. The dagger is linked to my magic, and it's staying with me.

"Perhaps it is now," the goblin says calmly. "But if you want me to lead you to the Blockhouse, then it will be mine. Unless…" He pauses, and I hold my breath, anxious for what he'll say next. "You have something more valuable to offer me? Like that necklace, perhaps?"

His gaze drifts to the cross pendant around Tristan's neck.

Dominic's necklace.

My heart jumps into my throat. Because I won't let Tristan give it up.

I can get another dagger. Tristan's necklace, however, is irreplaceable.

"You can have the dagger," I say quickly, and the hobgoblin smiles, pleased with himself. "*After* you drop us off at the Blockhouse."

"A fair request," he replies. "Now, if you'll kindly remove the weapon from my hand, I'll lead you to the place you seek."

"Do you promise?" I ask, wishing we had Zara with us right now so she could swear him into a blood oath.

His eyes narrow in suspicion. "We're fae," he says slowly. "We're bound to our promises."

"Apologies on Elysia's behalf," Tristan says swiftly, using the name of the fae I'm disguised as and stepping up next to me. "She sometimes forgets that your kind is… well, you know…" He rubs the back of his neck, as if embarrassed to say whatever he's insinuating.

"You forget that the non-gentry are held to the same laws as your lot." The goblin huffs and rolls his beady eyes. "Figures."

I assume that "gentry" means the fae who look humanoid—like Elysia and her friends. But I don't ask, since that would give away the fact that we're not fae at all.

It's probably best to let the others do most of the talking from here forward.

"Now, you realize I can't lead you anywhere with a blade pinning me to a tree, correct?" the goblin asks, eyeing me in particular.

"Correct," I say, and then I stride up to him and yank the dagger out of his hand in a single movement.

He winces, but doesn't cry out.

It was nice knowing you, little dagger, I think, although I don't place it back inside my jacket. I have no interest in getting goblin blood on myself.

We don't need a weapon, my wolf speaks up from inside me. *We have our magic.*

She's right. But my illusion magic can't be used to go all stabby on people. And since I can't use my earth magic right now, my elemental magic isn't particularly useful. Besides, I liked having a dagger. Once we're back in the human realm, I'm going to be in the market for one.

Although, once we're back, I have to deliver the key to the Blood Coven. And Gwen definitely won't be open to stopping by a weapon shop before leaving the city.

However, that's a problem for another day.

I have to take this one step at a time.

Right now, that means getting to the Blockhouse. Then getting the key.

The goblin rubs the hole in his hand, and just like when Tristan was stabbed in the cell, the wound grows smaller and knits itself back together. A minute later, you'd never know it was there.

"Much better," he says. "I take it you're all ready to go?"

"Lead the way," Connor says, motioning for the goblin to go first.

The little creature nods and takes us through the forest. This time, thankfully, we're not bombarded by other goblins trying to mess with us.

"So, what's your name?" Tristan asks, breaking the silence.

The hobgoblin pauses, glancing back at us with a slight frown. "Why do you want to know?"

"Common courtesy." Tristan shrugs. "We're making a trade. It seems fair to know who we're dealing with."

After a moment's hesitation, the hobgoblin says, "You can call me Kip."

"It's nice doing business with you, Kip," he says.

Kip rubs his now-healed hands and eyes the dagger, a greedy glint in his gaze. "I can't say I feel the same. Although, it'll be worth it once I get that little shiny of yours."

I press my lips together and say nothing.

After about five minutes, we walk around a hill, and there it is, right on top of it.

The Blockhouse.

It's the size of a small house, and vines crawl up the stone walls, which are moss-covered and weather-beaten. But the entrance isn't a door or a gate like I expected. Instead, a cascading waterfall flows down the front. Stone steps lead up to it and disappear behind it, which is the only clue that the entrance is somehow through the water.

And, as expected from Gwen's briefing, an empty podium stands next to the steps.

"Here it is." Kip motions to the Blockhouse, then looks to me. "Now, the dagger."

I hold his gaze, saying nothing as I walk over to him and hold out the dagger.

He snatches it with his bony fingers and grins.

"A magnificent blade." He admires it again, then fastens it to himself by placing it inside his tunic belt. "However, don't expect to make any progress from here. Everything in and around the Blockhouse is guarded by the strongest traps, riddles, and trials. Its secrets are known only to a select few." He pauses and eyes us with disdain, as if what he's seeing is subpar at best. "No arid fae has ever been granted access inside it. You might have knowledge, but without magic, you're likely out of luck."

He zips out of the clearing in a blur, leaving us no opportunity to ask for more information.

"It's a good thing we're not arid fae," Hazel mutters, and then she turns her irritated gaze to me. "And I see how much you cherished my gift."

"Would you have rather I offered him *your* blade?" I ask in challenge, knowing that Hazel probably would have offered him her left pinky before handing over the Blade of Erebus.

Maybe even a thumb.

"Fair point." She reaches inside her jacket, as if making sure her dagger is still there. "Now… I don't know about you all, but I think that podium is missing a stone tablet."

Ruby

THE STONE TABLET. The one inscribed with the Aquatic Riddle.

Finding it around the Blockhouse and placing it on the podium is the last thing Gwen knows about what we'll be encountering on this journey. Once we're inside the Blockhouse, it's going to be completely on us to locate, retrieve, and leave with the key.

"The tablet will be somewhere near the Blockhouse," Tristan reminds us. "If we lose sight of the Blockhouse, then we've searched too far."

"And we'll risk not being able to find our way back, thanks to those stunts from the hobgoblins," Connor adds.

"Correct." Tristan glances around the area, already searching for the tablet. "We need to make a complete circle around the house to make sure not to miss anything. Ruby and I will start in one direction. Hazel, you and Connor can go in the other."

Connor glares at Tristan and steps to my side. "I'm going with Ruby," he says, keeping his gaze level with Tristan's. "You'll go with Hazel."

"Absolutely not," Hazel says. "We can't risk the two of you running off together."

"Where, exactly, do you think we'd go?" I motion around the surrounding trees. "Trying to find our way around the forest didn't go over too well for us earlier."

"Connor has earth magic," she says—as if we could forget. "There's no way to know if he could have navigated the forest, but was holding back to delay us from reaching the Blockhouse."

From Connor's steely gaze, I can't help wondering—*did* he try to do what Hazel's accusing?

No, my wolf speaks up. *The hobgoblins were messing with our senses. Our earth magic couldn't override them.*

Connor tells Hazel the same thing, but Hazel scoffs in return, apparently not believing him.

"We're wasting time," I finally say, looking Connor straight in the eyes and holding his gaze. It's strange seeing Lorcan's green eyes there instead of Connor's brown ones, but

Connor's serious expression is his, through and through. "I'm going with Tristan. You'll go with Hazel."

Connor shakes his head. "No way. I'm not leaving you alone with him."

"I'm perfectly safe with Tristan." I don't have to think twice about it.

Meanwhile, Tristan's studying Connor curiously, as cool and collected as ever. "Do you truly believe I'd do anything to her that she didn't ask me to do?" he asks.

His underlying reminder is clear: Tristan's already drank my blood. And it was with my consent. Multiple times, even after we were released from that cell.

"You muddled her mind from the moment you sank your teeth into her neck." Connor's tone drips with more venom than Tristan's fangs, and I worry he's about to shift into a wolf and spear a claw through Tristan's heart. "You have no right to her. Not like I—"

"Enough!" I snap, throwing my hands up in exasperation and stepping away from both of them. I'd volunteer to go with Hazel, but leaving them alone together is probably the worst idea of them all. "We have a few hours to get that key. We don't have time for this. I'm going with Tristan. Connor, you're going with Hazel. That's final."

This, thankfully, seems to shut them both up.

"She's right," Hazel chimes in. "We have to get started. Connor—which way should we go? Right, or left?"

Connor doesn't look happy, but then, like a switch going off, he looks to Hazel and smiles. "Did it occur to you that without the hobgoblins messing with my senses, we don't have to waste time searching aimlessly for this stone tablet?" he asks.

Hazel opens her mouth to reply, then shuts it. "Oh," she finally says.

Of course.

The tablet is made of stone. Stone is part of the earth.

Connor kneels on the ground, presses his palms to the grass, and closes his eyes.

All is still. There isn't even a breeze rustling through the tree leaves, or (thankfully) any more word from the hobgoblins. It's like the world's on pause, and we watch Connor, holding our breaths as we wait for him to finish what he's doing.

His eyes snap open, and he looks straight ahead at the steps.

"There." He stands, marches toward the base of the steps, and pulls out one of the stones.

It's about the size of a book, and unlike the gray stones surrounding it, there's a blue-green tint to it. Now that it's in Connor's hands, I'm amazed none of us noticed it there to begin with.

"The Aquatic Riddle." Hazel rushes to his side and tries to take it from him, but he pulls it close.

"That was quick," Tristan says.

"It's a stone." Connor walks right past Hazel and back over to me. "I tuned into the earth and sensed it."

I wonder if my earth magic's strong enough to be able to do the same, but now isn't the time to try.

With no time to waste, we gather around the stone and look at it. There are detailed carvings of waves, raindrops, and rivers along the edges. In the center, there's a riddle inscribed in elegant script:

I am seen in the sea and the sky so blue,

In tears and in dew, I am in you.
In lakes, rivers, and rain, I am pure and plain,
Tell me, what is my name?

Ruby

I READ the riddle over a few times, thinking.

"The answer is clouds," Tristan declares, tracing a finger over the wavy carvings. "They float in the sky and are seen over the sea. They contain water, which is part of the rain cycle involving lakes and rivers, and they symbolize the 'crying' of the sky when it rains."

"That's too literal," Connor's quick to argue against him. "It's not something as obvious as 'clouds.' It's 'life.' Life is found in the sea and sky. It's associated with tears and dew—emotions and new beginnings. And all life requires water to survive."

Tension crackles in the air as their interpretations hang between us.

But there's one word in both of their ideas that stands out to me...

"It could be salt." Hazel shrugs, and I get a feeling that riddles aren't her specialty, and that she's well aware of it. "It's found in the sea and in tears. And even though not directly in the sky, I guess it could be connected through the evaporation process of seawater?"

There's that word again.

How can they not see it?

"It's water," I tell them, absolutely sure of it. "Water's seen in the sea and the sky, in tears and dew. It's found in lakes, rivers, and rain. Plus, it's the fae element. It's almost *too* obvious, when you think about it."

The silence that follows is deafening.

"Do you really think they'd make the answer that obvious?" Hazel asks.

"No, Ruby's right," Tristan says, and I give him a small smile, grateful for his support. "First of all, salt isn't always in lakes and rivers, so that's not the answer. And Connor—your answer is too metaphorical. Especially because water is directly visible in all the forms listed in the riddle."

"I do see your point," Connor says steadily, and I'm relieved that he's not turning this into an argument with Tristan when all of us need to be focused on the answer to the riddle.

"And clouds aren't generally described as pure and plain," I say, referring to Tristan's answer. "Usually the opposite, actually. Water's the right answer. I know it is."

Connor lowers the tablet, as if the discussion's over. "So, we're in agreement?" he asks. "Water's the answer?"

"Yes," Tristan says, and then he looks to me and adds, "Smart thinking."

Another wave of appreciation for him flows through me, warming my heart.

"Thank you," I say, and we share another smile.

Connor stiffens, and I brace myself for him to do something to assert his "claim" on me over Tristan.

Instead, he holds the tablet out to me.

"Do you want to do the honors?" he asks.

"I'd love to." I take the tablet from his hands, my fingers brushing his while I do. Fire rushes through me, and electricity crackles over my skin. I can barely think, barely breathe. My eyes lock with his, and even though they're Lorcan's green eyes instead of Connor's brown, it still feels like they're staring deep into my soul.

It's just like when he and I first touched in the woods—as if the universe is speaking to me, saying we belong together.

Because we do, my wolf chimes in.

"Ruby?" Tristan's voice pulls me back into focus, and I realize Connor and I have been standing there with our fingers touching for the past few seconds.

I shake myself out of my Connor-induced trance and pull the stone closer to me.

"Sorry," I say, and I look to Hazel, unable to meet Tristan's eyes. "What do I do?"

I know what I need to do next. I just need to say *something* to diffuse the tension buzzing in the air. And Hazel is the most neutral person to talk to.

I never thought I'd consider *Hazel* to be neutral in any shape or form. But yet... here we are.

"Put the tablet on the podium," she says.

I give her a single nod, grateful to her for not making a big deal about what just happened between me and Connor, then walk toward the empty podium.

Anxiety curls in the pit of my stomach. Not due to the riddle, but because of the uncertainty of what comes next.

I feel the others looking at me, but I don't turn back to them.

"Here goes nothing," I mutter, and then I steady myself and place the stone tablet on the podium.

I hold my breath, half expecting the earth to shudder or the skies to crack open. But nothing happens. The only sound is the rustling of the leaves in the forest around us.

Then, the tablet starts to glow, and another line of cursive text appears below the riddle.

State your answer.

Okay. That seems simple enough.

Keeping my gaze fixed on the stone, I square my shoulders and say, "Water."

The moment the word slips from my lips, the tablet trembles, glowing brighter. Its brightness is nearly blinding. But then everything goes still again, the light fades, and a single word is carved into the stone:

Accepted.

"It worked." I turn around to look at the others, and my eyes meet Connor's.

Every bone in my body wants to run to him and have him sweep me into his arms in celebration.

From the way he sucks in a short, startled breath, I have a feeling he wants the same.

Then my gaze goes to Tristan's, and guilt shadows my soul. Because *he's* the one whose arms I should want to run into. Not Connor's.

This would have been a lot less complicated if everything had gone as planned, and Benjamin was the one here with us instead of Connor.

If I didn't have to deal with the war raging inside my heart.

Still, I'm glad Connor's with us. I feel safe with him here—protected. I wouldn't trade his help and encouragement for anything in the world.

"Good job." Tristan stays calm and composed, although there's a certain strain to his voice, as if he knows the exact thoughts that just crossed my mind.

I don't have a chance to respond, because the waterfall slaps louder against the stones below, and a woman emerges from it. Her long hair cascades to her waist, her dress appears like soft waves, and her blue eyes are as deep as the ocean. There's something calming and soothing about her gaze, and I have an instinctive feeling that she's here to help us, not harm us.

"Well done, seekers of knowledge," she says, her voice as gentle as a raindrop. "I'm Nereida, the water sprite who guards the mysteries and artifacts of our realm. You have correctly answered the Aquatic Riddle, and have thus earned the right to prove yourselves directly to me, so I can decide if you're worthy of entering the Blockhouse."

Ruby

ANOTHER TEST.

Of *course* there's another test.

The Key of Hades has been in the Blockhouse for over a century, and not because no one has known to look for it.

We aren't the only ones who have tried this.

But we do hope to be the ones who finally succeed.

"How do we prove we're worthy?" I ask.

"Simple," Nereida responds. "You must use your magic to prove your connection to the element of water."

She watches us expectantly, and my heart sinks. Because her request might be simple for fae—at least, for the fae connected to their element.

But for us?

Kip's words about how we'd be out of luck without magic float through my mind.

I glance at the others. Tristan's eyes are stony, Connor seems lost in thought, and Hazel's chewing nervously on her lower lip.

"How?" Connor finally asks.

"By showing me your magic, of course." Nereida's laugh is melodic, like water. "Unless… you don't have magic?"

Hazel's glaring at Nereida as if she wants to shoot fire at the water sprite straight from her eyes. Connor looks so determined that I worry he's about to shift into his wolf form and try to rush at the sprite to use brute force to get through the door. Tristan's gaze is far off, as if his mind is whirring at a million miles per second, and I can't even imagine what's going on in there.

"Oh." Nereida frowns. "Are the four of you arids?"

"We don't have water magic," Connor confirms, steady and grounded.

"Then I'm afraid I can't grant you access to the Blockhouse. Thank you for your attempt, but it's not possible for anyone to survive what awaits inside without any magical abilities."

Disappointment crosses her eyes, and her form ripples, as if her edges are melting into the surrounding mist.

"Wait!" Tristan calls out, and he steps forward, his arms held confidently by his sides.

Nereida's form solidifies once more, and she tilts her head, curious about what he has to say.

"Yes?" she asks.

"We're not arids," Tristan says. "We do have magic."

"Eamon," Hazel hisses through gritted teeth, using the name of the fae he's disguised as.

Tristan turns to her, his eyes hard. "We didn't get this far to accept defeat now," he says, and then he looks back to Nereida and continues. "Do we specifically need water magic to gain entrance to the Blockhouse? Or will any type of magic suffice?"

The sprite raises her chin slightly, looking more intrigued than defensive. "You must use magic to prove your connection to the element of water," she repeats what she said earlier, giving no further explanation than that.

"So, no. And all the elements are connected," Connor says, and I don't know which is crazier—the fact that Tristan has all but revealed that we're not who we're claiming to be, or that Connor is backing up Tristan's decision. "We simply need to figure out how each of our elements connects with water, then focus on that aspect of our power in our demonstration to Nereida."

Our elements, his words repeat in my mind, and my heart drops.

Because none of them know that I have earth magic. And my illusion magic isn't technically an element.

Unless...

An idea crosses my mind, and it's not a terrible one.

Although it doesn't really matter yet, since Nereida still hasn't replied one way or the other.

"Clever," she finally says, giving us an encouraging smile. "Other supernaturals rarely enter our realm, and I've never had non-fae attempt to enter the Blockhouse. But you're free to try. One at a time, please."

Crap.

I can't use my illusion magic to keep up their disguises if they're in another room. Which we will be when we're entering the Blockhouse.

Then again, Nereida already knows we're not actually fae. We don't have anything to hide anymore, although I do feel like it's in our best interest to keep up the disguises for as long as possible.

"As alpha, it's my responsibility to make sure everyone gets through that door safely and no one's left behind," Connor says, his voice bringing me out of my wandering thoughts. "I'm going last."

"I'm first." Tristan barely misses a beat after Connor's done speaking. "Neither of you should be in there alone."

His message is clear: the girls need to be protected. And we don't have time for any arguments about if the guys are being insanely old fashioned or not, so it's best to just ignore the implication and get on with our task.

"Come forward," Nereida says to Tristan.

Tristan nods and steps forward, not appearing to second guess himself in the slightest.

I'm completely still as I watch him, bracing myself for anything. Because if Nereida tries to hurt him in any way, then I'm ready to fully embrace my inner wolf and get my claws out.

Nereida's eyes remain on Tristan as he crouches by the pool of water at the bottom of the steps and places his hands above it.

"Air and water share a symbiotic relationship in nature," he begins, his voice steady. "Where there's wind, there's the power to guide water."

His eyes take on a slight glow as he focuses on the water, and the air around his hands starts to swirl. Slowly, the water responds to his magic, and a waterspout spirals upward from the pool, gleaming under the moonlight.

He guides the waterspout, making it dance and sway, and it's positively beautiful.

"A vampire," the sprite eventually says. "Very interesting."

There's no judgment in her tone.

She seems to actually be... okay with it.

"The air isn't commanding the water," Tristan continues, his voice gaining even more confidence than before. "It's guiding it, just as the wind guides the tides. This is the connection between my air magic and the element of water."

Nereida watches him silently, and I hold my breath, bracing myself for her to reject Tristan's attempt.

If she does, what will we do? We need to get into the Blockhouse.

We could try pushing through her with brute force, but Nereida's only doing her job right now. She doesn't deserve to be hurt because of it, or worse—killed.

I glance at Hazel at the thought, the ashes of the fae flashing through my mind.

Her eyes are hard, and her hands are clenched into fists, as if she's prepared to unleash her magic at any moment.

I want to say something to her, to tell her not to do anything. But I also don't want to risk interrupting Nereida's decision about Tristan's presentation.

If she tries anything, we'll pounce, my wolf thinks, which sends a sudden rush of power through me.

She's talking as if I'll—no, *we'll*—be able to work as a team to shift again.

Hope rises inside me at the thought.

Finally, Nereida nods in what looks like acceptance. "You have proven your connection," she says, and she steps to the side, so the path up the stairs and to the waterfall is clear. "You may walk through the waterfall."

"Thank you," Tristan says, and his waterspout grows smaller, dissolving back into the pool. He glances over his shoulder at us, and adds, "I'll see you on the other side."

His gaze lingers on mine for a few seconds more, and then he makes his way up the steps and walks through the waterfall, his figure vanishing into the unknown.

It worked.

I can't believe that it worked.

At least now, if the three of us fail the sprite's test, Tristan will be able to continue forward. But I hate the thought of him in there alone. We're a team—albeit, an unlikely one—and I don't want any of us left behind.

We won't fail, I think. *If she accepted Tristan's loose interpretation of his connection to water, then she's open to all of ours as well.*

It's going to be fine. Because we're worthy, and just like she saw it in Tristan, she'll see it in us, too.

The moment Tristan's through the waterfall, Nereida steps back in front of it. "Don't try to walk through without my approval," she warns, her eyes sharper than they've been since we met. "Only those I permit can enter. Prove your connection to water, and you too shall pass. Now, little witch," she says, turning her attention to Hazel. "I believe you're up next?"

"How do you know what I am?" Hazel asks.

"You're powerful, but your magic is still ruled by your emotions," the sprite says. "I caught slight flickers of flames from your fists while you waited for me to pass judgment on your friend's presentation."

Hazel presses her lips together in irritation and relaxes her fingers.

Sure enough, I spot a spark of orange as she reins in her emotions.

Very interesting.

"Fire and water are traditionally viewed as opposite forces of nature," Nereida says. "But please, I invite you to show me their connection."

"I've been working with fire for my entire life," Hazel says. "I know how it interacts with *everything*."

Nereida motions to the space in front of her and gives Hazel a knowing smile. "Then you may begin."

With a determined fire to her eyes, Hazel walks to the pool of water and kneels next to it. She dips her hands into the water, collects it in her cupped palms, and looks back up to Nereida.

"Fire and water might seem like opposites, but when they interact…" She gives Nereida a mischievous smile, and orange glow comes out of her palms, shining through the water to light up her face.

In her fae form, with Aeliana's golden hair that flows down to her waist, she looks like some sort of goddess.

Nereida watches patiently, waiting for what's next.

Connor and I do as well.

The water in Hazel's palms ripples, and tiny bubbles form as it begins to boil. The fiery glow intensifies, and with a final surge of power, the water evaporates in seconds.

A cloud of steam drifts up to the sky, where it disappears into the starry night.

Steam.

The connection between fire and water.

I don't particularly like feeling impressed by Hazel. But I can't deny that it was smart, quick thinking on her part.

"Fire turns water into one of its three forms—steam," she begins to explain. "It's not a destructive relationship, but a transformative one. This is how my fire magic is connected to water."

Nereida gives Hazel the same knowing smile as earlier, and even before she speaks, I know she passed.

"That was an insightful display," the sprite says. "You've proven your connection to the fae element of water. I give you access to the Blockhouse, and you may pass through the waterfall."

Hazel stands up, brushes the dirt from her knees, and looks back at me. "Remember—we need you in there. You've got this," she says, and with those surprisingly encouraging words, she follows Tristan's path up the stairs and walks through the waterfall to enter the Blockhouse.

Tristan

THE FEELING of water rushes over me, but when I step inside the Blockhouse, I'm completely dry.

Looking at my hands shows me that my fingers are no longer the thinner, longer ones of the fae Ruby disguised me as. They're back to being mine. And luckily, there's no one inside this place to see my true form.

The Blockhouse is only a small space, about the size of an average living room, with stone walls, a dirt floor, and no windows. A pedestal about three feet tall stands in its center, and a large conch shell is displayed on top of it, with calming ocean sounds drifting out of its opening.

No Key of Hades.

Not surprising. If getting the key was as simple as passing Nereida's test out there, it would have been stolen centuries ago.

I should examine the shell and try to figure out what it does. But now that I'm alone, I can't stop my mind from wandering.

I can't believe *he* showed up.

Ruby's mate.

Connor.

She may have said back in the clearing that she was with me and not him, but I see the way she looks at him. It's the same way she looked at me many times when we shared that cell, and then when we were finally alone in the attic bedroom, before her wolf broke through and ruined the moment.

After I drank her blood and muzzled her wolf, she was back to being *my* Ruby. The one who loved me, and *only* me. If I'd kissed her one more time and we picked up where we'd left off instead of going to sleep... maybe her eyes wouldn't be wandering so much to Connor right now instead of to me.

I reach for my brother's pendant and rub my fingers over the gem, calming myself. Because when Dominic had a witch infuse the necklace with Jessica's DNA, and then drew her toward him with its magic, she chose him over her fated mate. And they weren't even blood bonded.

With the necklace's influence after Hazel infused it with Ruby's DNA, along with the blood bond between us, I have every reason to believe that Ruby will choose me. Especially because the connection that formed between us when we were in that cell was real. No necklace or blood bond can make two people know each other the way we got to know each other during all that time confined together.

But still, the way she looks at Connor…

No.

I refuse to believe she'll choose him. He rejected her and proposed to Autumn. She hates him.

I've been here for her. *Always.*

That has to count for something.

I don't have time to further contemplate it, because my thoughts are interrupted by Hazel walking inside.

She's back to her regular form—a young, plain-looking girl whose only hint of the strong magic inside of her is the fire in her eyes and the black leather jacket she wears.

"You look upset," she observes.

"My girlfriend's fated mate—who *rejected* her and broke her heart—forced himself along on our quest and is out there alone with her as we speak," I say. "So, yes. I'm upset."

"They're not alone," Hazel says simply. "Nereida's there."

"That's not the point." I glare at the waterfall door where Hazel just entered. It glows blue, providing the only light inside the Blockhouse.

"Don't worry about him." Hazel shrugs. "Do you really think we're just going to let him walk out of the fae realm with us after we get to the key?"

I hold her gaze and stare her down. "What, exactly, are you implying?" I ask.

I have a pretty good idea what she means, but I want to hear her speak plainly about it.

She grins wickedly. "As Kip said, we have many difficult trials ahead," she says. "It wouldn't be overly surprising if all four of us don't make it out alive."

As I suspected.

"You want to take out Connor."

"We'll make it look like an accident." She shrugs again. "Ruby will never know the truth."

"It would devastate her," I say.

"He already devastated her when he rejected her," she reminds me. "But here she is now, so willing to let him step back into her life."

She's trying to goad me. I know she is.

She wants me to help her murder my girlfriend's fated mate.

"I won't do it," I tell her.

She flinches back, clearly caught off guard. "What?"

"I won't help you 'take Connor out.' Ruby's going to choose me because it's *me* she wants—not because her fated mate is dead."

"How can you be so sure of that?" Hazel raises an eyebrow. "After all, mate bonds are exceptionally powerful things."

"So is this necklace." I reach for the pendant again, holding onto it like a lifeline. "So is a blood bond. So is *love.*"

She steps back and drinks me in, as if trying to figure me out. "You truly do love her," she finally says. "Don't you?"

"I do."

Tension buzzes in the damp air between us.

"Okay, Romeo," she says. "Let's see what develops between the three of you as the trials continue."

"And then what?"

"Do I really have to spell it out again?" she says, her voice thick with challenge.

My magic swells inside me, and a rush of wind blows in a circle through the otherwise still air.

Sometimes, I think Hazel forgets that wind can extinguish fire, and that fire needs air to burn.

She flexes her fingers, as if preparing herself to call on her fire, and I rein in my magic.

All is still again.

I glance at my watch. 2:44 AM.

"We have three hours and sixteen minutes to get the key," I tell her. "We have no idea what these trials will entail, and we're stronger as four than three. Especially because with Connor here, we have four types of magic at our disposal—air, fire, earth, and illusion."

The truth of it is that we're likely at more of an advantage with Connor here than Benjamin, since Benjamin and I share similar strengths with our air magic.

"Ruby won't be much use to us if she's distraught over the death of her fated mate," I add. "Plus, if she ever finds out that you had even a bit to do with it, do you truly think she'll still want to be your friend, let alone join the Blood Coven?"

Hazel chews her lower lip after I mention the part about Ruby not wanting to be her friend.

Luckily for me, I know exactly where the young witch's weaknesses lie. She wants friends. Desperately. And, for whatever reason—probably because she's fascinated by Ruby's star touched magic—she wants Ruby to be her *best* friend.

I don't blame her for it. There's something utterly fascinating about Ruby—like she's a black hole, pulling everyone around her into her orbit, and it's impossible to break free of her hold.

"Fine," she agrees, deflating slightly. "You have good points."

"Thank you." I give her a forced, appreciative smile. "Now, as we wait for the two of them to get in here, how about we take a closer look at that shell and figure out what to do with it?"

Ruby

NEREIDA'S GAZE turns to me after Hazel disappears through the waterfall. "I believe you're up next?" she asks.

I glance at Connor, who's watching me with those serious eyes that are so distinctively *his*.

Now that Tristan and Hazel aren't here, there's so much I want to talk to him about. Mainly, how he's holding up after everything that happened with Autumn. There's been an aura of pain around him tonight—one that I'm pretty sure I feel because of the mate bond between us—and I know he's struggling. Because even though he and I are mates, he truly did love Autumn.

Learning that someone you love betrayed you like she did to him...

It has to be devastating.

"Hey." Connor's voice is smooth as silk, guiding me out of the trance I always feel while looking into his eyes. "Do you need help figuring out how to use your magic to prove its connection to water?"

"No," I say. "I know what to do."

His lips curve into a small smile. "As I expected you would."

His belief in me sends butterflies through my stomach, but I force myself to turn back around and focus on Nereida.

"I'm looking forward to your demonstration," the sprite says with an encouraging smile.

"Thank you." I ground myself and prepare to show her what I've got.

Reaching for my magic is a rush, a feeling of power that courses through my veins like a riptide. My brain tingles, and the magic swells inside me, ready to be used.

"Rain," I say softly, and almost immediately, droplets begin to fall. They're illusions, of course—mirages conjured by my magic. But they're so lifelike that they blur the air around us, misting gently onto the water pooled around Nereida's feet.

The sprite's eyes widen, and she steps forward, lifting a hand to catch the illusory droplets.

Of course, there's nothing to catch.

She rubs her fingers together, and something that looks like disappointment crosses her tiny features.

I will *not* disappoint her.

So, I make the rain fall harder, faster. I ensure that the droplets appear to hit the surface of the water, causing tiny, shivering ripples that spread out and disappear.

I wish Hazel was out here to see it. After all our sessions together working on my magic, I know she'd be proud.

"Fascinating," Nereida finally says, pulling her hand back to her side. "This is unlike any magic I've ever seen."

"It's illusion magic," I tell her, even though it should be obvious by now. "I can make people see things that aren't there. Including water."

She says nothing for a few seconds, and I hold my breath, awaiting her verdict.

Connor gives me an encouraging nod that settles my nerves slightly.

"This is a beautiful display, truly." Nereida shakes her head, her eyes full of wonder and regret. "But it doesn't pass my test."

Confusion rushes through me, and the illusory raindrops disappear. "Why not?"

"Your magic is powerful, no doubt. And the illusion of rain you've created is nothing short of impressive," she says, gentle but firm. "However, the test requires you to interact with the element of water—to command it, manipulate it, and demonstrate a physical connection to it. An illusion, while it mimics the properties of water, isn't water itself."

Her words hang in the air, and my chest tightens with a feeling of failure.

But I'm not a person who fails. I never have been, and I never will be.

I can fix this.

Nereida turns to Connor, seemingly finished with me. "You referred to yourself as the alpha," she says. "I assume that means you're a shifter, with earth magic."

So are we, my wolf thinks, and I know instinctively that if I don't say something, I'll be left out here while the others continue forward. I won't have completed my promise in the blood oath to do *everything I can* to help retrieve the Key of Hades, and then Hazel won't reverse the curse.

Because there's something I can do right now to gain entrance to the Blockhouse.

"I'm not going in there without her," Connor says exactly what I knew he would.

"Then you'll have to wait out here," Nereida says. "Because her magic doesn't pass the requirements of the test."

I look at Connor, my eyes pleading. "Don't tell the others what I'm about to do," I tell him. "Promise me."

"You're my mate. My loyalty is to you above anyone else," he says, so assuring that I know he means every word of it.

My heart rises in my throat, and I want to run to him so badly that it hurts.

But I turn back to Nereida, determined to see this through. "Creating illusions isn't the only type of magic I have an affinity for," I tell her, and I walk to a grouping of multi-colored tulips next to the pool of water by the steps. Some of them are fully bloomed, some are still buds, and many are in-between.

Slowly, I kneel in front of them and cup my hands like Hazel did in her display, dipping them into the pool to fill them up with water. I glance up at Nereida, who nods for me to continue, then I let the water sprinkle down onto the tulips, wetting their petals and leaves.

Taking a deep breath, I reach inside of myself for my earth magic—the magic connected to my wolf.

Let's do this, my wolf thinks, and it feels so natural to connect with her and work with her as a team. Because we *are* a team, and we forever will *be* a team. She's part of me, and in that moment, I swear to myself that I'll never purposefully suppress her again.

I let the rest of the water fall onto the flowers, then hold my hands over them so my palms are facing the ground. Unlike my illusion magic, my earth magic is a quiet, warm pulse of life. As I continue to focus on it, it responds to my call, as if excited to finally be put to use.

Grow, I think, and I release the buzzing magic from my palms, so it surrounds the flowers and flows down into the soil.

The tulips respond in seconds. Their roots stretch and twine, their stems thicken, and their buds burst open, revealing a spectacular array of colors. They grow larger than any of the surrounding flowers, and they're more colorful—more *alive.*

Amazement fills me as I look down upon them. Because I created more than an illusion.

I created *life.*

I stand and wipe the remains of the water from my palms onto my jeans, stepping back to let Nereida see the transformation I just created.

There's a small smile on her lips as she waits for me to speak.

I gather my thoughts, and then begin.

"Water brings life to the earth," I tell her. "It's an essential part of the cycle. Because without water, there's no growth, no blooming, and therefore, no life."

She watches me carefully, and I realize that while it's a start, it's not enough. So, I think harder, searching for a way to strengthen my explanation of the connection between the two elements.

I've said why the earth needs water.

But why does water need the earth?

Ruby

I CAN'T MESS up this second chance she's given me.

I have to say something—quickly.

"Water and earth are connected in a cycle of giving and receiving," I say as I continue piecing my thoughts together. "The earth shapes the water, because without the earth to guide it, water would evaporate back into the air or flow aimlessly until it finds the sea. The water, in turn, brings life to the earth. Without one, the other can't fully exist. They're intrinsically linked, just as I'm linked to them."

Nereida's eyes move over the flowers, and she nods, sending relief coursing through me. "Well said," she tells me. "And, just like your illusion magic, it was a beautiful demonstration. You've proven your connection to water, and I admit you passage into the Blockhouse."

Triumph races through me, and I glance back at Connor, my breath catching at the pride burning in his gaze.

Pride... and amazement.

He walks toward me, looking me up and down as if he's seeing me in a new light.

"You have earth magic," he says, continuing before I can respond. "Why did you hide it? Why didn't you tell me?"

There's also another undercurrent to his questions.

Why didn't you trust me?

There is, of course, the fact that he rejected me and basically commanded me to leave pack territory forever. But somehow, that already feels like a lifetime ago.

"I didn't hide it," I say. "I didn't even realize I had it until doing the blood oath ceremony with the Blood Coven. They created the circle for the spell, and it connected with my earth magic, releasing it."

"Just like the blood moon released your wolf." From the mesmerized way he's looking at me, you'd think I was an angel fallen from heaven.

"Maybe." I shrug, not knowing the exact science behind it.

Because magic *isn't* science. It's not all facts and laws. If science is logic, then magic is emotions. It has a life of its own… just like the wolf living inside me, who shares my soul.

"If you can already make flowers bloom after one day, then with more practice, you're going to get even stronger," he says. "Maybe as strong as—"

He cuts himself off, as if just thinking the next word created a lump in his throat.

"As strong as Autumn," I finish for him.

"Yes."

His eyes are full of so much pain that I can nearly feel it as my own.

Of course we can feel it, my wolf speaks up. *His emotions are ours, and ours are his. He's our mate.*

From her tone, you'd think she didn't realize I knew it already.

I inwardly roll my eyes at her, then turn my attention back to Connor. We don't have time to get into an entire discussion about Autumn right now, but this isn't something I can just brush aside, either.

"You miss her," I say.

"It's complicated." He exhales and runs his fingers through his hair. "I think I miss the person I thought she was. Or the person she used to be back when we first started dating. Because her betrayal… well, it's unforgivable. I know I made a promise to her. I tried with every bit of my soul to stand by it. But I'll never be able to trust her again, and I don't think there's anything in the world that can possibly change that."

His eyes are far off when he says the last part, as if the reality of it still hasn't hit him.

Given that he learned about her betrayal less than a day ago, it likely hasn't. It'll probably take a while until it does.

And we'll be with him every step of the way.

I don't bother arguing with my wolf.

Because standing here with Connor, with the tulips I nurtured to life blooming by our feet, I know she's right.

"You gave Autumn every chance in the world. You don't have to defend your decision to me, because I understand completely, and I know the rest of the pack will as well." My gaze is locked on his, and as we move closer together, conflict tears at my soul.

Everything about him calls to me. His scent, his eyes, and the desire for his touch. He may look like Lorcan on the outside, but I can still see Connor on the inside. It's in the way he looks at me, and the way he moves toward me, as if he has no more control over the pull between us than I do.

My wolf all but purrs inside me, urging me to give into the connection and finally discover what it's like to feel Connor's lips on mine.

But I can't do this. At least not here, right now.

I've told him that I'm with Tristan. I *am* with Tristan.

If Tristan saw the two of us like this right now, he'd be devastated.

Needing to break the moment, I glance back at the tulips. They've maintained the life I gave them, even though I'm not holding onto my earth magic anymore.

"Do you promise you won't tell anyone about my earth magic?" I ask Connor, stepping back and trying to bury the electricity humming in the air between us.

"I swear it," he says. "You are my mate, and I'm as loyal to you as I am to the pack. Maybe even more so."

He glances down after saying it, as if he's ashamed for even suggesting that something could mean more to him than the pack.

I simply stand there in shock.

Because this is the man who *rejected me*. Who caused me so much pain that it shattered my soul.

Now he's telling me that I'm the most important thing to him in the world.

It's too much.

I can't deal with this right now. Not with so much else on the line.

"Thank you." I keep my voice cordial, as if speaking with a business partner instead of to my fated mate. "I'll see you on the other side?"

The hope in his eyes dims out.

"See you on the other side," he says, just as cordially as I did.

"Good luck."

"Thank you, but I don't need luck." He smiles confidently, reminding me of the Connor I first met—the one determined to show off his skills in the highly competitive sport of beer pong. "I've been training for this kind of situation for my entire life."

"Well, then. Knock her dead."

"I will."

"No one will be knocking anyone dead," Nereida chimes in, narrowing her eyes at both of us.

"Sorry," I say in a rush. "It's just a saying from our realm. To tell him to impress you."

She takes a moment to size us up.

My heart races, and I pray I didn't just mess everything up with a stupid saying that apparently doesn't translate well in the fae realm.

"Okay." She relaxes slightly, managing a small smile. "Then yes, please knock me dead. But before your mate can take his turn, you need to enter the Blockhouse."

My pulse quickens at her words, and I nod, suddenly feeling the nerves creep back in. But a quick glance at Connor sends a rush of calm rushing through me. Because no matter what we're about to face, we're going to face it together.

"See you soon," I tell him.

"You can count on it. You can count on *me*. Always."

My heart flutters at his words, but I snap back into focus and walk up the steps to the Blockhouse.

Nereida gives me an encouraging nod, and I take a deep breath, bracing myself for whatever might be waiting for me on the other side of the waterfall.

"Remember that the Blockhouse is a realm of water," she says, her tone serious. "It will test you, and it will challenge you in ways you've never been challenged before. But it will also reveal your true potential. And if you come out, you'll be a thousand times stronger for it."

If I come out.

I know she's trying to be encouraging… but there are other ways she could have put it that would have better done the trick.

I swallow hard, nodding my understanding. "I'm ready."

"Then go forth. And good luck."

"Thank you," I say, and with a last breath, I step through the waterfall and into the unknown, now dreadfully aware of the fact that I might never emerge again.

Ruby

WATER COVERS MY SKIN, although it's gone the second I step into the Blockhouse.

Tristan and Hazel—no longer disguised to look like the fae—are standing in front of something in the center of the room. Other than whatever they're standing in front of, there's not much to the inside of the Blockhouse. Stone walls, dirt floor, no windows, and a slight smell of must.

Hazel's carefully examining the object.

Tristan, however, is focused on me. His familiar golden eyes light up when he sees me, and relief fills me that he's okay.

He runs to me and wraps me into a huge hug, and I easily fall into his embrace.

"You did it," he says, pulling back and smiling proudly. "I knew you would."

He cups my cheek with his hand, and the next thing I know, his lips are pressed against mine and he's kissing me as if he hasn't seen me in years.

No, my wolf snaps at me. *This is wrong. We belong to Connor.*

We don't belong to anyone, I think back to her, and I stand on my toes to return Tristan's kiss. Just like every time I'm near him, there's something about him that warms my heart, pulling me toward him. A blanket of safety that wraps around me and promises to never let me go.

"I missed you, too," I say, smiling up at him in return.

"Good." His gaze moves to the waterfall, and from the seriousness that crosses his eyes, it doesn't take a mind reader to know he's thinking about the only member of our foursome who's still on the other side.

Connor.

My cheeks flush as I remember the connection that buzzed between us out there. It was different than my pull toward Tristan—more intense, as if every fiber of my being is urging me to trust Connor with my entire soul.

I don't need to hear my wolf's voice inside me to know it's because Connor is my fated mate.

He also might walk into the Blockhouse at any moment.

So, I pull away from Tristan and look to the center of the room, where Hazel is still standing.

"Let me guess—you created an illusion of water?" she asks.

"I did."

Not a lie.

The illusion of water isn't what got me accepted into the Blockhouse, but I *did* create an illusion.

Not wanting to go into further detail, I walk closer to the thing she's standing next to. It's a pedestal that comes up to slightly above my waist, with a giant conch shell on top of it. It's way larger than any conch shell I've ever seen—about the size of a bowling ball. There's a slight, blue aura around the shell, and sounds of ocean waves are coming out of it.

Seven words are written on the small, metal label below it.

The Aqua Echo.

Please speak your intent.

"The Aqua Echo," I repeat, wanting to shift the conversation away from the magic demonstration I gave to Nereida. "Have either of you ever heard of it?"

"No," Tristan says. "Gwen knew nothing of the quest after the part where we had to place the Aquatic Riddle on the pedestal."

"I know you didn't know it would be in here," I say, since Gwen told me herself during the car ride here. "I just thought maybe you'd read about it somewhere else."

"We haven't." Hazel glances at the waterfall, looking impatient for Connor to make his way inside. "Do you think he's going to pass the test?"

"Of course he'll pass the test." I can't believe she'd ever think otherwise. "This whole thing about the elements being connected to each other was his idea."

"It was also my idea," Tristan reminds me.

"It was both of your ideas."

They worked together pretty well out there, and I can't help but think they'd be friends if this entire situation was different.

But it isn't different, and I know they'll never be friends.

I look around the Blockhouse, trying to make conversation as we wait for Connor. "Did you guys find anything else in here? Any possible clues?" I ask.

"Nothing," Hazel replies. "Only the Aqua Echo."

Luckily, Connor passes through the waterfall a few seconds later.

He's back to looking like *my Connor*. Brown hair, tan skin, and dark eyes that always seem to be holding the weight of the universe inside them.

He gives me a nod of acknowledgement, as if I'm almost a stranger to him, then looks to the shell. "What have we got here?" he asks, and he strides toward it before any of us can answer, taking a few seconds to study it. "Speak your intent. Seems simple enough."

Hazel steps forward. "I'll do it," she says, squaring her shoulders and focusing on the shell. "We're looking for the Key of Hades."

Nothing changes, and her brow furrows in confusion.

Then, a memory of a day at the beach with my parents when I was a child sweeps through my mind, and I think I might know what we *actually* have to do next.

* * *

We were knee-deep in the sand, building an intricate castle that mirrored the ones we'd seen in fairy tales. They were creating a miniature kingdom, complete with the tiniest of details, and had assigned me the job of building the moat.

"Dad! Look at this!" I exclaimed, finding a beautiful conch shell buried in the sand.

With a smile that etched lines on his tanned skin, he held it up to the sun to examine it. "The voice of the ocean," he mused, and then he held it up to my ear, the soft whisper of the sea filling my senses. "Can you hear it speaking to you?"

"Yes." I smiled up at him in wonder, the shell feeling like magic itself.

"The shell is now part of the earth, but it was once part of the ocean," he continued. "And here, from the beach, we don't only hear the ocean from the shell. We can speak to it, too."

Eager to try, I took the shell from him and held it like a microphone, the open end of it toward my face.

"Go ahead." My mom smiled in encouragement. "Ask it a question."

I thought for a few seconds, wanting to choose the perfect question.

"What's your favorite color, ocean?" I finally spoke into the shell.

For a moment, all was quiet. Then the breeze stilled, the seagulls paused their squawking, and a beam of light from the setting sun broke through the clouds. It shimmered across the surface of the ocean, giving way to vibrant blues, which melted into greens, pinks, and purples.

It was as if the ocean had burst into a watercolor painting right before our eyes.

My mom reached for my dad's hand, the colors of the ocean reflecting in her hazel eyes. "Look, Ruby," she said. "The ocean answered your question."

"But those are a lot of colors." I frowned. "We're only allowed to have one favorite color."

Her eyes sparkled even more, her red hair shining under the light of the sun as if she was an angel or a goddess. "The ocean, like the earth, doesn't have one favorite color," she said gently. "It loves and appreciates all of them, because its beauty lies in its diversity, just like all of the colors in our world."

* * *

Suddenly, someone snaps a finger in front of my face, yanking me out of the memory.

Hazel.

"Earth to Ruby," she says. "Where's your head at?"

"I think I know what to do." I reach forward, pick the shell up from the podium, and hold the open end toward my face like I did all those years ago when I was a kid. "Ocean," I say, since it feels like I should address it first, to be polite. "The four of us are seeking the Key of Hades. How do we get to it?"

The last of my words echo into the shell, and a moment of silence stretches between us.

Hazel crosses her arms over her chest. "Looks like we need to try something else."

Disappointment washes over me.

I was *so sure* I was right. Nearly as sure as I was that the answer to the Aquatic Riddle was "water."

I glance to Connor, about to ask what he thinks. But before I can, the whisper of the sea coming from the shell transforms into a steady hum. It grows into a symphony of the sea, and the shell shimmers, glowing with a blue light that fills the Blockhouse.

I look around in awe, as if I'm a child in Disney World. It feels like we're at the bottom of the ocean, surrounded by the mystery and magic of the deep.

Hazel looks around uneasily, seeming incredibly uncomfortable to be surrounded by so much water. Tristan, with his air magic, is slightly on edge as well. I can tell by the way he absentmindedly rubs his thumb over the cross pendant of his necklace.

Connor's eyes are lit up as he gazes around the room, and he looks just as awestruck as I feel. It takes all my strength to stop myself from reaching for his hand so we can enjoy this beautiful moment together.

Instead, I place the shell back on the pedestal.

Immediately afterward, a strong and ancient voice echoes throughout the chamber.

"Only the strongest of magic users—both physically and mentally—are worthy of such a powerful artifact," he says. "You must pass three trials to earn access to the Key of Hades."

Before any of us can get a word out, a tide rushes in beneath us, swift and unexpected.

Water floods the chamber in seconds.

I share a startled look with Connor as it lifts me off my feet. I'm not even aware that I'm screaming until I'm pulled into the depths below, water filling my lungs so I can no longer make a sound.

Right before everything goes black, I realize: the trials have officially begun.

Ruby

I COME TO WITH A START, the rough ground beneath me and the cool night sky above. I'm flat on my back, heart pounding, lungs heaving. Water still seems to be in my ears, and I paw at them, needing to get it out.

My head pops, followed by the warmth of the water exiting my ears.

I can hear again.

Looking around, I see Tristan, Hazel, and Connor. They're also lying on the ground, just starting to stir.

"Is everyone okay?" I manage to choke out, pushing myself to sit up. I can taste the remnants of salt water on my lips, and I wipe at them with the back of my hand.

I've never been much of a water person. But after that experience, I never want to swim in an ocean ever again.

Tristan is the first to respond.

"I've been better," he groans, but he's sitting up, looking as confused as I feel.

Connor's by my side in seconds. He reaches for my face and pushes a strand of hair off my cheek.

Somehow, my hair is dry. As are my clothes, and my skin.

Like we were never in the water at all.

"Are you okay?" he asks, his eyes brimming with so much concern that it makes my heart swell.

"Yeah. All good." I force myself to move away from him and stand up, fully aware of Tristan's eyes tracking our every move.

"How long were we out?" Hazel asks. Her face is paler than normal, and while I think she's trying to sound calm, it's impossible to miss the way her hands are shaking.

Tristan glances at his watch. "Minutes, if even," he says. "It's 3:16 AM."

"More than enough time to get to the key," Connor says.

I'm not sure if two hours and forty-five minutes is "more than enough time" to pass three magical trials that will apparently test both our mental and physical strength so we can get the Key of Hades. But I don't say it, since it won't do any good to bring negativity down on the group.

Instead, I look around to get a handle on our surroundings.

My eyes catch sight of something behind Hazel, and I squint, my eyes still adjusting to the dim light.

It's a rowboat just large enough for the four of us. It's bobbing gently at the start of a river that stretches out ahead, the water disappearing into the distance.

"Looks like we have our first trial," I say, nodding toward the boat.

The three of them look around us. We're in some sort of cove, with cliffs stretching up toward the night sky. Unless we're supposed to scale them—which really wouldn't fit into the whole "water theme" we have going on here—then it's pretty clear that we're meant to get into the boat.

Hazel's doing a mix of pouting and glaring at the boat. "Are we sure we have to get on it?" she asks. "It could be a trap. After all, we're supposed to pass three trials. Testing us to see if we're impulsive enough to hop into the first boat we see could be one of them."

"Do you have any other ideas?" Connor asks, completely neutral as he waits for her to respond. He has every reason to hate her—he definitely *does* hate her. But he's an alpha through and through, looking out for the group above all else.

She looks nervously back at the boat, then calls a ball of fire into her palm, as if making sure her magic still works.

The light of the flames dances across her face, the sight of her magic seeming to calm her.

"Fine." She huffs, extinguishing the fire in her palm. "We'll check out the boat."

Tristan's already halfway there, and we follow in his footsteps.

Connor walks behind me and Hazel, and I know it's on purpose. He's watching our backs.

When we reach the boat, I stand by Tristan's side, which earns me a smile from him.

"Glad you're okay," I tell him.

"You, too."

I want to reach for him, to squeeze his hand, to do *something* to show affection. But I can't bring myself to do it with Connor watching.

Instead, I focus on the boat.

It's simple but sturdy, designed for river travel. However, there's one big thing missing…

"No paddles," Tristan says.

Connor walks around to examine every inch around the boat, but finds nothing.

"Maybe we're supposed to trust the water," I say, since again, it goes with everything I've seen of the fae realm so far.

"Trust the water. Great." Hazel rolls her eyes. "That's a very encouraging thought after it *almost drowned us.*"

"Technically, it *did* drown us," Tristan points out.

Hazel glares at him. "You're really not helping things here."

Sick of their arguing, I reach for the side of the boat, swing my leg over it, and jump in. It gives a slight lurch, but steadies quickly.

"We don't have time to waste. We have to keep going," I tell them. "Come on. Get in."

Connor's in the boat faster than I can blink, followed by Tristan. They flank my sides, as if they're ready to protect me from anything that might try attacking, whether from the sky or the water.

Hazel gives the boat one last wary look, then hoists herself inside, quickly sitting down on the bench closer to the front.

Each bench is meant for two people, so I sit down next to Hazel. She's not my prime choice—obviously—but it's better than possibly causing drama with Connor and Tristan.

I don't need to look back at them to know that they're not thrilled to sit next to each other, but whatever. They're old enough that they should be able to deal with it.

Key word: *should*.

The moment we're all situated, the boat starts moving. Slowly at first, then gaining speed.

"Hopefully it doesn't take too long to get to the first trial," I say, glancing over my shoulder at Tristan's watch.

It doesn't feel like we've gone that far, but the land behind us is gone now, swallowed up by darkness.

And is it just me, or has the light from the moon and stars started to dim?

"We'll be fine," Tristan says, even though we have no way of knowing that for sure.

Suddenly, the river rushes beneath us, and the boat picks up speed.

I turn back to face forward and grip the side of the boat.

Hazel's doing the same on her side, her face as white as ever.

She's terrified.

"You're the most badass witch I've ever met," I tell her. "We're going to be fine."

"I'm definitely pretty badass," she agrees, although the boat gives another lurch, almost flinging her off the bench.

I reach for her with my other hand, steadying her.

"Thanks," she says. "Glad to know you don't want me thrown overboard."

If you're thrown overboard, you won't be able to reverse the erasure spell, I think, although I don't say it out loud.

"You think I want to feed my friend to the sharks?" I say instead, light and teasing.

She smiles, seeming to eat it up. "Friends," she repeats. "I like that."

Just as I'm about to respond, the water rushes faster. My stomach flips as the boat rocks from side to side, like a bronco trying to shake us off, and I tighten my grip around the edge.

"It's started," Connor says calmly from behind me. "Because I don't think the boat is bringing us to the first trial. I think it *is* the first trial."

Ruby

As if to confirm his words, the boat lurches to the right, nearly flipping us over.

Hazel squeals and reaches for my arm to steady herself.

"We have to navigate this," Connor shouts over the roar of the water. "Whatever happens, try to stay on your side of the boat to keep it balanced. If we all end up on one side of it, it'll tilt and knock us overboard. Got it?"

"Got it!" I say back to him, relieved when Hazel listens and scoots away from me.

"And, most importantly, we have to be adaptable," Connor adds. "We move with the boat—not against it."

"I'm adaptable!" Hazel yells back, her voice tight with panic. "But I'm not sure I can adapt to drowning."

As if to punctuate her words, a wave crashes over the side of the boat, soaking us all.

Hazel squeals again and clings tighter to the side.

"Stay calm. I've got this," Tristan calls out, and I feel the boat rock a bit behind me.

A glance over my shoulder shows that Tristan's stood up, surprisingly steady on the swaying boat.

He holds his hands out in front of himself, and a gust of wind blows around us, steady and forceful. The violent rocking of the boat eases, and the river, though still rapid, becomes manageable.

Just when he seems to be getting it under control, we turn the corner and are on course to crash into a jagged rock.

"Look out!" I scream, and Connor holds his palms out toward it, and the rock *explodes*.

Some of the shards get into the boat, but thankfully, we're all still in one piece. As is the boat.

"Nice," Tristan says as he creates another gust of wind, steering us around a whirlpool on the left.

It was almost like the rock came out of nowhere.

"Hazel, can you keep a fire going?" I ask. "Help us see farther ahead?"

"On it." She breathes out in relief, glad to be able to do something other than sitting there in a panic.

Flames burst out of her palms, helping to light the way. The flickering shadows they cast across her face make her look more fierce than terrified.

Meanwhile, Tristan and Connor continue using their magic to guide us through the wild waters. Every time we're about to crash into a boulder or get sucked into a whirlpool, Tristan summons a gust of wind to steer us clear, and Connor uses his earth magic to manipulate the rocks around us.

They work together in perfect harmony, their magic complimenting each other's in a way I never thought possible.

Maybe they're not as different from each other as they thought they were.

Just when I think we're getting the hang of it, the river starts to narrow, the water rushing faster.

"Everyone hang on!" I call out, shifting my weight to steady myself.

We grip onto the sides of the boat as we're thrust forward at breakneck speed. The high cliffs surrounding us turn into a blurred line of green and brown, and the light from Hazel's fire flickers rapidly across the rough rock.

We break free from the narrow channel, and the boat shoots out into a massive, calm lake.

All is quiet.

Eerily so.

"Is that it?" Hazel asks, extinguishing her flames and slumping back in her seat.

I look around the lake, its mirror-like surface reflecting the moon and stars overhead.

"Maybe," I say. "It seems like it."

"It does," Connor agrees.

I turn around to look at him and Tristan, who've both sat back down on the bench.

"You guys did a great job," I tell them.

"So did you." Tristan's looking at me with so much pride that it makes my heart flutter.

"I didn't do anything." I shrug.

"You were calm and alert," he says. "You kept us on task. That counts."

"And besides," Connor adds. "You came up with the right answer for the riddle, and you stood by it. You were the first to hop onto the boat. You may not think much of it, but that's leadership. That's bravery. That matters. *You* matter."

His eyes are sincere and full of admiration.

Maybe even of love.

Heat creeps up to my cheeks, my breaths shallowing. "Well, someone had to get this show on the road," I try to joke, although he remains as serious as ever.

"And that someone was you," he says. "Without you, we might still be sitting on that shore, arguing about the boat."

I ache to move closer to him, to take his hand, to tell him how much his words mean to me.

My wolf wants the same.

But I can't. Not here, not now.

Especially not with the pained look in Tristan's eyes as he looks back and forth between me and Connor.

It's so quiet that I almost wish for the rushing river again.

"Thank you. Both of you," I say, meaning it from the bottom of my heart.

Neither of them has a chance to reply before Hazel screams, a piercing sound that makes me jump so much that it's a miracle I don't topple out of the boat.

Something's latched onto Hazel, wrapping around her forearm like a giant snake.

But unlike a snake, it's *glowing* blue.

"Get it off!" she shrieks, flailing her arm in a panic.

I reach for it, ready to wrangle it off her arm.

The moment my fingers touch it, it *jolts* me. It's like an electric shock, but a hundred times as powerful.

I scream, yank my hands off it, and flinch back into Connor's arms. He was apparently trying to stop me before I reached forward and touched the thing.

Hazel, on the other hand, seems unaffected by the electric shock. She's panicked—apparently the best training in the world wasn't enough to prepare her for real life attacks—but it didn't electrocute her like it did me.

But that's not true.

It *is* electrocuting her. Or, it's trying to.

She's simply immune to something that's attempting to fry her, thanks to her fire magic.

"Burn it up!" I yell at her. "Use your fire magic!"

Realization crosses her eyes, and she reaches for the snake with her other hand.

It combusts into flames, turns to ash, and falls to the floor of the boat.

She stares down at its remains in shock as she catches her breath.

"What was that?" I ask.

"Some sort of electric eel, from the looks of it," Connor says.

I search beyond Hazel at where it must have come from, but see nothing. In the dark of night, it's impossible to see even an inch below the lake's surface.

Another one jumps out of the water, flying toward the boat, but Hazel shoots a ball of fire at it and turns it to ash in mid-air.

"Nice," I tell her, and the two of us share a smile.

"Watch out!" Tristan points in front of the boat, and I follow his finger to see a small swarm of glowing bees skimming across the water, heading straight toward us.

The first of them are upon us before we have a chance to react.

One lands on Connor's shoulder, and he grunts in pain, his arm going limp. Another strikes Tristan's thigh, and he stumbles onto the bench. One almost flies into my cheek, but I duck before it can.

Heart pounding, I pick up a fistful of the shattered rock on the floor of the boat from earlier and throw it at the swarm, nudging the tiny stones with my earth magic to make sure they go where I'm aiming.

Most of them drop back into the water. The rest fly away, seemingly deterred by my attack.

"Nice aim," Tristan says.

"Thanks." I shrug. "I've played my fair share of beer pong."

Connor barely manages to suppress a laugh.

Much to my relief, the two of them seem to have recovered from whatever those things did to them.

But I'm so busy double-checking to make sure they're okay that I barely see it when a thing that looks like a black garden snake wraps itself around my ankle and sinks its tiny fangs into my skin.

Ruby

I curse and tear it off me, tossing it back into the water. But my ankle throbs from whatever venom it injected into me, and my vision starts to blur.

I stumble back and sit down on the bench. My mind feels hazy, and I cradle my head in my hands, massaging my temples to regain focus.

"Ruby," Tristan murmurs my name from next to me, his arm wrapped around my shoulders. "Are you okay?"

He's gazing down at me with those golden eyes I've come to know so well, so concerned for me that it warms my heart.

"Yeah. I'm fine." I shake it off as the brain fog starts to disappear. "That thing *bit* me."

Connor reaches for my hand and helps me to my feet. "Best not to get close to anything that bites," he says, although his tone is tense, his gaze is fixed on Tristan.

Tristan gives a dry chuckle, looking back at Connor with his familiar smirk. "Wouldn't want to catch fleas now, would we, Fido?"

"Hey," I warn him. "I'm a shifter, too."

"As if I could forget."

His expression hardens, and he looks back and forth from me to Connor, the rest of his thought clear.

As if I could forget when your fated mate is right here with us.

Connor scowls, although he quickly turns his attention back to the surrounding water. "We need a plan," he says seriously, barely flinching when I pull my hand out of his.

Another small swarm of those glowing bees flashes in the far off corner of my eye, but Tristan blasts a gust of wind at them, sending them flying off in every direction other than toward us.

"How about I blast us out of here?" he says, and he calls on his air magic to push the boat along, like he did while we were on the river.

We don't go any faster than before.

"What's wrong?" I ask him.

"It's like the boat's anchored down." He tries again, straining himself, but nothing happens. "It's some sort of water magic. We can't go any faster than the lake's letting us."

At the rate we're going, it's going to take at least ten minutes to get to the other side of the lake.

"We can't run," Connor says. "So, we'll continue to fight."

"Good plan." I reach down for another fistful of stones, ready to throw them at anything that tries getting in our way.

"I have an idea," Hazel says, and we all look to her.

Determination shines in her eyes, and the dangerous witch that I far from love is back.

But before she can enlighten us about her idea, Tristan reaches down near Hazel's feet, pulls up one of those dark snakes, and stretches it out like a rubber band until it snaps in half.

Oil-like blood drips out of both ends of the snake, and he tosses it back into the lake.

"Hopefully none of you were in the mood for sushi," he says, and I shake my head a little in amusement.

One of Tristan's superpowers is that he always manages to make me smile. It's one of the many ways he helped me get through all those days when we were stuck in that cell together.

Then, quickly remembering that there might be more snakes where that little guy came from, I swallow and look around the floor of the boat.

Thankfully, it seems to be empty of them.

I relax slightly, but not completely.

"You were saying?" Tristan asks Hazel as he wipes the snake's guts from his hands.

Hazel takes a deep breath, making sure she fully has our attention. "I can create a barrier of fire around us, to keep these creatures away," she says.

"It could work," Tristan muses, and he glances around the lake, keeping an eye out while we chat.

We're *all* keeping an eye out.

Connor, on the other hand, looks skeptical. "What about the heat from the fire?" he asks. "We'll roast alive."

A sensible concern for a shifter, since they tend to prefer cold environments.

We.

I'm one of them.

Now that my wolf's surfaced, I can't help wondering how I'll do in the Florida summers in the future. I never *loved* how hot it got in the summers back home, but now, just the thought of the intense heat makes my wolf scrunch her nose in disgust.

"I can control the heat," Hazel tells us. "I can make sure it emanates outward instead of inward."

"She can," I back her up, since it's exactly what she did back in Jax's library when she used her fire magic to stop anyone from being able to listen in on our conversation.

"Well, then." Connor gives her a nod of approval. "Light it up."

Hazel glances around, faces her palms to the sky, and a ring of fire erupts on the water's surface. The air warms, but as promised, it doesn't burn.

The creatures in the water retreat, hissing and squealing as they dive beneath the surface.

Hazel smiles as the fire continues to burn, traveling with us as the boat continues slowly making its way across the lake. The fierce expression in her eyes dares anything to try attacking us again.

It worked.

A wave of relief rushes over me.

But it's short-lived.

Because with the glow of Hazel's fire lighting up the water, we can now see what lies beneath the surface.

Hundreds—maybe thousands—of skeletal remains litter the lakebed. A graveyard of them. There are more bones down there than sand.

My stomach churns.

"Damn," Tristan says, looking as horrified as I feel.

"Now we know—don't fall off the boat." Connor's expression is grave, but he keeps his voice calm.

Hazel's so focused on keeping the fire moving along with us that she doesn't seem to notice the skeletons. Either that, or she doesn't care.

A chilling silence falls over us as we continue our slow journey across the lake, unable to keep ourselves from looking at the death beneath the water.

"I've seen a lot in my life," Tristan finally says, breaking the silence. "But this... this is something else."

I nod in acknowledgment, unable to find words strong enough to voice the horror I feel, and unable to stop myself from gazing down at the warning of death beneath us.

We will *not* be joining those skeletons.

No matter what more dangers the trials throw our way, I'm going to make sure of it.

Ruby

A FEW MINUTES LATER, we reach the opposite side of the lake and drift into a calm river surrounded by a dense forest.

"Do you think I can let go of the fire now?" Hazel asks. A few beads of sweat drip from her brow, as if she's starting to strain.

I know she's powerful. But magic isn't limitless. How much can she expend before she weakens?

As we continue into the final trial, I hope it's a lot.

Tristan glances over the edge of the boat. "There are still just as many skeletons at the bottom of the river," he says, although he studies Hazel, seeming to also notice that her hold on the flames might eventually wane. "But it's possible that those creatures were only in the lake—not the river."

"We can't know if you can let go or not until you try it," I say to Hazel, hoping to sound encouraging and optimistic.

"Start slowly," Connor adds. "But keep some fire in your hands—like you did in the first trial—so we can see ahead. Can you do that?"

Hazel scoffs, annoyance flashing in her fiery eyes. "Of course I can do that."

She does as asked, and we let out a collective sigh of relief when no more lake creatures jump out at us.

"Seems like we're out of the crosshairs," I say.

"Agreed," Connor says. "But we need to remain vigilant, just in case."

We remain seated, but on guard as the river takes us farther into the forest. The trees on both sides get denser, their canopies intertwining above us like interlaced fingers, and owls occasionally hoot from somewhere deep in the woods.

"What's the time?" I ask Tristan.

"3:40," he says.

"We were only in the lake for ten minutes?"

"Time really slows down when you're trying not to get electrocuted, or stung so your muscles freeze up, or bitten by venomous snakes," he says casually, as if he faces those challenges every day.

"Hopefully this next trial passes as quickly as the others," I say. "Then we should be able to get the key with time to spare."

"Hopefully," Connor agrees, although from his tone, I can tell he thinks it'll be more complicated than that.

Another minute or so passes, and then, it starts.

A white mist rises from the river. It snakes its way up the tree trunks, blanketing everything in a thick fog until we can't see more than a couple of feet ahead of us.

A chill breezes through the air, and a shiver runs up my spine.

"Anyone else seeing things?" Connor asks, squinting into the fog.

I strain my eyes, catching glimpses of figures moving in the mist. They appear and disappear too quickly for me to make out their forms, but they're definitely there.

This time, the chill seeps deep into my bones.

"We're being watched," I say.

"Like I said earlier—we have to remain vigilant," Connor replies, doing just that.

We remain on guard as we track the shadows in the forest, staying silent, as though any words muttered could incite some sort of attack.

Suddenly, Hazel extinguishes the flames from one hand, letting the ones from the other glow brighter.

"What's wrong?" I glance into the forest again, surprised to find that the shadowy figures are gone.

I'm not sure what's creepier—the fact that they were there to begin with, or the fact that they disappeared in seconds.

"I think I see something," she says.

"Where?" I strain to see through the fog, but there's only endless, swirling white mist.

"Not there." She lowers her gaze and points at the water. "Down there, in the river."

We all peer over the side of the boat.

Floating above the skeletal remains, I spot something glittering, submerged, and slightly out of reach.

Scrolls.

A feather is nestled between them, its tip gleaming with gold.

Hazel's eyes brighten with recognition.

Connor and Tristan are studying them, as if they feel like they should recognize them, but don't.

"What are those?" I ask Hazel, since she's the only one who seems to have the answer.

"I have no idea how they got here, but I'm close to positive that those are the Scrolls of Hecate," she says. "Ancient scrolls known of only by witches, said to contain lost lunar spells and secrets of the night sky."

"And the feather?" Connor asks.

"The Golden Griffin's Feather. A celestial token rumored to bring immense luck to whoever's holding onto it."

"And they're here…" Tristan says, full of skepticism. "In a river in the fae realm, while we're in the midst of our trials."

"They can help us." She leans over the edge of the boat, focused only on the objects below. "We have to get them."

A pit forms in my stomach as she leans farther forward. "What are you doing?" I ask carefully, not wanting her to do anything sudden.

"I'm going to get them." She lets the remaining fire she's holding onto die out, and rolls up her sleeves. There's enough of an eerie glow coming from the mist so we can see, but not as clearly as when Hazel was holding onto her flames. "The scroll and feather can help us," she continues. "We can't just leave them there."

I search for the figures in the woods again, as if they can guide us, but they've disappeared.

"But you hate the water," I say, desperate to get her to stop and think about this.

She turns and glares at me. "We're not leaving here without them."

The boat slows down, hovering near the objects as if it's testing us, waiting to see what we'll do.

"You can't jump in there," I say.

"We never know what we're jumping into," she shoots back. "That's the point of the trials."

I hold my breath, worried that if I move, she'll be in that water before I can blink.

"Let's think about this," Connor says, always the logical one, and we all quiet to listen. "We don't know the rules of this trial. It's possible that Hazel's right, and we're supposed to get those objects."

He has a good point, but something about those objects seems *off* to me. I can't put my finger on it, but I also can't shake the instinct that says Hazel absolutely shouldn't jump into the water, no matter what.

"But think about the skeletons," I press on, gesturing at the riverbed below us. "Clearly, the water didn't work out well for them."

"We're not them." Hazel's balancing so precariously near the edge of the boat that I worry that even if she doesn't jump, she'll fall right in. "And these scrolls... that feather. They can change everything for us. Not just us—they can help the Blood Coven as a whole."

She says it as if she thinks I actually want to help the Blood Coven after following through on the promise I made during the blood oath.

At least I'm apparently doing a good job convincing her that I'm on her side.

"Or it could be a trap," Tristan says, and I give him a grateful smile for backing me up on this. "It seems too convenient, don't you think? Two incredibly powerful objects just waiting for us to pick up. Neither of them being the key."

"Even if they're not a trap, we're still in unknown territory," Connor adds, his voice steady but serious. "Like Tristan said, neither of those objects are the key. Yes, they could be helpful, but we don't need them. And if this trial follows the patterns of the previous two, then our task is to get to the end of the river—not to fetch ancient objects from the water."

Uncertainty flickers in Hazel's eyes, as if she's considering what we're saying.

Then she straightens her shoulders, her stubbornness returning. "We won't win the trials if we don't take chances. And I'm willing to take the risk," she says, and she turns around, places her hands on the edge of the boat, and takes a deep breath in preparation to jump.

Ruby

I GRAB HAZEL'S ARM, using every ounce of strength inside me to stop her from jumping.

In that moment, as I glance back down at the scrolls and feather, the thing that's wrong with them clicks.

There are shimmers around them. Faint ones, but they're there.

"Let go," Hazel snaps, glaring at me like she wants to rip my head off my neck.

She flails her arm, trying to fling me off, but I hold tight.

Flames form in her hand, and they travel slowly up her arm, threatening to burn my hand. The heat's already so intense that I have to fight against every sense of self-preservation to not pull away.

"They're illusions," I say through the crackling fire. "They're not real."

She blinks and extinguishes the fire. "What?"

My hand is red and covered in blisters, but I still don't let go. I *won't* let go until I know for sure that she's not going to try to jump.

If she dies, then I'm erased from the memories of my parents, Luna, and the rest of the human world—permanently.

Hazel's going to survive the trials.

All four of us will.

"They're illusions. Like the ones I create with my magic," I explain steadily, hoping to keep her calm.

She glances back down at them—the boat has all but stopped by now—then refocuses on me. She's still glaring at me, but at least she's listening.

"How can we know for certain if I don't try to get them?" she asks.

Connor picks up a few stones from the bottom of the boat and holds them out to us. "We use these."

He drops the stones over the edge of the boat, and they move in slow motion, clearly being guided by his earth magic.

Hazel calls forth her fire so we can see more clearly. Thankfully, she doesn't try to burn my hand off this time.

As I expected, the stones meet no resistance, moving right through the feather and scrolls as if the two objects are ghosts. They settle on top of the bones below, and the scrolls and feather flicker and disappear.

She continues staring down below, as if the objects are suddenly going to flicker back to life.

They don't.

"Oh." Realization sets into her eyes at the same time as the boat starts floating down the river again.

I release her arm, convinced that she's come to her senses, and she massages the place I'd been holding onto.

"Wow. I can't believe I was about to…"

She backs away from the edge of the boat, her eyes wide with horror at the fact that she considered jumping into that water for even a second.

"You crave power," Tristan tells her, as if it's a fact. "It's the thing that tempts you most in this world."

Hazel frowns, but doesn't disagree.

"The river must have used your desire for power to try luring you in," Connor continues Tristan's thought. "If it wasn't for Ruby, you'd be in that water right now. And I think it's pretty obvious what happens when people jump in there."

The skeletons.

How could we forget?

"After this, I never want to get anywhere near water again," she mutters, sitting back down on the bench.

The rest of us take our seats as well, and quietness falls over us, broken only by the distant hoots of owls and the soft lapping of water against the boat.

"So," I say, wanting to break the silence. "Do you think the river will drop us off at the key's location?"

"Maybe," Connor says, although he doesn't look convinced.

"Time?" I glance back at Tristan.

"3:46."

Good. We're still on track.

The shadow figures flicker in the corners of my eyes from the forest, and I hold my breath, as if by not breathing, they'll ignore us. Unease pricks my senses, but the mist grows thicker, and somehow, it's calming. As if it's a blanket wrapping itself around my brain, telling me that everything is going to be okay.

We've got this.

"Dominic!" Tristan's shout cracks through the silence, and he's suddenly on his knees, gripping the edge of the boat so hard that his knuckles turn white as he looks down into the water.

"Tristan, don't—" I reach out, grabbing his arm in the same way I grabbed Hazel's.

His eyes don't leave the water. They're wide and filled with a kind of desperation I've never seen from him before, and panic floods through me, a single thought repeating in my mind.

I can't lose him.

My gaze follows Tristan's, toward a man struggling against the current, his eyes wide and panicked. His eyes are golden, and an identical cross pendant to Tristan's floats around his face. His features are slightly softer than Tristan's, his hair longer, but there's no doubt in my mind that this man is Tristan's brother.

Dominic.

Who was killed about twenty years ago.

The boat stops moving.

Tristan fights my grip, but I wrap my other arm around him, holding him close and using every ounce of strength inside me to keep him from jumping.

"It's an illusion," I tell him, since the edges of Dominic's form are shimmering, like they did on the scrolls and feather. "He isn't real."

Tristan relaxes slightly in my hold, and relief fills me that he's seeing reason.

At the same time, I dig inside of myself for my star touched magic, curious if I can dispel whatever magic is creating these illusions in the first place.

But it's just like when I try to change the color of my eyes. No matter how hard I focus, nothing changes.

Then, Dominic takes a pained breath inward. Water fills his lungs, his eyes rolling back as unconsciousness takes hold of him.

Tristan pulls himself out of my grip—hard.

Connor lunges forward, somehow managing to stop Tristan before he jumps.

His dark eyes lock on mine over Tristan's shoulder. "The stones. Now," he commands.

I gather the last of them and drop them onto the illusion of Dominic floating up toward the surface, using my earth magic to make sure they fall in the right direction.

Connor and I are close enough to each other that if either Tristan or Hazel asks, I can say he was the one directing the stones, and I was just the one who threw them.

Just like with the scrolls and the feather, the stones move right through Dominic, and the illusion of Tristan's brother flickers and disappears.

We all stare down into the water in silence.

"I'm okay," Tristan says, although Connor doesn't fully let go. "I said I'm okay," he snaps, and he yanks himself out of Connor's hold and moves closer to me.

"Tristan," I say, knowing that seeing Dominic like that must have been an insanely painful experience, and unsure what can possibly help him right now. "I'm so sorry."

I give his hand a squeeze, surprised by the coldness of his skin.

He pulls me close and buries his face in my hair.

"I love you, Ruby," he says, and while his voice is quiet, it's not so quiet that Connor and Hazel can't hear.

My heart stops.

A few days ago, I wanted to hear those words from him so badly. Even now, they send a certain warmth through my body, and I know with utter certainty that he's speaking from his heart.

But I can't bring myself to say them back.

A glance at Connor shows me that he's listening, his gaze focused on me and Tristan, his face impassive.

But this is about Tristan. Not Connor.

And I need to *say something* in return.

Anything.

"You, too," I finally say, the words coming out rushed and breathless.

It's not a declaration—not the kind of response Tristan might have been hoping for. But it's all I can give him right now.

Tristan gives my forehead a light kiss—the sweet kind that sends butterflies through my stomach—and manages to give me a small smile.

I squeeze his hand again to show him I'm here for him.

But my thoughts are somewhere else.
Because Connor easily could have let Tristan jump.
Instead, he chose to save him.
And that single act is something I'll never, ever forget for as long as I live.

Ruby

THE CHILLING SILENCE that follows Tristan's confession lingers in the air, heavy and unbroken.

I couldn't say it back. I couldn't fully tell him I loved him.

A few days ago, I would have. The pull I felt toward him was undeniable.

It's still there, but...

My gaze moves to Connor.

He's staring forward, refusing to meet my eyes.

Our feelings for Tristan will never match the mate bond, my wolf says.

She's right. I know it. Especially since it's been a while since Tristan's fed on me, and my wolf has resurfaced.

I'm continuing to glance at Connor from the corners of my eyes when a beautiful song weaves through the quiet night.

A woman singing.

Her voice is perfect—more so than any I've ever heard. It's smooth as silk, every note precise and full, with an ethereal quality that rings through the otherwise quiet night.

The boat turns around a corner, and there she is, sitting on the riverbank, bathed in the moonlight. Her long blonde hair flows around her, and her eyes, glowing with an otherworldly radiance, meet ours as she continues to sing.

And I don't think she's an illusion. There's no shimmer around her like there was around Dominic, the scrolls, and the feather.

"A siren," Hazel says, breathless.

Sirens.

I know what they are, from when I had to read the *Odyssey* in high school.

The mystical women who lure men to their deaths.

I glance at Tristan and Connor to see how they're doing.

Tristan seems okay.

Connor, on the other hand...

He's inching toward the edge of the boat, his gaze fixed on the siren, his expression utterly spellbound.

Crap.

"Connor!" My hand shoots out to grab his arm the same way I gripped Hazel and Tristan's. "It's a trick. It's part of the trial. You have to fight it."

He growls at me and tries to shake me off.

I don't let him.

Tristan jumps up next to me and grabs Connor's other arm, and together, we hold him back.

But Connor's strong. He's fighting us. And just like the other times, the boat's stopped. It's waiting to see what we do—waiting to see if we can pass this part of the third trial.

"What do we do?" I look to Hazel and Tristan, feeling helpless. Because this isn't an illusion. I can't make the siren disappear with a handful of stones.

I can make her invisible with my illusion magic, but being invisible won't stop her from singing.

What if…

"Hazel—create a ring of fire around the boat again," I say. "Drown out her singing."

"On it," Hazel says, and in seconds, a ring of fire ignites around us. It crackles and pops, and this time, I feel the heat more than before.

She must be doing it on purpose, to try to deter him from attempting to walk through the flames.

And unfortunately, while the siren's call is softer than before, it's still there.

Connor continues to fight us, and I'm glad I have Tristan's help, because there's no way I would have been able to keep him held down on my own.

He looks over his shoulder and glares at Hazel. "Stop," he roars, his voice so deadly that it sends chills through my spine. "Let me go to her."

Sweat drips down Hazel's brow. Her features pinch, like she's trying to hold on and failing.

"The siren's call is stronger than my magic," she says, straining to speak. She sounds shocked—as if it should be impossible for any magic to be stronger than hers.

Then, the fire starts to die down until it's gone completely.

Hazel's sitting on the bench again, trying to catch her breath.

She must have used up the last reserves of her magic.

Connor turns his gaze back to me, his eyes so full of hatred that it nearly shocks me into loosening my grip around his arm.

"She sees me, Ruby," he snarls, raw emotion etched in every line of his face. "She sees me for who I am, down to my soul, and she loves me. She won't betray me, like Autumn. She won't choose someone else, like you. No one can give me unconditional love like she can."

"That's not true." My voice gets stuck in my throat, like someone's squeezing my windpipe until it's about to break.

"I need to be with her." Desperation edges his words, and his gaze returns to the siren, who's still singing her beautiful, deadly song. "Let. Me. Go."

He tries to yank free with every word, but Tristan and I hold strong.

I can't let Connor go to her.

I just *can't*.

"Connor," I whisper, barely able to say his name. "You have to fight her. It's a trick to get you into the water—she's not actually connected to your soul. Not like I am."

Something softens in his eyes. Barely, but enough to give me hope.

I don't hesitate.

I close the gap between us and press my lips to his, giving myself over to him completely.

There's an initial resistance, his muscles tensing under my touch, but I persist. I pour every ounce of my feelings into the kiss, determined to break through the siren's spell.

Then, it's like a switch flips.

He relaxes, yielding to me, melting into the kiss as if he's been starved for it. His arms wrap around me, and he holds me tight, like he's afraid I'll disappear at any second.

It's like everything's right in the world, the last puzzle piece fallen into place, and I'm alive in a way I've never felt before. Even my wolf quiets, as lost in the moment as I am.

The siren's song fades to a whisper—a barely-there melody swept away by the wind—until it's gone completely.

When I finally pull away, dazed and breathless, the siren is nowhere to be seen.

In the quiet that follows, Connor stares at me, his eyes bright in the moonlight. The hatred in them is replaced by a softness, a vulnerability I've never seen in him before. His fingers are warm where they rest on my cheeks, and it's like time around us has frozen and we're the only two people who exist in the entire world.

"I'm sorry," he whispers, the words barely audible above the water lapping against our boat. He's gazing down at me as if he's seeing me—really, truly seeing me—for the first time. "Thank you."

I swallow, speechless, unable to find words to express the relief coursing through my body.

"You're okay," I finally say, and I hold him close, as if making sure he's still here with me—still real. "You're safe."

"I am. Thanks to you." He tears his gaze from mine and looks to the shore where the siren once stood, which disappears behind us as the boat continues along the river. "Her voice was unlike anything I've ever heard," he says. "More entrancing than even a witch's flames."

At the mention of the word *witch*, I pull away from Connor and glance to Hazel.

Color's starting to creep back onto her cheeks.

"I did my best," she says, her eyes begging for forgiveness. "I tried."

I press my lips together, unsure what to say to her. Because she could be lying. She has many reasons to not want Connor to make it out of these trials alive.

She also wants that key. And the loss of one of us could make every difference between our group failing or passing.

Connor sniffs the air, as if searching for the truth.

He nods in acceptance.

But what did she try? my wolf presses. *Did she try to save him, or did she try to make sure he had every opportunity to walk away, without being overly obvious about it?*

I have no idea, and I don't think asking her will go over very well right now.

Connor's safe, and that's all that matters.

Suddenly, an arm snakes around my waist, a force pulling me gently but firmly away from Connor.

Tristan.

His jaw is set, the muscles in it twitching as he works to keep his emotions under control.

A lump forms in my throat as I stare up at him. Because he saw every second of that kiss with Connor. He seems to be holding himself together, but I can't begin to imagine how much it must have hurt him.

"I'm sorry," I say, and his arm tightens briefly around my waist, his gaze never leaving mine.

"You did what you needed to do." His voice is steady, but there's something lurking beneath the surface that makes my stomach drop. "He was under her spell. You found a way to break it."

It's like he's saying it for his benefit instead of mine, and hearing the pain in his voice tears at my soul until it feels like it's going to snap in half, just like he did to that snake in the lake.

I stiffen, my heart pounding against my ribcage as I scramble for a response.

"I had to," I say, the words catching in my throat. "I couldn't let him..."

I glance at the shore again, and it's like my entire body drains of blood as I imagine what would have happened if Connor had gone to her—if he was now one of the grisly skeletons decorating the bottom of the river, drowned there for all eternity.

"I know." Tristan's words, cold and final, silence me. "I understand."

He doesn't sound angry. He doesn't look angry. But there's a stiffness to him that wasn't there before. One that distinctly reminds me of when we were locked in that cell together, and it was taking every effort of his not to feed from me.

Not to kill me.

I step away from Tristan and glance back at Connor, unsure what to do.

His eyes look as pained as Tristan's.

I'll never be able to make them happy. At least, not both of them. When this is all over, I'll have to break one of their hearts, which will end up breaking mine either way.

You know what we have to do, my wolf speaks in my mind.

My chest hollows, because she's right. I do know.

I'm just not ready to think about it. Not yet. Not when we still haven't gotten that key, and not when we have no idea if we're going to make it out of the fae realm alive.

That's all I can focus on right now. Succeeding, and surviving. Allowing myself to get distracted could be the difference between life and death.

I'm still frozen in place, trapped in my swirling thoughts and emotions, when a voice cuts through my mind.

"Ruby?" she asks, and I know who it is before I can even turn around and see her for myself.

My mom.

Ruby

It's not just my mom who's there by the side of the river.

My dad's there, too.

And, unlike the last time I saw them, they're looking at me like they *know* me. Not just know me—like they love me.

My heart constricts, tears pricking at the corners of my eyes.

I'm vaguely aware of Connor reaching for the rocks near my parents with his earth magic, getting ready to throw stones at them.

No.

I won't let him.

I reach back with my own earth magic, stopping his stones from reaching my parents.

I know they're not real. Even though they're speaking to me, it has to be a fae trick. They must be disguising themselves to look like my parents, and even sound like them.

But it's so realistic. And I have to see them—to hear them—just for a few minutes.

Digging deeper into my earth magic, I create a barrier around them, stopping *any* stones that might try to destroy them. I'm not sure if blunt force will make their disguises disappear, but I don't want to find out.

"Ruby," my mom calls my name again. Her voice carries across the water, as soothing as the lullabies she used to sing to me when I was little. "We've missed you. Come to us."

Beside her, my father's eyes are wide and hopeful. "We remember you. We love you. We can be a family again. You can come home."

A crushing wave of longing washes over me. I miss them so much that it hurts. A physical, tangible pain that gnaws at my insides, eating me alive. The need to reach out to them, to throw myself into their arms and pretend everything's all right, is overwhelming and consuming.

Suddenly, a familiar smell filters through the air.

Pie.

Specifically, strawberry pie.

It overwhelms my senses. Because illusions can't create smells. Whatever I'm seeing in front of me… it has to be at least *somewhat* real.

"Do you remember that Christmas when you were eight?" my mom asks, her eyes shimmering with unshed tears.

"The full moon, the carols, the joy in your eyes when you found the berries…" My dad adds, a nostalgic smile on his face.

Of course I remember.

I walk to the edge of the boat, needing to get a better look at them. I don't care if it's not truly them. After seeing my parents at the restaurant, I'd been living with the fear that they might never look at me like they know me ever again.

But right here, right now…

This could be the last time I see them like this.

"Ruby?" Tristan's voice cuts through my daze. "Ruby, you have to ignore them."

I can't ignore them. I have to see what will happen if I talk to them—say *something* to them.

"Mom? Dad?" My voice wavers, unable to hide the raw emotion I'm feeling.

"Ruby, it's not them." Connor's voice is sharp, like a slap to the face, and it stops me in my tracks. His hand is around mine, and he forces me to look at him, his dark eyes full of love and care. "Remember the trial. This isn't real."

"I know," I say trying to snap myself back into reality. "They just look so real. And that Christmas they're talking about—it actually happened. They know about it."

"We baked your favorite pie," my mom says, and there's now a picnic set up on the shore. "Can you smell it?"

I take a deep breath, the memory of that night clarifying even more in my mind at the sweet smell of the berries mixed with the warm buttery crust.

"I can," I say. "It was the best pie I've ever had."

My mom's smile broadens. But her eyes, brimming with tears, tell a different story—one of longing and loss. "Come, Ruby. Join us here. We can bake more pies, spend more Christmases together. We can be a family again."

It's the thing I've wanted most since first learning I wasn't allowed to return home.

Could a few minutes swimming through that water *truly* hurt me? After all, we don't know how all those people whose bones are down there died. Maybe something else killed them.

And I'm not them. I'm star touched. I have earth magic. I have my wolf.

If anyone can fight off whatever's in that water, it's me.

Behind me, Tristan reaches for my shoulder, grounding me. "Those people aren't your parents," he reminds me, and when I look hard, I know he's right. I can see the slight transparency around them—the illusion those people are using to disguise themselves.

"But the smell of pie…" I say. "It's *real.*"

"We waited to eat it until you got here," my dad continues. "Let's recreate that night—our family reunited under the moonlight."

"Do you not want to spend time with us?" The tears finally start to trickle down my mom's cheeks, and my heart breaks at the sight of her crying.

"I do." I swallow down a lump in my throat. "I've missed you so badly."

"We've missed you, too."

"Connor," Hazel hisses from beside me. "Use your magic to throw stones through them, like you did for me and Tristan."

"Those aren't illusions conjured out of thin air—like those magical objects and Tristan's brother. We can hear them. Like I heard the siren. They have to be fae, using illusions to disguise themselves, like we did earlier. Which means stones won't go through them." He pulls at my arm, spins me around, and tilts my chin up so his eyes are locked on mine. "Those people aren't your parents. They're fae, using illusions to disguise themselves as your parents. You're an *illusionist*. If anyone is able to see past this, it's you."

I blink a few times, his eyes bringing me back to focus.

"They have that haze around their edges, right?" he continues, and I nod in response. "Good. You saw it. If you want to see your *real* parents again, you have to fight this. Make the illusions disappear. Don't let them win."

Them?

The illusions? The fae? The Blood Coven?

All of them, my wolf growls in response. *Listen to our mate. Those are not your parents. We have to make the illusion disappear.*

My heart breaks at the thought of making them disappear.

At the same time... I know that Connor and my wolf are right.

"Okay." I take a deep breath, steadying myself. "I can do this."

"Yes. You absolutely can."

His belief in me strengthens my resolve, and I turn back around, focusing on the haze around the illusions of my parents instead of my parents themselves.

"I miss you," I whisper. "I'm so, so sorry."

I dig inside of myself for my star touched magic, my mind tingling as I get hold of it and direct it toward the illusions of my parents.

They try to say something to me, but I block them out.

You're not truly there. I won't let you trick me. I won't let you stop me from getting my real *parents back.*

Go. Away.

Slowly, the illusion falters. My parents' smiles waver, the pie in my mother's hands grows less vivid, the smell of strawberries fades. It's like watching a movie with the brightness slowly turning down.

Connor gives my hand another squeeze. "You're doing it, Ruby," he says, his voice thick with pride. "You're breaking the illusion."

The final remnants of them disappear, replaced by two people who look absolutely nothing like my parents.

Fae.

The boat slowly starts moving forward again.

"You did it," Connor says. "You fought it off."

"Did you expect anything less of me?" I shoot him a confident smile, even though I can still see the images of my parents in the back of my mind.

I *will* see them again.

The *real* versions of them.

"After we get the Key of Hades, you'll see them again," Tristan promises. "I'll make sure of it."

"Thank you." I look back and forth between Tristan and Connor, as aware as ever of the tension crackling between the three of us. "Thank you both. For your help."

"Always," Tristan says.

Connor only nods, but the look in his eyes speaks volumes.

He's my mate, and he'll never let me down. *Never.*

At least, not again.

In fact, I'd bet my soul on the fact that if I jumped into that river, he would have jumped after me. Tristan probably would have, too.

But there's no point standing here thinking about what might have been.

The only thing we need to be focusing on is finishing up this trial, getting the Key of Hades, and going home.

"We should pull up to the key soon," Hazel says, sounding insanely confident even though none of us have an actual idea about what's coming next.

As if replying to her statement, the boat lurches forward, picking up speed.

A monstrous roar fills the air from somewhere up ahead. It carries a primal fury, a raw power that cuts through to my core.

The river narrows, the water going faster.

"You don't think that's..." I look at the others in horror, unable to say the word out loud.

"A waterfall?" Connor's gaze remains fixed ahead of us, at the same time as I'm able to make out the sudden drop approaching.

Panic shoots through me. The current is pulling faster and faster. Even if Tristan was able to direct us with his air magic, there's nowhere to go but straight.

Plus, he needs his hands to use magic. And there's only one place where his hands should be right now—holding on for dear life.

We can't jump. The rapids are going too fast now. They'll suck us under, and it won't be long until we're rotting at the bottom of the river alongside those skeletons.

There's only one thing to do.

"Brace yourselves!" Tristan's voice cuts through the noise.

I grip the side of the boat and hold my breath in preparation for the inevitable.

Mist splashes up at us.

I force myself to keep my eyes open as we tip over the edge, my stomach rising into my throat as we plunge into the frothing waters below.

The world blurs around us in a chaotic blend of water, sky, and screams. But the entire time, only one thought echoes through my mind.

No matter what happens, don't let go.

Ruby

WE CRASH into the water below, gravity pulling us down and sucking us beneath the current.

My lungs scream for air.

Then, just as quickly as it began, I'm lying on some sort of hard floor.

The boat's gone.

Connor, Tristan, and Hazel sit up around me. Water drips from our soaked clothes, pooling on the smooth, cool stone beneath us. It's cold, but not so cold that I'm shivering.

I look around in a daze to figure out where we are.

It's a grand foyer of sorts, lined with large gray stones. Massive doors stand before us. The patterns etched into them resemble storm clouds, and the dim light reflects off what looks to be flecks of crystal embedded in the stone. It's eerily beautiful, yet terrifying at the same time.

Tristan stands and calls on his magic, using the air to dry himself off.

"Get up," he says to us. "It's 5:10. Less than an hour to go."

We do, and he dries us off as well. His magic caresses my body as it dries my skin and clothes, warm and welcoming, like a blanket of safety that can protect me from whatever's going to happen next.

I smile at him in gratitude, and he nods curtly in response.

"We passed the third trial," he says, refusing to hold my gaze for longer than a second. "We should be at the key."

"It's in there." Hazel tilts her head toward the massive double doors. "It has to be."

Connor moves toward the door and presses his hands to it. He closes his eyes, as if he's connecting to the stone with his magic, then opens them again. "No point in standing here staring," he says. "Are you all ready?"

His gaze lingers on mine, and warmth travels up my spine.

"Yes," I say, nodding for him to go ahead.

He pushes against the doors, and they creak open, a dull groan echoing through the room.

When they're open fully, we're staring into a giant super dome. The ceiling must be a hundred feet high, covered in intricate carvings that mimic roiling storm clouds, similar to the designs on the doors.

In the center, on another podium, is a glowing silver key. It's hard to see from this far away, but it looks to be about as tall as my hand, from my wrist to the tips of my fingers.

"The Key of Hades," I whisper under my breath.

"Do we just… go get it?" Hazel asks what I'm sure all of us are thinking.

A robotic female voice sounds through the arena, stopping us from answering Hazel's question.

"Welcome to the Chamber of Rains, and congratulations on passing the three trials," she says, her voice seeming to come from everywhere and nowhere all at once. "The Key of Hades is waiting for you in the center of the chamber. Good luck!"

Thunder sounds from up ahead, and the clouds carved on the ceiling start moving.

Rain starts to fall.

Each drop shimmers like a drop of starlight. I take a few steps forward and hold out a hand in amazement, watching as the rain patters onto my palm, feeling almost enspelled by it. The water is the perfect temperature, and it's positively mesmerizing.

A few seconds later, something glints in the corner of my eye, pulling me out of the trance.

I look to it and see Connor bathed in a strange, lavender glow. He blinks heavily, his steps staggering, as if he's suddenly bone-tired.

"Connor!" I call to him, by his side in a second.

He stumbles into my arms, and I'm barely able to hold him up.

"I'm okay," he says, but his voice is sluggish, his words slurred.

He pushes himself away from me, trying to prove he doesn't need my help, but he doesn't make it two more steps before collapsing to his knees. He barely manages to use his hands in time to stop himself from face planting completely.

I lower myself down next to him, feeling helpless as I cup his cheek in my hand, forcing him to look at me. His eyes are glazed and unfocused, as if it's taking every bit of his effort to stay awake.

I glance over my shoulder, where Hazel and Tristan are also gazing around at the rain, as entranced as I was.

"Hazel, Tristan!" I call out, and they snap to it, by our sides instantly.

Hazel crouches beside Connor and places her hand on his forehead while Tristan stands over us, his eyes darting between Connor and the incessant rain.

"What happened?" I ask them, praying one of them has the answer.

"It could be the rain." Hazel looks around uncertainly. "He could be having a bad reaction to it."

"I'm fine," Connor says again. He rubs at his eyes, but balancing must be too hard without using both hands, because he catches himself before almost falling completely to the floor.

"You're not fine," I say. "We need to get you out of this rain. Come on."

Hazel and I help him up, and we manage to make it the few feet back to the foyer. Once there, Connor sits back down and leans against the wall, taking a deep, frustrated breath.

"I'll be okay," he says. "Just give me a minute."

"We don't have time. I'm going to get the key," Hazel says, and she heads back inside the arena, not looking worried in the slightest as she makes her way through the rain.

"Wait." Tristan hurries after her, and they get about twelve feet before one of the sparkly drops hits his arm.

He screams in anguish and stumbles backward, holding onto the part of his bicep hit by the rain with his other hand.

Hazel pulls his hand off his arm to examine it.

The skin that was hit by the drop glows yellow, and he hisses in pain as Hazel takes a closer look.

She glances back at Connor, then returns her focus to Tristan. "Are you tired?" she asks him, her voice muffled over the patter of the rain.

"I'm okay," he says, although from how tight his voice is, he doesn't seem okay. "It feels like a couple of bee stings. That's all."

Connor tries to push himself back again, but he doesn't make it a few inches off the floor before falling back down.

"Is it getting worse?" I ask, praying that whatever the rain did to him, he's able to fight it.

He lowers his gaze, in deep thought, then brings his eyes back up to meet mine. There's a steely determination in them, and I know that whatever decision he's made is not up for debate.

"I'm holding you back," he says steadily. "The three of you have to go get the key. Watch out for the sparkly drops—they apparently have different types of spells in them. The one that hit me drained my energy, and the one that hit Tristan caused him pain. Avoid them at all costs."

"I can't just leave you here," I say.

"You can, and you will." His gaze bores into mine. "You need to go with them. You need to get that key."

Tristan comes back to us, wincing as he cradles his arm. "He's right, Ruby. We're on a time limit—we can't just sit around and see how long it takes for him to recover. We need to move. Now."

I swallow down a lump in my throat, knowing that they're right. Still, I stay where I am, praying that whatever spell hit Connor will dissipate any second.

It doesn't.

"Go with the vampire," he says. "Don't come back here unless it's with that key."

The key.

I have to get the key.

"Okay," I say, and even though it takes every ounce of effort, I pull my hand out of his and stand up. "I'll see you soon."

"See you soon."

He manages a weak grin, and I know I need to continue forward, but it's like my feet are glued to the floor.

"I'll use my magic to blow the rain away before it can hit us," Tristan says from next to me. "Come on. Let's go."

He reaches for me, but hesitates, as if he's afraid to touch me. My heart breaks a little, but I don't move to him.

Not with Connor watching.

"All right," I say. "Let's do this."

Hazel and I follow Tristan back inside, and we continuously scan our surroundings, watching out for sparkling droplets. As promised, Tristan walks slightly ahead, using his powers to direct the wind and create a vortex around us that repels most of the rain.

But not *all* of it.

Because a shimmering blue drop misses Tristan's protective barrier, hits my arm, and I gasp and stop walking as a wave of freezing cold blasts through me.

Ruby

It's worse than any cold I've ever felt in my life. It soaks me to the bones, and my teeth chatter, despite my attempts to rub my hands over my arms to warm myself up.

Tristan's in front of me immediately, pulling me close, his face inches from mine. The vortex he created continues to roar around us, blocking us from any more droplets, but it's too late for me.

"You're freezing," he says, his voice low and filled with concern.

"I'm fine," I say, but my words are broken, caught between my chattering teeth.

"You're not. You're getting colder by the second."

His arms wrap around me, and I lean into him, trying to absorb every bit of his body heat that I can. But it's not enough. The cold is turning my blood to ice, and I'm shaking so violently that I feel like I'm about to shatter.

It's exhausting.

I just want to sit down for a few minutes, close my eyes, and wait for my strength to come back.

Before Tristan can do anything more, Hazel's pulling him off me, her grip firm around my wrist and amazingly *warm* on my skin. "Move over and keep the wind from touching us," she says to him. "I need to be able to keep my fire going, and I don't want to accidentally cook you."

He must know that there's nothing more he can do, because he nods and steps aside, handing her the reins.

I want to thank him for trying to help, but I'm too cold to talk.

Determination flashes in Hazel's eyes, and she releases my wrist. "My friends will *never* go hypothermic on my watch," she says to me, and then she holds out her arms, and a crackling ring of fire erupts around us.

The heat creeps back inside me slowly, getting warmer, and warmer, and warmer…

Suddenly, it's like I've been sitting outside for far too long on a hot summer day.

"Stop!" I cry out, my skin feeling like it might peel away in blisters if exposed to her fire for any longer.

The flames die out in a second.

The heat's gone with them.

I examine my arms, relieved to find that they're not burned to a crisp.

"Better?" she asks, concern creasing her forehead as she takes a step back to look me over.

Much to my relief, the chill doesn't return.

"Better," I say, and then I add, "Thank you."

"No problem." She glances back to the key, and either the rain's picking up or the key has dimmed, because it's not shining as brightly as before.

Tristan's back to my side in a second. "I'm sorry," he says. "I tried blocking them all…"

The guilt across his face is soul crushing.

"It just made me cold for a little bit," I say. "It's fine. It didn't—"

I cut myself off, not wanting to jinx us.

It didn't kill me.

Because sure, that one didn't. But what about the next? And the ones after it? The one that hit Connor was a lot more potent than the ones that hit me and Tristan.

Although, without Hazel's help, I might be a popsicle on the floor right now.

"We need to get that key and get out of here as fast as possible," I say instead, and just as I do, the rain starts falling harder.

A few shimmering red drops fall in a cluster near Hazel. She jumps back, avoiding most of them, but one hits her finger.

It sizzles on her skin, but she doesn't as much as wince.

"I'm guessing those were supposed to burn me." She smiles sheepishly. "Good thing I'm fireproof."

Thunder rumbles louder overhead, and we all look up.

The rain starts falling harder. So hard that I can barely make out the glow of the key ahead of us anymore.

"We have to keep going," Tristan says. "Come on."

He keeps the vortex alive around us, but more rain keeps coming, an occasional sparkling droplet scattered between regular ones.

Yellow flashes in the corner of my eye, and I scream as pain stings my shoulder. It's like being stung by a giant bee, just like Tristan said.

Hazel flings her hand in front of Tristan's face to absorb a shining orange droplet before it can hit him.

My shoulder throbs, but I hold onto it tightly, breathing through the pain.

Tristan pulls Hazel out of the way before a sparkling gray drop falls onto her head.

Thunder cracks from the ceiling again.

My eyes dart around the room, catching sparkly droplets more frequently now. This isn't going to work for much longer. There are too many of them.

I don't have to be a statistician to know that the chance of all of us making it to the key are slim to none. And if any of us go down, we're not close enough to the exit to crawl back into the foyer like Connor did. We'll be down for the count, an easy target for any more cursed droplets that fall our way.

"Hazel!" I call over the roaring rain, an idea striking me like lightning. "Can you make the rain evaporate? Like how you make the water evaporate in your demonstration to Nereida?"

"I can try," she yells back, and she closes her eyes and raises her hands.

A surge of heat radiates from her. Fire burns overhead. I don't know exactly how it's interacting with Tristan's air magic, but the water that's not getting blocked by his vortex sizzles and steams, creating a thick fog that obscures my vision.

Tristan coughs beside me.

"Too hot, Hazel!" he shouts.

"Sorry!" She lowers the temperature, and the steam lessens, although it doesn't disappear completely. But it's easier to breathe now, and I can vaguely make out the key again.

"This is good," I say, amazed at how none of the raindrops are getting through their barriers. "This is working. Let's keep moving."

I'm sandwiched between them—Tristan in front of me, and Hazel behind. They're both quiet as we continue forward, and I can tell by the way Tristan's gradually slowing down and from the sweat running down Hazel's face that they're running out of steam.

I try to come up with a way I can help with my illusion magic or even my earth magic, but come up with nothing.

It's a total downpour now. Stronger than anything I've ever seen in Florida.

Then, something shimmers up ahead.

The key.

"Come on!" I tell them, deciding that being encouraging is the most I can do to help right now. "We're almost there."

But they're going too slowly. A shimmering lavender drop breaks through their barriers—the same type that sapped all of Connor's energy. It doesn't hit any of us, but it's close.

A sparkling blue drop—the type that almost turned me into an ice cube—falls in what feels like slow motion and lands on Tristan's wrist.

He screams, loses hold on his magic, and stumbles back into me.

"Help him!" I scream to Hazel, and then I make a bolt for the key.

I reach for it, only a few feet to go, when a sparkling white drop lands on my hand.

Mist curls into my vision.

It's blinding me.

"No!" I yell, and with one final burst forward, I push through the fog and make a bounding leap for the key, wrapping my fingers around it and yanking it off the podium a second before crashing down onto the hard metal floor with a bang that echoes through the entire chamber.

Ruby

I ROLL INTO THE FALL, keeping my grip tight around the key the entire time.

Eventually, I stop.

My vision clears.

I'm on my back, staring up at the chamber's ceiling. The Key of Hades is safely secured in my hand. And there's no more rain. It must have stopped the moment I grabbed the key.

I push myself up and look at it. Now that it's not glowing anymore, I can see it more clearly. It's a skeleton key made of dark gray metal, with swirling designs that lead up to its head, which is shaped like a literal skull.

Darkness radiates off it and into my skin.

There's no doubt in my mind that this is a key connected to death.

"We did it!" I hold up the key for the others to see.

As I do, the ground beneath us shivers, and the metallic floor vibrates with a hollow thud.

No.

Fear jumps into my throat. Because there can't be more to the trials.

Haven't we been through enough already?

Hazel and Tristan are huddled on the floor, and judging from the color on Tristan's cheeks, she's warmed him up from the cursed raindrop. Far away, beyond the open doors, I can barely make out Connor standing up, his hand pressed against the wall as he steadies himself.

But I can't focus on any of them for long.

Because the puddles throughout the chamber are floating off the ground, coming together to form a massive, watery monster.

I stare up at it in horror, a pit forming deep in my stomach as it fully takes form.

A dragon. It towers above us, swirling tendrils of water giving it life, its deadly eyes glowing a bright blue that sends chills to my core.

It opens its watery mouth and roars so loudly that the entire chamber shakes.

I curse and scramble to my feet. Clutching the key, I secure it inside the inner pocket of my jacket, where I kept the dagger before trading it with the hobgoblin.

Hazel's already up, fire dancing in her palm. Tristan's gathered wind around him, ready to strike at a moment's notice. I can't see Connor through the dragon, but I pray that whatever's going on with him, he's safe.

Apparently disliking the fire, a jet of water erupts from the dragon's mouth and shoots straight toward Hazel.

I tense, worrying she's about to freeze up, like she has many times tonight when faced with anything that required her to think on her toes.

Instead, she screams and throws a wall of fire in front of her. The dragon's water hisses against it and evaporates mid-stream.

It and the remnants of the fire disappear.

Go, Hazel, I think, surprisingly proud of her.

But the dragon's not done yet.

It turns its jet stream to me, its eyes glowing in preparation to strike.

I dodge to get out of the way. At the same time, I brace myself, unsure if I moved fast enough.

A split second later, someone's barreling toward my side, lifting me up and basically *flying* the two of us away, our feet barely skimming the ground.

Tristan.

He rolls on top of me and pins me down. His golden eyes stare down at me like they did when we were in that bed together what felt like an eternity ago, and my breath catches in my chest.

Not now, my wolf's thought snaps me back to focus.

"Thanks," I say to Tristan, and I squirm out from under him, since we have more important things to deal with than the way my heart races every time he touches me.

Such as *vanquishing this water beast* that formed basically out of thin air.

Hazel screams again, and when I sit up, it's to the sight of a beautiful black wolf running toward her and pushing her out of the way before one of the dragon's water claws can rip her to shreds.

I know that black wolf.

Connor.

He's the most magnificent creature I've ever seen in my life.

But I don't have time to gawk at him. Because the dragon's attention is back to me and Tristan, another surge of water ready to strike.

Tristan's wind magic whirls around us in a frenzied defense. The water hits it but doesn't get through, forced around the cyclone surrounding us and spraying off to the sides.

I hold my breath until the onslaught is over.

The air stills around us.

Connor howls so loudly that it fills the arena, and he lunges at the beast. But the dragon's ready, reforming its watery body so there's empty space in the places where Connor's claws were poised to rip through it.

The beast snarls at him and snaps his teeth.

Connor zooms out of the way before the dragon's mouth can clamp down on him.

No longer blocked by Connor's wolf, Hazel launches more fireballs. She's going all out, the fire magic bursting out of her in waves of fierce, fiery energy, like a goddess out for vengeance.

Then there's me, unable to use my earth magic in a room made entirely of steel. I *so* wish I still had the dagger I traded with the hobgoblin. I have zero doubts that if I connected with the gemstone embedded into it and flung it forward like a javelin or arrow, I'd nail the beast straight through the eyes.

Think, I tell myself, searching frantically through my mind for another idea.

There's nothing I can use to physically hurt the beast. But can I try to trick it?

Not wasting a second more, I create an illusion of the dagger and send it soaring toward the dragon.

The beast creates a hole in its watery forehead for the fake dagger to fly straight through, its head reforming a second later like it did during Connor's attack.

So much for that.

Hazel launches more fireballs, but her face is pale and shining with sweat. Tristan's managing to keep up the windshield, but his breathing is labored, his movements slowing. Connor prowls around the monster, still trying to get in strikes, but the dragon remains one step ahead of him.

They're tiring. And there's nothing I can do about it.

But wait. That's not true.

Because there *is* something I can do.

It's risky, but at this point, I'm willing to try anything.

I call forth the image of the Key of Hades to my mind. Slightly taller than my hand, made of dark gray swirling metal. A head shaped like a skull, with hollow eyes staring outward, cold and unseeing.

My magic tingles in my mind, and I project it outward, creating a perfect illusion of the key in my hand.

I raise it above my head, focusing on keeping the illusion in place and making it look like my hand is wrapped around the key.

"We surrender!" I call out so loudly that my voice projects through the arena, and then the dragon stops itself right before blasting another stream of water at Hazel and turns its deadly, glowing eyes to me.

Ruby

My heart hammers as I hold the dragon's gaze.

It motions with its snout toward the podium.

It wants me to put the key back.

Okay. I can do that.

Slowly, I walk backward toward the podium, careful not to make any sudden movements.

Keep the illusion, I repeat to myself with every step. I feel my wolf inside me, supporting me the entire way, telling me we've got this.

The dragon's gaze remains fixed on me. Its form quivers, as though ready to pounce at any second, but I stand strong, forcing myself to not allow a semblance of doubt to cross my features.

I reach the podium and lower the false key down to it. Remembering my training with Hazel, I concentrate on the details. The way the key sits on the flat surface, making sure its shadow is cast just right, and adding the silver glow around it that it had when we first entered the chamber.

It's perfect.

An exact replica of the true Key of Hades tucked inside my jacket pocket.

I hold my breath for what feels like an eternity, glued into place. The others do the same.

Finally, the dragon ambles forward slowly to inspect the key. His gaze is no longer on me.

It's now or never.

"Run!" I scream to my friends, making a bolt toward the door. But while I can run fast, my wolf can run faster.

Shift, I think to her at the same time as I take a giant leap into the air.

She eagerly takes over, bursting out of my skin and landing on all four paws. They thump against the metal floor as I pick up speed, and it's like I'm soaring at a pace I never dreamed possible.

Shifting on command is the most freeing thing I've ever felt in my life.

In the corner of my eye, I see Connor running beside me. We're going at the same pace, as if every beat of our souls is working in tandem.

Tristan's using his wind power to launch himself toward the exit.

Suddenly, the dragon growls, angrier than ever. Its roar grows louder as it gets closer to us.

It must have realized the key was a fake.

Faster, I think to my wolf, and we push ourselves harder, running faster than ever.

We can do this. The exit is in sight…

Hazel screams, and I glance over my shoulder in time to see that she's tripped in a puddle of rain and fallen to the floor.

Tristan hurtles toward her with the power of wind at his heels and shoves her out of the way a second before the dragon's watery tail can slam into her.

It slams into him instead, flinging him across the chamber and into the wall, which he crashes into with a heavy thud.

No.

Panic rips through my body.

Fighting back my wolf's instinct to keep running, I skid to a halt, whirling around to face the dragon once more.

Tristan is pushing himself up, blood trickling down his forehead. He looks shaken, but not overly injured.

If that had been Hazel, she'd likely have multiple broken bones from the impact. Witches don't have as accelerated of healing as vampires and shifters. She definitely wouldn't be able to stand up, like Tristan's doing right now.

Just as I'm about to leap into action, Connor stops running, howls, and charges. The dragon's attention shifts from Tristan to Connor, but it's too late. Connor is a black streak as he soars through the air, slamming into the dragon's chest and tearing through its watery body like a torpedo.

Water splatters everywhere, and the beast roars, its form wavering.

Hazel doesn't waste a second. She stretches out her hand, fingers splayed wide, and a fireball explodes from her palm. It's so bright that it nearly blinds me.

It shoots forward and catches the dragon square in the face.

The fire hisses and sputters as it makes contact with the water, but Hazel doesn't let up. She's forcing it, fueling the fire until it burns brighter and hotter, warming the entire arena.

Then, slowly but surely, it begins to evaporate.

Tristan shoots a burst of wind toward the fire. It combusts in an explosion of light, sending a shockwave throughout the arena and making the water inside the dragon bubble and churn.

The monster roars in agony while its body shrinks, steam billowing out of it as its form wavers, flickers, then dissipates into thin air.

The chamber goes silent.

The water dragon is gone.

Evaporated.

Connor and I give each other a knowing look, and we hurry over to Hazel and Tristan, shifting into our human forms before reaching them.

"Do you have the key?" Hazel asks me.

I reach into my jacket and pull it out with a triumphant grin. Its blank skull eyes are as ominous as ever, and darkness seeps out of it and into my fingers, but it's nowhere near strong enough to wipe away the victory surging through me.

"Right here."

Hazel visibly relaxes at the sight of it. "Good job with the illusion," she says. "We wouldn't have been able to get that running start if you didn't trick the dragon like you did."

"Says the girl who literally *evaporated* the thing," I say.

"With Tristan's help." She glances over at Tristan, who has blood smeared across his face from where he hit his head, clearly not wanting me to forget about what he did.

As if I ever could.

"Yes. With Tristan's help." I give him a grateful smile, then turn my attention back to Connor. "You jumped right through its chest."

"It was just water." He shrugs, as if it was nothing, and glances at Tristan's watch. "Time?"

"5:45," Tristan answers. "We have to go. Now."

We all move together, racing through the puddles toward the chamber doors. Every echo of our footsteps sends a fresh wave of adrenaline coursing through my veins, pushing me to run harder, faster.

Finally, we emerge in the foyer, dripping wet onto the marble floors.

Safety.

Sort of.

Because there's no obvious way *out*.

"Where now?" I ask, and then the doors slam shut, the world blurs around us… and we're right back where we started.

Inside the Blockhouse.

Ruby

It looks the same as before, with the Aqua Echo in the center of the room, and the waterfall in place of a door.

"Let's get out of here before six," Hazel says. "I don't know what will happen if we're still inside this place when our world stops overlapping with the fae realm, but I don't want to find out."

"Agreed," I say, but before we can decide who's going first, Nereida emerges from the water, as radiant as ever.

"Congratulations on getting the key," she says, looking at each of us in approval. "You used your magic in there as creatively as I hoped you would."

"You were watching us?" I ask.

"The entire time. And you were quite entertaining. I must say, there were many moments when I didn't think you'd make it. Specifically in the final chamber."

I shiver as I remember the Chamber of Rains. Specifically, the moment when that frosty droplet nearly turned me into a Ruby popsicle.

"People rarely get that far," she continues. "The few who do usually end up succumbing to the rain."

Succumbing.

Apparently a fancy word for "get brutally killed by."

"We got the key," Connor says, a slight edge to his tone. "We're ready to leave now."

She purses her lips and looks all of us over.

A knot of dread twists in my stomach.

"About that," she begins, and a hunger crosses her eyes that I didn't see—or notice—from her earlier. "There's one tiny thing I need from you before you can go."

We all shift uneasily, and I glance at Tristan, but he looks as clueless as I feel.

Connor's eyes are hard and focused, as if he's ready to shift and attack Nereida on the spot if it comes to that.

"What do you need?" he asks.

"Payment," she replies simply. "I'll let you leave... for a price."

"What sort of price?"

She turns her gaze to Tristan, her lips curling up into a devious smile. "Your freedom will cost you a trinket," she says. "Your necklace."

Tristan instinctively reaches up to touch the necklace resting against his chest, his face a mask of confusion and defiance. But then he lowers his hand back to his side, as though he's not bothered in the slightest.

"Why do you want this old thing?" he asks, although his voice shakes slightly when he speaks.

Nereida merely chuckles, the sound echoing around the room. "It's not just any 'old thing,'" she says. "But you already know that."

She glances at me and smiles knowingly, as if holding in a secret she's dying to share.

Tristan fumbles with his watch and holds it out to her. "Here," he says. "It's solid gold, worth far more than the necklace. Take it instead."

"I have no need of your watch," the sprite says calmly. "I want the necklace. The one that was created by the fae queen over a thousand years ago, was gifted to witches, and then somehow ended up in the hands of the vampires. The one whose magic you've been using to seduce your illusionist."

About the Author

Michelle Madow is a *USA Today* bestselling author of fast-paced young adult fantasy novels full of magic, adventure, romance, and twists you'll never see coming. She's sold over two million books worldwide and has been translated into multiple languages.

Michelle grew up in Maryland, then moved to Florida, and now lives in New York City. She wrote her first book in her junior year of college and hasn't stopped writing since! She also loves traveling, and has been to all seven continents. Someday, she hopes to travel the world for a year on a cruise ship.

Never miss a new release by signing up to get emails or texts when Michelle's books come out:

Sign up for emails: michellemadow.com/subscribe
Sign up for texts: michellemadow.com/texts

Connect with Michelle:

Facebook: facebook.com/MichLMadow
Instagram: @michellemadow
Email: michelle@madow.com
Website: www.michellemadow.com

CURSED MOON
Star Touched: Wolf Born 3

Published by Dreamscape Publishing

Copyright © 2023 Michelle Madow

ASIN: B0C54DX78N

This book is a work of fiction. Though some actual towns, cities, and locations may be mentioned, they are used in a fictitious manner and the events and occurrences were invented in the mind and imagination of the author. Any similarities of characters or names used within to any person past, present, or future is coincidental.

All rights reserved. No part of this book may be used or reproduced in any manner whatsoever without written permission from the author. Brief quotations may be embodied in critical articles or reviews.

Rising Moon

STAR TOUCHED: WOLF BORN 4

Ruby

"I WANT YOUR NECKLACE," the water sprite, Nereida, says to Tristan. "The one that was created by the fae queen over a thousand years ago, was gifted to witches, and then somehow ended up in the hands of the vampires. The one whose magic you've been using to seduce your illusionist."

My stomach drops to my feet as her words settle in.

Tristan's necklace—the one that previously belonged to his brother Dominic—has magic.

Seduction magic.

And he's been using it to seduce me. This entire time.

It makes a sickening amount of sense. The way I was immediately drawn toward him at the bar and let him kiss me in front of every other person there. The calming warmth the necklace radiates every time I'm near it. The way it enveloped me in safety the day I wore it, as if Tristan was there, looking out for me.

From the pain twisting in Tristan's golden eyes, I know Nereida's accusation is correct.

"It's true," I say to him simply—a statement instead of a question.

"It wasn't like that." Tristan wraps his fingers around the garnet pendant, as if protecting it, defending it.

"Then what was it like?"

Before he can answer, Connor snarls, shifts into his wolf form, and launches at Tristan.

Tristan jumps to the side, barely evading Connor's gnashing teeth and outstretched claws.

I glance at Hazel, but she's backed up to the wall, her hands held up to show that she's staying out of this fight.

"Connor. Stop," I cry out, but my words are drowned out as Tristan calls upon his air magic and blasts a gust of wind at Connor, strong enough to send him flying into the opposite wall.

Nereida watches with a cruel smile. Her gaze lands on me, triumph burning in her eyes.

Anger surges through me, and I jump between Connor and Tristan, raising my hands to hold them back.

"Stop!" My fury takes over, and the stones that make up the walls of the Blockhouse rumble, the floor quaking beneath my feet.

The four of them still.

I rein in my magic, but it's too late. I can't change what I've done.

Connor shifts back into human form and eyes Tristan like he's prey. "Let that serve as a reminder that I can collapse this entire place with my magic," he says, taking credit for what I did.

It works.

Tristan believes him, and he backs off.

He and Hazel don't know I can use earth magic, and I intend on keeping it that way. Connor and I *both* want to keep it that way.

I'm glad I kept the truth from Tristan. Despite the necklace and the blood bond, at least part of me was smart enough to not fully trust him.

That part was me, my wolf speaks up. *You're welcome.*

If she didn't live inside my body, I'd strangle her for how self-satisfied she sounds.

Now's not the time for this conversation, I tell her instead.

Luckily, she agrees.

Nereida's eyes flicker to the rumbling walls, then back to me. She clearly knows I was responsible for that display of power, thanks to my use of earth magic to pass her test a few hours ago to enter the Blockhouse.

I hold her gaze, daring her to reveal the truth.

She says nothing.

"We don't have long until six a.m." Hazel's voice slices through the silence. "We have to get out of here. Now."

6:00 AM—the time when Central Park will no longer overlap with the fae realm, and we'll be dumped back into the human world.

We don't want to be in the Blockhouse when that happens. Because this place feels different from rest of the fae realm. Like it exists on its own plane entirely.

It's too risky to be here when the transition occurs.

"Give Nereida the necklace," Connor says to Tristan. His voice is carefully measured, as if it's taking every ounce of control for him to not shift again and attack.

Tristan hesitates, conflict raging in his eyes, but then he reaches up and unclasps it. "Fine," he says, his gaze hardening as he drops it into Nereida's outstretched hand. "Take it."

The warmth that once radiated from it—the invisible thread that tied me to Tristan—evaporates in an instant.

But underneath it all, I still feel the pull of the blood bond. A soft whisper of longing that's distinct from the necklace's magic.

I refuse to listen to it.

I *will* resist.

Nereida grins, her conniving blue eyes gleaming in the light of the waterfall.

"That wasn't so hard, was it?" she asks sweetly.

Tristan glares at her, saying nothing.

Instead, his gaze flickers to me, dark with regret. "Ruby," he starts, but I cut him off, my voice cold.

"Not now," I snap, since we don't have time for this.

We have to get out of here.

Connor's by my side in a blink. "Come on," he says, speaking only to me. "Let's go."

Nereida moves over and motions to the waterfall. "One at a time, like earlier," she says. "Good luck."

"Thank you," Connor says, and then he looks around at us with the sort of confidence only seen in an alpha wolf. "I'll go first to make sure it's safe out there. Tristan and Hazel—I don't care what order you leave in, but Ruby's coming after me." He turns back to me, his eyes hard, his decision final. "Ready to go home?"

Home.

Where is that anymore?

It's not in Florida with my parents, whose memories are wiped of my existence. It's certainly not in Spring Creek with Tristan and the rest of the Blood Coven. As for Pine Valley—who knows? Jax distrusts my magic. Even if Connor accepts me as his mate, which I'm not sure how I'll feel about if it happens, Jax is the alpha of the pack. His decision is the only one that counts.

Home is with our mate, my wolf's thoughts break through my pain.

It's a nice idea, but that doesn't make it true.

For now, it's best to simply think of home as the human realm and take this one step at a time.

"Yes," I say to Connor. "Let's go."

He moves toward the waterfall, giving me one final glance before he steps through.

I follow without hesitation.

The air outside is warm and humid. There's greenery everywhere, and the giant flowers I grew to earn entry to the Blockhouse are healthy and strong. A breeze blows through the trees, and I swear I can hear the whispers of hobgoblins in the forest.

We're still in the fae realm, although it'll only be a minute or two before the human realm takes over again.

Hazel emerges from the Blockhouse, followed by Tristan.

Seconds after Tristan's feet hit the ground, the flowers wither and fade away. The hobgoblins fall silent. The air turns thin and cold.

I can't bring myself to look at Tristan.

Was everything between us a lie? Was there any truth in his web of deception? Or are these lingering feelings of hope just the blood bond talking?

The distant sounds of car horns bring me back to the present.

Where, strangely... there's snow on the ground.

A blanket of it.

And while my Floridian self doesn't know how quickly snow typically accumulates, it seems like far more than could have possibly fallen during the five hours we spent in the fae realm.

Autumn

I PACE around Connor's kitchen, the house disturbingly silent, unable to keep myself from replaying yesterday morning's incident in my mind. Mainly, the coldness in his eyes when he looked at me like I was a stranger he wanted nothing to do with.

I can only come up with one idea to explain the shift in his behavior.

He knows.

Somehow, he knows I turned Ruby in to the Blood Coven. I have no idea who could have told him, but what other reason could he have to look at me like that? With so much betrayal. Even hatred.

If I'm right, then he might never forgive me.

My heart twists with pain at the thought.

Deep down, I knew this day would come. I prayed it wouldn't, but Ruby's his *mate*. I never stood a chance against that kind of connection.

Although, I could be getting ahead of myself. His attitude shift could have nothing to do with either me or Ruby.

But I highly doubt it.

Realizing I'm on a downward thought spiral, I glance at the microwave clock. It's just past eight in the morning.

Morning training starts soon. Connor never misses training. When he doesn't show up, the others are going to realize something is wrong.

I have to do something.

Tell Jax, my wolf urges me.

I reach for my phone.

Don't call him, she continues. *Go to him in person.*

Why? I think back to her.

Because he's our alpha. He'll protect us, no matter what.

Her words are simple and pure. Comforting, even. Especially because while I don't know for sure, I think Jax is as wary of Ruby as I am. Maybe even more so.

There is, of course, the matter of what I promised the Blood Coven in exchange for when they break the mate bond between Ruby and Connor. But I won't tell Jax about that.

Plus, if he knew, he'd have already come after me by now.

Ignoring the knot of anxiety in my stomach, I take a deep breath, steeling myself for what I'm about to do. Then I grab my jacket and head out the door, leaving the emptiness of Connor's house behind me and shifting into my wolf form.

The morning breeze ruffles my fur as I dart through the forest trees, and I let my wolf take control for a blissful few minutes, her instincts guiding us to our alpha.

Jax's house comes into view, the mansion over twice as large as any other house in pack territory, and I shift back into human form.

Standing at his doorstep feels surreal, as if I've been swept up in a dream—or more appropriately, a nightmare. The knots in my stomach tighten as I lift my hand, and I hold my breath before bringing myself to knock.

It's only seconds before the door swings open, but it feels like an eternity.

Jax stands in front of me, his tousled hair hinting at a restless night. His sharp eyes meet mine, flickering with confusion, and then... desire.

I swallow, reminded of the last time he looked at me this way. It was during the engagement ceremony when Connor and I pledged our futures to each other.

Being close to him right now lights a fire inside of me that I'd been trying to forget.

Maybe I shouldn't have come here.

But there's no turning back now.

"Autumn." He studies me, concern marring his strong features. "What's wrong?"

"We have to talk." I stand taller, gaining control of my emotions. "It's Connor."

"What about Connor?"

"He left Pine Valley yesterday morning. He still isn't back, and he didn't tell me where he was going. I have no idea what to say to the others during training, so I just—"

"You came here," Jax interrupts. "As you should have."

His approval calms my racing thoughts.

"Come in." He steps aside, motioning for me to enter. "It sounds like this is a conversation that's best had over a few cups of coffee."

As I step past Jax into his home, I gaze around the grand entrance hall, with its lofty ceiling and curved staircase that leads up to the second floor. It's a house befitting our alpha, although its magnificence is eclipsed by the man himself.

"Coffee sounds great," I say. "Thanks."

He leads me into the kitchen and sets to work on the coffee.

"So," Jax begins as I sit down at the table, turning to face me as the coffee machine hums to life. "Connor disappeared. Has he done this before?"

"Not without telling me," I say. "And definitely not for this long."

"It's not something he ever did when he lived here, either. And he'd never put anything before his training."

"Never," I agree, since Connor's always been the pinnacle of responsibility. His devotion to our pack, to the laws of the Guardians, and to me is one of the many things I love about him.

"We'll figure this out," he says. "As is it, I'll tell the others that I sent him out of town to help me out with something."

"What sort of 'something?'"

"I'll figure out the details. This is for me to worry about—not you. You did your part by coming here and telling me. That's more than enough."

His eyes are full of conviction, and a flicker of something else. Something warm and inviting that makes me feel undeniably *safe* here with him.

From the way his breathing slows, I know he feels it too. But before I can analyze further, he turns to pour the now ready coffee.

I take a deep breath, trying to quell the fluttering in my chest.

I should go. I've told him what I need. Like he said, figuring out what to tell the pack about Connor's whereabouts is up to him now.

But when he walks over and hands over my cup of coffee, I accept.

Our fingers touch.

And it's enough to send a jolt of electricity up my arm, stopping my heart and freezing me in place.

Autumn

JAX'S GAZE holds mine for what feels like an eternity, and I can barely breathe. The warmth of his hand, the delicious scent of the forest coming off his skin, the electricity between us... it's intoxicating.

Then, in one swift movement, he bridges the distance between us, his lips capturing mine in a kiss that's as inevitable as it is unexpected. It's rough and hungry, as if he's been starving for air and I'm what he needs to breathe.

All rational thought disappears as he reaches for the coffee mug in my hand and places it on the table. Then he wraps his arms around me and stands, pulling me up with him so quickly that I'm barely able to process what's happening.

A flame like nothing I've ever felt before lights inside me, and I wrap my legs around his waist, every part of my body screaming at me to get as close to him as possible.

This is crazy, wrong, yet somehow *right* all at the same time.

But the craziest part is that my wolf isn't yelling at me to stop.

Because I *should* stop. I'm still technically engaged to Connor. But my heart and body betray me, and I give in to the kiss, returning it with an intensity that matches his.

He lowers me down so I'm sitting on top of the table, and my hands curl into his shirt, pulling him closer, wanting—no, *needing*—him.

When we finally pull apart, my heart's pounding so hard that it's echoing in my ears. My fingers are still tangled in his shirt, and I quickly let go, scooting back on the table as if his touch is a fire I need to escape.

He's staring down at me with so much darkness and desire in his eyes that I think my heart's about to explode on the spot. And from the way his eyes rake over my body, I have a pretty good idea about what he wants to do next.

I want it, too.

My wolf still says nothing to stop me.

I shouldn't have come inside. I should have just told Jax what he needed to know, and then left.

But I did go inside. Because deep down, I wanted this. I've wanted this ever since Jax said all those kind words about me at the engagement party.

The party to celebrate my engagement to Connor. My fiancé... and Jax's grandson.

Sure, Jax looks only a decade older than Connor, at the most. But that doesn't change the fact that they're related.

And it doesn't change the deal I made with the Blood Coven. The one that involves betraying my alpha, who's looking down at me like he's ready to eat me alive in the best way possible.

What on Earth am I doing?

"I can't," I say, my voice shaky. "Jax... I can't."

He pulls back, the space between us heavy with unspoken words. "Autumn, I—" he starts, but I cut him off.

"You can't tell anyone about this." The words spill out of my mouth in a rush. "I'm still with Connor. He hasn't asked to break our engagement. This was a mistake."

His expression twists with pain, and I want to take it back.

Instead, I jump off the table, smooth down my clothes, and take a few steps back.

"I understand," Jax says after a long moment. "I should never have—"

"It's okay." I give him a small, forced smile. "We both got caught up in the moment. It's... it's nothing."

It's quite possibly the biggest lie I've ever told in my life.

His gaze remains fixed on me, filled with so many emotions that it's hard to read. Regret, perhaps? Desire, definitely. But also a strange kind of sadness that's impossible to decipher.

A huge part of me wants to run to him and finish what we started.

Somehow, I resist.

"You should get going," he finally says. "Training starts soon. You don't want to be late."

"Right. Training." I move toward the door, but before I leave, I turn back to him. "Thanks for the coffee."

Not that I had a chance to drink any of it.

"My door's always open. Literally," he says, referring to the fact that everyone in the pack keeps our doors unlocked, to demonstrate our unwavering trust for one another.

He cracks a small smile that I want to kiss right off his dangerously beautiful face.

I'm never going to forget that kiss for as long as I live.

Snapping myself back into focus before I do something else that I regret, I let myself out. The cold, crisp air wraps itself around my skin, and I shift into wolf form without looking behind me. There's still a bit of time before training, and hopefully a run through the woods will clear my mind so I'm ready to show up and give it my all, like I always do, no matter what.

I'm going to walk onto those training grounds with my head held high, pretending I'm not falling apart inside. Because that's what Guardians do. And that's what I am: a Guardian, the fiancée of our future alpha, and the strongest magic user in the pack, even more so than Connor *and* Jax. They're both physically stronger than me, especially in wolf form, but my earth magic is a force to be reckoned with.

Everything is going to be okay.

Connor's going to come back. He'll assure me that whatever happened yesterday had nothing to do with me, and everything to do with him. I'll laugh at myself for even thinking that he was considering breaking our engagement.

I'll keep my distance from Jax as much as I can.

I'm going to figure this out.

I have to.

Until then, I'll train as hard as I can, keep my secrets hidden, my feelings buried, and my heart guarded.

If I don't, I might break.

And I absolutely refuse to break.

Ruby

Some patches of the snow are undisturbed. Others are dirty with signs of wear and footprints, none of which belong to us.

"This didn't pile up overnight," Tristan states simply.

"How long do you think it's been here?" I look at Hazel when I speak, since everything with Tristan—and Connor—is too complicated right now to deal with.

"No idea." She reaches for her phone, frowns, then taps the screen a few times. "It's dead."

"Mine, too," Tristan says.

I don't have a phone to check. Jax destroyed mine the morning after I shifted for the first time, and I haven't exactly had the opportunity to buy a new one.

Connor, however, is kneeling next to a pile of snow, examining the ground beneath it. "It's been here for a few days," he says. "Three, at the least."

"But we were only in the Blockhouse for a few hours," I say.

The answer for what happened is obvious. At the same time, it's absolutely crazy.

"No one said time works the same way in the Blockhouse as it does in the human world, or even the rest of the fae realm," Tristan chimes in.

Connor frowns and gets up to stand next to me. "Come back with me," he says, his dark gaze not leaving mine. "You controlled your shift for the first time in there. I'll talk to Jax and help him come around on his feelings about your star touched magic. He *will* come around. Because you belong with me and the rest of the pack in Pine Valley."

"Connor..." My heart breaks, since this is what I've wanted to hear from him since the moment he rejected me.

"The Blood Coven can't be trusted," he adds before I can continue. "You'll be safe with me."

It's so tempting to say yes.

But the images of my parents pass through my mind. Mainly, the blank ways they looked at me when they saw me at the restaurant, having no idea who I am.

"I'm sorry, Connor." My voice is steady, even though my heart is racing. "I need my parents to remember me. The Blood Coven is the only chance I have. I need to go back to Spring Creek."

"Then I'm going with you," he says, strong and firm. "We'll figure this out—together."

His words wrap around me like a warm blanket, and for a moment, I feel like maybe everything might turn out okay.

But I can't let him come with me. I can't put him in danger because of my decision.

And there's only one thing I can think to say to him to drive the point home.

"I choose Tristan."

Shock crosses Connor's eyes.

But he stands strong and takes a deep breath of the thin winter air.

He can smell lies, but I haven't lied to him. I've made a choice, yes, but not the one he thinks. My choice isn't about romance or loyalties. It's about keeping my mate safe, away from the danger that seems to follow me wherever I go.

Connor's gaze cuts to Tristan, who looks just as surprised as I feel.

"The necklace is gone, but the blood bond still exists between the two of you," Connor says simply, and then he turns back to me. "You're my fated mate. The connection between us isn't temporary—it's not forged by an enspelled necklace or by sharing blood. It's sealed by the gods. And no matter where you go, and no matter what happens, I'll be here for you. Always."

His confession nearly knocks me off my feet.

Go with him, my wolf urges. *Our mate is more important than your human parents.*

Her words send an intense wave of anger through me, and it doesn't take much effort to lock her up.

Yes, a huge part of me wishes I could take Connor's hand and go with him. But that's not an option. At least, not right now.

And the longer I stand here saying nothing, the more likely it'll be that he—and Tristan—will doubt my decision.

So, I step away from him and make my way toward Tristan, whose golden eyes are heavy with hope, caution, and love. He barely moves or breathes, as if one wrong step will break this moment in an instant.

Now that I know the truth, I feel like I'm looking at a stranger. But I can't let him know. I have to be convincing.

"I'm not choosing you because of the necklace or the blood bond." I select my words carefully, so Connor can't sniff out lies from the truth. "I'm choosing you because you comforted me when I was terrified, held me when I cried, and made me laugh when all I wanted to do was scream. You listened to me in that cell, and you shared yourself with me, too. Those moments were real. What I learned in the Blockhouse changes none of that."

To drive my point home, I step forward, stand on my toes, and press my lips to his.

His body tenses. But then his arms come around me, hesitant at first, growing more certain as I don't pull away.

It feels empty and hollow compared to the kisses we shared before, back when I thought he loved me. But I need it to look real. It has to look like a choice made from love, not strategy.

When I finally pull back, his eyes are dilated, and he's staring down at me with hope and adoration.

I do think he believes he loves me. But he doesn't truly know me. He only knows a version of me—the one that was captivated by the magic in his necklace and that trusted him because of the blood bond.

He stole my ability to make my own choices.

I will never, ever forgive him for that.

Behind me, I hear Connor's heavy breaths and Hazel shuffling her feet, but I don't look away from Tristan.

"Are you sure about this?" he asks.

"I am." I do my best to keep my voice steady. "We've been through a lot, and I want to see where this goes. In Spring Creek. With the Blood Coven. And maybe, once they get their memories back, with my parents. I don't know if humans can ever be accepted in the coven, but if they can be—"

"I can talk to Zara and Gwen," Hazel cuts me off, and I turn to face her, unable to look in Connor's direction. "If they're open to it, there's definitely a way."

"What kind of way?"

I feel sick at the thought of my parents joining their cult. But if I'm going to sell this, then I need to make it convincing.

"The Blood Coven doesn't accept humans," she says slowly. "But we do accept vampires. Humans can be turned into vampires…"

She lets the sentence hang, since it's obvious where she's heading with it.

"You want to turn my parents into vampires."

Ruby

THE THOUGHT of the Blood Coven turning my parents into vampires makes me sick.

Guardians believe people lose their souls when they become vampires.

Given what I learned about Tristan and the necklace, and what I've seen of Gwen and Benjamin, it doesn't sound like they're far off.

"Thank you," I say instead, my stomach twisting at each word. "It would mean a lot if you talked to them."

"Happy to do it." She smiles.

Tristan wraps his arm around me, and even though my skin crawls at his touch, I force myself to lean into him. "Ruby, I promise to make this up to you," he says. "I'll protect you and your parents. I swear it."

There's a sincerity in his eyes that catches me off guard.

But it doesn't matter. Nothing can change what he did.

Finally, I look to Connor.

His body is tensed, his eyes hard, his every emotion held in check like the Guardian and future alpha he is.

But he says nothing to me.

Instead, he turns to Hazel.

"Who are you trying to raise with the Key of Hades?" he asks, all business now, as if he flipped a switch.

"Classified information," she says. "Sorry."

She sounds far from sorry.

"By the way, I advise that you don't send the Pine Valley pack to us." She ignites tiny fires from the tips of her fingers, playing with them in what's clearly supposed to be a warning. "The Blood Coven is more powerful than you know. Plus, Ruby was never an actual member of the Pine Valley pack, so we've done nothing to break the law by bringing her to us. Retrieving an ancient artifact from the fae realm doesn't break the law, either. You have no grounds for an attack."

"Besides the fact that a member of your coven fed on a supernatural," Connor says, his gaze locking on Tristan's.

"She gave me permission," Tristan says, even though it was far more complicated than that. "If anyone finds out, she'll be punished as well."

Great. No one ever told me *that*.

I would have let Tristan drink from me anyway—since he might have ended up killing me otherwise—but it would have been nice to have known that before I made the decision. However, Tristan doesn't seem to be a fan of letting me make decisions without his influence or control, so I'm not surprised in the slightest.

Connor's eyes narrow, and I prepare myself to get between him and Tristan again if they turn this into another fight.

"I'll never tell anyone what the two of you did," he promises, his eyes dark and haunted. "I swear it."

"Then, like I said, you have no grounds to attack," Hazel says with an uneasy smile.

"Ruby's made her choice," he says. "I might disagree with it, but it's her choice to make, and I'll do whatever it takes to protect her. Even if that means keeping the truth from my own pack."

"Thank you, but I'm going to be okay," I tell him, since I won't accept anything else for myself. "Tristan's not going to let anything happen to me."

Despite everything, I do believe it.

Connor reaches for me, and I flinch. Not because I'm afraid of him, but because I don't want to cause him further pain.

The tension between us is thick and suffocating.

"Um, guys?" Hazel breaks the silence. "It's dawn."

Tristan checks his watch. "It's six twenty," he says. "Dawn isn't supposed to break for another twenty-five minutes. Which means—"

"More than a few days have passed since we entered the fae realm," Connor completes his thought.

We all stand there for a few minutes, shock and horror crossing our faces as we take in the full implication of what this means.

"How long has it been?" I finally ask.

Weeks?

Years?

"There's only one way to find out," Connor says. "We have to find someone and ask."

I glance around, and a distant figure down the path catches my attention. It's a man walking his dog, bundled up against the cold and listening to something through his earbuds.

The four of us hurry toward him, and his head jerks up in surprise as we approach.

He pulls one earbud from his ear. "Yes?" he asks, taking a cautious step back.

"Could you tell us what day it is?" I ask, trying to remain calm and normal.

"It's Sunday." He offers a friendly smile, but there's a wary edge in his eyes.

Sunday.

We left on Wednesday night.

It explains why there was enough time for snow to pile up on the ground.

But there's still the question of why dawn's breaking way earlier than it should. And while I'm no astronomer, I don't think the time of sunrise can change by twenty-five minutes in a few days.

"And the date?" Hazel asks.

His smile fades a little, and he glances down at his watch. "February twenty-sixth."

A full month since we left.

My stomach drops, and I can't bring myself to ask the next obvious question.

"Year?" Tristan asks calmly.

"Is this some sort of joke?" He takes a step back, looking at each of us as if we've lost our minds.

"Not a joke. We just need to know the year." Tristan attempts to offer him a reassuring smile, but the furrows in his brow deepen with uncertainty.

After a long moment of silence, he finally mutters the year under his breath.

Relief floods me.

The year is the same.

Sure, a few weeks have passed. But it could have been so, so much worse.

"Thank you," Tristan says. "Hope you have a nice day."

"Sure. You, too." The man gives us one last strange look, then turns around and hurries away as fast as his little dog's legs can handle, glancing over his shoulder a few times as if he's worried we might follow.

We stand in silence for a moment, taking in the news.

Then, without a word, Connor turns and bolts into the woods.

He's gone before I can process what happened or scream his name.

No. My wolf tries to burst out of my skin, but I use the memory of my parents not recognizing me to hold her back.

I have to remember what I'm fighting for.

"Let him go." Tristan watches me carefully, like this is a test to see how serious I am about choosing him over Connor. "You don't need him. You have us."

"I didn't get to thank him," I say the first thing that pops into my mind. "He risked himself with that water dragon back in the Chamber of Rains. He could have died. And I never thanked him for it."

"We all could have died," Hazel says gently. "We all risked ourselves."

"I know." I stare sadly out at the trees, as if Connor might come bursting out of them at any second.

He doesn't.

He's gone.

And it feels like he's taken my heart with him.

"It doesn't matter." I bury my feelings, just like I've been burying my wolf. "I have the two of you. We succeeded in getting the key. So, how about we get out of here and head back home?"

"Home." Tristan smiles and squeezes my hand. "Yes. Let's go back home."

Ruby

WE FIND A CAR RENTAL PLACE, rent a car with cash, and head out of the city with Tristan at the wheel. Because firstly, neither Hazel nor I are comfortable driving in the city. Secondly, vampires need the least amount of sleep of all supernaturals, and it's been a while since we've slept.

I don't even realize *how* tired I am until I'm situated in the passenger seat.

As Tristan expertly maneuvers the car through the city traffic, Hazel fusses with her phone in the back seat. The car came with a charging cable, and now her phone is plugged into the USB port, sucking up power like a thirsty vampire.

She keeps checking it, waiting until it has enough power to turn on.

"Finally." She stares at the screen in relief. "I'm calling Benjamin first."

She taps the screen a few more times, turns on the speakerphone, then places the phone on the center console as it rings.

As it does, I realize—there's no one for me to call. Not my parents, not Luna... no one.

No one cares if I'm alive or not, because most of the world has forgotten I was alive in the first place.

The emptiness the reminder gives me hurts like a thousand tiny pins poking into my lungs.

Just when I think it's going to voicemail, the phone stops ringing.

"Hazel?" Benjamin says softly, as if he can't bring himself to believe it.

"It's me," she says. "I'm alive. We all are. Me, Tristan, and Ruby. They're here right now."

"We have the Key of Hades," Tristan says. "We're driving back to Spring Creek."

"You didn't come back." Benjamin sounds shellshocked, like he's talking to a ghost. "We thought you were dead."

"We almost died a few times." Tristan chuckles, even though it's far from funny. "But it seems like time passes differently in the Blockhouse. We were only there for a few hours. But here it's been weeks."

"And Connor?" Benjamin asks, and I can practically feel his anger radiating out of the phone.

I don't particularly blame him, given that Connor drugged him and took his place on our mission.

"He made it out as well." Tristan's grip tightens around the steering wheel, and he keeps his eyes locked on the road.

"Where is he?"

"He ran off when we got back," I chime in. "But it doesn't matter. We have the key."

"Good," Benjamin says. "Gwen and I have been looking for alternatives, and we haven't come up with much. She thought we might be able to find *something* here in Greece, but it's one dead end after the other. Unsurprising, since she's been obsessed with this for centuries and has done research in nearly every place imaginable, but I think she needed something to keep her occupied while she processed… everything."

"Like the fact that she thought we were dead," Tristan says at the same time as Hazel says, "You're in Greece?"

"We are. I'm going to get Gwen now, and then we'll be on the first flight out of here to New York."

"Good," Tristan says. "We need the two of you here."

"Stay safe. And try not to lose the key," he adds with a hint of humor in his voice.

I reach for it inside my jacket, the cold metal keeping me somewhat grounded. It's the key to the world remembering me. I'm guarding it with my life.

"Don't worry," I say. "It's safe with me."

With that, the call ends, and Hazel moves on to call her parents.

I lean my head against the window, watching the city lights fade into the darkness of the countryside. It's peaceful out here. A stark contrast to the turmoil raging inside me.

Not just mine, but also my wolf's.

Once Hazel's done calling her parents, she puts her phone down and leans her head against the back of her seat. Her eyes close, and her breaths gradually become deeper, slower.

Tristan glances over at me and gives me an encouraging half-smile. "Get some rest," he says. "I can get us home."

I don't reply. Instead, I run my fingers along the key again and look out the window. The sun is fully risen, casting a warm golden glow over the snow-covered hills, and despite everything, I feel the faintest sense of hope.

The Key of Hades is my key out of this mess. Spring Creek isn't my home, but I *will* find a home. Once I do, I'm never letting it go.

"We'll get through this," I whisper, more to myself than to Tristan. But he hears me, and his soft reply echoes my sentiments.

"Yes, we will. We always do."

And then I lean my head against the window, my eyes slowly close, and I'm pulled down into a deep sleep.

* * *

I'm jolted awake by gravel crunching under the tires of our car. For a moment, I forget where I am, but then it all comes rushing back.

The Blockhouse.

The Key of Hades.

The Blood Coven.

Telling Connor I don't want him, then watching him leave me in his dust.

I pray I didn't make a horrible mistake.

But I push the heartache away—I've been getting good at that recently—and look around. It's midday, so the sun is shining high above the Blood Coven's Victorian mansion. The house belongs to Calliope—the leader of the Spring Creek coven—but the three blood witch sisters along with Tristan, Benjamin, and Gwen have been living there with her since bringing her in as a member of the coven.

There's also Lindsay and Jason, the humans they've been keeping in the basement as food for the vampires.

Dread pools in my stomach at the thought of them. I pray they're okay, since it's been a month since we left.

Hazel wakes with a giant yawn, stretches in the back seat, and checks her phone.

"Benjamin and Gwen found a flight back," she says. "They'll be here by tomorrow night."

"Good," Tristan says.

I don't bother with a response. They both know precisely how fond I am of Benjamin and Gwen.

"How are you feeling?" Tristan asks me.

"Hungry," I say, since I can't remember the last time we ate. We talked about stopping for food on the way back, but Hazel and I were sleeping so deeply that I assume Tristan didn't want to wake us.

"Figured you'd be hungry," he says. "I asked Willow to have lunch waiting for us."

He parks in front of the house, and as we make our way to the entrance, my wolf stirs at the smell of cooked meat.

When my parents remember me and I see them again for the first time in weeks, they're going to be appalled that I'm no longer a vegetarian.

The door swings open just as we reach the steps, and there, standing with a bright smile on her face, is Morgan.

"I knew you'd be back," she says.

"How?" I ask.

"Divination," she reminds me about her blood magic ability. "I didn't know timing or anything like that, but I still knew."

"Benjamin thought we were dead," Hazel says simply.

"I tell the fewest amount of people about my visions as possible," Morgan explains. "The more people I tell, the more likely it is that the future will shift in unpredictable—and possibly dangerous—ways."

I glance inside just as Willow hurries barefoot across the room to greet us. "Tristan!" she says, and she stops in front of him, studying him as if making sure he's real. "You look… thirsty."

I look at him—really *look* at him—and can't believe I missed it. Dark, hollow circles have spread beneath his eyes, and his skin is even paler than normal. He fed before we left for the fae realm, but given how strangely time moved while we were there, there's no saying how it affected his body.

"The humans are still downstairs." She points her thumb in the direction of the basement door. "You can go—"

Tristan moves in a blur across the living room and disappears down the hall before Willow can finish her sentence.

I feel the emptiness of his absence. The blood bond. It's still inside me.

But it doesn't matter. Because now that I know the truth about him, I'm going to control the blood bond.

I won't accept anything less from myself.

"How are Lindsay and Jason?" I ask Morgan as Hazel and I step inside, glancing down the hallway where Tristan disappeared.

"They're hanging in there." Guilt flashes in her eyes, and I feel like she doesn't like the thought of locking people in the basement any more than I do.

Before I can ask any more, Zara enters the living room. All three blood witches are beautiful, but there's a regal quality to Zara that makes everyone basically stop breathing when she enters a room.

"I hear you successfully retrieved the Key of Hades," she says.

"We did." I step back, protective over the key in my jacket.

"Show it to me."

Zara's obviously not going to take no for an answer, and angering the Blood Coven isn't going to get me anywhere. So, I reach into my pocket and bring it out. The dark gray metal glints under the soft light, and the intricate etchings leading up to its skull head seem to dance and move.

Zara moves forward to take it, but I pull it back instinctively, wrapping my fingers around it tighter.

"It's safe with me," I tell her.

The air crackles around her—like she's going to unleash her fire magic at any second—but then she glances to Morgan, who nods in assurance. "Very well," she says, and she turns her sharp eyes back to me, the flame tattoo on her cheek glimmering like a warning. "But remember, Ruby, we're all on the same side here."

"We are," I say. "And I'll prove it to you by keeping the key safe."

She stares me down like a cat about to pounce, but I hold my ground. Because I'm a wolf, and I refuse to back down.

"All right. I'll let you keep it for now," she says, and I place the key back inside my jacket pocket in relief. "But given that you're technically not a member of our coven yet, Gwen might not be as understanding when she gets here."

"I thought you were the leader of the Blood Coven?" I ask.

"I am. But Gwen's the one who brought us all together. She has a unique connection to that key."

"What sort of 'connection?'"

I doubt she'll tell me, but it's always worth it to ask.

"You'll find out soon." She gives me a thin smile. "But Calliope's been preparing lunch, and it seems like you both could use some food."

With that, she turns around, her dark hair swirling around her as she leads the way to the dining room.

I follow with my head held high.

I'll eat, I'll rest, and I'll prepare. Because the battle is just starting, and after everything in the fae realm, I'm ready to face anything this world throws at me.

Connor

THE WOODEN FLOORS of my home creak beneath my weight as I step inside. I've been awake for more than a day, and after everything that happened in the fae realm, my magic feels depleted. My emotions, too. Like a phone battery running on one percent, begging for a recharge.

My entire *life* could use a recharge. Or a total reboot.

As it is, a night of sleep will have to be enough.

I don't even change into my pajamas before my head hits the pillow, sleep overtaking me in seconds.

When I wake, I almost expect Autumn to be next to me. But of course, she's not. I don't *want* her to be. After what she did, I'll never be able to look her in the eyes again.

Still, I did love her. And even though that love wasn't the same as a mate bond, it meant something to me. I wouldn't have tried to make it work with her if it didn't.

There's also the important fact that it's been a week since her birthday. I wasn't there for it. And it wasn't just any birthday. It was *the* birthday. Her nineteenth birthday—the age when she'll finally be able to meet her mate.

I hope she does.

Then, hopefully she'll stop going after *my* mate.

As it is, I have to tell her that I'm breaking our engagement and get the ring back.

So I take a much-needed shower, then run in wolf form to Jax's place, pausing only to hunt for breakfast on the way there.

Nothing hits the spot like fresh meat.

Jax comes to the door quickly, opens it, and stares at me like he's seeing a ghost. I can't tell if he's excited to see me, or angry at me for disappearing for a month without telling anyone where I was going.

It's probably both.

"Where have you been?" he asks, straight to the point.

"Long story," I say, and he opens the door, motioning for me to come in.

Inside the familiar confines of Jax's home—the house where I grew up—the scent of old books, strong coffee, and pine fills the air. I make myself comfortable on the couch in the living room, getting ready to fill Jax in on the parts of the story I want to share.

Meaning, the ones that won't put Ruby in danger.

"You disappeared for a month, Connor. An entire *month*." Jax remains standing, glaring at me like he wants to rip the truth out of my throat. "I had to lie to the pack about where you went. I was beginning to think you might be dead."

"I wasn't dead," I tell him. "I was in the fae realm."

He stares at me like I lost my mind, and I give him a few seconds to let it sink in.

"You went to the fae realm. Alone," he says slowly.

"I wasn't there alone."

"Then who *were* you with? Because I know it wasn't Autumn. She's been devastated by what you did to her."

What I did to *her*?

She has no idea what it feels like to be truly shattered by someone you loved and trusted.

But I'll deal with Autumn in a bit. I want her to be here for that.

"Hazel is working with the Spring Creek coven," I tell him. "She brought Ruby there so they could use her magic to help them retrieve an artifact from the fae realm."

Jax pauses for another few seconds, thinking.

"And Ruby chose to stay with them and help them?" he asks.

"They blackmailed her into it," I say. "Hazel did more than make Ruby's parents and everyone who knew her in the human world think she was dead. She made them forget about her entire existence."

"That's not possible," Jax says.

"Hazel's the strongest witch in centuries. I assure you that it *is* possible. She promised Ruby that she'd reverse the erasure spell if Ruby helped them successfully retrieve the artifact."

Jax is silent for a few seconds, his expression unreadable.

"How did you get involved with all of this?" he finally asks.

"There are those in Spring Creek who don't support what their leaders are doing," I say, being purposefully cryptic about it. "They wanted to strengthen their alliance with the Pine Valley pack. To gain my trust, they came to me and told me what was happening to Ruby."

"So, you chased her into the fae realm."

"Not just her. Hazel and two vampires were going with her. I knocked one of the vampires out and took his place on the mission."

This catches him even more by surprise. "How did vampires get involved?"

"They're working with the Spring Creek coven."

"Of course they are." He huffs. "The witches and shifters of Spring Creek have always been too accepting when it comes to vampires. It's unnatural. Just like Ruby's magic."

"Do *not* talk about my mate that way," I growl.

He doesn't apologize.

I didn't expect him to.

"It's not our place to interfere with the business of the witches," he says instead. "If Hazel wants to work with Spring Creek, and if Spring Creek wants to trust vampires, then those are their decisions. They haven't done anything against us. And Ruby doesn't count as one of us, given that your mate bond hasn't been consummated."

"I'm aware of that," I say steadily. "But I wasn't going to let my mate enter the fae realm without me."

"So, you left without telling anyone where you were going."

I hold his gaze, not backing down. "I couldn't risk anyone trying to stop me."

His jaw clenches, and he starts pacing around the room. "And now you've come back," he says. "After a whole month."

"Time moved differently in the fae realm," I explain. "We were only there for a few hours."

He stops pacing. "Interesting. I'm glad you made it back safely," he says. "Where's Ruby?"

"She went back to Spring Creek to complete her promise to them."

I refuse to tell him that she chose to be with a vampire. Like I told her, I'm not going to put her in danger.

"And the artifact?" he asks.

"It's called the Key of Hades. We successfully retrieved it, and they brought it back to Spring Creek."

"The Key of Hades," he says thoughtfully. "I've heard of it."

"So, you know it can be used to resurrect the dead."

"That's what the legends say," he confirms. "But it's not against the law to retrieve artifacts. We have no grounds for attack."

"I'm aware. I know our laws."

I've only spent my *entire life* devoted to them.

He releases a long breath, his gaze never leaving mine. "You're playing with fire, Connor," he warns. "And what about Autumn? Your *fiancée?*"

It almost sounds like he struggled to say that last word.

"She did something unforgivable, so I'm ending our engagement," I tell him. "But she needs to hear it from me. And I want to have you, our alpha, as a witness."

Connor

JAX MAKES coffee as we wait for Autumn's arrival. He asks me for more details about the fae realm, and I happily fill him in, glad to have something to talk about that won't risk the truth coming out about Tristan and Ruby.

Autumn lets herself in as if she lives here. Which it felt like she did back when we were dating, before I moved out last year to live on my own.

Her eyes go wide when they land on me, then harden. She's lost weight in the past month, her red hair hangs limply down her back, and she looks so frail that I have no idea how she's managing to keep up in training. Especially since the hollows under her eyes make it seem like she hasn't slept in weeks.

"Connor." She fiddles with her engagement ring, which is still slightly too big on her. "You're back."

She knows what's coming. I can feel it in the air and see it in the way she's looking at me, as if she's readying herself for me to break her.

From the looks of her, I already *have* broken her.

Before I found out about what she did, I would have run to her, taken her in my arms, and told her that everything was going to be okay. But the version of me that loved her died when I learned about how she turned Ruby in without any thought of the possible repercussions of her actions.

Looking at her now, all I feel is angry and betrayed.

"Yes. I'm back," I say, keeping it simple.

She glances at Jax again, as if searching for support, then turns back to me. "You ran off without telling me where you were going."

"Sort of like how you ran to the Spring Creek coven and told them the truth about Ruby without telling me where *you* were going?" I shoot back, allowing my anger to rise to the surface.

She flinches at my words. "I did what was necessary."

"And how, exactly, was it 'necessary' to put my mate's life in danger?"

"Your precious Ruby isn't one of us, and she never will be," she hisses, the words exploding out of her like a missile. "She's a danger to our pack and to our kind."

"Her magic is a gift from the gods." I growl and stand up, slamming my hand on the table so hard that coffee spills over the top of my mug. "She's my mate. You had no right to decide what was best for me or for the pack."

"Your mate bond blinds you to the truth about her," she insists. "But the Spring Creek coven might be able to break the bond without killing her. Then you'll be able to see clearly again."

"I see this situation perfectly clearly." I remain calm, since nothing she does or says will change my mind. "I was blinded to the truth about *you*. You were so hell-bent on getting what you wanted that you didn't think about the consequences. Ruby could have been killed because of what you did. She still might be. As it is, she's chosen to join the Spring Creek coven. If it wasn't for you, she'd still be here in Pine Valley, which should have been her home. But she's not, and I will never, ever forgive you for it."

We stand there in silence, the tension so thick that it's impossible to breathe, and regret flashes in her eyes.

Regret that she got caught.

Not for what she did.

"I need the ring back, Autumn," I say, unprepared for the relief that floods through me after I do.

Her hand instinctively moves to the engagement ring on her finger, like she's trying to protect it. She glances at Jax again, but he's watching, waiting, unwilling to interfere.

She keeps looking at him like she expects him to jump in and help her. But he's her alpha—not her savior.

She's not getting out of this one.

Finally, she removes the ring, her movements slow and robotic. Her eyes are empty as she stares down at it.

"What about us, Connor?" She meets my gaze again, sounding and looking smaller than ever. "What happens to us?"

"There is no 'us' anymore, Autumn. Not after what you did."

She walks toward me and opens her hand, revealing the ring. "I'm sorry, Connor," she says. "I truly am. I wasn't thinking. I'm so incredibly sorry."

Is she so deluded that she actually expects forgiveness?

I snatch the ring out of her fingers, the cold metal against my skin a stark reminder of our broken relationship. "Sorry doesn't change what you did," I say, and she sucks in a sharp breath, as if I punched her in the stomach.

Good.

She deserves it.

"You still haven't told me where you went these past few weeks," she says.

"It doesn't matter," I reply. "All that mattered was that I was away from you."

It's harsher than I intended. But by this point, I don't care.

She backs away, as if I'm a snake ready to bite her. "Were you with her?" she asks. "With Ruby?"

"I was."

"In Spring Creek?"

"No."

I stare her down, daring her to challenge me again.

She fights it for a few seconds. Then she trembles, and she breaks my gaze.

I toss the ring down onto the table, since I have no need for it anymore. "I'm leaving," I tell her—and Jax. "Again."

"Where are you going?"

I look at her, really look at her, and for a moment I almost feel sorry for the desperate, lost girl standing before me.

Almost.

"I don't owe you that information," I say. "Just like you didn't think you owed me the truth about what you did to Ruby."

"I was going to tell you. Once the mate bond was broken, and you could think clearly, then—"

"Enough," I say. "I've said what I needed. We're done here."

"But Connor..."

"No, Autumn," I cut her off. "You made your choices. Now you have to live with them."

She closes her eyes, the tears falling freely now. But this was a long time coming. So, I turn to leave, ready to walk away from her, from all of this.

Before I can, Jax clears his throat, drawing my attention.

"You're correct that you don't owe Autumn that information," he says. "But I'm your alpha—and your family. You do owe me."

"Fine," I say, since I'm more than aware how protocol goes around here. "I'm going back to the city for a bit. I'll stay with the Guardians there."

"You can't just go stay with the Guardians in the city," Jax says. "You have your pack here. You have training."

"I can train there."

"That's not how things are done here."

"I didn't think the way things are done here was for my grandfather to look at my ex-fiancée with *lust* in his eyes," I snarl. "And yet, here we are."

I stare him down, daring him to tell me I'm wrong.

He doesn't flinch.

Autumn doesn't fight the statement, either.

In fact, she looks... guilty. More guilty than she did when I told her I knew the truth about what she did to Ruby.

"All right," Jax says, calm and steady. "I'll call the Guardians in the city and let them know to expect your arrival soon."

That was easy. *Too* easy.

Which means I'm right.

Jax and Autumn...

I've known it since our engagement party. I've tried not to think about it, but deep down, I knew.

My stomach clenches simply from looking at them.

"I hope you both find what you're looking for," I say, since it's the closest thing to a civil goodbye I can manage.

I let the door close behind me with a soft click, and as I shift into my wolf form to head out, I feel a sense of relief. Because I'm moving forward. From Autumn, from Ruby... from all of it.

At this point, I have nothing left to lose.

And I'm going to pour every piece of my soul into becoming the best Guardian this world has ever seen.

Autumn

The door closes behind Connor with a soft click that sounds through the room, and I stare at it in shock.

For the past month, I thought he might be dead. That I'd never see him again. When he didn't come back, the world went from technicolor to black and white, and I grieved harder than I thought possible. Time barely existed. I simply did everything I needed to survive, and was proud of myself for waking up in the morning and making it through the day without breaking down completely.

But he came back.

And he broke up with me.

He doesn't want to marry me.

I feel like he just took an ax to my heart.

Because he's still alive, but our relationship is dead. He ripped our planned future out from under my feet. He's so blinded by Ruby that he doesn't even *see* me anymore.

Now I feel Jax's gaze on me, watching as my emotions tear through my body.

The electricity from our kiss still fizzes under my skin every time I think about it. But I kept a safe distance between us, the ghost of our betrayal hanging heavily over my head every time I saw or thought about him.

Now we're alone, and the space feels tight. Crowded by our shared memories and guilt.

He starts to speak, but hesitates.

I pick up the engagement ring from where it sits on the table and throw it across the room so hard that it dents the wall.

"The years we were together meant *nothing* to him," I say, releasing the anger. "I knew this was going to happen the moment I found out they were mates. He tried to fight it, but it didn't matter. The mate bond always wins in the end. I know that. It's why I tried…"

I can't bring myself to say it. Jax already knows what I did. And, if he asks more about it, the full truth about my deal with Calliope and the Blood Coven might come out.

If it does, I might not just lose Connor. I'll lose my place in the pack as well.

The ultimate betrayer.

I wish I could go back in time and stop myself from going to Spring Creek. Maybe Connor would have been strong enough to fight the mate bond. It rarely happens, but at least I'd have had a semblance of a chance.

"Autumn…" Jax's voice is soft as he approaches me. But then he hesitates, like he's unsure if he's crossing a line or not.

I should leave. But I'm frozen, staring at the dent in the wall and the ring on the floor.

"What have I done, Jax?" I finally say, meeting his eyes for the first time since Connor left.

"You questioned Ruby's heritage and whether or not she's truly one of us," he says. "You were right to do so. Because she is *not* one of us. But you should have come to me with your suspicions—not gone to Spring Creek."

"You're going to banish me." The hollowness in my chest worsens after I say it out loud.

"Ruby isn't a member of our pack," he says. "You'll be punished for turning her in to Spring Creek, because the knowledge about her magic wasn't yours to share. But you won't be banished. I would never—"

He cuts himself off, as if he can't believe what he was about to say.

"You would never do what?" My breath hitches at the realization that we've been gradually moving closer together, and there's only a few feet of space left between us.

"I would never do that to you."

His admission hangs in the air between us like a lifeline I'm not sure I have the strength to grasp. And the way he's looking at me—like he wants to scoop me into his arms again and do whatever he can to take away my pain—makes it impossible for me to look away.

"Jax…" I start, but my words falter, my voice shaking.

He steps closer and reaches out a hand to tentatively touch my arm.

His fingers brush against my bare skin.

The contact is like a lightning bolt, shocking and sudden. It's like our skin is fusing together, making us one and the same. My breath hitches as something new ignites between us, a powerful and ancient force that curls inside me and seeps into my soul.

Then his eyes start to glow, smokey magic traveling between his eyes and mine, and my world shifts on its axis. Because Jax is no longer just my alpha, and the man who raised Connor.

He's my mate.

Our hearts beat in time together, and he's watching me with the same shock and wonder that I feel.

This can't be happening.

But it is. And so, I just stand there, staring up into his burning eyes, rendered totally and completely speechless.

"You're mine," he growls, and then he pulls me to him, crushing his lips against mine before I can comprehend what's happening.

This is worlds above the first time we kissed.

It's like a forest fire, consuming and untamed. I can't fight it. I don't *want* to fight it.

So, I melt into him and kiss him back, pouring all my anger, sadness, and desire into every movement.

He matches my intensity, his hand releasing mine to move up to my hair, pulling me closer. His other hand wraps around my waist, anchoring me to him. It's wild and raw, and the most alive I've felt since the day Connor left.

He backs me up until I'm pressed against the wall, his body covering mine, with no space left between us. His kiss is hard—almost punishing. And I'm completely at his mercy. Yet, I feel so incredibly safe in his arms, and I never want this moment to end.

When we break apart, his eyes bore into mine, the glow of the mate bond fading as it settles into his soul.

"Jax," I say his name, the sound of it making my heart leap in my chest.

"Autumn," he replies, and he goes to kiss me again, but I cup his face with my hand to stop him.

His breaths slow, and from the way he's looking at me—like he wants to eat me alive—I know this is going to happen. Tonight.

My alpha is my mate, and nothing else in this world has ever felt so incredibly *right*.

"You're not leaving here until I make you fully mine," he says, and it's like a wild beast has taken over his soul, making the fire inside of me burn higher and brighter.

But I gather myself together and lean into him, pressing my forehead against his chest and listening to the erratic beating of his heart.

"How's this possible?" I ask, searching for answers only he can give.

"You're my mate," he says. "You're made for me, and I'm made for you."

"But you already…" I trail off, feeling incredibly awkward about the entire thing, but he simply watches me, waiting for me to finish. "You already have a mate. Well, *had* a mate."

She was killed on the same night as Connor's parents, with Jax as a witness.

He snaps himself out of the lust buzzing between us and moves away slightly, giving both of us a chance to cool off and breathe.

"Margot was never my mate," he says simply.

"I don't understand."

"Margot was a strong, incredible woman, and I loved her deeply. She was a loyal wife, and a devoted mother to our children." His eyes search mine, like he's begging me to understand. "But she and I weren't mates."

"You let everyone think you were."

"No one ever asked," he says. "They assumed, and I let them. I'm their alpha, and I don't have to validate my choices to anyone. At least not until right now, with you."

Because I'm his *mate*.

I can hardly believe it's true.

Especially because the promise I made to the Blood Coven is a million times worse now that I'm mated with Jax.

My stomach sinks at the thought of it. Because no matter what I choose to do from here, he and I are doomed, before we even have a chance to begin.

I can't fulfill my promise to the Blood Coven. I'm going to be forced to join them.

Maybe this is the universe's way of punishing me for what I did to Connor.

It's crueler than any punishment Jax might have given me before the mate bond formed between us—before I belonged to him.

But the mate bond isn't consummated yet. If I leave his house now, it'll be far less painful for him when I leave the pack forever.

"What are you thinking?" he asks with a surprising amount of patience given the fire between us that's a second away from combusting completely.

"I can't stay," I whisper, but as I say the words I know that this man—my mate who's also my alpha—has power over me that I never imagined possible. "After everything that just happened with Connor—"

"Once I'm finished with you tonight, you're going to forget that Connor even exists," he growls, and then his hands are on my face, brushing away the tears I hadn't realized I was shedding.

Without another word, he picks me up and wraps my legs around his waist, pinning me against the wall and kissing me harder, deeper, pushing his hips against mine in a promise of what's to come. Every touch sends a thrill coursing through me, the tension between us building to an almost unbearable level.

Finally, when I think I'm going to explode, he carries me into the living room and throws me down onto the giant couch so hard that it nearly knocks the wind out of me.

I'm at his mercy. And not only does he know it—he revels in it.

Still, he keeps his gaze locked on mine, and I know that he's giving me a choice.

Get up and walk away, or submit to the mate bond buzzing between us.

Desire for him burns through me like a fire I can't control. It's not one I *want* to control. It's one that I need satiated, right here, right now.

So I give him a single nod of consent, and then his lips crash against mine with even more passion than before, until I'm giving into the most primal instinct of all—the one to be claimed by my mate.

Ruby

A FEW HOURS after returning to Spring Creek, I'm back in the attic suite that the sisters declared as mine, finishing up getting ready for bed.

Memories of Connor refuse to leave my mind.

Mainly, the memories of when I kissed him. The fire that burned between us was like nothing I've ever felt in my life, and the way he looked at me before bolting into the woods makes me ache for a future together that might not ever exist.

Eventually, I make my way back into the bedroom, where Tristan is reading in bed where I left him, as if nothing in the fae realm ever happened. As if everything between us didn't change the moment Nereida revealed the truth about how he used the necklace to seduce me—to get me to trust him.

Now that he doesn't have the necklace and the blood bond is basically gone, the sight of him makes me feel like there are bugs crawling up and down my arms. After everything he did, I can't even trust my own feelings around him.

I hate it, and I want him to leave.

But I need him to believe the lie that I've chosen him over Connor. Telling him to leave will hardly help my cause. Especially because we didn't spend much time together yesterday due to Gwen and Benjamin's return, and last night, I avoided conversation with him by telling him that I was exhausted.

Now, as I situate myself in bed next to him, his gaze is intense and expectant.

He closes the book and places it down on the nightstand, and I know instinctively that he wants something from me.

"Are you okay?" I ask him, although I keep distance between us, not wanting to scoot closer and encourage anything I'd rather avoid.

He nods, his eyes never leaving mine. "I'm fine," he says. "I'm more interested in how *you're* holding up through all of this."

In that moment, I see a flash of the man I was falling in love with.

No—the man I *thought* I was falling in love with. It was all a lie. I won't let myself be tricked again.

My feelings aren't facts.

He made sure of that when he manipulated them to his will.

"I'm fine, too," I say, my voice tight. "Just tired."

He reaches out to touch my arm, but I pull away before he can. A mistake. Because his golden eyes flash with pain, and he sits completely up in bed, twisting his body so he's facing me straight on.

"Ruby," he pleads. "You can talk to me. I know we've had our… differences. But I want to make things right between us."

Differences?

That's quite the unique way to put it.

"I'm truly okay." I give him a smile that I hope is convincing. "We got the Key of Hades. We're alive and safe. It's a relief to be back here, at home, with you."

It takes every ounce of self-control to not cringe when I call this place my *home*.

"You know that I'm here for you, right?" he says, his voice barely above a whisper. "Anything you want. I love you, and I'm here. Always."

Before I can reply, he leans forward and kisses me. It's gentle and sweet, the exact opposite of the explosive passion of my kiss with Connor… and I feel absolutely nothing as I force myself to kiss him back.

I pull away after a few moments, and his eyes search mine, trying to figure me out.

"It's been a long day, Tristan," I tell him, wanting to say something before he has a chance to call me out on that soulless kiss. "Let's get some rest."

"Okay." His expression falters, but he quickly recovers. "I just can't help but wonder…"

"Wonder what?" I ask, instantly on guard.

"You've been thinking about Connor."

It's a statement—not a question.

"Tristan," I say gently, needing him to believe everything that's coming next. "Connor rejected me from the day he met me. He handed me off to the witches and didn't want me to ever return to pack territory. He tried to *get rid of me*. The only reason he came after me was because he broke up with Autumn. If she hadn't turned me in, he'd still be engaged to her. But you chose me. You love me, and you're here for me. I want to be here, with you. Always."

He searches my face for any trace of deceit.

I meet his gaze head on. Because for now, for the sake of everyone I love, I need to keep this act up. And it *is* an act. I thoroughly intend on turning against the Blood Coven… *after* Hazel reverses the erasure spell.

But am I wrong to do it? Now that the key is here, and the Blood Coven can use it on the next full moon, it feels so much more real than it did when it was simply a mythological artifact we needed to find and retrieve.

Everything's happening so fast. I've been on such an emotional roller coaster that I've remained focused on the one thing that's been keeping me grounded—doing whatever's necessary to make sure my parents remember me. I've taken no time to look beyond myself and my own desires.

I still don't know what the Blood Coven truly wants.

What if, in delivering the key, I'm bringing more harm to the world than I ever imagined possible?

Finally, your thoughts are making sense, my wolf thinks.

I hate that she might be right.

A side effect of the necklace and blood bond wearing off? I'm horrified at the thought, but also can't deny that it might be true.

It's possible, she thinks, and then I do something new.

I acknowledge her, while also keeping her at bay.

She's part of my soul, but my mind and body are *mine.*

"There's something else on your mind, isn't there?" Tristan's voice snaps me out of my darkening thoughts, and he reaches for my hand. "I see it in your eyes."

I force myself to not pull away. Because I need to end this conversation, and there's one main way I can think to do that.

"You're right." I hold his gaze and brace myself for the lie that already feels sour on my tongue. "I love you, Tristan. But I want to take this slow. I want us to build this relationship up again without the influence of the necklace or the blood bond. And I need you to be patient with me while we do."

Lies.

So many lies.

It's amazing that I can keep them straight anymore.

"I understand," he says, his voice quiet. "I'll be patient. And I'll prove to you that my love for you is real."

I sit there, stunned, waiting for him to add something else. Some sort of caveat, or another doubt about the strength of my mate bond with Connor, or another attempt to get physical.

He doesn't.

"I know that your love for me is real," I lie again. "I just… need some time."

"I'm an immortal vampire. I have nothing *but* time," he says, flashing me the familiar smile that I know and *thought* I loved.

"Thank you, Tristan," I say, feeling like I can breathe for the first time today. "Goodnight."

"Sleep well." He turns off the lamp, but I can tell he's still upset as he lays back down and faces away from me.

However, there's not much more I can do for him right now. So I close my eyes, trying to will myself to sleep, but my mind keeps racing with thoughts of the Blood Coven and the Key of Hades.

Bringing the key here was a mistake.

I feel it deep in my bones, and I have no idea how to fix it. Tristan won't help me. Connor most certainly won't. My parents don't remember my existence. I'm completely and utterly alone, and the emptiness in my soul is so suffocating that I'm drowning in it.

I'm finally drifting off when I hear my name whispered through the window, so soft that it could be mistaken as a breeze pushing its way through a crack in the glass.

"Ruby…"

It's barely there.

But I know that voice.

My wolf stirs, I sit up, and I glance at Tristan to see if he hears it. But he's still lying there, his back toward me, sound asleep.

I don't want to wake him. But I have to know who's there. I have to know if my suspicion is correct.

Quietly, I slip out of bed and pad barefoot over to the window, pulling the heavy velvet curtain aside to look out into the night.

The garden below is bathed in silver moonlight.
And there, standing in the middle of it, is Luna.

Ruby

My best friend is ethereal, her pale skin glowing under the moonlight, a cascade of silver hair falling down her back. She must have dyed it since the last time we saw each other. Her eyes, the color of the moon at its brightest, meet mine and she smiles, beckoning me to join her.

Is this a dream? Or a trick? It has to be. It's impossible for Luna to be here. Firstly, she has no idea that I exist, thanks to the erasure spell. Secondly, how would she know to find me here? How would she get here? How could I hear her whispering from the garden to the attic?

It has to be a dream.

But I don't remember falling asleep.

Then again, who actually remembers falling asleep?

It doesn't matter. Because if this isn't a dream, and Luna's really here, then she's in danger. I have to go to her.

But how? Even though this house is huge, there are seven people staying here—not counting me, Tristan, Lindsay, and Jason. If I go downstairs, one of them will hear me. And we're three floors up. I can't leave through the window.

Or can I?

My gaze drifts back to Luna, who's still waiting patiently, her soft smile unwavering.

I lean forward to find a way to climb down, but there's nothing. Besides, opening the window and leaving through it will definitely wake Tristan.

What if…

Taking a deep breath, I tiptoe to the bathroom, open the door, and go inside. Tristan shifts in his sleep, but he doesn't wake up. Holding my breath, I click the door shut as quietly as possible, waiting a few seconds to see if Tristan says something.

He doesn't.

Now that I'm safely out of the bedroom, I look over to why I came in here.

The window.

It's an old house, and we're high up enough that when they built the bathroom, modesty wasn't taken into consideration.

Much to my relief, Luna's still out there. She gives me a mischievous smile—reminding me of the times she was about to do something that would get her in trouble in college—and I know she's waiting for me to figure out how to get down.

Opening the window seems like a good start. It releases a low moan as I do, and after making sure Tristan doesn't call out to ask what I'm doing, I peer out at the sheer drop below.

My breath catches in my throat. There's no way.

We can jump, my wolf says.

I gape at her in our mind.

Are you crazy? I think back to her. *We're three stories up.*

We have earth magic at our disposal, she retorts. *The ground is not our enemy.*

All right. Fair point.

Kind of.

Because I've never been a fan of heights, and the thought of falling makes my stomach twist with nausea.

But I swallow it down. Luna's waiting. The longer she's out there, the more likely it is that one of the others will see her. I have to protect her from them. I have to tell her to leave Spring Creek and go back home.

I glance back at my reflection in the mirror, taking in my wild, anxious eyes. As I do, the image of a sleek, powerful white wolf—*my* wolf—springs into my mind.

She's communicating with me. Attempting to show me how we can pull this off.

Her idea is nuts.

I know, she replies. *Isn't it exciting?*

Despite myself, I smile. Now that she's stopped fighting the choices I make, and now that I'm getting better at stopping her from taking control over my body, I'm finding that I actually sort of like her.

And so, with a final deep breath, I hoist myself onto the window ledge.

Luna nods in encouragement.

It's now or never.

Trying to give myself the most momentum possible, I launch myself into the night.

Panic surges through me, and I let my wolf take over, shifting mid-air. For a moment, we hang suspended. Then gravity takes hold, my stomach rises into my throat, and we plunge down to the garden.

Our magic, my wolf thinks to me, panicked. *Use our magic.*

I dig inside myself for my magic, focusing on the earth below. It blossoms inside me, bending to my will, surrounding and cradling me in tendrils of warm energy.

When we use elemental magic, we release it through our hands. So, in this case, I let it flow through my paws.

Just before crashing to the ground, I soften the dirt, letting my momentum bury me slightly into it. It's like being caught by a trampoline.

But it's not perfect.

Pain explodes up my paw, forcing a whimper from my throat. It's sharp and hot, and when I look at it, I see bone jutting from my fur.

It takes all my effort to not get sick at the sight of it.

It'll heal, my wolf thinks, although from the way her voice is strained, she's in just as much pain as I am. *Shift back.*

Following her command, I grit my teeth as the bone shifts back into place, the skin stitching itself back together. The pain ebbs, leaving a dull throbbing in its wake.

I hold my wrist out to inspect it. Blood's smeared across my skin, but there's no more bone sticking out of it.

I rise to my feet, wincing slightly. But I'm whole. I'm okay.

I survived the jump.

And, most importantly, Luna's waiting for me.

However, now that the rush of adrenaline is waning, doubt creeps through me.

Is this person in the garden actually Luna? Or is this a trick? The Blood Coven testing my loyalty? The fae somehow breaking through into our realm to take back the Key of Hades? Not like they'll have much luck, since I stupidly left the key in the nightstand, and I can't think of a good way to go back up there and get it without getting caught.

But standing here wondering all of this isn't accomplishing anything.

So, pulling myself together, I walk the final steps to where Luna's waiting in the center of the garden.

For a moment, we simply stand there, staring at each other. There's something sharper about her—stronger. She's practically glowing in the moonlight, and now that I'm closer to her, another memory crashes through my mind.

The last face I saw before passing out in the woods after my first shift. The face of the goddess who star touched me. I was so out of sorts that I couldn't take in the details of her features when it happened, but now that I'm seeing her again, I can't believe I didn't put it together sooner.

"Luna?" I say softly, my voice barely a whisper in the cold night.

Because she isn't really Luna. Yet, at the same time, she is.

Her lips part, as though she's about to say something, but then they close again. Instead, she shushes me and waves her fingers at the empty space next to us.

I watch in awe as a chariot fit for Cinderella on her way to the ball materializes out of thin air, pulled by a pair of horses that look like they've been plucked from a fairytale. Crafted of a material that seems to both absorb and reflect the moonlight, it casts a gentle glow over everything within its reach. It's beautiful. Like a piece of the night sky has descended from the heavens and taken a physical form.

Luna opens the door and motions for me to get in.

I glance back at the mansion, relieved that all the windows remain dark. Somehow, throughout all of this, no one woke up.

I return my focus to the ethereal woman in front of me.

"Are you really Luna?" I whisper, not wanting to get inside her magical chariot without making sure.

"In a manner of speaking, yes," she says, quiet but confident.

"Prove it."

She rolls her eyes, like the Luna I remember. "You press the snooze alarm exactly three times to get out of bed for morning classes. You organize your closet by color. You lost your favorite purple pen in the beginning of the semester and didn't find it until we packed up for winter break. You eat Bagel Bites and Easy Mac when you're studying for a test. And you think it's a sin against the universe when I microwave my Bagel Bites instead of using the toaster oven."

I study her in shock.

Only my college roommate, my best friend, could know those things.

"Luna," I breathe out in disbelief, looking from her, to the carriage, and back again. "How...?"

"I'll tell you everything on our way there." She reaches for my hand and pulls me closer, her touch sending a wave of calm through my body. "But we have to leave. Now."

"Where are we going?" I ask, letting her guide me into the chariot.

"Do you trust me?" she asks with that familiar twinkle in her eyes.

"Who do you think you are? Aladdin?" I ask in response.

"No. But I know that's your favorite Disney movie. You tear up during the whole magic carpet ride bit. Now, are you coming, or not?"

If I walk away from her now, will I ever stop wondering what would have happened if I didn't?

"I guess I trust you," I mumble, and then I situate myself in the carriage, she takes the reins, and the glimmering horses fly us smoothly up toward the moonlight.

Ruby

THE RIDE IS SMOOTH, but my heart hammers in my chest as I clutch the edge of my seat, holding on for dear life.

Don't look down, I remind myself, and as I turn to Luna, my heart thuds even wilder as what's happening truly sets in.

She isn't just my best friend.

She's a goddess. The one who star touched me.

At least, I'm close to positive that's what's going on here.

"Luna," I begin, figuring it's best to just be out with it. "You're a goddess."

It's no crazier than everything else that's happened to me these past few weeks. But, at the same time, it's the most insane thing I've learned yet.

She simply nods, not taking her eyes off the path we're soaring through. "Yes. Specifically, a moon goddess."

"Okay. A moon goddess," I repeat, as if saying it again will make it less surreal.

It doesn't.

She turns to face me, her moonlit eyes soft and welcoming. They're different from the eyes of the Luna I knew, but still somehow the same. "Yes, Ruby. But I'm also your friend. That hasn't changed."

As I watch her, waiting for her to elaborate, anger replaces some of my shock. "Why didn't you tell me?" I ask.

Luna sighs, her gaze returning to the open skies. "What would you have preferred I do? Introduced myself as a goddess when we first met? When you were still living in ignorance of the supernatural world, and of your place in it?"

It's a fair point.

"Maybe not when we *first* met," I say. "But you could have eventually. If you showed me your magic, I'd have no choice but to believe you."

"You always have a choice. Besides, you weren't ready then," she says simply. "Now, you are."

"Where are we even going?" I accidentally glance down at the world below, blinking away the vertigo as I force myself to look away.

"We're going to get you the Lunar Crescent."

She says it as if I should know what she's talking about.

"What's the Lunar Crescent?" I ask, humoring her.

"A weapon," she says, and after my brief experience with Hazel's old dagger, excitement buzzes through me at the thought of getting my own weapon. "I forged it myself over a thousand years ago, for the one I'd eventually choose to bless with my magic."

"Your magic," I repeat. "You have illusion magic."

"I do." She raises her hand, and a flicker of silver light sparks to life above it, expanding into a miniature moon that orbits around her fingers. Before I can say a word, her fingers weave through the air, and the tiny moon dissipates, replaced by a white wolf.

My wolf.

The wolf takes a step forward, pauses in front of me, and vanishes.

"You gave me your magic," I realize.

"More like a *taste* of my magic." She laughs, light and musical. "Your magic is just a fraction of what I can do. But back to the Lunar Crescent—it's a bow and arrows. Magical ones. You'll learn more as you gather its pieces during your trials."

Trials.

Of course there are trials.

Nothing in the supernatural world ever seems to come easy.

"Where are the trials?" I ask.

"We're heading to the starting point right now. You'll find out soon enough."

I frown and lean back in my seat, having enough sense to stop myself from looking out the window again.

A hint of a smile plays on Luna's lips. "Sometimes the journey is just as important as the destination," she continues. "You'll have to face whatever comes your way with bravery and wisdom. No hints, no cheats. Just you, your magic, and your wits."

"You're not coming with me?"

"I'll be there every step of the way," she promises.

"Metaphorically, or physically?" It doesn't hurt to ask, given that she's a goddess and all.

"Physically. But as a guide—not as a partner. I can explain your goal for each trial, but not what you have to do to complete it. Otherwise, it would defeat the purpose of you proving you're strong enough to handle the Lunar Crescent."

"Okay," I say, even though I'm far from okay.

I'm about to face mysterious trials, gather pieces of a magical weapon, and do it all under the guidance of my best friend, who I just discovered is a powerful goddess.

Luna. A goddess.

It's going to take a while to get used to that.

How much power does she have…?

"Can you reverse the erasure spell?" I ask, sitting straighter as I wait for her answer.

"That's not in the realm of my abilities," she says sadly. "The spell didn't affect me—obviously—since a goddess's memories can't be erased by a witch. As for the rest of the human world…"

"They won't remember me until Hazel reverses the spell."

"Correct."

"And where are we going after I finish the trials?"

I have so many questions that I feel like I might explode from them.

"Back to Spring Creek," she says, like it should be obvious. "You have unfinished business there."

"But my reasons for going back there after getting the Key of Hades were selfish," I tell her. "I helped the Blood Coven because I wanted my parents to remember me more than I wanted anything else in the world. But I'm not on their side. I never *will* be on their side. I don't know what they're going to do with the Key of Hades, but I should be trying to stop them—not to help them. Even if that means…"

The rest of the sentence gets stuck in my throat.

Even if that means that my parents—and everyone else in the human world—never remembers me.

"Sometimes, the best way to stop something from happening is to do it from the inside," she says. "By becoming a part of the entity you wish to alter, you understand it better. You discover its weaknesses, its strengths, and its core. Once you've done that, you have the power to shift the tide of fate to the side of righteousness. You're currently in an excellent position to make that happen. You've worked too hard to back out now."

"Understood." I risk a glance behind us, where the Blood Coven's mansion has long disappeared into the darkness, and realization crashes over me like a wave.

"Tristan," I say. "What do I tell him when he realizes I'm gone?"

"I have it handled," she says.

"What do you mean?"

"One of my sisters is taking your place for tonight," she says. "I used my magic to make her look like you. You'll return before sunrise, and Tristan will be none the wiser."

"You never told me you have sisters," I say.

"Your best friend Luna from college doesn't have sisters. The moon goddess Luna, however, does. Many of them."

"Forty-nine of them," I recall from the book I read in Jax's library. "Fifty of you total."

"Yes. Although, only three have magic as strong as mine. And, like I said—my magic is far stronger than yours. I can create permanent illusions."

"My eyes…" I realize.

"The turquoise suits you better," she says with a smile. "But they'd make you stand out too much. You didn't tell anyone—right?"

"No one."

"Good."

The horses slow as we begin our descent, gliding from the open sky to the earth below. The mountains here are far larger than the ones in the Adirondacks—it's like their peaks are touching the stars.

And, most amazingly, there isn't just one moon brightening the sky.

There are three.

"Welcome to the Valley of Moons," Luna says, guiding the horses to land in a sprawling valley bathed in the purest moonlight I've ever seen. Flowers bloom in abundance, and silvery streams wind through the landscape, their water reflecting the countless stars above. "This is where your trials begin."

There's also a pile of clothes and boots waiting for me, and I'm relieved I won't have to do whatever's coming next in my pajamas.

I gaze around the valley and pray the trials aren't as hard as the ones in the Blockhouse. Especially the Chamber of Rains. That was a complete nightmare, and I doubt I could have gotten through it without help from the others.

"What sort of trials should I expect?" I ask, since it's always best to be prepared. Or, to try to be.

"I don't want to tell you too much. But I will say that they're going to test your mastery in all areas of your magic."

"Mastery." I scoff. "I've only had my magic for a few weeks."

"And you've gotten better at using it in those few weeks than most do in an entire lifetime," she says. "You're a natural. I wouldn't have chosen you if you weren't. Now, how about we hop out of this carriage and get started on our hike?"

Autumn

After our time on the couch, Jax and I enjoy ourselves in many other places around his house. Eventually, we reach his bedroom, where we spend the remainder of the day and night.

The mate bond is complete.

It's like nothing I ever imagined. It's like my entire being has expanded, my soul now large enough to hold not just one person, but two. My wolf is more content than she's ever been. It's like we never knew true happiness before today, and now, with Jax, we've found it.

He turns to me, his eyes sparkling with an intensity that leaves me breathless. "You always knew you were destined to mate with an alpha." He uses his thumb to trace tiny patterns on my cheeks that leave electricity buzzing in its wake, and I know in that moment that I'll do anything he ever asks of me. "It's because you've always been destined to be *mine*."

I can't believe that my soul is tied to this beautiful, amazing, confident, strong man. It's like a bridge has been constructed between us, and I want to fully let him in so we can explore this invisible thread that binds us together every day for the rest of our lives.

I don't want secrets between us.

Which means I have to tell him what I know—what I learned that night in Calliope's house. Along with the deal I made with her.

If he hates me afterward, then at least he'll have heard it directly from me. But, if he's willing to help me, we might figure out a way through this awful mistake I made.

He's my mate, and I trust him with my life.

So, I take a deep breath and say, "There's something important you need to know. Something I learned the night I went to Spring Creek and turned in Ruby."

The mood shifts to one far more serious, and he sits up in bed, watching me and waiting.

"What did you learn?" he asks.

I sit up as well, brushing through the tangles in my hair as if doing so will calm my nerves.

"I learned the truth about Ruby," I tell him. "Well, not specifically about her. I learned the truth about her parents."

"Her parents live in Florida." He watches me carefully, on edge, like he's preparing himself for anything. "They're human. Powerless."

"They're not human," I say.

"They are," he insists. "Rafe and Lowell tracked them down with our witches. They're two of the most loyal men in this pack. They wouldn't lie to me. And, even if they tried, I'd smell it."

"They didn't lie," I say, and he relaxes slightly. "Ruby's parents are currently human. But they weren't born that way. They used to be shifters. Then, almost twenty years ago, they chose to have their magic stripped. They presumably moved to Florida because there aren't any packs that far south, and where they are in Naples is far enough from Miami that they wouldn't run into any trouble with the Guardians there."

His eyes harden.

He doesn't believe me.

"Who told you all this?" he finally asks.

"Calliope."

"Interesting." He stares out the window for a few seconds, then returns his attention to me. "However, I sent photos of Ruby's parents to the alphas of every pack in the country to see if anyone recognized them. No one did. Ruby's parents were never shifters. Calliope is giving you false information. You cannot trust her."

Too late for that, my wolf interrupts my thoughts. *But you're right to trust our mate. We can always trust our mate.*

"Those photos aren't what Ruby's parents truly look like," I say, eager to get out with it.

His brow furrows more, like he isn't sure what to make of my statement. "I can assure you that they are. My men took the photos themselves."

"The photos are what Ruby's parents look like after having their magic stripped," I continue, despite how crazy it sounds. "Calliope stripped their magic, and that night, they prayed to the moon goddess for help. She granted their wish by using her illusion magic to create permanent disguises for them."

"Illusion magic. *Ruby's* magic," he says slowly, working through it in his mind.

"Yes. Ruby's mom was pregnant with her when this all happened. Even though her mom was stripped of her magic, Calliope suspects that Ruby was able to hold onto some of hers, although it didn't awaken until the night of the blood moon."

"It's unprecedented," Jax says, visibly uncomfortable by the thought of something that goes against every law our kind has ever learned.

"It explains why the moon goddess might have chosen Ruby to star touch," I point out. "She's had her eye on her since before she was born."

I can barely breathe as I wait for his reaction, dreading everything I have to tell him next.

"It's a fascinating story," he finally says. "But why were her parents running from the supernatural world in the first place? It's highly frowned upon to choose to have your magic stripped, but it's not a punishable offense. No longer having magic and no longer being part of the pack is punishment enough."

"This is the part that shocked me the most." I take a deep breath and brace myself, knowing that Jax is going to be a hundred times more surprised than I was when Calliope dropped this bomb on me. "Ruby's parents are Xavier and Abigail Hightower."

I don't need to spell out the next part. Jax can easily put it together, and I see the horror on his face when he does.

Because Xavier and Abigail killed Jax's wife, son, and daughter-in-law.

And were presumably taken care of immediately afterward by Jax's own hand.

Autumn

Jax's expression morphs from confusion, to pain, and finally, to a fury I've never seen on him before.

"Xavier and Abigail Hightower," he says, each syllable sharp enough to cut glass.

"Yes."

"They killed my family." His voice is barely a whisper, the words heavy with grief and bitterness. "With the help of Xavier's traitor sister Jessica."

Jessica, who chose to turn into a vampire instead of accepting her shifter mate, so she could live forever as an immortal with her vampire lover. It was a stupid plan, since it's a criminal offense by both the vampire and the supernatural who agrees to be turned. I've heard the story many times, and I've never understood why she did it.

Jax stares straight ahead, shellshocked, as if he's experiencing his grief all over again.

I reach for his hand and hold it. It's the little comfort I have right now to offer him, and I'm relieved when he doesn't push me away.

There is, however, one huge thing about the story that doesn't add up.

"Jax," I say cautiously, watching as he comes back to me. "What really happened that night in the caves?"

"I didn't kill Xavier and Abigail, like everyone thinks I did," he admits. "They wanted to kill me, but it's against a wolf's nature to kill their alpha. So, they ran. I was too stricken with grief, surrounded by the bloodied bodies of my family, to run after them and give them what they deserved."

The heartbreak, the pain, the unfathomable loss... I can't imagine what that was like for him. I've seen Connor's grief for the grandmother and parents he never got to know. But to have actually *been* there, to have seen them killed and been unable to stop it...

"I wish I'd run after them," he continues, his eyes dark and haunted. "Not a day goes by that I don't regret letting them live."

Then, the darkness in his expression twists into something else.

The thirst for revenge.

"You're going to go after them, aren't you?" I ask.

"I am."

"Then I'm going with you."

"No," he all but growls. "You're absolutely not."

There's so much alpha willpower in his tone that it rumbles through me. It can't control me, since I'm his mate, but I can still sense it. Which means I can feel how adamant he is about this decision, and how it's something he needs to do alone.

"I understand," I say, since I really, truly do.

"Thank you." He pulls me close, his heart thundering against his chest, matching the rhythm of my own. "They took everything from me. *Everything.* And now, they're finally going to pay for it."

I don't answer right away. I don't know what to say. I can't promise that everything will be okay, because I don't know if it will be. But I can give him something else.

More of the truth.

Before he can hear it from someone else.

"Jax, there's one more thing I need to tell you," I say slowly, knowing this will change everything.

He pulls back, his eyes searching mine. "What is it?"

I swallow hard.

He's our mate, my wolf reminds me. *He'll understand. He'll help us. He'll figure out how to make this right. But, for him to do that, we have to trust him.*

She's right.

Still, that doesn't make this any easier.

"When I went to Calliope about Ruby, it was because I wanted the Spring Creek coven to break her mate bond with Connor," I say, even though this was heavily implied when Connor marched in here to break our engagement.

"It sounds like she was open to the idea," Jax says steadily.

"She was," I start, feeling sick about what's coming next. "But it was for a price. She wanted to make a deal."

"What kind of deal?" He stiffens, on edge again, preparing himself for anything.

But there's no way he can possibly prepare for *this*.

"Calliope's not just the leader of the Spring Creek coven," I say. "There are others there now, living in that house with her. They call themselves the Blood Coven. And they're not just witches. They're vampires and shifters, too."

Quickly, I fill him in on everything I know about the Blood Coven, which admittedly isn't much.

"What did you do?" he asks when I finish.

"She asked for you." My eyes wander to look down at my hands, but I force them back up, so I'm looking at Jax face-on when I come clean. "She asked me to deliver you. To them."

His eyes harden. "And what did you say?"

"I agreed to the deal."

Shock flashes across his face, then hurt, then a deep, simmering anger as he pulls his hand out of mine.

"I'm not going to do it," I add, even though I know it won't fix what I did.

"You were going to betray me."

"I wouldn't have been able to go through with it." I hear how desperate I sound, but I don't care. "And, when I made the oath to them, it was before we were mates."

"I was still your alpha," he seethes. "I *am* your alpha."

There's a rumbling below us, and the paintings on the wall start to rattle and shake. So does the wolf figurine on his nightstand, and the TV mounted on the wall across from us.

His earth magic.

"Jax..." I clutch the sheets as the tremors under us intensify.

He barely seems to hear me.

The room shakes even more violently. The force of his magic is too powerful, too wild to contain.

Alphas aren't supposed to lose control like this.

If I don't get him to focus—to control his magic—then it's going to spread through pack territory. Others will know something's wrong.

I need to do something—fast. So, I take a deep breath, gather my magic, and ground myself in the Earth's energy. It heeds my call in less than a second, a buzzing warmth that fills my body, ready for me to command it to do anything I please.

But there's something different this time. Because I can feel him.

Jax.

Acting on instinct, I merge my magic with his, clashing and fighting against the energy he's unleashed. I've never gone against such a strong magic user, and my body feels heavy and drained. But I keep pushing, keep pulling, until the last of the tremors subside and the room falls back into silence.

He watches me with a mix of awe, caution, and anger.

"I would never give you up, Jax," I say, praying to get through to him. "I'd rather join them than betray you like that. I swear it."

"You already betrayed me," he says with a calmness that makes every nerve in my body go on edge.

"I know."

For a moment, he's silent.

"I'm going to take a shower." His voice is so flat that it sends a shiver down my spine. "Stay here."

As he walks across the room, he passes a stone sculpture on his dresser—a wolf carved intricately in granite. It wobbles, then crashes onto the floor, shattering into a thousand pieces.

He doesn't glance behind at the mess. He simply disappears into the bathroom and turns on the shower.

Needing something to focus on, I reach for the shattered pieces of the sculpture with my magic. One by one, the fragments rise from the floor, and I guide each shard back to its rightful place.

Finally, the smallest piece—a tiny sliver that forms the tip of the wolf's ear—completes the sculpture. It's whole again, but it's not the same. The cracks, though invisible, are still there. They'll always be there.

"I'm sorry, Jax," I whisper to the room, and the relief that came from fixing the sculpture fades, replaced with fear and guilt.

He's going to reject me.

He's going to banish me from the pack.

My heart hollows at the thought.

Although, I suppose being banished won't matter, since I have to leave Pine Valley anyway to join the Blood Coven.

Finally, the shower turns off and he comes out to join me. He's in only a towel, and the drops of water trickling down his chest and abs light me up inside with a need that can only be satisfied by my mate.

My wolf purrs inside of me, but I push her down. This is hardly the time for that sort of distraction.

Jax meets my gaze, and a muscle ticks in his jaw. But then his expression softens slightly. It's a subtle shift, but right now, I'm clinging to any sign that he won't cast me away.

"I won't let them take you," he finally says. "I won't lose you. We can figure this out. Together."

I blink, stunned by his words. "What?"

"You heard me. We'll deal with this. There's a way out of every situation. We'll figure out what that way is, and we'll make it happen. Because you're mine, and I'm yours. Nothing changes that. Not even a blood oath with the most powerful witches in the world."

I sit there speechless, shocked and relieved at his words.

"Even after what I did?" I ask.

His gaze softens as he walks over to the bed and sits down beside me. "Even after that," he says, taking my hand. "I've already lost one woman I love. I'm not losing my mate, too."

My heart melts.

Because he loves me.

He pulls me close, his warm scent grounding me and giving me strength.

Being with Jax feels like coming home.

"I trust you," I whisper into his chest. "Whatever's coming next, we'll face it together."

"We will," he promises. "But first, I'm taking care of Xavier and Abigail. I'm leaving in the morning. It'll only be two days. Three, at the most."

I nod, still processing everything that just happened.

"Anyway, it's been a long day," he says, tracing tiny patterns along my arm that leave electricity buzzing in their wakes. "And I think you can be of great assistance with tiring me out so I can get some sleep."

"I can be *amazing* assistance," I say, and then I look back up into my mate's eyes, melt into his kiss, and let him take my troubles away—at least, for tonight.

Ruby

LUNA and I don't have much time to walk together in the Valley of Moons—maybe ten minutes, at the most—before turning around a hill and into a lush meadow.

It sprawls out in front of us, an expanse of green framed by towering mountains. And, gathered in groups in the meadow, are clumps and clumps of sheep.

Their wool glitters like diamonds under the moonlight, their horns sharp and glistening.

"These aren't regular sheep, are they?" I murmur to Luna, not wanting to bring attention to us.

"They're all male sheep," she explains. "Rams."

"Named because they like to ram into people with their horns?" I chuckle at the attempted joke, although I can't shake the feeling that it might be true.

"Yes," Luna says, and I step back, instantly on guard.

I don't want those horns anywhere near me.

Unfortunately, it seems obvious by now that these rams are going to be part of my first trial.

"And why are we here, exactly?" I ask, trying to untie the growing knot in my stomach.

She glances at me, a sharp, calculating look, then gestures toward the center of the meadow. "See that stone? The one shimmering under the moonlight?"

I squint, following the line of her finger.

Nestled deep within the meadow is a large stone, radiant under the night sky.

"I see it."

"The silver essence—the heart of the Lunar Crescent—is tied to the stone," she explains. "When you infuse the essence into the weapon's bow, you'll link its magic to yours. Only then will you be able to unlock its unique power."

"And what type of power is that?"

"Be patient." She gives me a knowing smile, with a sort of quiet wisdom she never showed me when she was pretending to be a regular college student. "You'll learn it all in time. First, you need to complete this trial."

"All right," I say. "I suppose I can make myself invisible and dart around the rams. If they give me any trouble, I can use my earth magic to hold them down, or to trip them up."

"Look up," she says, and I do as asked.

A blanket of stars stretches across the sky. It's beautiful and magical, especially under the light of the half moon.

But one constellation in particular catches my eye.

A wolf standing on a cliff, its head raised to the moon in a permanent howl.

"That's Canis. The constellation of the wolf," Luna explains, following my gaze. "It's always there, watching over the Fleece Rams. They respect the spirit of the Canis immensely."

"The wolf," I murmur, tracing the stars with my eyes.

It feels strangely fitting.

Of course it's fitting, my wolf thinks. *In case you forgot, you can use more than your illusion magic and earth magic in these trials. I'm here for you, too. Would you have been able to get out of that house without my help?*

I know. Guilt fills me at how I'd valued the help of my magic over the help of my wolf. *I'm still adjusting to all of this. I'm sorry.*

Apology accepted, she replies.

"Do you know how sheep are herded?" Luna asks, bringing me out of my inner conversation with my wolf.

Before I can answer, one of the rams bleats, low and threatening.

The nearest group of them are advancing. Their diamond-hard wool gleams in the moonlight, their eyes burning with hostility.

They're like demons.

Demon-rams.

I curse internally and take another step back, even though it's too late.

They've seen me.

Then, all at once, they charge.

"Luna!" I call out, my stomach dropping when I see she's moved away from me, leaving me to handle this without her. "What do I do?"

"Remember the wolf! The Canis!" she shouts back.

If she says anything more, I can't hear it. The rams trampling the earth drowns out not just her words, but my thoughts as well.

I stand there, shellshocked.

I will not be trampled by demon sheep, I think, and then I reach for my earth magic and blast it outward, spraying dirt into their faces.

They stop so abruptly that the ones behind them crash into them.

And then, they roar.

It's a loud, powerful roar that hits me with a wave of terror and shakes me to my bones. I can't move. I can't think.

My chest tightens so much that I can't even breathe.

We're not prey, Ruby. Especially not for sheep, my wolf's voice breaks through. *We're a predator. Get yourself together and act like it.*

I glance at the Canis constellation again, and it hits me.

Dogs herd sheep. Specifically, *sheepdogs.*

But these aren't your average sheep. They need something more powerful than a dog to herd them.

Yes, my wolf thinks, excited now. *Let's herd them.*

Reaching out to the moon and stars overhead and the ground below, I embrace the wolf inside me and *release* her like I did when we jumped out that window.

She explodes out of me, and I let out a howl, a call that ripples through the meadow.

The rams falter. Their charge slows, and their eyes dim, apparently confused by my transformation.

But it only lasts for a second.

The first ram breaks away from the herd, his eyes glowing with defiance as he charges towards me.

I crouch low to the ground, preparing to strike, and growl.

The ram doesn't stop. Instead, he opens his mouth so wide that I can see his sharp teeth, and he lets out another roar.

It crashes into me like an actual sound wave. A physical, painful thing that knocks me to the ground.

I whimper, use my illusion magic to make myself invisible, and jump out of the ram's path.

He crashes to the ground with an echoing *thunk.*

But he quickly recovers, growling at the place where I just stood, his sharp teeth shining in the moonlight.

I don't know much about sheep, but I'm close to positive they're not supposed to have teeth like that.

I look around the meadow, searching for a way through the rams. But they're prowling in a circle around me, like predators about to pounce.

It doesn't matter that they can't see me.

Somehow, they can sense me.

No more invisibility or earth magic, my wolf reminds me about what Luna told me earlier. *We have to herd them. Guide them. We can't do that if they can't see us, or if we're attacking them.*

Kind of hard not to attack them while they're attacking us, I think back.

We're outnumbered, but we're not their enemy, she replies. *Stop thinking like a human, and start acting like a wolf.*

She's right.

I need to shake myself out of it. I can't scare them away, deflect their attacks, or pin them down.

I have to become their leader.

Okay, I say to my wolf, steadying my nerves. *Let's do this.*

Dropping the illusion, I reveal myself and scan my eyes around the group of them circling me, daring them to defy me.

I am a wolf.

They are sheep. Scary-looking sheep that look like they belong in Hell instead of a peaceful meadow, but sheep, nonetheless.

I've got this.

I prowl inside the circle they've created around me, maintaining a careful distance, but also asserting my power and authority.

They follow me with their glowing eyes. Their gazes are still intense, but no longer hostile.

I bare my teeth slightly, and they move closer together, breaking their circle and forming into clumps once more.

Good. This is progress.

It is, my wolf agrees. *We're making excellent progress.*

Not just me. Not just my wolf.

Because as we work together, the two of us are one.

Ruby

TAKING A RISK, I howl again, low and authoritative, my call echoing in the silence.

The rams clump closer together.

Time to go for the stone, retrieve the lunar essence, and get out of here.

Slowly, I walk toward the stone, holding my gaze with any ram that so much as tries to break formation.

They shift, adjusting their positions to make way for me. Some even lower their heads in deference.

My heart races as I continue forward. This is absurd and thrilling, all at the same time. And crazily enough—now that I've gained the respect I deserve—I love it.

Right now, I don't need earth magic. I don't need illusion magic. All I need is my wolf.

A sudden snort breaks my concentration.

The biggest ram, a massive creature with a set of twisted, dangerous-looking horns, blocks my path. His eyes blaze with defiance, and his body tenses, ready to strike.

Crap.

I can't let him get to me.

Instead of stepping back, I meet his gaze and growl, stopping him before he can release one of those bone-shattering roars.

He charges forward, hooves thundering on the earth as he makes his way closer and closer.

Screw this.

Just as he's about to reach me, I launch myself to the side, agile and quick. His horns miss me by mere inches.

Almost instantly, he twists his body to face me again.

The other rams are in a circle around us now, watching us like we're facing off in a boxing ring. If I lose, this is over. All respect I earned will be lost.

So, I growl again, louder this time. Then I lower my head, emulating the challenging gesture the alpha ram showed me.

A clear message: *I am not your prey, nor your enemy. I am your leader.*

I have no idea how long we stay there, eyes locked, challenging each other. The other rams are as still as statues. I remain aware of them, ready to defend myself if necessary, but keep the majority of my focus on the alpha.

Finally, his stance relaxes. Then, after what seems like an eternity, he lowers his head. Not in a threat, but in submission.

We've got this, my wolf thinks. *It's now or never.*

Not wanting to make any sudden movements, I slowly pass him, not once breaking our silent conversation.

It's working.

A demon-ram is acknowledging me as his superior.

I've had a lot of crazy experiences, but this might be the most surreal of them all. Especially because for the first time ever, my wolf and I are finally one. No more bickering, no more fighting. Just the two of us working together, as we were born to do.

Turns out you do have some sense, after all, my wolf thinks.

I smile inwardly. Maybe the bickering is just part of our relationship. I don't mind, since it keeps me on my toes. But the fighting and having my body taken over part is something I'm glad to leave in the past.

I make my way to the stone, eventually having no choice but to turn my back on the alpha and the other rams. The silver essence glimmers under the moonlight, its warm, pulsing magic inviting me to come closer.

As I do, I get a better look at the details of the essence. It's a small clear quartz about the size of a grape. The silver liquid fills it, sparkling and swirling like a galaxy of stars.

I can't pick it up while in my wolf form. I need hands—not paws.

So, I shift back to my human form, the transition coming easier than ever. No bones crunching, muscles pulling, or tendons twisting. Just a pleasant tingling as I go from wolf to human.

Not wanting to waste a precious second, I reach forward until my fingers skim the surface of the stone.

Cold, lunar energy pours inside me, the magic of the stone entering my bloodstream and filling up my soul. It's like the essence recognizes me, and the connection is instant and unbreakable.

Suddenly, a shadow falls over me.

My stomach drops, and stone in hand, I turn back around to face whatever's threatening me now.

It's far from what I expect.

Because the alpha ram from earlier is gone. Now, I'm looking up at a man with an impressive physique, dark hair, and sharp eyes that glow with an otherworldly light. The fur hide he wears look ancient, and I suspect he's as old as the stars above.

He's a shifter, just like I am.

"Canis constellation." He drops to a knee to show reverence to me, and the rams behind him lower their heads, also showing their respect. "My brothers and I thought you were a tale—a myth among us. Yet, here you are. A goddess from the heavens, reclaiming the moonlit essence we've been protecting for ages."

I glance at Luna for help, but she simply nods at me, encouraging me to respond to the man standing before me.

Refocusing on him, I swallow hard and find my voice. "I'm Ruby," I correct him, and his confusion shows on his face. "My wolf and I are one, but we're not the same Canis as the one in the stars."

"But you wield its essence." He gestures toward the stone. "You have shown us your leadership. Your strength. If you're not Canis, then who are you?"

"I'm Ruby," I repeat, more firmly this time. "I'm a wolf shifter blessed by the goddess of the moon."

"Interesting." He watches me more carefully now, and I brace myself for another attack. "We shall respect you as we respect our Canis constellation. Ruby the wolf shifter, a daughter of the moon and stars."

The rams lower their heads more—a testament to his words.

I'm not sure if they're correct or not about my connection to the Canis constellation. But if it convinces them to let me leave their meadow with the lunar essence, then hey, I'll take it.

He turns to the rams and raises his voice. "The Canis has returned!" he says, and they bow their heads so low that their horns touch the ground, as if I'm some kind of deity.

However, while I'm powerful, I'm not the true deity in this meadow.

Luna steps out of the shadows, pride shining on her face. "Well done, Ruby," she says. "You have earned the respect of the Fleece Rams, claimed the lunar essence, and therefore, have passed your first trial—as I always knew you would."

Ruby

Luna gives me a satchel where I can keep the lunar essence and leads me out of the meadow, with the Fleece Rams trailing behind us until we cross a bubbling stream that will presumably lead us to the next trial.

As we make our way through the forest, I try getting information from her about the magic of the essence, the Fleece Rams, the Canis constellation—basically, anything I can think of. But she reveals nothing.

She looks like the Luna I know. But now that she's not hiding her identity, she's very different from my chatty roommate-turned-bestie that I used to know.

I don't mind it. I'm glad to have her back in my life. It's just… different.

Our journey through the forest feels both too long and too short. Too long because Luna remains frustratingly silent. Too short because before I know it, we're standing at the edge of a grove so enchanting that it takes my breath away.

Gems of all colors and sizes dazzle in the moonlight, sparkling like stars brought down to earth. Each one is more precious and beautiful than the next, their magic so strong it nearly knocks me off my feet.

"What is this place?" I ask in awe.

"The Glimmering Garden," Luna replies. "Home to the most powerful and beautiful gemstones in the world."

"And home to my second trial," I guess.

"Correct."

She doesn't say more, which I take as a hint that I should be the one asking the questions. Not that I got many answers to my questions during our walk through the forest, but this feels different, since Luna promised to guide me through each task.

I trust her.

Sure, she lied to me from the beginning about who she was. But still, I trust her. Because at the heart of it all, she's my best friend.

"What task do I have to complete in the garden?" I ask.

"One of them is the gemstone meant to be embedded in the Lunar Crescent," she says. "Your task is to find it."

"Got it." Again, I sweep my gaze over the countless gems scattered around the garden. "What does the one for the Lunar Crescent look like?"

"I'm afraid I can't tell you that. But you can figure it out on your own. All you have to do is let your magic be your guide."

"Great," I say sarcastically, since it feels like she's being far vaguer than she was with the Fleece Rams.

"There's one more thing you should know," she adds, her expression turning serious. "Some of these gemstones absorb magic. The longer you spend here, the weaker you'll feel. Be aware of that as you go about your task."

The garden suddenly feels far more dangerous than it did when I first set eyes upon it.

"So, not only do I need to find a needle in a haystack, but I'll be steadily losing power as I do?"

Luna's answering smile is far from reassuring. "It's time to begin. Good luck, Ruby."

With a sigh, I step forward, the grassy earth crunching under my boots as I make my way toward the grove. The magic radiating from the gemstones thrums against my skin, like a heartbeat echoing my own, and they pulse with a soft, eerie light.

There's something else as well.

Whispered words carried by the wind, coming from the gems themselves. They curl around me like invisible tendrils of smoke, growing more distinct by the second.

"You'll fail them," one hisses, its icy touch sending chills down my spine. "Just like you always do."

"Your parents don't even remember you," another taunts. "You're just a forgotten memory."

"Who will you choose, Ruby?" another asks, and I swivel to locate its source, but find nothing. "The wolf who rejected you, or the vampire who can't be trusted?"

I clench my fists, my nails biting into my palms.

"Stop," I say to them. "You're not real."

It makes no difference. The whispers continue. They're closing in on me, like a tourniquet around my lungs getting so tight that I can barely breathe.

I press my palms to my ears to quiet them, but it makes no difference. Because they've crawled inside my brain. They're like bugs, invading every crevice, and they're not stopping.

But I can't let them get to me. I'm here for a purpose, and I won't be distracted.

"Enough!" I call out, and my earth magic quakes out of me, shaking the ground so much that some of the gemstones fall from their perches and into the dirt, their lights dimming out.

All is silent.

Good job, my wolf thinks, and her voice is a relief—a reminder that I'm not alone.

But my body feels heavy. Tired.

I need to find the gemstone, and fast.

Let your magic be your guide, Luna's advice echoes through my mind, and as I center myself, I close my eyes and focus. The cool grass beneath my boots, the rocks lining the path, the trees surrounding the garden—they all pulse with the life force of the Earth.

Then there are the gemstones. Each one has a unique pulse, like a song sung only for me.

However, their wavelengths are all different. It's subtle, but there's a pattern. A rhythm.

A heartbeat.

They're speaking to me.

Listen, my wolf thinks. *Really, truly listen.*

Okay. I can do that.

So, I dig deeper inside myself and quiet my mind. It takes a few seconds, but eventually, I notice something.

Only the rubies match the exact timing of the Earth's heartbeat.

Given my name, it now feels stupidly obvious. The gemstone that belongs in the Lunar Crescent is a ruby.

The problem is, there are dozens of rubies in the garden. How am I supposed to know which one to get?

I gaze around, discounting all the other types of gems, and there's a subtle shift in the air around the rubies. A haze. It's slight, but it's there.

Illusion magic.

They're not all what they appear to be.

Excitement bubbles inside me. I'm on to something.

So, I stretch my magic further, weaving tendrils of energy around the gemstones to dispel them.

As I do, the colors of the rubies shift. Some of them pale, barely holding onto their pinkness. Others deepen, turning into a dark burgundy that almost seems black. Others, however, maintain the rich, healthy glow that rubies are supposed to have.

Those are the true rubies. The others are imposters trying to throw me off.

It's progress. But how am I supposed to know which is the *right* ruby?

I can do it.

I just need to *think*.

Minutes pass like hours, my energy draining from the continuous use of my magic. I'm weakening, my movements becoming more sluggish, my thoughts harder to hold onto.

Frustrated, I glance up at the moon for guidance. Its silvery glow bathes the garden, and it feeds my magic, restoring the strength that the gemstones have been sucking out of me.

I scan the garden again. All of the rubies glisten under the moonlight, but one reflects it differently.

Somehow, its color is both the natural red of a ruby and the silvery sheen of the moon at the same time.

Moonlight, my wolf whispers in my mind. *Of course.*

Then, she adds, *Don't hesitate. We have no time for that.*

Trusting her, I reach out and wrap my fingers around the brilliant stone in front of me.

It doesn't drain me, like Luna warned me to expect from the gemstones. Instead, it fills me with a pure, harmonious energy that's unmistakably *right*.

I found it.

The gem for the Lunar Crescent.

"Congratulations, Ruby," Luna says, stepping out of the shadows. "You tuned into your earth magic, illusion magic, and the wolf inside yourself to locate the correct gem, and therefore, have completed your second trial."

"And hopefully the last?" I ask hopefully.

Her laughter rings through the garden. "You're proving yourself worthy of a weapon created by a goddess," she says. "Do you truly think it'll be that easy?"

"I wouldn't call these past two trials easy…"

"Add the ruby to your satchel." She motions to the pouch where I'm keeping the lunar essence, not bothering to counter my statement. "Because as beautiful as this garden is, it's time to go. I have some friends I want you to meet."

Ruby

I SECURE the ruby inside the satchel, the air between the brilliant gem and the lunar essence crackling with power.

"Who are these friends of yours?" I ask Luna as we leave the garden.

"You'll see," she says simply, leading the way out of the garden and back into a lush, green forest she calls the Emerald Woods.

We follow the bubbling stream from earlier. Luna, once again, falls silent, wrapped in her own thoughts. This new Luna is harder to read, with her playful, chatty demeanor replaced by a thoughtful, distant one.

I miss the best friend I used to know.

She's still the same Luna, my wolf reminds me. *She's just not hiding her true self anymore.*

I want to believe it's true. But right now, as we make our way through the thickening forest, I'm not sure it is.

Eventually, the trees part, revealing a massive clearing bathed in the moonlight.

Frolicking in it are creatures I only thought existed in myth.

Centaurs. Humans on the top, and horses on the bottom. There are seventeen of them in all.

Sensing our presence, they stop their socializing and turn to stare at us.

After a few painfully long seconds, the largest one steps forward. He oozes authority and power, and he keeps his eyes locked on mine, clearly trying to intimidate me.

But he's a horse. I'm a wolf. Wolves trump horses. So, I hold his gaze, strong and steady, making sure he knows exactly who he's dealing with.

He turns his focus to Luna, and I relax slightly, proud of myself for not backing down.

"Moon goddess." His deep voice echoes through the clearing. "What brings you to our lands?"

"We've come for the arrows of the Lunar Crescent. Rather, Ruby has come to claim them." She motions to me, making me the center of his attention once more.

He looks me up and down, sizing me up.

Again, I don't back down.

"You are star touched," he finally says.

"I am."

"As I'm sure you know, in order to earn the arrows we guard, you need to prove your worth," he tells me, and I nod for him to continue. "To do so, we will make a high-stakes wager. Win, and you'll have your passage through our lands, along with the arrows for your Lunar Crescent. Lose, and you'll serve us for an entire year."

A year.

He wants me to potentially give up an *entire year* of my life to serve him and his little centaur kingdom.

"You ask a lot of me." I don't want to show my worry, but at the same time, I look to Luna for help.

Back when we were roommates, she understood what I was thinking without me having to speak a word. I don't know if that was because we got to know each other so well after sharing the same living space, or if it had something to do with her abilities as a goddess, but right now, I would appreciate her guidance.

"The Lunar Crescent is a powerful, dangerous weapon," she tells me. "A person shouldn't wield that much power if they're unwilling to make sacrifices. Andros's wager is fair."

Great.

That was *not* the answer I was hoping for. But the lunar essence and the ruby hum in the satchel that hangs from my hip, and I'll never forgive myself if I turn my back on this opportunity now. Especially because Luna wouldn't be here by my side if she didn't believe I could succeed.

Still, I'm not going to say yes before I know exactly what I'm getting myself into.

"What sort of competition will we be entering?" I ask the centaur—Andros.

"You're here for arrows," he says. "Therefore, it's only fitting for you to pass a test of archery."

My heart sinks. Because even though I'm proving my worth for a bow and arrow, I've never actually used one before. I figured that once I claimed the Lunar Crescent, using it would come naturally, since it's apparently meant for me and all.

How am I supposed to face off in an archery competition against this majestic creature and come out victorious? He's likely immortal, with who knows how many years of experience with archery.

He wouldn't look so smug right now otherwise.

All is not lost, my wolf thinks. *Remember Hazel's dagger, and how you threw it in the fae realm to pin the hobgoblin's hand to the tree?*

As if I could forget. I scoff inwardly, even though I immediately understand my wolf's point.

It's the same principle.

Sort of.

"What materials will the bow and arrows be made of?" I ask.

"Are you allergic to certain materials?" Andros raises an eyebrow and gives me an arrogant smile.

It's a clear jab meant to provoke me.

But I'm not biting.

"No," I reply calmly, despite wanting to use my earth magic to rip the ground up from under his hooves. "I'm asking because every material resonates differently. I want to know what I'll be handling."

A murmur sweeps across the assembled centaurs, surprise coloring their faces.

Andros' smile falters, and his eyes turn deadly serious. "The bow will be made of sturdy yew, and the arrows of ash."

"And the tips?" I ask.

"Pure silver."

Not ideal, since my earth magic doesn't control silver. It does, however, control wood.

I can work with this.

As if replying to my thoughts, the satchel pulsates against my hip. It's like the ruby and the lunar essence are rooting for me, filling me with a warmth that seeps into my veins and strengthens my resolve.

"If I accept, then the trial will begin now?" I ask, since I have no time to waste.

"Indeed." He nods. "There's no time like the present."

"Then I accept your challenge."

With a swift movement, Andros whistles a sharp, high note, and a young centaur steps forward. He's carrying a long, sleek bow, and a quiver filled with arrows.

He trots forward and holds the weapon down for me to take. The bow is heavier than I anticipated, its smooth surface cool to touch. But, as I run my fingers over it, energy surges through me.

My earth magic.

"The terms are set," Luna says from beside me. "Now, the trial will begin."

Andros snaps his fingers, and six centaurs emerge from the forest. They're each holding a target, which they arrange on the ground at varying distances in a matter of seconds.

"A true test of skill," he says. "You must hit each target in the right order, starting from the nearest to the farthest. Miss one, and the trial is lost."

As he speaks, my eyes move across the targets, trying to calculate the distances.

They're so far away. Throwing the dagger through the hobgoblin's hand was child's play compared to this. Especially because it's the dead of night, with only the shine of the half-moon to light my way.

But the weight of the bow in my hand grounds me. With each breath, I feel the texture of the yew, and the veins of life running through the wood.

This is *my* element.

And I'm no one's servant. Not now, and certainly not for a year.

I will not fail.

No—we *will not fail.*

My wolf's encouragement sends a wave of confidence through me.

"Ready, Star Touched?" Andros asks.

"Ready," I say, and the centaurs fall into a hush, every eye on me.

Ignore them, my wolf thinks. *Pretend they aren't there. It's just us, the bow and arrows, and the targets.*

It's so quiet that all I can hear is my heart pounding, and the wind whistling through the forest.

But, listening to my wolf's advice, I reach over my shoulder and pull an arrow from the quiver. It feels unnaturally light in my hand—almost fragile—but I know it won't break.

I take a deep breath, nock the arrow, and draw the bowstring back. My arms shake slightly, and I feel the stares of the centaurs on me, heavy and expectant, anxious for a good show.

And I'm ready to give it to them.

Ruby

I REACH for my magic and let it flow from my hands into the arrow.

Then, I release.

The arrow sails through the air with a hum, hurtling toward the first target. As it does, I don't break my connection with it. It's just me, my magic, and the arrow. Nothing else.

It embeds itself in the center of the target, earning gasps of surprise from the centaurs.

Yes.

The ruby and the lunar essence thrum in response, a reassuring warmth pulsing through my body.

Andros digs a hoof into the ground, irritation coming off him in waves.

Luna's eyes shine with approval, and she nods at me to continue.

I refocus on the targets.

One down, five to go.

I reach for the next arrow, pausing for a second to feel its weight. It's slightly lighter than the previous one. I'm not sure if Andros is trying to trick me, or if it's just a true variation in the craftsmanship of the arrows, but it doesn't matter either way.

I have my magic on my side.

And so, with another deep breath, I let the arrow fly.

Another perfect shot.

I do the same with the next, and the next, and the one after that. It's like my earth magic is one with the bow and arrows, making it impossible to mess this up.

Now, only one target remains.

The farthest. The hardest.

I've got this.

My hand is steady as I pull the last arrow from the quiver. This moment determines if I can continue forward, or if I'll be stuck serving these conceited, horse-bottomed jerks for a year.

They will not win.

I close my eyes for a moment and feel the cool breeze against my skin, the weight of the bow in my hand, and my own heartbeat. I can barely feel the difference from where my fingers end and the arrow begins.

I draw the string back, breathe out, and release.

As I do, a centaur whistles loudly and charges across the field.

My connection with my earth magic snaps. Broken.

The arrow drifts off course, heading wide of its target.

No.

Desperate energy rushes through me, and I claw for the magic of the Earth. But my fingers slip through it.

The arrow soars above the target.

But it hasn't hit the ground yet.

And so, connecting with the wood of the arrow, I will it to shift, and bend, and turn. I call upon more magic, strengthening my hold on it and letting it fill me. My focus will *not* be broken again. I will not let the centaurs win.

The arrow loops through the air like it's on a rollercoaster, turning around on itself and coming back for a second chance at hitting the target.

Gasps and murmurs ripple through the clearing. But I won't look at them. Not until this is finished.

The only thing I'm looking at is the arrow.

I force it downward with all the strength and willpower I possess, and it thuds into the final target.

Dead center.

I lower the bow and stare at the row of targets—all of them pierced with arrows.

I did it. I really, truly did it.

A loud cheer breaks through the silence, and I pull my focus away from the targets to look at my four-legged audience.

The centaurs, despite their obvious surprise, are clapping and hooting. Andros looks stunned, and while he doesn't join the clapping, there's a sheen of respect in his eyes as well.

Luna runs up to me and gives me a giant hug.

For the first time since seeing her outside Calliope's mansion, I feel like I'm with my best friend instead of an immortal moon goddess.

"Well done." She pulls away, a bright smile on her face. "I knew I chose well with you."

"That was… incredible," I say as the rush of adrenaline fades away.

Andros approaches, his hoofbeats heavy against the grass. "Impressive showing, Star Touched," he says. "You passed the trial, and therefore, earned the arrows of the Lunar Crescent."

A weight lifts off my chest at the fact that I won't be forced into a year of servitude.

As if we wouldn't have figured out a way to escape, my wolf scoffs, and I smile inwardly, loving her more and more with each passing minute.

"Thank you, Andros," I reply, trying to keep my voice steady.

"You've earned it," he says, and then he looks over his shoulder toward the forest. "Gideon! Bring forth the arrows."

A few seconds pass in silence. Then, a centaur far older than any of the ones in the clearing walks out of the forest. His gray hair falls past his shoulders, and his skin is wrinkled with age.

The others part as he walks by, allowing him ample space to approach.

"Star Touched," he says, and I nod my head in respect, since it seems like the proper thing to do.

When I look back up, he reaches inside the quiver strapped to his back and removes one of the arrows to inspect it.

Its shaft is dark as night, and it's tipped with a ruby. A pure, vibrant red ruby that gleams under the moonlight.

I stare at it in awe.

"It's beautiful," I say.

"The arrows of the Lunar Crescent were crafted by the moon goddess under a rare alignment of celestial bodies." He pauses to look at Luna, places the arrow back in the quiver, then hands it to me. "Each one contains a piece of magic from the night sky."

"You'll learn more about the Lunar Crescent when you piece it together," Luna adds. "The arrows respond to intention, but depending on the moon phase, the effect will vary. Most importantly—the deadlier the intent, the more of your magic it will use. So, be sure to use it wisely."

"I understand." I sling the quiver across my back, letting the weight of the responsibility settle on my shoulders. The arrows are powerful, but it's up to me to not put *so* much of my magic into them that I drain myself in the process.

"I know you do. I wouldn't have chosen you if I doubted you." Luna smiles, her eyes reflecting the moonlight. "Now let's get you to that final part of your quest so you can show it who's boss and return to your realm before sunrise."

Ruby

THE CENTAURS BOW their heads as Luna and I cross the clearing—even the obnoxious one who tried to mess up my final shot.

As we make our way through the forest, she tells me more about how to use the Lunar Crescent, and it isn't long until we exit and find ourselves in the center of a perfectly formed hilltop.

Before us lies the bow of the Lunar Crescent, its crescent shape shimmering under the moonlight.

It's breathtakingly beautiful, crafted with rare, celestial wood and finished off with a smooth leather grip. The space where the large ruby should rest is empty, awaiting its final piece.

"Combine all the elements. Let the power of the Lunar Crescent become one with you," Luna instructs.

I nod, trying to steady my racing heart.

Because this is the moment I've been working toward all night.

The one where I claim the Lunar Crescent as mine.

And so, I reach for the pouch hanging by my side and remove the large, radiant ruby I retrieved from the Glimmering Garden. It pulses with life, beckoning me to place it on the bow.

Gently, I set it into its spot in the center of the grip, where my palm will rest when I use the weapon. It clicks into place, and a soft light glows from the point of contact, melding the bow and the gemstone together.

Magic hums through me, the weapon becoming more alive.

Next, I reach back inside the pouch for the quartz that contains the silver essence.

There's no obvious space for it. So, I look at Luna for guidance.

"Hold it above the bow," she says, and keeping my eyes locked on the quartz, I do as told.

The silvery liquid inside the orb streams down and merges seamlessly with the crescent bow.

Then it explodes in a silver light so blinding that I have to close my eyes.

Power surges through me. So much of it that it burns through my veins and sears itself into my bones, as if it's transforming me into something *else*.

Something powerful enough to use a weapon imbued with magic from the moon.

Finally, after what feels like the most torturous few minutes of my life, the pain stops. The light behind my eyes is gone.

When I open them, Luna's no longer standing next to me.

I scan my eyes across the hill, searching every inch of the horizon for some sign of her. There's nothing.

All I hear is the rustling of the leaves and the creatures chirping in the forest.

Anxiety coils in my stomach. I spin around, faster now, gripping the bow of the Lunar Crescent tighter.

"Luna!" I call out, but no one answers, minus the hoot of an owl.

I swallow down a ball of fear in my throat.

Where is she?

Why did she leave me here alone?

You're never alone, my wolf thinks. *You have me.*

It's only somewhat comforting. Because it's not the same as having someone physically *with* me.

Where am I supposed to go from here? I don't know how to get out of this realm. Without a guide, I could get stuck wandering alone, forever.

Something must be wrong. Luna wouldn't leave me like this.

But that's not totally true, is it? Because she left me in the woods after my first shift. She star touched me, then left me there when I was cold, alone, and more lost than ever.

"Luna," I say again, and I glance up at the moon, praying for guidance.

A soft, mocking laugh echoes behind me.

I clutch the Lunar Crescent, the weight of it grounding me, and turn around to see who's there.

A shadowy figure emerges from the darkness.

I hold the bow up and string it with an arrow, ready to strike.

But then, the figure becomes clearer.

Connor.

My heart leaps, and I lower the bow, running to him. But I stop when I'm halfway there, my blood turning to ice at the look in his eyes.

Cold indifference.

The same way he looked at me each time he rejected me.

I step back, nearly tripping over my feet, and the figure in front of me shifts and morphs.

Tristan, his smirk filled with deceit, with Dominic's cross pendant hanging around his neck.

"Did you really think you could trust me?" he says, low and teasing as he walks slowly toward me. "That I could love you? That *anyone* could love you?"

"Get away from me." I raise the bow, hoping to ward him off. "You're not real."

He laughs, and now Connor stands before me. "You're an abomination of nature. Did you really believe I could ever accept someone like you?"

Before I can reply, Tristan replaces him. "You're so gullible, Ruby," he sneers. "Did you really think I'd ever be honest with you? That I'd ever care for you?"

His words slither around my skin like ice, and the ground's so unsteady that I'm afraid if I move, I'll fall over and sink into it.

"You're not real," I repeat, and I hold his callous gaze, as if I can intimidate him into submission.

It doesn't matter. He—Connor, or Tristan, or something else entirely—grows larger and more menacing by the second.

"See, Ruby?" he growls, his voice a blend of both of them. "You're alone in this world. Nobody loves you. Nobody wants you. Not even your precious Luna."

His words tear my heart apart.

"I'm loved," I whisper, holding on to the belief as if it's my last lifeline.

"Your magic is a curse." Connor sneers, not hearing me—or not caring. "The Blood Coven hunts you because you'll never belong anywhere, so they think they can bring you into their little band of misfits."

"Even your wolf is a chain that binds you," Tristan adds. "Making you lose your humanity with every passing day. Turning you into a killer. A monster."

The memory of my wolf attacking Tristan in the attic bedroom crosses my mind, and guilt squeezes my lungs. Because as much as I hate what Tristan did to me—as much as my trust in him was shattered when I learned about that necklace—I don't want him *dead*.

My wolf, on the other hand, doesn't feel the same.

The shadow figure's now impossibly massive, and the landscape around me changes. I'm no longer standing on a hill, but on an endless expanse of cold, barren ground. The sky is a swirling abyss of black and gray, and it's suffocating me, drowning me.

But no.

This isn't real.

I ground myself and take a closer look at the shadow creature. Really, truly look.

Those eyes aren't Connor's. Yes, I've seen him reject me. But when he did, there was always something else in his eyes—longing, guilt, and regret. I didn't see it then, but compared to the malicious way this false Connor's looking at me, I see it now.

Tristan's sneer isn't his, either. Because despite all his lies, I don't believe he truly got pleasure out of tricking me. It doesn't make it more forgivable, but I know in my heart that he didn't enjoy it.

"You're right," I say, stronger now, wiping a tear off my face that I don't remember falling. "I'm afraid of being alone. I'm afraid of not having a home. I'm afraid of the Blood Coven, and of making the wrong choices. I'm afraid of my wolf taking over."

The shadow smirks. "Then come to me. Let me take away your fears. Let me make you strong. Powerful. Unbreakable."

"What you don't understand is that these fears don't make me weak." I step forward, and he stills, caught off guard. "They give me something to fight for. I might not be unbreakable, but I *am* resilient. And I will fight for the people I love. No matter what."

I gather all the strength I have, focusing on the Lunar Crescent in my hand. It's warm and alive, ready to fuse with my will.

"I have fears and doubts—everyone does—but they don't define me." I hold the weapon high, letting its light pierce through the dark. "I won't let them."

The shadow shudders at my words, retreating a bit. "You're the one who doesn't understand. I *am* you, Ruby," it says. "I'm every doubt you've ever had, every insecurity, every fear."

"No." I move forward, refusing to let this demon break me. "You're a manifestation of them, but you're not truly me. You'll never be me."

A young girl appears in the center of the shadow, turquoise eyes filled with doubt and insecurities. Me, when I was younger, before the magic, before everything. That girl didn't know what major to study in college, let alone what she wanted to do for the rest of her life.

She thought she was in control, but she had no purpose—no true goal. She was lost, and she didn't even realize it.

I'm not that girl anymore. I won't let her hold me back.

And I will destroy this demon.

Intent rushes through me, flowing out of my palm, and the ruby under it pulses with energy.

I drown out the shadow's words. I have only one goal now, and nothing will distract me.

Focus on my target.

Breathe in, pull the warm earth magic up through my feet, and gather my strength and power.

Release.

The ruby on the arrow's tip glows as it soars through the air.

Time slows, and the arrow strikes the shadow straight where its heart should be.

A loud, shattering scream fills the air, and the shadow figure writhes, trying to resist the light piercing its chest. But it can't win. The light crackles through its body like electricity, consuming it from the inside out until it dissolves into millions of shimmering particles and fades into the night sky.

As it does, the dark landscape around me shifts, becoming the beautiful moonlit hilltop once more.

A soft clapping sounds from behind.

Luna, her silver eyes filled with pride.

"You've done well," she says. "Confronting one's own darkness is the hardest challenge any of us can face, but you stood strong against your fears and emerged triumphant. *That* is the true power of the Lunar Crescent. It's a reflection of your heart, your soul, and your strength. And you just embraced them all."

"It's not the bow, or the rubies," I realize, examining the weapon with newfound awe. "They're conduits of my magic, but they don't create it. The core of my power lies in believing in myself."

"Correct," she says. "And now that you've proven yourself worthy, it's time for you to finally learn about the true darkness you're destined to face."

Ruby

"What sort of 'true darkness?'" I hold the Lunar Crescent closer, as if it can protect me from whatever Luna's about to tell me next.

"How much do you know about the original vampire?" she starts.

"Ambrogio," I answer, since I read about this weeks ago, in Jax's library. "He fell in love with the moon goddess, Selene. Your mother?"

"Correct." She nods. "He fell in love with her while he was human, and they were going to be wed. However, not all the gods supported their future union. They cursed him, turning him into what we now refer to as a vampire. He wanted to turn Selene so they could be vampires together, but she was horrified by what he'd become, and she didn't want to be a monster. So, she deceived him by telling him she wanted to get permission from her family before promising herself to him forever. But she lied. And when she went to her family, she had Ambrogio banished to Hell."

Slowly, the pieces click together.

Ambrogio's in Hell.

The Blood Coven wants the Key of Hades so they can raise someone from Hell.

"The Blood Coven is going to try raising Ambrogio from the dead," I say, and Luna nods, confirming my suspicion is correct. "But witches and shifters don't like vampires. Why would they want to bring the original, and presumably most powerful one, back to Earth?"

"For love. You see, Selene wasn't Ambrogio's first love," she says. "He loved a human woman before her. They had three sons together. He couldn't bear the thought of being immortal and eventually seeing his sons and their mother die. And so, when Selene went to the gods to speak with her family, he sought out his previous love and their children and turned them into vampires, so he'd never be forced to live in a world without them in it."

"Thus, unknowingly assuring that the vampire race continued after he was banished to Hell," I conclude.

"Yes," she says. "His ex-lover—the mother of their children—loved him deeply. She spiraled into despair after he was banished to Hell, and she made it her personal mission to bring him back to Earth. Then, when witches created shifters in the Dark Ages to hunt vampires, all three of her sons were killed. Her grief grew. She disappeared for centuries, and many thought her dead. But at the turn of the twentieth century, she stumbled across three men who reminded her of her sons. She turned them into vampires and emerged from hiding. But it wasn't enough. Her love for Ambrogio is an obsession, and she's continued to search for a way to resurrect him to this day."

One female vampire who's been alive for centuries.

Three men she turned into vampires in the early twentieth century.

"This woman Ambrogio loved before Selene," I say, knowing deep in my bones that I'm right before even speaking it out loud. "Is she Gwen?"

"She is," Luna confirms.

I stand there for a few seconds in shock.

"But Ambrogio loved Selene," I finally say. "He chose Selene over Gwen, even though he had three children with Gwen. Even if she manages to resurrect him, why does she think he'll take her back?"

"Because she believes that since Selene is now with my father, Ambrogio will see that she was always meant to be his true love—not Selene."

"Your father is Endymion," I repeat the story I read in Jax's book. "Zeus cursed him into an eternal sleep and Selene joined him so she could be with him forever."

"They have many daughters together—myself, obviously, included. They're happy together," Luna says. "There's no chance she would ever choose to be with Ambrogio. And if he wakes her from her eternal sleep—if he pulls her away from my father and turns her into a vampire—her rage and despair will drive the world into darkness. The Blood Coven doesn't understand the true scale of the danger they're involving themselves in. They *cannot* be allowed to succeed. And you have the magic—and the weapon—that can end this."

"But if I stop the Blood Coven from raising Ambrogio, then I won't be following through on my oath to them. Hazel won't reverse the erasure spell."

The thought of my parents never remembering me tears deep at my heart in a way that makes me feel like I'll never be whole again.

"Not necessarily," she says, and a bit of hope sparks inside me.

"What do you mean?"

"I'll get to that in a minute. But firstly, if Gwen and the Blood Coven don't get a chance to use the Key of Hades, they won't give up. They'll do everything they can to get their hands back on it and try again. Stealing it from them won't be enough."

"You want me to kill Gwen."

It's not impossible. Shifters and witches slay vampires all the time. The trickiest part will be getting her away from the rest of the Blood Coven so she's as vulnerable as possible.

"Killing Gwen would make sense if she was the only one trying to raise Ambrogio," Luna says. "Unfortunately, she's convinced all the members of the Blood Coven to join her cause. Which means Gwen isn't your target. It's Ambrogio himself."

"But he's locked in Hell…"

"Which is why you're going to have to wait until *after* the Blood Coven starts the resurrection," she explains. "Once his body is returned to Earth, one of the witches will give him her life force to complete the process. It will be Calliope, since she's the oldest. Your job is to stop her while she's transferring her life energy. She'll be vulnerable and weak, as will Ambrogio. It will be the perfect time to strike."

"You want me to follow through on my oath to help the Blood Coven use the Key of Hades to raise Ambrogio," I realize. "And you want me to be with them when they do."

"Precisely," she says, and from there, she fills me in on the rest of the plan.

It's doable. Tricky, but doable.

"I know it sounds dangerous, and it is," she says when she's done. "But you won't be alone. As for this..." She reaches out for the Lunar Crescent resting on the table beside us, and the bow shimmers, transforming into a stunning necklace with a radiant ruby at its center. "You can wear it next to your heart, and no one will know it's there. All you need to do is touch the ruby, think about what you want it to do, and it will transform into the bow and arrows. Do the same thing to turn it back into a necklace, but with the large ruby in its grip."

"Can I try?" I ask.

"Go ahead."

I reach for the gleaming ruby. It's cool to the touch, and it pulses lightly, like it's alive.

As Luna instructed, I gather my magic and communicate with the gemstone to turn the necklace back into the Lunar Crescent. It responds instantly. Turning it back is just as easy.

"Amazing," I say.

"Thank you. I designed it myself." Luna smiles, although she quickly turns serious once more. "You'll always have its power at your fingertips, but you must be cautious. The Blood Coven is not to be underestimated. They're powerful, and they'll stop at nothing to make sure Ambrogio's return is a success."

"I understand." I clasp the necklace around my neck, its weight settling against my skin. It's the weight of the responsibility of what I need to do—the responsibility given to me by a literal goddess. "Thank you, Luna. I won't let you down."

"I know you won't," she says. "But always remember, while the power of the Lunar Crescent is great, the strength that lies within you is even greater."

"I hope so," I say.

"I know so."

I glance up at the moon, its light giving me hope, then focus on Luna once more. "Before the Blood Coven raises Ambrogio, there's one thing I'd like to do," I tell her, since if I don't ask for this favor right now, I'll always wonder what would have happened if I did.

"Yes?" She watches me carefully, waiting for me to continue, and I tell her exactly what I want to do—and who I want to see—before the next full moon when the world possibly goes to Hell.

"I'll see what I can do," she says when I'm finished. "But it's almost sunrise. We have to get back."

"Okay." Sadness pulls at my heart, even though she's right. "Thank you again. For everything."

I change back into my pajamas, and we fly back to Spring Creek in her chariot, with only minutes to spare.

She drops me off just outside the bathroom window. It's still open from when I jumped out of it earlier, and I climb back inside without making a sound.

Before re-entering the bedroom, I stop in front of the mirror. The ruby necklace is stunning, but I can't have anyone else see it. I had no necklace before, and they'll be suspicious if I have one now.

Good thing I can easily use my illusion magic to make it invisible.

It's so beautiful that I hate hiding it, but there's not much else of a choice right now.

Readying myself, I open the bedroom door and peek inside.

As Luna told me, there's someone else in the bed with Tristan. She looks asleep, but she's instantly alert, and I startle at the sight of my face staring back at me.

Luna's sister. The one she used her illusion magic on to disguise her as me.

As quietly as a ray of light, she hops out of the bed and meets me at the door. We say nothing to each other—we can't risk waking Tristan—but she gives me a small smile of approval before striding past me and hopping out the window to join Luna on her chariot.

I stay in the bathroom for a minute and flush the toilet, just in case Tristan was even slightly aware when Luna's sister got up. Then I head back into the bedroom and slide back into bed next to him.

I've only been gone for a few hours, but it feels like an eternity.

Once I'm situated under the covers, he wraps his arm around me, pulls me close, and I fall into a deep, exhausted sleep.

Ruby

THE NEXT NIGHT, I find myself at dinner again with the three blood sisters—and with Gwen. They only wanted it to be the five of us, and as I sit down at the lavishly set table, I brace myself for anything.

"Thank you for joining us tonight," Gwen tells me, pausing to take a sip of her red wine. "I haven't had time to dine with you yet, and I thought it would be nice for us to get to know each other over a meal."

After everything I learned about Gwen from Luna, she looks different to me. She's beautiful in the way that all vampires are, but there's a sadness in her eyes I didn't see before.

"The food smells delicious," I say simply.

Morgan flashes her playful green eyes in my direction, the golden strands of her hair bright under the candlelight. "It's an old family recipe. I hope you like it."

"I'm sure I will." I relax slightly, since there's something warm and welcoming about Morgan that always puts me at ease.

"The weather has been lovely lately, hasn't it?" Willow gives me a tight smile that isn't quite as welcoming as her sister's.

"I guess." I help myself to some bread from the basket. "I'm still getting used to the snow."

"Then it's a good thing you have company at night to keep you warm," Zara adds with a knowing smirk.

My cheeks heat, and I stuff a piece of bread in my mouth, which is just as buttery as it smells.

The sisters keep at it with the chitchat as we start on the chicken and potatoes, but I can't shake the feeling that there's a bigger conversation looming on the horizon.

Finally, as if reading my thoughts, Gwen sets down her wine glass, her violet eyes serious and probing.

"Ruby," she begins. "You did an impressive job retrieving the Key of Hades from the fae realm and bringing it back here. Tristan has spoken quite highly of you. And, given the fact that he's like a son to me, it's time for you to learn the truth about the Key of Hades and what we intend to do with it."

All eyes turn to me, waiting for my reaction.

"You want to use it to raise someone from the dead," I say carefully, since that's information they've already told me.

"Yes." Gwen takes another sip of her wine. "But not just *someone*. We want to raise the original vampire. Ambrogio."

Shivers crawl up my spine when she speaks his name.

And then, much to my surprise, the four of them tell me everything Luna shared with me last night. Gwen and Willow say the most, but Morgan and Zara occasionally hop in with a thing or two.

"Ambrogio and I loved each other deeply," Gwen finishes. "When he returns, we will wed, and we will rule the coven together."

Morgan looks down at her lap and fiddles with her rings under the table.

Morgan, who specializes in blood scrying. Who can *see the future*.

Something's off with her.

But Gwen, Zara, and Willow are watching me expectantly, and I can't just sit here saying nothing.

"I can't imagine how hard it's been for you here without him," I say to Gwen, figuring it's a decently neutral response that won't make her suspect my feelings one way or the other.

She gives a faint smile, touching the silver locket around her neck. "The years have been long, but love endures. Especially when it's as deep as ours. I've always known he'll eventually return to me, which is what's kept me going for so long. And now, thanks to you, it will finally be possible."

"I did what I could," I say, continuing with my goal of neutrality. "And I'm glad to have helped. I'm only just starting to learn about love, but after spending these past few weeks with Tristan… well, I can't imagine a world without him in it."

"You love my son," Gwen says with a motherly smile.

"I do."

Luckily, there are no shifters in the room to smell out my lie.

"Then I'm sure you know there are options for you to share a long, happy future with him," she says. "Although, given your unique magic, I understand why you've had your reservations."

"What do you mean?"

I have a pretty good idea what she means, but I want to hear it straight from her. She's so deluded about her love for Ambrogio, and so full of gratitude for me retrieving the key, that she's a fountain of information tonight. I won't let that go to waste.

Zara raises an eyebrow and speaks before Gwen has a chance. "Surely you've wondered why my sisters and I—along with the other witches of the Blood Coven—are supporting Gwen in her mission to raise Ambrogio?"

"Given that witches typically hate vampires, it's certainly been on my mind." I meet her gaze straight on, unwilling to let her intimidate me.

"We're not typical witches. We all have burdens to bear." Willow sounds proud and sad at the same time. "My sisters and I have to live in hiding from those who consider our blood magic to be unnatural and dangerous. Hazel's immense power makes other witches hold her at arm's length. Calliope is so old that she won't be long for this world, and the few remaining members of her coven aren't strong enough to survive without her."

"Obviously, we have a lot of power," Zara continues, smiling dangerously. "But not enough to safely come out of hiding. To do that, we need more. And Ambrogio can give us that power—if we let him turn us into vampires."

I lower my fork back down to my plate, since I wasn't anticipating *that*.

Morgan picks at the remainder of her food, refusing to meet my gaze.

So, I turn back to Zara, who's watching me expectantly.

"I thought witches—and all supernaturals—lose their natural magic when they're turned into vampires?" I ask.

"That's the general belief, yes," Gwen replies smoothly. "But Ambrogio is different. He was the first. Any supernatural he turns will gain the abilities of a vampire and keep their natural magic as well."

"More than keep our natural magic. He'll amplify it," Willow adds. "We'll be more than just witches, or shifters, or star touched. We'll be *Revenants.*"

The room silences, the echo of her final word hanging in the air.

I shudder at the thought of what the Blood Coven could do with that much power.

Zara leans in, her gaze intense as it locks on mine. "You've only had your magic for weeks, but you've already had a taste of what it feels like to be different. To be feared. To be rejected by your own kind."

Those final words cut deep, as she knew they would.

"I've never felt a pain as awful in my life," I say honestly.

"You don't want to go through the rest of your life feeling this way." Gwen's eyes soften, making her look downright vulnerable. "Trust me, I know."

Willow takes a sip of wine, and the phoenix tattoo that wraps around her wrist glimmers in the candlelight. "If there's even a sliver of chance to change our fate—to finally get the respect and freedom in this world that we deserve—then we're willing to take it," she says. "You should, too."

"Plus, when life gives you love, you need to hold onto it," Gwen says. "If you join us and become a Revenant, then you'll be with Tristan. Forever. You'll have power. You'll have love. You'll have family. Isn't that exactly what you want?"

I swallow hard, feeling the weight of their eyes on me.

She's not wrong.

I just don't want it like *this*.

"This is... a lot to take in," I say, struggling to keep my voice steady.

"We're not asking for an answer tonight." Morgan reaches forward and places her hand on mine. Her eyes go wide for a second, but she neutralizes her expression and pulls back, continuing before I can ask what's wrong. "Think about it. Consider what's important to you, and what you want for your future."

There's a beat of silence before Gwen speaks again, her voice gentler than before. "And remember, we're not your enemies. We've presented you with an opportunity—a gift. The choice to take it or not remains yours. You have until the full moon to decide."

And what if I don't make the choice you want?

"I'll remember that," I say instead. "Thank you."

Dinner continues with lighthearted chatter, and despite the underlying tension, Gwen and the sisters steer the conversation toward neutral grounds. Stories of past adventures, memories of family gatherings, and even opinions on popular television shows and movies.

If I didn't know any better, it would all feel so... normal.

As the night winds down, and the candles burn low, Gwen stands, signaling the end of the evening. "Thank you for joining us tonight, Ruby," she says with a graceful nod. "If you need to talk with us any further—if you have any more questions—you know we won't be far."

"I'll remember that," I say, and as we make our way out, Morgan falls into step beside me.

"Ruby, a moment?" she whispers, guiding me away from the others.

They glance back at us, but continue down the hall and split ways, not saying a word.

"What is it?" I ask once we're alone.

She hesitates, looking around to double-check that we're not overheard. "Be careful, and trust your instincts," she finally says, her voice low and urgent. "There's more at stake here than you know."

A part of me wants to ask her to tell me more. Because I like her. I want to trust her.

She's one of them, my wolf speaks up for the first time since before dinner. *We can't forget that. Plus, even if she's truly trying to help, we don't need her. Luna's already told us everything we need to know.*

She's right.

And I'm not going to risk messing up everything I've done to gain the trust of the Blood Coven on the off chance of making a new friend.

"I will," I say. "Thanks, Morgan."

She gives me a quick, tight smile before rejoining the others.

But her message—especially after everything I learned from Luna—is clear.

I'm treading on dangerous ground, and the choices I make next could shape not just my own future, but the fate of the entire supernatural world.

Connor

Fluorescent lights flicker above me, casting a dim glow over the empty subway platform.

In normal hours, a good number of people would be waiting here for the train.

At 3:00 AM on a Wednesday night? Not so much.

NYC, with its unyielding energy, offers the distraction I desperately need. I want to be here, to make a difference in the way I've been training to do for my entire life: keeping the city safe from vampires.

Sure, I haven't had my final test yet to pass training and join the Guardians. But I'm close. And when Jax told them to expect me, they had no choice but to welcome me with open arms. They even gave me a private studio in one of their buildings downtown. It's a walkup on the top floor, but I'm not in a position to be picky right now.

As the two other Guardians and I prowl through the subway, searching for the vampires who have been killing humans in these off-hours when the night owls have already gone home and the early birds have yet to wake up, my thoughts inevitably wander to Ruby.

Mainly, to the kiss we shared in the fae realm.

Then to when she shattered my heart by choosing Tristan.

She didn't mean it, my wolf speaks up, like he always does when I think about her. *She's doing what she needs to get Hazel to reverse the erasure spell. She wants us. That kiss spoke louder than her words ever could.*

On one level, I understand his point.

On another, she kissed the vampire in front of me. She made it clear that she doesn't want or need my help.

I can't force her to choose me. To love me. The void she's left feels like a gaping wound that refuses to heal, and given that we're mates, I don't think it will *ever* heal.

Then there was the lust in my grandfather's eyes when he looked at my girlfriend.

Ex-girlfriend.

Ex-*fiancée.*

Whatever. None of it matters.

Because despite how painful it all is, I have to move on.

Which is exactly what I'm trying to do. Here, in NYC, fighting for everything the Guardians believe in—keeping humans safe and ensuring the supernatural world stays hidden.

"I've got a scent," Maria, one of the senior Guardians, whispers. She's short, but built like a tank, every inch of her sculpted from years of training and battle. I've learned a lot from her in the brief time I've been here.

"It's them," the other Guardian with us, Derek, confirms, nostrils flaring.

We spread out, using the shadows to our advantage. My wolf is restless beneath my skin, eager for a fight. In these tunnels, we're limited with what we can do with our earth magic—which the vampires are aware of—but that won't stop me from trying.

Two dark figures step out of an adjoining tunnel.

Vampires.

Their eyes are cold, their hunger evident, and my heart beats faster. Not out of fear, but out of excitement.

This is the test I've been waiting for.

I've never killed an actual vampire before, but I feel more ready for this than I have for anything in my life.

"It's go time," Maria says, and then she shifts, lunging at one of the vampires with a snarl.

He produces a slender, gleaming dagger and dodges Maria's attack. "You really think you can take me, wolf?" he sneers, gathering air magic in his palms.

Without a word, Maria pounces.

For now, I stay human. In a cramped environment like this, my human form grants me a unique precision and deftness that I can't quite get as a wolf.

The vampire hurls a concentrated gust of wind at Maria, knocking her backward.

She growls and attacks again.

Derek's locked in combat with the second vampire, who's handling a chained weapon that moves so quickly it seems to disappear in the air.

"Fancy toy," Derek remarks, ducking out of its way. "But it won't save you."

I choose my moment, diving into the fray to help Derek out.

Our weapons meet in a storm of sparks.

"You're the new Guardian," the vampire observes, his chain whipping toward me.

"You've done your homework." I jump away from his chain a second before it can turn my brain into mush.

That was close.

Too close.

Derek, however, isn't as lucky.

The chain connects with his shoulder, creating a wound so deep that he whimpers and shifts back to his human form. His blood pools into a puddle on the floor. Luckily, it wasn't a fatal strike, which means the wound will heal.

But he's losing blood quickly.

This is on me now.

The vampire turns back to me and snarls. He tries using another burst of wind to unbalance me, but I dig deep, drawing on my earth magic to ground myself.

Shift, my wolf urges, but I have to trust my instincts.

I catch the vampire's blade with my own, and with a calculated flick of my wrist, I make sure that the chain does more than clash with my dagger.

Instead, it wraps around it.

"You can't win, Guardian," the vampire hisses, his face inches from mine, the scent of fresh blood on his breath.

"I already have."

I twist the dagger in my hand, using the vampire's own chain against him, yanking him forward.

He stumbles, and that split second is all I need to pin him down and slam my dagger into his chest to pierce his heart.

His eyes widen in surprise, and he turns to ash beneath me.

One second he's there. The next, *poof*.

Gone.

The rush of adrenaline is unlike anything I've ever experienced in my life.

Because I did it. I killed a vampire.

It's what I've been trained for—what I've been waiting to do for as long as I can remember. And now that I've done it, it's like a weight has been lifted off my shoulders.

I'm ready to take on anything thrown into my path.

Maria, meanwhile, has the first vampire subdued. With a swift, merciless move, she ends him with a clamp of her jaws around his neck.

His head rolls to the floor. When it stops, his face is toward me, and his eyes blink.

Actually *blink*.

Then he turns to ash.

I stare at the dust for a moment. I already knew that decapitated heads stay alive for a few seconds after being split from their body, but learning it and *seeing* it are different things entirely.

I'm looking forward to seeing many, *many* more of those monsters face the last seconds of their existence for the rest of the time I serve as a Guardian. Meaning, for the rest of my life.

Derek's standing up now, his wound fully healed, grinning despite his disheveled state. "Hell of a first kill, Connor."

Maria approaches, nodding in agreement. "I've seen lots of fights, but taking down a vamp in human form for your first kill? That's impressive."

"It's a small space, and I'm good with a blade." I wipe it clean, sheathe it back inside my jacket, and glance at the chain weapon near my feet. "Haven't fought against one of those before though."

"If you want it, you can take it," she says. "He's certainly not using it anymore."

I shake my head. "No, thanks. It's not my style."

I've had my dagger for years, and I'm not parting with it anytime soon.

"Suit yourself." Maria shrugs and takes the weapon, a dangerous gleam in her eyes as she studies it up close.

As she does, I pull my phone out of my pocket and check it.

There's a missed FaceTime from an unknown number, and a text message a minute later.

Call back ASAP. I have important information about your mate's parents.

"Something wrong?" Derek asks.

"Nothing," I say quickly. "I'm going to walk back. Alone. Need some air after my first kill."

He takes a second to size me up. "All right," he says. "Whatever you want."

As I thought. Even though I'm new here, I'm still Jax's grandson. I'm still the future alpha of the Pine Valley pack. They're not going to fight me on this—or on anything.

As if on cue, the next train arrives at the station.

Perfect timing.

Derek gives me a single nod, and he and Maria get on board. She watches me carefully, as if she's hoping I'll change my mind and go back with them, but I stay put.

The doors shut, the train pulls out, and I head up the steps to the street. As I emerge aboveground, the weight of the message on my phone feels like a brick in my pocket.

I need a quiet corner, away from prying eyes, where I can return the call.

And I hope to the moon above that whoever's on the other end has genuine information and isn't leading me into a trap. Because if there's a chance I can help Ruby, even from afar, then there's not a question in my mind that I'm going to take it.

Connor

THE COLD WIND rushes around me as I find a dark, quiet residential street lined with brownstones to make the call.

The person on the other end picks up halfway through the first ring. A woman who looks to be in her early twenties, with sun-streaked hair and green eyes flecked with gold.

I've never seen her before in my life.

"Connor?" She keeps her voice low, and it's full of urgency.

"Who are you?"

"I'm Morgan." She shifts uncomfortably, as if embarrassed. "I'm a witch. I know your mate. She might have told you about me when you were in the fae realm…?"

"She did," I say. "You're one of the blood witches. You're in Spring Creek with her right now."

"I am."

"How did you get my number?"

"I found it on Hazel's phone," she explains. "She's always leaving it places around the house, and I've seen what her password is, so it was easy to get into it and grab your number."

That's how Thalia got my number, too.

Even though Hazel's a powerful witch, she's still a sixteen-year-old girl who leaves her phone around the house. It's not surprising in the least.

"What do you know about Ruby's parents?" I ask, bringing us back to the point.

"Last night at dinner, I accidentally touched Ruby, and I got a feeling that I needed to use my magic to scry for something about her," she starts, and I remember what Ruby told me about Morgan—that she can use her blood to see the future. "I was able to get away for a bit tonight to do it."

A chill passes through the air, and I stand straighter, more on guard. "What did you see?"

"It's about Jax." Morgan's voice trembles. "He's planning on killing Ruby's parents."

"What?" The words hit me like a freight train. "Where? When?"

"Tomorrow night," she says. "Naples, Florida. I'll text you the exact address."

"Thank you," I say. "But I have to ask—why are you helping me?"

"I like Ruby." Darkness crosses Morgan's eyes, and she takes a deep breath. "But there's more to it. You see, when I was younger, my parents were killed."

My heart stops for a beat. "What happened?"

"They were killed by other witches." Morgan's voice cracks, and I see the grief in her eyes. It's a pain I know well, given the deaths of my parents when I was a baby. "They were our parents' closest friends. When they found out we were blood witches, they tried to kill us, too. My parents died protecting me and my sisters."

"I'm so sorry, Morgan."

It's one thing *knowing* your parents were killed.

But seeing it happen in front of your eyes...

That's a pain I wouldn't wish on anyone. Not even on Tristan.

Well, *maybe* not on Tristan.

"We managed to survive." She looks away for a second, her eyes shimmering with unshed tears, then turns back to me. "And my sisters killed our parents' murderers. I was there. I saw it. I wouldn't wish that on anyone."

"You and me both."

I can't smell lies unless I'm physically with someone. But my gut tells me to trust Morgan.

So does mine, my wolf chimes in.

With that, my decision's final.

"I'm in the city right now, but I have my car with me," I tell her. "I'll leave now."

"No," she says, her eyes wide. "Jax left last night. Driving won't get you there in time. You have to fly."

My chest tightens. Flying is about as far from the ground as we can get, so because of our earth magic, shifters stay as far from planes as possible.

"The flights don't leave until early tomorrow morning," I say, staying calm despite my panic.

"It's three thirty in the morning," she says. "By the time you're at the airport—go to JFK—you should be able to catch the six fifteen flight out of there."

"You looked it up already?"

"Of course I did," she balks, as if offended. "I always plan for the future."

"Right," I mutter. "Divination."

"Exactly."

"Thanks, Morgan," I say, and I feel a shared connection with her—the type you only feel when you've experienced a similar tragedy.

"Anytime," she says. "Good luck."

The call ends, and Morgan's words echo in my head.

Flying. A plane.

The thought churns my stomach, but there's no time for hesitation. I can't fail Ruby.

We won't *fail Ruby*, my wolf thinks.

I hurry to a busier street where the headlights of cars flash by, quickly spotting an available taxi. Heart pounding, I step as far out into the sidewalk as I can manage without getting run over, stick my arm out, and the taxi slows down.

"Airport," I say as I slide into the back seat. "JFK. Hurry."

The driver's eyes narrow, concern etched on his face. "I'll get you there as fast as I can."

"Appreciate it."

The buildings pass in a blur, and my wolf paces inside me, uneasy with the thought of flying but also understanding the necessity of it.

"Managed to shave fifteen minutes off the ride for you," the driver says as he pulls up to the terminal. "Good luck."

"Thanks." I hand him the fare in cash, plus a lot extra. "I mean it."

He nods, understanding in his eyes. "Whatever you're doing, be safe."

"I will," I say, and then I race into the terminal, ready to do anything it takes to stop Jax from doing something unthinkable to the parents of my mate.

Even if it means changing the entire pack order as we know it.

Connor

THE PLANE TOUCHES down in Florida mid-morning, and the drive in the rental car toward the address Morgan provided is a blur.

Finally, I arrive.

It's an abandoned warehouse so far away from the main area of town that it's basically in a swamp.

I swallow down a lump in my throat.

Because this is bad. Really, really bad. I can't shake the feeling that I'm about to walk into the set of a horror movie.

I park far enough away that there's no risk of being heard, then circle around the warehouse, searching for an entrance. A loose window eventually catches my eye, and I pry it open with careful precision. There's no room for error here.

The smell of sweat, blood, and something metallic fills the air as I slip inside, and I prowl in the direction it's coming from, going utterly still as I take in the scene before me.

Jax is there, his back to me, and what he's done makes my stomach turn and my fists clench.

Ruby's parents, who I recognize from photos, are strapped to rickety wood chairs. The rope cuts into their flesh where it binds their arms and legs, preventing escape, and their faces are twisted in pain. Their eyes are bloodshot and swollen, their hair matted with sweat, blood, and grime. Jax has ripped half their fingernails off, and there are so many tiny cuts on their bodies that it looks like the start of a horrific impressionist painting on their skin.

But, most impressively, even though they're in pain, they don't look broken.

The sight before me would make most people sick. Not me. I've studied the art of torture. It's part of our training as Guardians.

It's a great way to get information out of your enemies when you need it badly enough.

But it's not being used right now to get information from a soulless vampire, or another enemy who needs to be stopped. It's being used to get information from Ruby's very human mom and dad. And I'm going stop Jax from going any further, no matter what it takes.

He paces in front of them, dagger in hand.

"Oh, you'll talk, Xavier," he says, his voice dripping with malice. "You'll admit to the truth about who you are. About what you did that night in the caves."

Xavier.

I don't understand.

Ruby's dad's name is Kevin.

Xavier is the name of the man who killed my parents and grandmother. I've seen Xavier's picture before. This man isn't him. He *is* Kevin. And the woman is Ruby's mom, Jane.

Has Jax lost his mind?

Kevin's deep brown eyes are filled with defiance. "Never," he says, his voice strained but firm.

Jane's glaring at Jax like she wants to kill him with her bare hands. From the ferocity in her gaze, I might actually believe she could.

As I lurk in the shadows, my mind races, working through scenarios, strategizing my intervention. Rushing in without a plan could be fatal. Not only to me, but also to Ruby's parents. I need to be smart, precise, and most of all, silent.

Jax saunters over to Ruby's mom with a maniacal grin on his face.

I've never seen him like this before. Yes, he's an alpha. He's commanding. He's strong, powerful, and a force to be reckoned with.

But he's always, *always* in control.

Not now. There's a gleam in his eyes right now that makes him look possessed. Like he's no better than the vampires we hunt.

He moves closer to Ruby's mom, dagger raised. "You ran," he snarls. "You could have stayed and fought until the end, but you ran."

Instead of replying, she bucks back into the chair with so much strength that it slams back into the floor.

Her head smacks onto the concrete, and her body goes limp.

It doesn't deter Jax. He saunters over to her, kneels next to her, and uses his dagger to carve a line into her cheek.

She comes to and gasps for air, as if breaking through to the surface after minutes underwater.

"You killed them." Jax lowers his face to hers so there's only an inch between them. *"Admit it."*

He puts so much alpha willpower in that last part that even I feel the waves of it cross my skin.

My hand tightens around the handle of my dagger—which, thanks to the fact that it was forged with magic by witches, made it through airport security. My muscles are coiled like a spring.

Jax's back is toward me. The time to strike is now.

Kevin's eyes dart to me, widen slightly, and then narrow, understanding flashing through them. A silent communication passes between us—an unspoken promise that I'm going to help them out of this.

I step forward.

"Jax!" I roar, my voice echoing through the warehouse. "Step away from them. *Now."*

He flinches, and I suddenly realize what I've done.

Alpha willpower.

It's in my voice. Barely. But it's there.

Slowly, he stands and turns to face me.

His eyes, once filled with authority and wisdom, now dance with madness.

What *happened* to him?

"You shouldn't be here," he growls. "Get out."

"They're Ruby's parents. They're human. They have nothing to do with any of this." I keep my eyes fixed on his, my body poised to move. "Let them go."

"Human?" He throws his head back and laughs. "Your mate is a shifter with demon magic. You really think her parents could possibly be *human?*"

"The witches checked them out." I somehow remain calm and steady even though he's looking at me like he wants to run his dagger through my stomach. "They're human."

"Lies!" he yells, but then he quickly gathers himself together. "You don't understand, Connor. You don't know what they've done. They're imposters. Murderers. These are the people who killed your parents. They're Xavier and Abigail. Betrayers of our pack."

Ruby's mom struggles against her restraints and twists her head to look in my direction.

My stomach drops at the look in her eyes.

Guilt.

But no. It doesn't add up. It doesn't make sense.

I return my focus to Jax, who's watching me, waiting for my reaction.

"Xavier and Abigail are dead," I say slowly. "You killed them that night."

"He didn't." Ruby's dad chuckles—a low, hollow sound. "We ran, and he didn't try to stop us."

My blood runs cold, and Jax's face turns a shade paler, his eyes widening.

"I don't understand," I say, to Jax, to Ruby's parents—to all of them.

Kevin's eyes fix on mine, hard and unflinching. "He's right. We're Xavier and Abigail. We had our magic stripped. We changed our names and our lives to leave behind the world that believed my sister had to die for choosing love and becoming a vampire. I didn't agree with her decision, but she had the right to make it without being *killed* for it."

The words hang in the air, thick and heavy, choking the breath from my lungs.

"You're lying," I finally manage. "You're playing a trick to save yourselves."

"It's the truth," Ruby's mom says. "We never wanted to kill your parents or your grandmother, but they were going to kill us. We did what we had to do to get out of that cave alive."

"No." My world tilts off its axis, and I pray for them to *stop*. To take it back. To say they're lying.

"We fought for Jessica," Xavier continues. "They wanted to execute her for her choices. We had to protect her. We failed, but we survived. We left the supernatural world and haven't looked back since."

"But you don't look like them. Like Abigail and Xavier."

"After the witch stripped their magic, a goddess changed their forms," Jax fills me in. "A moon goddess with illusion magic. The one who star touched Ruby. These people are Abigail and Xavier. They killed your parents. They killed my wife. They deserve to die."

He's telling the truth.

The room falls into a tense silence as I look into the eyes of the people who killed my family.

They're Ruby's parents, my wolf whispers in my head. *Don't allow our mate to experience the same pain you've felt for your entire life. Don't make her pay for her parents' mistakes.*

Ruby's face flashes through my mind.

She's done so much to fight for her family, to get them to remember her. Her parents are everything to her.

If I don't stop Jax from getting his revenge, it will break her.

"They're murderers, Connor," Jax insists. "They're going to pay for what they've done."

No, my wolf thinks. *We can't allow this.*

"They've paid," I reply, heavy with resignation. "Look at them, Jax. They've been hiding for years, stripped of their wolves and their magic, their lives destroyed. They're weak. They're *human*. They can't heal from their injuries, they can't escape from these chairs, and they can't defend themselves against supernaturals. That's punishment enough. Some might say it's worse than death."

Jax's face contorts with rage, and the earth shakes slightly beneath his feet. "No," he says, taking a step closer. "It's not enough. Not after what they did."

"It is enough." I stand steady, holding my ground.

"They killed our family," he repeats, as if I didn't hear him all the other times. "And you're defending them?"

I tighten my grip on the dagger, my heart pounding. "I'm defending *Ruby*. She had nothing to do with any of this, and she's my mate. You know what that means. I have to protect her."

His lips curl into a sneer. "Ruby's tainted, Connor," he says. "Her magic is dark, devil's magic. And whatever magic transformed her parents' appearance is the same. You've been blinded by the mate bond. You won't see clearly until it's broken."

His words cut through me like a knife, but I stand my ground. "And how do you plan on breaking it? By killing her?"

Jax's eyes flash with something cold and calculating. "If that's what it takes."

"You wouldn't."

"She'll never be a member of our pack," he says, his eyes burning with hatred. "But I'm going to kill these two first. Like I should have all those years ago."

Every nerve in my body goes on high alert. Because with those final words of his, the challenge I've been contemplating is inevitable.

If I don't do it, he's going to kill my mate.

And so, my voice is firm and unwavering as I speak the words that will change everything.

"Then I challenge you, Jax. I challenge you for your position as alpha."

Connor

THE WORDS HANG in the air, and Jax smirks, as if I'm twelve years old again and am reaching too high, too quickly.

Then his expression hardens.

"You really want to do this, Connor?"

His question is mocking, but I know him well enough to hear the undertone of surprise.

"I do," I reply. "I have no choice. You threatened to kill my mate, and therefore, are forcing my hand with this."

He circles around me, sizing me up, as if he's seeing me for the first time.

I'm not his grandson anymore.

I'm his opponent. His enemy.

And I will win. Whether that's from getting him to forfeit, or from doing the unthinkable, I *will* win this.

Preferably the former. The thought of anything else makes a sickness rise in my throat that I know I'll never be able to recover from.

I take a quick glance at Ruby's parents. Her mom's eyes look tired. Her head slammed too hard against the ground, and she might have a concussion. Her dad's eyes are narrowed at Jax, as if he'd kill him himself if he wasn't bound to the chair.

A wave of disgust passes over me. But, seeing them in such a weakened state gives me a sense of satisfaction.

They've paid, my words to Jax from earlier repeat in my mind. *They're weak. They've been human for twenty years. They're not our enemy anymore.*

The thought calms me and helps me focus on the true task at hand.

Making sure Jax is unable to set the entire Pine Valley pack on a mission to kill my mate. If I'm alpha, I'll be able to use alpha willpower on him to stand down. Plus, it'll be as unnatural for him to kill his alpha's mate as it would be to kill his alpha. Just like how Ruby's parents couldn't bring themselves to kill him back in those caves.

He snarls, baring his teeth, his power pulsing around him. But the challenge has begun. His alpha willpower can't influence me until it's finished.

I'm on my own now. No safety net, and no going back.

Let's do this, my wolf thinks, and his determination fills me, empowering me.

I take a moment to size Jax up as a true opponent.

He's bigger than I am. Physically stronger. Not by much, but we both know he is.

However, I'm faster, in both human and wolf forms. I'm better at using earth magic than he is.

I can—and will—use that to my advantage.

I lunge forward and shift in the air, claws extended, aiming for Jax's throat. But I can tell as I do that my angle is off. It'll hurt him, but not kill him.

Dodging my attack with ease, he spins around and delivers a powerful kick to my side, sending me flying.

I hit the ground hard.

The impact knocks the air out of my lungs, but I gasp for breath and get back on my feet.

Jax circles around me, a cruel smile on his face. "Is that all you've got?" he taunts. "I thought you were better than this."

He hasn't even bothered to shift into wolf form. That's how confident he is that he's going to win.

I bare my teeth at him and growl.

He laughs—a dark, menacing sound. "You're a fool, Connor. You've always thought you're better than you are. I supported you—encouraged you, even—but look where it led you. Your arrogance is going to get you killed."

The words sting, but I push the hurt away. He's trying to rattle me.

I won't let him.

So, I charge at him again, this time using my earth magic to connect with the stone floor, so it gives me more power to propel myself toward him.

I connect with him before he has a chance to react. My claws dig into his flesh, and his blood dampens my fur.

He grunts in pain and answers with a fierce blow with his knee that sends me flying once more.

He follows me, shifting into his wolf form as he does. He's bigger than I am—a massive, dark-furred beast with power emanating from every muscle. His eyes, a deep, unyielding blue, fixate on me with predatory intent.

Doubt crawls over my skin, but I push it down.

I can't afford doubt. Not now.

We circle each other. His growls are deep, resonating in his chest, his teeth gleaming with menace.

He wants to kill me.

I lunge again, but he's ready. Our bodies collide with a bone-jarring force, teeth snapping, claws tearing. He's relentless, powerful, each of his blows threatening to end me.

I fight back with all I've got, but it's not enough.

He gets me in a hold, his jaws closing around my neck. The pain is searing and blinding, but it's the cold, calculated look in his eyes that terrifies me more.

I'm losing.

No, my wolf growls, and Ruby's face flashes through my mind. The electricity that crackled between us when we kissed, and the strength she showed during every single one of those trials.

Once I'm alpha of the Pine Valley pack, I'm going to show her that the conniving vampire doesn't deserve even a sliver of her heart.

I twist free from Jax's grip and stagger back, gasping, blood dripping from my wounds. My body screams in protest, but I can't stop.

I won't stop.

"Shift back!" Ruby's dad calls to me. "He used a lot of magic when he was trying to show off to us. Enough to weaken his power. Use it against him."

I can't believe it.

Xavier Hightower is trying to help me.

On my flight here, I imagined a bunch of ways this rescue mission could go down. *This* certainly wasn't something that crossed my mind.

But he's right. I have to shift back into human form. I can use my earth magic more effectively that way.

With a growl that tears through my body, I shift, my body morphing and twisting, pain lacing through me.

It doesn't last long. Because my magic surges, connecting with the stone floor, grounding me as my injuries start to heal.

Jax pauses, his wolf eyes narrowing.

He charges, but this time, I'm ready.

I call upon my earth magic, digging deeper than ever before, and a wall of jagged rocks erupts from the stone floor to block his path.

He snarls and tries to break through it. But I control the rocks, making them sharper and more resilient. They cut into his pelt, leaving deep gashes that slow him down.

He howls in pain.

The ground around him trembles. He's trying to loosen my rocks, but I hold on tight, not letting him use his magic to overpower mine.

He shifts back into human form, his eyes wild with rage. "You can't defeat me," he snarls.

"I can, and I will."

He raises his hands to loosen the rocks from the ground again.

This time, I let him.

He smiles with glee. "Not as strong as you thought, are you?"

I don't reply.

Instead, I throw out my magic, reach with it for the rocks he thinks he's controlling, and send them flying toward him.

They crash into him all at once and force him to the ground, beaten and broken.

Not wanting to waste any time—every second is a moment longer he has time to heal—I hurry toward him, my hand clenched around my dagger.

I spring forward, blade raised, and drive it deep into his chest.

It pierces his flesh and sinks in up to the hilt.

The scent of his blood fills my senses. It's metal coating my throat, the smell traveling to the bottom of my lungs.

I'm close. The blade is a millimeter away from pressing into his heart. One tiny motion, and I can end this.

I can be alpha of the Pine Valley pack.

I can make sure Ruby's safe. Forever.

"Do it," Xavier urges. "End him."

But as I look into Jax's eyes—the man who raised me and taught me everything I know—it's clearer to me than ever that I can't follow through with this. I'll never be able to live with myself if I do.

Sweat dampens his brow, dripping down his face.

"You're not the only one of us with a mate," he says slowly, breathing through the pain.

"What are you talking about?" I wiggle the dagger a bit, reminding him that if he tries even one thing against me—if he so much as *moves*—then he's dead.

"Your grandmother and I loved each other, but we weren't true mates." He smiles knowingly, confident that what he's going to say next will change my world as I know it. "I know who my mate is now. We completed our bond on the night you skipped town to join the Guardians."

"Who?"

"I think you know *exactly* who I'm talking about."

"No." Sickness fills me to the core. I knew there was something going on between them—some sort of twisted fantasy of theirs—but *mates*?

He's perfectly still, watching me as I put it together, and it's clear he's not going to be the one to say it.

"You and Autumn," I say slowly, keeping the dagger buried in place as I do.

"I knew you were a smart one."

The way he continues to taunt me when I have a blade to his literal heart amazes me.

"You love her," he continues, his breaths slow and level. "Maybe not the way you love a mate, and I know you're angry at her for her betrayal, but you've known each other for your entire lives. A part of you will always love her. Do you really want to be the one responsible for killing her mate? For doing the exact same thing to her that she tried to do to you?"

I don't want him to be right.

But despite everything, I will always be tied to Autumn—even though I'm leaving those ties in the past. She was my first kiss. The woman I lost my virginity to. The one who supported me through thick and thin, until Ruby flashed into my life like a bolt of lightning and the love I felt for Autumn became a distant star. A star that likely died long ago without me even realizing it.

I don't forgive her. I never will. But I know what it feels like to have a mate, and I don't wish the hollow pain that comes with their death on anyone.

More than that—I will never be cold enough to kill my own kin.

But I can't let Jax know that.

And, thanks to how shallow he needs breathe to stop my blade from piercing his heart, he can't take a deep enough breath to smell my lie.

"Forfeit your alpha power and give it to me," I demand, poking his heart with the tip of my blade for added measure. "Then you live. Refuse, and you die, here and now."

He stares at me, hard, his face a mix of emotions.

I don't back down.

Then, something within him shifts.

"I forfeit my alpha magic." Hatred shines in his eyes as he speaks. "Take it from me now and do with it as you will."

Connor

JAX'S ALPHA magic surges into me, filling every crevice of my being with a raw, untamed energy. It's a jolt of electricity running through my veins, and while it's not exactly painful, it's something else.

Overwhelming.

I feel the strength, the dominance, and the leadership that comes with it. The power feels endless. Like a storm I have to wrangle under control.

Luckily, I've always been in control.

Managing this power is basically second nature to me.

The final bits of Jax's alpha magic leave him, and the fire in his eyes dims.

It's done.

I withdraw the dagger, my hand surprisingly steady. It's coated in blood. So, in a move of dominance, I use Jax's shirt to wipe it clean.

He brings his hands to the wound on his chest, which is already starting to stitch itself together.

"You've won," he says, his voice low and empty of the arrogance it held less than five minutes ago. "You're the alpha now. I hope you're ready for it."

"I've always been ready." I'm surer of it than anything else in my life.

He laughs, but there's no humor in it. "We'll see, Connor. Being an alpha isn't just about power. It's about making decisions that affect the lives of the entire pack. Decisions that can mean life or death. It makes you do things that you previously thought were unthinkable."

"Like being willing to kill my own kin?" I sheathe my blade and stand up. "Because for the record, I wouldn't have done it. Not now, and not ever."

I look down at him and his wound finishes healing, the raw power of the alpha magic pulsing through me.

I've never looked down at Jax in my life.

And, right now, I can't stand the sight of him.

"Get out," I command, pushing alpha willpower into my words. It comes naturally, like a muscle I've been dying to flex for my entire life. "And don't do anything that might harm Ruby. Ever."

He stands, but his body trembles, more sweat beading on his forehead as he fights the force of my command.

"You can't control me," he says, although from the way he curls his fingers into fists as he tries to resist, I'd beg to differ.

"I said *get out.*" It's like a mix of my wolf and me speaking at the same time, and my head buzzes from all the power I'm pushing out.

Jax's face twists in pain and anger, but finally, he stumbles back. "This isn't over, Connor," he snarls. "I promise you that."

Then, with one last hateful glare, he turns and leaves.

If he was in wolf form, his tail would be behind his legs.

Dizziness rushes through me, and I close my eyes for a few seconds, breathing deeply to center myself.

I guess alpha willpower is harder to use than I thought. Or maybe it's the rebound from the magic I expended in the fight against Jax.

It's probably both.

"A little help here?" a woman says from nearby—Ruby's mom.

Abigail Hightower.

The resentment I feel toward her and Xavier forces its way to the surface, but I push it down. All of this will be for nothing if I lose my temper on them now.

I untie their restraints—Abigail first, then Xavier. Their injuries look painful, but they'll live. Jax was calculated enough in his torture methods that he hadn't done anything fatal before I arrived.

After they're both free, they rush to each other's sides, checking each other over to make sure the other is okay.

Eventually, they turn back to me.

"You have every right to want us dead," Xavier finally says. "Thank you for showing mercy. You're a true leader, and you're going to be a fine alpha for the Pine Valley pack."

"I didn't do it for you," I say steadily. "I did it for your daughter. Ruby. My mate."

Abigail leans into her husband, unsteady from her head injury. "I think you have us mistaken for someone else," she says. "We don't have a daughter."

"You do." I don't bother with alpha willpower. I'm too exhausted, and they need to believe this for themselves—not because I forced them to. "She's a shifter, like you two used to be. She's my mate. You raised her human, but she shifted for the first time on her nineteenth birthday, while on vacation in Pine Valley. We brought her into the pack while we tried to figure out her heritage, but when the witches investigated you, they determined you were human."

"Because we *are* human," Xavier says. "At least, we are now."

"I obviously see that." It takes everything in me to not completely snap at him. "The witches did, too. But they decided that Ruby's magic made it too dangerous for her to return to the supernatural world, so they did a spell to erase her existence from human minds."

"A spell that strong is impossible," Abigail says.

"Not for this coven of witches," I continue.

"No," she says. "We'd know if we had a daughter."

"You wouldn't. Not even if you saw her, which, you did. She went with a witch and two vampires to your restaurant while you were both there, so they could prove to her that you didn't remember her."

Quickly, I tell them what Ruby, Hazel, Tristan, and Benjamin look like.

Recognition dawns in Abigail's eyes.

"I know who you're talking about," she says. "But I'd never seen any of them until that afternoon."

"Because the spell made you forget her existence..." I run my fingers through my hair, frustrated.

Time to try another angle.

And so, I search my mind for something—anything—that might help them realize I'm telling the truth.

"Strawberry pie," I say quickly, and Ruby's mother flinches, as though it means something to her. "When Ruby was eight years old, she picked strawberries from your garden on Christmas Day. You baked them into a pie for her. Then, you took the pie to the beach and ate it under the moonlight."

She blinks, confusion swirling in her eyes.

"We *did* do that for Christmas about a decade ago," she says slowly. "But it was just the two of us. I picked the berries. I baked the pie."

"You did bake the pie," I say. "But *Ruby* picked the berries."

Abigail glances at Xavier in question, but I continue before they can fight me further.

"Then there was the sandcastle and the conch shell," I say, remembering the story Ruby told us right after we hopped onto the boat, before the first trial began. "You were on the beach making sandcastles, and she found a conch shell. You told her that she could speak to the ocean through the shell. She asked the ocean to tell her its favorite color."

Abigail stills in surprise.

"And then a beam of light came through the clouds, reflecting a variety of colors," she continues with a far off look, as if she's seeing it happening again.

"Ruby said that the ocean should be allowed to have only one favorite color." I smile at the thought of a young Ruby thinking she could tell nature what it should and shouldn't be allowed to do. "Then you said—"

"The ocean, like the earth, doesn't have one favorite color. It loves and appreciates all of them, because its beauty lies in its diversity, just like all the colors in our world."

Connor

Relief and amazement rush through me. "You remember."

"I remember that day," she says sadly. "But it was just me and Xavier on the beach. I found the conch shell. He told me to ask the ocean a question. I asked what its favorite color was, Xavier said it was only allowed one favorite color, and then I answered him about how it loves every color because it appreciates the diversity of the world."

"That's not true." I'm so frustrated that it takes all my effort to not put alpha willpower into my voice to force them to believe me. "*Ruby* found the shell. *Ruby* asked the question."

"I believe you," Xavier suddenly says.

"What?" I'm happy, but at the same time, I wasn't anticipating him to say that.

"Abigail and I were the only ones there—at least, as far as we remember. You have no way of knowing the details about that day," he continues. "Yet, you do. Same with Christmas and the pie."

Abigail's eyes widen, and she looks from Xavier to me, her face pale.

"You weren't the only ones there," I press on, finally feeling like I'm getting somewhere. "But with the magic of the witches erasing Ruby from your memories, you simply replaced her with yourselves."

Abigail shakes her head, tears welling in her eyes. "But how? Yes, witches can compel people with their flames. But to erase someone's existence… it's impossible."

"It is with *these* witches," I say, and then I proceed to tell them everything I know about the Blood Coven.

They listen quietly as they take it all in.

"They want Ruby to help them use the Key of Hades, and eventually, to join their coven," I finish. "They're using the fact that they can restore your memories of her as leverage."

"Who, exactly, are they trying to raise with the Key of Hades?" Xavier asks cautiously.

"I don't know," I admit. "But your daughter needs you. And I need her."

Silence fills the room as Xavier and Abigail absorb the enormity of what I'm telling them.

Finally, Abigail takes a shaky breath. "How can we help?" she asks, and relief fills me to the core at having gotten through to them.

"You need to remember Ruby," I say. "She needs her parents."

A tear escapes her eye, and she wipes it away quickly. "I want to. But it feels like grasping at smoke. How can I remember something that's been erased?"

"Vampires," Xavier suddenly says.

My guard goes up immediately, especially because I know they're both vampire sympathizers. "What about them?"

"You specified that the witches only erased memories of Ruby from the non-supernatural world. From humans."

"I did." I hold his gaze, waiting for him to continue.

"If we become vampires, we may be able to remember Ruby." His voice shakes slightly, and I can tell he's struggling with the idea, but he keeps going. "Plus, with the air magic they possess, we'd have the strength to fight back against the Blood Coven. Because let's face it—we're no good to Ruby as humans."

"And becoming a vampire is the only way to go from human to supernatural," Abigail finishes his thought.

"Exactly." He gives her a single nod, as if it's already decided.

I don't like it.

Not one bit.

"But that means giving up your humanity," I tell them—as if they don't already know.

"We spent time with Jessica when she was a vampire," Xavier says, firm with resolve. "She was still herself. Her soul wasn't lost. It's why we fought for her."

He doesn't say it outright, but the meaning behind his words is there.

It's why they killed for her.

I cringe inwardly at the fact that their *fighting for her* was the same thing as their *killing my family*.

"It's true." Abigail bites her lower lip, thinking. "We've always known it's an option if something happened that made it too dangerous for us to be human. It's not one I like, but given that we turned against our own kind to defend a vampire, they have a good reason to listen to our request."

"That's true," I agree, since while I don't love the idea any more than she does, their logic is far from faulty.

Plus, if turning into vampires will make them remember Ruby and make it easier for them to help her, then I'm all for it.

"There are six more nights until the full moon, when the Blood Coven can use the Key of Hades to unlock the veil between our two worlds," I tell them. "As you're well-aware, the uptown clan in the city has an alliance with the Pine Valley pack. I can bring you to them. Given that I'm now the alpha of the pack, they'll have to hear us out."

A shared understanding settles in the room.

"We'll need to move quickly," Xavier says. "We'll fly to NYC and go to them tonight."

"But your injuries…" I look them up and down, taking in the bloodied cuts, the bruises, the ripped-off fingernails. "They're going to draw attention in the airport."

"We have an emergency fund," he says. "Enough to fly private. Given our history, we've always known it might be necessary someday."

"Very sensible," I say, since it might be the highest level compliment I'm willing to give the two of them.

And even though I want to hate them, I see their resolve—their need to fight for a daughter they don't even remember, and for a world they tried to leave behind. It fills me with both admiration and a strange kind of hope.

I extend my hand to Xavier, and he shakes it firmly. "We'll do this together," I tell him. "We'll save Ruby, and we'll stop the Blood Coven."

He nods, his eyes glinting with determination. "Together. And Connor?"

"Yes?"

"I may not remember our daughter. But I do know that no matter what happens, I'm proud that she's able to call you her mate."

Connor

We soon find ourselves on a private jet, bound for New York City.

I help Abigail and Xavier clean up from Jax's abuse as best as we can. We can't risk there being any fresh blood on them when we go to the vampires. Abigail then spends the remainder of the flight gazing out the window as she ices the bump on the back of her head, while Xavier and I pore over every piece of information we have on the Blood Coven.

Eventually, the bright lights of the city at night come into view. Despite my hatred of flying, there's no denying that the city from above is beautiful. From here, I can see it all. Downtown Manhattan, where the Guardians live—where we defend the city against rogue vampires who find joy in pushing our limits until we have no choice but to stop them in the best way we know how.

Then there's uptown, with its sparkling skyscrapers built around the massive dark rectangle of Central Park. One of the tallest skyscrapers directly south of the park is home to the uptown clan. They're the "civilized" vampires—if any of them can be considered such a thing.

Upon landing, we call for a car and head straight to the uptown clan's luxury high-rise building. The Fairmont. The place reeks of opulence, the air smells cold and sterile, and I can't help the twinge of discomfort as the doorman opens the door for us and we enter the marble-floored lobby. It's too clean, too shiny, and too quiet.

It feels more like a museum than an actual home.

We approach the receptionist, a vampire with pale skin and light gray eyes, who arches an eyebrow at our appearance.

"May I help you?" she asks.

I meet her gaze straight-on. "We're here to speak with Damien."

"And you are?"

"Connor Ward, alpha of the Pine Valley pack," I reply, my voice steady. "And these are Xavier and Abigail, known allies to your clan."

She narrows her eyes at me. "The alpha of the Pine Valley pack is *Jax* Ward," she says. "You're his grandson."

"The alpha of the pack *was* Jax Ward." I gather as much alpha willpower as I can, pushing it into my tone. "As of this afternoon, I'm the new alpha. Tell Damien that I'm here to see him, and that it cannot wait."

Her eyes widen, and she picks up the phone, murmuring something into the receiver.

"Very well," she says. "Please, make yourself comfortable. You'll be escorted upstairs in a few minutes."

As we wait for our escort, tension crackles in the air. Abigail paces back and forth, while Xavier appears calm and collected. I, on the other hand, channel my inner alpha, making sure to appear as confident and in control as ever.

Finally, a tall, muscular vampire dressed in an impeccably tailored suit arrives to escort us to Damien's apartment. He says nothing as he takes us into the elevator and presses the button for the penthouse.

A penthouse. So high up that it can literally be in the clouds.

Breathe.

I can do this.

My ears pop as we whoosh up faster than I imagined could physically be possible. Then the elevator doors slide open, and we're greeted by a sleek, modern penthouse with high ceilings and floor-to-ceiling windows overlooking the park.

Damien Fairmont stands at the far end of the room, his icy blue eyes regarding us intently. He's dressed in a tailored suit that probably costs more than the chartered flight from Florida to New York, making him look like he's stepped right off a fashion show runway—not like someone who's been alive for centuries.

"Connor," he greets, his voice calm but authoritative, with the sort of aristocratic accent expected from a vampire turned in England centuries ago. "I hear you're now the alpha of the Pine Valley pack?"

"I am."

His eyes flick to Abigail and Xavier, a hint of curiosity in his gaze.

"You brought humans with you," he says simply. "An offering to show that the alliance between my clan and your pack will continue under your leadership?"

"Something of the sort," I say, since I suppose it could be spun that way.

"Very well. I see we have much to discuss." He walks to a long, sleek buffet bar at the side of the room, opens a bottle of what appears to be a very expensive liquor, and pours himself a drink. "Would any of you care for a drink? Or perhaps something more fitting for the shifter and human palate?"

"I'll have what you're having," I say, remembering my training. It's polite to accept a drink when in the presence of an ally, especially in the supernatural world. A refusal could be seen as a slight. "Xavier, Abigail?"

Xavier nods. "Beer, if you have it. A lager."

"Wine for me, please," Abigail chimes in.

Damien selects the bottles with care, then pours our drinks and hands them to us with a slight nod. "To alliances," he says, lifting his glass.

"To alliances," we echo, clinking our glasses together.

With the formalities observed, we settle into the plush seating area, drinks in hand.

"So, Connor," Damien begins. "It seems you have much to share."

His message is clear.

Tell him everything I know, or…

I'm not sure I want to know the end of that sentence. I'm a brand-new alpha who just almost killed my own grandfather for the title, then marched into the headquarters of the most powerful vampire clan in the country with no warning whatsoever and two traitorous shifters-turned-humans in tow.

I need to explain, and I need to do it *quickly*.

"What do you know of a group of witches who call themselves the Blood Coven?" I ask.

Damien's eyes narrow, and he leans back, swirling the liquid in his glass. "The Blood Coven," he muses. "I've heard whispers, but nothing concrete."

He says nothing more. I suspect he knows more than he's letting on, but I'm not exactly in a position to push him.

"The Blood Coven is a group of witches who have gathered in Spring Creek," I tell him. "Three sisters able to do blood magic. Calliope, the leader of the Spring Creek coven, along with the few witches left there. Hazel and her parents, of the Pine Valley coven. And, most surprisingly, three vampires. Gwen, Benjamin, and Tristan. All three have lived in the city in the time you've been here. I expect you've heard of them?"

He sips his drink, his expression neutral. "I have."

"They've acquired an ancient artifact," I continue, not allowing myself to be shaken by Damien's cold behavior. "The Key of Hades."

I watch his face, searching for any sign of recognition or deception.

"Interesting," he finally says. "Many might say the Key of Hades is a myth."

"It's not a myth," I tell him. "I know because I've seen it myself."

Connor

I SUMMARIZE the basics of what's happened since Ruby arrived in town, including everything that happened in the fae realm.

Damien listens, asking the occasional question, but he gives no sign that he has any information of his own to share.

"Ruby returned to Spring Creek," I tell him when I'm done. "The Blood Coven has the key now."

He takes another sip of his drink—he's almost finished it now. I can see him weighing my words, considering the enormity of the situation.

"A fascinating story," he finally says. "But retrieving ancient artifacts isn't a criminal act on its own. What they intend to do with it is the real concern."

"It's not going to be anything good."

"Agreed. As for the humans…" His gaze drifts to Abigail and Xavier, calculating and predatory. "It's a pity that your memories of your daughter have been erased. She sounds like quite the… enigma. But you weren't always human, were you?"

His words are more statement than question.

Abigail and Xavier shift uncomfortably in their seats, but they maintain their composure.

"No," Xavier replies, firm but hesitant. "We were once shifters in the Pine Valley pack. We defended my sister, Jessica, after she was turned into a vampire. We were… killed in the process. At least, that's what everyone was meant to believe."

A sly smile spreads across Damien's face. "Yes, I remember the story. My people admired your change of heart, along with your brave sacrifice." His eyes narrow, and he leans forward. "So, how is it that you're now seated in my penthouse, very much alive, and very much *human*?"

"We had our magic stripped," Abigail says, and then she fills him in on everything I learned in the warehouse.

Damien tilts his head thoughtfully after she finishes. "And now you'll do anything to remember your daughter," he says. "Even if that means being turned into the very thing you were born to hate."

"It's the only way for us to have our memories of our daughter restored, regain our supernatural abilities, and fight against the Blood Coven," Xavier says. "And, since we're now human, the law that vampires can't turn other supernaturals won't be broken."

Damien leans back in his chair, considering it.

"An intriguing proposition indeed." His eyes glint with a mix of curiosity and something more dangerous as he refocuses on me. "Turning two former Pine Valley Guardians into vampires would solidify the alliance between our clan and your pack. Far more so than if they were human offerings, as I first believed when the three of you stepped through my door."

I nod, maintaining my composure. "Exactly. Given that Ruby is my mate, it would be a merging of families, so to speak. Reminiscent of how nobles married into alliances back in the day."

Since Damien was a British aristocrat before he was turned, I hope he'll appreciate the statement.

"An apt comparison," he says. "But even though Ruby is your mate, she didn't choose to be with you."

The reminder is a knife to my heart. "She didn't," I say slowly, refusing to let Damien rattle me. "But she's still my mate. She'll always be tied to me, and I'll always protect her, whether she likes it or not."

"You love her."

"She's my mate. Of course I love her."

He nods, apparently satisfied with my answer. Then, his icy blue eyes drift to Abigail and Xavier.

Neither of them looks away.

They might be humans now, but they're still shifters, through and through.

"And you two are willing to forsake your human lives to become what you once fought against?" Damien asks.

Xavier's jaw clenches, but he nods firmly. "If it helps us remember Ruby and gives us the strength to fight the Blood Coven, then yes."

"And what about you, Abigail?" Damien asks. "Do you share your husband's convictions?"

She takes a long breath, looking deep into his eyes, and in that moment, I see Ruby's fierceness in her. "I want to remember my daughter. I want to help her. I'll do whatever it takes to make that happen."

Please work, I think. *Please say yes.*

My wolf is silent. He's not thrilled to be in this vampire lair, but he's not opposed, either.

Like me, he'll do anything to ensure Ruby's happiness.

Damien's calculating smile deepens, and he raises his glass, swirling the contents thoughtfully. "You have courage, both of you. Something I respect. Your sister would be proud."

He directs the last part to Xavier.

Xavier's eyes go far off for a moment. "The situation with Jessica was complicated, to say the least," he says. "But I know with my entire soul that she didn't lose her humanity after she was turned. I'm confident that Abigail and I won't, either. If you do this for us, we will be loyal to your clan. I swear it."

Silence settles over the room, and I feel the weight of Damien's contemplation.

Finally, he sets down his glass and rises to his feet. "Very well, Connor Ward, new alpha of the Pine Valley pack," he says to me. "I agree to your terms. I will turn Abigail and Xavier, solidifying our alliance and ushering in a new era of collaboration between our people."

Relief washes over me, but I keep my face neutral, standing and extending my hand to Damien. "Thank you, Damien. You won't regret this."

His grip is firm, his smile chilling. "I certainly hope not. But remember that alliances can be as fragile as they are strong. Betrayal will not be tolerated."

"I understand." I hold his gaze, like the alpha I am. "The Pine Valley pack is loyal. We will honor the continuation of our alliance. I swear it."

"Good," Damien says, releasing my hand. "Then let us unite against the Blood Coven and move forward together. I'll make the necessary arrangements, and we'll proceed with the ceremony at midnight."

Autumn

I STARE DOWN at the book spread open before me, the faded words blurring and shifting as I attempt to concentrate on my studies.

With everything that's been happening, burying myself in books has a calming effect. Nearly as much as when I go on runs or practice my magic.

Somehow, I've kept everything that's happened the past few days from my parents. Connor's return. His breaking our engagement. The truth about Ruby's parents, and what Jax set off to do to them.

And, most importantly, our mate bond.

Because Jax is our alpha. He'll make the announcement when he decides it's right for the pack. I just have to wait, be patient, and somehow, stay sharp and focused as I do.

Suddenly, my phone vibrates on my desk, yanking me out of my studies.

Jax.

My heart leaps into my throat, and I quickly answer.

"Jax? Where are you? Is everything okay?"

"Autumn." There's a heaviness in his voice that I've never heard before, and it sends a cold chill through my body. "I'm back in Pine Valley. I need you to come over. Now."

"I'll be right there."

I end the call and rush outside, shifting into my wolf form in a fluid motion. My paws pound against the earth as I race toward Jax's house, my heart thudding in my chest with a mix of relief that he's back, anticipation about what happened while he was gone, and dread that it's something that will change everything forever.

Xavier and Abigail are dead.

They *must* be.

I reach his house in record time, shifting back into human form as I approach the door and let myself inside.

He's waiting for me in the foyer, his face etched with lines of stress and exhaustion that makes him look like he aged years overnight. But he relaxes the moment he sees me, pulls me close, and kisses me so intensely that it's like I'm air and he hasn't breathed in days.

My body's instantly on fire, and I melt into his embrace, responding to his kiss with equal passion and desire. It feels like coming home after a long time away, like nothing else in the world matters except for the two of us.

But as he pulls away, I see the sadness in his eyes. Sadness and… shame?

Something's wrong.

Very, very wrong.

"What happened?" I ask, my voice barely above a whisper.

He takes a deep breath, his grip on my hand tightening. "I need you to sit down. There's something I have to tell you."

I follow him into the living room, my heart pounding louder with each step, and sit next to him on the couch.

"Connor somehow found out where I was going, and he followed me there," he says, his eyes empty, his voice hollow of emotion. "He challenged me to be alpha of the pack."

"That's insane. Is he…?"

I can't bring myself to say the final word.

"Dead?" Jax chuckles—a dark, empty sound. "No. He's not."

"Then he forfeited. He left. He went rogue."

It's the only thing that makes sense.

Because Jax is… well, he's *Jax*. Our alpha. My mate. A seasoned warrior, magic wielder, and leader.

"Connor is the new alpha of our pack," Jax says, the words falling heavily between us.

This has to be a joke. Or a trick. Or *something* other than the truth.

But why would he ever make something like this up?

He wouldn't.

"I don't understand," I finally say. "How could this happen?"

"I'd been using my magic to… intimidate Ruby's parents before giving them the end they deserved," he says, and then he continues telling me what happened—every single gory detail of it.

When he's finished, a long, heavy silence hangs in the air between us.

The shame in his eyes makes my heart break.

I reach out and place a hand on his cheek, forcing him to look at me. "I'm here for you," I tell him. "Whatever you need, I'm here."

He kisses me again, soft and slow, and I feel the weight of everything that's happened in the way he holds me. The way his lips linger on mine, as if he's trying to memorize every inch of me before the world falls apart completely.

"I love you," he murmurs against my lips, and I know it's not just a statement of affection. It's a promise. A plea for me to stay by his side no matter what happens next.

"I love you too," I say, and I mean it with every fiber of my being.

Jax is my mate.

I will stand by his side, always.

His eyes meet mine, filled with pain and determination. "Before you, I would have rather died than forfeited my position as alpha," he says. "But I have a mate now. I can't just think about myself anymore."

Tears well in my eyes as the weight of his sacrifice hits me. "You gave up everything for me."

"I already lost one woman I love," he says. "Facing a world without her in it was nearly an impossible weight to bear. The thought of you going through the same thing—

but worse, since it would be the loss of your *mate*—made the decision easy. I sacrificed a title. But I will never, *ever* sacrifice your happiness."

My heart leaps at the intensity in his gaze, and it hits me just how willing I am to do anything for this man who gave up everything he's ever known for me.

"I love you," I repeat, and then I kiss him again, my hands roaming his body to explore every inch of him, so I can show him just how much I mean it.

He responds eagerly, his hands tangling through my hair as we fall back onto the couch. I cling to him, savoring the feel of his skin against mine, the taste of his lips, the sound of his voice as he whispers my name.

The weight of everything that's happened lifts off his shoulders as we lose ourselves in each other, and for a moment, it's just us. Our love. Our passion. Our bond.

But reality comes crashing back all too soon.

We're lying on the couch together, his arm around me as I snuggle into his chest, and I want to freeze this moment and live in it forever.

"I couldn't have done it." He keeps his eyes on the ceiling, not looking at me.

"Done what?"

"Killed him."

"I know," I say softly. "He's your family. And, despite whatever happened back there, he couldn't have killed you, either."

He takes a deep breath and turns to look at me, his eyes filled with an emotion I can't quite place.

Resolve?

"I'll get us some water," he says, and he heads to the kitchen as if he's carrying the weight of the world on his shoulders.

When he returns, he hands me a glass of water and sits down next to me.

"There's something else we need to discuss," he says.

Whatever it is sounds serious, and I place my glass down on the coffee table, giving him my full attention.

"What is it?"

"I don't want to stay here," he says. "I won't submit to Connor. We'll be of better use serving as Guardians in the city."

"You want us to leave Pine Valley," I say slowly, my mind racing with the implications of his words. "But what about our families? Our friends? The pack?"

"The only member of my family just came within an inch of killing me," he says, bitterness lacing his tone. "Your parents can visit the city whenever they want. Hell, they can move there too. As for the pack… they're not my responsibility anymore."

I take a deep breath, trying to process it all.

It's a lot.

On the other hand, none of it feels wrong. Quite the opposite, actually.

"I was going to complete my training this summer and end up in the city for the next twenty years anyway," I say, making sure to sound bright and positive—for him. "Heading there a few weeks earlier barely matters in the scheme of things. And you know I've always wanted to be a Guardian. Maybe even more so than I wanted to be alpha."

The crazy thing is—it's true. My dedication has always been to my studies. My training. My magic.

All those things are more useful for warriors. Not for rulers.

A smile tugs at his lips, and some of the heaviness releases from his shoulders. "Really?"

"Yes." I smile and take his hand, squeezing it gently. "I think this is the path we were meant to take. Together."

"Then we'll leave tonight."

"Tonight?" The word catches in my throat.

"Yes, tonight. I'll gather the pack in an hour and let them know about the... changes. I want us to be gone before Connor returns."

I nod, feeling a mix of emotions—excitement, fear, determination. But mostly, I feel alive.

Like I'm about to start off on the life I've always trained for.

"Okay," I agree. "Tonight it is."

He tucks a stray strand of my hair behind my ear, his eyes soft and caring. "No matter where we go, or what we do, I'll always stand by you," he says. "My heart belongs to you. Forever."

"Forever," I repeat, and something deep inside me shifts. Because even though my entire world is changing, I feel more grounded than ever.

This is the fresh start I need. That we *both* need.

The city will be our home. The Guardians will be our family.

And I'm going to make it my mission to be the best Guardian this world has ever seen.

Connor

I PACE around the apartment Damien provided for me while I wait for Xavier and Abigail to complete the change. The apartment is on the second floor, close to the ground, as requested. It's small—a studio—but that's more than enough for me.

I wasn't permitted to watch Xavier and Abigail's vampire transformation ceremony. But now the sun is just starting to set, and it will soon be complete.

Meanwhile, I've been planning what to say to the pack when I return to Pine Valley. I've declined all calls from my friends, but I know from their texts that Jax announced to the pack earlier today that he and Autumn are mates and he's no longer alpha.

He hasn't told them who's taken his place.

I have to get this right. If I say the right words—if I can make sure they believe in me and the future I want to lead them toward—then the pack can be stronger than it ever was before.

No pressure.

Eventually, there's a knock on the door.

I take a deep breath, walk over, and open it.

Damien stands in the doorway. A moment of silence and understanding passes between us, and he steps aside, revealing two people I don't recognize... at least, not at first.

Xavier and Abigail, both now vampires, their human disguises lifted.

Xavier's blond hair is now dark chestnut, wild and slightly wavy. His deep brown eyes are now a piercing blue, and he now appears to be in his upper twenties, youthful yet intense.

Abigail's bright red hair is now rich brown, and it cascades in loose waves down her back, just like Ruby's. She's now graceful and athletic, her skin smooth and flawless, and she also appears to be in her upper twenties.

But there's one change that's most startling of all.

"Your eyes," I whisper to Abigail, captivated by their familiar shade. "I know those eyes."

"I imagine you do." Abigail gives me a warm smile. "They're the same color as Ruby's."

My heart swells with relief the moment she speaks my mate's name. Because that means…

"You remember her."

"Yes," Xavier confirms. "The transformation negated the spell, just like we hoped."

We did it.

It worked.

But my happiness is quickly replaced by a tug of conflict on my heart. Because these are the people who turned on my pack. I've imagined revenge on them for my entire life.

A part of me still wants it, despite what I told Jax in that warehouse.

But they're Ruby's parents. She loves them. I won't allow myself to forget that.

Damien clears his throat. "Sorry to intrude on your moment, but this is hardly a conversation to be had in the hall," he says. "May we come in?"

Given that it's his building, he doesn't technically have to ask. But I appreciate the gesture, nonetheless.

I step aside to allow them entry. "Of course. Please, come in."

They situate themselves in the main area, vampiric grace in their every movement. Damien remains standing, his eyes flicking between us, as eerily calm as ever.

I keep my eyes on Xavier and Abigail, analyzing every detail of their transformations. The striking blue of Xavier's eyes, the richness of Abigail's hair—it's all so surreal.

But her eyes…

"Ruby's eyes are brown," I say. "They were turquoise—the same shade as yours—on the night we met. But then she shifted for the first time, and she lost her contacts. Not like she needed them anymore, since her vision became perfect after she shifted, but her eyes are definitely brown."

"As her mother, I assure you that Ruby has never needed contacts, and her eyes are not brown," she says. "If they are now, it's because of an illusion."

"But *why*?"

"Jax knew the two of us well, and Abigail's eyes are unforgettable," Xavier speaks up. "If Ruby was walking around Pine Valley with eyes identical to her mother's, I suspect he would have put the truth together sooner rather than later."

"The moon goddess must have cast an illusion on them to help keep Ruby's heritage secret," Abigail continues Xavier's thought. "If Jax realized the truth, then he would have… well, he was quite clear with us in the warehouse about what he intended to do to her the next time he saw her."

Anger rises inside me at the reminder.

But there's no time for anger right now. I have to remain calm and focused.

"Jax will never lay a hand on her. I made sure of it," I say. "And after Ruby gets word that you remember her, she'll have no reason to keep helping the Blood Coven."

Minus the fact that she said she loved Tristan.

No, my wolf growls. *She'll never love Tristan. He tricked her. He used her. She's our mate, and we'll bring her back home, no matter what it takes.*

I can call Morgan. Ask her to get me on the phone with Ruby so I can tell her that her parents remember her. We can figure out a plan to get Ruby out of Spring Creek. Maybe with Thalia and Gunnar's help, too.

"I wish we could help you get her out of there," Abigail says. "But the bloodlust… it's too strong."

"It's worse than I imagined." Xavier's face twists with pain, his eyes darkening. "If we go out into the world this soon, we'll risk killing humans. You know what the Guardians will do to us if that happens."

"More than anyone."

I look to Damien, hoping for a way around this. But his expression is grim.

"They're right," he says. "Given Xavier and Abigail's history as shifters—even though they were human when they were turned—the bloodlust is likely stronger for them. It takes time to master. We can't risk a tragedy. It would speak poorly of both my clan and your pack, and it would mean the end of our alliance."

As he speaks, my attention returns to Ruby's parents.

"So, neither of you will see her," I say.

"It's not that we *won't*. It's that we *can't*." Abigail's voice trembles, anguish in her eyes. "It's up to you to get her away from the Blood Coven and out of Spring Creek. You have to bring her home. To Pine Valley."

My wolf howls inside me in agreement.

But my human side knows it's not entirely up to me.

"I'll do everything I can," I say, choosing my words carefully. "I'll get the message to her that you remember her. But even though she's my mate, she has free will. I can't force her to leave the Blood Coven. I'll do everything in my power to get her home, but Ruby can be… stubborn. You, of all people, should know that."

A silence settles in the room, thick and heavy, as they process my words.

"Your feelings for her have grown beyond your mate bond," Abigail finally says. "You love her."

"With everything I have."

I'm starting to think there's nothing I won't do to ensure Ruby's happiness. Even if it means sacrificing my own.

Xavier reaches for me, but quickly stops himself, apparently thinking better of it. "Thank you for saving our lives, and for giving us the chance to remember our daughter," he says. "We owe you a debt we can never repay."

"Yes, thank you, Connor," Abigail says, tears shimmering in her brilliant turquoise eyes. "We'll do everything in our power to support you and Ruby, in whatever way we can."

Looking into Abigail's eyes and seeing the love she has for her daughter, I know I've made the right choice.

Damien breaks the silence, his voice steady and purposeful. "This alliance is a new beginning for all of us," he says. "I look forward to what the future holds, and to working together in ways we never thought possible."

"As do I," I reply, meaning it. "There's much we need to do, especially concerning the Blood Coven, but I'm confident that this alliance will be beneficial for us all."

His expression hardens. "Yes, the Key of Hades. I've already begun looking into what they plan to do with it. I expect you to do the same once you're back in Pine Valley and have taken control of your pack."

"I will." I nod, feeling the weight of responsibility on my shoulders when he refers to the Pine Valley wolves as *my pack*. "With Jax out of the way and my pack looking to me for leadership, I'll do everything I can to uncover the Blood Coven's plans and stop them."

After Hazel's betrayal, the rest of the witches in Pine Valley can't be trusted. But Jax's library is huge. There has to be something in there that can point me in the right direction.

And let's not forget that I have Morgan, Thalia, and Gunnar as contacts on the inside.

Xavier looks back and forth between me and Damien, his body tense. "We need to be cautious," he warns. "The Blood Coven is dangerous, and with Ruby entangled in their schemes, we can't act recklessly."

"But we know you'll do what's right," Abigail adds. "We trust you with our daughter's life."

"I won't let you down," I promise, since no matter how this ends, I'm going to make sure it's with Ruby alive. "I'll head back to Pine Valley tonight. I need to take control of the pack, reassure them, and begin our investigation into the Key of Hades."

We spend the next hour discussing our plans. The weight of the tasks ahead feels immense, but the shared purpose and unity in the room gives me confidence that we'll bring the Blood Coven down before they can put the Key of Hades to use.

Meaning, before the next full moon.

Finally, as the meeting comes to an end, Damien turns to me, his expression serious. "Connor, remember that trust is hard to earn, and easily broken," he says. "We've come a long way, but shifters and vampires are not friends, and this alliance is fragile. Let's make sure it grows into something strong and unbreakable."

"I couldn't agree more," I respond. "And, as I'm sure you'll learn as we continue to work together, I'm a man of my word. Always."

"Very well." He nods, and I can tell that despite everything, he believes me. "I'll see you out."

He leads me to the door, and I exchange last glances with Xavier and Abigail, unable to shake the uncanny feeling of looking into the faces of the people who killed my parents. But it's Abigail's eyes—those turquoise eyes, filled with gratitude and concern for her daughter—that truly stay with me.

We reach the lobby, and Damien holds out his hand to shake mine. "Take care of your pack," he says. "And of Ruby. She's at the center of something bigger than all of us."

"I know," I reply. "And I will."

He gives a satisfied nod and releases my hand.

"Safe travels, Connor. We'll be in touch."

I make my way to the street, where the city's nightlife is just beginning to awaken. But my mind is already miles away, in Pine Valley with my pack, my responsibilities, and with Ruby.

I will lead. I will protect. And I will love.

For Ruby, for my pack, and most importantly—for all our futures.

Ruby

It's been two nights since my dinner with Gwen, Zara, Willow, and Morgan. Two nights since Luna took me to her realm so I could earn the right to wield the Lunar Crescent.

I haven't seen her since.

Morgan's been pretending that whatever warning she tried to give me didn't happen. She's avoided being alone with me, and I've just about given up trying.

Tristan has continued to stay in my room each night.

As I finish getting ready for bed, I gaze out the bathroom window one final time, hoping to find Luna there. But there's nothing.

She'll come for us before the full moon, my wolf thinks. *We just have to be patient.*

And so, I brush my fingers against the ruby pendant hanging from my necklace, reach for my magic, and make it invisible again.

If I keep Tristan waiting for any longer, he's going to wonder if there's something wrong.

I re-enter the bedroom, finding him where he always is while I get ready for bed—propped up against the pillows with a book.

He glances up at me, his eyes scanning my body. I feel his hunger, his desire, and I glance down at the floor, my cheeks heating.

How much longer will I be able to hold him off without him realizing that he isn't the one I want to be with? How much longer will I be able to keep him believing my lies?

As I sit on the edge of the bed, he sets his book aside and reaches out to trail his fingers down my arm.

I remember the time when I would have responded to his touch—when I wanted more. When I wanted to be with him, fully and completely. But now that the blood bond is basically gone and he no longer has Dominic's necklace, that feels like a lifetime ago.

I stop myself from pulling away from him, forcing myself to meet his eyes instead. He's gazing at me with so much love that I almost feel bad for deceiving him.

Almost.

"What's wrong?" he asks. "You seem distant."

"Nothing." I force a smile. "Just tired."

A mischievous smirk plays on his lips. "Good thing I know the perfect way to help you relax," he says, and he leans forward, desire flashing through his eyes as he glances at my lips.

Before I can stop him, he kisses me, soft and hesitant.

Just like every night he's tried this since we got back from the fae realm, I feel nothing. But I kiss him back anyway. It feels mechanical—robotic—and a pit forms in my stomach as he curls a hand around the back of my neck and pulls me closer.

"I want you, Ruby," he murmurs against my mouth, his hands sliding down my back.

I don't want you.

As if he can read my thoughts, he pulls back, his eyes searching mine, frustrated and confused.

"You've been different since we got back from the fae realm," he finally says, and then he lets out a long breath and leans back into the pillow. "It's him, isn't it?"

I don't do him the disservice of pretending I don't know which *him* he's speaking about.

Instead, I twist around to look at him straight on.

"I chose you, Tristan." I keep my voice steady, unable to afford his not believing me. "I chose you because I want to be with you. Not Connor. *You.*"

"Then what's going on?"

My heart pounds, and I see the hurt in his eyes. He's looking for reassurance, for love, for connection. And I'm failing him.

I have to turn this around. Quickly.

Luckily, there's one more card I have left to play.

"I've been doing some thinking," I tell him. "About my future. *Our* future."

He reaches for my hand, and I feel the warmth of his touch, but not the spark that used to be there.

Because there never was an actual spark there. Only lies and betrayal.

"And?" he asks.

We've already talked about Ambrogio, and what the sisters told me at dinner the other night.

We haven't talked about what will happen after the ceremony is complete.

It's not going to *be* complete—not if I have anything to do with it—but I can't let Tristan know that. If I do, all will be lost.

"I've made my decision," I tell him. "After Ambrogio is risen, I want him to turn me into a vampire."

My lie hangs in the air, silence filling the room as Tristan's eyes widen with a mixture of surprise and elation.

"You mean it?" he asks, his disbelief giving way to excitement. "You want to be like me? *With* me?"

"I do." I swallow down the thickness of the lie. "I've been thinking about it ever since learning that if Ambrogio turns me, I can keep my magic. I can have a family, with the Blood Coven. And I can be with you. Forever."

Dread swirls in my stomach at the final word.

Tristan seems troubled as well.

"When you turn, your mate bond with Connor will break," he says slowly, carefully, watching me as if whatever I say next will change everything.

"I know," I reply. "I want it gone. That's part of why I'm making this choice. I'm choosing my path, and it's with you. With the coven. I don't need or want my stupid bond with Connor weighing me down for any longer."

He grins and pulls me close, kissing me with more passion than ever before.

As he does, I try to pretend it's Connor I'm kissing—not Tristan. The way Connor's lips felt against mine, the warmth and love that radiated through our mate bond and into me when I kissed him for the first time in that boat.

Tristan's hands slide down my waist, and for a moment I can almost believe it's Connor holding me.

But it's no use. The kiss is empty and cold—at least, it is for me.

Not so much for Tristan. He pushes me down onto the bed, and I know he wants more.

No, my wolf thinks. *Absolutely not.*

She doesn't have to say it twice.

I push him away, gently but firmly. "Not tonight, Tristan."

His face falls, and he pulls himself off me, sitting up and leaning back into the headboard.

I sit up next to him, searching my mind for a way to do damage control before this can spiral into potential conflict.

"This is all just so much," I continue, and from there, I don't even have to lie. "Everything I thought I knew about my life—about who I am, and the world as I know it—turned upside down a few weeks ago. In a few days, it's going to change even more. I'm… on edge, to say the least. My thoughts feel like they're everywhere all at once, and I can't be in the present for even a minute, let alone for an entire night."

His eyes search mine, as if he's waiting for something else.

I know what he's waiting for.

It's time to lie. Again.

Good thing I've lately been spinning illusions with my words as easily as I've learned to do with my mind.

"I love you, Tristan." My voice catches in my throat, and I pray he thinks it's because I'm overwhelmed with love for him instead of by the guilt of what I'm doing. "I want our first time to be when I'm fully here with you. You deserve that. *We* deserve that."

He takes a few seconds to process what I'm saying.

Please, I think, praying to every goddess out there that he believes me.

Then his face softens, and he pulls me into a warm embrace that I remind myself not to move away from. "I understand, Ruby," he says, but when he looks back down at me, disappointment lingers in his eyes. "We're going to have all the time in the world. I'll wait for as long as you need."

"Thank you," I say. "I appreciate it. Truly."

"And I'm here for you. Always."

I force myself to smile, letting my face relax into what I hope appears to be contentment. "I know," I say. "I expect you to be right by my side when I tell the others about my decision tomorrow."

He takes my hand, his fingers intertwining with mine, looking at me with more intensity than he has all night.

"Ruby, I want you to know something," he begins, and I nod for him to continue. "No matter what happens in the coming days, no matter the chaos and uncertainty, my love for you will never waver. My life began the moment I found you, and I'll stand by your side through eternity. I swear it."

A lump forms in my throat, and I swallow it down. The words of love and devotion he's offering are everything a girl could want.

But they're not meant for me. Not really. Because he doesn't know the real me.

It's impossible to truly know someone when you've been forcing them to bend to your will from the moment you met them.

"Thank you, Tristan," I manage to say, and then I lie to him again. "I love you."

"I love you, too."

We settle into bed, and he wraps his arms around me, holding me close.

For the first time in days, he seems truly content. Like he did before all of this, when he had me under his spell and his bond.

I don't like sharing a bed with him. But after all that time in the cell together, I'm used to it. And so, eventually, sleep claims me.

It's restless and filled with dreams of magic. A wolf's howl, and the moon's embrace.

Ruby, someone whispers in my dreams, and I float back into consciousness, my heart leaping at the sound of the voice I'd been praying to hear again soon.

Luna.

Ruby

She's come for me.

Finally.

I slip out of bed and hurry to the bathroom, not waking Tristan, my heart pounding in anticipation.

Just like the other night, Luna's waiting for me in the garden. Her silver hair blows in the wind, and the nearly full moon casts light down upon her that makes her look even more like a goddess than she did the other night.

She glances up, her eyes meeting mine, and gives me a small, knowing smile.

Time to get out of here.

I nudge the window open, call on my wolf form, and soar out into the night without a second thought. Like last time, I call on my earth magic. I'm far more successful this time, and the earth cradles me as I land next to Luna in the garden without breaking a paw.

The moment after shifting back to human form, I give Luna a giant hug.

"Hey." She pulls away and gives me a warm smile. It's like I'm seeing two people in her at once—my best friend, and the moon goddess—and I suppose she and I are similar in that way now. Two in one.

Don't you forget it, my wolf thinks.

As if you'd ever let me, I think right back to her.

Concern etches Luna's brow. "All okay?" she asks.

"All good." I glance back at the dark windows of the house, relieved it doesn't seem like anyone's seen us. "Want to get out of here?"

"My chariot awaits." She waves a hand, and her carriage and horses shimmer into existence next to us. They shine with a light that seems to come from the stars themselves, and, like last time, I can't help but stare in awe.

"Come on," she says. "Get in."

"Where are we going?" I hold my breath, praying her answer will be what I want.

"To Connor, of course."

My heart leaps at his name, and I jump in without hesitation.

The ride is a blur, and before I know it, we're landing outside Connor's house. Back where all of this started.

Looking around the backyard now, it's almost impossible to remember the life where Luna and I were college students at a party during winter break and I was crushing over the mysterious, cocky guy who challenged us to a game of beer pong.

Suddenly, a light turns on in one of the second-floor windows.

Connor's room.

I barely have time to register what's happening before a shadow moves behind the window, and a wolf I'd recognize anywhere launches himself through the open frame.

My wolf sings with happiness at the sight of him, and Luna and her carriage disappears into the night.

Connor's wolf form lands effortlessly on the ground, his dark fur catching the silver glow of the moon. He's beautiful. Majestic.

He's ours, my wolf purrs, and I can feel that she never wants to return to Spring Creek.

A second later, he shifts back to human form.

"Ruby." He gazes at me like I'm a star fallen from the sky. "You're here."

"Yes. I'm here."

He strides forward with purpose, closing the distance between us in a heartbeat. My breath catches in my chest, and before I can comprehend what's happening, he pulls me close and crushes his lips to mine with a hunger that just about brings me to my knees.

The kiss is fiery and all-consuming. It's like nothing else exists in the world but him, me, and the mate bond singing within us, tying us together in a way that feels both ancient and new.

I can also sense something more in him. A strength and command that wasn't there before.

He breaks the kiss, his forehead resting against mine, our hearts pounding in time with each other's.

"I've missed you," he says, his voice rough with emotion and desire.

From the way he's looking down at me, it's like he wants to claim me as his mate right here, right now.

Let him, my wolf urges.

Heat rises inside me, but somehow, I push down my desire and step back.

"You're different," I tell him. "You're..."

Alpha, my wolf answers in my mind. *He's our alpha now.*

"I am different," he confirms. "I challenged Jax. I've taken over as alpha of the Pine Valley pack."

"But how?" I ask. "Why?"

"It's a long story." He runs his hands through his hair, looking at me as if I'm a ghost. "But first... how are *you* here? Where did you come from?" He glances behind me, into the woods, as if he might find his answer there.

"That's also a long story," I say.

He nods in understanding. "Then let's sit down and start from where we left off."

* * *

"My parents," I say in shock after he tells me everything that happened in that warehouse with Jax. "They're..."

"They're vampires now," he says. "Damien agreed to turn them to solidify our alliance."

I sit back in the lounge chair on the deck, glancing up at the moon as I take everything in. It's a lot, to say the least.

Connor's sitting in an identical chair next to mine. "I'm going to talk with Damien and work something out to bring you there," he tells me. "I'll call him now."

"No." I pull him back down, stopping him from getting up to make the call. "I can't see them. Not yet."

It hurts to say, and I can't believe the words coming out of my mouth. Seeing my parents is all I've wanted. It's what I've been working toward.

What I *was* working toward.

"You don't have to go back to the Blood Coven," he says softly, as if he doesn't think I understand the full meaning behind everything he just told me. "Your parents remember you. The oath doesn't matter anymore."

"I know. But this isn't just about me anymore," I say. "It's bigger than that. Much bigger."

"What are you talking about?"

"I'm talking about the Key of Hades. I know what the Blood Coven is going to do with it. I know who they're trying to bring back."

Connor's quiet as I fill him in on everything I learned from Luna and the Blood Coven. He's a good listener, and it's a trait I admire in him.

It's one of the many qualities that I know will make him a great alpha.

"I have to stop them," I say after I've caught him up. "They can't be allowed to raise Ambrogio. As I said, this isn't just about me anymore. It's about the future of the world."

He looks me over as if he's seeing me in a new light.

"You've changed," he observes. "You're stronger, more determined. Not that I didn't think you were strong before. I did. It's just..." He gazes at me, like he's searching for a word and can't quite find it. "You're beautiful."

I can't help but smile at the fact that this strong, smart alpha is not only my mate, but stumbling over his words around me.

"Thank you," I say, feeling my cheeks warm. "So are you."

He leans forward and captures my lips in a searing kiss, one that leaves me breathless and dizzy.

"Be with me, Ruby," he says, his eyes burning with desire. "Be my mate. Fully and completely."

Ruby

I'M FROZEN IN PLACE, gazing into the eyes of my fated mate, knowing that this moment could change both of our lives forever.

And you know what? I'm sick of fighting fate.

This is what I've wanted—really, truly wanted—since he first touched me in those woods and ignited the mate bond between us all those weeks ago.

"I want that, too," I say on instinct, and the moment I do, it's like something *releases* inside me. Something I've been trying to suppress and have finally set free. "But I can't stay. I have to return to the Blood Coven before sunrise, and I don't know when I'll be back in Pine Valley again."

"I don't care. I don't want to wait any longer," he says before claiming my lips again, and my wolf howls inside me in agreement, sealing my decision.

The kiss is wild and frenzied, just like the connection between us. My hands are everywhere, gripping his hair, pulling him toward me, as I try to get closer to him in every way possible.

Finally, we break apart, breathless.

"Have you ever…?" He pauses, like he isn't quite sure how to pose the question.

"I had a boyfriend for a few months in high school," I say, understanding what he's trying to ask. "It… wasn't that great."

"Poor boy." He smirks, his eyes lighting up with a newfound determination that sets my heart on fire. "He didn't realize he needed to tame a wolf."

I tilt my head and look up at him under my lashes, feeling bolder and more empowered than ever. "So, are you going to show me how it's done?"

"You can count on it." He takes my hand and leads me down the stairs of the deck, finding us a spot near the trees where the earth is soft and welcoming.

He kisses me again, slowly and deliberately, and then he stops to take off his shirt, revealing the chiseled muscles of his chest and abs that I've only ever seen teasers of before.

I can't help but stare and appreciate this beautiful man in front of me.

My mate, and my alpha, who I'm allowing to claim me as his.

"Like what you see?" he asks, a crooked grin on his face.

"Very, very much."

Without hesitation, he takes me into his arms and kisses me again, his touch igniting every nerve in my body. He's gentle at first, but the kiss deepens as the heat between us intensifies.

We sink to the ground, and he reaches for the bottom of my shirt, ready to yank it up above my head.

But then, he stops.

"What's wrong?" I ask, breathing heavily, wanting *more*.

"I know we haven't had much time together, just the two of us," he says, and I can tell from the urgency in his tone that it's taking every ounce of control for him to not take me right here this second. "I haven't had time to take you out on dates, to run through the woods as wolves with you, or anything else that a woman as amazing as you deserves. But I love you, Ruby. I've loved you since the moment I saw you. And I'm the luckiest man in the world to be able to call you my mate."

His words are so powerful, so intense, that tears well in my eyes. I'm afraid that if I blink, this moment will vanish, and I'll wake up to find that it was all a dream.

"You're not the only one," I say. "I love you too, Connor. But you need to hurry up, or I'm going to explode."

He smiles so big that it lights up his face, and it's the most beautiful thing I've ever seen. Then his eyes run up and down my body, and before I know it, he's pushed me down to my back on the ground, pinning me beneath him.

"Are you challenging your alpha?" he growls, his eyes hot coals that make me squirm under his hold.

"You bet I am."

Clothes come off in a rush, and as we strip away our layers, it's like we're peeling back everything that once held us apart until there's nothing standing between us anymore. Each touch sends a pulse of electricity rippling through my body, and the earth trembles beneath us, the wind whispering through the forest. It's the most amazing feeling of my life, and I can't get enough.

We lose ourselves in each other completely, and a rush of energy surges through me—strong, warm, and comforting—the ground quaking as a string between us tightens and solidifies, binding us together forever as mates. It's a strong, powerful force, and the magic of the earth glows around us, the air sparkling and shimmering as our souls are seared together as one.

As the last of the magic fades, he collapses beside me on the ground, catching his breath we stare up at the stars.

"You're mine now," he says. "I love you, Ruby. And I'm never letting you go."

"I love you, too," I reply. "Forever."

"Forever," he repeats, and then his lips are on mine again, and we lose ourselves in each other once more.

Together, Connor and I are unstoppable.

And we don't stop until hours later, when I'm covered with earth, bathed in moonlight, and linked with my mate for all eternity.

I'm going to have to shower before returning to Spring Creek. I can't go back covered in dirt. But we lay there for a bit afterward, holding each other and basking in the reality of the fact that our mate bond is consummated.

Then, after a while, he props himself on an elbow and looks down at me, his eyes so full of love that it makes me want to cry.

"I will protect you, and I will love you," he swears. "You don't have to face what's coming next alone. We have each other. We have our pack. We can stop them, together."

Our pack.

Because he's the alpha.

What's his is mine.

"I can't stay for much longer." I sit up, the reality of what's coming crashing down all at once. "But I have an idea. A plan. And I need your help to make it happen."

"I've been training for these situations for my entire life. And I'll do anything for you," he says. *"Anything."*

And so, we strategize, our minds working in tandem as we consider every move, every detail.

The world may be on the brink of darkness, but as long as we're together, there's hope.

We'll stop the Blood Coven. We'll make sure that Ambrogio never fully rises to see the light of day. And we'll do it together. As mates, as powerful magic wielders, and as leaders of the Pine Valley pack.

Ruby

FIVE DAYS HAVE PASSED since the night Connor and I were together. Luna hasn't appeared to me since, and I haven't gotten to see him again.

My heart longs for him. My soul aches for him.

But everything's going to be okay. Because we have a plan, and I believe in it.

The Blood Coven was thrilled when I informed them about my decision to become a vampire. I managed to avoid making a blood oath with them on the grounds that if they want me to join them, they need to show that they trust me.

Morgan backed me up.

Thanks to the fact that her ability is divination, her sisters trusted her and agreed not to push me into entering into a blood oath.

Crisis averted. From what Connor told me, I know she's on our side. But we haven't talked about anything yet, we can't risk anyone overhearing.

Tristan stopped pushing me as well. Now that he believes I've chosen him and thinks we're going to spend the rest of our lives together, he no longer feels a need to rush our relationship.

Now, the night is here.

The full moon.

Its silvery light bathes the garden outside the Spring Creek mansion in an ethereal glow, casting shadows that dance and flicker like restless spirits.

I'm standing in a circle with all the members of the Blood Coven. Zara, Willow, Morgan, Hazel, Hazel's parents, Thalia, Calliope, Tristan, Benjamin, and Gwen. The witches stand closer to the center of the circle, since they're the ones who will be casting the spell.

We're all wearing flowing robes of deep crimson embroidered with skulls, bones, and celestial symbols. Crowns of black roses and thorny vines rest on our heads. Having pieces of the earth on my head calms me, as if it's reminding me that my magic is here for me.

The Spring Creek shifters are scattered around the perimeter, a living barrier between us and the outside world. They're in the all-black gear of warriors, guarding us, ready to stop anything that might stand in our way.

Glancing up at the moon, I replay the plan Connor and I came up with.

We've got this.

"Ruby," Tristan murmurs from next to me. "Are you with us?"

I snap out of my thoughts and gaze into his eyes, seeing the trust and love he believes we share. "Yes," I say, my voice steady. "I'm ready."

"Good." He reaches for my hand and squeezes it, and I resist my instinct to pull away. "Soon, it's going to be you and me. Forever."

My heart drops at his words.

Because for him, it's a dream.

For me, it's a nightmare.

Zara's fiery eyes meet mine, a knowing glint within them, and she raises her arms, signaling the start of the ceremony.

Everyone quiets, and the air is still.

"Hear us, Hecate, goddess of witchcraft," she begins. "Safeguard our ritual tonight, for it is wrought with power and peril, born of truth and blood."

The same tingles from our previous ceremony crawl over my skin, but this time they're sharper, more insistent.

The air thickens with the weight of our intent.

Willow and Morgan move to the edge of the circle, drawing forth their ceremonial daggers. Zara removes a dagger from her robe as well.

The blades gleam in the moonlight, and I swallow hard as I watch them slice their palms.

Their blood drips onto the earth, and spirals of fire erupt from the blades, following Willow and Morgan as they trace the perimeter. Every witch's eyes glow orange as flames leap up from the circle, creating a barrier and searing it into the ground.

Gwen's eyes gleam hungrily as she focuses on the center of the circle, at the ground that just absorbed Zara's blood.

"Guarded by flame and guided by starlight, we protect this sacred space, an unbroken circle, bound by fire and by blood," the sisters chant, their voices echoing through the circle.

Owls hoot from the forest, as if they're acknowledging the spell.

The earth beneath me rumbles. The sensation is stronger this time—even a bit unsettling. But it grounds me, reminding me of my connection to the Earth.

We've come this far. We've got this, my wolf reassures me.

I want to believe her.

But I'm also aware of the risks I'm about to take.

The fire pulses three times, the air shimmering as it settles into the ground. The wind picks up. The temperature drops.

Zara, Morgan, and Willow look paler than normal. More vulnerable.

Which is exactly how I want them to be.

"Now, the blade," Zara says, looking to Hazel.

Hazel, her face set with determination, removes the Blade of Erebus from her robe and makes her way to the center of the circle. Its edge catches the moonlight as she slices into her palm, and my breath catches in my throat as her blood falls to the ground, meeting the spot where Zara's own blood was spilled.

The fire flares in a burst of heat, reacting to her offering, then calms once more.

"By my blood and by my soul, I give my offering to the God of Darkness," she says, her voice full of so much power for someone so small and young. "May our will be done."

"May our will be done," the rest of the witches repeat.

The air grows colder, the energy in the circle shifting as it becomes more concentrated and potent. I shiver as the magic crawls over my skin.

Calliope joins Hazel and Zara in the center of the circle, her silver hair glimmering in the moonlight, and looks to me. "The key," she says, her gaze hard and unblinking.

I reach into the folds of my robe, hands trembling, and retrieve the key. It feels colder now, as if it's aware of what we're about to do with it.

I don't want to give it to her. But I have to.

So, I move to the center of the circle and hold it out for her to take.

She snatches it from me in a second.

"Thank you," she whispers, her hand closing around the key. "Return to your place."

She doesn't have to ask twice.

Once I'm back to Tristan's side, he gives me a nod of approval.

I give him a half-smile back, since it's probably going to be the last time he looks at me with approval again.

Calliope clutches the key tightly. Then she takes a deep breath and kneels to the ground. Her eyes narrow as she begins to chant, the words in an ancient tongue that makes the hair on the back of my neck stand up on end.

"Portas inferni aperi." Her voice resonates with power, and the wind whooshes as it picks up around us. "By the Key of Hades, by our blood, and by our intent, I call upon the darkness to open the gate between Earth and the Underworld."

Ruby

THE GROUND SHAKES, the flames flicker, and a thunderclap sounds through the night.

A crack tears through the center of the circle.

It splits the earth in two, and a guttural roar echoes from the depths, a sound so haunting it chills my soul as shadow creatures flood out from the darkness below. Grotesque and terrifying, they emerge in frenzied howls, soaring up in the air and dispersing themselves out toward the town. They push us back, and suddenly Tristan's arms are around me, keeping me steady.

None of the others are surprised or scared by these shadow creatures.

They knew this was going to happen. They knew the extent of the horror they were unleashing.

And, apparently, they didn't care.

Calliope's standing now, pushing out her magic and pouring it into the gate to the Underworld. Her body's trembling, sweat glistening on her forehead, her face twisted in concentration and pain.

The shadows twist and writhe as they form a dark vortex, a tunnel into the depths of the Underworld.

Gwen's eyes widen, and she steps forward, hungrier than ever as she watches Calliope pour her magic into the pit to Hell.

"It's time," she says. "He's coming."

My heart pounds as Calliope turns paler by the second, my senses alert, waiting for what I know is about to happen.

And then, it does.

I step away from Tristan as a figure emerges from the heart of the darkness in a slow, agonizing process, as if the Underworld is reluctant to let him go. But inch by inch, Ambrogio's body floats upward, surrounded by a twisting halo of dark magic. His skin is ashen, his eyes closed, and he looks every bit the corpse he is.

A collective gasp escapes our lips.

"He's beautiful," Zara says, tears in her eyes. "He's just as the legends described."

"Yes." Gwen gazes up at him as if he's a god. "He is."

I can't deny that they're right. There's a terrible, mesmerizing beauty to him, a grace that defies his lifeless state. But there's something else there, too. Something dark and twisted that makes my stomach churn.

This is wrong.

I knew that coming into this. But knowing it and *seeing* it are two entirely different things. And, as I glance at Morgan, I see caution in her expression as well.

Calliope's eyes are glowing red, a sign of the magic—the very essence of her soul—she's giving to Ambrogio. She's sacrificing herself, lost to the madness of their cause. If she succeeds, the empty shell of her that'll remain will be nothing more than Ambrogio's puppet.

Any trace of humanity she had was lost the moment she started giving him her magic.

Focus, my wolf snaps at me. *It's time to act—before it's too late.*

I look up at the moon and reach for my magic, spreading it through my body to become invisible.

Then I touch the ruby hanging from my neck.

Transform, I tell it, and then I'm holding the bow of the Lunar Crescent, its quiver of arrows on my back.

I nock an arrow, its ruby tip glowing with an inner light.

Time seems to slow as I draw back the bowstring. I aim high, making the arrow visible as it soars into the sky, the ruby lighting up like a flare.

It's a signal. A beacon that it's time to strike.

"Ruby, stop!" Tristan's voice is filled with betrayal as he searches for me, but I can't look back. I can't hesitate.

I draw another arrow.

Kill, I think, letting my intention flood through the arrow and into its ruby tip.

"Calliope!" I yell, and her burning red eyes dart to where my voice is coming from, and the arrow is flying, speeding straight toward her heart.

It pierces her chest.

She releases a blood-curdling scream, the light in her eyes fades away, and she falls to the ground.

Dead.

Ambrogio's body crashes down next to hers.

"Traitor!" Zara screams, aiming fire toward me.

I dart out of the way just in time, but my invisibility falters.

"Ruby, behind you!" a familiar voice rings through the air.

Connor. He made it.

I turn just in time to see the alpha of the Spring Creek pack—Riven—shift into a wolf and jump toward me, his jaws open wide, ready to strike.

Adrenaline surges through me, and I infuse an arrow with death, shooting it straight into his open mouth.

His blood splatters all over my face, and he crashes to the ground.

We're on a ROLL, my wolf cheers me on in my mind.

But the chaos escalates around me, the triumph short-lived.

I glance in the direction where Connor's voice came from, searching for him. He's shifted into wolf form, and he's leading the Pine Valley pack against the wolves and witches of the Blood Coven, their bodies colliding in a whirlwind of fur, teeth, magic, and blood. The Pine Valley pack—*my* pack—has the upper hand. Their determination and unity is giving them strength against the now leader-less Spring Creek wolves.

Then, my eyes meet Tristan's over Riven's dead body.

His expression is twisted with heartbreak and betrayal.

"I'm so sorry," I tell him, because despite everything, I don't hate him. "I had to."

His face hardens, and the wind around us picks up, whirling and howling. "You've chosen your side," he says, his voice cold. "Tell me—did you ever really love me?"

"Tristan…" my voice breaks, as does his expression, and I can see that he already knows my answer.

Then he's blasting wind at me, a focused, brutal force that knocks me off my feet and sends me crashing to the ground.

Pain shoots through my body. But I force myself up, my eyes never leaving his.

He doesn't spare me another glance. Instead, he turns, moving to defend Benjamin and Gwen, who have Ambrogio's body and are retreating toward the forest.

I throw off the stupid crimson robe and run after them, although after all the magic I used with the Lunar Crescent, they're far faster than me. I've used more energy that I realized. But I can't let them get away.

I just need *one more shot.*

So, I nock the arrow and infuse the ruby with intent to kill, my wolf howling inside me as I tune into my target.

Ambrogio.

Gwen's carrying him on her back, his ashen body as limp as a rag doll. If she gets away with him, she'll do anything to revive him. But it's not too late to stop them. They're not to the forest yet…

I aim and release, the arrow singing through the air. My earth magic stretches out with it, a part of me riding along its path, willing it to find its mark.

The arrow embeds itself into Ambrogio's body with a sickening thud.

The death magic activates.

Gwen stumbles. But she doesn't drop him.

Instead, the four of them—Gwen, Benjamin, Tristan, and Ambrogio—disappear in a blur into the forest.

They're gone so fast that I don't have time to call the arrow back to me.

But the death magic hit Ambrogio. The resurrection failed. He's not coming back.

And now, I need to make sure that my allies, my pack, and I take down our enemies and get out of this hellhole alive.

Ruby

I WIPE MORE of Riven's blood off my face and turn back to the chaos.

My wolf thrums with satisfaction as I hear the howls of our enemies, their bodies falling to the ground. Connor tears anyone who comes at him to shreds, his fur matted with their blood.

My mate is sexy as all hell in battle.

Then I see a movement out of the corner of my eye.

Zara.

Her eyes blaze with fury as she sends fireballs toward me. But I dodge them with ease, using my earth magic to create barriers around me and suffocate her flames.

An anguished scream pierces the air.

Hazel.

She's fallen onto her knees, her body wracked with sobs, hunched over two people on the ground who look very, very dead.

Her parents.

I don't like Hazel. That's no secret. But what I'm seeing right now isn't something I'd wish on anyone in the world.

Willow and Zara rush to Hazel's side, protecting her from attacks. I don't see Morgan anywhere, but the Pine Valley pack knows she's on our side. Same with Thalia and her shifter boyfriend, Gunnar. Connor made it explicitly clear that if anyone touches the three of them, they'll answer to him.

The ground quakes.

Fire lights up the garden-turned-battlefield.

Darkness moves in shadows around us.

I turn back to the fight... where Connor's facing off against three large Spring Creek wolves. He's dodging them and holding them off with teeth and earth magic, but he's outnumbered.

Help him, my wolf thinks, but I'm already on it.

I reach for another arrow and nock it, focusing on my target before releasing it with all the power I can muster. I'm getting too weak for death magic, and my hold on the Lunar Crescent is waning, likely because the shadow creatures leaking out of the crack in the ground are dimming the light from the moon. But I can still cause pain. And, if I strike at the correct angle, I can still kill.

The ruby glows as the arrow streaks toward its mark—the wolf closest to Connor.

It pierces the wolf directly into its flank. He howls in agony, his body contorting in pain before he falls to the ground, dead.

That's what he gets for trying to kill my mate.

Connor charges forward and tears into the other two wolves with a ferociousness that takes my breath away — all while dodging their lethal blows.

It doesn't take long for him to kill them both.

But we don't have time to celebrate. Because bright orange light flashes out of the corner of my eye, and I turn to see what's going on.

Zara, Willow, Morgan, and Hazel are standing back-to-back in a ring of fire, sending wave after wave of fireballs at anyone who tries to attack. Hazel's in a rage, her body crackling with energy, like an angry fire goddess.

Morgan uses her magic to create a fiery shield around the group while also defending against any attacks. But even though she's defending her sisters, she doesn't kill, or even maim.

Willow creates blazes that keep attackers at bay, while Zara hurls fireballs from within the flames.

I reach for an arrow, ready to aim at Hazel, but I can't do it.

I've been through too much with her. And she's not evil, like Calliope and Gwen. She was misled. Vulnerable. Impressionable. She's hardly my friend, but I can't bring myself to kill her.

"Stop!" I call out to her, infusing something into my voice that I didn't even know I had until now—alpha willpower. *"Yield."*

Hazel's eyes narrow.

"That doesn't work on witches," she snarls, and then she looks to the others, gathering strength. "We need to get out of here. Help me."

The fire grows around them like a living, breathing thing. It crackles and pops, smoke filling the air, joining together at the top like it's trying to touch the stars.

It extinguishes in an instant.

The only one left standing is Morgan, alone in the circle of charred earth, looking after her sisters with tears streaming down her face.

"Morgan!" I call out, and I lower the Lunar Crescent to my side, running to her.

When I get to her, I see something shining in her hand.

The Blade of Erebus.

"Hazel was distracted by what happened to her parents," Morgan says, gazing down at the weapon in shock. "I... took it from her. At the last second."

"It's yours now." I gaze around at the charred ground—any greenery that was on it before is gone. Wiped out. Just like Hazel, Zara, and Willow. "Did they...?"

"Kill themselves?" Morgan asks, and I nod slowly. "No. They fire jumped."

"Fire jumped?"

"Teleported. In a burst of fire."

"I didn't know that was possible."

"It's rare magic," Morgan says. "But Hazel is powerful, and her emotions were heightened. Magic feeds off emotions."

"Right. Of course it does." I want to ask more, but too much is happening at once.

Over where the shifters are still fighting, only two of them left are from Spring Creek.

Connor sinks his teeth into one of their necks, and Thalia blasts fire at another—holding him off for long enough that Gunnar can fully take him down.

Wow.

Connor told me that Thalia was more powerful than she let on. But I didn't realize she could do *that*.

One by one, the Pine Valley shifters look around and shift back into their human forms. Connor is the last, and the relief that crosses his eyes when they meet mine makes my heart leap into my throat.

It's over.

We won.

We run toward each other, meeting in the middle, and he checks me for injuries. It's unnecessary, given how fast we can heal, but it's sweet, nonetheless.

"You were amazing," he says, and then he crushes his lips to mine, as if verifying that I'm truly all right.

"I struck Ambrogio with one of my death arrows," I tell him. "The vampires left with his corpse, but they can't bring him back."

Suddenly, Morgan screams.

I jump out of Connor's arms, reach for an arrow, and raise the Lunar Crescent.

Brandon—Connor's beta—is charging towards Morgan in his wolf form with a crazed look in his eyes.

No.

I can't aim to kill. He's a member of our pack. It goes against every alpha instinct to turn on our own like that.

Pain, I think, and then I release the arrow, using my earth magic to guide it into Brandon's shoulder.

His anguished howl echoes through the night, and he falls to the ground.

Morgan is feet away from him, a fireball burning in one hand, the Blade of Erebus raised with the other.

Anger swirls in Connor's eyes. *"Shift,"* he commands, and when Brandon returns to human form, he's curled on the ground in pain.

The arrow's still sticking out of him.

Connor and I march over to him, and I kneel next to Brandon, but don't pull out the arrow.

He grunts and groans, his eyes closed tight, his teeth clenched in agony. Beads of sweat drip down his brow all the way to his chin. The skin around the arrowhead is red and inflamed, but he's so paralyzed with pain that he can't move to pull it out.

"You attacked one of our allies," I say slowly, carefully.

"Not... an... ally." He strains to get out each word.

His face is so pale that I wonder if he's going to pass out from the pain.

"Look at me!" I command, and when he does, his eyes are wild and crazed. "Why did you attack Morgan?"

His chest heaves, and instead of speaking, he releases a long, deep groan.

His eyes roll into the back of his head.

"That's enough," Connor says. "Take it out."

Personally, I think Brandon deserves a few more minutes of this torture. But I remove the arrow with a sickening suction sound, wipe it off on my pants, and stand back up.

Brandon releases a guttural scream and reaches for the wound, holding it tightly. Eventually, his breathing slows, and his muscles relax. The pain is still there on his face, but he should be able to speak.

"Why did you attack Morgan?" Connor asks again, his voice low and steady.

"She's not one of us," Brandon says. "She can't be trusted."

Morgan's by my side, gripping the Blade of Erebus as if she's ready for Brandon to attack again.

The other members of the Pine Valley pack watch behind us in silence.

As all of this is happening, more and more shadow creatures are leaking out of the crack in the ground. It's eerie, especially now that the battle's ended and I can hear their hushed whispers in the night.

"I am your alpha," Connor seethes down at Brandon. "I decide who can and can't be trusted."

Brandon tries to sit up, but Connor forces him back down with a foot on his chest.

"You have no right to question my decisions. Especially in the heat of battle."

"I follow my alpha." Brandon struggles to breathe under Connor's hold. "But I don't follow blindly."

The air grows tense, and I feel the pack's eyes on us, their breaths held, waiting for Connor's decision.

Connor remains focused on Brandon, his gaze hard and unyielding. "You were my beta," he finally says. "I trusted you. I've trusted you for my *entire life*. But you betrayed that trust less than a week after I assumed command of this pack."

"Connor, please," Brandon pleads. "The witch played a part in raising that... *thing*. I did what I thought was right."

"The witch's name is Morgan." I string the bow with the arrow, enjoying the way he flinches when I do. "We didn't give her our trust lightly. She earned it by risking herself not just to help the pack, but by fighting by our side to stop that *'thing'* from fully rising."

Morgan steps closer to me, supporting me.

"I'm sorry." Brandon quivers under Connor's boot, tears glimmering in his eyes.

"You disobeyed a direct order," Connor says, unmoved by Brandon's pleas. "You attacked an ally. You cannot be trusted as my beta."

"What are you saying?" He glances at the other pack members for help, but none of them speak up.

Connor presses down on his chest harder, forcing him to look back at him.

"I want you to leave and never return," he says, strong and sure. "Because by the decree of your alpha, you're banished from the Pine Valley pack."

Ruby

BRANDON'S FACE GOES WHITE, and a sob escapes his lips.

"Connor," he cries, but Connor simply gives him another push with his boot, releases him, and turns to look at the rest of the wolves in the pack.

"Tyler," he calls out. "Come forward."

A strong, dark-haired shifter who looks to be around our age steps forward, uncertainty in his eyes.

"We've known each other for our entire lives, and during that time, you've proven your loyalty, power, and wisdom," Connor says. "I choose you as my new beta."

Tyler's eyes widen in surprise, but his expression quickly shifts to one of understanding and acceptance.

"Thank you, Alpha," he says, bowing his head. "I won't let you down."

"I know." Connor gives him a single nod, and Tyler steps back in line with the others.

I can't help but feel a rush of affection and attraction toward my mate as he asserts his dominance as alpha.

Brandon stumbles to his feet, the tears now streaming down his face. He looks at Connor one last time in a mixture of betrayal, confusion, and grief. Then he turns and walks away, alone and broken, into the night.

But this isn't over.

Those dark, creepy, smoke-like demon things are continuing to writhe and escape into our world. They need to be stopped.

"We have to close the Hell Gate," I say, irritation rushing through me at the fact that Brandon's disobedience resulted in the crack staying open for longer than necessary.

Quickly, I use my magic to transform the Lunar Crescent back into its necklace form.

I don't need it for what's coming next.

"The Key of Hades." Connor turns to Thalia, since this was one of her assignments. "Do you have it?"

"I do." She steps forward and presents the key.

"Thank you." I give her a grateful smile and take it from her, feeling its cold, metallic surface against my palm.

I don't know why, but having it back feels so insanely *right*.

Connor reaches for my hand, so we're both holding the key, and the power of our mate bond surges through me. "Let's do this," he says, and we focus on our earth magic, connecting it with the essence of the key.

The air thickens, and the whispers of the shadow creatures grow louder.

I visualize the Hell Gate sealing shut. The key glows in response, and a tremor rumbles through the ground.

"Now," I say, and we hold our free hands up, our palms facing the Hell Gate, blasting it with as much earth magic as we can.

It rushes out of us in identical streams of bright green brilliance, lighting up the night and flooding into the gap in the ground.

But it's harder than I thought.

The Hell Gate doesn't want to close. Instead, it fights against us, pushing back.

"We're not strong enough," I gasp, somehow managing to hold onto the magic as sweat beads on my forehead.

"We can do this," Connor says. "We have to."

He's right.

And so, we push harder, our earth magic merging with the Key of Hades. I continue picturing the ground bending to our will, projecting the image out of my mind with as much strength as I'm using to force my magic out of my palm.

Finally, the crack begins to close, the shadows hissing and clawing in desperation to escape.

"It's working," I breathe, my hope rekindling.

But then a sudden, powerful resistance pushes back against our combined magic.

I cry out, almost losing my grip on the key.

"Focus!" Connor says, and with a final burst of effort, we scream and release all the magic we have.

The ground quakes. And then, with a deafening roar, the crack seals shut.

We fall to our knees, our breaths ragged, our bodies drained.

"It's done." Connor's dark brown eyes gleam with triumph, despite all the magic we just expended.

I look at the now-sealed Hell Gate, but something doesn't feel right. There's a lingering darkness, a subtle distortion in the air.

"No," I say slowly. "Look."

Connor follows my gaze, realization dawning in his eyes. "It's sealed, but not completely."

Dread settles over me. Because a tiny fissure remains, a place through which evil can still seep.

A frustrated curse escapes my lips.

Morgan steps forward, her eyes narrowed as she assesses the situation. The Blade of Erebus glints ominously in her hand.

"What are you doing?" Connor asks, alarm creeping into his voice as he sees the intense focus in Morgan's eyes.

"Cauterizing it," she says simply, and she raises her hands, flames dancing at her fingertips.

A torrent of fire erupts from her palms in a bright, burning inferno that races towards the Hell Gate. It collides with the crack in the ground, and the roar of the flames mingles with the howls of the shadow creatures in the crisp night air.

We watch in awe as the flames rage, the fissure in the Hell Gate glowing bright red as the fire does its work.

The cries of the shadow creatures grow fainter and fainter.

And then, finally, they're silenced.

After what feels like an eternity, Morgan lowers her hands, and the flames die down, leaving behind glowing embers and the smell of burnt earth.

The Hell Gate is still there, an ugly scar on the landscape. But the shadow souls are no longer slipping out of it. The threat is contained.

We've protected our world, our pack, and each other.

But as I look around, I'm reminded that the casualties weren't all on the side of Spring Creek.

There's a man I recognize on the ground, his lifeless eyes staring up at the night sky. Penny's dad. I haven't thought much about Penny since I left to live with the Pine Valley witches, especially given everything that happened with Hazel taking me to Spring Creek and the craziness after that. But Penny's mom is on the ground, weeping in front of him, and my heart hurts for the girl who's waiting for her parents to come home after this battle.

The girl who's always wanted to be a Guardian, but who wasn't allowed to come here tonight—along with everyone else under the age of eighteen. After all, the Pine Valley pack is large, and we need to continue to the next generation.

And her father is far from the only one.

We've won the battle, but at a cost that weighs heavily on our hearts.

Connor wraps an arm around me, giving me strength.

"We did it, Ruby," he says. "We stopped them. We saved the world from the Blood Coven, and from Ambrogio."

I know he's right, but the loss still aches.

From the heaviness in his eyes, he feels it, too.

Of course he does. He's known everyone in this pack for his entire life. If I can feel the loss of our pack members—as someone who's barely spent any time with them yet—what must this be like for him?

Devastating, my wolf answers my question.

And yet, Connor shows no signs of breaking.

"Wait. How did you...?" Tyler frowns at me, looking like he's putting the pieces of something together. "You're an omega. But you used earth magic."

The other members of the pack turn to stare at me, eyes wide and confused.

"Yes," I confirm. "I have earth magic."

"But omegas don't have earth magic," someone mutters from the crowd.

"I was never an omega," I start to explain. "My earth magic was suppressed for most of my life, as was my wolf. And that's not the only magic I have. Because on the night when I shifted for the first time, I was star touched by the moon goddess."

More confused mutters pass throughout the crowd, and some of them even look angry.

But as one of their alphas, I owe them the truth.

And so, I tell them as much as I can. The only thing I keep to myself is the truth about my parents. Because we've been through a lot tonight, and I have an instinctual feeling that the story about my parents is best kept for another time.

Plus, this isn't about my parents.

It's about me, and who I'm going to be to the pack I'm going to help lead for as long as I'm lucky to live.

As I speak, I feel their astonishment and disbelief, but also a growing sense of acceptance and admiration. They're seeing me… and they're not rejecting who and what I am.

I've never felt more welcomed by a group of people in my life.

Connor steps closer to me and takes my hand, his voice strong and clear. "Ruby is my mate, and she will lead by my side. Her strength, her courage, and her love have saved us all. She is the future of our pack, and she will help me guide you and keep you safe from this day forward."

His words resonate through the clearing, met with nods and murmurs of agreement.

My heart warms.

And then, as if to drive the matter home, he kisses me. Long, hard, and slow, for everyone to witness.

The Pine Valley pack is strong, and we're only going to get stronger.

Our future is a bright one. It's filled with hope, magic, unity, and love.

And we're ready for whatever comes next.

As the pack surveys the damage around us, my eyes are drawn to the woods, where Tristan, Gwen, and Benjamin disappeared with Ambrogio's corpse.

Memories of the time I spent with Tristan haunt my mind. The way he looked at me, the way he made me feel, the way he tricked me… it all swirls around in my head, a chaotic dance of fondness, betrayal, and anger.

"You're thinking about him, aren't you?" Connor asks.

"I can't help it," I admit. "He was part of this journey for me. A complicated part, but despite everything, I don't fully hate him."

"The two of you went through a lot, and you're a compassionate, caring person," he says, full of so much understanding that my heart basically melts. "That's one of the things I love about you. But remember, Tristan chose his path. Now it's time for us to focus on our pack, our family, and our future."

My family.

Connor, who became a part of my family the moment we completed the mate bond. My parents, who I feel like I'll have to get to know all over again, but who thankfully remember my existence. Even, to some extent, Luna.

Plus, the entire Pine Valley pack.

Tristan's chapter in my life is closed. It's time to move forward. But I'll always carry a piece of him with me, a bittersweet reminder of the time we spent together while I was learning who I am and what I'm capable of doing.

Now, as I look out over the pack, I see the faces of those who've come together, who've fought and survived in the face of overwhelming darkness. I see the hope in their eyes, their determination, and their strength.

I see our future.

"We have a lot to do," I say, turning back to Connor. "But we'll do it together."

"Always," he promises, sealing it with another kiss.

This, with him, is right. Because our story is just beginning, and I know in my heart that it's going to be an incredible journey.

Ruby

The warmth of the bonfire dances against my skin, casting shadows around the circle of people gathered for the ceremony that will celebrate Connor and me as mates, and as alphas of the Pine Valley pack.

The witches are here, too.

Plus, two others. Jason and Lindsay. We rescued them from the basement of the Blood Coven's mansion before leaving Spring Creek and brought them back with us. They're pale and gaunt, but at least they're alive.

The three of us are standing off to the side, near the forest, trying to have a bit of privacy.

"So, you're really going to join the uptown clan in the city?" I ask Jason, doing my best to keep the concern from my voice.

Because he's not going there to be turned into a vampire.

He's going to live there as one of the humans they regularly use for their feedings.

That's one of the key points of the already existing alliance between the Pine Valley pack and the uptown clan. Their vampires only feed from humans who've volunteered to be there, and they never kill them. The humans are well-provided for, but at the end of the day, they're still servants to the vampires.

Jason grins, his blue eyes twinkling in the firelight. "It's not every day you get an offer like this. Besides, I've seen firsthand that not all vampires are evil."

He still thinks he's in love with Gwen, and nothing we say will convince him otherwise.

Lindsay, thankfully, has made what I think is a much better decision. She's going to allow the witches to erase her memories of the supernatural world so she can return to her life, her family, and her boyfriend.

"How are you feeling about everything?" I ask her, noting the conflict in her warm brown eyes.

She hesitates, biting her lip. "I'm scared, Ruby. What if something feels off? What if I know something's missing, but I can't figure out what?"

"You're making the best decision for yourself." I reach out and squeeze her hand, which seems to ease her tension. "The witches are skilled in this kind of magic. They'll make the transition as smooth as possible. And remember, no matter what, you're strong and loved, and my pack and I will be watching out for you from a distance."

"You mean you don't want to be friends?" She chuckles, but it's hollow and sort of sad.

"No—I do," I say quickly. "I won't be able to tell you the truth about what I am, and we'll have to start fresh, since you won't remember me at all. But I'd love to be friends."

"Good." She gives me a warm smile. "I'd like that, too."

I glance at Connor, who's standing across the fire with Tyler and some of the others. As the pack's new alpha and beta, neither of them will become Guardians in the city. Their responsibility is here, to the pack. And Connor, always one to value duty above all else, is happy to remain in Pine Valley, where he's most needed in the supernatural world.

Tyler's still adjusting to this sudden shift of his future path, but he'll get there. He's honored to stand by Connor's side as his beta.

I'm giving Lindsay some more assurances that everything's going to be okay when a gentle breeze sends a shiver down my spine.

Luna shimmers into existence next to me, accompanied by three beautiful women I don't recognize. Each of them is graceful, their presence filling the air with a hum of magic, and I instinctively know they're not from this realm.

"A moment?" Luna says to Jason and Lindsay, and they bow their heads, hurrying off to refill their drinks.

"Hi," I say to Luna, although I keep glancing at the three other women, having a pretty good idea about who they might be.

"Allow me to introduce my sisters," Luna says. "Celeste, the star goddess. Sunneva, the sun goddess. And Tempest, the storm goddess."

"Wow," I say, speechless for a moment. "It's an honor to meet you all. Thank you for coming."

A bunch of the others in the pack are glancing our way—including Connor—but they know better than to interrupt or stare too obviously.

Celeste, with hair like spun silver, extends her hand to me in greeting. "Your courage has inspired us. Stopping the Blood Coven from resurrecting Ambrogio was no small feat."

Sunneva's eyes, full of mischief, sparkle as she looks at me. "And I was more than happy to provide you with my assistance the other night," she says.

"What do you mean?" I ask, since as far as I'm concerned, this is the first time we're meeting.

"Sleeping in bed with Tristan… well, it wasn't so bad. He's excellent at cuddling."

A gasp escapes my lips.

Luna chuckles, nudging her sister playfully. "Sunneva!"

"What?" Sunneva protests, her grin never fading.

A small bit of dread forms in my stomach at the implications of what Sunneva said. "You didn't…" I start, although I feel like if she actually *did* do anything with Tristan while she was disguised as me that night, he would have mentioned it.

Specifically, mentioned wanting to do it again.

"Nothing happened." She holds up her hands in innocence. "We just slept."

"Vampire lover." Tempest rolls her eyes, but the sun goddess simply tosses her long golden hair over her shoulder, as if she's proud of it.

"They're fascinating," Sunneva says. "Their immortality, their grace. Besides, they can be very charming when they want to be." She winks at me after that last part, as if we share a secret.

"Maybe," I say, since despite the complexities of my relationship with Tristan, he did know how to turn on the charm.

Luna steps forward, ending the conversation. "Ruby, we've come to bless Pine Valley and thank you for your bravery," she explains. "Our blessing will keep the town safe from any darkness that might threaten your territory. We hope Pine Valley will serve as a refuge not only for your pack and coven, but for any supernaturals in need of protection."

Suddenly, Connor's by my side, taking my hand. "Luna," he greets my friend with a teasing smile. "I believe we're due for a rematch."

She raises an eyebrow. "Connor, I'm a goddess. Do you really believe your beer pong victory was thanks to anything but my generous concession?"

"I can hope." He smiles casually, as if he's unfazed that we're chatting with four goddesses.

Not wanting them to have it out here and now, I introduce him to the others and fill him in on what Luna just told me about blessing Pine Valley.

"Your blessing and your presence here are an honor to Pine Valley and all who call it home." He lowers his gaze, deferring to them, then meets their eyes once more. "Our doors will forever be open to those in need."

The sincerity in his words resonates through the air, and pride surges through me for my mate and the leader he's become.

No—the leader he's always been. Because he's trained for this his entire life.

I'll learn as I go, with him by my side.

Luna's eyes soften, and a smile graces her lips as she acknowledges his words. "Your wisdom and compassion are evident," she says. "We trust that Pine Valley is in capable hands, and we look forward to witnessing the great things you and Ruby will accomplish."

Connor bows his head slightly, accepting her praise with humility and grace.

"I believe they're ready." Celeste glances over my shoulder, and I realize that the others in the clearing have silenced, watching us with a blend of excitement and anticipation.

They make way for us as we walk toward the fire.

The goddesses form a circle around it, and they raise their arms, hands intertwined. Their eyes close, and they begin to chant in a language I don't understand. The words flow like music, soft and mesmerizing, and I'm drawn closer, pulled into their spell.

Luna's voice rises above the others, and her energy connects with the land, which is drenched with the soft light of the moon. Sunneva's warmth radiates from her like the sun's rays. Then there's Tempest's magic, which sends ripples through the air, summoning a gentle breeze.

Above us, the sky shifts, the stars sparkling brighter, as if acknowledging Celeste's dominion.

It's a breathtaking sight, and I gaze around in awe, lost in the wonder of it all.

The world seems to hold its breath for one long moment.

Then the goddesses release their magic, and it washes over me—and the entire town—in a wave of love and protection that fills my soul.

Slowly, the four of them lower their arms, and their eyes open.

"It is done," Celeste says.

"Now, we must depart," Luna says, calm and gentle. "But our blessings will remain with you for as long as the stars shine, the moon waxes and wanes, the sun rises and sets, and the storms weave their wild dance. May your bravery be an inspiration to us all."

"Thank you." I nod, tears prickling my eyes at the enormity of what they've done for us. "We won't let you down."

"I know you won't," she says with a twinkling laugh. "Do you think I would have star touched you otherwise?"

"Fair point." I give her one last smile, and then the goddesses join hands once more and vanish into the moonlight.

Ruby

"They were incredible," Connor finally says, breaking the silence.

"They were," I agree. "We're lucky to have them on our side."

He smiles, leaning in to kiss my forehead. "We're lucky to have each other."

"Yes." I gaze up into his eyes, love for him filling me so much that I feel like I'm about to burst from it. "We are."

"Now, I think it's time to make this official," he says. "Thalia? We're ready."

Thalia steps forward, and the flames grow higher, responding to her magic. She's positively stunning in her long green dress, and the fire pendant on her ring shimmers under the moonlight.

Connor and I kneel before her.

"Both of you, rise," she says, motioning for us to do so.

There's a slight murmur among the gathered crowd, but Thalia's unwavering gaze silences them.

"This ceremony is done kneeling," Connor says, firm and steady, staying where he is.

I remain in place as well.

"It used to be. But now that I'm the head witch of this coven, the days of shifters being viewed as inferior to witches in Pine Valley are over," she explains. "Now, you will stand before me as equals."

Her words resonate with me, and I glance at Connor, relieved when he gives a nod of approval.

We rise together, standing tall before Thalia, who meets our eyes with compassion and grace.

"Tyler," she says, looking to Connor's new beta. "The crowns."

He steps forward and passes them to her before resuming his place in the crowd.

Carved from the ancient trees of Pine Valley and shaped to resemble antlers, the crowns are even more beautiful than I imagined. Their beauty lies in their simplicity, mirroring the strength of our pack and our connection to the earth that grounds us. The magic humming through them is so strong that I can feel it.

"Connor and Ruby, you've proven yourselves to be wise and courageous leaders," Thalia begins. "You've faced great challenges and emerged victorious, showing compassion and strength in equal measure. You're worthy of the honor and responsibility that comes with leading the Pine Valley pack. Are you prepared to accept this duty?"

"We are," Connor and I answer in unison, our hands clasped together.

"Then let it be known," she says, her voice ringing clear in the night, "that from this day forward, you're bound together as alphas of the Pine Valley pack, united in purpose, love, and strength. May you lead with wisdom, protect with courage, and rule with grace."

With those words, she places the crowns upon our heads.

Energy courses through me, connecting me to the land, the pack, and the magic that surrounds us. It's a current of electricity between my body and Connor's, and I feel more at home and at peace than I ever have before.

When I glance over at Connor, the love shining in his eyes shows me that he feels the same.

"Thank you, Thalia," he says. "Your leadership is an inspiration to us all, and we're honored to stand with you as equals."

"And I'm honored to stand with you," she replies, her eyes softening. "Together, we'll usher in a new era of understanding, acceptance, and harmony."

The crowd erupts into cheers and applause, the warmth of the bonfire grows brighter, and the celebration begins. It's a wild night, full of revelry, and for the first time in a long time, I feel like I belong.

We only start winding down when the soft pinks of dawn are peeking over the horizon.

Eventually, there's only one person left, apart from me and Connor.

Morgan.

Her green eyes are full of resolve, and she's holding the Blade of Erebus, its dark metal gleaming ominously in the first rays of sunlight.

"How are you doing?" I ask, worried about her after everything that happened last night. She slept in Connor's guest room upon our return from Spring Creek, and we heard her cries as she tossed and turned in bed for hours on end.

She turns the blade over in her hand, watching the light reflect off it. When she looks back up, there's a fire in her eyes as wild and untamed as the flames that have been burning all night.

"I'm going to learn its secrets," she says, dancing around my question. "It's not enough to have the blade. I need to master it."

"We'll help you," I say. "We'll search Jax's library for information. Thalia's going to look through the coven's references as well. And there's got to be something in Hazel's house. We just have to—"

"I'm leaving," she interrupts.

"What?" I say. "Why?"

"There's a whole world out there that I haven't explored yet," she says, and there's a fierceness to her that wasn't there before. Or, if it was there, she never showed it to me. "I can help people with my magic. I know I can. I've seen it in my visions."

As I process what she's saying, sadness makes its way through me. I was looking forward to getting to know Morgan better. I thought that in her, I had a friend.

She is our friend, my wolf speaks up from inside me. *Friendship isn't measured by distance. It's measured by trust, support, and love. Morgan has given us all those things, and more.*

"I understand," I finally say, because I do. "Where will you go first?"

A light breeze stirs the air as Morgan takes a deep breath, her eyes searching the horizon as if she can already see the path she's chosen.

"There's a village on the Grecian coast, along the Aegean Sea," she says. "Something's there for me—calling me. I have to find out what it is."

"That's so far away." I look over her small frame, unable to imagine her going across the world alone.

But my duty—and Connor's—is to the pack.

Offering to go with her is out of the question.

Although, I feel like if I did offer, she'd turn me down.

"It is far," she says. "But I'm ready to change the world. To make it better. And this is the first destination on my journey to do just that."

I don't have a chance to get in another word before she draws the blade across her palm. Her blood flows freely, dripping to the ground, so much of it that she goes pale as a ghost.

And then, before I can blink, she disappears into a burst of flames.

The scent of burned earth and magic lingers in the air, and I stand there frozen, staring at the spot where she'd just been standing.

"Well," Connor says, breaking the silence. "That was quite the exit."

"Morgan's quite the witch," I say with a smile.

"She is, and she's going to keep getting stronger," he agrees. "We're all on a journey, Ruby. Each one is unique, but hopefully, it's filled with the same desire and determination to be the best version of yourself you can be, and to make the world a better place. Like what we're going to do here, in Pine Valley."

I rest my head on his shoulder, allowing myself to be enveloped in his love and strength as we watch the sun creep up the horizon.

Eventually, hand in hand, we walk back home, ready to face the adventures that lie ahead. And somewhere in the distance, on a path that winds its way to places unknown, I know Morgan is doing the same. Her spirit is strong, her resolve unbreakable, and her journey is only beginning.

Just like ours.

But for now, our paths diverge, and Connor and I are ready to embrace anything the world decides to throw at us.

Because we're powerful.

We're alphas.

And, most importantly, we're *mates*.

Ruby

CONNOR'S ARM is warm around me as we lie together in the soft darkness of his bedroom.

No—*our* bedroom.

This is my new home.

It'll take some time to adjust. But eventually, I'll get there. For now, I nuzzle into his arms, my wolf happier than she's ever been since she emerged all those weeks ago.

Just as I'm about to drift into sleep, a whisper dances through the window, calling my name.

Luna.

My heart leaps. I didn't think I'd see her again so soon.

Careful not to wake Connor, I go into the guest bedroom and throw on a sweatshirt and yoga pants. They were Autumn's—she kept a bunch of clothes here—but it doesn't bother me at all.

She was Connor's past.

I'm his present, and his future. And, to me, that's all that matters.

The night air is cool against my skin as I step outside into the backyard.

Luna stands near the edge of the forest, her silver eyes glowing in the moonlight.

Two people who look to be in their upper twenties—a man and a woman—stand in the center of the yard.

The man is tall and lean, his dark chestnut hair wild and untamed, his blue eyes strong and confident.

The woman's hair cascades down her back in rich brown waves like my own. But it's not her hair that makes everything click into place.

It's her eyes.

Bright, turquoise eyes that I'd recognize anywhere.

"Mom? Dad?"

Her face breaks into a smile, a mixture of joy and sorrow. "Ruby," she says, and that's all I need before I'm running across the yard and into her arms.

Her touch different, yet unmistakably hers. My father is there too, his eyes full of a strength and determination I've never seen before.

"You're here." My brain's going a million miles a minute as I try making sense of it all. "I thought you had to stay in the city. That it was too risky for you to be around humans so soon after your transformation…"

"Does it look like they're around humans?" Luna asks, her eyes dancing in amusement.

"She brought us here in her… chariot," my dad says slowly, as if he's still processing the journey. "We met on the roof of the uptown clan's building and came straight here."

"We can't stay," my mom says quickly. "But we had to see you. To know that you're safe."

"I am now," I say. "But these past few weeks have been…"

How can I even begin?

"Luna told us everything," my dad says, and I glance at my best friend, grateful I don't have to live through everything again by catching them up.

As for my parents—it's surreal to see them like this. Yes, their mannerisms are mostly the same, as are their ways of speaking. But they're so much younger. And they look so different. Yet, at the same time, they're the same parents I've known my entire life.

Turning into vampires hasn't made them lose their souls. I can *feel* it.

"We're sorry for keeping our true selves from you," my dad continues. "For lying about who we are. About who *you* are."

"We never meant to hurt you," my mom adds. "We just wanted to keep you safe from those who hunted us."

"I've missed you both so much," I say, since while I still need time to process the fact that they lied to me for my entire life, they're still my parents. I love them, and I don't want to spend a second of this time we have together fighting. "For weeks, I didn't know if you'd ever remember me. And when I saw you at the restaurant, it was…"

I search my mind for the proper word.

Heartbreaking?

Soul-crushing?

Devastating?

"I know." Tears glimmer in my mom's eyes, understanding my feelings despite my inability to find the right words. "But we're here now. And we'll continue to be here for you. Always."

"Literally, since we're immortal now." My dad laughs in an attempt to make light of it all.

The weight of their new burden crashes down on me with his words. Because while shifters have a far longer lifespan than humans, my parents are now frozen in time. Eventually, they'll still be here, and I'll be gone.

But for now, we're here together, and that's what matters.

"We brought you something," my mom changes the subject, unclasping her bracelet and handing it to me.

It's silver and delicate, with turquoise stones and a pendant hanging from it of a wolf's paw.

"My parents made it for me a long, long time ago," she says, and I realize that I know nothing about any of my grandparents.

"They all passed before you were born," my dad adds, apparently sensing my thoughts. "We didn't lie to you about that."

I feel like there's more there, but that it's a story for another day. So, I don't press for more information.

"They gave it to me when I moved from Spring Creek to Pine Valley after mating with your father, as a symbol of my strength and courage," my mom continues as I run my fingers over the cool metal. "Let me put it on you."

"It's beautiful," I say as she does, tears in my eyes as I admire it on my wrist. "Thank you."

"It fits you perfectly," she says with a smile.

Luna steps forward, joining the three of us. "There's one more thing that needs to be set right," she says to me.

Curiosity tingles in my veins.

"What do you mean?"

"You'll see." She raises her hand, her fingers glowing with the light of the moon as she presses them to my forehead.

Electricity buzzes through my head, and a warm breeze passes through the air, settling over my mind. But it's finished as quickly as it began, and I blink as the world returns to focus.

Luna reaches into her jacket, pulls out a compact mirror, and opens it so I can see my reflection.

My eyes.

They're turquoise again. Just like my mom's.

"Brown never suited you all that well." Luna shrugs and gives me a playful grin.

Despite everything, I laugh.

"Then you could have chosen blue!" I say. "Or violet."

"Because violet would *really* help you blend in." She rolls her eyes.

"Hey, in a world filled with magic, nothing's too outrageous, right?" I counter, still smiling, but my attention shifts back to my parents. There's an unspoken understanding in their eyes. A gratitude that words can't express.

But my mom finds a way.

"You looked after Ruby when we couldn't," she says to Luna. "You guided her, protected her, blessed her with magic from the stars, and were the friend she needed. I don't think there are words that can properly express what we owe you."

"You owe me nothing," Luna says. "It was my honor to do it. And trust me—Ruby more than proved her worth along the way."

"Understatement of the century," I say, thinking about all the challenges I had to overcome to get to this point.

My dad steps closer to Luna, extending a hand to her. "You're family now," he tells her, sounding like he's talking more to the Luna who was my college roommate than the goddess standing before us now. "Whatever you need, we're here for you."

"I'm a bit too used to looking after myself, but I'll keep that in mind," she says, and then she turns back to me. "It was an honor getting to know you, Ruby. I must admit—I wasn't looking forward to pretending to be a college student. But you made it all worth it. Thank you for your friendship. I'll cherish it, always."

Tears well in my throat, and I try to swallow them down. "Will I see you again?" I ask.

"You can count on it." She smiles, the moonlight playing in her eyes, then turns to my parents, serious once more. "It's time."

Their faces fall, and a pang of loss spread through my chest.

I hug each of them as we say our final goodbyes.

"This isn't forever," my mom promises me. "We'll see each other again soon."

I nod, tears blurring my vision. "I love you both. More than anything."

They step back, joining Luna at the edge of the forest, where her horses and carriage have reappeared.

I stand frozen, watching as they get situated inside. Then Luna takes the reins, and the chariot rises, the wheels leaving trails of shimmering light as they ascend and disappear into the night sky.

Once they're gone, the moon seems to shine brighter, as if it's telling me that whatever comes next, I'm ready for it.

Life is still filled with unknowns, and there will be challenges ahead. But as I gaze up at the moon, I know without a doubt that I have the strength, courage, and support from the people I love to help me face anything the world throws my way.

Tristan

ONE MONTH LATER

GATHERED around Ambrogio's lifeless body with Gwen, Benjamin, Hazel, Zara, and Willow, I look down at my watch as the second hand hits midnight.

We're in a long-abandoned cathedral, its decayed beauty the perfect place for our hideout. Stained glass windows that once depicted scenes of holy reverence are now fractured and dull, silently bearing witness to our dark, forbidden rites.

Ambrogio's ashen face is illuminated by lanterns of flickering candles, his body lying on a cold stone altar. The arrow Ruby used, still buried in his flesh, is just as dull and lifeless as the original vampire's pallid complexion.

Ruby.

Every time I think about her—and the eternal life I believed we were going to share—my heart aches.

But it gets better each day. Enough to make me believe that there might be light at the end of the tunnel, after all.

"Are we ready?" Gwen's voice is steady, but I catch the mix of hope and fear in her eyes.

If this doesn't work, she might never be reunited with her true love.

"It's time." I lower my watch to my side in preparation to begin.

Willow reaches for the dagger laid upon the altar and picks it up. Its hilt is wrought from blackened silver, the blade forged from a metal that refuses to shine. It's like it was carved from a void.

Her fingers, gentle and healing, seem almost at odds with the dagger's cruel elegance.

"Go on," Zara encourages her with a hungry smile. "Do it."

Willow gives her sister a firm nod, then slices the blade across her palm without a flinch.

Her blood flows down onto Ambrogio's body, right on the spot where Ruby's arrow enters his flesh. More and more of it, so much that her face turns a ghostly shade of white that makes me want to reach out and stop her before she loses too much.

I don't.

She's strong and powerful, and she knows what she's doing. So, I silently watch as her blood seeps in Ambrogio's wound, which has black, decayed veins flaring out of it like spiderwebs inked upon his skin.

Hazel begins to chant in an ancient language, her voice weaving through the cold air, intertwining with the faint rustling of the tattered tapestries lining the walls. Her words are a dark melody, and the flames on the candles grow stronger as she speaks.

Soon, the others join in.

"Let the darkness unbind," Zara says, her eyes fixed on Ambrogio's body.

"Let death unwind." Willow, her hand still dripping blood, reaches for the arrow. Her face contorts with concentration, and it's like the entire room is holding its breath as we watch her focus on bringing the death magic out of Ambrogio's body and back inside the arrow.

Wind howls through the broken windows.

The glass of the fire-filled lanterns explodes.

And then, a movement.

A twitch in Ambrogio's finger.

Just a twitch. But it's enough.

Gwen leans forward and reaches for Ambrogio's face, brushing her finger against his ashen cheek and gazing down at him as if he's already returned. "Come on," she pleads. "I need you. Come back to me."

Willow's face is straining now, her forehead covered in sweat, her hand trembling as she pushes more and more magic into the spell.

Tears fall from her eyes, joining with her blood on Ambrogio's body.

"Willow, that's enough!" Zara's voice pierces the thick air. "You're killing yourself."

"I can do this," she says, but her voice is faint, and she sways slightly, as if she's about to pass out. "I'm so close."

"No." Zara rips the dagger out of Willow's hand, and the wind around us stills. "I've already lost one sister. I'm not losing another."

Morgan, lost to the flames. To her own element.

Hazel's magic wasn't strong enough to save all three of the blood witches. Every supernatural has limits—even her.

Every victory comes with a sacrifice.

Gwen hisses, and I worry she's about to pounce on Zara for forcing Willow to stop.

I hold her back.

"Leave it," I growl. "We have to stop for now. We can't keep trying in the future if she kills herself while attempting to heal him."

Willow gives me a small, grateful smile and mouths a "thank you" across the altar.

The wound on her palm begins to close. Her face regains some color, but she still looks exhausted.

On instinct, I reach for her hand.

She doesn't pull away.

And, in that moment, as I gaze into her warm, amber eyes, something shifts between us. It's subtle, but it's there. A promise of something more.

"We'll get through this," I tell her. "We'll bring Ambrogio back. And we'll do it together."

She smiles, and warmth spreads through me.

It's the spark of a new beginning. Of possibility. Of love.

I'm still not over Ruby. I don't think I'll ever be.

But maybe—with enough time—this beautiful witch in front of me will be able to heal my heart.

From the Author

Hi! I hope you enjoyed the *Wolf Born* series.

If you liked the series, I'd love if you wrote a review. (One or two sentences is fine!) Reviews are extremely important to authors, because they encourage more readers to pick up the book. Plus, I read every review I get, and they motivate me to write faster!

A review for the box set is the most helpful.

* * *

CONNOR AND RUBY EXTENDED SCENE

The original version of the scene where Connor and Ruby have sex for the first time was much steamier than what made it into the book. Since I have readers of all ages and preferences, I decided that the full version of the scene works better as a bonus scene for those who choose to sign up for it.

Read the Connor and Ruby extended scene:
michellemadow.com/rising-moon-bonus-scene

* * *

The next series in the *Star Touched* universe—*Vampire Bride*—is complete!

Get it now:
mybook.to/vampirebride1

You can also turn the page to see the cover, description, and to read the exciting first chapter.

Black Sun

STAR TOUCHED: VAMPIRE BRIDE 1

Embark on an adventure filled with magic, romance, and epic twists in the first book in *USA Today* bestselling author Michelle Madow's *Vampire Bride* series—a fresh and enchanting take on the classic love story of Hades & Persephone.

Amber Benson has no idea what to do for the rest of her life, let alone what major to pick for college. So when she inherits an apartment in Manhattan from a grandmother she never knew, she moves there faster than a New York minute.

Her plan to find herself is soon derailed—on the subway, where she's attacked by demons.

Even crazier? She defends herself with something she never knew existed: magic.

But it's not her newfound ability that saves her. It's the intervention of a mesmerizing warrior with otherworldly grace… who then proceeds to kidnap her to a supernatural kingdom hidden in the heart of the city.

Because Amber's savior—Damien Fairmont—is a king. A *vampire* king.

And he's just declared to his entire kingdom that Amber's destined to be his bride, whether she wants to be or not.

But trying to escape her so-called destiny as Damien's queen isn't Amber's only problem. Because dark forces are rising in Manhattan. And now that they've gotten a taste of her powerful magic, she's not just a target for Damien's affections, but also for the sinister shadows that lurk in the underworld of the city.

Welcome to *Black Sun*, a fast-paced adventure perfect for fans of fierce heroines and brooding vampire royalty that will leave you turning the pages late into the night, until the very last twist.

Get it now:
mybook.to/vampirebride1

Or turn the page to read the exciting first chapter!

Amber

THE BASEMENT STUDIO apartment in New York City that I recently inherited from my grandmother is basically a dungeon.

Scuffs and scratches line the hardwood floors. The slit of a window barely lets in any natural light. And the manager's tip for when it gets cold in the winter? Stay near the hot water pipe.

Luckily, it's the start of summer.

But even though the apartment is tiny and falling apart, it's *mine*. And it couldn't get more different from the home I shared with my mom in Vermont if it tried.

"Different" is exactly what I need right now. Because even though a nineteen-year-old is supposed to know what they want to do with the rest of their life—mainly, what to major in for college—I don't.

This gap year in the city might be what I need to figure out who I am and what I want. Thanks to the grandmother I barely knew, who—for some unknown reason—left me everything she had.

I'm placing a pile of shirts in the rickety dresser when a knock at the door yanks me out of my thoughts.

My heart jumps into my throat.

I didn't order delivery. No one knows where I live.

I don't even know anyone in the city.

My eyes dart to the kitchen counter, spotting a knife. Next to it, there's a small pink canister of mace—a parting gift from Mom.

"Just in case," she'd said with a wink.

Mace it is.

Grabbing the mace, I approach the door slowly, trying not to be heard.

They knock again. Harder, more insistent this time.

"Who's there?" I call out, trying to sound more confident than I feel.

"Eva," a bright, airy voice says from the other side. "Your neighbor?"

I instantly relax.

Not a serial killer. A neighbor.

That makes sense.

I take a deep breath to shake off my nerves, unlock the bolt, and open the door.

The woman in front of me has sparkling blue eyes and hair that shines like spun gold. There's a timeless quality about her, but if I had to guess, I'd say she's in her mid-twenties.

"Hi," she says with a radiant smile. "I saw you pull up earlier. Welcome to the building! I'm Eva—but you know that already."

"I'm Amber." I go to push a strand of hair behind my ear, and that's when I remember—the mace. "Sorry about the…"

I motion to the pink can, heat rushing into my cheeks.

"No need to apologize," she says with a warm chuckle. "It's always better to be safe. The city can be overwhelming at times."

"It's definitely a lot to get used to," I agree, glancing over my shoulder at the rundown apartment. "Everything's so different from my hometown."

She tilts her head, studying me. "Maplewood, Vermont. Right?"

I blink in surprise. "Yes. How did you—"

She waves a hand dismissively, her bracelets clinking along her wrist. "I knew your grandma," she says. "She was always talking about her hometown, and how happy she was to get out of it. She talked about you a lot, too. How she hoped that when you inherited this apartment, you'd love living here just as much as she did. When I heard she died, I figured…" She shrugs and looks around. "Well, I hoped you'd move here instead of selling it and staying in Vermont."

"Thanks," I say, and she gives me another encouraging smile. "This apartment may not be much, but I feel like it's a fresh start for me. A chance to find my path."

A knowing look crosses her eyes. "Then you got here on the perfect day. Because there's something happening this afternoon that you shouldn't miss."

"And what's that?"

"A solar eclipse." She just about bounces on her toes from excitement. "It's been on the news for weeks. The view from the rooftop is going to be incredible. Want to join me? In an hour?"

A solar eclipse.

I've read about them—the rare alignment of the sun and the moon. But to witness one in the heart of New York City?

"That sounds amazing," I tell her. "I'll be there."

It's not like I have any other plans.

"Perfect!" She beams and takes a step back. "See you there. It's a walkup building, so just take the stairs all the way to the top. You can't miss it."

With that, she turns on her heels, disappearing down the hall before I can ask her anything more.

Sort of weird.

But also interesting.

Happy that I've already met a friend, I close the door again and return to unpacking. The time seems to fly, and before I know it, the hour is up.

The old stairs creak under my weight as I make my way up the building. But, like my new apartment, there's a certain charm to it. Like the floor is sharing its history and secrets with my every step.

Eva's already on the roof. She's having a hushed conversation with another woman, whose back is turned to me.

I hesitate, not wanting to interrupt.

Before I can figure out how to break in without being rude, Eva catches sight of me and waves me over with a grin. "Amber! You made it!"

The other woman turns around, her gaze meeting mine. It's both unsettling and magnetic, filled with a depth that pierces straight through me.

She's younger than I expected. Maybe my age? A year or two older?

"This is Morgan," Eva says, quick with the introduction. "She's an old friend."

"Hi," I say, still not walking toward them. "Nice to meet you."

"You, too." She gives Eva a knowing look, then turns back to me. "I was just leaving."

"Already?" I glance up at the sky, where the sun is already starting to get covered by the moon. It looks like someone's taken a big bite out of it.

"I told another friend I'd watch the eclipse at their place," she says. "Have fun. And good luck."

She rushes past me and down the stairs, leaving me alone with Eva, who gives me a bright smile and holds out glasses that look like the ones people wear for 3D movies.

"Eclipse glasses," she explains. "It's not safe to look directly at the sun. You don't want to burn your eyes out."

"No. I definitely don't." I walk over to her and take them. "Thanks."

She puts on her glasses, I do the same, and we situate ourselves on lounge chairs facing the skyline. The skyscrapers beyond our downtown West Village apartment spread out around us, and the sound of heavy traffic comes from the street below. It's an endless sea of steel and glass, and the city's frantic heartbeat syncs with my own, a ripple of excitement coursing through me.

"So, Amber." Eva makes herself comfortable and faces me. "Tell me about yourself. What do you like to do? What do you *want* to do?"

"Um…" I bite my lip, thinking.

"I like reading. And music." I search my mind for something more, since I'm not exactly coming across as the most interesting person on the planet. "I'm good at sports, but I don't really enjoy playing them. I also bake, but that's more of my mom's thing than mine."

"Interesting," she says, and we continue to chat as the moon crawls across the sun.

Eventually, the sky takes on a twilight hue, even though it's mid-afternoon. There's a final sparkle of light, and then the sun turns black, minus a ring of fire in a halo around it.

It's like it went from day to night in a few seconds.

"We can remove our glasses now," Eva says, sounding as awe-struck as I feel.

The eclipse, when the sun is completely covered by the moon, is even more breathtaking without the screens of the glasses dimming my view.

But as I gaze up at the covered sun, Eva remains focused on me. There must be something strange going on with the reflection of the light, because it's like her pupils are mini eclipses, the sunbursts around them glowing on their own.

"Are you okay?" I ask slowly.

She doesn't respond.

Instead, she reaches forward, touches my forehead, and it's like the power of a million electric shocks travels through her fingers and into my mind.

The pain is blinding. It's like the worst migraine of my life, amplified beyond anything I could ever imagine, and I gasp, struggling to breathe.

"Relax." Eva's voice is distant, yet clear. "I know it hurts. But you're going to be okay. I promise."

The world tilts, my eyes burn, and before I can ask what she means, I fall back and tumble down into the darkness.

* * *

I awake to a soft light filtering through the window, the smell of roses, and something spicy, like cinnamon.

It's nothing like the pine scent of home.

Because I'm not home, I think, and the memories of recent events crash through my mind. Arriving at my grandmother's apartment, Eva introducing herself, and the eclipse that all but burned a hole through my brain.

And, judging from the fact that there's an actual *window* in here, I'm not in my basement apartment.

Luckily, the window looks out to my new street. Which makes it safe to assume that I'm currently in Eva's apartment. And if it's already sunrise, that means I just slept for… over twelve hours.

My head throbs, but I force myself up in the bed.

Eva's sitting on the chair at her vanity, with two mugs in front of her. "You're up," she says, giving me that radiant smile of hers. "How are you feeling?"

"Like my brain exploded and then melded back together." I press my fingers to my forehead, remembering how she did the exact same thing to me during the eclipse. "What happened?"

"There must have been some defect with the glasses," she says. "I'm so sorry. You experienced some solar retinopathy, but we caught it early."

"Solar what?" I ask.

"Solar retinopathy," she repeats. "The sun burned your eyes a bit."

"That… doesn't sound good."

Understatement of the century.

"Don't worry—you're totally fine now," she says quickly. "I didn't have a chance to tell you much about me, but I'm a nurse practitioner. I checked your eyes, and all was well." She picks up one of the mugs and holds it out to me. "Here. Drink this. It'll help you feel better."

It does smell good. And my throat is so dry that it hurts.

"What is it?" I ask.

"Chamomile tea."

It's exactly what my mom always made me when I felt sick at home.

"Thanks." I accept the mug and take a sip. "Is this your apartment?"

"It is. I couldn't just leave you on the roof," she explains, and I nod slowly, taking another sip of the tea. It grounds me. I feel warm. Safe.

At the same time, I don't want to stay here any longer than necessary. I have a lot to do with the move, and I need to get it all done, on top of having to search for a job.

Anxiety tightens in my chest at the thought.

"Thanks for everything, but I have to go," I say, grabbing my bag from the nightstand. "See you around?"

"Of course." She flashes me another smile. "Oh, and one more thing."

"Yes?" I stop midway to the door and turn to face her.

"I won a ticket to a show tonight. *Wicked*—the musical," she says. "But work called earlier and let me know that one of the nurses is sick, and they need me to take over an extra shift. Do you want it?"

"What do you mean that you 'won' a ticket?" I ask.

"Have you ever heard of the Broadway lottery?" she asks, and I shake my head no, waiting for her to continue. "It's a system where anyone can enter to win tickets for Broadway shows a day in advance at a much lower price. I enter every day and win a decent amount of the time. But I can't resell it, and I don't want it to go to waste. So, do you want it?"

"How much is it?"

I know she said a "much lower price," but I'm on a pretty strict budget over here.

"I'm gifting it to you," she says. "So… it's free."

"Are you sure?"

"Yes. I'm sure," she says, and then she adds, "Please take it. It would be a shame for it to go to waste."

I pause, thinking. I feel bad taking it without paying. At the same time, she *is* offering…

"That would be great," I finally say.

"Cool—I'll text you the ticket," she says. "Let me know how you like it!"

"Will do," I say, smiling again. "And, thanks."

"Anytime."

The rest of the day passes in a blur as I work non-stop to situate myself in the apartment. Eventually, it's time to head out for the show. And I leave *extra* early. It's my first time using the subway, and despite all the instructions I've read online, I don't want to mess up and get there late.

It all goes… surprisingly smoothly.

The show is amazing.

When I exit the theatre, the city is alive and buzzing, even at this time of night. Everyone in Maplewood is probably home and getting ready for bed right now.

Maybe I should hail a taxi to get home. I have no idea if the subway is safe this late.

But taxis are expensive. I have no job yet. Sure, my grandmother left me a bit of money, but I need to save it for apartment fees and anything else that might go wrong and need fixing.

So, the subway it is.

I follow my phone's directions to the station and head down the steps, hurrying to the platform at the sound of the train approaching. With a final sprint, I dive into the back car, just as the doors slide closed behind me.

Victory.

Catching my breath, I lean against a pole and scan the subway car. There are only a few other passengers inside. They're engrossed in their own worlds, headphones in or phones out.

Then, my eyes lock with a man's at the opposite side. Blond hair. A perfectly tailored suit. He radiates power and wealth, seeming entirely out of place here.

No way does he need to save money by taking the subway instead of a taxi.

Or instead of being driven around by a chauffeur.

I should look away. By now, he's totally realized I'm staring. Well, he's doing it right back, but still—it's probably because I looked at him first and he's wondering why a stranger is staring at him on the subway.

Before I can shake myself out of it, the train jolts, and I stagger, gripping the pole tighter and miraculously avoiding falling on my face.

The lights flicker.

My heart jumps into my throat, and I glance around at the others in the car, checking to see if this is normal, or if the train's breaking down.

As I do, coldness wraps around my bones. Because there's something not right about the others in the car. Their eyes are eerily vacant. Hollow. Hungry.

And then, their bodies and faces stretch and contort, shifting into something twisted and grotesque.

No, I think. *This can't be real. My eyes are playing tricks on me.*

A side effect from what happened during the eclipse?

I shouldn't have trusted that Eva could properly diagnose me and know I was okay. Why *did* I trust her?

I need to go to a doctor.

I try blinking the visions away, but then one of the ghoulish creatures lunges at me with an inhuman speed, his eyes fixated hungrily on mine.

My scream gets stuck in my throat.

From the corner of my eye, the blond man from earlier leaps into action, plunging a dagger into the attacker's chest.

"Stay behind me!" he shouts as the ghoul disintegrates and melts into a sticky puddle on the floor.

He doesn't have to say it twice.

I scramble backward, into the corner. My eyes dart around, searching for a way to escape. But there's nowhere to go. I'm trapped.

I turn back around, my breaths shallow, watching in horror as the ghoulish things try coming closer.

Luckily, the man in the suit and a bigger, broader man with silver hair keep using their daggers to ward the creatures off and disintegrate them.

This can't be happening.

I have to be seeing things.

Before I can come close to processing it, one of the creatures breaks through the men's defense. A darker, more menacing one than the rest, with dead eyes and long fingers that reach out to wrap around my throat.

His touch is as cold as death.

I gasp for air, trying to pry away his icy grip, but it's useless. His gaze burns into my soul. And as he grins down at me, his sharp teeth glinting in the flickering light, a haze creeps into the corners of my vision.

It feels like he's trying to suck the life out of me.

But whatever this thing is trying to do to me... I won't let it. I might not know what my purpose in life is yet, but it sure as hell isn't to die at the hands of a monster in the subway on my second day in the city.

Determination fills me, and something stirs within me. A deep warmth—a vibrant, burning energy. It starts in my chest, radiating outward, rushing through my veins like liquid fire.

The creature's eyes widen in surprise, and he hisses, recoiling in pain.

And then that warmth—the one I felt building inside me—*comes out*. The blinding orb collides with the creature's chest, so bright that it fills the car with a radiant, golden light.

The ghoul releases a blood curdling scream, his face twisting and distorting even more, and then he dissolves—*melts*—into a brown, sticky puddle on the floor.

As I stare down at it in shock, the two men finish off the other creatures in the car.

The last one dissolves, and the world silences for the first time since the lights started flickering.

Now that it's over—or seems to be over—exhaustion hits me like a truck. Every muscle, every fiber of my being screams in agony. I can barely stand, let alone speak as the darkness at the edges of my vision closes in. I reach for the wall behind me, but it's no use.

I'm slipping, sliding.

The blond man rushes over, catching me just in time.

I try to focus on his face, to find some comfort in the ice blue eyes of the man who just saved my life, but everything seems so distant. Whatever just happened—that monster sucking my soul out, the light that burst out of me—it's like it drained every bit of energy out of my body.

Amidst the impending darkness, a phone rings.

"We found her," I hear, and then the world fades to nothing.

Get *Black Sun* on Amazon and keep reading now:
mybook.to/vampirebride1

About the Author

Michelle Madow is a *USA Today* bestselling author who's sold over three million books worldwide, with translations in multiple languages.

She writes what she loves: young adult fantasy where girls with no magic discover they're more powerful than they ever dreamed—and it's up to them to stop dark forces, with a broody supernatural man by their side. Her books are packed with enemies-to-lovers slow-burn romance, found family, elemental magic, forbidden love, fated mates, epic quests, and twists you won't see coming.

Writing has been her passion since childhood, and she wrote her first novel in college. Now, she's thrilled to share her worlds with readers every day.

When she's not writing, she's probably reading, exploring magical settings, or dreaming up her next big twist.

Never miss a new release by signing up to get emails or texts when Michelle's books come out:

Sign up for emails: michellemadow.com/subscribe
Sign up for texts: michellemadow.com/texts

Connect with Michelle:

Instagram: @michellemadow
Facebook: facebook.com/MichLMadow
Email: michelle@michellemadow.com

Printed in Dunstable, United Kingdom